THE SIXTH LABYRINTH

REBECCA LOCHLANN

ERINYES PRESS

THE SIXTH LABYRINTH

REBECCA LOCHLANN

ERINYES PRESS

BOOK FIVE

THE CHILD OF THE ERINYES SERIES

MOTHER

Note to Readers

Almost all the Gaelic in this book is translated immediately or within a few paragraphs or pages. The dialect is usually clear via context. But I have included a glossary at the end for those who prefer it.

PRONUNCIATION OF NAMES IN THIS BOOK:
SEAGHAN – SHAWN
DIORBHAIL – DER-VAHL
EAMHAIR – EE MER
RUAIRIDH – ROOREE

He sings the morn upon the westward hills
Strange and remote and wild;
He sings it in the land
Where once I was a child.

He brings to me dear voices of the past,
The old land and the years;
My father calls for me,
My weeping spirit hears.

~~~~Robert Louis Stevenson
~~~~

LOCATIONS IN THE SIXTH LABYRINTH

Prologue

GLENELG, SCOTLAND

NOVEMBER 1853

"IT LOOKS TO BE A HARD LABOR," BEATRICE SAID.

Isabel squinted at the woman from the corner of her eye. Beatrice Stewart never wasted words. If she opened her mouth to say *It looks to be a hard labor,* well, it was no doubt going to be the worst labor ever seen in Inverness-shire.

The forest pressed in, heavy and watchful, the shadowed trees looming like baleful black giants.

Beatrice seized Isabel's arm. "Fetch water."

Grateful for a distraction from brooding thoughts and growing panic, Isabel carried a wooden bucket to the nearby burn, using a fallen tree limb to break the ice. She wasn't so far away that she couldn't hear Hannah Lawton's awful moaning as the poor lass struggled to give birth. The babe was a full two months early. Nothing could save it. They'd be lucky to save the mother, with no midwife.

She fought off tears as she knelt to fill the bucket. Hannah had endured much this day. So had the rest of Glenelg. The entire village, Isabel's friends and kin, all those she'd ever known, had been evicted, forced to watch without recourse as every building, even the old kirk, was burnt to the ground. The men hired to carry out the landlord's wishes had inflicted many cruelties.

Terror, devastation, and now this unrelenting cold—brought by the worst storm she could remember blanketing the entire coast in snow—surely these things would curse the coming infant and its mother.

The bucket was cracked, but didn't seem to leak. Isabel tripped through frozen loam, snow, and hidden tree roots, handing it to Beatrice then standing there, not knowing what else to do. She glanced through bare branches and sweeping evergreen limbs into an ominous patchwork of clouds. *Lord, help this woman,* she prayed. *Help us all.*

If God ignored her, they would die, either of slow starvation or painful freezing. How many days could this pitiful band survive? Her instincts declared, *Not many.*

Hannah screamed, "Seaghan! Seaghan!" The circling trees magnified her cry.

Isabel looked at each of her companions, those who had gathered here after the destruction of their homes. Yesterday, over two hundred people lived in and around Glenelg. Now she counted seventeen. Six were children.

She turned away, not wanting these wounded, weary souls to see the defeat she couldn't hide, or her conviction that they would all die here together.

WAKE UP, DAUGHTER.

Isabel rose on one elbow, rubbing at her eyes. Mist eddied, eerie and opaque. She half-expected a unicorn or dwarf to appear.

A miracle comes. Why do you sleep?

Shivers ran over her, though she was oddly warm. "Miracle?" She peered in every direction, though she was almost certain the source of the voice was inside her own head.

The mist split like a tattered sail, framing a woman who observed her in a curious yet arrogant way. A lady with long, curling black hair and pale skin, rather like an Irish lass. But she wasn't dressed like any Irishwoman Isabel had ever seen. A narrow silver band ran across her forehead; in the center was an ornament shaped like a boat with high-pointed prow and stern, or a crescent moon propped on its spine. Her white gown, sleeveless and bound with silver ribbons, rippled about her ankles. Isabel, who loved fabric and needlework, couldn't help admiring such an uncommon article of clothing, or a twinge of envy at how it fit.

The holy child comes.

Envy vanished beneath apprehension. "Who are you?"

Handmaid of Areia Athene, she who brings life and death to men. The crown flashed as the lady inclined her head. *She brings life now, sacred life. Wake. See the child who suffers for your sake.*

"Suffers? For me?"

For you and all miserable mankind. Though you cursed and abandoned her, my Mistress loves you still. She returns her daughter, who will live among you as she prepares for her future destiny. Here, in the sixth life, she shall be known as Morrigan, the very name my Lady was called in these islands once, though few now living remember it, any more than they remember her, for she has long been discarded in favor of newer gods.

Isabel wanted to listen to this woman for the rest of her life. Pure, warm as spring breezes, her melodious voice cast away fear as well as hopelessness. But the phantasm was undulating as though she stood behind a waterfall.

"Wait!" Isabel cried.

You were once a queen, and gave her life. Grace and forgetfulness surround you for that. Go and look upon her. She is the finest miracle you will ever see.

Isabel sat up with a startled gasp. Someone had thrown a frayed cloth over her. It sagged around her waist as she stared wildly. Where was she? Why was it so cold? There was no mist. No lady. She'd simply had a dream.

Light from the nearby fire sent shadows dancing across the face of her brother's ill-fated wife. The woman's moans recalled tales of the *bean-sìth*, ghostly female spectres who appeared, shrieking, when someone was about to die.

Beatrice knelt between Hannah's legs. Isabel's mother was there too, her hand cupped over Hannah's knee.

It all returned in a torrent. The storm. The stench of flaming thatch. Screaming children. Folk ejected violently from their homes. One of the landlord's hired outlaws had shoved Hannah, causing her to fall. She'd landed hard on her belly.

Isabel's brother, Douglas, refused to let them board the ship for Nova Scotia. He'd said he would not be cast off like rotted fish, nor so easily forgotten. Instead he'd dragged them to this forest, and who could say in the end which choice would turn out worse?

His wife's labor had gone on and on now, for hours. Isabel had smoothed Hannah's hair and murmured nonsense meant to convey encouragement. At some point, there came a time of silence, of stillness. Hannah fell into sleep or unconsciousness and eventually, Isabel drifted off as well.

Now the labor was intensifying again. Something was wrong. The two women helping Hannah wore worry on their faces like black storm clouds on the summit of Ben Nevis.

"Why did you do this to me?" Hannah muttered. "I hate you."

Isabel said, "Wheesht, dear, you'll be fine," and stroked her cheek, but Douglas had heard.

"*A shiùrsach!*" The father of the coming child leaned over his wife, his hands bunched into fists as though he meant to strike her. "You and Seaghan thought you could make a fool of me. Now see where you are. You've made your bed—"

"Stop!" It was wee Nicky, Douglas's son by his first wife. He was only three, but he broke away from the man who held him and ran forward bravely. "Don't hurt her!" He began to sob.

Isabel had always been afraid of Douglas. She was afraid now, but she swore if that fist rose, she would put herself between them. If Nicky could stand up to him, then so, by God, could she. Bad enough to call your wife a whore to her face while she was giving birth to your child.

But Douglas turned away. He picked up his son and carried him off into the dark.

Hannah sounded like a beast caught in a steel trap, the kind that broke bones and left its captive to die in agony. Her hair hung lank. Strands clung to her thin, pale face, and her eyes were huge, black with terror. Was this what giving birth did to a woman? By the good Lord in Heaven, Isabel would never make such a mistake. No man could speak sweetly enough to make it worthwhile.

Douglas returned without Nicky and reached out, catching Beatrice's arm. Isabel started to rise, intending to throw herself over Hannah. But, "Save her," was all he said, his voice hoarse. "Don't let her die."

Isabel stared. Never in her life had she heard such misery in Douglas Lawton's voice. She couldn't trust her own ears. Perhaps he did care, after all.

"I'll do my best." Beatrice brushed his cheek with her fingertips, turning back to Hannah without expression when Douglas jerked away from her touch.

Gloaming crept into frigid night. "Saint Brigit spare the lass," one of the villagers cried, making the sign of the cross.

Beatrice slapped Hannah. "Push, or this wean'll kill you!"

Hannah sucked in a deep breath and bore down, screaming.

Desperation glimmered in the women's eyes. They moved swiftly now, sweat dappling their foreheads, though above them, ice encased the tree limbs. Blood slicked their arms to the elbows.

Hannah's flush faded to greenish-white.

At last the babe was born. The cord was cut and Isabel's mother smacked it on the rump, prompting a shaky yowl. Beatrice fought to stem Hannah's bleeding while Isabel's mother swaddled the newborn in a scrap of singed blanket.

"Ibby," her mother said, "hold this child."

Hannah's eyelids fluttered. She opened her mouth and tried to speak, but no sound came.

Black clots of blood splattered the snow. There was a hot earthy smell. Steam rose from between the new mother's legs. Isabel's empty belly lurched when Beatrice wiped sweat from her forehead, leaving behind a glistening streak of scarlet.

Back in the spring, before all these troubles, Isabel had watched Hannah wade in a mountain burn, her skirts kilted above her knees, hair trailing in the water. Laughing, she'd flicked the wet ends at some enraptured lad. With her rich red hair, wicked blue eyes, and voluptuous body, she'd left great men fair stammygastered.

It remained a mystery why this bonny girl had accepted Seaghan MacAnaugh's proposal only to break the engagement and marry Douglas Lawton instead, without waiting even the barest interval to save Seaghan's wounded pride.

Gossip had enflamed the village. Snatches trailed through Isabel's brain as she held the baby and regarded her sister-in-law.

She's a slut.

Seaghan is well rid of her, and Black Douglas Lawton has finally got what he deserves. Hope he takes her far from Glenelg.

Nothing remained now of Glenelg but smoldering ruins. Burned, like their grasping landlord wanted, cleared of crofts and bothersome humans, ready for an influx of more profitable sheep. Almost everyone Isabel had ever known, including Seaghan MacAnaugh, had sailed away to a country on the other side of the ocean. She'd never see any of those folk again. Her village, her world, had been pared down to fewer than twenty people.

Douglas kissed Hannah's forehead. "*Beannachd leat, a ghràidh,*" he said, and drew the blanket over her face.

Isabel cradled the newborn. Wee thing, light as down. Her niece. Fluids, blood, and pasty goo covered the baby's skin. Her elfish crimson face screwed into a plaintive whine.

"My sister would no' want us sniveling over her," Beatrice snapped. "Give me the child, Isabel."

Unnerved by the woman's scowl, Isabel handed the babe over.

Beatrice unwrapped the blanket. "She appears healthy, though born before her proper time. Come, Douglas, see your daughter."

Douglas, still kneeling beside his wife, glanced up. After a moment, he took the baby. He looked confused, like he'd already forgotten the cause of Hannah's death.

"Would you name her Morrigan, after our mother?" Beatrice asked.

The wee one's cry was weak and pitiful, bringing tears to Isabel's eyes. Douglas returned her to Beatrice, shrugging. "It doesn't matter."

Morrigan.

Isabel crossed herself.

PART I

The Reunion

Chapter 1

STRANRAER, SCOTLAND

1872

MORRIGAN CROUCHED BEHIND A BOULDER, WILLING HERSELF TO VANISH INTO IT. She heard a scrape, as of a shoe against stone, and tensed. Silence descended, so deep and thick it beat against her eardrums.

With a sharp flutter and startled cry, a grouse rose from the sedges to her left. She squinted, trying to make out details, but all was disguised in predawn shadows.

There was no time for hesitation. She must be bold. Drawing in a breath, she leaped, loosing a warlike shout, and slapped the flat of her blade against the tall dark figure standing with his back to her. He toppled, breaking apart in a most unwarrior-like fashion. She stared. Her Viking attacker was nothing but a crude stook of weeds, roped together like a massive corn dolly and propped upright.

A hand squeezed her shoulder, bringing her around with a stifled shriek. "Thought you had me, didn't you?"

"Damn," she said.

"Don't you know by now you'll never best me? You're a female, cursed by God and nature. Sneaky, that's what you are, just like your hair, until the sun comes out and reveals the truth. Lucky for you Scotland has many cloudy days."

She couldn't help it—she nudged her braid over her shoulder and out of sight almost guiltily.

Nicholas Lawton's sardonic laughter echoed into the heavens. "No one with any wit is fooled," he said. "Red hair on a lass is unlucky, and dark red's the worst."

Nicky never tired of these well-worn taunts. Having learned long ago that to argue only worsened things, Morrigan changed the subject. "Where were you?" She dropped her clumsy wooden sword on the ground, disgusted with it, herself, and most of all, her smug brother.

"Here...there...in the sky, the ground...." He poked her chest. "In your soul." He hooked his thumbs under his braces, cocky as a Spanish matador, then plunged his own sword into the damp soil, where it quivered like a naked girl.

Nicky polished his nails on the front of his grimy sark and threw out another round of derisive laughter. It echoed off cotton-wisp clouds and frightened a covey of partridges from their nests.

Goaded to fury, Morrigan bent and grabbed her sword. She thwacked at her brother, longing to rattle his unquenchable amusement, or at least inspire his respect, but he caught her around the waist, lifted her with no apparent effort, and, dodging the blade, tossed her into a patch of gorse.

She shrieked again.

He dusted his hands, planted them on his hips, and grinned. His teeth flashed briefly, framed as they were by ill-shaven cheeks covered in black stubble. "Mind what I tell you," he said, shaking a finger before whistling at his horse. "The world's designed for men, so you're pretty much buggered." He swung onto his nag and perused the sky.

A sharp throb diverted Morrigan's attention as she untangled herself from the gorse. She knew what it was even before she looked. A thorn, embedded in her right index finger.

She pried it out, watching a crimson drop of blood balloon from the puncture.

When the gorse is not in flower, love is out of season. So the saying went.

Instead of calling him some name he would only laugh at, she heard herself say, "Is that the way of love then, bonny, sweet, yet ready to sting when you least expect?"

He looked puzzled until he saw the blood. "If you don't get home to your chores, you'll never have the chance to find out." His ready grin held a hint of devilry, as though he half-hoped she would defy their da and his temper.

"I'll be back before the train comes. Stay, Nicky. I'll read you the tale of the labyrinth, and the black Minotaur. There's plenty of time."

"Jesus, one of these days you'll fancy yourself Helen of Troy and we'll have to put you in an asylum." He leaned towards her. "Truth is, your head is full of mince. You're far more trouble than use." He shrugged. "Don't greet to me about your bruised backside. You make your own bad fortune like you cannot bear a day of peace."

That was Nicky, always trying to protect her from their father's wrath. But in the end, he never told her what to do. He let her make her own choices.

As he galloped away, Morrigan opened her satchel and pulled out her beloved, dog-eared book, *A Translated Greek Mythology*. She settled on the grassy slope overlooking Loch Ryan, glancing with appreciation at the water's indigo surface. "In truth, I'd love a day of peace," she said, studying the sky, where a rosy blush trellised the eastern horizon, sweet with promise. It couldn't yet be seven. The first train, on the Port Road from Castle Douglas, didn't arrive till eight-thirty. Papa was in his fields, where he went every morning before dawn. As long as she made it home before him, he would never know she'd left at all.

Widdie pricked her ears and nickered after Morrigan's brother. The sound was half-wistful, and the way the mare swung her head around and stared at Morrigan suggested reproof. Oh, she was imagining too much again. A reproving horse? Nicky loved to claim pagan faery blood ran through his sister's veins, and this was what caused folk to stare at her in confusion half the time, lifting their eyebrows and giving each other those *I told you, didn't I* glances.

Sometimes it did feel like she'd come from the stars rather than the Highlands. Perhaps she suffered from insanity as Nicky often suggested...but she preferred to think herself possessed by magic spells.

Maybe Hannah Stewart Lawton had been in truth a faery, a changeling...a witch. That would explain Papa's reasoning in never allowing anyone to speak of her, or of their old life in the North Country. Could she be living up there still, enchanting virile men in the forest, making them forget their pious Christian roots? Maybe, just maybe, the sorceress had managed to bequeath a few fey tricks to her daughter. Tricks the wild girl who lived inside Morrigan used often enough. That hidden, depraved lass caused nothing but trouble for hapless Morrigan, daring her to while away hours on the cliffs and moor and goading her into flirting with the lads in town. The girl's fierce voice proclaimed these rules and constraints no more than muck to be shoveled away. The two Morrigans battled incessantly, the secret one haranguing her to mischief, while the other, the outer Morrigan, longed to make everyone, especially Douglas, happy and proud.

Impossible task. No one could please him.

Morrigan opened the book and ran her fingers over the faded lettering.

Papa's sister, Isabel, had given it to her on her tenth birthday. The title page held a message, written in fine, trembly script.

> *Someone once called you the finest miracle I'll ever see, and I've come to believe it. I was told yours is the name of a goddess, dear Morrigan. So here is a book about Greek gods and goddesses. Perhaps you will see yourself in these ancient tales.*

Page sixty-seven, to which the book opened naturally, carried the chapter heading "Theseus and the Minotaur of Crete." Though she'd read it hundreds of times, the names *Theseus, Minotaur,* and *Crete* still awakened a faint involuntary shiver.

Theseus was young, the account began, *when shipped along with six other youths and seven maidens to the isle of Crete as slave-payment to King Minos. These doomed prisoners were to be fed to the gruesome Minotaur—half-man, half-bull, the product of an ungodly physical union between Minos's wife, Pasiphaë, and a magnificent white bull sent by the god Poseidon.*

Morrigan pictured the scene: lasses weeping as dark-skinned Cretan soldiers prodded them onto the vessel. Heroic Theseus, though, would never give in to such weakness.

Chewing on a fibrous stem of grass, she rested her head in the crook of one arm, hearing the enticing murmur of weeds. *Stay…relax…dream.* She closed her eyes and slipped into the old familiar fantasy of beloved Greek characters and their grand adventures.

The Athenian prince swaggered off the Cretan pier, not bothering to hide his contempt. Among those watching was Minos's daughter, Princess Ariadne, who would soon fall in love with this barbarian from the northern lands. Could she help it, when moonlight and magic brought a god's statue to life, transforming it into the foreigner's likeness? As it crossed the clearing it changed from cold marble to living man, and this man lay upon her like a lover. *For longer than you can imagine,* he promised, *I will be with you, in you, of you. Together we bring forth a new world, and nothing will ever part us. Aridela, open your heart.*

Morrigan settled more comfortably into her grassy nest. The statue called the princess Aridela, not Ariadne. Yet Morrigan knew it was no mistake. Aridela was the older name, the origin from which transpired the fable of Ariadne. She also knew, though she couldn't remember how, that Aridela's father was listed in the oracle logs as Damasen, royal consort who met his death bravely, that her mother was Helice, renowned queen of Crete, and her sister the courageous Iphiboë.

Morrigan loved to pretend she was Aridela, her hair no longer giving hints of unlucky auburn highlights but black as night-sky, her eyes not brown but exotic ebony, lined with a substance that made them appear mysterious and seductive. As Aridela, she watched the marble statue transmute into a living being. How wonderful he felt, stone warming into smooth flesh against hers, breath ardent and sweet on her cheek. She would love him forever. For as long as wayfaring stars sailed the midnight sky.

For as long as the pyramids stand in Egypt.

Morrigan scrambled from her springy bed, blinking to clear her sight. The hillside was empty but for her pony and a foraging pair of linnets, which flew up, crying in alarm at the human's sudden movement.

She must have fallen asleep and dreamed the words…but they'd sounded clear and close, as if a man spoke right next to her. Maybe the loch washing against the shore had done it. The sea could make uncanny sounds.

Reassured, she lay back in the grass and closed her eyes. It was a bonny saying. Aye, the princess would love her Theseus that long, maybe longer.

She sighed. Now she was in an arena. Hot sand burned the soles of her feet. Rising onto her toes, she ran, buoyed with the lightness of a butterfly, the swift danger of a wasp. The gate creaked behind her. A snort, heavy and challenging, was followed by the thud of massive hooves. *Aridela!* the people thundered.

She turned, laughing. The bull trotted into view. *Her* bull. It pawed the sand and lowered its head.

The crowd's chants lengthened into a continuous roar as she ran towards her destiny, what her people called *moera*.

The bull's breath heated her face then vanished as she soared, propelled by the upward jerk of his head. She turned a graceful somersault, losing herself in the rush of wind. Everything slowed. Cheers echoed, fading into an angry snort that reverberated through her eardrums. There was an instant of vertigo as the sky yawed below and sand stretched above. Then she righted herself, landing on the bull's hindquarters, her toes searching for hold in its bristly hair. She made a quick, final leap into the arms of her primped and painted half brother, who placed her safely on the ground and made a grand flourish to impress the audience. What was his name? *Isandros.*

The cheering and foot-stomping intensified until she thought the bullring would collapse. Only her mother, the queen, refused to join in.

Aridela…Aridela…Daugh…terrrrr of the Calesssiennnda!

Morrigan started, blinking against bright light striking her full in the face. There it came again. Shrill, accusatory, the whistle shivered over the moor, announcing the train as it raced to Stranraer. She should be at the Wren's Egg, helping Aunt Beatrice prepare breakfast. If hungry travelers came to the inn and she wasn't there, her da would be furious.

But what did it matter? He was always furious, no matter what she did.

Widdie nuzzled her cheek with damp, grass-stained nostrils. "We're late."

Morrigan rose, brushing at the weeds and thistle clinging to her wool skirt. The sky had gone as pale as a shallow bowl of water. Looking at it, she knew with a sinking sense of dread that she would be flayed livid.

She mounted her pony and headed for the inn on Neptune Street. Then she paused. She was already damned. Why not make a pleasant memory for later, after the thrashing?

Kicking the mare to a gallop, she careened along the ridge above the loch, pretending she and Theseus were escaping enemy soldiers, making for a ship that would carry them to a secret bothy on the hazy isle of Ailsa Craig, where none would ever find them.

"Hurry or they'll catch us," she cried, looking over her shoulder at imaginary pursuers.

A gust of wind tugged at her green velvet hat, the one Aunt Isabel had given her last November for her eighteenth birthday. It flew into the air, long plaid ribbons fluttering.

Morrigan pulled up the mare and jumped off, but the hat dropped away to Loch Ryan. It would be a dangerously slick climb to retrieve it.

"Feck! Damn this bloody wind!" If Aunt Beatrice heard her speak such language, she'd rip every last hair from her head and slap her raw, but Morrigan went on spouting the words she often heard her brother and his comrades use. That hat was her favorite.

There it lay, on a narrow stretch of beach, against a stone. A grey seal gave it a curious sniff before tidewater reached out, grabbed it, and dragged the wretched thing into the loch.

Premonition crawled through her spine. The seal gazed up at her.

Come to me.

Morrigan pivoted in a breathless circle. There was nothing but waving grass, gorse, and thistle.

I need you.

She closed her eyes, hard, and when she opened them, gasped at the shimmering, almost transparent image of a man standing where the seal had been. His white knee-length tunic, topped by a leather cuirass, fluttered at the hem. Sunlight glinted against the hilt of a sword at his waist. One hand rested on his chest, and waving golden hair framed an uncompromising, sun-bronzed face. He seemed to stare directly at her.

The sea claims final possession, and leaves nothing behind.

Morrigan clapped her hands over her ears, shut her eyes, and counted to ten. When she opened them, she saw nothing but bright sunlight and a network of spider web clouds. There was the seal, rubbing its nose with one flipper. Loch Ryan washed against the shore and a curlew called sadly. It was a typical country scene, no different from a hundred other mornings.

She'd heard no voice. Wind, swirling through weeds, had fooled her. As if in confirmation, the seal barked as seals do, not sounding remotely human, and slid into the sea.

For years Morrigan had wondered if other people dreamed like she did, of places, people, and events that often left her twisting in her bedclothes and waking in a sweat. She never asked, for she was too afraid of being locked away in some ghastly place with mad folk.

She'd heard those words before, but never so clearly. She'd dreamed of that man, too, with his long golden hair and green eyes. They could be pitiless or tender, depending on his mood. *Theseus,* she'd long ago started calling him: magnificent, larger-than-life barbarian from Greek fable. Whenever she experienced the dream, she longed for…something. Her arms felt empty. Her heart ached. She knew none of it was real, but the beloved dream gave comfort, something to wish for.

She could almost believe, though she'd never even been kissed, that out there in the enormous, fathomless world, love waited. Impatient, ardent love. It came from a honey-haired man, who searched for her, called to her, spoke to her deepest recesses. When, *if,* he found her, he would snatch her out of this unhappy life. He would give her a castle with turrets that punctured the clouds. He would banish the demons from her soul.

The sea had sucked away her hat, but Morrigan felt it would like to seize her as well, yank her into its abysmal, inscrutable reaches.

Come to me, her dream-lover urged. *I've waited so long.*

Oh, find me, her heart cried. *I need you, too!*

Curran Ramsay stifled a sigh of boredom. How he'd managed to get roped into being Isabel MacLean's traveling companion quite escaped him. Somehow she'd contrived it, the moment she'd glimpsed him yesterday at the Glasgow station and waved her handkerchief, screeching to draw his attention. He remembered having a fondness for her, and he hadn't seen her in…well, he couldn't remember the last time. He knew her husband had died. No doubt she was lonely. He should invite her to Kilgarry for a change of scene. But she never stopped talking, and this morning, he found listening to her with the required expression of interest almost too exhausting to bear.

If only they'd met some other day. He would have dealt with it in a much more gentlemanly fashion. Today, however, he was thickheaded, bleary after a night of disruptions, moments of rest interrupted by long stretches of a persistent dream, or nightmare. He'd spent most of the night tossing and turning, and had to lock his jaw to keep from yawning in her face.

He'd planned to hide behind a copy of the *Dundee Courier* and spend the journey dismembering the dream. It always began with a spiraling sensation, like he'd been pushed into a hole or over a cliff, and was falling end over end. Then he would see himself carrying a child up out of the ground, a young girl bleeding profusely from a wound in the stomach. The staircase seemed endless, the girl's eyes huge in a pinched little face, and his feet were so heavy he could hardly lift them. He always kissed her forehead in an effort to reassure her, and to hide how terrified he was that she might expire in his arms. Sometimes the dream ended there as he hurtled out of sleep, gasping. Other times it continued, with him running into a large open space, being surrounded by men and women, all shouting in a language he couldn't begin to understand. They'd rip the child from him and carry her away, leaving him trapped by soldiers who held sharp blades against his throat.

That particular dream never went any farther. He never knew if the child lived or died. Maybe it was the not knowing that filled him with this awful sense of guilt.

"I sold the gown to the lady and she showed it to her kin and acquaintances. I have so many orders coming in I may have to hire an assistant. What d'you think of that, Mr. Ramsay?"

"What? Oh...aye, Mrs. Maclean, it's bonny news. You'll soon be designing ballgowns for the royal family."

Her gaze narrowed, making him fear he'd said something wrong. "I swear you look as though you've lost your home and livelihood. Where is it you're off to, again?"

With determined effort, he smiled. "Larne, Mrs. Maclean, to buy a puppy. The owner has promised to hold the best of the litter for me. And what of you? You said you're traveling to Stranraer?"

As easily distracted as a two-year-old, she said, "Aye, to visit my brother, my nephew, and my niece. My brother is Douglas Lawton. He's an innkeeper now, you might recall. Your papa arranged for the fee, mind?"

"Of course, I do remember Mr. Lawton. I hope they are well?"

"Indeed they are. Thank you for asking."

The time passed sluggishly as Mrs. Maclean waxed into ecstatic descriptions of how breathtaking her niece had become and what a prodigy she was with music. "She first sat at a piano when she was three," Isabel claimed, "and played complex pieces of music by simply listening to others perform. It's truly astounding." She continued with stories of her braw young nephew, and how desperately frustrated she was by her brother's refusal to allow his children any of the finer graces in life. He'd even cut off Morrigan's music instruction, though Isabel was the one paying for it. It was a crime against art! She told Curran she often traveled to Stranraer to give the wee things a diversion from their perpetual chores. Douglas treated them like servants, slaves, or hired hands, and she was not exaggerating.

He forced himself to pay attention, to nod, smile, agree when it was needed, and to show the proper concern at the dreary life her niece and nephew were forced to live. His memories of Douglas Lawton's children were blurry; all he could picture was a vague image of his mother fawning over the infant.

"Is that hurting, Mr. Ramsay?" She pointed to the scar by his eye. "You're rubbing it rather vigorously."

He hadn't realized. The scar did hurt. Truthfully, he could hardly see through the haze of pain, and drew his fingers away prepared for blood, but there wasn't any. He couldn't remember the last time the old wound had caused such discomfort—not for years, not since the attack in the desolate wilds up by Loch Torridon. He'd always been self-conscious about the disfigurement, though it wasn't so bad—a simple defect that sliced through the outer edge of his left eyebrow and curved in a crescent shape past his eye to end at the top of his cheekbone. Women seemed to find it fascinating.

This had been a long journey. He was tired, and would be grateful to get home again. Maybe it was the pain that caused him to voice such an ignorant statement. As soon as the words left his mouth, he wished he could unsay them, but, of course, it was too late.

"I am lost, Mrs. Maclean. I often have this feeling, but it's much worse today." As he spoke, he thought of the other dream, for it, too, involved a scar. In this dream, he held a woman. He lifted her hand and turned it, kissing an odd, reddish mark on the inside of her wrist, a scar of some kind, or a blemish left by an old burn. The woman pulled him closer, saying, *Kiss me. Kiss me again.* He never could recall her face when he woke, though he spent countless hours trying, and couldn't be sure if this was someone he knew, or a fabrication shaped wholly in his head.

Simply thinking of it made his heart speed up and shortened his breathing. He turned away from the prim and proper Isabel MacLean, carefully refolding the newspaper on his lap while tamping down an almost overwhelming erotic hunger.

Thankfully, before she had a chance to give him stern, commonsense platitudes about the healing power of tea and toast, and how one must never eat cheese before bed, or how he needed a wife to be happy, the train whistle blared, disintegrating the last remnants of desire.

They'd arrived in Stranraer.

Chapter 2

"Morrigan! Morrigan Lawton!"

An insistent, rather braying voice carried over the rush and bustle of busy townsfolk, arriving passengers, and resting growl of the train engine. Reining in Widdie, Morrigan glanced over her shoulder.

"Here…over here!"

A white square handkerchief waved, vanished behind a group of tall, solemn-frocked gentlemen, then reappeared as they passed.

She squinted. A short, squat woman, dwarfed by an enormous feathered hat. Why, it was Aunt Isabel, Papa's sister from the Highlands.

Morrigan wheeled her mount. She'd be even later getting home, but it couldn't be helped. Maybe the arrival of his only sister would soothe Papa's anger.

As Morrigan dismounted, brushing hair out of her eyes, Isabel pulled her into an exuberant, perfumed hug, released her, and gave her a thorough examination, going so far as to turn her niece in a circle.

"Where is your hat? How many times must I remind you that a lady never goes out with her head uncovered? And will you look at this? We'll be hours on these snarls. You're seventeen, Morrigan, a lady of marriageable—"

"Eighteen, Auntie, I'm halfway to nineteen—"

"Old enough to mind a hat, then. I've made you enough to suit a countess. Surely one of them appeals. There is simply no excuse. Why has Beatrice allowed you to ride out half dressed?"

Humiliation burned Morrigan's cheeks as the last departing passengers sent varying glances of disapproval or amusement her way. Aunt Isabel's voice tended to carry.

"I left before she woke up. And I love the hats you've made me, Aunt Ibby. I love them, truly."

"You need to spend more time with that lass, what's her name…Enid. She could teach you a thing or two about the habits of a proper lady."

Morrigan sighed. Enid Joyce was blessed with wealth, an impressive home, and, as she often boasted, an introduction to the queen's youngest daughter. Her finest accomplishment in Morrigan's opinion was a tongue so sour it could blacken a pickle, and she used it freely to belittle others. Aunt Isabel, forced to take up a trade after the death of her husband, had become a seamstress, and did quite well. For years, she'd showered her niece with fine, hand-sewn clothing. This had drawn Enid's scrutiny to one she never would have deigned to notice otherwise. Over the last three years or so, Stranraer's bachelor gentlemen had begun to openly admire the innkeeper's daughter, they being so much less discriminating than Enid. In response, Enid's castigation had escalated into the righteous outrage of the wellborn against peasants who dared ape their betters.

Morrigan thought it best to move on to another topic. "Does Papa know you've come?"

"No." Isabel's stern expression melted into an unpretentious smile. "It's a surprise. I've brought a friend, and he's fair anxious to meet you. Now where's that lad gone off to? He was right behind me a moment ago."

Morrigan's thorn-pricked finger stung. She stuck it in her mouth, tasting bitter remnants of yellow gorse and the slightest mineral hint of blood.

"Did you see where my traveling companion went?" Isabel asked a nearby porter.

"No, mum." The man was blandly polite, yet Morrigan caught the brief narrowing of his eyes, the flicker of annoyance. *I have no idea who your companion is, and moreover, I do not care,* his frown suggested.

Isabel, oblivious to such subtleties, replied tartly, "Well, help me find him. We don't have all day to stand about. And where is my trunk?"

The porter half-ran to keep up with Isabel's rotund figure as she hurried along the platform, chastising him all the way.

"She's a remarkable lady, your aunt."

Morrigan turned towards the nearest car. A figure stood there, still and dark, little more than an outline. The fine hairs along the edge of her scalp lifted, and she hastily removed her finger from her mouth, tucking it behind her. "Aye," she replied.

"You must be Miss Lawton." His voice reminded her of how a field of barley whispered in a warm breeze.

Thinking something had gone wrong with her sight, she blinked. A mist of color surrounded the being on the step, like a rainbow glimmering through watery clouds, but this rainbow offered only the blue spectrum, with hints of violet.

She managed to contain a desire to reach out and ruffle the colors like the surface of a pool. "I am," she said, taking a half step backward. There was nothing to fear. She heard her aunt berating the porter a few cars away. Nevertheless…. She lifted one brow. "How d'you know that, sir?"

"Forgive me." He descended the steps. A shaft of sunlight, finding its way through a hole in the station's wood and glass ceiling, pinned him in a halo of light.

For one instant that seemed unending, the world stopped. The train engine's pant faded into the overpowering pulse of her blood.

"Beg your pardon, Miss Lawton?"

The words sank into her brain as though slogging through mud. "Wha-what?"

"Did you say, 'Theseus'?"

For an instant more, she remained trapped in muffling cotton. Then the world burst apart. Her heart lurched. A surge, what a lightning bolt must feel like, streaked through her, almost drawing her up on tiptoe, as though she'd lain dormant her whole life until now. She wasn't at all certain her heart could handle the strain. Along with a thousand other mental pictures, gone too quick to make any sense of, she saw herself clutch her chest, fall, and expire, right before the physical embodiment of her long-cherished illusion.

A breeze lifted his unruly blond hair, fair begging for a woman's smoothing hand. Supple skin, mouth curving on one side, bringing out a playful dimple. Alert twilight blue eyes beneath dark brows, hinting at confidences and merriment he'd like to share. Clean-shaven. Five and twenty? Older perhaps, the direct gaze and confident stance hinted; maybe younger, said the unlined skin, riotous hair and generous mouth.

Her frozen muscles grew hot and began to tremble. *Daftie. He's a man, not a Greek hero come to life.*

"Miss Lawton, are you well?" He stepped closer, lifting a hand as though in contemplation of grasping her shoulder.

Her gaze locked on a scar marring his otherwise perfect face, curving around his left eye. It was shaped like a miniature crescent moon, or one of those Moslem curved swords: a scimitar. "Aye, I'm well, Mr.—Mr.?"

"Ramsay." He inclined his head. "Curran Ramsay."

"You're the…my aunt's traveling companion?"

"I had that pleasure, aye."

"There you are, Mr. Ramsay." Isabel's voice intruded with the hearty insistence of a magpie. "I've located our bags. Have you met my niece?"

"If this young lady is your niece, Mrs. Maclean."

Throughout her aunt's dialogue, Mr. Ramsay kept his gaze on Morrigan. The undisguised admiration in those vivid blue eyes helped her dismiss the notion that in her many ardent reveries, she had always created her hero with eyes of green. She supposed she was like most females, and couldn't resist a man canny enough to reveal his appreciation.

The strange colors that had sparkled around him were gone, banished perhaps by the light of the sun. He smiled as though he and Morrigan shared some private, affectionate joke about Aunt Ibby, and Morrigan's knees turned to butter. The smile was angelic, yet to charm her so, it must be diabolical. She clamped down on her wayward thoughts, fearful of spouting more half-witted nonsense. *Theseus.* For the sake of blessed pity, had she really said that out loud?

"And is she not all I claimed?"

"Indeed, Mrs. Maclean, you failed to do her justice."

Morrigan glanced from the gentleman to her smirking aunt and thought her cheeks might erupt in flames.

"Mr. Ramsay's an acquaintance of yours, my dear, though you couldn't possibly remember. He hails from Glenelg."

She returned her scrutiny to him. Light glanced off his gold tiepin, a fancy scrolled "CR," one wee diamond separating the two letters.

No, she could not have actually met and forgotten this sun god, the male who'd haunted her daydreams for as long as she'd been alive. Everything about him seemed to shout, *I am here to rescue you.*

She cleared her throat. "Aye?" Her voice sounded faint and tinny through the drumbeat of blood in her ears. *Theseus.* In the flesh. The golden dream-lover.

Yet he wasn't exactly the same. His hair wasn't nearly as long, and he was dressed like any other proper gentleman, in striped trousers, tie, and waistcoat, not in leather armor and greaves. She nearly laughed out loud as she imagined what would happen in conservative Stranraer if a man stepped off the train adorned in such a costume. Now that she put cold logic to it, she realized he didn't resemble the hero in her fantasy, really, except for the color of his hair. She must have been half asleep, still floating in her dream spell, to think it. The stench of acrid smoke, windblown rubbish, and sullen porters were returning her to common sense and drab reality.

There was no denying though, that part of her longed for him to exclaim his own happy knowledge, to clasp her in his arms and refuse to let her go.

But he merely bowed like every other gentleman she'd ever been introduced to. "Pleased to meet you, Miss Lawton."

"And I you, Mr. Ramsay." She'd never worked so hard to keep her voice steady.

Isabel tugged Morrigan towards the street. "Will you join us, Mr. Ramsay? Come and break your fast at my brother's inn."

"I'd love to," he said.

She gave the porter detailed instructions on what to do with their luggage then swept towards Stranraer proper, heels clicking on the cobblestones. "D'you care if we walk?" she asked. "It's only a bit up the road and I feel the need to stretch my legs."

"Certainly." Mr. Ramsay took Widdie's reins and offered Morrigan his arm. His left brow came up, causing two horizontal lines to crease his forehead, and elongating the crescent scar.

What would it be like…to touch it?

She curled her hand obediently around his forearm, hoping he couldn't feel her nervousness through his coat sleeve.

Enid Joyce, enthroned on the seat of a shining victoria drawn by two matched bays, chose that moment to pass. Her well-fitted jacket, strung with lace, accented an hourglass figure. Blue eyes, beneath a head of perfectly coiffed hair, narrowed as the lass observed her rival so neatly ensconced on the arm of this handsome stranger.

Morrigan had almost forgotten her shortcomings beneath Ramsay's admiring regard. Now she remembered her bare head, snarled braid, and bitten fingernails. Her homespun dress, still littered with a few stubborn stickseeds and patches of dust, offered evidence of her time in the wild, and she was sure she smelled of horse. Next to Enid's slim figure, Morrigan felt as cumbersome as an elephant seal. She shriveled, much like a blossom left too long without water.

Of course Aunt Isabel had to pause and say good morning. Enid replied with easy smiling grace, as though she and Morrigan were lifelong comrades. The lass displayed her saucy dimple and for good measure fluttered long black lashes as she extended a hand encased in a lace-trimmed glove.

"Now there's a born lady," Isabel said as Enid ordered her driver on. "See how her parasol draws attention to her hat? You'd never catch *her* without a hat."

Perhaps she noticed how her niece flinched, for she patted Morrigan's shoulder, adding, "Still, you've a charm she lacks. I cannot put a name to it, really…." She gave their companion a roguish wink. "Don't you agree, sir?"

"Aye, indeed," he replied. "A most intriguing and singular charm."

Isabel's face exuded satisfaction, and Morrigan realized what was truly going on. Her aunt had dragged this poor, unsuspecting fellow here, using trickery, no doubt, for the sole purpose of meeting her. She'd die if he perceived he was being paraded as a candidate for marriage. His fine suit proclaimed his wealth and his manner of speech almost screamed *expensive education.* Heaven knew what Isabel thought he'd find appealing in a penniless innkeeper's daughter who'd only been allowed eight years in an unpolished, rural school.

She lowered her face to hide her mortification.

Aunt Isabel would drag Crown Prince Edward himself to Morrigan's door if she could manage it. Aye, she would.

And no doubt she would expect the prince to display humble appreciation over his good fortune, since he was, after all, naught but a damned Englishman.

—————————————————

Chapter 3

—————————————————

"Where the devil have you been?"

It took all of Morrigan's will to keep from seizing her skirts and running at the sight of Douglas Lawton's scowl. His eyes were as icy as half-melted slush.

"Widdie n-needed a run. I meant to be home sooner."

Mr. Ramsay's arm tightened, squeezing her hand against his ribs. The gesture lent her a momentary sense of courage, and was accompanied by a feeling of sparks, like wool blankets being rubbed together.

"I waylaid her at the train station and made her wait for us," Isabel snapped. "Are you no' going to acknowledge that I'm here?"

His brows lifted. No one in his own household would ever dare speak to him in such a tone. "I see that you're here, Isabel," he said, and bent so his sister could kiss his cheek, but the scowl remained, lingering so pointedly on his daughter's hand resting upon the gentleman's forearm that she released it and stepped away.

Isabel's love of drama was clearly on display. "See who I've brought? It's—"

"I've no' gone blind," said Douglas. The two men shook hands. "You've changed. Grown into your height."

"It's good to see you again, Mr. Lawton, and doing so well for yourself," Ramsay said.

Morrigan stared. They knew each other. Aunt Isabel had claimed this Mr. Ramsay knew her, too.

Could she have formed her imaginary hero from forgotten memories of

Curran Ramsay? Perhaps it would all come clear in time if she kept her mouth shut and her ears open.

Beatrice appeared at the front door, stout, firmly corseted, her grey hair pinched into a bun, a white apron covering her ample breasts and stomach. "Your breakfast is going stone cold." She paused, observing the newcomers with no change in her dour countenance. "I see you've come again, Isabel."

The lift of one brow and subtle emphasis on the word *again* revealed Beatrice's annoyance. Her aunt had said it out loud more than once. *Why does she come here so often? Extra cooking, extra cleaning. Don't we have enough to do?*

Isabel ascended the steps, holding out her arms. The women embraced briefly, without much warmth. "How I've missed all of you," Isabel said. "Mallaig is too lonely and quiet without my Gregor." She turned to Mr. Ramsay. "Mind you Beatrice Stewart? She makes a grand kidney pie, Mr. Ramsay."

"Good day, Mrs. Stewart," Ramsay said, smiling. "It's a pleasure to see you again."

Beatrice frowned as she regarded the stranger, then she blinked as she recognized him.

"Aye," Isabel said, "it really is the same pale skinny lad. He's turned out well, eh? No longer all elbows and shinbones."

Morrigan's maternal aunt quickly regained her composure. "You thought he might turn out poorly?" she said. "I didn't."

"Come, sir," Isabel said.

Ramsay handed the mare's reins to Morrigan. "I hope you'll join us," he said.

She kept silent, her father's fury bombarding her like a tangible thing.

Isabel waved the gentleman up the steps and led the way inside, rambling on without pause.

Hoping to escape, Morrigan brought Widdie around, but as she did, the satchel slipped off her shoulder; *A Translated Greek Mythology* slid out and fell to the ground. A gust of wind ruffled the pages, causing Widdie to snort and prance. Morrigan tried to quiet her, which gave Douglas time to retrieve the book. Smearing the cover with his grimy fingers, he looked at it then his gaze lifted to Morrigan. She pressed into the pony's solid, comforting side.

"So this is what you were doing. Leaving Beatrice to prepare breakfast alone."

She said nothing, knowing better. Inwardly, she gave thanks that she and Nicky had left their wooden swords by Loch Ryan, under a stone. Outwardly, she appeared contrite.

"Get your bloody arse inside." He jerked Widdie's reins out of her hand and looped them around the post. "Lazy glaikit."

His calling her names wasn't anything new, but what would he do to her precious book? No doubt he was jealous, since he'd never been taught how to read, and couldn't decipher more than the simplest script.

Her sneaked morning rides had always vexed him, but today he was like a boiling thunderstorm. She couldn't decide what had set him off. Isabel's arrival? The gentleman friend?

It's you. The mere sight of you is all it takes.

Misbegotten leeches, he called women. *What use have they ever been?*

The wild, secret Morrigan spoke up. *Well, if it weren't for women, how would males get their precious rose-scented arses onto the earth?*

They probably had an answer for that, as well.

Bacon, eggs, and deviled kidneys filled the dining room with a delicious, crackly-hot scent. Morrigan poured tea into china cups, holding herself stiff as wood beneath the paternal stare boring through her scalp.

With the excuse, "I must tend my cakes," Beatrice vanished into the kitchen.

"Mr. Ramsay's away to Ireland," Isabel said, spooning eggs onto a plate. "He's aye kindled about some dog."

"Sometimes I race them," Ramsay said, "but mostly I breed them and sell the pups. A lad I know in Dungarvan deals in greyhounds descended from Master McGrath."

"Oh, aye?" Morrigan said without thinking. "The three-time winner of the Waterloo cup?"

Ramsay rewarded her knowledge with an appreciative smile. "That's the one."

Laughter crinkled the skin around his eyes and deepened winsome lines on either side of his mouth. He seemed to savor every aspect of life. When had she ever enjoyed anything half this much?

She'd swear a June morning sat on one side of the dining room while a January blizzard darkened the other.

Could laughter be as contagious as fear…as catching as the dread and misery in this place?

"You'll take the new ferry," she said, solemn-faced, holding on with both fists to cool reserve, as Beatrice had taught her she must always do. "The *Princess Louise.*"

"I've read about it." Mr. Ramsay glanced from her to her father, his brows creasing into the slightest frown. "I hear it makes the crossing in less than three hours." He sat at the table with a small helping of bacon and eggs, and sipped the tea Morrigan had poured for him.

Douglas Lawton remained in the doorway, a sickle dangling from one dirty hand. Morrigan, who had several more books of Greek myths tucked away under her bed, thought he looked uncannily like Charon, the ferryman who rafted dead people across River Styx.

"Douglas, will you have your breakfast?" Isabel gestured to a chair. "You're making my flesh creep, standing there like that. My brother seldom takes time for conversation," she added. "He's fair preoccupied with his crops. From the look of him, he's labored since before sunrise, and seems to have forgotten about washing before coming into a dining room."

Grey irises glittered between a wealth of black lashes as Douglas stared at his sister. He looked as though he might be contemplating throwing her across the room.

Not for the first time, Morrigan wished Isabel possessed more tact. One would think his own sister would know he often vented his rage on those who hadn't necessarily annoyed him. Well, Ibby was eight years younger. Douglas had already taken a fee to support his mother and sister while Ibby was still a suckling babe.

She continued on, unaware or uncaring. "And I expect you'll begrudge me any time with your children, though I've come all this way. Where is Nick?"

"In the fields, where he is every morning. We haven't a woman's leisure."

She snorted. "I daresay leisure is something Morrigan and Beatrice would find unfamiliar. Go on, then." She gave a dismissive wave. "But be warned, I'll steal them when you're no' looking. I'll force them to giggle, sing, and dance, and think of anything other than toil."

Douglas's jaw clenched. He turned, but before he left, he sent Morrigan a glance she couldn't decipher. On anyone else she might have named it uncertainty, but she didn't imagine her father capable of such an emotion.

Why was he leaving? He hadn't yet had anything to eat. Somehow this was her fault, she knew it.

"He works them half to death," Isabel grumbled, then seized Morrigan's hand and pulled her into a chair. "Mr. Ramsay has a grand old manor house in the hills outside of Glenelg. It's called Kilgarry. You can see the turrets from the Sound."

"Aye?"

"The estate borders Glenelg to the south," he said. "The central tower is one of those drafty old keeps, built by the Macleods in the 1600s, but various owners added onto either end, and my father updated it as well. It's fairly modern now."

"I'll never forget the *cèilidh* of…1860, wasn't it?" Isabel said. "It was the only time we returned to Glenelg after the troubles, and the last time we were fortunate enough to see your dear father and mother."

"Oh, aye," Ramsay said. "There was a snowstorm, and everyone stayed until the roads were passable. We made a bonny long holiday of it."

Isabel nodded, smiling. "Thomas Ramsay—" she leaned closer to Morrigan to say, "that's Mr. Ramsay's father—loved to throw parties, especially at

Christmas. Kilgarry's windows reflected the sunlight as we sailed by, like great diamonds...."

Strange, the expression in Isabel's eyes. Sad. "What's wrong, Auntie?"

"Nothing." Yet Isabel's fingers tightened against Morrigan's, and a tear spilled over her plump cheek.

"Auntie?" Morrigan jumped to her feet.

Ramsay stood too, proffering a handkerchief from his waistcoat pocket.

Morrigan rubbed her aunt's hand. "Are you ill? Shall I call Beatrice?"

Isabel wiped her cheek. "Of course not. I'm a daft old woman, giving childhood recollections more power than they deserve."

"Can I do anything, Mrs. Maclean?" Ramsay seemed truly concerned.

"No," she said. "I mind Glenelg, you know, and my childhood. Forgive me, both of you."

"They weren't happy years," he said. "Perhaps they're best forgotten."

"Were such a thing possible," Isabel snapped. "None but a soul who'd not lived through that would suggest they could be."

Ramsay's face revealed his anxiety and regret.

"Nevertheless," Ibby continued, "I've a few cherished memories. You'd be surprised. Though we were poor, often hungry, we enjoyed good times before the coming of the sheep. We'd sing the most outlandish ditties. Lasses learned much of life from those songs...." Waving the handkerchief, she added, "Your grandmother used to send me to scratch dulse off the sea rocks to flavor the soup. It gave a nice salty flavor. But after the clearings, for days and days, dulse was the only thing we could find to eat. It got aye wearisome, I'll tell you, and was scarcely what you'd call filling."

"What does Mr. Ramsay know of your childhood?" Morrigan hadn't missed the color blooming in their guest's face. "And how did sheep destroy your good times?"

"I apologize, Mr. Ramsay." Isabel returned his handkerchief. "My niece doesn't know a thing of course, being an infant at the time. My brother's never told her what happened. He won't allow anyone to speak of Glenelg or those awful days. Maybe he doesn't want her to be sad. He seems a harsh man, but I remember him before...when he was young, married to Nicky's mother. I still believe there is a good heart in him, buried deep down inside."

She patted Morrigan's cheek. "Life was hard in those cold mountains, as Mr. Ramsay knows. He was only seven when Thomas moved them to Glenelg, and just eighteen when his father slipped away, isn't that right, sir?"

"Aye," he agreed softly.

"You lost your folk too soon." Her eyes refilled with sympathetic tears. "Mr. Ramsay is a fine example of an indomitable spirit. Not yet twenty-six, but responsible for an estate, a shipping business, and, I might add, the livelihood of a good number of folk."

"Mrs. Maclean, please. You flatter me."

"No more than you deserve." Squeezing Morrigan's hand, she said, "Tea, that's what I need. Pour me another cup, would you, child? I can't wait to show you the hat I brought. It has a plume of ostrich feathers. Lord knows where you'll wear it. Oh, and will you play for Mr. Ramsay? I bragged about you all the way from Glasgow. Chopin...everyone loves your Chopin." She sent their guest a speculative glance. "No doubt you thought I exaggerated, Mr. Ramsay, but I can prove it. My niece possesses a gift from the angels, as you'll hear for yourself."

Though Isabel's cheery personality had rebounded, Ramsay's constraint remained. "The ferry departs too soon for me to appreciate Miss Lawton's playing," he said, consulting his pocket watch. "Perhaps when I return...?"

What secrets did Aunt Isabel, this man, and her father share? Mr. Ramsay appeared too distressed to ask, but Morrigan vowed she'd get the tale from her aunt at the first opportunity.

"I'd best check on Beatrice," Morrigan said. "I should've helped with breakfast, but...." She shrugged and made her escape.

The scent of a golden-white bannock, cooling on the worktable, sent her stomach growling. Beatrice was washing dishes out of sight in the scullery, so she gouged a chunk from the edge and bit into it. Light as a cloud, warm and yeasty, it melted like butter on her tongue.

Before she could filch more, her aunt appeared in the doorway, wet skillet in hand. "Why d'you test your father's patience, again and again?" she said, frowning. "I'm beginning to think you enjoy being strapped."

"I didn't hurt anything." Retrieving a blue-striped towel from a hanger beside the worktable, Morrigan took the skillet, finished drying it, and put it away on the shelf above the range.

"Your chores were left undone," Beatrice said.

"I would've been home long since, in plenty of time to help, if Aunt Ibby hadn't stopped me at the station. Must I spend every moment I breathe doing chores?"

"Maybe you'd prefer to starve."

Sighing her defeat, Morrigan collected the basket of dirty linens and started out to the close, but Beatrice stopped her.

"Before you do that, go and freshen a room for Isabel. Then I suppose you should spend a bit of time with her. I have better things to do than listen to her complain about being ignored."

"But I thought...you said—"

"Keep a civil tongue, Miss, and do what I tell you."

The woman was beyond comprehension.

"I've done it this time, Mama," Morrigan said as she climbed the narrow rear staircase to the second storey. Conversing with Hannah lent a fancy that the one person she longed to know above all others might not be so completely lost as death implied, and had become a habit so long ago she'd lost its beginnings.

When she reached her bedroom, she unplaited her hair and worked a comb through it. "To hell with him. I'll ride again as soon as he turns his back."

She knew she was bluffing, though. Experience had long ago taught that bravado, undaunted in her bedroom with the door closed, would thaw like an icicle against her father's angry stare and the warning slap of the leather tawse, forked at one end, that he kept hanging in the barn for disciplining his children. She suspected the tawse was only meant to instill fear, as he most often used his fists.

She changed her dress, donned a clean white apron, and rewound her hair into a proper knot. A few months ago, Beatrice had carelessly mentioned that Morrigan's hair was much like Hannah's, probably never realizing how from that moment, every time Morrigan put it up, she would think of her mother, and suffer pangs of loss all over again.

Morrigan often searched Beatrice's face in hopes of glimpsing something of Hannah. They'd been sisters, after all. But Beatrice's lined, dour, heavy features never came close to the description Nicky had offered, though his own memories were vague at best, or Morrigan's own fantasy. Maybe it wasn't fair to compare the two women. Hannah had died young, still resonating with youthful ardor, and would remain fresh and beautiful forever to all who had known her.

"I wish you were here," she said as she hung up her discarded skirt and brushed it vigorously. "Papa wouldn't be this way if he still had you, would he?" Surely Douglas hadn't considered his own wife a misbegotten leech.

Nothing happened, no ghostly voice or any other spectral sign of comfort. Jingling the keys on her chatelaine, she went off to tidy one of the guestrooms, replaying Mr. Ramsay's smooth manner of speech as she plumped the pillows on the creaky four-poster. Maybe he'd attended one of those grand old English universities, she thought with envy. Though his accent couldn't compare with good Lowland Scots, it was inviting, like drowsing in a meadow on a sunny day. How strange, when she'd always been told Highland folk were coarse and ignorant. Beatrice often said she should count her blessings to have grown up in the Low Country.

How would it feel, to be married to such a braw young gentleman? Would being a wife, in the end, be no more pleasant than being a daughter? She was expected to trade her father for a husband, to never strike out on her own or create her own destiny. Sometimes it made her want to punch a hole in the wall. There was no doubt a good reason for all the rules and expectations surrounding females, but what was it? Women possessed no means to threaten men. A woman's entire existence, whether fine or not, depended solely on the goodwill of the males in her life.

Such thoughts would probably never have occurred to her if it weren't for school and the dominie, and the books he'd given her to read, and the hours they had spent talking about ancient civilizations. He'd suggested there may have been places, in long lost times, where women made the laws. And he'd laughed at the way her initial shock had transformed into captivated imaginings.

Beatrice's polish, made of beeswax and a drop of chamomile, lent the room a sweet apple scent. Morrigan arranged cut daisies in a glass vase and placed it on the commode. She checked the coal box, cleaned a dead spider out of the china basin, and filled the spill holder with splints, though the weather was grand and there would be no need of a fire.

Mr. Ramsay doubtless had servants to perform such mundane duties. His wife would have no more to fill her days than deciding what to serve for dinner and which jewel to fasten about her pampered white throat.

Part of Morrigan's imagination urged a coward's retreat until he'd gone, while another embellished a picture of herself freed of drudgery, dressed in silk, one languid hand resting on his capable arm, the other extended to welcome admiring guests.

Without a dowry, title, or land, no woman could hope to achieve such a status, and certainly not a country wench with chapped hands and bitten fingernails. Though gentlemen seemed to enjoy flirting with Douglas Lawton's daughter, they always left without any sign of regret.

She had been a plain child. When she'd been sent into town, not even the bullies noticed her. She'd liked being invisible. It gave her freedom to observe folk without them knowing. She had overheard bitter arguments between husbands and wives who would have kept silent had they realized someone was listening. She'd watched couples in dim wynds, amazed and shocked at the nasty things they did. She'd seen the bullies take out after boys they wanted to persecute, and harass girls they thought pretty, or ugly, or different.

Nowadays, she couldn't take a step in town without drawing attention. She'd developed a habit of walking quickly with her head down, her shoulders drawn up, though the sense of having done something wrong, or of being wrong, merely because of the way she looked, made her inwardly blaze with indignation.

It felt as though she was more appreciated yet less appreciated at the same time.

The stares of men told her she was no longer a skinny lass with tangled plaits. It was unnerving, especially when low whistles accompanied the stares, or murmuring was followed by coarse laughter. Only the shameless inner Morrigan wanted to flaunt and flutter and use folk. Even now, as she descended the stairs, the sinful lass suggested that if she would turn the force of her beauty on Mr. Ramsay, she might win her longed-for escape.

But no. She was not so daft. Gentlemen married to benefit their stations, and lasses who thought they could change that paid a heavy price.

Theseus didn't exist. He'd never really lived. He was a myth, a legend, as was her dream-lover, a fantasy of her overzealous imagination.

In an hour Curran Ramsay's elbows would be propped on the ferry rail, his face turned to the wind, and it wasn't likely he would ever come back. In fact, he might thank his God for the narrow escape from marriage-obsessed women and their penniless spinster nieces.

When would Aunt Isabel relinquish these hopeless matchmaking efforts?

Morrigan paused on the front stairs as she glimpsed Isabel's young golden male through the open doorway into the dining room. Light poured through the window, making a halo of his hair, and a signet ring glinted on the little finger of his right hand. The man outright dazzled, like the sun had come alive and slipped into their home.

For a moment, she was confused by a sense of familiarity. She derided herself for the fancy, yet it persisted, this feeling that someone very dear, missing for an ungodly length of time, had at last returned.

Her aunt was regaling him with tales of an Edinburgh holiday she'd taken with Uncle Gregor. Mr. Ramsay's expression was so politely engaged Morrigan couldn't hazard a guess to his thoughts.

If she could travel, maybe she would acquire the ability to engage in sophisticated discourse with handsome gentlemen. Oh, to have confidence. It would be grand. Whenever Beatrice or Douglas ordered Morrigan to entertain their guests in the parlor, she spent the whole time damning her blushes, straining to think of the next stilted topic, and trying to remember not to bite her fingernails, which she always ended up doing anyway.

Seldom had the task of determining a man's designation been so easy. She watched him laugh at something Isabel said and felt her lips curve in response, though she hadn't caught more than a word or two.

Years ago, while reading about Robert Burns, she'd learned Scotland's beloved poet put men into two categories: grave and merry. She'd adopted the game, and ever since grouped whatever male she met into one box or the other. Nicky was merry. Though he had dark interludes, they never suffocated his innate cheerfulness for long. Douglas landed with ease into an ominous container labeled "graver than grave."

Curran Ramsay was definitely merry.

"There you are," Isabel said when she entered. "Mr. Ramsay and I are sharing tales of Edinburgh."

"I've never been farther than Ballantrae," she admitted.

"Believe it or not," Ramsay said, "I spent the first seven years of my life here, in a house on Rose Street. Three cousins live there still. I can't believe I've never noticed the Wren's Egg before." He smiled and his eyes subtly darkened as he added, "I must remedy that error in the future." He paused, then drew in a decisive breath and stood. "Mrs. Maclean, Miss Lawton, if you will excuse me, I believe I should make my way to the ferry."

"I'll fetch you something for the trip over." Morrigan wanted to show, in an unobtrusive way, how much she appreciated his kindness to her aunt. She added, "You're welcome to take our trap and leave it there. My brother can fetch it later."

Isabel said, "No need to bother Nicky. I'll go with Mr. Ramsay and bring it home myself."

When Ramsay looked at her, Morrigan didn't lower her face but smiled for the first time. It felt braw to allow it, like water bursting free from a broken dam. He returned the smile, and for one instant, Ibby, the inn, and her life vanished into a golden wave of warmth and comfort.

She turned and fled to the kitchen, fearing utter loss of self-control.

Cheese, a cold kidney pie, and a half-bottle of decent Strathisla went into a wicker hamper cushioned with a towel. As she approached the barn, she saw Nicky had escaped the fields after all and was harnessing Widdie to the trap. The difference between the two lads struck her: one black-headed, ragged, sweat-stained, and grimy, the other elegant and clean, bright as the brass bell atop the Presbyterian kirk on Bridge Street.

"Thank you, Miss Lawton." Ramsay relieved her of the hamper. "I look forward to our next meeting."

Was that a blush on his cheeks? Aye, it was slight, but there. She'd always thought she was the only fool on Earth cursed with that betraying affliction. She'd never seen Nicky, her father, or Beatrice show any sign of embarrassment.

A longer visit would've been pleasant. She imagined him sharing tales of swift dogs and diamond-crusted Highland castles. But there was no help for it. She didn't believe his promise to return for an instant, and knew she'd never see him again.

"Goodbye," she said, adding, "Good luck with the puppy."

He frowned almost imperceptibly before swinging up onto the seat beside her aunt and taking the reins.

Isabel clapped one hand to her hat and waved with the other. "Don't run off, dears. I'll soon be back, and I'll want to hear your news."

As they rolled away, turning towards the wharf, an eagle swooped overhead; it soared past the barn, flying so low Morrigan heard the wind through its wing feathers. She stared at it, charmed by its grace and beauty.

"Seems a fair sort," Nicky commented. He scratched his earlobe and waved off a bumblebee.

"She said she met him in Glasgow. His name's Ramsay."

"Didn't she tell you who he is?"

"She said something about knowing him when he was young."

"Curran Ramsay babbed you on his lap when you were an infant." Reaching for a shovel, he scooped up Widdie's leavings and tossed them on the midden heap. "Da half-feared he'd drop you on your head."

She didn't much care for the picture of that sophisticated gentleman carrying her about in her hippins. "Where? Glenelg?"

"Aye. Curran Ramsay's father is the one who found Da this innkeeper's fee."

She cuffed him on the shoulder. "I knew you were lying. Sir MacAndrew's our landlord."

His eyes narrowed and she saw revenge coming. "We wouldn't be here if it weren't for Thomas Ramsay, who wrote the letter of recommendation. No doubt we'd have starved long ago in whatever's left of that sorry pile of rubble."

"Nobody told me."

He leaned close with a fiendish grin. "Because you're a daft, useless karriewhitchet," he mocked. Lifting his thumb and forefinger, he flicked her cheek.

"Don't call me that!" She rubbed at the sting. "I'm almost twenty and I've run the Wren's Egg for at least ten years. You should respect me."

Laughter brightened his eyes, but he blocked her threatened punch. "You turned eighteen not six months ago, you run nothing and never have, and you must *earn* respect by cultivating a modest air, producing fourteen weans, and learning how to cook."

Beatrice scolded from the kitchen door. "Morrigan, can you be bothered to finish the washing?"

"The washing," she said. "And if it's no' the wash, it's dusting, or the bloody milking, or boiling the jams...."

"Well, you'd best show Da you've done *something*." Nicky ladled water over his head then rested one big hand on her shoulder. "Have ye seen our unicorn?" he said, close to her ear. "She comes out when the moon is full... stands right under your window, polishing her horn on an arse as white as milk and glittery as a star. You should look for her."

"If she's not careful, everyone will see," Morrigan said, "and they'll make us change the name of the inn to the Silver Unicorn."

"Like it always should've been." Tightening his grip briefly, her brother gave her a cockeyed grin and sauntered off to his labors.

A fanciful poet—that was the Nicky nobody ever saw but Morrigan. Not Papa, not Beatrice, not even his closest cronies, she'd wager. Especially not them.

In the close, Morrigan removed her shoes and stockings. She'd taught herself to enjoy the washing, as she could do it without giving it much thought, and could allow herself to stray into flights of fancy. She was re-envisioning Curran Ramsay's face before she had her sleeves rolled up.

In her imagination he dropped to his knees, overcome with emotion. Kissing her palms, he expressed undying love. She must leave with him this very day and become his wife and ally, his partner in the trials of living. Like Theseus and Antiope, the great Amazon queen, they would remain loyal, passionate until death forever separated them....

Depending, of course, on which version of the myth one learned. The one where Antiope died defending Theseus and Athens against an Amazon army, or the version where Antiope survived, only to be betrayed and murdered by Theseus after he decided he wanted to marry the daughter of the Cretan King Minos.

Morrigan and the dominie had spent much time discussing the myths and tales from ancient Greece. He'd told her she knew more about those old stories than most anyone else in Southwest Scotland, including Carlisle. She was his prize student, and she reveled at the gleam of pride in his regard. She was careful to never breathe a word of how often she was skelped for getting home late, or how she had to hide the books he gave her then sneak them into her bedroom after her papa fell asleep. When Douglas put an end to her schooling she had wept bitterly for weeks. The dominie even came to the inn to personally try and reverse Douglas's decision, but his efforts had failed.

She saw her father exit the barn and gesture to her brother. They spoke, and then disappeared within. When Nicky reemerged, he waved at her.

"Help Da, will you?" he said. "The foal's coming. I'm away to fetch the veterinary."

At last! Leo's foal out of Cloud, their finest mare. Morrigan ran to the barn, leaving the sheet she'd been washing half in and half out of the tub. She couldn't wait to see it. Sometimes when she sneaked away and everyone thought her traipsing the moors she was actually in Leo's warm stall, tucked in the hay near his enormous front hooves. She liked to read to him while he crunched his oats. He'd nod his massive head, nickering like he understood. Now his first foal was coming. It would be so fine if Papa would let her halter-break it.

"What do you think you're doing?" Douglas left the stall, latching the door behind him.

"Nicky told me to help you."

"You'll try any excuse, won't you? Prancing about like a bloody princess." His fingertips ground flesh against bone as he grabbed her arm and bent, his stale breath laden with the aroma of boiled turnips. "God, what will it take to break you of that?"

She stared into his unblinking eyes, longing to scream at him. But she kept her mouth closed, forcing down her resentment. Long ago she'd learned that defiance made matters much worse with Douglas Lawton.

Something changed in those grey depths. There was an odd intensity she didn't understand. His gaze dropped. His hand tightened, pulled her closer, too close, before he drew in a breath and shoved her away.

"Get back to your washing. This be men's work."

She ran from the barn, rubbing her arm. Fury and hate coiled in the pit of her stomach. *Damn him.* She was so tired of his contempt, the way he always looked at her like he wished she were dead.

She scrubbed the bedclothes as if the Devil himself writhed under her fingers. Dizzy breathlessness brought an explosion of starbursts through her eyes, and an uncomfortable stuttering of her heartbeat. No, she would not swoon. No, by *God*, she would not.

It was that crazed bitch hiding inside her making all this trouble. Morrigan always had to choke down her rage for fear of repercussions. The wild inner girl, though, never suppressed anything. Morrigan felt her seething, cursing, throwing things.

The old delusion spewed…crystallizing into images of worldwide carnage and a suffocating drench of blood. *No,* she thought. *Push it away. Drive it out. Don't see it. Refuse to hear it. It's merely a picture, not real.*

The eagle brought her back. Lodged in the silver birch at the edge of the close, its yipping cries penetrated the screams and moans of her hallucination. It fluffed its magnificent wings and hopped about in anxious fashion.

Next was the vicious stinging. She stared, breathing hard, for a moment not comprehending how she'd come to be crouched on the dirt, her trembling hands immersed in warm water. The sheet lay mangled, a great tear across the middle. She'd ripped two of her nails on the washboard clear into the quick. Blood mingled with the soapy water, turning the froth of bubbles pink.

Chapter 4

Morrigan rose from her laundry when she spotted the vet and his son, Kit. Kit and Nicky had met long ago at the school on High Street, before Douglas insisted Nicky needed no more education. An impatient scholar at best and tired of the dominie's eternal haranguing, Kit had stopped going as well. He'd skipped classes more often than not in order to paint his pictures, and blamed the dominie for being too pinheaded to teach him what he needed to learn.

The vet and Nicky disappeared into the barn, but Kit paused to wave when he saw Morrigan, and veered towards her.

She took a few deep breaths and labored to present a calm demeanor as she dabbed at her torn fingernails with a cloth from the laundry basket.

"What've you done, lassikie?" With a snort of laughter, he held up her wounded hand, glancing from it to the torn, blood-spattered sheet still draped across the washboard. "You're a hopeless excuse of a woman. It'll be a miracle from God himself if you ever find a husband."

Snatching her hand from his grasp, she said, "Papa won't let me help with the foal," and tried to swallow a cloying suffocation in her throat.

He bent and kissed her cheek. "Wee simplehead, to him you're a scullery wench, and Nick his ploughman. Don't you understand he'd rather shove bamboo in his eyeballs than allow you a moment's pleasure?"

Euphoria swelled through her chest, submerging the rage and dread.

From the moment Nick first brought his new mate home, thirteen years past, to sample Beatrice's girdle scones, Morrigan had fallen hard. Ever since that day, Kit of the gangly arms and bold brown eyes teased her mercilessly, but some instinct she didn't quite trust had marked changes in his behavior over the last year or so—the same sort of change she'd seen in almost every other male, young and old. His teasing had acquired an edge; she'd caught him eyeing her in a way that made her nervously aware of odd things always taken for granted...the way inhaling lifted her breasts...how breezes caused her skirts to frolic at her ankles. Somehow his furtive observations kindled a desire to preen and parade, though she never did, not having a clue how to do it and too afraid of being laughed at.

She was sure they belonged together, though he hated Scotland. *What can a body do with himself in this damned country?* he often complained.

Her cheek burned where he'd kissed her. She longed to return the kiss, forget tiresome manners and self-restraint. They must marry and run so far away she'd never again see her father's scowl. Somehow Kit would make his fortune. They'd live like kings, sleep till gloaming, and dance through the night.

She swayed closer. He put a steadying arm around her shoulders and laughed into her upraised face, but the moment was ruined by Beatrice's voice, echoing from the kitchen door like a thunderclap. "Stop bothering that silly besom. It's plenty of trouble she's found herself in this day without you to make it worse."

Kit would never risk vexing one of Stranraer's finest cooks. "I'll away to this birth, then. Don't let him spoil your day, you daft nuisance." With a meaningful backward glance and cocked brow, he whistled, "My Love She's But A Lassie Yet" as he sauntered off.

Ibby returned soon after, red-faced and breathless with her recent triumph. She seized Morrigan's wrist and pulled her into a hug. "Mr. Ramsay sends his best wishes. He said you've too much work to do, and should have some help. I knew it would happen. What a fine catch, Morrigan. He's aye rich, and you've seen with your own eyes how handsome he is, and kind. I didn't want to embarrass him so I said nothing before, but he's commonly known in the north as 'Laird of Eilginn.' It's not a formal title—nevertheless, when he marries, his wife will locally be called *Lady Eilginn.*"

"Oh, Auntie." Morrigan blushed, wondering if she'd ever felt as mortified. Thank God she would never see him again. It would be too, too awful.

THE NIGHT BECKONED WITH LINGERING WARMTH AND SOFT BREEZES. A FINE COLT had been born, long-legged, according to Nicky, blood-bay like his sire. Since she'd first heard Cloud was expecting, Morrigan had eagerly awaited the arrival of Leo's offspring, and she would see him, with Papa never the wiser.

An hour passed. Morrigan paced to her bedroom door and edged it open. Grating snores echoed through the corridor.

Holding her breath, she crept down the stairs and let herself out. Above her, a milk-white crescent moon rested on a vast bed of diamonds. Warm dirt muffled her footsteps as she ran across the close. Victory infused her, made her feet as light as elf-wisp. She'd fooled the old man, and could spend the whole night with the foal if she wanted, while Papa snored—but the sight of the open barn door stopped her cold. Yellow lamplight flickered within and she heard quiet voices.

Poised to flee if she recognized her father's gravely rumble, she inched forward. But it was Nicky. A laugh followed. *Kit*. Kit, of course. One of them idly plucked the strings of some instrument, creating a harmonious sound.

She stepped through the gap.

"You're daft, you know," her brother was saying.

"No, you are," Kit replied, "to think you could ever be anything but half-starved and penniless if you stay here."

"I'll not starve, and I won't be penniless. I'll have respectable work with *The Scotsman*, while you'll be freezing in the wynds of Paris. You couldn't choose a more miserable profession if you tried."

"Tell me again what you'll be doing? Writing about rich old women and giggling debutantes?"

"Shut your bloody gob."

"I can see you covering the Winter Ball to Benefit Our Puir Masses."

Morrigan stepped into the circle of light, startling Kit, who leaped from his bale of hay; his father's prized mandolin slipped from his lap and struck the floor with a raucous jangle, prompting a horrified gasp from Morrigan. She could only hope the fact that it fell on straw saved it from damage.

Though his father would have his head if the mandolin came to harm, he barely glanced at it. "Hist," he cried, his eyes traveling over her. "I thought you were a ghost." Coming closer, he bowed and offered his hand like a gentleman, then ruined it with, "You're no' dressed properly, you floozy."

He'd be right about that, since she wore nothing but her nightgown. "It's the dead of night. You're the one who shouldn't be here. I want to see the foal, and I won't be put off."

They obediently led her to Cloud's stall. Morrigan fed the mother lumps of sugar she'd filched and stroked the colt's velvety black nose. He stood on spindly legs, eyes bright, droplets of milk clinging to the baby whiskers about his mouth.

"You smell so new," she said, kissing him.

The lads said *Och*, and *Females*, and returned to their whisky.

"Sing to us, Morrigan," Kit called, his words half-slurred.

"Whisht...you'll wake Da," Nicky said. "Do you want a dishing?"

"Bollocks! I'm sick of your da. You treat him like he's God in Heaven, and he'd never lay a finger on me. He can't afford to lose the good will of the only veterinary in Stranraer." Kit wandered back to the stall. "Morrigan, come away."

"I don't want to sing." She stepped out of the stall, now self-conscious. "I'll go."

"Aye, well. I'll sing to you then." Kit placed the whisky bottle on the bale of hay with great care, picked up the mandolin and gazed into the rafters, weaving like a ship's captain caught in rough seas.

"Bonny wee thing, canny wee thing,
Lovely wee thing, wert thou mine...."

A thrill fluttered through Morrigan's breast. The way he lowered his gaze from the roof to her eyes, the way his brows lifted, made it clear he was singing to *her*, sending yearning and wishes from his soul to hers. His mouth moved softly over each word as though caressing a lover's face.

"Wishfully I look and languish
In that bonny face o' thine..."

She opened her mouth, wanting to say something...but she didn't know what.

"...And my heart it stounds wi' anguish," he finished,
"Lest my wee thing be na mine."

He strummed a few more chords. Their eyes locked. Then he leered, and the spell was shattered.

"What you'll never do, Christian Lindsay," she said, "is sing on key." Yet her taunt sounded weak and shaky.

Man's love for woman. It stirred anticipation...for caresses. For ardent promises.

She pictured the warrior. He could throw a spear straight and strong—decapitate an enemy without care or emotion. Yet he could also kiss a woman's lips with unparalleled tenderness in the dark green of a summer night.

How she wished the fantasy could be real.

"I asked you to do it, didn't I?" Kit said. "Would you care to dance instead?"

In truth she was a simplehead. Where was the sense in languishing over an imaginary lover when right before her stood this fair fellow with warm hands and canted smile? She could see and touch Kit. He'd be here tomorrow, the next day, and the next, waking and sleeping. He was *real*.

"Let me do the singing," Nicky said, "else the dogs'll howl and poor Burns'll rise from his grave and curse us." He cleared his throat and strummed the mandolin. When had he learned to do that?

"Wit and grace and love and beauty..."

Kit caught Morrigan's hands and pulled her into the yellow wash of lantern light. He watched her, eyes half-closed, the hint of an indecipherable smile on his lips.

"In ae constellation shine..."

Holding up the hem of her nightgown, Morrigan followed his lead though he stumbled twice and trod on her foot.

"To adore thee is my duty,
Goddess o' this soul o' mine...."

He bent to kiss her cheeks, and Morrigan returned the gesture with a formal curtsy, as though they stood in Queen Victoria's court.

Nicky yawned loudly. "I'm to thin the onions and turnips tomorrow, and God only knows what Morrigan must do. Away to bed, ye doxie, you've scorned decency enough for one night."

Morrigan scrutinized her brother's comrade as he held out his hand for the mandolin.

Christian Brynmor Lindsay, the veterinary's son. He'd make a fine husband, and he loathed Papa, which displayed unerring good sense.

Grand day we're having, Mistress Lindsay. Could your fine husband tear himself away from you to see my sick cow?

Aye, dark-eyed Kit. He was the man for her.

THEY WENT OUT INTO THE BRILLIANT, STARRY NIGHT. "I'M NOT A BIT TIRED," Morrigan said. "Are you, Kit?"

He shrugged.

"Will you stay awhile?"

Darkness disguised his expression, but after a slight pause, his shoulders again lifted. "A moment, maybe," he said in an offhand way.

"Fools, the both of you." Nicky made a rude gesture and disappeared. The kitchen door squeaked behind him.

Time to put away childish dreams of women leaping over wild bulls, of arrogant Greek princes and aye, of blond Highland lairds. She was a Woman, as Aunt Isabel so often pointed out, and must act like one. If she did not compose her future, Papa surely would. Let others conjure handsome faces, silk gowns, and castles. Long ago she'd relegated Kit to the category of "merry," and when contemplating a spouse, merriment was her foremost stipulation. If she somehow got stuck to a grave man, she might as well stay with her father: that or slit her own throat.

It was time to use what the stares of men told her she had—beauty, and willingness to work hard. The latter was more valuable than the former, but it was the former that would get her where she wanted to be.

Leaning against the side of the barn, Morrigan turned her face to the sky and tried to think of something witty to say.

She could swear a god had abandoned his celestial game of jacks on a great black velvet cloth. The moon had risen higher, and was brighter. The night seemed perfectly constructed for bringing Kit around to her way of thinking. Not even the pungency of manure could spoil such magic. Robert Burns must have chosen a night like this to write his *Bonny Wee Thing*. The air was alive with delicate patterings, distant hooting, and the susurration of breezes dancing through grass.

"A bonny night," Kit said.

She started and returned her attention to him, wishing she could see his face better. His voice gave nothing away.

"Look at the moon," she said. "A jewel upon a woman's forehead." The dissolute inner Morrigan must be awake. Only she would dare speak such improper poetry. "Can you see her, the black-haired queen against the starlight?"

"Aye, almost," he said, with more than a hint of mocking laughter. "Daftie."

A gliding shadow became the queen's sweeping arm, followed by a hollow cry. An owl on the hunt. At once there was fluttering as all wee creatures took cover.

The storybook vista caught Morrigan's imagination. She stared, her skin livening as though stroked by a hundred fingertips. She saw herself lying beside a bright fire, beneath stars much like these, kissing the dream-lover, whose tawny hair was so long it draped her face. But then the earth exploded. The ground heaved. Ancient trees were uprooted. All was chaos, and fire burned the sky....

An arm slipped around her waist and a hand, smelling of hay and sweat, clamped over her mouth. "You've been asking for this, I think," Kit said, and she felt the hammering of his heart as he nuzzled her temple.

She could hardly breathe with his hand covering her mouth and half obstructing her nose. Panic reared, and her own heartbeat thudded, fast and shallow. Succumbing to instinct, she seized the fleshy side of his hand in her teeth and bit, hard.

"Damn it, Morrigan!"

Oh my God.

They stumbled apart. He shook his hand, wrung it, and squinted at the damage.

"Did I hurt you?" she asked, trembling.

"What the hell d'you think?"

"I don't know why I did that. I wasn't expecting…I didn't…I thought—"

"Pity the man who ever does try to kiss you." He stalked into the barn.

Morrigan followed. She found the tinderbox and lit the lantern. In ominous, frowning silence, he inspected his hand.

"There's no blood." Morrigan shifted from one foot to the other. "I didn't break the skin."

Kit abruptly snorted and caught her to him, pressing her cheek to his chest. His laughter reverberated through her head. "God save us poor louts from virgins and the Kirk," he said. "I had an idea you wanted…well, more fool me. I suppose I got what I deserved. What else would you do?"

"I don't know," she answered, closing her eyes, savoring a renewed sense of happiness and safety. Heat radiated through his sark, and beneath was a structure of iron, kept pliant and alive by the strong, steady beat of his heart. His scent, that which always reminded her of the sea-wind off Loch Ryan, and currently redolent of whisky, drifted around her. She inhaled with enthusiasm.

When he bent to give her his usual amicable peck, she turned her head, placing her mouth in line with his. He started to jerk backward, but she flung an arm around his neck and held on tight.

For one long moment he remained motionless. Then he seized her arms. His mouth pushed against hers, forcing her lips open.

Nothing she had ever experienced could compare to this. She rolled her tongue against his, thinking she might well get drunk from the whisky she tasted. For the first time she thought she understood those couples in Stranraer's wynds, why they'd done things, with only the barest privacy, that they weren't supposed to.

She felt herself being lifted then deposited on a bed of straw. His body lay heavy upon hers. She heard herself protest when he stopped his kisses, but he'd merely lowered his mouth to the side of her neck, which instigated an entirely new level of delight.

"Oh, Morrigan," he said, covering her breasts with his warm hands. "You're so braw."

The panic that ignited at this intimate touch disintegrated under the rare, longed-for endearment, and she tightened her grip, squeezing her eyes shut to keep out unwanted reality.

No rigid corset or petticoats separated them—nothing but her muslin nightgown. The barn, nearby horses, fear of discovery, all vanished. Again, the daydream floated through Morrigan's head; it felt as though two men made love to her, one young, inexperienced and clumsy, yet warm and real, the other demanding, sure in what he wanted but insubstantial, like a ghost. Behind her closed eyelids she saw the flicker of a fire. She heard the sigh of wind in nearby trees and caught an unfamiliar, exotic scent, similar to the spices Beatrice kept on a shelf in the kitchen.

Impatiently, Kit—or was it the dream-lover—fumbled with the front of her gown. Eventually the two conspirators had her buttons undone, and oh, the feel of their mouths, the way their teeth pulled her skin…she could never have imagined such sensations existed.

Where was she? In the barn with Kit…or in a meadow, embraced by wind and dreams? Two realities fought for ascendance, one clear when she opened her eyes, the other bursting with life when she closed them.

"I can't stop," he said into her ear, and though she recognized Kit's voice, was there another, underneath, hardly more than an echo?

Even death won't break our bond.

"I've never wanted anything so much in my life." His hands crept beneath her, pulling her hips closer. "Please, Morrigan, don't make me stop…."

Hearing her name severed the fantasy. She was in her father's barn. There was but one man, one mouth, one set of hands. The aromatic crackle of burning embers and nearby murmur of oak leaves diffused into dry straw, hot lamp oil, fresh manure.

Everything recoiled as she realized he'd bunched her nightgown up around her waist, and was settling between her legs with determination. *No,* she screamed inwardly. *Stop him, don't let him, he can't….* Her thoughts were disjointed, but the overwhelming terror wasn't. She had to get away. *Oh God, help me.*

She pushed at his chest, yet he didn't seem to notice, and he was so heavy she despaired of having any effect. "Stop! Kit, stop!" She craned away desperately, even resorting to balling a fist and striking him on the cheekbone, then the side of his head. Where a moment ago she had succumbed with unthinking joy, now her stomach churned with revulsion.

Oddly, the wild girl inside her agreed. *He's not the one.*

Kit's breath tore in ragged gasps. She cringed, fearful he'd be vexed enough to strike her. Could she stop him? If she didn't, it would ruin everything. This was not right. *He* wasn't…right.

He opened his eyes. Stared at her face then her breasts. Shame brought her hands up; she tugged the opened edges of her nightgown together.

"You taste grand," he said, touching her neck where he'd chewed her almost raw. His eyes narrowed. "What's wrong? Why are you stopping me? *Damn* you, Morrigan."

"I…we can't do this. It-it's a mistake."

Shuddering, he turned his face away. His eyes closed; he sucked in a deep breath.

Pushing at him again, she managed to roll out from underneath and scramble to her feet. She wished this night had never happened. She wished she could die. She wished herself into her squeaky, miserable bed.

Kit stood too, and grabbed her elbow. "Playing a whore's game with me, then? Is it coin you want, or marriage? You think you can tease me into giving you whatever you want, don't you?"

"No, I-I don't want anything. I'm sorry."

"Jesus and Mary! You think you can put a man aside like a goddamned book? Damn it! I knew you'd do this to me."

She couldn't think of anything to say.

He stared at her, his jaw clenching, then he surprised her. "Well, you did the right thing," he said coldly. "Not you or any other lass will keep me from what I want. I'm away to France, and there will be no wife, no scraiching infant, to tie me down. Do you hear?" He shook her. "D'you hear me? Not you or any…other…lass. I don't care what happens to you!" Shoving her roughly, he hissed and paced towards the door.

She stumbled. Her shoulder struck the gate of the stall behind her. "D'you hate me, Kit?" Behind her, the mare shuffled and snorted.

He was her only friend besides her brother. Look what she'd done. She'd never felt so awful, ashamed, guilty, humiliated, and frightened, all at the same time.

Two more steps he took, and she thought he would leave without saying another word.

"*Shite.*" He hunched his shoulders and wheeled.

Morrigan held her breath.

With swift, heavy strides he returned and lifted her from the ground. He kissed her, long and hard, then lowered his head. He rubbed his bristly cheeks against her chest until the sting left her gasping, her eyes tearing. Then at last, he set her down.

"I suppose I understand," he said. "You didn't know what you were doing, and we went too far. In a few days, no doubt, I'll thank God you stopped us."

"But, Kit, are we, has this…is everything spoiled?"

"I won't marry you, Morrigan, if that's what you're wanting. If you think about it, you'll realize it's for the best. I have nothing to offer."

"You'll be a veterinarian, like your da."

"I'd die first. I'm leaving this damned place. I'm away to Paris and Rome, and nothing, *nothing,* will stop me. Now go to bed, damn you, or I-I'll make you wish you had." The way he was staring at her, gritting his teeth, gave his threat menacing weight.

She wrung the front of her nightgown. "Aye. Whatever you want."

He squeezed her shoulders until they nearly pressed against her jaw.

"And…don't you ever do this again. D'you hear? One of these days, some man will make you sorry you played such a game. Give me your promise."

"I didn't mean to. I'll never do it again. I promise."

He turned away, cursing under his breath.

"Will you wait for me, Kit?" she asked. "I need more time, is all. Will you wait for me…to grow up?"

He stood there, clenching his hands into fists, releasing them, and clenching again. She could see a portion of his cheek; his jaw was clenching too.

"I do…I think I—" Morrigan choked. She wanted to say she loved him, but she couldn't. The word *love* caught like a burr on her tongue.

He didn't look at her. "You are grown up, Morrigan," he said. "It's only you can't see it." Then he left, slamming his fist into the big door, sending it flying against the wall with an awful crack and studder.

After the door settled, there was silence but for the *whish* of the mare's tail and the sucking sound of her nursing colt. Weak and defeated, Morrigan slumped to her knees. "I'll never get away." She struck her fists against the floor. "This *is* my madhouse."

Chapter 5

When Morrigan rose in the morning, all the previous night's seductive warmth had vanished, replaced by fine grey mist alternating with drumming rain and growling thunder.

"Mama," she said, low. "I've ruined everything."

Her reflection in the window, wavery and indistinct as it was, revealed the darkening bruise Kit had made on her neck. She rubbed it, flinching at the sting, thankful she had plenty of collars high enough to cover the evidence of her wrongdoing.

Her cheeks were reddened from his unshaven face, but she didn't think anyone would notice that. Who would suspect her of meeting a man in the barn and nearly coupling with him like a witless animal? No one, not even Douglas, surely, though he was always eager to think the worst.

Morrigan didn't need Hannah's ghost to warn her about the risk she'd taken, the consequences she'd barely escaped. The ugly word "whore" said it all.

Stranraer could claim one whore of its own. Though the woman was despised and shunned, abused by gangs of unruly boys, forced to live in an awful shack on the outskirts of town, she stubbornly remained. Originally from somewhere in the Highlands, Diorbhail Sinclair wore clothes that were hardly more than rags, as did her fragile, bony daughter, but every time Morrigan had seen them, the wean's face was clean and her hair combed.

When Diorbhail first came to Stranraer, she'd passed herself off as a widow, but someone discovered she'd never been married, and that was the end of that. Her child had no father.

Morrigan felt a certain wary kinship with Diorbhail's bastard.

Beatrice had instructed Morrigan to look the other direction if she happened upon Diorbhail, to cross the road so they wouldn't come within speaking distance.

Succumbing to an odd fascination, Morrigan often peeked anyway. *Where is your man?* she longed to ask. *He should be here to protect the mother of his child from torment.*

Douglas had spit on the ground when Diorbhail passed by. Morrigan knew mere spitting wouldn't satisfy him if he found out about Kit and his daughter in the barn.

She hid her face among the dresses in her wardrobe, breathing the comforting scent of cloves and wool. "I know you're gone, and maybe you never cared about me anyway, Hannah Lawton. But there's no one else I can talk to. None who could understand."

With a last wishful glance at her bed, she smoothed her skirts and trudged down the stairs, following the scent of new-baked scones. Once when she was little, she'd pilfered four wedges, covering each with so much of Beatrice's heather honey she'd made herself sick. She couldn't smell them baking without thinking of that day and suffering a twinge of queasiness. But she still loved honey.

"Morning, Auntie," she said as she entered the kitchen. She slipped on the jacket hanging by the close door, and stepped outside.

Sharp air stung her cheeks and clouded her breath. The rain slackened into drizzle, and she paused to scrutinize the muddy road. Mist prevented her from seeing much beyond the carriage house, but she mentally followed that road as it wound away to the east and the veterinary's door.

Before she'd regained her sense of decency, there had been an instant where Kit's touch felt better than anything she'd ever known…better than the taste of honey, or the softness of summer rain, or the brush of wind on the moor. That part shamed her the most. For several moments, she'd lost all notion of right and wrong.

Yesterday she'd imagined herself Curran Ramsay's wife. Fourteen hours later, she'd lured Kit into kissing her, and more.

What about the long-held, impassioned dream of the warrior she'd fondly dubbed "Theseus"? She shook her head and faced the truth. The pleasure she'd felt with Kit had really been for that fantasy. She'd kept her eyes closed so she could pretend it was her imaginary lover touching her, kissing her, pressing her into the hay. When confronted with the reality, she'd only wanted to escape.

How daft was that? Would she spend her life wishing for a man who didn't exist?

"Have you too few brains to get in from the rain?" Douglas had come around the corner of the byre, leading their Clydesdale. Leo nickered and bobbed his head at the sight of her.

"It doesn't bother me," she said bravely, though as she spoke, she realized the shoulders of her jacket were soaked, as was her face.

"Aye?" His callused thumb swiped at her cheek. "Are you wearing paint?"

"Where would I get such a thing?" She jerked away from his touch.

His eyes narrowed and he cuffed her, hard, with his knuckles.

"It's the cold air!" She rubbed her cheek. Her jaw felt half-dislocated. There would be a bruise later, and it would hurt to eat.

"You should've had the milking done an hour past." With a scowl and a curse, he went on about his business.

"Someday," she said, "I'll have a life free of beatings, and no one will tell me what to do."

"Sit down," Beatrice said when she returned to the kitchen. "I have things to say before Isabel wakes and our day is thrown to the wind."

Morrigan hung her jacket on the peg, carried the egg basket into the larder, and wondered what she'd done now.

Her aunt gestured to the other chair at the worktable and joined her, frowning as she glanced at the spot Douglas had cuffed. Morrigan could feel it swelling.

"Yesterday, when you were doing the wash...." Beatrice regarded her teacup and sighed, grimacing as though she'd tasted something bitter.

Morrigan waited, chewing on the rim of her thumbnail.

"Christian kissed you," Beatrice said finally. "Bold as could be, and you let him."

A blush flooded Morrigan's cheeks clear to her scalp. She knew Beatrice saw it from the way her aunt's eyes narrowed.

"Are you ignorant, or deliberately wicked?"

Damn you, Morrigan. Kit's furious sneer materialized along with a wrench of shame.

"Your father would never consider that lazy, penniless lout good enough for you." Her voice escalating, Beatrice added, "I hope you don't think to trick him into marriage by lying with him."

No one could accuse Beatrice Stewart of not saying what she meant. If she were to find out about last night, she would tell Douglas, and he'd skelp the hide from her bones. He'd throw her lifeless body into the loch and consider himself well rid of her. Fish would eat her eyeballs. Eels would play in her ribs....

"I shouldn't have to remind you that you must never allow a man to touch you, I don't care who he is or how long you've known him. Gossip of any kind will ruin you, but d'you think the tarnish rubs off on the man? You alone must be spotless, or no man will ever have you, and no decent woman will speak to you." Beatrice's unblinking gaze burned halfway through Morrigan's forehead. "When you marry, you must be untouched. Ignorant. After you wed you'll find out the hard way what's expected. Married women must suffer it, suffer and suffer for the rest of their lives, in misery and pain, as the Bible demands." She rapped her knuckles against the table. "After you're wed, then you'll submit, even when what he does makes you wish you were dead, and it will. This is woman's sorry lot."

Morrigan stared at her aunt. If suffering was what came of marriage, then why were women expected to want it? Dismay crept through her memory of the night. Kit had been like a stranger, almost violent when he'd pushed against her. He'd *bitten* her. There had been a moment when she wasn't sure he would stop, no matter what she said or did.

"I hope, if he ever does make advances, that you'll have sense enough to put him in his place. Listen to me or not, I cannot always be there to turn you back to righteousness. But undoubtedly, if you choose to ignore me, you'll get everything you deserve."

With that last bit of sage advice, Beatrice returned to wiping grease off the stove. The talk was over.

Morrigan drew in a deep breath and closed her eyes as the old rage sparked, curling from toes to scalp, a low smoldering at first, then accelerating, leaping into consuming flames.

The faded flowers in the smoke-stained wallpaper shifted and began to whirl. She had to get away, before her truth, her madness, was betrayed. She must run and run until exhaustion and the primal need to breathe deadened everything else.

Her chair squealed as she pushed it back. Ignoring Beatrice's sharp, "What are you about, mutchit!" she ran outside. Drizzle had made everything muddy and she slipped, but she stumbled on, not stopping until she'd climbed over the stone wall and entered the little forest that butted up against their property on the south side.

Water dripped from the branches. Leaves sighed as they brushed wetly against one another. *Come inside. Rest. Here you are safe*, they seemed to suggest. Morrigan bent over, gasping until she regained a semblance of control and no longer felt she was about to throw up, then she followed the overgrown path to her secret place: a pool, half-hidden under long grass, lush bracken, and moss. She sank to the ground, hugging her knees to her chest.

Someone shouted, but the sound was far away. "Go to hell," she said.

Images of the inn's usual patrons crowded her thoughts. The Wren's Egg generally played host to well-dressed, polished Englishmen, who poured into Scotland nowadays since the queen had made it so popular. Some came to hunt deer. Others were on their way to Ireland. Many sought to buy up cheap tracts of land. The Wren's Egg had few local customers, partly because it was so favored by the English, and partly because most everyone hated Douglas Lawton.

Two and a half years ago, just after she turned sixteen, Douglas told Morrigan she was to sit with these guests in the parlor after the evening meal. When she'd asked him what she was supposed to do, he'd shrugged. "Use those lessons Isabel paid for and play the piano. Ask them about themselves. Smile, if you can. Make them enjoy their time here, so they'll recommend us."

She knew the income from paying guests kept the family from destitution —barely. The crops Douglas grew and sold brought in hardly anything. But as much as she longed to please him, she hated that chore above all others. Shy, seldom at ease unless she was alone or with Nicky, Morrigan had no talent for idle pleasantries. Playing the piano only worked for a half-hour or so. Then silence would fall and conversation would falter. Men traveling alone had usually spent an hour or two in the taproom and were tipsy, some downright drunk. They wanted to be entertained. They wanted to flirt, and be flirted with. Sometimes these men seemed to assume her presence meant she was willing to give more.

Once, after a long evening fighting off an inebriated lout from Yorkshire, Morrigan had come downstairs and overheard Beatrice tell Papa that his daughter was what brought those rich Englishmen out of their way to stay at the Wren's Egg. "The hussy's paps alone make men forget their wives and Christian reputations," she'd said. "If we can catch the right man in the act, Morrigan's loss will purchase a lifetime's comfort for us. You'll never have to plough another row, Douglas."

Looking into the bright kitchen from the shadowed corridor, Morrigan saw her aunt rub her thumb against her fingers.

Papa had shrugged and snorted. Morrigan expected him to blast Beatrice for suggesting such a thing, but he didn't. He merely called her a born swindler, and added that he could hardly believe how she and Hannah were raised. "Everything that redheaded bitch told me was a lie," he'd said. "Why am I surprised that you're no different?" This caused Beatrice to turn away with an impatient huff.

As she blindly stared at the brown surface of the pool in the forest, Morrigan knew what had sparked her rage. Beatrice had looked her square in the face and said she must never allow Kit to take liberties with her. She'd implied an awful punishment for ignoring her advice. Meanwhile, when she didn't know her niece was listening, she suggested their lives would be improved if Morrigan were raped.

Oh, aye, Beatrice might think her ignorant but Morrigan knew how things were done. Men and women coupled, the same as dogs, kye, and horses. Men made water inside a woman. The same water they spilled onto the ground magically started a babe when it was deposited in a woman.

Aunt Beatrice wanted to use Morrigan as bait for blackmail, and Douglas hadn't seemed overly disturbed by the idea. The only reason Beatrice warned against Kit was because he didn't have coin enough to make it worthwhile.

Morrigan pressed her face against her knees. Would she ever be loved by anyone? Was any part of her worthy of it?

She brushed one hand over the pool's surface, watching the ripples spread and diminish.

Mud oozed over her other hand where it was pressed to the ground. Strangely entranced, she made a fist, squeezing the mud between her fingers, watching how it covered her chilblained skin and bitten, ragged nails.

What if the mud could draw out her flaws? She saw herself emerging, perfect, new, unspoiled, like a butterfly from a chrysalis, rage sucked from her soul like poison from a bee sting.

Tentatively, she dabbed a little on her cheeks and across her nose. "You really are daft," she said mockingly.

It will cleanse you. Purify you. The wild inner Morrigan now, urging her on.

She fought the compulsion, yet she knew it would win in the end. All she need do was let the spell consume her.

She stood and stripped off her dress, corset, and petticoat, leaving only her chemise and drawers. The mud was thick, very wet, and there was plenty of it, more than enough to cover her chest and arms and comb it through her hair.

Like the phoenix, she would rise, filled with the inexhaustible strength of Gaia, Mother Earth. A book she'd seen once on the dominie's lectern carried a fanciful etching of that goddess. Hills and mountains formed her abundant breasts and rounded belly. The entrance to her womb was a yawning black cave mouth, outside of which a tiny, naked, terror-stricken male cringed.

She hadn't heard the dominie come into the room. He'd been angry; he'd slammed the cover closed and told her never to pry into his things.

A blush ran through her cheeks. She knew the etching was improper, and that she shouldn't have looked at it. Many times since she'd wondered what the artist had been trying to suggest.

She looked into the pool. There *she* was, the hidden secret lass, smiling and triumphant. The girl who bedeviled with counsel no one else could hear, who forced the flesh and blood Morrigan into defiance that brought nothing but punishment. The mud hadn't eradicated her at all. It had freed her.

"Bitch," Morrigan said.

The fetch smiled and made a moue of her lips. *I'm the only thing keeping you sane.*

Morrigan's hair, heavy with mud, fell over her shoulders and struck the water, sending those turbulent dark eyes into the world of chimera.

A MAN RUBBED THE BIRTHMARK ON HER WRIST. *KISS ME,* MORRIGAN WHISPERED, dissolving against him. *Kiss me again.*

Then the sudden *kitti-wee-wit* of a sandpiper's cry brought her up from the ground with a gasp.

Leaves rustled. Branches creaked. Dappled greenish light blinded her one moment and the next caressed her in drowsy shadows. The smell of damp soil permeated the air.

Her dress was carelessly draped on a bush. As she stared at it, she remembered dancing in nothing but her underthings, calling upon long-dead female deities to share their secrets.

"God help me," she said, though she'd long known man's mysterious creator never bothered with women.

The sound of a twig snapping alerted all of her senses. If anyone saw her like this, covered in dried mud, they really would lock her away in a madhouse. She might belong there, but she didn't want to go.

She waited, fighting the urge to bolt like a startled partridge. Silence stretched; when she heard nothing else she slipped into the pool, keeping close to the protective cover of long reeds. At last, convinced the sound had been caused by nothing more dangerous than a foraging bird or cat, she floated to deeper water and began scrubbing, humming an old ditty as she used her fingers to comb the last of the mud from her hair.

She'd almost forgotten her reasons for running away by the time she dunked her head for a last rinse, only to see Nicky reclining against the trunk of an oak, one arm slung atop a propped knee, a stem of grass protruding from his mouth.

"Awake at last," he said, as calm as if they'd just sat down to breakfast.

"How long have you been there?"

"Long enough to know you've lost what little wits you ever hoped to claim."

He'd seen her, covered in mud like an aboriginal.

"You should've let me know you were there."

He shrugged. "And miss this?"

"Turn around so I can dress." Not bad, the casual tone she managed. She hoped it hid the mortification. After he'd obligingly scooted to the other side of the tree, she climbed from the pool and wrung out her hair. "Were you sent to drag me home?" She shook out her dress, but it was no use. It would need time with a hot iron before it would again be presentable.

"Maybe you'd prefer I bring Da here. He'd appreciate this new sport you've invented, don't you think?"

"I'm sure he'd join us for a swim." Though the day had grown sultry, a shiver ran down her spine as she fastened the top two buttons at her throat.

After a long moment, he asked, "What happened?"

She frowned at the ragged earth where she'd dug up piles of mud. "I don't know. I never know."

"Did you swoon?" His voice was carefully neutral.

While she could usually hide her bouts of explosive rage, there was no way to disguise the fainting spells. The only warning came in a blinding flash of light and a piercing stab of pain through her left temple. Time and awareness fell away into a fathomless hole, leaving nothing but shadows, echoes of voices, and lingering vertigo when she woke. So far, only Beatrice, and once, Nicky, had been present when it happened. Morrigan lived in fear that one of these swoons might overcome her when she was in town shopping, walking along the shore, or serving guests their dinner.

After the third spell, Beatrice told Douglas, and suggested Morrigan should see the apothecary. But Douglas, squinting at Morrigan contemptuously, said she would "grow out of it," and a doctor would be a "waste of coin."

"No," she said. "Not this time."

Nicky sighed. She heard him rip up a fistful of grass. "I mind him carrying you around on his shoulders, calling you his 'wee mouse.'"

Douglas, carrying her, giving her a nickname? She couldn't imagine such a thing. Anyway, it hardly mattered. He hated her now.

Robins warbled overhead. A pair of dippers swooped down to splash beneath the baleful eye of a goosander.

"You can come out now," she said.

When he did, he gave a derisive laugh. "Bloody Christ. Here...." He brushed, rough-handed, at her skirt, but soon gave up, shaking his head. "It's no use. I swear, when he sees this...." His gaze landed on her jaw. He frowned and put two fingers on her chin, turning her face gently. "Bastard."

"Is it bad?"

"Swollen. Bruised. You've had worse." He paused. "Will you visit me in Edinburgh?"

"Take me with you."

He kept his regard steady. "Da would have me thrown in prison if I did that."

"But, after you've set yourself up, why couldn't I come on my own? I could cook and clean. I could find a fee. Laundry, or sewing. If he comes searching for me I could hide."

He hesitated, gnawing at his lip. "Why d'you give him so many reasons to beat you? If you'd wait till you've finished your chores before you run off to the moor, you could be happier. Then he'd ignore you."

"My chores are never finished. You know that. You don't care what happens to me. All you care about is yourself and your own freedom."

His heavy black brows knotted. "That's not true. You can't live with me because I don't have a clue what'll happen, or what my life will be. I've never been to Edinburgh. No doubt I'll struggle, for a while at least. I can't be fashing over you as well as myself." He dropped his gaze to the ground, scuffing at the mud with the worn toe of his boot. "I can't thole this anymore."

Washed in guilt, she said more gently, "Aye, you're a man and can make your own way. Of course I want you to go. I'm envious, is all."

"I do want to bring you with me. I'll try to think of a way…."

"Perhaps another lad will solve the problem."

"Well." He grinned and cocked a brow. "I'll not tell all I know about that."

"What? What d'you know?" She grabbed his arm.

His smile was satisfied and mocking. "I know what lass one of my best mates is so taken up with the fool can scarce speak of anything else. I almost broke his nose over it."

"Is it—"

"I'll betray no confidences."

"You wouldn't say a word if—"

"Come, jo, time to face your punishment." His expression gave nothing away as he asked, "Has that unicorn let ye keek it yet? All silver-white… standing beneath your window?"

She couldn't help laughing. "You know I haven't, because I haven't the eyes of a madman."

"Speaking of madmen," he drawled, "I'd suggest you make certain Da never sees that mark on your neck."

Her cheeks grew hot as brushfires. "Aye…" she said weakly. "That's good advice. We'll be brave, won't we?"

"We will."

Like the fields he ploughed, Douglas's face was deeply furrowed. It was a testament to over fifty years of strife and labor, of the fight to survive. Though grey now dominated, his hair and beard had once been deepest black, or so Isabel claimed. The one feature on Douglas that never seemed to change were his eyes—for as long as Morrigan could mind, they had been as cold as a winter sea. She could hardly remember a time when they hadn't sent fear springing through her.

He was sitting in the kitchen with a cup of tea when she and Nicky returned. Beatrice was there as well, and Aunt Ibby. Morrigan made a downcast apology, speaking faintly around the lump of terror in her throat. Douglas's gaze flickered over her then veered to her brother. "You were sent to bring her home, not play in the mud," he said. "Where have you been all this while?" He paused only an instant before jerking his head at the door. "Go and wait for me in the barn."

This was his well-worn method of letting his children know they were about to be whipped. But Douglas hadn't touched his son with hand nor lash in years. Nicky was nearly twenty-two, far too old to be punished like a misbehaving wean. Morrigan watched her brother's face whiten. "What are you on about?" he asked, his eyes narrowing. His hands clenched though he kept them at his sides, and the air nearly crackled with threat.

"You're right." Douglas rose. "It's her punishment to take. Be off. Do whatever you please." He shrugged, grabbed Morrigan's arm, and began pulling her to the door, his grip tightening as she tried to free herself.

"Stop it." Nicky's jaw worked. "You've already blackened her jaw. Beat me then, if you must beat someone." Grimacing, he lowered his head and went out, striding across the close.

Morrigan didn't have the courage to tell her father what a monster he was, though the words shrieked inside. She wanted to tear his face open with her nails, but she could only stand, frozen, disbelieving.

"What are you doing?" Ibby was no coward. She got right up in Douglas's face. "You can't mean to beat Nicky."

He turned from her and went out the door, not bothering to reply.

"No!" She went after him, grabbing his arm. "He's a grown man. It's humiliating!"

"Get off me, Isabel." He flung her hand off his arm.

"Beast! You're an inhuman, uncaring beast!" She stopped and stood, wringing her hands. "You don't deserve to have children!"

There soon came the distinct crack of a leather strap against skin. Ibby returned to the kitchen, dabbing at her eyes with her handkerchief.

"You enjoy listening?" Beatrice said coldly to Morrigan, who remained by the door.

"He does it to punish me," she said.

"Your mischief brought this about, aye. Maybe he thinks it's the only way you'll learn."

Morrigan ran from her aunt into the close, stopping outside the half-open barn door.

She heard six sharp cracks, followed by a strangled gasp, and imagined herself ripping Douglas Lawton's eyes from their sockets, hearing *him* scream. Feeling *his* blood pour, warm and sticky, over her fingers.

Douglas came out, scowling as though the lashing had only increased his anger. There was so much hatred there, in his eyes, on his face.

She wished she could explode, leaving nothing but a mess of blood and slivers of bone.

"Tend your brother," he said, and walked away.

She ran into the barn. Nicky lay on his stomach, unmoving. For one instant, she thought he might be dead. The strap marks crisscrossed his back, red and swollen. A few were bleeding. They seemed an enigmatic roadmap, leading the way to some dismal place no one with any sense would choose to go.

"Nicky?"

"Why does he hate you so much?"

Stretching out next to him, she wiped tears from his cheek with her thumb.

Beatrice brought a bowl of warm water, clean cloths, and her special deadening liniment. Morrigan cleaned the welts and applied the ointment.

Dust motes careened through shafts of light. At last Nicky put his hands in the straw and pushed up. Using one of the wooden beams, he dragged himself to his feet, releasing a harsh sound of pain and almost losing his balance as he reached down for his sark.

Morrigan grabbed it and gave it to him. She rose, putting her shoulder under his arm.

His face was different. There was no light in his eyes. Always generous with smiles, his mouth now lay flat, tight and colorless. Douglas had extinguished his merry spark, what she'd loved most about him.

The rage that had sent her to the forest reared again, but this time it twisted inward like a bitter poison.

"I'm going," he said. "Tonight."

She covered her mouth with her hand.

"I'll send for you." His teeth grated and he shook his head. "Be careful until I do."

He draped his sark over his shoulders, grimacing.

No beating on earth could have matched the one Morrigan proceeded to give herself in the dusty barn. Which was, no doubt, her father's plan.

Chapter 6

THE HONEYED SCENT OF WOODBINE FLOATED THROUGH THE OPEN WINDOW, bringing memories of lost summers, of wrapping barley into fat droopy stooks and Nicky carrying her cockerdecosie around them. Morrigan leaned against the casement and observed her world.

Peewits chirped and a hidden dove cooed. The sun peeked over the roof of the barn, throwing peach-stained streaks across a cobalt sky. In the meadow, Leo kicked, snorted, and shook his black mane. With a half-rear and a whinny, he raced to the stone wall and carved a trench in the soil with one gigantic hoof. The more sedate old mare, Widdie, ignored her restless companion as she ripped up mouthfuls of grass.

Such a peaceful scene offered encouragement after the dreich weather of two days ago, when the skies had wept for Nicky.

He'd slipped out like he said he would, in the night. When Douglas discovered it, he'd raged through the house, cursing his son, his daughter, the rain, the crops. Morrigan had hidden, frightened yet triumphant. This was one time events hadn't bowed to the cruel bastard's demands.

Douglas let her know he blamed her by pointedly leaving whatever room she entered, sometimes with a disgusted growl.

She had seen her brother off, pressing her hoarded two shillings into his hand, and a packet holding three thick sandwiches, for he was always hungry, and one of her books, to keep him company on the train, and finally, the unicorn he'd carved for her tenth birthday. He'd stood for several moments in the doorway, his forehead pressed to hers, before he sighed, kissed her, and went off into the night.

She pictured him arriving in Edinburgh, looking for a place to stay, maybe starting his fee with the newspaper. He'd planned to go anyway, after the harvest. Now Papa would have to hire a strong lad or two to help him get the wheat and barley in, unless he added that to her chores as well.

"You're lucky to be gone," she said. As for his promise to send for her, she wouldn't let herself hope.

Thankfully, there were no travelers who would be perturbed by the shouting and tension. She would finish the laundry and hang it in the sun to dry. Beatrice planned to roast a chicken or two and would expect her help. Today she would try to be what Nicky had so often advised: quiet and industrious. It might help soothe Douglas's anger.

Not a hair lay out of place nor a crease marred her skirts when she finished her toilette. *Nick is well away*, she chastised her selfish grief. *No one will ever lash him again.*

With a firm pinch on each cheek to coax some color, she descended to the kitchen, where her aunts were slicing leeks and peeling potatoes.

Ibby gave Morrigan a sad, subdued glance and patted her hand. "Good morning, sweet," she said when Morrigan bent to kiss the older woman's soft, wrinkled cheek.

After the wash was finished, Morrigan simmered vegetables, wrung the necks of two chickens, and set herself down in the close to pluck the feathers.

Ibby joined her. "I ordered a bolt of velvet last month," she said, settling onto a three-legged stool. "Cisele, it's called. Also a good dimity and I couldn't resist two yards of Spanish lace, though I fear lasses have small need of a lace shawl the way the wind blows off the Sound. I should've ordered tartan, but there you have it. Your aunt is a wretched daft woman."

A feather floated against Morrigan's cheek.

"But I've found that lasses don't always use their heads when they fancy something," Ibby added more cheerfully. "Did I tell you I've had a few customers clear from Fort William?"

"I'm happy you're doing so well." Morrigan didn't reveal that after Uncle Gregor died, Douglas had predicted Ibby would soon be on their doorstep, destitute, and he'd have another mouth to feed.

Pulling a handkerchief from her sleeve, Ibby wiped her nose and regarded the frolicking horses. "My bones long for a warm place." She gave an embarrassed laugh. "Sometimes I dream I live on a tropical island. Kings trust me. Folk bow to me wherever I go. I still have dreams where you're my child."

"You do?" Morrigan smiled. It was too bad Ibby had never given birth. She loved steadfastly, and would've made the grandest mother.

"Aye, every few months." Her aunt's laughter faded into reflection. "For years I've thought I should pack up and move here so I could be closer to you and Nicky. Now he's gone, and you're alone."

"Don't fret, Auntie. I'll make do."

Ibby picked up the other chicken and plucked a few feathers. "Of course you will...but I'm thinking I want you to come with me to Mallaig." She paused. "I can't in good conscience leave you here."

"You want me to leave the inn? To live with you?" She could hardly believe it. After a lifetime of bondage, two tenuous avenues of escape had been broached in a matter of days.

"You'd be a great help to me, though it's a shame you've never learned to make a straight seam, and your mending is..." she shook her head. "A sight is what it is."

Morrigan hated sewing. Delicate, painstaking work appealed to Ibby, but Morrigan invariably snarled the thread, broke the needles, and ended up wanting to set fire to the whole mess.

"It was different when Nicky was here," Ibby said, low. "He watched out for you. I knew he wouldn't let things go too far."

"You really mean it?"

"D'you want me to ask?"

"It's useless. He'll never agree."

"We can try, *isoke*."

The pet name was one Ibby used only when they were alone. "I don't know where it comes from," she'd admitted when Morrigan first asked, "or when I first thought it. But it's always there, every time I think about you."

Once the chickens were basted and roasting in the oven, Beatrice asked Morrigan to go to town and buy a sugarloaf so she could make fruit pastries, adding that maybe on the way home she could pick some wildflowers for the dining room table. The invitation to dawdle was kind and rare. Perhaps Ibby had suggested it. Morrigan seized gloves and a bonnet and ran before her aunt could reconsider.

After she'd made her purchase, she strolled to the seafront to watch the gulls soar, marveling as she always did at how much their cries sounded like sad, lonely babies. A half-buried shell twinkled, prompting her to brush it clean and listen to the surf inside.

Led on by the earthy fragrance of bracken, gorse, and open moorland, she came to the edge of town and turned inland, climbing the hill that would give her a view of Loch Ryan and Stranraer. At the summit she watched the *Princess Louise* glide to the wharf, and the tiny black figures swarm along the pier like ants emerging from an anthill. The way the light struck the humped isle of Ailsa Craig to the north made it appear closer than it was, nearly close enough to swim to.

She rambled on into undulating moor that soon hid all evidence of Stranraer, giving an impression of vast, uninhabited expanses. Up and down over rough ground she clambered, taking off her boots and stuffing her stockings inside them so she could wade through a burn. Away in the west, a lochan sparkled in a froth of blue-green, and the only living things she saw were grazing sheep and an eagle, gliding joyously. Roving wind stirred about her feet, sparking an urge to dance, blowing away fear and sadness and all dark things, away into the wild, empty land she loved.

The wind sharpened, billowing her shawl. She removed it and folded it over her arm; her gloves and bonnet soon followed, so she could feel the warmth of the sun on her hair.

Remembering Beatrice's suggestion, she picked bluebells, campion, colts-foot, and yellow rattle. Then she spotted a patch of tormentil and farther on, purple mallow. It was too bad there was no heather. Beatrice would be dissatisfied with this pitiful cluster, and would no doubt inquire why she hadn't gone to the meadows and woodland, where wildflowers of every type and hue abounded.

As she shaded her eyes, searching for color, she spied a figure approaching from the direction of Stranraer, and with a jolt of surprise recognized Curran Ramsay, the Highland gentleman who had gone to Ireland days ago to acquire a puppy. His golden hair, being blown about by the wind, gave him away.

He waved and quickened his step. "I saw you from the pier," he said, "standing on the hill like a statue."

"You've good eyesight, Mr. Ramsay." Morrigan held out her hand. He appeared highly pleased; it seemed cruel to wish he hadn't spotted her. She'd so wanted some rare time alone.

"Aye." He clasped her fingers as he shrugged a bulky leather knapsack off his shoulder. "I was on my way to the inn to show you something."

Sunlight brought out the diverse shades in his hair, from gold and honey to wheat and flaxen. It reminded her of a watercolor rendition of the Greek god Apollo in his sun-chariot, which had hung on the dominie's schoolroom wall. Curran Ramsay could have been that painting brought to life.

Belatedly she remembered she was barefoot, bareheaded, and gloveless. Would she ever be prepared when something like this happened? Enid Joyce would never tramp about on the moor at all, much less without shoes.

A white pup with dark grey patches on its face and ribs popped its head out of the open flap, its mouth open in a grin, and she forgot her shortcomings.

"Oh!" She fell to her knees, carelessly dropping everything: the wildflow-ers, her boots, her shawl, and the sugar cone. The pup jumped on her lap and licked her face, whining as though she was a long lost friend. Morrigan fondled velvety ears and soft new paws. At last she set it on the heath and wiped her hands on her apron, blushing as she glanced at its owner.

But Mr. Ramsay didn't appear to notice what a fool she'd made of herself. He gallantly picked up her sugar and shawl so they could follow the youngster's curious meandering. Morrigan gathered the flowers and tucked them into one of her boots.

"Choose a name for her, Miss Lawton."

Morrigan considered. The pup's owner had at first reminded her of the Greek hero, Theseus, who, according to the tale, had wed an Amazon queen, a lass no doubt slim, graceful, and strong, much like this greyhound would become in a year or so. One title almost forced its way out of her. "Antiope."

He tilted his head and murmured, "Odd."

She remembered that a proper lady was expected to appear refined without seeming bookish. He'd think her uncouth, if he didn't already. His gaze was keen, searching her face as though he would like to pierce her flesh and invade her brain. "Antiope was a great queen," she said, trying not to sound defensive. "Strong and free. I've always admired her."

"Have you, then?" he asked softly.

Damn these blushes she couldn't control. She'd like to sink into the ground. Now he'd lost any respect he may have entertained for her. If she would only learn how to keep her mouth shut.

But he interrupted her mental scolding with, "Antiope it is. Thank you, Miss Lawton. Tell me, has your aunt returned to Mallaig?"

"No, she's still here. She's going to ask Papa if I can live with her."

His face lit, or maybe it was his smile, so devastatingly arresting. "Would that be possible? You appear invaluable to the workings of the Wren's Egg."

She barely stopped herself from snorting. "Oh, aye, I'm fair important, but she's going to try anyway."

They walked on. Loving the feel of coarse grass and warm earth beneath her feet, Morrigan continued to carry her boots. It was too late to make a better impression, and no doubt they'd cross another burn sooner or later. Besides, she much preferred being barefoot.

They climbed a knoll. The day was so clear she felt she could see forever. "Look," she said, pointing. "There's Ireland."

"And Ailsa Craig," Ramsay said.

Nodding, she turned the other direction. "And the Galloway Hills. What a bonny day it is."

"Aye."

"It'd be grand to go wherever one wished," she said. "Have you traveled, Mr. Ramsay?"

"Oh, aye. My father was in shipping. I set sail at a young age."

"Where have you gone?"

"India, Europe, China, Australia. One day I hope to visit America."

She stared, trying to comprehend being to so many foreign countries. "Paris?" she asked. Kit's image loomed. She hadn't seen or heard a word from that stripling since the night of kisses in the barn. With Nicky gone, and having offended him so badly, she might never see him again.

"I was ten the first time I went to Paris," Ramsay said. "You'll think me a fool, Miss Lawton, but I've yet to find anywhere in this world that compares with home. Every time I go, I only want to get back to Kilgarry, to my garden, my dogs, my blue mountains."

He spoke as though all the Highlands belonged to him alone. *Such arrogance comes easily to rich, powerful men,* she thought.

"Where would you go, Miss Lawton, if you could?"

"I don't know. I would like to see an elephant."

"Maybe you feel as I do. Few places compare to Scotland."

Wouldn't Kit jeer if he overheard Ramsay speaking of their country with such appreciation?

"Have you heard of a fellow named Heinrich Schliemann?"

She shook her head.

"He's digging up the coast of Turkey, hoping to excavate the fabled city of Troy."

Could it be? Would the ancient tales she loved so dearly be proven real, not fanciful myths at all? "Och, aye? How I'd *love* a keek of that!"

So much for her effort to appear refined.

But he didn't display a bit of contempt at her country bumpkin dialect. "I hope you can," he said.

"That'd be a right miracle." Inwardly she reeled at his expressive sincerity. "My future's been planned by others, down to my last dying breath."

His grin held a hint of deviltry. "We're a rebellious lot in the Highlands. We do what we wish. If anyone's bothered by it...we cut off their heads."

Morrigan laughed. "You cannot say you are one of those 'Highland savages,' as my Aunt Beatrice calls them. Not after telling me you were born in Stranraer."

"I've lived in the north since I was seven. My mother and father are buried there. Something about those mountains changes you, makes you see and think differently. You'll understand if you visit."

She remembered suddenly that he was a laird of sorts. He behaved so naturally, as though there was no difference between them. He'd managed to make her forget wanting to be alone, as well. Being in his company rejuvenated her.

"There's a man in my village," he said. "Seaghan MacAnaugh, a fisherman. He believes the whole world would come to the Highlands if they knew of its magic. Many years he traveled, for he was cleared in '53, and only managed to get home ten years ago."

"Oh, look, the pup!" Morrigan sprinted to snatch it from the edge of a burn, but she was too late. It fell in, yipping. She fished it out, laughing at it for looking so startled.

Raindrops spattered from a heavy black cloud. They'd gone too far by now, and couldn't possibly reach town before getting soaked if this sprinkle turned into a storm. Morrigan met Mr. Ramsay's gaze and determined from his expression that he didn't want their afternoon to end any more than she did, so she led him to an abandoned shieling she knew of, which sat at the edge of a small coniferous wood; they squeezed beneath the half-rotted lintel-piece and overhanging section of lumber that had once supported thatch. It soon began raining in earnest, but she didn't think it would last, as bright rods of sunlight were arcing and wheeling through the clouds to the west and south.

"I would like to visit your Highlands." Morrigan leaned against the jamb. "I can see how you love it."

"Love." He contemplated the downpour then he shrugged. "Somehow it's more than that. Mallaig is an easy sail down the Sound from Glenelg. I hope your aunt succeeds in her request." His eyes acquired such intensity that it sent a shiver through her.

"You should have an alternate plan." His gaze broke from hers as though he, too, was unnerved. "We could snake you away in the middle of the night. Or we might simply announce it. Tell your father he'll have to run the inn on his own. Come; practice a haughty tone and look down your nose at me."

Having experienced such an expression leveled at her more than once, Morrigan knew exactly what he meant, and laughed again. When was the last time she'd so enjoyed a conversation, or laughed with such abandon? "While he's sleeping would be best, I think," she said. "I'd leave a note informing him I've gone to dig up Troy. I wonder what he'd make of that?"

The gentleman smiled. "You've a bit of thistle near your eye." He brushed his thumb over her cheekbone.

Amidst a rush of startled apprehension, she realized she was alone with a man in this empty countryside, giggling as they made plans to run away. No one knew where she was, or that he was with her. Beatrice's warnings played through her brain, slowly and distinctly.

Yet it was impossible to be afraid. At this moment she believed if she and Enid Joyce walked side by side down the street and Mr. Ramsay came along, he wouldn't spare a glance for the lass touted as Stranraer's greatest beauty. His manner made Morrigan feel nothing could distract him. For the first time in her life she experienced elation rather than shame as a sense of power ran through her. She was glad she'd made such an impression upon this man that he'd come searching for her. She had his undivided attention, and she didn't want to release it. Just for this afternoon, she would revel, enjoy, and damn the consequences.

I would leave with him right now if he'd take me. Reckless, dangerous thoughts, but the beguiling vision of freedom made almost any risk worthwhile. Would she be free, though, or merely trading one master for another? Vivid imagining faded beneath depressing common sense. He was such an obvious gentleman. He'd never do anything to harm or compromise her. She sensed it, as clearly as she saw the rain subsiding and the return of sunlight.

Widening sunrays flared across the landscape. Antiope barked at birds until a raven swooped and clawed at her. With a yelp she scrambled beneath Morrigan's skirts.

"Dinna moolet and cringe, lassie-wean," she said soothingly. "Never show how feared you are."

"Are you promised?" The color in Curran's cheeks heightened as he blurted out the question. "Ha-have you any suitors? You're old enough, aren't you?"

"None of that for me, thank you," she replied lightly. "Why should I exchange one gaoler for another?"

"It's freedom you want, then?"

How quickly he saw beneath her words to the core of truth. "Surely that is every creature's desire, after food and water."

"What would you do with freedom, if you had it?"

No one had ever posed such a question to her, not even Nicky. Heady as a dram of whisky, it lent all possible answers vast importance. She wanted to say something profound, but in the end, she gave her imagination free rein. "I'd live in a blackhouse, as far from civilization as I could get. I'd read poetry by a fire...." With clarity came craving and swifter speech. "I'd ride my stallion in the morning mist. I'd swim in lochs...." The vision expanded and she almost forgot she wasn't alone as ideas crowded one upon the next. "I might fall in love," she said, "and maybe have babies, but no' unless I was sure I'd always love them. No man would own me, like horses or kye. And I suppose I'd be pagan, since I know nothing of God anyway. At the full moon I'd frighten folk who thought they saw me in the shadows, but couldn't tell if I was real or a ghost."

He said nothing for a while then seemed to collect himself. "That's why you chose Antiope," he said quietly. "You've a wild Amazon heart, Miss Lawton, and the soul of a poet."

Feeling much like a lass caught in nothing but a petticoat, she blushed furiously. She'd called herself a pagan. Said she knew nothing of God. Desperately she tried to think of a witty response that would undo the damage, but while she floundered, he leaned forward and kissed her.

Initial surprise and alarm liquefied into that odd familiarity. *I know this. I've missed this.* It was like falling into warm, luxurious water and relinquishing all care. Shame and guilt slipped away and the inner Morrigan burst free with a stunned cry.

His mouth against hers caused a tingling sensation, like infinitesimal sparks were being ignited between them. She heard a faint silken murmur, and only realized it came from her throat when he turned his head and his kiss intensified. His mouth opened, coaxing hers to open as well. Their tongues met, and the sound escaped again, involuntarily. As though on command, his grip tightened upon her shoulders and she felt the tingling there as well, streaming from his hands, bringing her skin to life.

At the very moment she thought she might melt clear away or be absorbed into him, he stopped. Clasping her hands, he drew them away from his face, rubbing his thumbs over her palms before releasing them. She stared at her hands mutely. She could remember the feel of his hair, his earlobes, and a hint of stubble along his jaw, but not lifting her hands to his face. How could she do something like that and not remember it?

He stepped back, blinking as though coming out of a dark cave into glaring sunlight.

The only sound, for one long, tense moment, was a lonely curlew's seeking cry.

"Forgive me," he said, pushing hair off his forehead. "I had no right. I cannot believe I…I apologize, Miss Lawton."

He wasn't unaffected. His pupils were large, consuming the blue of his irises. His breathing was uneven. She saw him swallow as though something was caught in his throat, and his hands fisted at his sides.

Oh…aye. Her senses sluggishly returned from that place of heat and craving. With him, with this *stranger,* she'd forgotten what he'd done was a bad thing. Lowering her face, she fought to slow her breathing and banish the flush from her cheeks, but they only seemed to grow hotter, betraying her further. She should have screamed the instant he touched her. That's what a proper miss would have done—not that a proper miss would have accompanied him to this forgotten shieling in the first place.

"You hate me," he said, low.

Beatrice's warnings reverberated. *You must be spotless, or no man'll ever have you, and no decent woman will speak to you.* She'd said more, about how Morrigan must be ignorant if she wanted respect. Surely, the way she had returned this man's kisses, she had forfeited all hope of that.

Taking a deep breath, she gave him a clear, steady regard. "I don't hate you," she said, surprised at how cold and calm she sounded. He mustn't sense how she had to clench her hands to stop from reaching out to draw his mouth back to hers, or how she had to choke down the words rising through her throat. *Kiss me. Kiss me again.*

"You are vexed, Miss Lawton, and I cannot blame you. I'm deeply ashamed." The crescent scar next to his eye stood out, white and defined.

"I am angry, aye." She stepped out of the doorway into the fitful sunlight, picturing Douglas spitting on the ground at a mere glimpse of Stranraer's fallen woman, Diorbhail Sinclair.

"Allow me to escort you home, I beg you." He spoke quickly. "I'll not touch you in any way…I swear. Can you forgive me?"

Long shadows stretched across the ground. The air had turned chilly.

Morrigan bent, hiding her face while she slipped on her boots and buttoned them. Ramsay picked up the sugar and her wilting flowers.

"Antiope," she called, draping her shawl over her arms. The pup bounded over. Morrigan swept her up and cuddled her, holding her so close the poor beast squirmed and whined.

She felt raw, inflamed, as if she'd swallowed a nest of raging bees.

ACRID SMOKE SPEWED FROM THE TRAIN'S ENGINE. IT GROWLED, A HUNGRY BLACK tiger impatient to be off.

Mr. Ramsay held out his hand then haltingly lowered it. Morrigan gave him the pup and at the same time took pity.

"Please," she said, and smiled. "I forgive you. I'm not vexed. What must I say to convince you?"

"Do you mean it, Miss Lawton?"

"I do, Mr. Ramsay."

"You don't know what this means to me."

The whistle screeched. He glanced over his shoulder.

"You'd best get on the train."

Hesitantly, he said, "I'm traveling to Edinburgh in a fortnight. May I stop at the Wren's Egg? Or would you prefer never to see me again?"

"Please come." She touched his lapel, making it appear she was innocently brushing away a spot of lint. "But isn't it fair out of the way?"

Smoke belched. The train lurched and squealed. He ran, grasping the attendant's outstretched hand. "Of course not," he shouted when safely aboard. He waved and grinned. "Thank you!"

Men desired intimacy; that much was clear. Yet at the same time they feared it, thought it evil, something to be ashamed of. It was pure confounding. Why was this thing between men and women so queer and complicated?

Morrigan knew no one she could ask.

A LETTER ARRIVED FROM NICKY. NOT ONLY HAD HE FOUND LODGINGS IN Edinburgh, he'd begun his fee. They were pleased he'd come four months before schedule and he was buried with work. His brain had never felt so weary, but his body was enjoying the rest.

Beatrice gave Douglas the news. She had a way with him, a talent for subduing his rages. He listened when she spoke, almost as though she were a man. For years Morrigan had suffered jealous torment over their closeness, wondering why he liked Hannah's sister so more than his daughter, but long ago she'd closed away that pain, for it ached like a rotted tooth.

Two days after her encounter on the moor, Ibby broached the subject of taking Morrigan home with her. She picked her time carefully. Nicky was now known to be safe. Sunlight balanced with rain showers had urged their barley and wheat into vibrant sprouts. The new colt was healthy, a fine, strong beast, delightful to watch, and a group of men on their way to Ireland had spent a small fortune in the taproom.

While Morrigan placed his dinner before him, Ibby sipped tea and said, "I'll soon be going home."

"Aye," Douglas replied.

"What would you think of me borrowing Morrigan for a few months?"

He examined first his sister, then his daughter, who dawdled nervously by the door. One eyebrow lifted. "What are the two of you plotting?"

"There's no plot, Douglas. I've more orders coming in than I can take care of without help. You're doing well here. A lass from town could lend Beatrice a hand on washday. It wouldn't cost you more than a penny or two."

Oh, that was a mistake. Her aunt should never have mentioned the financial repercussions of his daughter being absent.

"No." Douglas returned to his bread and butter.

Ibby glanced at Morrigan then ventured on. "Morrigan is of weddable age. 'Tis past time she learned a few of the accomplishments that impress marriage-minded men. You do want her to marry well, don't you?"

"She's naught but a dawless wean. Beatrice will teach her whatever she needs to know."

"She's eighteen…hardly a wean, and anything but lazy. Many girls her age are married, mothers as well. Have you no pride?" Ibby's voice rose. "And the way you leave her with your guests—with *men*—after you and Beatrice have gone to bed. You know what that will do—may have already done—to her reputation."

Morrigan sighed. She almost turned and left, not wanting to see poor Ibby get her comeuppance.

"Who d'you think we are, lords and ladies? I've labored my whole life and so will she. I've been a fisherman, a crofter, and a soldier. Now I'm an innkeeper, and she's an innkeeper's daughter." His voice lowered to a dangerous rumble. "It was you insisted she learn to play the bloody piano. It's me what uses it to bring in coin. You do want her to eat, I suppose?"

Morrigan's spine quivered uneasily.

Yet her aunt barreled on. "Are you telling me you don't think it's wrong to leave her unchaperoned with men?"

"She's perfectly safe. I'd hunt and kill any bastard who dared touch her. Don't think they don't know it."

"No man, rich or poor, will ever ask her to marry him if he hears such gossip! She'll never have the chance to be happy, to be a mother."

He rose from his chair, his face mottling. "Mind your own affairs or take yourself from this house. The hissy will bide for as long as I say. Bring you a hundred louts from Glenelg—it'll change nothing. If I wanted to be reminded of that cursed spot, I'd go there." He tossed his napkin on the table and stalked out.

"He's a hard man." Ibby fumbled for her handkerchief. "Lord knows how you've lived with him these many years."

"It's not as if I had a choice," Morrigan replied, but Ibby acted like she didn't hear. "Don't fash over me, Auntie. Maybe one day, things will change."

Ibby departed on the late afternoon train, so vexed she refused to say goodbye to her brother, but before she left, she gave Morrigan the ostrich-plumed hat she'd made, the very height of London fashion. "I love you," she said with a kiss. "And I will get my way. I promise. I need to think on it."

Morrigan watched the train lumber off. People passed, talking, laughing, causing her to wonder if they ever considered the freedom they possessed, or took it for granted.

When one looked at the coil from every angle, Douglas made more sense than Ibby. Morrigan *was* an innkeeper's daughter, not a lady. No amount of ostrich feathered hats or piano lessons could change that.

The train's roar faded. A ball of crumpled newsprint blew across the deserted cobbles. Sighing, Morrigan turned to make her way home. She set her gaze upon the exit and froze, gasping. Douglas stood there, seemingly at ease the way he leaned against the wall, arms crossed. Yet she knew why he was there. He'd suspected she might run off with Ibby despite his forbidding it. If she had stepped foot on the train, he'd have been there, dragging her home by her collar. It made no sense. Not a day passed where he didn't clearly demonstrate how much he hated her. Why not let her go, then? Be rid of her?

Spots of color burst before her eyes. She saw herself fruitlessly shaking the steel bars surrounding her, longing for a freedom that remained out of reach.

Without speaking a word, he turned on his heel and walked away.

Chapter 7

Devil curse all men.

With days to ponder, Morrigan realized Curran Ramsay had taken advantage of her innocence. Every time she thought of the way he'd coaxed her into responding to his advances, she burned with embarrassment. Then, once he knew she had no decency, he'd left! And what about Kit Lindsay? She hadn't seen him once since the night in the barn. *There will be no wife, no scraiching infant, to tie me down,* he'd shouted. *I won't marry you.*

Both had humiliated her. Nicky had abandoned her. Then there was Douglas Lawton, the man who could never for an instant stop hating her. Everything Curran and Kit had done only reinforced what Douglas had made clear long ago. She was not worth caring about.

She yanked weeds from her kailyard while the angry inner Morrigan created pictures of them all kneeling in abject remorse, their knees stuffed in piles of fresh manure. Douglas, Nicky, and Curran Ramsay were beyond reach, but each day, as she went about her chores, she scanned the road, hoping to catch sight of Kit, his arm raised in a loose-limbed wave. May passed into June, but the only people who approached the inn were strangers in need of lodging and meals.

During a violent nighttime storm, Morrigan quaked in her narrow bed and wondered if God was venting his rage upon Stranraer, or more probably her. The next day they heard a ship had almost foundered near land's end at Corsewall, but managed to escape the fate that had so often occurred there before the lighthouse was built.

Remnants of pride stopped her from ringing the bell at Ian Lindsay's veterinary practice on Charlotte Street, though she constructed a few excuses that might make it seem natural.

Thanks to Aunt Ibby's generous efforts, she was exquisitely garbed whenever she entered Stranraer proper. Young men gowked, wide-eyed as lemurs, on those rare occasions. Sometimes an extra-brave lad would come forward with an offer to carry her parcels or hold her arm.

Their muttering and blushes irritated her. Those same louts who stumbled over themselves in her presence, their Adam's apples bobbing like frantic netted toads, took vicious pleasure in persecuting Diorbhail Sinclair and her unfortunate daughter. Morrigan had seen them throw rocks, any one of which could maim or kill the child. Diorbhail shielded her offspring with her own body, and suffered many injuries.

The woman obviously loved her wean. Once Morrigan had seen her shriek at the bullies. *Coarse devils*, she called them. Then a stone struck her forehead, knocking her half over. The lads whooped with laughter as blood gushed over her face.

Yet *she* was considered evil, worthless, damned, and the frail wee paddler along with her.

Kit would never be so cruel.

Oh aye? The inner lass smirked. *Then why are you so miserable? Kit's no' the one for you. A man is what you need, not a namby-pamby boy.*

How Morrigan wished she could control her thoughts.

July burgeoned, hot and dry. Morrigan helped Beatrice bake loaves of barley bread and a loaf or two of white for their snobbish English guests. Life spiraled on, unchanged. Curran Ramsay never returned and she began to forget what he looked like but for that infectious smile, making him seem like Mr. Carroll's Cheshire Cat. They received no letters from Ibby or Nicky, and the earth had swallowed Kit. Her hopes for escape faded. Beatrice had stated that no man would want her if she allowed him liberties. It must have been the truth.

She brushed butter over hot bread crust and considered whether other women ever longed to create their own fates. Nicky left when he couldn't bear it any longer. But when Morrigan thought of running away, fear made her heart skip and stutter. Douglas would hunt her. He would never give up until he found her and he would beat her lifeless. Besides that, the world outside the inn loomed cold and huge, full of unseen dangers she instinctively knew she wasn't prepared to confront. When she imagined herself alone, without these walls to hide behind, it was never as that wild spirit she had described to Curran Ramsay. She was always starving, dirty, being tormented like Diorbhail

Sinclair. At least this life provided a bed, food, and shelter, no matter how insubstantial, from unknown cruelties.

"Yonder colt's grand," Beatrice remarked as she slid another loaf in the oven.

"Aye." Morrigan dried a bowl and swiped a thin veil of sweat from her forehead. "Ian Lindsay says he'll be seventeen hands or more." Before she could lose her nerve, she asked, "Do you know what's become of Kit?"

Beatrice's eyebrows rose, emphasizing the grooves across her forehead. "He'll never set foot in this house again and you're not to speak his name. He's ruined a lass, exactly as I predicted he would."

"Ruined...."

"Her father caught them. He's demanded they marry, and who can blame him? Not what he was hoping for, though, and no doubt that prideful chit wanted more for herself as well. Since you'd not mentioned him lately I thought you'd heard. Folk in town speak of little else these days."

The bowl Morrigan was drying fell to the floor and shattered. She stared at it, uncomprehending.

"You've gone pasty as an unbaked scone." Beatrice pushed Morrigan into a chair and fetched the broom. "No doubt he planned it this way. He wouldn't waste his precious self on any ordinary lass. It had to be one of the wealthiest. Lazy mad daftie."

Could this be her fault? If she hadn't stopped Kit from having what he wanted that night in the barn, would it be her own wedding Stranraer was gossiping about?

Dropping the dishcloth on the table, she left the inn, determined to find him. She would do it for Nicky, she told herself. But damn it to hell, he owed her the truth as well. He'd more than implied he cared about her.

He wanted what all men want, and you almost gave him that. He never said he cared about you. Just the opposite.

The housekeeper at Ian Lindsay's told her Kit had gone out and she didn't have the slightest idea when he would return. Morrigan searched the lanes one by one until at last she spotted him leaning against a lamppost outside a ladies dress shop on George Street, his hands shoved in his pockets, a pinched, cheerless expression on his face. He tapped the heel of his boot against the post, a gesture Morrigan knew was something he did when bored or impatient. At nearly the same instant she saw him, his gaze met hers.

He straightened and took a few steps towards her. "You heard."

"It's true?"

"My da and hers are up in arms." He ducked his head. "They've put me through hell over this."

The door opened behind him. A bell chimed as a girl came out of the shop.

"Kit?" she called.

Morrigan's mouth opened like a beached fish. It was Enid Joyce.

Enid walked swiftly to them and clasped Kit's arm, giving Morrigan a coldly curious stare. Close behind her, an older woman wrestled armfuls of parcels and hatboxes.

"What d'you want?" Enid asked, squeezing Kit's arm. "Trying to make me jealous already, love?" Her chin went up in a contemptuous manner, recalling Ramsay's advice on the moor. *Come; look down your nose at me.* It was such a perfect example of the expression he'd urged, in different circumstances Morrigan would have laughed.

Enid's cultivated voice, hardly betraying a hint of Scots, continued. "If you ever do want to make me jealous, you must do better than this...the daughter of a slut and an illiterate crofter. Daughters of whores, it's said, usually turn out whores themselves."

Kit's cheeks reddened. "Miss Lawton," he mumbled. "It was good to see you. Please give my regards to your brother." He wheeled, half-dragging Enid away, but not before his intended launched a triumphant sneer at Morrigan.

I won't marry you, he'd said that night, flatly, decisively. But he would marry Enid Joyce.

Three young boys who'd been eavesdropping broke into peals of laughter. They pointed at Morrigan and shouted, "Daughter of a slut...daughter of a slut makes a slut!"

She's the one who sinned, not me! But what good did righteous indignation do? Enid's wealth would bring her through this scandal. Kit would take her with him to Paris and Papa Joyce would finance his son-in-law's every desire.

The boys' taunts rang through her head all the way home.

MORRIGAN HAD TO CHECK THE LAMPS THREE TIMES, AS SHE KEPT FORGETTING whether she'd cleaned the soot from the chimneys. Later, as she gathered up the dry linens in the close, Beatrice sent her off to dust the parlor, saying she couldn't stand it another moment. Morrigan wandered through the room, carelessly giving the clutter of knickknacks, china figurines, bowls, and books haphazard swipes with a feather duster that simply moved the dust around.

Kit would never marry Enid. He abhorred her; he and Nicky had ridiculed that proud, snooty witch without mercy. Morrigan minded their hilarious mimicking of her, how they'd pranced and preened and pursed their lips. She'd laughed so hard her sides hurt.

She had to speak to him without Enid being there. There was no other way to get the truth.

Silence descended in the dining room after Beatrice gave up trying to make conversation with the Irish couple headed to London.

Morrigan put away the clean dishes, carried water to the guests, and retired to her room. She undressed and put on a wrapper. Beatrice usually said good-night on her way to bed, so Morrigan needed to make it appear she had no intent other than going to bed herself. She would dress again when she was sure Beatrice and Douglas were asleep.

As she suspected, Beatrice soon knocked and opened her door. "You left the wash outside," she said, "and it smells like rain."

"Oh." Grateful for the reminder, Morrigan nodded. She eyed her discarded corset, petticoat, and nightgown.

"The guests are in bed," Beatrice said, deciphering her glance. "Your wrapper's decent. Away with you, hurry before Douglas comes in."

Folding the collar up around her throat, Morrigan tiptoed down the stairs.

The sky was fading to deep bluish black. Peewits flitted and squeaked, and the rich scent of woodbine thickened the air. Morrigan flung the bedclothes over her shoulder.

Kit hadn't appeared pleased. Maybe he'd like to form a new plan. He and Morrigan could leave it all behind, all they hated. True, she had recoiled from him in the barn. But that wouldn't happen again. It was nothing more than a virgin's fear of the unknown. She refused to compare it with Curran Ramsay's kiss, and how she'd longed for that to go on and on forever. Ramsay was gone. Kit was still here, at least for the moment, and Kit understood her like no one else but Nicky ever could. Life with him would free them both from intolerable futures, and she would force herself to enjoy his touch.

"*Bonny wee thing, lovely wee thing, was thou mine....*"

She spun around. "Kit!"

He stepped out from the shadows by the carriage house.

"What are you doing here?"

"When I saw you today, I knew I had to try and explain."

"Are you going to marry Enid Joyce?"

"What would you have me do? She claims she's expecting." He rubbed a hand roughly over his cheek.

"I cannot believe this. Not *her*."

He came closer. "I thought I'd die for want of you. I couldn't thole it. She was willing, and her father found us out. See what you've brought me to?"

"What did you do?"

A humorless laugh escaped him. "Must I explain the details of my crime? Sweet Christ! If I didn't love you so, I'd—"

"You love me? I thought you hated me."

He came right up to her, grabbing her cheeks and stroking the hair from her temples. "I love you, for whatever good it does me. Have you not listened? I lay with her, and I caused a child to root inside her. Now there'll be no Paris for me, no Rome. We've booked passage on the emigrant ship to America, for her father's disowned her. He's keeping up appearances, but he's told us he doesn't want to see us again after the wedding. I'll have to become a vet like you wanted."

"I don't understand."

He shook her. "What don't you understand? How babes are made? You sweet, daft goose. It's the same as the bull and the cow, the stallion and the mare, the dog and the *bitch*, damn you!"

"I know that," she said scornfully, though thinking of it made her blush and turn away.

She'd seen plenty of mating dogs and sheep through the years, and had watched Leo and Cloud in the stable yard. Leo had mounted Cloud's hindquarters, snorting, his powerful haunches working, that long, spotted thing hanging ugly and obscene when he finished. Morrigan had heard her father's voice and had gone quickly about her business, knowing he'd thrash her if he caught her.

When she was young, she'd thought the sole purpose of that appendage was to make it convenient for men to piss, a wee gift, in a way, from their God. But eventually she'd worked out the truth.

Cloud hadn't acted overly pleased with the stallion's attentions. One of Leo's great hooves had managed to slice a bloody gash on her side.

"I did it for want of you," Kit said, breaking into her unhappy thoughts. "You stopped me, Morrigan, and I couldn't get over it. I thought I might go daft." His jaw clenched. "I couldn't have you, but Enid was…more obliging."

"Papa would've killed us. You know it."

He dropped his arms to his sides. "I'm glad you stopped me," he said. "I'd never shame you, not for anything!"

There it was again, this shame that was always connected to love. Hot anger flared. "But you didn't care about shaming her, did you? And now you're marrying, though you said you never would. Marrying a lass who means nothing to you, a vicious shrew you've always loathed, and you're going away to America, destitute." The absurdity hammered the inside of her skull and found its escape in bitter laughter.

He chafed his hands through his hair and turned away. "I meant to leave without seeing you again," he said. "But when you came to town today, I knew I had to…one more time. I swear, Morrigan, if it was you I had to marry, you I had to give up my dreams for, I think it would be worth it."

His misery and hopelessness broke her. He looked like he might start weeping. "Kit…" she cried. She stretched out her arms and he wrapped her in a hard embrace, stroking her hair.

"Tell Nick goodbye for me," he said.

Maybe with his troubles he didn't know about Nicky. She started to speak against his chest, to tell him Nicky was gone, but he flew backward and sprawled in the dirt, leaving her clutching nothing. A raven's harsh cry echoed through the close as it fluttered from the midden-heap, disturbed by the abrupt violence.

With a grimace of pure rage, Kit scrambled from the ground. Morrigan saw Douglas, his curved sickle upraised like a weapon.

"So one ruined family isn't enough for you," her father said in a growl. "You'll wish you'd never laid eyes on what is mine, you coarse young bastard." The last glitter of light reflected against his blade, and Morrigan experienced a horrible vision of Kit's head lopped off and rolling on the ground.

"I was telling her goodbye," Kit said, "but of course you think the worst. You're a beast, you know that? She'd be better off if you were dead."

He leaped. Back and forth the two men tottered. The sickle flew, thudding against the carriage house wall when Kit smashed Douglas on the chin with his fist.

Douglas returned the blow, knocking Kit clear off balance. He sprawled once more. Douglas threw himself on top of Kit and started pummeling. Morrigan clutched her father's braces from behind and managed to pull him off, but he landed on top of her and ground a boot-heel into her shin.

Kit struggled to his feet, blood flowing from his nose and lip, his cheekbone reddened and swelling. "Are you hurt, Morrigan?"

"No," she gasped, rolling away as Douglas stood.

"I didn't shame her," Kit said. "Believe us or not, it's no difference to me. I'm away to America, and pleased to never see you again in this life, you damned useless mucker."

"Papa," Morrigan said. "He was only saying goodbye!"

Douglas swung on her so sharply it brought a small scraich of fear from her throat. "Don't you speak." His narrow-eyed stare burned her skin. "Panting after him. In your nightclothes."

"Christ," Kit said. "It's a waste of breath. Let him think whatever he wants." He stalked away but paused at the edge of the road. "If you hurt her, you'll see me again, Douglas Lawton, and I'll kill you. D'you hear?"

"Kit…are you going?" Morrigan asked.

"I love you…." His words floated so low through the honey sweet air she could almost believe he spoke directly into her heart.

Douglas seized Morrigan's arm and dragged her into the barn.

"We didn't do anything wrong," she cried.

He slapped her, causing a tooth to cut her lip.

"Whores…" His scowl was like a stabbing blade. "That's what you are, all of you." His voice dropped, becoming quiet, the voice she most hated and feared. "You, especially."

Knowing defiance would make things worse, she stamped out her thoughts. The barn smelled of hay and dung and horses, pleasant, homey aromas, but for times like this, when Douglas strapped his children. He lit the lantern. Morrigan backed away from him, stopping in front of the nearest stall. Cloud nickered at her, and the foal nosed her hand through the slats.

"Bend over," Douglas said, low and raspy.

She gripped the top pole and bent over the gate, dull apprehension stiffening her muscles. The tawse hummed then landed and she met the mare's dark gaze, instantly terrified. Something about this strapping was different. It felt like she'd been slashed with a white-hot knife blade. She'd always had the protection of her clothing. This time, her corset and petticoat lay on her bed and the wrapper she wore was simple muslin, with nothing beneath but a chemise and drawers.

Again he struck her, and she had to fight to keep silent. He'd enjoy that, hearing her cry, knowing he hurt her. It was what he wanted. But when the strap lanced across other forming welts, a small, involuntary shriek escaped. She ground her mouth against her arm and bit, hard.

Two more times he lashed her. Then there was a pause. He said something, but she couldn't hear what through the screaming in her throat.

He whipped her around. "Did you hear me? I said take down your dress."

In the shadows and lantern light he resembled a beast dredged from blackest nightmare. He stared at her as though she was a stranger.

Because she hadn't wailed or wept, he must think her unhurt. He stood there, holding a lash wet with her blood, as much as promising he wouldn't stop until she screamed, begged for mercy, or died.

"Thrawn...." He spat. "Just another bitch in heat."

"Don't call me that!" She crossed her arms over her chest, pressing her hands over her shoulders.

"A hoor then?" He grasped her collar and tore her robe open to the waist. Buttons popped and flew. Only the knotted belt around her waist prevented it from being pulled clear off.

Flinging away the tawse, he grabbed her wrists and forced them down, restraining both in one hand. His skin was splotched. His breath wheezed and his lips contorted into a feral grimace. "Now you'll see," he said. "You'll see."

Morrigan pulled and wrenched against him until she managed to free her hands. She clutched at the shreds of her wrapper and chemise as he backed her against the planks of the stall.

"Don't play the innocent," he said. "You think I can't tell this is what you've been wanting? The vet's son saw it. You probably think he cares, stupid cow. All he cares about is between your legs."

She gagged, suffocating in his close, hot breath. She strained and fought, trying to push past him, but he grabbed her by the hair and jerked, hard.

Stop, make him stop, she prayed, but there never was any answer to her prayers, and this time was no different.

Resolve formed like an iron spear. *I'll kill you for this, Papa. I swear I will.*

He lifted his free hand, reaching for her, and she angled away, slapping him as hard as she could. He yanked her hair so brutally she screamed.

The big door gave a harsh squeak. Morrigan looked up, half-afraid and half-hopeful Kit had come.

But it wasn't Kit. "Douglas." Her aunt sounded calm, soothing. "Come away now."

Her father's hand dropped, releasing her hair, and she stumbled out of his reach.

"I've made tea," Beatrice said. "It's fresh and hot."

The lantern's yellow glare impaled them all like insects. The mare crunched her oats and stamped.

From the periphery of her vision, Morrigan saw her father slump. His breath seeped in a long wavering sigh.

"I...I shouldna...have done that," he said. "I don't know what...."

Their eyes met. His were shuttered, his skin deeply flushed. He spun like he couldn't bear the sight of her, and she knew. He considered this her fault—this, as well as being born.

Beatrice held out her hand and they left the barn together.

———————————

Chapter 8

———————————

Morrigan held her bloodstained wrapper up to the light, putting her fingers through the splits made by Douglas's lash.

A mysterious, shadowed being had disgorged from Hell and possessed her father. She could almost smell the burning, sooty stench, could almost see crimson-tinged, leering eyes.

These were foolish thoughts. Only Beatrice had witnessed the horror. Why would the Devil waste time on her if God did not?

Unnerving silence blanketed the inn. She hoped the Irish couple hadn't heard the disturbance. She tried to remember if she had screamed, but wasn't sure.

She put on an old skirt and a loose blouse that could be worn with no corset. Rolling up her sleeves, she went downstairs.

Beatrice sat alone in the kitchen with tea and bread. "Your father's in the fields," she said when Morrigan entered.

Morrigan nodded and poured a cup of tea.

"You're in one piece then, *a luaidh?*"

"Aye." Morrigan eased into a chair. Steam rose from the teacup, warming her cheeks.

It must have taken courage to confront Douglas when he was in such a rage. Morrigan felt guilty for the times she'd doubted Beatrice. At this moment her aunt seemed the only person in the world standing in defense of her. What would have happened if she hadn't come to the barn?

As if to prove the point, Beatrice rose and fetched the old green tin of deadening liniment from the cupboard. Morrigan unbuttoned her blouse, lowering

79

it enough in back so that Beatrice could smear the balm over the welts. It burned at first, but soon helped diminish the worst of the sting.

"Would you care for some gruel?" Beatrice asked as she put the tin away. Her eyes held familiar blankness. She wanted them to pretend nothing had happened. They were to have gruel, drink tea, and perhaps discuss their chores.

Morrigan shook her head and buttoned her blouse.

Once she'd seen an old woman being pushed in a wheeled chair by her tight-lipped maid. A dowager's hump forced the old lady's head down between her shoulders. The expression of hatred and pain in those colorless eyes told a bitter story. The woman had become a burden, even to herself. Morrigan had walked on, picturing her as she might have once been: bonny and sweet, with an eager entourage of young men.

Morrigan too, was a burden. Papa hated her. Beatrice thought her spoiled and held her to blame for her own misfortunes. Nicky feared for her.

Daughters of whores usually turn out whores themselves.

She wanted to weep, but her eyes remained dry, gritty as though sprinkled with sand. She had often wished she'd never been born, or could die. But it had never coalesced so clearly or strongly. She saw herself in a coffin, peaceful...quiet...arms crossed, lilies wound through pale, translucent fingers.

When Beatrice touched her arm, Morrigan flinched.

"You don't understand," her aunt said. "He's not evil. He has suffered."

Morrigan leaped from her chair and fetched a skillet. "Our guests'll be hungry."

An hour later she told the travelers goodbye and climbed the stairs to clean their room. It had been hard to smile, to speak of the weather and other nonsense while wondering what they might have seen or heard, and she fancied they'd leveled several curious glances her way.

The front bell jingled. More travelers. No matter her situation, she was obliged to put on a welcoming face, to pretend she longed for nothing more in life but to serve this endless dribble of strangers.

Halfway down the stairs, her arms spilling over with bed linens, she stopped. A fresh, accursed blush crept over her cheeks and her heart began to hammer.

Curran Ramsay held a confection of flowers, the like of which she'd never seen, a riot of blue, purple, white, pink, and red. His smile almost touched her it came so warm and easy. Somehow, it managed to blow the night clear away. Before she could stop herself, her lips curved up in return.

Had she really forgotten this handsome face, so bonnily put together, bringing with it not only pleasure but also a glorious sense of safety and trust?

"Mr. Ramsay," she said. "Didn't you mention you'd be seeing us again in June?"

"Trouble has a way of interfering with our most determined plans." He scrutinized her, not making the slightest effort to disguise how pleased he was. "One of my ships wrecked off the coast of India. I was obliged to meet with the buyers in Liverpool. Thankfully, everyone on board survived."

His smile increased. He looked almost…gleeful.

"I see." She descended three more steps. "Are those for me?"

"D'you like flowers?"

"Of course. I love flowers, like any female." Leaning over the bundle of laundry, she closed her eyes and breathed in the scent of a warm garden, of buttery sunlight and the velvet bellies of honeybees. "What of the cargo?" She met his gaze, made bluer by the rich petals he held. That white scar curved so close to his left eye. There must have been concern about it threatening his sight.

"The cargo was lost, unfortunately." His hand inched forward on the banister.

She straightened. "I'm sorry to hear it."

"I far prefer losing cargo to people," he said with a shrug.

Yet another thing to like about him. "How is our pup?"

"Pining for you."

She came to the last step, watching the pupils in his eyes expand.

"Along with her master," he added, as low and warm as a libation of simmered whisky.

Morrigan tossed the linens carelessly to the floor and dusted her hands. Giving him a smile Beatrice would've named her a *jillet* for employing—accompanied by a cuff for good measure—she accepted the bouquet, cupping one gloriously petaled red flower into the palm of her hand. "I fancy a stroll on the moor, Mr. Ramsay," she said, not quite believing her boldness. It was that other lass speaking, the wild secret girl who flickered sometimes in her looking-glass or smiled from the pool in the forest. "Would you care to walk with me?" What was she doing? That wicked siren had some half-baked plan…but this time Morrigan welcomed the interference. The girl reminded her of the imaginary Princess Aridela, bravest of females, who laughed as she seized the horns of a charging bull. She lent her mistress purpose and strength, sensations the surface Morrigan all too often lacked.

"I am at your service, Miss Lawton." Turning, he swept one arm towards the door and offered her the other. They exchanged smiles and strolled out, away onto the upper braes, into a cleansing wind.

"Why didn't you bring Antiope?"

"I came straight from Liverpool. She's doing well, and entertains herself by chewing everything I own to bits."

Morrigan steered them with unobtrusive intent towards the same ruinous shieling they'd used as a refuge on their last encounter, though she refused to think beyond that. "I miss her."

"And her master…I hope?"

"Aye…." One side of her mouth lifted in a most improper smile and the welts throbbed as though in warning. "And her master." Ah, it was good to possess a face fine enough to draw this man's attention. Papa couldn't take that away from her, no matter how much he might wish it.

She sat and removed her boots at the first burn they came to. He held her hand as she crossed, then went on holding it for a while longer.

"You've cut your lip," he said at the following burn. He ran the tip of his index finger next to it, kindling a warm fire that followed the path he traced.

"It's nothing. I was…bending over the foal and it-it hit me with its forehead." He would think her blush the result of shy innocence, but it came from a chilling realization. Douglas Lawton could indeed strip the beauty from her face if he so desired. A few well-placed strikes with his fists or the leather strap would easily accomplish it, and no man's eyes would ever again light with admiration.

The need to escape her father filled her muscles with a tense, overwhelming urge to flee, but to where?

They approached the shieling at the edge of the wood. Morrigan dropped her boots in a shady spot and laid the bouquet beside them. She leaned against the doorjamb, protecting her back by folding her arms behind her and barely touching her shoulder blades to the wood.

He joined her in the doorway, so close she caught his intoxicating scent, which reminded her of clouds draped across the hills, approaching rain, of leaves turned dry and crackly and air that burned one's cheeks to scarlet.

"Have your circumstances changed since I last saw you?" he asked.

"Life never changes for me."

"Your father didn't agree to send you to your aunt's?"

She shrugged then wished she hadn't. As delicate as her chemise was, it still chafed. "No. I suppose he can't survive without me after all."

"It may be time to plan your flight." One brow lifted, daring her.

He resembled her dream-lover so much. It made her knees weak. Well, there was the matter of the eyes, which were the wrong color, and the hair, which in her fantasy was longer. Her dreams always designed her warrior more huskily built than Curran Ramsay, too, not as tall, and not nearly so polished.

Resting her palm on his lapel, she said, "I do long to see your Kilgarry," and looked at him through her lashes.

"You've ruined everything, you know." He frowned. "I can't go anywhere without wondering what you would think of it…without wanting to show you the spots most dear to me." His frown deepened. "Miss Lawton…I…." One after the other, he placed his hands against the timbers on either side of her head and lowered his face to hers. Sounding almost vexed, he said, "I can't remember my own name...."

This time she would allow no misunderstandings, hesitation, or belated gentlemanly propriety. She clutched his lapel and pulled him in. Even before they kissed, she felt the incandescent glittering leap between them, like a river of invisible sparks.

"Pretend you love me." She was so close she saw the wee speckles of green and violet interspersed with a thousand variances of blue in his eyes. "Just for this one day. This moment."

His lashes shadowed his eyes as he stopped her from saying more.

Languor scattered everything: the breeze, the pain, and the awful memories. All burst and flew away, leaving nothing but a downpour of shared passion.

So. That was the wild girl's plan. As it turned out, it was a damn fine one.

CURRAN RAMSAY WAS GOLDEN AND BLITHE, WITH A MOUTH DESIGNED FOR KISSING, and eyes like the gloaming. But now he was changing. The crescent-shaped scar at his left eyebrow lengthened, forging downward to his mouth, disfiguring the entire side of his face. His hair spilled over his shoulders, darkening like a waterfall in shadow. His features transformed as well; they turned hard, almost cruel, and his bare chest carried more scars. He looked like a man who spent more time in battle than out. Only his eyes were the same, and made him recognizable.

Morrigan lay near a radiant ember fire. Water dripped off stalactites with a steady *ping, ping, ping*. Damp, the smell, confined, the scent of a deep cave, of the underworld.

Though he looked different, she saw Curran Ramsay tempting her from behind this bearded stranger's face. His touch, his longing, made her want to give him everything he asked for, and more, but something stopped her. Though she yearned to share the gifts of the goddess with him, she couldn't.

He was angry. *I will bind you to this pallet until the day of your death.*

You'll tether me like a goat? That is your image of victory?

I will have victory, Aridela.

His oath echoed through the dream, then there was silence.

HER BACK WAS STINGING. FOR A MOMENT SHE WONDERED IF SHE HAD MANAGED TO fall asleep on thorns before she remembered.

Douglas's face. The thrashing. His unbearable words. *Take down your dress.*

She smiled. Aye, it felt good to defy him, to become what he'd accused her of being. The *hoor*.

Her papa thought her so bad? Well, now she was, and he could never undo it.

Warm and inert, Curran lay comfortably against her side, one arm flung over her stomach, his cheek on her chest.

She wished she could savor this moment, but she couldn't bear the pain. She rolled, pushing at him. His head lifted and his eyes opened drowsily, reminding her of a dozing cat's. He gave her a sweet kiss she wanted to enjoy, but when his hand slipped around her waist, she flinched.

"What's wrong?" he asked.

"It's my back. It hurts."

He rose on one elbow, turning her onto her side, and spoke some Gaelic word she didn't know as he pushed at her chemise.

"You're bleeding." He sat up and so did she. "These are whip marks."

She sighed. "Aye." Through the throb and burning, she attempted a smile. "To be honest, I nearly forgot." She stroked hair from his eyes and touched his lips with her index finger.

"Who did this?" he asked insistently, but clasped her hand.

"God and Country give a father the right, I believe, to discipline his offspring. What should I call you now? I wager we know each other well enough for Christian names. Unless you prefer 'Mr. Ramsay.'" She pressed her palm to his jaw. "Your cravat's missing, Mr. Ramsay."

He would not be distracted. "Why did he do it?"

She paused, looking away over the rolling moorland. "I vexed him. My brother's run away because of the whippings. I don't know if I'll ever see Nicky again, and he was my best friend. My only friend."

His eyes darkened, stilled. He pulled her close, carefully, and kissed her in the hollow between her collarbones.

Swallows and blackbirds broke the silence as they probed for insects. From far away came the plaintive sound of the train whistle. Breezes rustled through the heath. In this wild place, it was easy to imagine invisible faeries ridiculing these two ungainly humans who wore little more than sunlight.

"The cut on your lip," he said. "It wasn't the foal."

She inclined her head. "Please. Our afternoon. You're spoiling it."

"And that bruise on your jaw, the first time you and I were here. I wondered then who had struck you, but thought I must be wrong."

"Is this the best you can do for wooing? I don't want to think of those things. Not now, not today."

His frown suggested he might argue, but then he plucked a few sprigs of miniature white flowers from the bouquet and presented them to her. He shook out his frock coat, which he'd gallantly placed beneath her earlier. She inhaled the seductive fragrance and thanked him with a kiss, but that was a mistake, wasn't it? Next thing she knew, he'd thrown the poor abused coat down again, and pulled her on top of him.

She giggled.

He was tender now. His kisses and hands cajoled her into incoherent response. The first time, she'd been nervous, fighting guilt, trying not to show fear and not sure what to do. For her at least, it hadn't ended as pleasantly as it began, and seemed to suggest Beatrice's warnings had some merit.

This time, she didn't think about sin or suffering. She gave herself to breathless fascination and the erotic response of her skin as he stroked it. She observed him as he reached his fulfillment. His face expressed a strange mixture of pain and joy.

Why was this a thing to worry over, to endure? It wasn't something she couldn't live without, but it was nice. The kissing, especially. She'd be sorry if she never got to do that again. Poor Auntie Beatrice. Having never married, she obviously didn't understand.

Kit's face intruded, his desolate expression when he said, *Don't you know how babes are made? It's the same as the bull and the cow, the stallion and the mare, the dog and the bitch, damn you!*

"Oh God," she said as her lover pressed kisses to her throat. "What have I done? Am I going to have a child?"

His eyes flew open. He blinked several times and she felt him wince. "I...ah...."

"Isn't this the way children begin? When you make water inside me?"

"It isn't like that," he said, flushing. "I mean...it is the way...but I don't...." He stopped. She was sure he was holding back laughter from the way the skin around his eyes crinkled.

"He'll kill me," she said before thinking better of it.

"No he won't." Curran's eyes flashed like blue and white lightning. "He'll never touch you again."

Chapter 9

Billowing clouds framed a single dark speck that soared and circled. It was high above them, but Morrigan recognized the glorious wingspan of an eagle, and heard its singular screeling call.

She'd just started to wonder if it could be the same eagle she'd seen several times at the inn when Curran, who had been gazing contentedly into the sky at her side, turned to face her.

He caressed her cheek. "You've never been with a man, have you?"

She shook her head, embarrassed, wondering what she'd done that made it so obvious.

"Did I hurt you?"

"Hurt me?"

"When we…when I…. I've heard there's pain for a girl, the first time."

"Really?" She shrugged. "Maybe. I don't remember."

He smiled, and she knew her answer relieved him. He truly didn't want to hurt her. She could see he didn't want her to regret what they had done—what *she* had done.

She tucked in closer and pulled his face down. "Kiss me," she said, happy to speak the words she'd stopped herself from saying the first time, and as soon as he did, demanded, "again. Kiss me again."

Another word formed, sliding through her thoughts. *Menoetius.* But she put it aside as his kisses took precedence.

She wasn't sorry. Yes, her reckless act had come from a need to punish Douglas Lawton. But there was more to it. She'd been driven to experience one act of her own making, something beyond her father's control.

"The strangest thing happened the day I met you," he said, much later, after kissing led to other things.

"Aye?" His mouth was captivating. She was certain she would never tire of kissing.

"Aye." The obliging lad seemed to sense her wish and did kiss her, on the mouth, the jaw, and finally, her shoulder.

She was sore by now, after three times, but maybe she could manage it once more.

"Colors surrounded you." He spoke low, next to her ear. "I've never seen anything like it…well, only a few times. And another thing. Once, when lightning struck a tree, I was near enough that every hair on my head stood up; the heat of it went through me, as though I was lit from within. I felt I was being lifted off the ground. When I saw you at the train station, something very similar happened."

"What colors did you see?" she asked, her voice nearly lost beneath the pounding of her heart.

"Pure gold, in a glitter like you were swimming in a sea of mica, with hints of lavender. It faded after a moment and I wondered if it happened at all. But a while ago, I saw it again."

Yours was blue. Every color of blue that's ever been dreamed. She didn't say it, though she wasn't sure why. She felt frightened, as though something of great import was happening. Nervous and jittery, she jumped up, straightening her chemise, and fetched the bouquet he'd brought her.

"See that cloud?" Curran pointed. "Zeus and his thunderbolts."

"Zeus?" Morrigan gazed into the sky. "A child's plaything, made up by foolish boys. Look into that one, there…." She used one of the flowers as a pointer. "The one all dark blue underneath, like it's full of rain. Can you see her?"

Curran lit a cigar and exhaled a cloud of aromatic smoke. "A horse?"

Morrigan gave him an affronted scowl and a cuff on the shoulder. "It's the Great Goddess. Athene. Are you blind?"

"Maybe…a horsey-looking woman with long hair. But there's no helmet or shield. It can't be Athene. Oh, wait. That might be a sword, going off to the right."

"Don't be daft. She was beautiful. And it's a snake, not a sword. See how it curls around her arm?"

Curran sat up. He grabbed her wrist and kissed her palm, murmuring, "You really are an unco lass." Then he frowned. His head tilted. She followed his gaze. She'd forgotten the ugly red birthmark. She tried to pull her hand away, but he wouldn't let go.

"What is this?" He turned an intent stare to her face.

"Nothing." Again she tried to pull her hand free, but he wouldn't release it.

He bent his head and kissed the mark then covered it with his hand, so gently her embarrassment dissipated.

"Tell me about these flowers," she said. "Did you choose them especially for me?"

He grinned, mocking her desire for flattery, but said, "Of course. Look." He separated a spray from the rest. "Bluebells, for gratitude. I'm grateful you didn't hate me after the last time." Releasing those, he touched the lavender, then the periwinkles. "Lavender for the scent, mostly—"

"They mean devotion," Morrigan interrupted.

"Aye." He grinned again. "They do. Periwinkles, for sweet memories." He sobered. "I haven't stopped thinking of you, of *us*, of the last time we were together, and the memories have been sweet."

"Tell me more. What are these?"

"Camellias. The pink is for how I've longed to see you again, and the red… perhaps I shouldn't say.…"

She didn't answer, but her gaze demanded.

"That you're a flame within my heart," he said with a slow smile. "Red is for how you hold my destiny in your hands." He brushed a strand of hair from her eyelashes.

"No one's ever given me flowers," she said, working hard to keep her voice steady.

He took that as the invitation it was, and the bouquet was placed to the side.

She traced the crescent scar where it severed his left brow and traveled around his eye. "How did you get this?"

It was his turn to blush. His gaze faltered.

"I'm sorry," she said. "I didn't mean to—"

"It's ugly, and reminds me of a time I wish I could forget."

"It's not ugly. It's interesting, but if you don't want to speak of it.…"

With a short laugh, he ran a hand through his hair and regarded her, his blush intensifying before it faded away. "Perhaps you, with your imagination, could put a meaning on the bloody thing. I don't really know how I got it."

What a wondrous sensation of importance he granted her, and how kind to suggest she possessed a finer wit than his own. She would give her life now to solve the puzzle, whatever it was. "Tell me."

Resting his forearms on his knees, he said, "My father thought me weak, or so he said. I believe his true purpose was to weed out a certain…disquiet… about the forest."

Morrigan watched a fresh wave of scarlet rise in his cheeks. Whatever the source of his injury, it still caused strong emotions.

His fingertips pressed against the scar. "He and I found the survivors of the Glenelg clearings shortly after we moved to Kilgarry. You and your brother... your father and aunts...the others. We rode out one morning and stumbled across them, some dead, most close to it. Several lay in two old ruins. More were in the forest. I'd never seen a dead person before that day."

Clearings. Every time she'd heard that word, it had been spoken in a hush or an angry hiss, and she'd learned young that to ask questions brought anger and censure, sometimes a clout or a beating, if Douglas's mood was bad enough. So she'd stopped asking, and she didn't now. The shadow in his eyes warned her.

Yet the question rose in her throat. *You found me, and my kin, half dead in a forest?*

"That started it," he went on with a shrug. "What my father never knew was how the woods spoke to me after that day. I heard those dead folk, and I began to avoid the outdoors." He glanced at her and made a sound, halfway between a laugh and a sigh. "Don't look so troubled. I don't think I'm ready for the madhouse."

Her heartbeat stuttered; for one instant that seemed to flip her upside down, she felt as though her soul flew out and touched his. In that instant, he wasn't the wealthy laird and she the penniless innkeeper's daughter. For the first time, she realized how devastated she would be if he left and never returned.

She swallowed. "I wasn't—"

"I know." Rocking forward, he kissed the frown between her brows. "When I turned eleven, he sent me into the northern wilds with a primitive chieftain from the Shetland Isles named Fearghas. God only knows where he met the man or how he convinced him to nursemaid me." He shook his head with a disgusted, one-sided smile. "Fearghas knew no English, and I hadn't fully mastered the Gaelic, at least not his version of it. Gibberish, more likely—the language of Sholties. Anyway, I had no warning. My father thrust me out next to this tall thin hairy fellow and told me not to come home until I was as comfortable in the woods as my bedroom."

"Oh." Was there no end to what fathers were capable of? *What a piece of work is a man,* Hamlet had astutely stated.

He nodded, surprising her by adding, "I'm grateful now, but I hated him as Fearghas dragged me from the courtyard. It worked, as my father somehow knew it would. I vanquished my fear."

"Was it this man, then, who hurt you...?"

"No, not Fearghas." He slipped the tender stem of a weed from its stiff fibrous sheath with a faint *eeek* and chewed the end. "He often left me, though, days at a time, to fend for myself. One night when I was alone, up near Loch Torridon...d'you know where that is?"

She shook her head.

"It's a bleak, lonely place north of Glenelg. I fell asleep beside a half-frozen tarn, and...." Again he stopped. He yanked another weed, glanced at her, and looked away. "It's difficult to describe."

Morrigan caught his restless fingers and caressed them. "Please?" Perhaps he'd murdered someone...Fearghas, no doubt.

He faced her again; his expression warmed her like a bottle of strong spirits.

"I say I was asleep," he went on, "but it's so vivid, and there's this...." He flicked the scar. "I have a memory of waking and rising. The moon was full. Everything had a glow about it—the water, the rocks. I could see a glow around me as well. I walked to the tarn—and jumped in."

He laughed, and Morrigan admired this image of him. Supple flesh, the stain of color in his cheeks, the way light seemed to adore his lashes, brows and hair, the warmth and pressure of his hand, and the indentations on either side of his mouth put there from an endless accumulation of smiles.

She wished she could capture this moment, fold him up, slip him into an envelope and carry him, tucked in her chemise next to her heart.

Only after this breathless moment of reverence did she comprehend what he'd said.

"You what?"

"As naked as the day my mother bore me."

"But...you said it was half-frozen."

"It was, but I don't remember feeling cold. I saw a palace. The moonlight shining on it made it seem like layers of pearls. I swam towards it and a set of gates swung open. Should I stop now? I've never told another soul this, not my father, my mother, not anyone. I was afraid they'd think me...mad."

"Don't stop."

"A lady was waiting, a beautiful lady with long red hair." He gave her one of his slow, luxuriant smiles with the lowered eyelids. "Near bonny as you, I'd say."

"Oh." This feeling he caused...the fluttering, shyness, and yearning...was it love? Could one love another so quickly? No, no. *No.* Such a thing was impossible.

There would be time to contemplate that later, when she was alone.

"She took my hand," Curran said, "and led me into the palace, all turrets, terraces, balconies, enormous chambers. We came to a long hall, and at the far end there was a throne. A woman sat there, holding a staff. She told me she was keeping the throne in trust for the rightful queen. These two ladies, one dressed in silver, the other white, led me to a door inlaid with pearl and carvings of runes, and snakes, and trees. The queen opened it. I could see only a few steps in—the rest was blackness. She told me I must enter, and conquer the beast. If I did, the enchanted palace would rise to the surface and be restored to its rightful place."

"Could you breathe?" Morrigan asked.

Curran laughed. "Bless you." He cupped her cheeks. "You haven't once said I was dreaming or daft. I could breathe, I suppose, or I didn't need to. I stepped through and they closed the door behind me. A candle was burning on a shelf; beside it was a knife, a wicked-looking thing with a curved black blade and ivory handle. I picked them up and followed a corridor through many twists and turns, and always, in the distance, I heard roaring."

"The minotaur. The labyrinth on the isle of Crete. You were…you were Theseus."

He smiled but his brows lowered. "Didn't you call me Theseus once, the day we met? At the train station."

"Aye." She fought to halt the inner reeling, to display a calm demeanor though inside she was crying, *Theseus. My Theseus.* Even the inner lass seemed startled into rare silence.

For the first time she realized something that now seemed profoundly important. Not for a moment, not from the first kiss to the removal of her clothes, nor when their bodies joined, did she experience that inner revulsion that had sent her recoiling from Kit. With Curran, she'd wanted more and more, to go deeper, and deeper yet. Now that she thought about it, she remembered the wild inner Morrigan shouting, *It's him. It's him!*

"Well, you're right," he said. "I was attacked in this maze, not by a man with a bull's head, but a lion." He paused. "Every time I thought I'd killed it, it sprang up again with more strength than ever. I was so tired. My wounds were bad, this one in particular." He touched the crescent scar. "Never in my life have I wanted so much to give up, to lie down and die."

"And then?"

"I heard weeping. I saw a woman behind the lion. She was chained at the wrist inside an oak tree upon a hill, and somehow," he shrugged, "I could see through the wood. She was trapped, imprisoned inside the tree. Then the answer came. I dropped the knife."

"You…but how could you…."

He shook his head. "The lion killed me, and it was as though I consented. It ripped out my throat."

"Oh. Oh."

"I was dying, but I saw the knife beside me. I picked it up and stabbed the lion through the heart."

"So you both died?"

"It fell on me. I felt its breath on my face, the heaviness of it. Then…nothing. I floated, and the lion's blood washed over me."

Morrigan shuddered.

"His spirit entered me with his blood," Curran said, "and I could breathe again. He and I were one. I'd never felt so strong and alive, and violently hungry. I ran up the hill and clawed through the oak. The woman welcomed me, and we drank wine from a chalice. Together, he and I…the lion, and me, we…."

She smiled, seeing what he couldn't quite say.

He smiled too, and blushed. Oh, how she adored his shyness.

"So the lion made the scar?" Morrigan asked as she remembered the point of the tale.

He nodded. "I've never known such joy as that night, lying on the grass with her. I would've gladly stayed forever. She…that girl…." He stopped.

"What?"

"My God." He was suddenly pale.

"What, Curran?"

He grabbed her hand and turned it, tracing the birthmark at her wrist. "I'd swear. Not the same, but somehow, you. *You* were the woman inside the tree. Your hair was black, you wore a crown, but you had this mark on your wrist."

"Fate brought you to me, then." She tried to be casual, but her smile was unsteady, and she suspected she might be as pale as he.

He contemplated her, emotion running swiftly across his face. "Fate." After a moment he said, "I fell asleep with her, but when I woke, I was alone beside the tarn, in the darkness of old night. Yet another lady stepped from the water. Not the lass from the oak, not the queen or the gatekeeper. This woman's hair was the color of the moonlight. She seemed familiar, and very solemn. She held up the knife I'd used in the maze, and the chalice I'd drunk wine from. I wanted to run away, but snakes were crawling over my arms and legs, binding me to the ground. The wounds were still there. I was in terrible pain, and screaming."

"Did she hurt you?"

He shook his head. "Of all the wounds, even the one in my throat, this one beside my eye hurt the worst. She pressed the blade against the wound and it cauterized. She soothed me and wept over me, and then she said, 'Do the same in the real world. Return honor to men if you would be reunited with us.'"

Morrigan watched her lover contemplate the horizon. A thrill raced through her as she recognized how seriously he considered the quest. A would-be hero sat here with her…a knight of old, like the Black Douglas or King Arthur. She had no doubt that he would give his life for the sake of the task.

Curran's voice was low and hesitant when he continued. "She told me the wound would never fade, that it was my mother's mark, to remind me of my origins." He appeared confused for the first time. "I've never understood that, or what she said after. 'Follow the sacred one, though she travels far and brings grief beyond endurance.'"

"You memorized it."

"Aye, and gone over and over it until I...." He broke off another tall stiff stalk and rolled it between his palms until nothing remained but a damp green smudge. "Riddles. She held the chalice to my mouth and I drank. The wine tasted somehow like the lass I'd been with. I pledged myself to her, and every wound healed instantly." He drew in a deep breath and regarded Morrigan. "Next I knew Fearghas was shaking me, gobbling about sleeping the whole day. Blood all over me, but no wounds, no sign of the lion fight, except for this scar, as you see it now."

Morrigan propped her arms on her knees and cupped her chin in her palms. "Mark of the lion. Not the moon after all."

"Moon?"

"When I first saw your scar, that's what it seemed to me. A crescent moon." She rubbed his hand between hers. "'Tis a fine vision, Mr. Ramsay."

"Vision...."

"Well, if it was real, I want to go there. Will you take me?"

He laughed. "You're not afraid?"

"No." She grinned. "I'd like to see this lion."

"I tried to find it again. I threw myself into the water—Fearghas thought I'd gone clear daft. He dragged me out, shook me like a dog, said in broken English that my father would roast him alive if anything happened to me. I realized for the first time my father hadn't really deserted me."

"And your quest? What is it?"

He shrugged. "I've searched...it's made me half mad, knowing there's something I need, and I can't find it. I've felt empty and useless...." He stared at her, his voice faltering.

"Curran?"

"Oh aye." Wonder again underlaced his voice. "It's gone."

"What?"

"That emptiness. It's gone."

A moment passed. He touched each of her fingertips, one by one, with his own. Closed his eyes tightly, frowning. "Morrigan," he said. His voice caressed her name.

"Curran? Are you ill?"

He shook his head. "I think I'm finally well."

WHEN THE SLEEPY HAZE OF LATE AFTERNOON STAINED THE SKY, MORRIGAN SIGHED and said she must go. Amazement and misgivings buffeted her as she thought of what she'd done. He might leave now, simply abandon her to her fate. Yet hadn't he promised a moment ago to bring her a copy of the *Iliad?*

She sat on his frock coat and rolled her stockings over her knees. Four times she had taken him into herself and she knew she'd given him much pleasure, yet his enthralled expression as she held up her hair and asked him to fasten the buttons on the back of her apron suggested he wouldn't refuse another round.

She stood, unable to block out the memory of Douglas and Kit as they struck each other, their faces ugly with hatred.

At last, fear blossomed. She stole another glance at the setting sun. Incriminating wrinkles creased her skirt and his frock coat. Though they tried to smooth them, both seemed to cry out, *You'll be lashed until you're dead for this.*

Curran's roguish smile implied the afternoon was worth any number of wrinkles. What wonderful, easy confidence. How she admired and envied it, and wished he could wrap some up and give it to her.

As they strolled towards town, Curran told her about his father. "His memory is cherished to this day," he said. "He bought Kilgarry in '54, right after the clearings, and rebuilt homes for those who'd survived. Until the day of his death he oversaw everything, from the draining of peat bogs to the lashing of the thatch on his shepherds' cots."

"Is it a rich estate?" she asked, before remembering her Aunt Ibby admonishing her that a lady never discussed money in polite company.

"Hardly. It devours time and currency like a sinkhole. There are many who claim the Highlands provide little of value besides sheep and soldiers."

He told her that Thomas was orphaned at ten and grew up alone, so poor there were times he'd survived on rotted food he picked up in alleys. Yet he made a fortune in the expanding railway business by working himself up the line from rough laborer to a respected engineer of the Caledonian Railways. He branched out and founded a shipping company he named *Uisge-Mor,* and joined in the tea and silk trade, using clipper ships. "Samuel Cunard and my father enjoyed their rivalry," Curran said. "But they remained good mates. Ship owners always try to outdo each other. For instance, one old seaman—Jock Willis—spent a fortune a few years ago building his dream ship, the *Cutty Sark.* She's sailing right now, racing the *Thermopylae* on the China run. Last I heard *Cutty Sark* is ahead." He gazed over the rolling moorland, pushing hair out of his eyes as though he had no idea how beautiful it was with the wind dancing through it. "My father adored the sea and his clippers. It's almost a shame steam has ousted them."

Pride and love underscored his words. Strange. She couldn't imagine loving a father. Surprising sensations of loss and envy darted through her, but she shoved them away. Life was what it was, and no amount of wishing would change things.

They stopped at the edge of town. "We can't return together," she said.

"I won't leave you."

"This is one day Papa won't have a word to say about where I've been."

"Why?"

She stared at the ground. He must never know, never, what Douglas Lawton had tried to do.

"He's been ill," she said, faltering. "Bedridden. He won't know I was gone."

Curran reluctantly conceded. They agreed he would wait to come to the inn until the arrival of the late train.

Morrigan stole into the Wren's Egg. All was quiet but for the ticking of the grandfather clock. Plucking up her courage, she crept along the narrow corridor to the kitchen.

Beatrice stood at the table, rolling out dough. A smear of flour whitened her cheek and dusted her bosom.

Her brows lifted as she absorbed Morrigan's wrinkled dress and untidy hair. They'd lost most of the pins in the rough undergrowth. Too late, Morrigan realized she should have gone straight up the stairs to her room. She could have changed, with no one the wiser.

But the woman, unreadable as ever, said only, "Are you hungry?"

"Starved."

Her aunt wiped a corner of the table while Morrigan fetched a cold sausage pastry and cheese scone.

Her stomach growled. She devoured every bite, along with strong tea and a hefty slab of shortbread.

"Where've you been?"

"Walking on the moor." Morrigan pumped water to wash her dishes. "I'll be half the night on these tangles. I forgot a hat again."

"Alone?"

"Who would I be with?" *No blushes.*

"You left your chores undone and said nothing to anybody. You're an inconsiderate wench. I was fashed about you!"

"I needed to clear my head."

"You think I don't know you ride up to Finnarts Hill, where the cliffs are high and the rocks sharp?"

"I went the other way, nowhere near the sea. Besides, no matter where I go, I know the moor like my own bedroom." The unintended picture the words created brought a hysterical giggle to the edge of her lips. She had to clamp her teeth together to keep it contained.

Beatrice crimped the edges of her dough and shrugged. "Your father was worried too."

Morrigan sucked in a breath.

"If you'd seen his face, you would've been ashamed. I think he feared you ran away like Nicky."

"So what if I did?" She spun around to face her aunt.

"Are you trying to make things worse for yourself and him?"

"Oh, aye. We must spare his poor feelings."

Her aunt straightened and wiped her hands on the towel. "Since the day of your birth he's labored to put food in your wame and clothes on your back. Do you think he enjoys scraping to the English? He's here because this is where he can provide. Both his wives died in childbirth. Could he save them? Yet here you stand, grown so fine you can mock him, aye, the spoiled, well-dressed lady. D'you know how hard it was to lose Hannah? Do you have any idea how it tore him apart?"

Redheaded Hannah? *Witch*, Douglas called her. *Whore*, Enid had sneered.

Beatrice shook Morrigan's arm. "He greeted like a wean when she died. We feared her death would kill him too."

"Do you want me to say I wish it'd been me? I do, I always have. It's abundantly clear he hates me because I made her die."

"Have pity!" Astonishment lifted the woman's brows. "Where d'you get such ideas?"

"I can't help it if I live and she's dead. Should I kill myself to make up for it? Could he be happy then?"

"Selfish besom!" Beatrice's grip tightened. "He never blamed you."

"I've known like he shouted it in my face every day. *I killed my mother*. And he'll never forgive me for it."

Ripping her arm free, Morrigan fled from the rage. If it caught her she'd suffocate. The world would expire. The air would blacken. Rivers would run with blood. She clawed at her throat.

Shadows swirled past her. There was a flash of blinding light, the stab of pain that always came right before she lost consciousness. Every sound was amplified: the creak of the steps, her breathing, her heartbeat.

She made it to the top of the stairs before it carried her away.

Chapter 10

Morrigan rolled over and buried her face under the pillow.

Luxurious, seductive pleasure came with images of Curran Ramsay. But then Beatrice's face interfered, the argument, and a slow-motion memory-fragment of running up the stairs. The echo of a scream reverberated. *He'll never forgive....* After that, nothing.

The unpredictable loss of consciousness was terrifying. It was as though her blood froze in an instant. She never knew when it would happen, and she was helpless to avert or control it. When she woke and tried to remember details, nothing came but disjointed colors, voices, and images that would surely frighten the most cynical, bloodthirsty soldier.

She threw off the bedclothes. All she wore was her chemise from yesterday.

What had happened at the top of the stairs? How had she ended up here? Curse this body. Damn her lunacy.

Leaping up, she rubbed her temples, trying to soothe away the dizziness, and paced from one end of her room to the other. Three times she made the circuit before noticing the flowers. Someone had put them in a vase. "He did come," she said. The blooms were drooping, hurried to their demise by the hours left on the ground without water. She doubted they would last another day. Her angry heartbeat slowed as she brushed the camellia's petals against her cheek, inhaling remnants of scents that returned the afternoon and all its delight. *You're a flame within my heart.*

Beatrice opened Morrigan's door without bothering to knock. She held a steaming cup of tea and the container of liniment. "I thought I heard you moving about."

Morrigan accepted the cup. "Is it late?"

"Not yet seven. Your father's locked in the parlor with Curran Ramsay."

"He's come again?"

The suggestion of a smile flitted across her dour aunt's face, and Morrigan knew she'd said it too fast. "Says he's bent for Edinburgh. I wonder why he traveled so far out of his way, when there's a train direct from Glasgow?"

Morrigan shrugged.

Beatrice crossed to the commode and rearranged the blooms. "He brought these for you. They're fading already. You'd think, since he went to the bother, that he'd bring fresh ones."

"He was kind to think of me at all."

"Oh, there's no doubt about his kindness." Her aunt sat on the edge of the bed. "What you said last night isn't true. Your father doesn't blame you for Hannah's death." With a glower she added, "Now don't go off into one of your tantrums. I'll admit Douglas has faults. But there's good reason."

Morrigan took a deep breath and unlocked her jaw. "I should get dressed, don't you think?"

"There's something I want to show you first."

Reaching into her big apron pocket, Beatrice withdrew a stiff, old daguerreotype. She glanced at it, her lips pursing, before handing it to Morrigan.

It was a photo of a girl in a hard-backed chair, tartan shawl draped over one shoulder, the fringed edge folded beneath her hands on her lap. Long-lashed eyes peered at the world from a solemn, delicately boned face, a face like any other human's, yet on this one so exquisitely arranged that it was hard to look away.

"Aye." Beatrice nodded. "It's your mother. This is before she met your father. Here, she's seventeen."

"Seventeen...." Frightening, this feeling of being turned inside out, of flying end over end. "Younger than I am."

"The years have gone by."

"Where is she buried?"

"The kirkyard at Glenelg. Ibby brought the Ramsay lad here on purpose. You've no idea how it scunnered your father. He wants no reminders of home. Ibby has never understood him. I believe she thinks she can convince us to go back there." With a decisive shake of her head, Beatrice murmured, "He'll never do that. Never."

"Why?"

"The memories...."

"What memories, Auntie?"

"The deaths, of course. Nicky's mam died there as well as yours."

"Neala Grant," Morrigan said.

Beatrice nodded. "I didn't know her, but everyone said she was the sweetest lass ever born. That's more than we can say for Hannah. Your mam was selfish, as selfish as a woman can be. Douglas's wives were aye different."

Morrigan stared at the portrait, remembering Enid Joyce calling Hannah a whore. Why had she done that? What could have given her such an idea? Enid was the whore, in spirit if not flesh.

Beatrice paused. When she continued, she sounded deliberately brisk. "Nicky was but two months old when Neala found herself expecting again. Both Neala and the new baby died in childbirth. It was such a tragedy in the parish; they were still grieving when we came, two years later. Folk thought Neala a saint. Didn't she tame Douglas Lawton, and he the black-tempered devil, always, even as a lad? I heard all about it, endless clishmaclaver over that unlikely romance. No one could believe such a tender, devout lass would want him. But when it came to Neala, the sun rose and set with Douglas Lawton. And he loved her. I mind how whenever the women spoke of it, they'd start greeting. They felt that sorry for him. After Neala died, Douglas raised Nicky alone, until Hannah came along."

"Why do you say it that way? You make it sound…bad."

"Hannah was bonny and well she knew it. Spoiled rotten. Everyone coddled her. With men it was worse. They'd do whatever she asked simply for a smile."

Beatrice fingered the long plait hanging over Morrigan's shoulder. "You're like her. That's part of the problem. You have her voice. Douglas is reminded of her every time he sees you or hears you speak. There are times I'd swear she's in the room. I've caught myself looking about for her."

Morrigan swallowed and clamped her teeth together so she wouldn't interrupt this singular talkative spell.

"Hannah could have made a fortune if she'd been born in London. She could've been another Ellen Terry. It's sure she put on a right good show at home. Few could deny her, your father included."

Beatrice continued to stare at Morrigan's braid for a moment, then she blinked and rose. "Can you manage a corset yet? I'll help you lace it."

When they finished, Beatrice crossed to the door. "We've squandered enough of this day," she said. "I've no' begun breakfast."

"What made her die?"

"You know that already. Have you a yen to hear an account of how she suffered giving birth?"

"No. I just want…to know everything about her."

"There is no more. But it would be nice if you showed your father a bit of mercy. His crime is that he cannot forget the life he lost. Now I'd appreciate your help downstairs." The latch clicked behind her.

The memories Beatrice offered were like exquisite miniature paintings, packed in a beautifully wrapped gift box. Morrigan wanted to separate the layers of gauze and examine each image, one by one. All her life she had wondered about her mother, yet fear kept her from asking, the walls of stone in the eyes of Beatrice and Douglas. Somehow she'd always known she was not to mention Hannah Stewart.

Or the *clearings*.

Or Glenelg, that place of secrets.

She thrust back the ivory curtains to let in more light and perched the daguerreotype beside her looking-glass. Feeling equal measures of trepidation and anticipation, she compared the face in the daguerreotype to her own wavy reflection, seeing immediately that her eyes were deep-set, like her mother's, and that she could imitate Hannah's expression.

She touched the solemn, still face. Hannah Stewart. *Redheaded witch.*

Everything she'd ever heard her father say about her mother was the lie. It was right there, in Hannah's face. She was simply a lass perched on the verge of womanhood, eyes serious but hopeful, mouth unsmiling but serene, ready to smile. The whole together gave an impression of dreamy imagination, and her steady gaze seemed to cover vast distances. This girl longed for the same things as other women. Happiness. Freedom. Love.

Then Morrigan searched for some kind of revelation in the mirror. What had Curran Ramsay thought of her? What sensations had she roused in him? She ran her hands over the places he had touched, her mouth, her throat, her breasts, and lower, where an ache lingered. It was a mysterious place, a place of power, the one spot on a woman's body to be hidden and protected at all times, a place that didn't belong to the woman who was born with it, but to her future husband. She had allowed Curran Ramsay, almost a stranger, to ransack it, not once but four times.

Slow heat spread, lifting the hair on her scalp, turning her cheeks scarlet. What was it she felt? What she'd done was the worst thing a woman could do. She stared at her face, wondering if her sin would be visible to others.

Diorbhail Sinclair was persecuted, reviled, and shunned. Morrigan was sure Diorbhail hadn't announced her crime when she came to Stranraer. She remembered hearing that Diorbhail tried to pass herself off as a widow. Yet her secret had been uncovered.

Would Curran desert her as the father of Diorbhail's child had done?

Curran! He's with Papa!

She finished dressing in a rush, certain they'd slaughtered each other. But the gentleman was sitting alone in the dining room with a cup of tea, studying the local newspaper. At the sight of her, he dropped the paper, rose to his feet, and blushed like a wayward schoolboy.

Somehow his shyness made everything bearable, and routed all hint of embarrassment and shame. Morrigan leaned across the table with newfound confidence and gave him a kiss.

He clasped the back of her head and returned her smile. Then, pleasure fading into worry, he came around to her side of the table, asking formally, "How are you? When I arrived last night you'd fainted on the stairs." He removed his pocket watch from his waistcoat without looking at it, snapped open the lid, and absently polished the crystal with his handkerchief.

"Oh. I wish you hadn't seen that."

"Miss Stewart allowed me to carry you to your bed since she couldn't manage." He lifted a frowning gaze to hers. "What happened? Was it…was it something I did?"

"My aunt and I had a disagreement." She spoke dismissively, though she was mortified to realize he'd seen her in a swoon. "Nothing about yesterday. When I ran up the stairs, I got breathless. I'm fine now." With a sideways smile, she added, "Perhaps our stroll left me in a weakened state."

One side of his mouth twitched. "I cannot get enough of you, Miss Lawton," he said, caressing her fingers.

"I am happy to hear that, Mr. Ramsay. It's you I'm worried about. Beatrice told me you had words with Papa."

"Aye." His face acquired a harder demeanor, unlike any she'd seen on him before. "I believe I made my point."

"What the devil have you done?"

He sat on the edge of the table and leaned over to fetch his teacup. He sipped as he looked her over, neat bun to black boots, the picture of proper decorum. "Have I told you you're the bonniest lass I've ever laid eyes on?" His gaze was half-smiling, half-serious.

"You've laid more than eyes on me." She could scarcely believe her audacity. It was the inner Morrigan, kicking and feisty as the colt, awakened by his appreciation.

He grinned; through it she saw lust spring. He liked her wicked tongue. "There are other things I'd tell you," he said, setting down the cup, "but I suppose they can wait for a better time." Though surely he must recognize this was not that time, he glanced at the doorway. Upon seeing no one, he caressed her shoulders then lowered his hands to her waist.

Morrigan was sorry she'd allowed herself to be talked into a corset. She wanted to feel his caress, plus, as the numbing power of the liniment declined, the thing chafed; the welts were throbbing.

"I confess I prefer you as you were yesterday," he said.

"Hush. Tell me what you said to my father…and maybe I'll reward you."

He obediently removed his hands. "That his landlord, Sir MacAndrew, has received complaints from folk who've stayed at the Wren's Egg. They accuse him of battering his children in a most vile manner, which they find cruel and affronting."

"No."

"Since I planned to stop here, Sir MacAndrew entrusted me with a message for Mr. Lawton, which would save him from sending his factor. If there are any more complaints of this nature, Sir MacAndrew, who enjoys a fondness for children, promises to dismiss Mr. Lawton without reference."

"Is this true?"

"MacAndrew and my father were close. I've sent him a telegram and I know he'll support what I've done. He is fond of children. I promised you your father would never beat you again. I intend to see he doesn't."

Morrigan fell into one of the chairs. "Do you know what you've done?"

"Overstepped my bounds?" His forehead creased.

She gave an impassioned shake of her head. "You've given me hope."

He smiled, slow and seductive. Yielding to an unexplainable urge, she grabbed his hand and pulled him closer so she could touch the scar by his eyebrow. *Lion scar. Moon-marked.*

"You've a sweet smile, Curran Ramsay," she said. "And you well deserve your reward."

THE NEXT DAY A LETTER ARRIVED FOR CURRAN, FORWARDED FROM GLENELG.

"It's from my aunt's doctor in Edinburgh," he said. "She is dying, and I'm her nearest kin."

"I'm sorry," Morrigan said.

"She's been ill a long time. Consumption." He crumpled the paper. "This is bad timing. I have to go right away. What about you?"

"All will be as it always is for me."

"Your father was angry after I spoke to him yesterday."

"Truly, Curran, I'll be fine," she said with a confidence she didn't feel. She couldn't tell him she hadn't glimpsed Douglas once since he had attacked her. It was a fine holiday, after a fashion, but there was a chance he was biding his time, waiting for Curran to leave.

"Then I'd best pack my things," he said.

They parted on the road beyond the inn. Morrigan wanted to kiss him but something of that nature would outstrip the wind in its eagerness to reach every ear in town. Giving her hand a quick, unobtrusive clasp, he promised to return at the first opportunity.

She wanted to believe him, but the practical part of her warned she might never see him again. Wealthy lairds didn't return to country girls. They probably didn't even remember them for long. Yet, no matter how coldly she thought it, no matter how rudely she sneered at her female notions, Morrigan couldn't completely stamp out a hollow sense of loss, twined at the edges with anticipation, as she mended a tear in her father's trousers. She tried, but Mr. Ramsay's winsome smile and the blue spark in his eyes kept returning, offering promises she couldn't quite expunge.

Boys were always throwing stones at Diorbhail Sinclair, shouting obscenities, and laughing at her.

If anyone discovered what she'd done, Morrigan understood that she would suffer the same fate—before Douglas took her life.

They hadn't been so far from town, though the rolling hills and vast skies made it feel like a different world. What if someone had seen them?

Kit wed Enid a fortnight after, on the twenty-second of July. Creeping unseen among the well-wishers at the terminal, Morrigan watched Kit wave jauntily and Enid give an affected smile. They may have suffered disgrace, but Kit had redeemed himself, and the lass, through marriage.

The train reversed from the station. Never again would she see him, never this side of death.

She pressed one gloved hand briefly to her stomach. The risk she had taken and its possible consequences sent her heart thumping erratically.

Curran held every playing piece in this game. If indeed a child sprouted, her future and the child's depended solely on his whim. Misery, poverty, shame…or marriage, a home, security.

She'd made herself hostage to a virtual stranger. His pleasing demeanor could have been a trick. He might turn out worse than Douglas Lawton.

With a determined shake of her head, she set out for the inn but someone blocked her way. The instant her eyes met Diorbhail Sinclair's, the woman averted her face, gripped her daughter's hand, and retreated towards the arched exit.

"Wait." Morrigan blinked, astonished, at the appearance of a faint white mist around the woman. She watched it twirl and rise, almost as though it was trying to draw her attention. It extended outward, assuming a pale pink hue before it disappeared into the gloom at the terminal's ceiling.

First Curran, the day she'd met him, and now Diorbhail Sinclair. Were her eyes tricking her, or had it really been there?

Diorbhail stopped. She turned, looking at the ground.

Morrigan glanced around the station. There would be no end to the punishment if word ever reached Beatrice that her niece had conversed with Stranraer's whore.

An inner warning sounded. *Don't go too close.* "Were you here to see off Kit Lindsay?" *Because it surely couldn't have been Enid.*

"Aye." Diorbhail continued to study the ground in front of her.

"You know him?"

With a quick, furtive glance, Diorbhail said, "No' so well as you."

"What-what…." Morrigan forced her mouth shut to stop the betraying stutter. Who could've told her what they'd done but Kit himself?

"Be careful. What you do can haunt you the rest of your life. It could turn you from your path, and change everything."

Not giving Morrigan a chance to recover her equilibrium, Diorbhail turned and walked away. But she slowed as she reached the exit. She stood there a few seconds then again faced Morrigan. "I feel I know you. There's something…" she struck her chest with a fist, "makes me want to help you." A ragged laugh escaped. "Fine joke, that. Me, helping anyone." Sunlight from outside touched her face and Morrigan saw that her eyes were both blue and green, like Loch Ryan's shallows could be in certain conditions.

"They say Satan rules women," she added. There was a red jagged scar on the woman's forehead, a memento from a well-thrown stone. "Do you believe it?"

"Men or Satan. What's the difference?" Morrigan spoke on a crest of anger she hadn't known was simmering so close to the surface.

Diorbhail blinked as though Morrigan's words shocked her, too. "Everything that steps from the cave throws a shadow. Within the shadows are lessons, if you listen. If you look." She paused. "Men fear the shadows women throw. They fear we'll win back our power. It's why they submerged us." She approached Morrigan again, still holding her daughter's hand.

Morrigan snorted. "We've all seen how much men fear *you*."

Diorbhail let go of her daughter to reach out gingerly and touch Morrigan's forearm. "Avatar," she said, frowning. Her eyes stared intently. "Learn of those who cleared the way for you. The warriors." She drew in a breath. "The shadow you throw is long…it will swallow you up if you're not careful."

Abruptly turning, Diorbhail held out her hand. Her daughter clasped it and together they walked away, leaving Morrigan struck and saddened by the child's grave dark eyes and solemn face.

Chapter 11

MORRIGAN LAY IN BED, CONTEMPLATING THE CHANGES THIS SUMMER HAD wrought, wishing for a wind to move the curtain…a storm, anything to break this endless stretch of hot, clear, motionless days. If it rained, something might happen. Maybe Nicky would write, telling her it was time to come to Edinburgh.

Right now, were she in Enid's place, she'd be far from the Wren's Egg and Douglas Lawton. No one would lash her or call her worthless, not ever again.

She and Kit would hold hands as they climbed onto a ship bound for America. What a grand adventure it would be. She continued on, seeing them in the American wilds, maybe friends with the savage natives she'd read about.

She knew she was dreaming about Kit to avoid thinking of the absent and silent Mr. Ramsay.

"Morrigan!"

Beatrice's voice ricocheted up the stairs. Morrigan had lazed too long and now must hurry. Flinging off the bedclothes, she leaped out of bed, took two steps, and doubled over, clutching her abdomen.

Oh…*mucker*.

She barely made it to the washbasin before losing last night's dinner. The room spun, bounced, yawed.

A second wave of nausea returned her to the basin. She retched helplessly. Any moment her entire stomach would heave from her mouth.

When the gagging subsided, she slid to the floor. Sweat beaded on her forehead. Her muscles trembled.

105

"Morrigan! Get your lazy dowp down these stairs afore I come away and skelp your arse! The kye are cryin' for a hand to milk them."

Morrigan pushed herself onto her knees and worked her way upright, using the legs on the commode. She staggered to her wardrobe and dressed. In wee measures, the nausea lessened until she could straighten and walk with a modicum of dignity.

Beatrice gave her a sour stare as she entered the kitchen. "Did you plan to spend the day in bed, m'lady? Get to your chores. You're aye lucky your father left early."

"Sorry, Auntie. Bellyache."

Queasiness rumbled the entire day, along with two more violent bouts of heaving. When she refused breakfast then wanted nothing at midday, Beatrice sent her a narrowed, piercing glance and asked if she'd been snaking the honey again.

The next day brought nausea even more severe. Morrigan hoped she wouldn't die still wishing to hear from Curran.

She finally received a letter from him on the twenty-sixth, then one from Nicky on the twenty-eighth. Curran said his aunt wasn't expected to last the month, and faded more each day. After her death he'd have to arrange the funeral. Would Morrigan please write at once to assure him of her continued safety?

Morrigan searched for something in his words that would indicate his feelings, other than a gentlemanly concern for her health.

Nicky's letter shared news from the last two months. He'd composed his first story and enclosed a clipping. It was all about a new Stevenson lighthouse at Dhu Heartach, which had been under construction for five years and was now nearing completion. Due to the unpredictability of the weather, the workmen had spent their summers living on site in an iron drum-like building, set atop narrow stilts high above the tumultuous sea. Night and day they labored on that treacherous rock, a place notorious for wrecked ships and lost lives. Nicky wrote that he'd been given permission to spend three nights in the barrack; that was enough to convince him of what terrible power the ocean possessed, had he ever doubted it. Waves slammed against the high-flung metal sides. Echoing, thunderous booms offered hints of what the workmen had endured during construction. His letter added that Thomas Stevenson's son had made a brief appearance and they'd struck up a friendship. *You'd like him, I think,* Nicky wrote. *His health isn't good, but he's the opposite of morose about it, and has a fine disregard for pious convention. I think, next to Kit, he's become my closest comrade. He's off to Germany and asked me along, but I have too much work and had to refuse. You'll meet him when you come.*

On his next assignment, he was traveling south with a more seasoned writer to cover the *Cutty Sark-Thermopylae* race. Imagine being fee'd to travel! By the way, he'd met a lass who didn't seem to hate him, could she believe it?

Oh, and had Da disowned him? Not that he cared…. The bastard could go fuck himself.

I miss our walks on the moor, Morrigan wrote to Curran. She tore the letter up then wrote it again on new stationery. To Nicky, she sent sage advice: *Bring your new friend for a visit when Papa isn't so vexed, and your lass, if she hasn't come to her senses.*

They had a larger than usual number of guests, many of whom were proper couples, and not inclined to drink away the evenings in the taproom, so she was ordered to entertain them at the piano.

Performing for strangers made her fingers clumsy and sweaty. To ward off fear and the mistakes it caused, she'd developed an intricate game. She closed her eyes, imagining her body diffusing through the window-glass and floating up over the inn. Chopin's romantic nocturnes lent themselves nicely to such flights of fancy. Higher and higher, into fleecy clouds, the wind pulling her hair free of its knot, she glided across her father's barley fields, above spreading oaks, stately beeches, and forget-me-nots half-hidden in velvety moss. Her eagle—the one that seemed so interested in her—swooped close, gazing at her from one fierce yet curious amber eye, and stayed with her, soaring away but always keeping her in sight.

She coasted across Loch Ryan, cold waves slapping her outstretched hands, then along high wet cliffs, over braes covered in gorse and heather. There was Nicky…working the fields, leather straps draped over powerful bare shoulders as he called to their great Clyde Leo to *move on.*

The eagle came so close she could touch its wing as she skimmed over green-checkered fields, ancient fortresses and villages, up to craggy mountains laced in mist. Switching easily from Chopin into the last movement of the *Allegro Assai,* her favorite Mozart sonata, she soared faster above dazzling snow as her fingers danced upon the keys. She usually imagined Loch Ness below her, but this time she pictured moody Loch Torridon, where Curran had fought a lion in an underwater castle made of pearl. The eagle's cry, high and shrill, echoed across still water and off somber mountains.

Along came the old town of Inverness and the green, fertile field of Culloden where so many brave champions lay buried. She flew across the sea, coming in due course to the iridescent Mediterranean, and an island. Once upon a time, she'd heard, this was where the moon lived when it left the heavens. All praised an Immortal Mother and oracles made prophecy to the dangerous roar of bulls. Here it was that Ariadne fell in love with golden, green-eyed Theseus. In this magical, forgotten place, women lived freely, powerfully, and were never punished or made to suffer for loving.

The eagle yipped repeatedly the closer she came to the island.

Clouds of dust drew Morrigan to the northern coast. Below her a bloody warrior supported a wisp of a girl on his arm. Hundreds of triumphant fighters, male and female, were lifting swords and cheering.

Kaphtor's great hero! the crowd shouted.

One man would never again wield a weapon. His severed head was shoved onto the end of a spear. Other foes lay strewn like trampled seaweed across the sand.

Held securely against the prince's sturdy shoulder, the woman smiled and wept.

Though Morrigan had never before envisioned this odd scenario, her fingers didn't pause. She knew the music well enough to perform it in her sleep.

The warrior was the man from her dreams, Theseus, and the woman he held must be the queen, Aridela. She had fought alongside her companions and was wounded, yet she ignored the pain and participated in her people's victory.

Such a woman could never be defeated.

It is truth, my daughter. You will rise and rise again, until Earth is redeemed.

Morrigan wasn't alarmed by the gentle voice. She accepted that the eagle had found a way to communicate.

With a farewell nod, Morrigan returned to Scotland, sweeping above white-blue clouds in a loose fitting garment that rippled and flowed. The eagle left her as she drew near to the town at the foot of Loch Ryan. Down she circled over windy moorland to a stretch of sand by the water, where a snowy seal pup with large melting eyes sat quiet and dear as she stroked its soft head.

Applause startled her out of her illusion, back into the inn's cramped parlor.

WITH HARVEST UPON THEM, DOUGLAS LEFT EVERY MORNING BEFORE BREAKFAST and didn't return until after Morrigan had gone to bed. In his stubborn way he'd refused to hire any help, so it wasn't surprising that she seldom saw him.

Strange, persistent aches tormented her. The slightest rubbing of her shift against her breasts was difficult to bear. Perhaps her body was rebelling at the loss of Curran's lovemaking. Though he'd seemed to receive more enjoyment from it than she did, still, each night, she wanted the things he'd done, especially the kissing, and his warm hands holding her. No wonder folk were told to wait until after the marriage vows. Once a couple experienced such intimate delights, they'd want to again, wouldn't they, and again…and again? What a convenience to have lovers in their beds every night and the approval of religion and law.

Another letter arrived from Curran. His aunt had died. He would return after the funeral and oh, his letter said, like an afterthought—*Tha gaol agam ort, Morrigan Lawton*. She stared at the words, wondering whom she could ask to decipher them, but then, when she turned the paper over, she saw he'd added, *It means I'm in love with you.*

She gave the crisp stationery a kiss and slipped it into the commode beneath her drawers and petticoats, secret and safe.

That night she dreamed again of Theseus, but this time he didn't resemble either the blond warrior or Curran. Nevertheless, she knew him.

He was grimly striking rather than handsome, pale and dark at the same time, familiar in a way that made her want to weep. She saw his mouth move. At first she couldn't hear what he was saying, but gradually it came to her, a dusty, distantly echoing, anguished cry. *Where are you? I've waited so long. I need you. I need you!*

The words faded when she woke, but for a long while the anguish remained, a faint unceasing reverberation she didn't want to let go.

One of Morrigan's small joys was tending the vegetables that would help feed their guests through the winter. A brief uncomfortable memory intruded when she dug out a clump of weeds from the damp soil. Her body covered with mud...the amoral inner lass giggling, Douglas beating Nicky. Everything had changed that day.

She didn't hear the boy come up behind her. He spoke politely and she turned, wiping her hands, to take the telegram he held out. She fetched him a coin kept for such things and watched him race to the road. He swung onto his pony and sent it galloping, his brown hair flowing in a breeze of his own creation.

Someone had printed her father's name on the envelope. There wasn't much use writing to Papa, as he'd never learned to read. She carried it inside, not knowing what else to do.

"Come with me," Beatrice said. "We'll take it to him."

"Is it important?"

"We'll not know until you've read it to us, will we?" Almost to herself, she added, "Though I've never yet seen a telegram that brought good news."

Beatrice's foreboding enfolded Morrigan as they walked through the fields. When they saw Douglas, Beatrice called and waved.

Sweat trickled down his temples. His sark was stained with dirt. He gave Morrigan a curt nod, indicating she should open the missive.

She tore the envelope and strained to read the splotched, uneven writing.

*Deeply regret to inform you that Nicholas Lawton passed away third of
August. Arrangements Proceeding. Contact Captain Marshall, Edinburgh
Ferry Road.*

Morrigan stumbled over *Deepest Condolences*, at the end.

It didn't say how. Though she turned the paper over, there was no other explanation.

Beatrice's face crumpled. Her mouth opened in a silent cry.

Douglas would call this daftness. He'd rip the note to bits. Nicky would write to inform them of his latest adventure.

But her father said nothing. When Beatrice tried to embrace him, he jerked away, grimacing.

Nicky…dead.

"It's a mistake," she said, hearing an odd ringing in her ears. The sough of barley grew as loud as thunder.

No one answered. Beatrice stepped away from Douglas and wiped her eyes. Everyone had loved Nicky, the poet with a flashing smile and far-seeing eyes.

Douglas squinted across the fields, his jaw working.

"Papa?" Morrigan asked.

He swung his head towards her, glowering like a bull preparing to charge. For one long instant he stared at her, eyes narrowed; then he strode away, yanking Leo's halter.

"Why d'you never shed a tear over anything?" Beatrice shouted. "You're indifferent…fair heartless, I suspect. Do you no' care that your brother's dead?" She dabbed at her eyes with the ever-present dishcloth.

Not a word to Papa, and was he weeping? "Who d'you think taught me never to greet?"

She ran away, through the amber fields and into her forest. Throughout the rest of the day she hid in dense green chambers walled by branches and leaves.

Nicky had painted vibrant images with words, delicate watercolors and robust oils. They were etched into her memories, and thickly populated with unicorns. *They're the happiness that just escapes us,* he'd told her. *Though fools try to rope them, unicorns can never be captured. They scatter and dissolve, fade into wind over the moor.*

Now he, too, ran swift and free with his horned companions across invisible open moorland.

First he'd left, now he'd died. Wherever he was, she hated him for stealing himself from her. He'd been her one bastion. Now there was nothing—only empty air, a sense of falling.

Wind fluttered among the high branches, knocking leaves loose. They fell, pattering like raindrops. *I wish it had been you,* her father's wordless stare had shouted.

Why hadn't she felt her brother's death? How could it have happened without her knowing?

She dug in the soil, unearthing pebbles and tossing them into the pool. Gradually, sensation returned, bringing the ache in her breasts, the nausea. She was still alive, not rotting. Not like Nicky.

Night had fallen when she at last left the forest for an open meadow, where moonlight spilled white and thick, as though a pitcher of cream had been overturned. Morrigan wasn't startled when a unicorn stepped from the shadows. Streaked with alabaster, lean and graceful, it paused to test the air for danger. Two smaller forms stumbled into view, and she realized she hadn't been given a glimpse of magic after all. It was simply a roe deer and her fawns. Mother nosed her hungry offspring away.

An owl swooped, calling *whoo, whoo,* as it landed on the stone wall. Morrigan held her breath, remembering that in some countries, owls carried spirits of the dead with them.

"Nicky?"

Its enormous round eyes rested upon her as it ruffled its wings. After a moment it glided away, selfishly keeping whatever secrets it held in confidence.

She slipped through the gate into the close. The kitchen door squeaked and a peewit twittered in reply.

The pale, pockmarked moon hung right outside her window, its white light turning her blanket to sea-foam. "Bring me visions," she prayed. "Share what you know."

Slipping under her bedclothes, she watched the moon and it watched her.

A dark figure separated from the shadows and crept into bed with her.

Nicky, you're so cold.

I suppose it was a mistake to be born. I've never felt a thing but want and rage. Who knows? Maybe I put myself in his way on purpose. Life's dreary, and I didn't want to see my wean's face when I hit it.

You wouldn't've done that!

Who knows? I felt it in me, the violence. It strangled me sometimes fighting to come out. You've fought it. I know.

Never! I'll kill anyone who tries to harm my weans....

I thought that too, but I couldn't be sure. Listen. Mind you the poem I taught you. 'One too like thee: tameless, and swift, and proud.' Always mind it if you think of me.

Morrigan slept late in the morning, haunted by images of Nicky, of fears, promises and poems, of two warriors, one dark, one gold, and mystifying words. *Death cannot stop the thinara king. He will slay me until time wears out.*

Not even the train's piercing whistle managed to wake her.

Chapter 12

Curran drummed his fingers against his thigh as he stared out the window at blurred scenery. The rhythmic *cli-clung cli-clung* of the wheels transformed into the girl's voice. *Cur-ran…Cur-ran. I fancy a stroll on the moor, Mr. Ramsay.*

"I won't let her go." He would never have realized he'd said it out loud but for the gentleman in the other seat glancing at him then giving his newspaper a snap to show he wouldn't tolerate any unorthodox behavior.

Curran rubbed his left temple. A headache drove stakes of pain underneath the scar.

Dogs and horses, crofting, traveling, shipbuilding…many interests kept him busy and he'd managed, thus far, to avoid female entanglements.

Why should I exchange one gaoler for another? she'd asked, displaying a too-jaded outlook for one so young.

No matter. He would have her, by God, one way or another. Even if he had to abduct her, like Paris and Helen, or Theseus and Ariadne, to coin her pet myth—she was devilishly intelligent. And he'd show her how pleasant certain prisons could be.

His thoughts circled. Was he considering marriage? To an innkeeper's daughter? A lowborn, displaced, penniless survivor of the Glenelg clearings? Was he ready to discard his plan of an heiress born into deeply moneyed pockets, someone not too unpleasant to look at, who could further his efforts to bring prosperity to his village? He pictured a few of the ladies he knew, those who had made their willingness clear. But no matter how beautiful or wealthy they were, he'd never been able to take that final step.

Curse it. Curse the damned dowries and titles. If he could have Morrigan, they didn't matter. He'd find some other way to finance his Highland estate.

Plan who you wed like a business venture, his father had instructed. *Believe me, son, if she provides enough silver, you'll find you can live with a stoat. And if you can no' bring yourself to bed her…well, there's plenty of bonny lasses who'll ease that ache, for you've your mam's pretty face, and it's a proven fact women are weak-willed.*

What would Thomas Ramsay say if he could see his beloved son so stupefied that he heard his lover's voice in the clatter of the rails?

When the train drew at last to a screeching halt in Stranraer's terminal, Curran immediately purchased a massive cluster of flowers from a canny street urchin who extorted twice their value. He tossed the grimy lad a few extra pennies and felt curiously rewarded by the grin he received.

It felt good to be here…at last. He inspected what he'd bought. Simpler than his last bouquet, it contained only red roses, woodbine, and baby's breath. He didn't know what meaning the woodbine carried—the woman who helped him last time had known everything about flowers, and had enjoyed a good laugh over his determination to create a bouquet with both the perfect meaning and beauty—but he knew red roses implied passion, and the scent of the woodbine was intoxicating.

He walked to the inn, only half noting how empty the lane was. When he opened the door, the bell jangled. Quickly he reached up and muffled it, giving in to a desire to surprise her.

What was this odd silence? He ventured along the corridor, glancing into the parlor, taproom, and kitchen. All stood empty. Pausing at the bottom of the staircase, he wondered how badly he'd be flouting etiquette if he ascended.

Bother. Where could she be? The grandfather clock in the parlor sounded the half-hour as he climbed the stairs.

Closed doors lined either side of the hall, but he remembered her room from the night he'd carried her there, limp and pale after the fight with her aunt. He hoped she didn't possess a sickly disposition. Then he remembered the energy she'd displayed during their intimate afternoon, and told himself Morrigan Lawton had never known a day of illness in her life.

The door swung open at his hesitant push. His paramour lay on the bed, tangled in coarse sheets, her braid stretched across the pillow. After cautious admiration of the naked ankle and foot peeking out from the edge of the bedclothes, he snapped open his pocket watch. Nine thirty-two. Why was she asleep? Where were Beatrice and Douglas? With a glance down the hallway, he entered, laid the flowers on the bed, and bent over her.

"Morrigan." He kissed her ear and twined the plait around his fingers. The girl damn well stole his reason. It had to be more than lying with her. He hadn't had much trouble enjoying female companionship since the age of fourteen, when a crofter's daughter from the next parish had lured him into an abandoned blackhouse.

No female could spellbind him because of one afternoon of simple pleasure. *Spellbind.* Interesting choice of words. It revived an old memory of gossip he'd overheard as a young lad. There had been tales of Morrigan's dead mother. Mention of Hannah never failed to bring on dour headshakings and a heartfelt *tisk* or two.

Witch, some had declared, crossing themselves. Fionna Dunbar had stated that Hannah held a strange power over men, and could make them do almost anything for a chance of winning her favor.

Too bonny for her own good, he remembered Fionna saying. *Shameless, through and through.*

Satan took her home, someone else had ventured.

Curran slipped the tie from the end of Morrigan's braid and unraveled her hair. It sprang to life, full of waves, undulating like sand dunes on the Sahara. Today it was as dark as coffee, but the day they'd spent together on the moor it had displayed seductive glints of red, like slow-burning embers, and had felt warm, sumptuous, in his hands.

Perhaps Hannah's daughter had cast a spell on him.

His old friend, Seaghan MacAnaugh, remained unmarried to this day, rumor claimed because he hadn't forgotten Hannah Stewart or recovered from their broken engagement. Curran never asked and Seaghan never broached the subject, but every month since the man had returned to Glenelg, flowers appeared on the gravestone of the woman who had given birth to this enchanting creature.

Had Morrigan's mother performed witchcraft? Had she been as beautiful as the rumors claimed?

Time had no doubt enhanced everyone's memories. After all, how bonny could Hannah have been, judging from her sister, Beatrice?

Besides, he didn't believe in witches, spells, or Satan, though he was careful not to offend folk by admitting it. Religion seemed more a business of power and practicality than anything else.

But if not Hannah, whom did Morrigan resemble? Not her father, him with his silver-smudged black hair and frigid grey eyes, while every inch of his daughter exuded warmth, from her hair that turned incandescent in the sun to the tentative smile he'd swear could revive the heart of a drowned sailor.

She seemed a charming potpourri of women combined into one. There was the first he'd seen, when Ibby brought him to the Wren's Egg in May. The windblown, sea-scented, scarlet-cheeked moor lass, with damp untidy hair and burrs on her skirts. That rustic girl disappeared into the cool, corseted lady in prim grey who'd later brought him a basket of food. Before he'd finished absorbing those two faces, another had appeared. The flushed seductress, giving off a delectable essence of musk, speaking entreaties against his mouth.

That one sealed his doom. But which was the real Morrigan? Moor sprite? Proper lady? Temptress?

No. Something more than her face caused the torment he'd endured in Edinburgh. Something about Morrigan—did she have a middle name? He longed to know—tore him apart even as it soothed him into a tranquility he'd never before experienced.

And there was that birthmark. The one he'd dreamed of. *Dreamed of.* How could he have done that, before ever meeting her?

"Morrigan," he repeated, picking up a lock of her hair. Memories of the strap marks flamed his senses into teeth-clenching rage. No one would harm her from this day on. No other man would touch these white limbs, in rage or lust. The idea ignited ferocious jealousy.

In truth, loneliness and edgy discomfort—the *searching* he'd described—had gnawed at him all his life until he'd spent the afternoon ravishing Hannah Stewart's daughter. The incessant pins and needles had dissipated much like a raincloud emptied of water. They hadn't returned, not even while he was away.

Morrigan brushed at her ear. Here was another face…snaring him closer yet. Not wind-kissed, remote, or impassioned. Innocent rather, a warm sleepy girl. This face awakened subtle memories of the baby his father rescued after the clearings, weak and malnourished, pathetically skinny, with sadly chilblained skin. Curran's mother had embraced the infant, vowing she would not die.

He pressed his mouth to the pulse beneath her jaw, tracing with his tongue to her collarbone, and she woke at last. "Curran." She blinked uncertainly. Her hands slid up. When she turned upright, her nightgown caught underneath her; he had to unbutton it, did he not, to make her more comfortable? Wicked, the way she roused him, fair wicked. Maybe she *was* a witch.

Morrigan dragged him onto the bed with her. Tumultuous thoughts fled, leaving only the conviction that if he didn't have her right now, this minute, he'd spill his seed on her sheets.

"Love me," she said, voice catching, eyes darker than he remembered, almost black, as deep and mysterious as the ocean.

He pushed up her nightgown and gave himself to the drowning.

I will love you, Menoetius, until only dust remains of my bones.

He swam through a stygian sea, searching for the surface, following the sound of that adored voice.

"Curran...."

I pray she'll reunite us somehow, somewhere, if I do what she wants. Wherever she sends me, I will wait for you.

"Curran? Please wake up."

He opened his eyes, letting go of the dream with reluctance. Stretching luxuriously, he smiled into his lover's face, so close to his on the pillow. He opened his mouth to say her name, yet for an instant, the name he wanted to say was not hers. It was something else...something that now escaped him.

Her expression routed any remaining pleasure. Passion no longer flushed her skin. Instead her eyes were webbed with grief. "My brother. He's...dead." The last word was spoken in incredulous disbelief.

The fleeting notion that she might be joking was eliminated by the obvious sorrow in her voice and expression. His entire body roused in protest. He couldn't bear her pain. He must right it, *protect*. But how? What could he say? "Morrigan." He pulled her face to his throat.

Before he could ask what had happened, the door flew open, crashing against the wall, eliciting a squeak from the girl and a startled surge of apprehension in him.

Fury quivered in every line of Beatrice's unpleasant face. "Is this how you carry on the very day after you've been told your brother's dead? You truly are a hoor!"

To Curran, she cried, "Get off from her!"

She sprang at him, fingers curved into claws. He had no choice but to grab her wrists and push her away before she could rake those nails over his face. His skin crawled as he stood and buttoned his trousers, glad he hadn't removed them. "Calm yourself, madam," he said.

Morrigan yanked her nightgown over her knees. She sat up, staring from her aunt to her lover. Fear etched her face. Terror, more like.

"Don't you speak to me of calm. How dare you? You've taken all she had that might persuade a decent man to marry her." Beatrice gasped and pushed her fists against her eyes. Her shoulders rose. For an instant, Curran thought she was weeping, but no, it was a convulsion of anger she fought to keep in check.

"Am I not decent enough?" he said. "I intend to wed your niece. I'll speak to Mr. Lawton today. Now."

"Curran!" Morrigan blinked at him as if he'd turned into a seahorse.

"You." Beatrice turned on her. "Spreading your legs for any lout what winks at you. How dare you act this way in your father's house! And Nicky not even cold—"

Curran seized Beatrice's arm. "Don't blame her. It's my fault. She was asleep when I came in. She didn't do anything wrong."

Beatrice's mouth fell open. Horror made her stagger. "You forced her?"

"No. Listen." He shook her arm. "I will marry her. We aren't the first who haven't waited for the wedding night. Aye, it was wrong, but no real harm's been done." *Marry.* The word rippled through the air, or was it him, trembling as he threw away his freedom?

He didn't care. The realization made him feel he could fly to the stars. *She'll be mine. Mine.* A shiver crept over him, as it had when he'd written *I'm in love with you, Morrigan Lawton* in his letter. He'd stared at the words, words he never intended to write; yet he couldn't make himself discard the paper and start over. He wanted to say them. He almost felt as though he had to. She was beyond his control, perhaps beyond his reason.

"Oh, aye?" Beatrice's narrowed eyes riveted on him. "You're so sure you're the first? Certain, are you, that you're the father of that bastard in her belly?"

A stifled moment passed as he glanced from one to the other. "Bastard?"

Morrigan shook her head. "I don't know what she's talking about."

Beatrice snorted. "You may no' understand it, silly mutchit, but you're breeding. Why do you think you've been puking your guts out?" To Curran, she said, "In a man's selfish way you took what you wanted. Now she, barely grown herself, is with child, too innocent to realize what's been done to her. Yet you say 'no harm done.'"

He couldn't stop the betraying flush. Clenching his muscles, he fought the urge to flee from the woman's penetrating eyes, or put his fist in her jaw. "Have you been ill, Morrigan?"

"Aye."

She was trembling. He wanted to touch her cheek, reassure her.

"Sick to my stomach," she added. "But what would a child have to do with that?"

I will marry you. His thoughts still careened, up and down, in anxiety and elation. *You'll be mine. You'll be my wife.*

Then Beatrice's *you're so sure you're the first?* echoed through the shock. It did seem incredible that Morrigan would prove fertile the first and only time she'd ever been with a man. As he regarded her, cold speculation reared. When he'd given in to what she so obviously wanted, he'd told himself she knew what she was doing. He surely wasn't the first. There was something in her eyes, knowledge that seemed the opposite of innocent. But he'd been wrong. For the first time in his life, he'd taken a girl's virginity.

Could that be why he felt responsible for her? Was it merely his upbringing that made him offer marriage to a girl he'd ruined?

No. He knew it in his bones. He had to have her. No matter the cost. Whether or not she was a virgin. Even if she bore another man's child.

"Damn it," he said, shoving away ridiculous fears. He strode around the bed, pulling her into an embrace. That cow Beatrice could choke on her spit. "This proves we should marry, doesn't it?" He gave her a smacking kiss then returned her to the bed and knelt in front of her. "Marry me," he said, clasping her hands. "Will you, my Morrigan?"

She stared at him, pale and shocked.

"Be my wife," he said. "Be mine, forever."

She started to smile, but almost immediately it faded. Her eyes darkened.

He couldn't sweep away this pain, couldn't make everything perfect though he would rip out his eyeteeth if that would do it. Nicky's death must chafe like a raw wound at the edge of every other thought. He knew it, for he'd experienced the same ache the night his mother had died, and for a long time after.

"Oh, I canna thole any of this right now," she said. She glanced at Beatrice, standing there like a fiery demon.

It was a terrible way to propose. He rose and stroked her cheek. "I know, *a ghràidh*. We'll go. Later I'll bring you tea and toast. Rest."

She nodded and lay back, her hair fanning out on the pillow. He kissed her temple and stepped away from the bed.

Beatrice sighed sharply. She held the door, forcing him to exit first.

"What happened?" he asked. "How did Nick—"

"Our affairs are not your concern."

"I'm not your enemy, Miss Stewart. I apologize for what I've done, but I will make her my wife. Everything I have in the world will be hers. And you. You'll always have a home with us."

Giving him a long, measured glare, she spun away and descended the stairs. "Trying to purchase my silence?"

"No. I mean it." He stopped her at the landing. "You're Morrigan's kin. That alone makes you welcome."

She stepped away from him and continued to the front hall. "We don't know what happened. A telegram came. It said Nicky was dead. Nothing else. Douglas has gone to Edinburgh to bring him home."

They entered the kitchen where the long unattended kettle was furiously steaming. She brewed tea.

"I'm sorry." Curran sat at the table. "Was he in good health?"

"Aye."

"Edinburgh can be rough. I hope—"

"There's been too much. And now this." Placing the pot and two cups in front of Curran, she sat in the opposite chair and rubbed her forehead.

He could think of nothing to say.

"I trust you're not planning to accost Douglas with your schemes. It's pure evil, to think you can steal away his daughter before he's had a chance to bury his son."

"You're right, now isn't a good time. But what of the…the baby?"

"You should have thought of that before you made a slut of my niece, aye?"

She drummed her fingertips against the table. "July had scarcely begun when you and that hissy snaked off together. It doesn't bear recalling, the condition she came back in. Her dress, her hair…like a slattern."

"The seventh," he mumbled, inwardly writhing like she no doubt wanted. Yet through the shame he couldn't help picturing Morrigan lying on his frock coat, holding a sprig of periwinkle to her nose. He stiffened helplessly, already wanting her again, but he sensed his sexual desire was changing into something more. Every thought of her, every remembered detail of expression, scent, and touch in Edinburgh had caused physical *thrills* to run through his limbs. He'd never experienced such a thing, and if asked, would have called the notion romantic tripe.

Antiope, she'd said. *She was a great queen, strong and free.*

What other female in the world would have said such a thing? He'd assumed she was simple, because most country girls were. But now he was beginning to realize. She was a depthless well. There was fear in her too, hesitation, and that distrust he sensed so strongly. Was it because of her father, or was there something else?

He wanted…needed…to know.

With a caustic smile, Beatrice said, "So she's near a month along, and will give birth, if all goes well, next April." Her gaze upon him was nerve-racking, as cutting as a blade. "You'll not have the luxury of waiting if you don't want your bride at the altar showing the world what you did." She plucked a lump of sugar from the bowl and stirred it into her tea.

"You needle me like an old sock, Miss Stewart. Are you sure you're not a missionary, sent to reform my sinful ways?"

"I need no church to explain right from wrong."

"Morrigan doesn't seem to know how we all originally met."

"We never speak of it. What would be the purpose? Folk died, Morrigan's mam for one. Douglas flees his pain sure as the wind over the Sound."

"She knows nothing?"

"I've told her a few things about her mother. Other bits she may have put together herself or found out from Nicky."

"D'you remember Seaghan MacAnaugh?"

Beatrice's spoon stilled then started stirring again, more slowly than before. "He was betrothed to my sister. Of course I remember him."

"He's back. Did you know? From the moment that ship…the *Bristol,* wasn't it? landed in Nova Scotia, he took any fee he could, saving to come home. He's told me about the clearings, and the promises your landlord made."

"He claimed Nova Scotia had fertile soil. That every child would have shoes and go to school. He made it sound like heaven."

"Seaghan told me that near three quarters of those on the ship died without ever setting foot on land. More died after, of smallpox and dysentery. When they arrived, there was no land. No shoes for the weans…what weans were left. Randall Benedict lied."

Beatrice stood so abruptly her chair tumbled over. "Don't."

He saw her trembling. "Forgive me, Miss Stewart. I've done nothing but vex you. It wasn't my intent."

She gave a shaky laugh. "What a brave speak, that Douglas flees from his pain. I suppose I'm no better."

"Who could live through such horror without being affected?" He picked up her chair, and after a short pause, she resumed her seat.

"Seaghan spotted a man in the ocean, just off the cliffs of Berneray," he said as he mopped up spilled tea. "He talked the captain into a rescue, pumped water from the man's lungs, and sewed up his wounds. Saved his life, but there were consequences. To this day, Aodhàn cannot remember how he came to be in the ocean, or much of anything else, not even where he was born. It's all gone but for his name, and I don't think he's completely sure about that. Seaghan brought Aodhàn home with him, and they built a blackhouse by Glenelg Bay."

She smiled slightly, but it held no warmth or affection. "Seaghan always did adopt wee homeless beasts."

"Aodhàn's hardly a 'homeless beast,' though there's some who might say so. He's rumored to be a selkie, trapped in a man's body as punishment for some crime. I'm certain Agnes Campbell started that tale. You wouldn't know her. She and her husband came along a few years after the clearings, bound for Fort William, but in the end, they stayed."

"What's this man done to cause such gossip?"

"He's quiet, which is understandable, with such a big hole in his life; but his worst crime, at least with the villagers he lives among, is that he adamantly refuses to attend church…any church. I've managed to become his friend, but it took effort." Curran paused. "I saw him once, staring out to sea." Even now, far away and obsessed with Morrigan, he remembered the agony on Aodhàn's face, and felt compassion for his bedeviled friend. He'd often wondered why he had such an urge to protect Aodhàn. It was a similar need to the one that had more recently galvanized, more powerfully, towards Morrigan. "I've never known anyone so miserable," he said. "But there are other things as well. From time to time he disappears. Agnes claims he rejoins the seals. You know how superstitious village folk are."

An awkward silence fell. He sounded like a pompous ass. No doubt he'd offended her again. It appeared so, the way she stared at him—like she fancied picking up one of her meat cleavers and parting his head from his neck. She and Hannah were city bred and raised, the offspring of a well-to-do Inverness merchant, but they had come to Glenelg meaning to live there after Hannah married Seaghan, to become, as it were, village folk themselves.

He rubbed the scar at his brow. "It isn't my wish to disrespect Nicky's memory, but you know I need to ask for Morrigan's hand."

She rose and paced. "You'll take her to Glenelg."

"Well, naturally," Curran said. What bothered the old witch now? "It's where I live."

"Seaghan will be there," she said, staring out the window.

"Aye." Curran wasn't entirely sure she was speaking to him. Why did it matter?

"Douglas will hate that."

Oh, aye. With everything else, he'd forgotten. Hannah Stewart had jilted Seaghan. She'd run off in the middle of the night with Douglas Lawton, leaving Seaghan heartbroken.

It would be Seaghan who would suffer at the living reminder of her betrayal, but Curran sensed he should keep silent on that detail. "I know it'll be hard." He tried to sound sympathetic rather than exultant. If Douglas hated it so much, perhaps they would never see him. "I understand why Mr. Lawton wouldn't want to be reminded of home."

Beatrice stared blankly. Then she faced Curran, a thin smile playing about her lips. "Maybe it will be amusing," she said. "Aye. Maybe it will."

"Pardon me?" Curran put on an impassive expression, but inside he felt uneasy. The woman must know many things about Glenelg and its history, many old secrets Curran wasn't privy to.

Then he was distracted as he remembered the strange halo of colors he'd seen floating around Morrigan. That glitter of gold, the watercolor wash of lavender. He couldn't even concentrate on this important conversation with her aunt. Truly, he'd turned into a mooning calf.

If Seaghan or Aodhàn ever discerned this, they'd flay him raw with mockery.

Beatrice's eyes cleared and she returned to stand beside the table. "She'll be in mourning for six months," she said coldly. "It'll be the speak of Stranraer, her running off to marry on the heels of her brother's death. I cannot fathom how we'll drag ourselves through the shame. Maybe Douglas should send her to Isabel. At least she'd be out of sight."

"And she'd be closer to me, away from him—"

"What are you suggesting?"

Curran silently cursed. If he had a knife right now, he'd slice out his tongue, damned if he wouldn't. He was as stupid as a sheep today. Yet the image of those strap marks infuriated him. "You know what I saw that day we were together."

"The chit needs more discipline than most."

"She'll carry the scars for the rest of her life."

"She can be shameless, as you have learned. It didn't bother you when it was to your advantage."

"Watch yourself," he said quietly. "Do you think Douglas Lawton would care to put the strap to me?"

"If he discovers how you've sullied his daughter, that'll be the least of what he does to you."

"I doubt he'd have the courage. It's more his manner to prey on those unable to defend themselves, isn't it?" He clenched his hands. "When did the beatings start? How young was she?"

"Don't you dare malign Douglas in his own home! That glaikit girl showed in every measure she would shame us, aye, from the youngest days. We tried to make her into a decent lady." With a harsh laugh, she added, "Yet here she is, with child, unwed. Exactly what we feared. Do you know what shame you've brought on us? Do you care?" She walked to the kitchen door, pausing to scowl at him. "You must be gone when Douglas returns. I'll not have him more upset. When Ibby brought you here he saw right off what you wanted. Now we know he had good reason not to trust you, don't we?" Giving him a final scowl, she left.

Curran slammed his fist against the table. He'd like to strangle her, the bitch.

Surely he deserved a few barbs for what he'd done. But he couldn't quell this vicious fury. His fingers itched to smash every bone in her face. Well, damn it, she could go to hell. No one would keep him from Morrigan, no matter what they said or did. Desire for Morrigan outweighed any annoyance caused by her ill-begotten kin.

Not for the first time, he relived her expression when he'd shared his whimsical experience in the northern wilds. She'd absorbed his story with the rapt, open acceptance of a child, without any hint of suspicion or cynicism.

Through mere chance, because he'd decided to travel to Larne for a puppy, because he'd struck up a conversation with Ibby Maclean, because he'd allowed her to drag him to the Wren's Egg, he'd found the one woman he knew he had to marry.

I'll be your Theseus. You'll be my Ariadne. I won't ever abandon you like he did, and I'll defeat a hundred Minotaurs—even if they all look like Beatrice.

It took several minutes to diffuse the simmering anger sparked by the dour, plainspoken aunt. At last, when he felt calmer, he trudged upstairs to tell Morrigan he must again leave her.

Chapter 13

Some damned stranger beat Nicky to death.

Apparently he had come to the defense of a barmaid who was being harassed by three drunken patrons. A fight had ensued, three against one. Before it could be broken up, one of louts picked up a stool and struck Nicky in the head with it. He never regained consciousness and died the next day. The men who started the fight retained enough sense to vanish into the bowels of Edinburgh; they hadn't been seen since, though the barmaid had given the police detailed descriptions.

Nicky, murdered, after swearing he would never be abused again. Morrigan was glad no one could see the inner fount of uncontrollable laughter, followed by horror and grief so overwhelming she wasn't sure she could bear it.

Douglas resembled November's fallen leaves, dry and brittle, like a gust of wind might blow him away.

The fatal blow left half of her brother's face disfigured. Beatrice had no choice but to cover it with a white shroud.

Aunt Ibby arrived, looking as though she'd wept all the way from Mallaig. The news that Mr. Ramsay had proposed marriage was received with subdued happiness, and a low, "I knew he was smitten."

Among those who gathered to say goodbye on the day of the funeral was Eddie Christopher, the mill owner's son, a staunch Tory who reminisced about their political arguments. The baker and his wife brought whisky and bread; Mrs. Forbes, the florist, pressed Morrigan's hand as she wiped her eyes. Kit's father, Ian Lindsay, kneaded his old felt hat and shifted uncomfortably. One by one they filed past the coffin, touching Nicky on the breast, not only in farewell but also to gain protection from ghostly visits.

Matthew Weir, the minister of the nearby Free Church, had offered to speak at the gravesite, a kind gesture, Morrigan thought, since neither Douglas nor his children had ever attended his services.

Just before the men left with Nicky's coffin, a stranger in a black suit approached the inn and hesitated in the doorway.

Morrigan came out of the kitchen at the sound of the bell. "We're closed," she said, drying her hands on a towel. "There are other places you can stay… the Sea Bank, the King's Arms…the Albion."

"Miss Lawton?"

"Aye?"

"I came to pay my respects."

She held out her hand. He took it, gripping firmly, his steady gaze never wavering, his eyes luminous with grief. "I am Louis Stevenson," he said. "Nick and I met—"

"Oh, aye. Nicky wrote to me about you."

"May I come in?"

She stammered some apology and led him to the coffin. He gazed upon the shroud and finally said, "We knew from the moment we met we would be grand mates. We seemed to have the same ideas about everything."

He gently traced the edge of the coffin Sir MacAndrew had provided. This man knew a Nicky she would never meet, one who made his own decisions and didn't fall asleep dreading the dawn.

Beatrice came to the doorway. "It's time," she said.

As the men gathered around the coffin, Morrigan heard Nicky's voice quoting his favorite poem, Shelley's *Ode to the West Wind*.

If I were a dead leaf thou mightest bear…

He had gazed into the sky when he spoke that line, as though imagining himself floating on a wayward breeze.

If I were a swift cloud to fly with thee;

And something, something…she always forgot the next part.

The comrade of thy wanderings over heaven…

"Freedom," he'd said, when she asked what the devil it meant. "Untouchable freedom."

One too like thee: tameless, and swift, and proud.

Her heartbeat slowed. The daft trembling in her fingers stilled. *Aye, Nicky. That's where you are. That's where you've gone, to the moor. I'll feel you there now.*

He was free. He could swim in and out of rainbows and touch her face on the high braes. No chains would ever again subdue him. None could ever catch him much less hurt him.

Douglas would sooner put a knife to his throat than allow grief to show, but Morrigan thought she caught a glazed stupor, as if from some old nagging injury, and she wondered what he was thinking. Perhaps he fought regret. Maybe he remembered Nicky's mother, the girl who had loved him.

Then her heart hardened. If it hadn't been for him, Nicky might still be alive.

The coffin lid was closed, sending waves of frantic, impotent rage coursing through her. The men were taking him. Never again would she set eyes on the lad. She wanted to scream at them to let go of her brother.

Ibby, with a discerning glance, tucked Morrigan's hand beneath her plump arm and held on tight. "Be strong, isoke," she murmured, tears running down her face.

Six sturdy souls carried the coffin on their shoulders. A line of men followed. Morrigan listened to the stamp of their boots fade in the distance.

She'd asked to go along, but Douglas had refused. She and Beatrice were to stay behind and prepare a meal. It had never been said but she knew women were considered bad luck; their impure presence would harm Nicky's journey to heaven.

Sometimes she wondered why God had created females. They did nothing but tempt, thwart, and harm his precious males. Perhaps he should have given men the ability to bear their own offspring, so there would be no need for the despicable weaker sex. Surely that lack of foresight was a failing on God's part.

Or maybe not, she thought as she crossed from oven to table, from scullery to pantry. No doubt he'd fashioned women to perform those tasks men weren't interested in. Who would do the cooking, mending, cleaning, and washing if not females? Perhaps the motive was well planned, after all. But why then give them souls, if they were designed only for tedious labor and bringing sons into the world?

Maybe women didn't have souls. Since she didn't know what souls were, she wasn't sure, but she felt there was something inside her more than beast or slave.

Douglas couldn't stop her from going along in her thoughts. She pictured the procession coming to the kirkyard, lowering Nicky into a hole beneath the yews. Matthew Weir would read from his Bible. Douglas would drop a handful of dirt on the coffin. There was even a stone grave marker, thanks to Sir MacAndrew.

Her eyes and jaw ached. Her bones were leaden and weary.

Daft words spoken, a prayer or two, and folk would disperse, leaving him alone in the dark. A hundred years from now, would someone enter the kirkyard, read his name and know how dear he'd been?

They closed the inn for a few days, a short respite before they must put on their pleasant *guest* faces and continue earning their livelihoods. The other crofters worked together to finish Douglas's barley harvest. No one liked the cold, disagreeable innkeeper, but social rules couldn't be ignored.

Two days after the funeral, Morrigan escaped to the woods, hoping to spend an hour in solitude. She came across a patch of forget-me-nots clustered in the shade, and knelt, thinking how the color nearly matched Nicky's eyes.

Mama, is he with you now, or with his own mam, Neala Grant?

No answer came but the weeping cry of a curlew as it passed overhead on its way to the shore.

Muffled footsteps broke the silence. She looked up, surprised to see Nicky's friend, Louis Stevenson. She stood. Without speaking, he embraced her, pressing her head against his chest, over the slow, steady beat of his heart.

His unspoken understanding lifted her from the dizzying abyss and placed her on firm ground.

She took him to her spot by the mossy tarn. "It seems like yesterday," she said. "Nicky and I sat here and spoke of his plan to go to Edinburgh. My father had forbidden it. He thought he could use Nicky as unpaid labor forever. They fought and fought...."

"In my family, the men become engineers. We build lighthouses and bridges. My uncle built the Cairn Point lighthouse, down the way. My grandfather designed Corsewall."

"I ride to Corsewall sometimes," Morrigan cried. "Fancy your kin building it. That lighthouse is an old friend."

He smiled wryly. "I feel that way about a few of them." He sighed, staring into the curtain of trees, running his palm over a patch of new grass stems poking through the mud furrows she'd made last time she was here.

Belatedly, she remembered her habit of categorizing men. Louis was merry, judging from the lines beside his eyes and the upward mobility of his lips. But graveness lay beneath.

"I heard my father rebelled once or twice," he said, "but he finally became a partner as expected. Imagine when I told him I wanted to spend my life writing stories. Sometimes I wonder why parents feel they must burden their offspring with their own ambitions. Long ago, I asked him about his youthful aspirations. He denied wanting to be anything other than an engineer, but his irritation gave him away. I'd caused him to remember something he wished to forget. Sometimes, what folk don't say tells the most."

"What did you do?"

"I compromised. I'm studying law in case my writing fails to support me. I've a premonition—" A fit of coughing forced him to break off. The skin under his eyes darkened and he shivered, though the day had grown almost sultry.

"Are you ill?" she asked. "Should we go?"

"It's nothing. A stubborn cold."

"What is your premonition?"

His smile transformed his face, lending his eyes a dark radiance. He wasn't handsome, but there was something fascinating about him. Morrigan could almost hear whispers of poetry in the rustle of his coat sleeves.

"That I'll never be grand or rich," he said. "My only real hope is to have a child. I desperately want children. I've...never told anyone that, but for your brother. He wanted bairns too, did you know?"

Oh, it hurt. It was like a stone lodged in her chest, pressing against her ribs every time she breathed. Nicky's dreams would never be fulfilled, but perhaps he could survive, in some way, through this man. It comforted her to think so. "No, I didn't know that," she said. Then she blurted, "I'm having a child. So I've been told."

She'd said it. Aloud. To a stranger.

His expressive face betrayed his thoughts. Concern became delight then reverted to concern. "My dear." He touched her cheek and his frown deepened. "Your father...."

Ah, so Nicky had shared that secret. Aye, indeed, they must have been close. If Nicky trusted him, then so would she.

"He doesn't know." Picturing him when he found out turned her blood to ice.

"Miss Lawton," he said. "Morrigan...how can I help?"

She wished, in the futile way of a child, that she could take back her revelation. "Every morning when I wake, I realize all over again this is no dream. It's there, growing. Soon there'll be no hiding it."

"What of the man? Could you marry? Do you love him?"

Curran's bright image brought an involuntary smile and a sense of warm safety. The braw lad, her braw, brave Theseus, who slew the lion and saved the world, at least in vision. "He seems willing. I...don't know what love is, or how to make it happen."

Surprise danced across his features, then something else, something deliberately erased.

Christ. He thought her depraved.

She ducked her head, fighting the urge to give in to a self-indulgent tantrum, and regarded the smooth brown surface of the tarn. Water would always ripple in whatever direction the wind compelled. It had no free will, no choices to make. Her desire to spite Douglas hadn't made him suffer, and soon, when the babe's presence could no longer be hidden, she'd be the sorry one.

Louis's fingers twined around her fist and she faced him, bracing for the only emotion he could in good conscience show: repulsed Christian condemnation.

His head tilted. "A light came over you just now, when you spoke of him.

I've seen such things from time to time, like the air is vibrating." His eyes narrowed as though he had something else to say, but he didn't, and they sat in silence. Then he shook his head. "I understand now what your brother meant. He compared you to an alder. No gale can break its branches. Nick claimed you're much stronger than he. If he were here, what would he tell you? The rest of your life is a long time, and far too many men are like your father."

"I won't have a choice," she said, flooded with gratitude at his acceptance. "If I don't marry him I'll end up like the local...." She paused, unable to say the word *whore*. "Fallen woman, having rocks thrown at me. Unmarried mothers are hated. Her fate could be mine no matter what I want. It's up to him, isn't it? The father."

"There's the other side of the coin to consider. Are you strong enough to suffer a lifetime of unhappiness as wife to a man you don't love?"

"I couldn't be unhappy with Curran. Oh, I do love him...." She rose, pacing from the water's edge to the nearest tree, staring blankly at a beetle scurrying around its base. "Surely I do. I'm fortunate he asked me to marry him. He didn't have to. He might as easily have blamed me." Glimpsing the soft petals of a violet, she bent and plucked it, holding it to her nose. Flowers held an intoxicating hint of the earth in their scent, sending her into calmer contemplation. "What is love?" she asked. "How d'you know it?"

His laugh was hardly more than an exhalation. "That I cannot answer, Miss Lawton. I think it must be different for each one of us."

This man made her feel at ease, unafraid of ridicule or censure. "What about hate? Why do folk hate weans who have no say in being born? Hate women who mean no harm? Yet judgment is never passed on the man."

"My father often says women should be able to divorce their husbands whenever they please, without hindrance, but as for men, they should not be allowed to divorce their wives for any reason. There are some of us who don't agree that the fairer sex is to blame for the world's ills." Louis remained silent a moment, frowning. "I see the fighter inside you. Her heart recognizes injustice. She wants to destroy it, to demand that equity be given to every being, highborn or low, male or female, young or old. But, disagreeably, there's another part that fights the fighter. She believes she should mold herself to the requirements surrounding her. You are at war with yourself, my dear Miss Lawton. At some point, someday, you'll have to make a choice. Which path will you follow?"

Louis's discomfiting observations brought a memory of Diorbhail Sinclair's odd words at the train station. *Avatar. Learn of those who cleared the way for you. The warriors.*

The word sounded foreign, certainly not Scots, unless perhaps it came from the Orkneys or the Shetlands, from which Curran's tyrant-protector Fearghas hailed. She'd heard folk from those islands were as far removed from Scotland as if they'd spawned at the North Pole.

"D'you know what an 'avatar' is?" she asked, adding hesitantly, "Louis?"

Creases deepened in his forehead. "It comes from India, I believe, and has to do with reincarnation."

"What's that?"

"The belief that folk return again and again, each new life reflecting how they lived before, until, hopefully, they grow beyond the need for bodies and achieve *Nirvana*, the Indian version of Heaven."

"Nirvana," Morrigan repeated, testing the word. A smile passed over Louis's face, but she felt too absorbed to ask what he found amusing. "And avatar?"

"I'm no expert on these matters, mind you, but I believe that is the human incarnation of a deity. Why do you ask about these things?"

"I heard it and wondered. But what does that mean? *Incarnation.*"

"The form a god takes when masquerading as a human. Rather like Jesus, I suppose. Human and divine in one."

What had Diorbhail meant, calling her that? And what women, other than her mother, and perhaps Beatrice, had cleared the way for her? Beatrice could hardly be considered a warrior.

Human incarnation of a deity. Morrigan felt as though the Norse god Thor was smashing his hammer against her skull, shouting *Listen! Listen, you vexing girl!*

She looked into the canopy of leaves, clenching her hands and fighting an angry sense of helplessness. "If I were a man, and had freedom...."

"No. Don't use that excuse. You'll be lost before you begin, and the fighter's soul will wither. Aye, for a woman, it's harder. But give yourself honor anyway, even if no one else does. Respect the strength inside you."

She pondered the name she'd chosen for Curran's dog. She'd thought it fine and bold. But Antiope had broken faith with her tribe for love of Theseus. She'd fought at his side against her clan, her people, only to be forsaken by him, the king who desired a new wife.

At every turn those mythical females had collapsed beneath the Greeks. If any lesson survived, it was that women could never triumph against male authority.

Yet even loyalty, conforming, and submitting brought abandonment.

"Is my only choice Penthesilea, then?"

"I don't understand."

She started. How far her thoughts had traveled from this shady pool, back in time to the beloved tales taught by a dominie as Greek-mad as herself. In Morrigan he'd found the perfect pupil, one willing to delve into ancient myth for as many hours as she could escape her father and her chores. This particular tale had been the source of much discussion between them. At first, when Morrigan was young, the dominie had been circumspect. Later, around the time Douglas stopped her schooling altogether, he'd revealed more.

"Penthesilea…" Louis murmured. "I know that name."

"The Amazon queen."

"She was defeated by Achilles outside the walls of Troy."

"Some think she killed *him*."

"Aye." Louis nodded. "And Zeus brought him back to life…."

"So he could kill her."

Louis's gaze faltered and he turned once more to regard the water.

"She was wounded, at the end of her strength," Morrigan said. "It was underhanded. Unfair. And after Achilles defeated her, he attacked her again… in the vilest manner."

He tossed a pebble, watching it skip across the water. "I misjudged you, Miss Lawton," he said. "This makes me more certain than ever. Because you understand the power, the lessons in the tales of our past. Whether or not they're true doesn't matter. They hold messages for all times, all people. That fighter inside you? She's an Amazon. I think a bit of Penthesilea has lived on in you, lass."

"Curran said…." She didn't finish. First Curran—*You've a wild Amazon heart* —and now Louis Stevenson, the poet. She gazed at him, wondering what these men saw that she couldn't. Perhaps the secret wild girl inside her was becoming more visible. She had to admit she'd done things over the last few months she never would have considered doing before, risky, reckless things. Was that what Amazon women did?

He regarded her, waiting for her to continue. What use was there in encouraging her to choose her own path, when the whole world was carefully designed to humiliate or destroy women who tried? "You haven't answered me," she said.

"How can I? It's too easy for me to advise you this way or that, when the outcome will no' affect me in the slightest. I'll only broach a question for you to ponder. Who assigns women their place? What happens to you, to your daughters, if you allow it? No, don't answer. Follow your path, whatever it is, wherever it leads. I've a notion your heart will steer you rightly."

"What if I submit, and take the easier path?"

Louis's next words struck deeply. Morrigan knew she would never forget them. He said, "Then that is the lesson you needed to learn." After a moment, he added, smiling slightly, "This man of yours is lucky."

And so will any lass be who wins you. She wanted to say it, but wasn't sure she should, and the moment passed.

Though Louis offered singular comfort, a sense that everything would turn out all right, he couldn't stay. He had companions waiting for him in Germany. He left on the late train, promising to write.

Remember to mix in a smattering of Athene with Penthesilea, and you'll be unstoppable, he said next to her ear, and kissed her cheek. His kindness promised friendship, and she had few enough friends. The fact that he'd been Nicky's first made him even dearer.

FOUR DAYS AFTER NICKY'S FUNERAL, MORRIGAN RETURNED FROM TOWN TO FIND A crate propped against the sideboard, covered in heavy brown paper and addressed to her.

"Two lads brought it an hour ago," Ibby said. "What do you think it could be? Open it, do, Morrigan."

As tall as she, wider too, and so heavy it couldn't be budged, the mysterious container gave no indication of its origin.

"Hurry!" Ibby cried. "Don't you want to see what it is?"

Morrigan ripped the paper. It fell, crackling, revealing slats of nailed plywood. Using a pry bar, they loosened the nails and wrenched the beams apart.

"Michty me," said Beatrice.

Morrigan herself gazed out at them, painted in oils, so real and responsive that the living, breathing girl who had inspired the work wondered if her likeness might step from the frame, bringing a burst of sea-drenched wind.

Her image sat on a slope next to Loch Ryan, in a dress fashioned of water and spindrift. Meadowsweet, fairy ink cap, and a perfect conch shell were scattered across her lap. One bared shoulder, a low-dipping bodice, and the direct gaze suggested daring. Innocence was there too, in the gown's virginal color and the blush layered upon the lass's cheeks.

The skirt foamed like a wash of tide onto a beach. Water drops, flung by the wind from her phantasmal costume, were forever trapped in midair, reflecting fine-spun rainbows. The girl's mouth was solemn, her brows feathered and low, lending an impression of gravity. Her hair, loose and blown by the wind, revealed her face in minute detail, from forehead to the subtle cleft in the chin. Finally, Morrigan saw webs of flesh between the girl's fingers, and knew what fantasy the artist intended to create.

"That is the most beautiful thing I have ever seen." There was a catch in Ibby's voice.

Beatrice said, "It reminds me of your mother, the way she was when we first went to Glenelg. It reminds me of the legends I learned there, on the far side of the Five Sisters." Her voice, when she spoke again, was low. "The foam-born goddess."

"Who did this?" Ibby asked, after glancing askance at Beatrice.

"It has to be Kit." Morrigan knew it without looking at the scrawl in the corner.

"The veterinary's son?" Ibby asked.

Beatrice plucked an envelope from the base of the container. She glanced at it then passed it to Morrigan. There was her name, neatly inscribed. Morrigan tore it open and read the enclosed note aloud.

Dear Miss Lawton,
I found this painting in my son's room, and thought you should have it. I do
not know his desires concerning the work, but as we are unlikely to hear from
him for some time, I send it on to you, trusting it will not cause embarrassment
or distress.
Again, my deepest condolences on the passing of your brother.
Most sincerely,
Ian Lindsay

"But why would he paint you?" Ibby asked.

"I don't know," Morrigan said. An aching sense of loss washed over her. "He's gone. Those I love all die, or leave."

"You loved him?" Ibby now appeared shocked as well as puzzled.

She caught herself. "No," she said. She'd looked upon Kit as a means of escape, as a bright spot of romantic excitement in an otherwise dull existence. But love? Love was something terrifying. "I liked him. He was blithe and bonny, and made me laugh."

"Well, I have not left you, and here is Beatrice. We've both been with you your entire life, and that will never change." Ibby put her arm around Morrigan's shoulders. "There must've been more to that lad than I ever imagined. The work...the hours he spent on this." She brushed her fingertips over the painted lass's cheek. "It will be an heirloom. Your great-grandchildren will know you through it."

"This is how he sees me," Morrigan said, marveling. "As he learns how to help kye give birth. He swore he'd never do that."

"Maybe someday he'll come back and you can thank him properly." Ibby used her *let's be cheery* voice. "I feel a need for Beatrice's strengthening tea. What about you?"

They left the oil painting there, propped against the sideboard in the dining room. Giving off a blue-green flash of prismatic light, the lass observed all from between slats of wood, ready to catch the eye of any soul who might happen along.

DOUGLAS SLAMMED THE DOOR AGAINST THE WALL AS HE STRODE INTO THE KITCHEN, shouting, "Who brought that shite into this house?"

Morrigan jumped halfway out of her chair and nearly tipped over her teacup.

"Christian Lindsay's father," Beatrice said. She, too, looked wary. "The boy painted it, we think."

"That rutting dog! He still wants to shame her, and me." He rammed his fist against the table, making the china clatter and pitch.

The sight of his crimson face sent Morrigan's heart palpitating. She ducked her head and gritted her teeth to keep from saying *It isn't my fault. I didn't ask for it.*

He bent over her, cutting off the light through the door. "Why d'you never look at me? At least she did that. Hannah wouldn't have feared a lion."

She kept her eyes downcast as she realized what had set him off. In the painting, she resembled too much the woman in the daguerreotype.

"You let him have his way, didn't you? Virtue did no' paint that bloody hoor picture."

"Damn you!" She did meet his gaze then and slammed her own fist against the table. "Damn you for always thinking the worst of me!"

His head reared. He grimaced and seized her shoulders. "Foisting bastards on innocent men, driving us daft over your shameless ways. You deserve what you get. You well deserve it." His breath wheezed and spittle struck her cheek. "Your brother would be alive but for you. It was *your* punishment he took, your fault he left, your fault he died."

"Have you lost your senses?" Ibby pried at his fingers. "Get away from her, you foul man."

Douglas slapped his sister so hard she stumbled. A drop of blood glistened on her lip and her cheek turned bright red.

"Don't you ever come between me and mine." He dragged Morrigan from the chair, pinning her against the table. The next thing she knew, he had slapped her as well. Exploding stars and a blood-red flower of pain burst through her cheek. Her teeth jarred. For an instant, all went black.

"You're thinking of Hannah." Beatrice gripped his forearm, forcing it down, but she spoke calmly. "This is Morrigan, *a luaidh*. Hannah cannot lie to you anymore."

Douglas abruptly released Morrigan. He stared a moment longer then stalked out of the room.

"Why...why did he do that?" Ibby turned on Morrigan, tears spilling from her eyes. "What am I saying? I know what he's like...I've always known." She began weeping in earnest, and fell into a chair. "Ever since Neala died."

Morrigan fetched a dishcloth and bent over her aunt, dabbing gently at her lip. "No harm done, Auntie. I'm used to it."

"But you shouldn't be!" Ibby propped her elbows on the table and pressed her cheeks against her palms as though she was too weary to hold her head up. "Plenty of harm's been done if you ask me."

"Go to bed," Beatrice said to Morrigan. "I'll give your aunt some tea. She'll be fine."

Morrigan started to protest, but exhaustion washed over her and she couldn't find the strength to argue. She hugged Ibby and climbed the back stairs, closing her bedroom door behind her, only realizing how badly she was shaking as she unfastened the buttons on her blouse.

She pulled on her nightgown and crossed to her window, leaning out. Low, heavy clouds released a spatter of rain and there were intermittent rumbles of thunder. She closed the window so she wouldn't have to wake up later and do it.

MORRIGAN WAS LOST IN DREAMLESS SLEEP WHEN HER DOOR WAS THROWN OPEN. It struck the edge of the wardrobe hard, startling her awake. At first she couldn't place where she was. She seemed to be falling through endless black space, punctuated by the warning pummel of thousands of tiny fists against glass.

Hands pulled her off her pillow. She couldn't see anything, but she felt a close presence, looming over her like an incubus. She cried out, terrified.

"Long past time," the darkness said. She knew then who it was, and instinctively began fighting. It was oddly easy to shove her father. He took several rapid steps in an effort to keep his balance. Wasting no time, she scrambled across the bed and off the far side, retreating until she could go no farther, and was trapped against the cold window. Behind her, rain drummed furiously.

He spoke from across the room. "Time…to pay for what you did to me. Did you think you would never face the…consequences?"

She wished for light but not a hint came through the window. She could smell though, a noxious aroma of strong, coarse whisky and sweat.

"Go to bed, Papa." She tried to keep her voice calm, like Beatrice did. "Leave me alone." But her voice shook in spite of her effort, like a frightened child's.

She heard him coming around the bed. He grabbed her, yanking cruelly on her arm as she fought to escape. "You thought no one would ever make you pay for what you did? Well I'm pure weary of waiting." He placed both hands around her throat and squeezed.

She clutched at his hands, pulling, ripping with her nails, but his grip was inexorable. Stars exploded before her eyes. She scrabbled, clawing his face, and gouged four deep furrows in his flesh.

Cursing, he released her. She sucked in a lungful of air and screamed.

He grabbed her by the shoulders and shook her violently. "It was that bastard's wean! You only used me to protect Seaghan, didn't you? Tell me! It's my right!"

Morrigan gasped. How had he discovered she was carrying a child? No wonder he was enraged. He truly would kill her for this, and no doubt go unpunished. She struck the side of his head and fought to twist free of his grip, though his violent shaking made her dizzy.

Light flickered at the open doorway and there were her aunts in their night-clothes. "What's happened?" Ibby cried. Beatrice lifted her candle, sending a wavering flare over the tableau.

Douglas turned his face as though the light hurt him. Keeping a pincer-like grip on Morrigan's shoulder with one hand, he rubbed his arm with the other, up and down, repeatedly. His upper lip lifted like a snarling dog's. His face was darkly shadowed, evil, the skin drawn in around his eyes.

She ducked and nearly freed herself before he swept his hand to her throat and again throttled her. She fought him blindly, or thought she did. She was no longer certain of anything beyond the whine in her ears and bursting spots of color disrupting her vision.

"Sweet Brigit," she heard Ibby scream. "He's trying to kill her!"

"He'll listen to me," Beatrice said. "I've always protected her. You've never known, never. Be quiet, Isabel. You're making it worse." She set her candle on the commode and approached him. "Douglas…Douglas. Do you know what you're doing?"

He glared at her. "Get out," he said, his voice thick and slurred.

Morrigan rallied, a desperate will to live flooding like fire through her. "Don't leave me!" she rasped, and again tried to gouge his face, but he struck her arm away.

His skin was sheened with oily sweat. "Did you think I would no' recognize the bastard? She's turned out like you, a hoor, her soul as black as sin."

Beatrice pried at his hand. Ibby grabbed his other arm, half-sobbing. "Dear Lord, I'm to blame for this. I'll never forgive myself."

Douglas shook his head and grimaced, much like a bull tormented from too many directions. His shoulders hunched. He released Morrigan and staggered. "What the devil…."

His eyes rolled up. He groaned and pitched forward, slamming into Morrigan and knocking her into the window. Glass exploded like a shotgun blast, drowning Ibby's screams.

Awareness faded in and out as her father's weight bore down on Morrigan's spine and pressed her into glass splinters on the windowsill. He lay motionless, his arms hanging limp on either side of her head. She pushed at him but he was so heavy, and she had no balance, no strength. Vertigo swirled through her head, making everything spin drunkenly.

A large, triangular-shaped chunk of glass swung above him, shooting out reflections of candlelight. *Free me,* Morrigan thought; before the words finished forming, the shard dropped, swift and silent as a dagger blade into Douglas's spine.

His body jerked. Blood trickled over Morrigan's throat.

She couldn't hold her head up any longer, and closed her eyes against pelting rain. Had he not been on top of her, the shard would have pierced her, and possibly the babe inside her. But if Douglas hadn't begun this sorry attack, the window wouldn't have broken. She wouldn't be here. She'd be asleep.

"Help," she gasped, without any hope.

"I'm getting him." Was that a man's voice?

The suffocating weight vanished. Morrigan slid off the sill and onto the bedroom floor, drawing in lungfuls of air. The circulation slowly returned to her legs, making them prickle and sting.

Strong arms picked her up and placed her on the bed. Gentle fingers removed bits of glass from her hair.

"What happened here?" Again, she heard a man speak.

"It was an accident," Beatrice replied.

"My eye...oh, it hurts." Morrigan hardly recognized her voice.

"Hold still."

A heavy weight settled beside her and a face bent over her. This must be a nightmare. Could it really be Matthew Weir, the minister? "Bring the candle closer," he said, and there was Beatrice, holding a glaring light.

"There's a bit of glass in there," he said. "Hold still, aye still. Don't blink. There, I've got it. You're in need of a surgeon."

An awful rattling sound brought her head up. Every breath burned, grinding over the damage in her throat.

Ibby stood in the doorway, wringing a handkerchief as she sobbed, for once making no effort to appear polished.

Beatrice set the candle down and knelt beside Douglas. His eyes bulged. The odd rattling noise was coming from him.

"He's hurt." Morrigan coughed. She remembered the glass falling, piercing him. Yet he was still alive, still breathing. Here was proof of what she'd always suspected. Her father was indestructible.

"It's his heart, I think," the minister said. "My wife's gone for the surgeon, but...I fear, Miss Lawton...." He clasped her hand. "He's asking for you, lass."

"No," Ibby cried. "Keep him away from her! He's a beast! A beast!"

Beatrice rose swiftly. She grabbed Ibby's arm and dragged her out of the room, hissing something in her ear.

"Aye," Morrigan tried to swallow. "Please help me."

Supported in Matthew Weir's steady arms, she dropped to her knees beside Douglas. Glass embedded in her hair and skin made her feel she was scoured raw everywhere. It hurt like the devil when she blinked, but if she didn't, she couldn't see through the blood. Without the minister holding her, she thought the shuddering, the chattering of her teeth, might tear her apart.

Beatrice returned alone and knelt on Douglas's other side. She picked up his limp hand and caressed it.

"I thought it was her," he said faintly, his face bloody from the grooves she'd scraped into his cheek. "Hannah. The painting. Seaghan.... Mocking me. I...I know I've sinned." His free hand found and seized Morrigan's in a surprisingly strong grip. "I wasn't always this way. Don't let anyone make you forget.... *Beannachd leat, mo nighean.*"

Air whistled from his lungs. The guttural breathing choked and stopped. His eyes went blank. Empty. No longer terrible. No longer anything.

Beatrice fell upon him. "No," she cried. "Don't leave me, Douglas."

Matthew Weir pried Morrigan's hand from her father's. Raising her, he said, "There, child," and patted her forearm.

Morrigan's heart was hammering. "He hated me," she whispered.

"Oh, lass. The man was ill. I saw he didn't want to leave you."

Morrigan stared at her father's face. It still scowled, even in death. "You can't die."

Beatrice worked her way to her feet. "It isn't so easy letting him go, is it? Never let anyone tell you otherwise."

"Come to the kitchen," the minister said. "I'll brew you both a cup of tea."

"Tea?" Morrigan laughed. "Tea." God had abandoned her, but there would always be tea.

Chapter 14

NO MATTER HOW MANY HUNDREDS OF TIMES SHE PICTURED HIM GONE, SHE COULD not accept it.

Douglas, Nicky, Hannah…her father, her mother, her brother, all dead. She had no kin left but her two aunts.

Yet whenever she retched into her washbasin, she was forcibly reminded that another life was coming.

Since he couldn't forbid it as he had with Nicky, Beatrice placed Douglas on a board in the Highland manner. She covered his body with scalloped linen and set a wooden platter on his chest holding two mounds, one of earth, the other salt.

"The earth is his body," she told Morrigan. "The salt his indestructible spirit."

Ibby refused to see Douglas, much less give him honor, so it was left to Beatrice to sit with him through the night in the candlelit parlor singing his eulogy, her voice eerie and unsettling. It was odd how the woman so suddenly returned to the language and customs she had long discarded. The only Gaelic Morrigan had ever heard from her were a few rare endearments, and all she'd ever said about the Highlands was dismissive and rude.

White cloth shrouded the mirrors and windows. The grandfather clock stood silent, stopped at the hour of death.

Any moment Papa would open his eyes and demand to know why she hadn't finished her chores. Irritation flamed as Morrigan brushed her fingers against his temple. His flesh was cold, a rotting shell, all that remained of what she'd believed eternal. Trembling settled in her muscles, spiraling inward, digging a chasm she feared might swallow her.

"He's dead." She said it, over and over. Yet the words were meaningless. She tried to see death on the person of Douglas Lawton, but the picture wouldn't form. Death couldn't sit on his body. In truth, wouldn't it be feared to try?

He was the force that pushed her from bed each morning, directed her every movement, even her thoughts, more often than not. Tall and dark, always frowning, he had created her world, and never allowed her to forget his supremacy. He was the possessor of knowledge she could never hope to understand, of beginnings, the first ray of earth's sunlight, the initial gasp of human lungs. His death was incomprehensible. She could more easily believe he'd simply deserted them to lord over some other realm. From the moment of her birth his had been a force as powerful, as uncontrollable, as a blast of wind. If he could die, what did that say about everything else? Perhaps tomorrow she would wake to find all of life a fantasy…the sun, the moon, the ground she walked upon.

Yet at the same time, she couldn't help but wonder if she had murdered her father by wishing the glass shard to fall.

The surgeon assured her, and a hovering, anxious Ibby, that her eye would heal. Had the glass punctured her cornea, he said, it might have gone differently; she should thank providence it hadn't. He bandaged it, telling her she could remove the gauze in three days, after the funeral. The bruises on her throat caused his brows to lift and his gaze to meet hers searchingly, but he said nothing other than to advise the application of cold water and vinegar, combined with rest, and promised her voice would soon return. He tended her cuts and scratches, accepted a cup of tea and slice of cake, and left them to their dreary business.

"Morrigan," her aunt said when he was gone, "we think it best Curran not be told what happened. We'll say you tripped on a floorboard that wasn't properly nailed and fell into the window. I'll make you more collars to cover your neck if necessary, and we'll wait until after the funeral to send him a message."

Morrigan took a deep breath and met Ibby's troubled gaze, knowing her aunt was afraid Curran would withdraw his proposal if he discerned the truth.

For the second time in one month, the residents of Stranraer gathered at the Wren's Egg for a funeral. Morrigan felt their curious stares and overheard some of the careless gossip. *Why does the daughter stand so stiff and silent, with no' a tear for her father? What are those cuts? Why is her eye covered?* Morrigan sensed malicious gratification beneath their conjectures. *You've heard the rumors…what goes on at this godforsaken inn. Didn't the son run off? The minister's wife told me the daughter has never entered a kirk in her life, ever!*

Matthew Weir didn't once ask about that night. He and his wife had been taking their customary predawn stroll, discussing additions to his sermon, when he'd heard the screaming. He'd broken the door to get in.

He visited Morrigan after the funeral. As he prepared to leave, he grasped her hand, closed his eyes, and spoke a prayer. His sincerity left her tongue-tied, shamed at her ignorance of religion.

Beatrice sent a letter to Sir MacAndrew, asking for his instructions, and another to Curran.

Workmen repaired the broken door and replaced the window. No doubt they would go home, and over tea would help spread tales about the devil's lair on Neptune Street.

Ibby took the bandage off Morrigan's eye. "It's no' so bad," she said, adding, "You'd be surprised how quickly folk will forget this."

Each day in the cusp of dawn, Morrigan walked. Sometimes she saddled Widdie and rode to Finnarts Hill or the other way, to the Corsewall lighthouse, astounded at the realization Papa could never again punish her for taking a morning ride. But the world of newfound freedom remained indistinct. Douglas's voice drowned it. *Your brother would be alive but for you.*

If she hadn't fought him, would he still be here? Should she have let him kill her? When she considered such questions, the bruises around her neck, in the shape of her father's fingers, throbbed, and it hurt to breathe.

She lived in a fog where nothing existed but endlessly circling impressions. Ibby and Beatrice had to sit her down to eat—she never felt the slightest pang of hunger or thirst. Neither attempted to stop her from walking or riding. At Finnarts Hill she relived stolen mornings when she and Nicky watched the sun rise or played at war with their wooden swords. He had listened to her read from her mythology book until he knew the stories as well as she, and he'd accused her of believing in them like they were fashioned from true history.

She sat on the slope above Loch Ryan, staring at one brilliant, poppy-colored sunrise after another.

Nicky wouldn't have been pushed into fleeing had I not run away to the woods in a fit of rage. It doesn't matter that I didn't intend to cause it, or that Papa was wrong in his vengeance. Nicky is dead. Papa is dead. Both died because of me, and I can never make it right.

Widdie grazed and Morrigan plucked wildflowers. She tore the petals without looking at them, then gazed, confused, at her damp, stained fingers.

At sunset of the seventh day after Douglas died, she returned to the inn and glimpsed a hazy figure sitting on the front steps. His head was down, arms resting in a weary manner upon his knees. She stopped. Gloaming's shadows made the figure nebulous, a phantom...a ghost. Blood rushed from her head, leaving her dizzy and breathless. She reached out to the rock wall to keep herself from falling. *Is he going to drive me mad for what I did to him?*

The figure's head lifted. He rose and approached her. "Morrigan."

A hard, aching lump formed in her throat. "You've come."

"I have." Curran folded her in against him. "And I'll never leave you again."

Tenderly scolding, he urged her to eat. "Feed my son, *a nighean*. I want him strong and healthy."

"What does that mean...*a nighean?*" she asked, a memory sparking.

"'My lass,'" he said. "Do you not know any Gaelic?"

"Hardly any. But Papa...he said that word, *nighean*, before he died."

"From him, it would've meant 'daughter.'" Curran frowned.

"He said something else. 'Byan-ach lat.' What does that mean?"

"He was blessing you, telling you goodbye."

Douglas's last words, as kind and out of character as they were, didn't soften Curran's ill will. He quickly steered them back to baked halibut and barley bread, and how important it was that she have some.

Was a child truly growing inside her? Her corset fit no differently, and her abdomen seemed as flat as ever. If it weren't for the nausea, the cessation of her monthly courses, the tenderness in her breasts, and the fact that she could no longer bear the smell of cigar or pipe smoke, she'd never believe it. Yet wasn't Curran dear, the way he touched her, kissed her hand and stroked her hair—like he found her extraordinary. As though he believed her the only woman on earth capable of providing his offspring.

To please him, she ate.

Thankfully, by the time he came, most of the superficial cuts and scratches left by particles of glass had healed over, and the injury to her eye had improved. The bruises on her neck had turned an ugly greenish-yellow, but that didn't matter, as they were hidden beneath her collars and he never saw them. The three women kept to their tale of her falling into the window, and he accepted her peculiar clumsiness.

Citing the double shock she'd suffered and her lethargy, he convinced Aunt Ibby to let him take her for a drive, to imbibe the "reviving fresh air." With a basket of food tucked between them in the trap, he sent Leo eastward. In due course they came to a muddy turn-off that rambled through open country and woods.

And oh, the hills...one over the next they rolled, draped with purple heather that resembled vast coronation robes for an unseen deity. Wildflowers burst from every crevice.

Leo's uniform hoof-beats lulled Morrigan into forgetful peace—or perhaps it was this lad beside her, gifting her with generous smiles, urging her to breathe, making her feel irreplaceable.

The track led them around the edge of a loch and they found themselves on a narrow isthmus, glimpsing the upper tines of a citadel through a leafy frame of trees.

"I've never been here," Morrigan said to Curran's inquiry. "I always go to the coast. Let's see what it is."

Leaving Leo to graze, they clambered over a low wall into a clearing. The stone fortress before them soared high and forbidding; the window openings were blackly menacing. Not a breath of wind or a single birdcall broke the silence.

Showers of ivy covered the ancient stronghold. Leaves brushed Curran's shoulders as he stepped through the doorway. He turned, held out his hand and smiled, never to know how the image of him there, crowned in ivy, reminded Morrigan of Dionysos, Greek god of wine. Vibrating with emotion, she put her hand into his and returned his smile, letting him draw her into a chamber bright and shadowed, a place of immense, watchful silence, bursting with invisible memories of lost lives. She tiptoed, fearful any sound or misstep might bring the old keep tumbling onto their heads.

Curran went off to explore. Morrigan, listening for his footsteps, instead heard subdued laughter and a distant, echoing beat of drums. Staring at a wall still webbed in shadow, she gave herself over to envisioning what it might have been like to live here, once upon a time. A carved throne near a roaring fire, a man with a full black beard, holding a goblet. Next to him, spackled in firelight, a tall, solemn-faced lass, her knee length hair braided with ribbons. Morrigan smelled roasting game, heard the sizzle of dripping fat. Thrusting the point of his dagger into a hunk of meat, the man ripped off a mouthful with his teeth and laughed as juices ran through his beard.

Morrigan closed her eyes to better visualize the spectacle. This man was a powerful chief. He had waged battle, enriched his clan, and won cattle through canny raids. His face wore pride, selfishness, and more than a dab of cruelty.

An old child's ditty trailed through her memory:

Frae Wigtown to the town o' Ayr,
Portpatrick to the Cruives o' Cree
Nae man need think for to bide there
Unless he court a Kennedy.

Curran appeared at her side, laughing when she jumped and released a startled shriek. Her fancy dimmed and she stood once again in an empty, echoing ruin, housing only mice and spiders.

They walked outside, fetched the basket, and spread a blanket beneath the branches of a great old oak. Curran lay beside her, whistling as he spooned jam on a scone and held it to her mouth.

She nibbled. "You'll have me big as a house."

"That's my plan. You're far too appealing. I don't want to spend all my waking hours fighting off Glenelg's lusty men."

"Oh, Curran."

"You don't know, do you, how bonny you are?"

A flush crept through her cheeks. She laughed and unwrapped a wedge of cheese. She knew too well it was beauty that brought Curran back from Ireland, then from the Highlands. He'd probably tried to forget her and couldn't. That would explain why he hadn't appeared in June, as he'd promised. There was power in beauty. Because of it she sat on this blanket being fed by an ardent lover who declared his willingness to marry.

Though she was gratified to possess the magic requirement that pulled him to her, she also wanted to demand more of him. But he wouldn't understand if she tried to explain. How could he, when she didn't understand herself?

"Morrigan." He clasped her hand, turned it, and rubbed the birthmark on her wrist almost absently. "You're the bonniest girl I've ever seen in my life… and I've seen a few. There's more pretty flattery I could say, but you'll have to marry me to hear it."

What if, that day on the moor, she'd had a missing tooth, a wandering eye…or was simply ordinary?

Had her nose been longer, or pointed…her eyes a wee fraction closer…lips half-a-heartbeat thinner…he might've spilled his seed then refused to marry her. He would have gone on with his merry life while she and his unwanted child joined the fate of women like Diorbhail Sinclair.

Beauty put this babe in her womb. Beauty carried her to this place. Beauty would see to it she remained unscathed by her reckless choice.

The paths that stretched from the hub of birth, some thorned, some smooth, were fair mischancy. *Beauty* seemed a flighty, insubstantial thing. Strange to think that, in the end, suffering or joy could be created by the way a woman's face and body were molded, rather than her ability to love, her loyalty, or her day-to-day efforts to make a worthy life.

Years of hard work and trying to be good brought Morrigan sorrow and pain, but beauty would transform the path to one of warmth and sunlight.

What if it vanished, this sole ability she possessed? No, she couldn't call it an ability, for she'd done nothing to achieve it.

"Why d'you stare at me like that?" Curran traced the frown between her brows. "You can be fierce as an eagle sometimes."

He didn't wait for an explanation. Light and quick, he dropped his hand down and stroked her stomach. "Our son will show before long. I'm scunnered by this waiting."

"It isn't me," she said, struck by his vehemence. "It's Aunt Ibby. She insists on a year of mourning."

"You know you can't wait that long. You'll have to tell her." He rolled on his back and rested his head in her lap, his golden hair a bright pool against her onyx-black skirts.

"I want to show you off. Glenelg's men'll be aye jealous. Seaghan has hounded me for years to get myself married and start a family. Doesn't make much sense. He's older than I by at least thirty years, yet never wed."

"Seaghan?"

"The fisherman who lives in Glenelg. I told you of him before."

"Oh, aye, the one who thinks the whole world would move to the High-lands if they could." Something about the name nagged at her. She frowned, concentrating, and was chilled as she remembered. Douglas had accused her of protecting a "Seaghan" during his attack.

"That's the one," Curran said. "There's a whole village to prepare you for. Seaghan, for instance, shares his home with another bachelor, a man he saved from a watery death."

She put away the memory and returned to the blithe, sunny day. "I don't know whether to ask you why Glenelg men never marry, or to explain the tale behind this near-drowning."

"Oh, plenty are wed, and no doubt rue the fact daily—bloody hell!" Laugh-ing, he grabbed her wrist to stop her from punching him again. "Sheathe your claws and I'll tell you about Aodhàn. It was the day Glenelg was burned to the ground. The landowner had a ship at Loch Hourn, the *Bristol*, ready to take his evicted crofters to Nova Scotia. They'd passed the cliffs of Berneray when Seaghan spotted Aodhàn in the water. He hauled him on board, pumped the water from his lungs, and stitched up a wound in his chest. They've stayed together ever since…almost nineteen years. He's told me he thinks of Aodhàn as his son, though there's only about ten years difference between them."

If Seaghan was in his fifties, and had lived in Glenelg when the village burned, that would make him Douglas's contemporary. He'd been in Glenelg when she was born. He and Douglas must have known one another. She wanted to ponder this, but it was hard with Curran kissing the birthmark on her wrist and changing the subject.

"So, my love, will you tell your aunt, or will you let your expanding belly notify her?" A quick flip brought him upright and facing her.

She saw his intent. He pushed her, slowly, inexorably, backward.

"You promised my aunts you'd behave…." *Take me and be quick about it,* she left unsaid, though it fair beat at the confines of her throat trying to come out.

His unruly hair made her think of the underwater castle, of the lion he'd fought and died with. Yet, undefeated, he'd risen from death and joined with the woman in the oak tree. Morrigan trembled with lust and longing, like the woman in Curran's underwater world must have done. Curran had absorbed the soul of the lion into his body and both had revived. Together, he and his deadly foe made love to the woman. She pictured it so clearly...the lion's warm breath, his tawny mane shutting out everything else, flashes of Curran infused with victory....

I will have victory floated through her imaginings, the phrase somehow familiar, recalling her daydreams of Theseus and his Cretan lover, the one she always wanted to call Aridela rather than Ariadne.

"Shall I leave you alone?"

Many scathing answers rose to the surface, but in the end they evaporated. She considered what that other woman might have said. "Kiss me." When he rose up from that, she whispered, "Love me, please, love me, Curran, I can no' thole it."

So he did.

ON CLEAR DAYS, MORRIGAN COULD LOOK OUT THE WINDOW IN THE CRAMPED ROOM she shared with Beatrice above Ibby's shop, and see the jagged black summits of the Cuillin of Skye in the west, across the Sound of Sleat. She often walked to the harbor, a few hundred or so steps from her aunt's shop, to watch Mallaig's ferries as they departed for Skye, or the blue humps of Eigg and Rum. The sough of water and shriek of gulls, the barking of seals and the odor of fish filled every hour of the day and night.

She at last gathered enough courage to confess her secret.

"You're what?" Ibby's face collapsed into disbelief then horror. "Sweet Saint Brigit, how could such a thing happen? Who is the man? It had better be the Laird of Eilginn."

"Of course it is." Shame caused Morrigan to dip her head. If her loyal aunt could contemplate her being with more than one man, she was lost. "I'm sorry, Auntie."

Then that is the lesson you needed to learn.

The memory of Louis Stevenson's words brought confusion, fear, even guilt that she'd chosen marriage. He was a man who would always follow his own way. But what else could she do? Defy society? Condemn her innocent child to starvation and suffering? Give birth in some shack or barn, beside a road, and maybe, like Hannah, die?

She shuddered. There was another truth as well, one she hardly dared examine. She couldn't bear the possibility of never again seeing Curran Ramsay, of never laughing with him, never feeling his hands upon her, never seeing that light in his eyes that made her feel so safe and cherished.

Ibby fanned her face with her handkerchief, fluttering her eyelids like she was going to swoon. "And I brought him to meet you. I brought him! How could he do this to me? If this gets out, I'll lose my patrons. I'll be ruined."

"They've caused a fine scandal," Beatrice said. "Thinking of themselves, no' the others who'll be blamed for their actions."

"How far along are you?" Ibby asked.

"Two months." Morrigan wadded her own black-edged handkerchief in clammy hands. Poor Ibby. Here they were in deepest mourning. Weddings should be the furthest thing from their thoughts.

Not for the first time, she imagined them as a coven of ravens. Ibby allowed no more than the smallest hint of white at the throat and black jet beads to decorate their bodices. Even their handkerchiefs and fans had broad black borders. Morrigan was weary of it already. How did the queen go on year after year, eleven since Albert had died, yet Victoria still wore black and lived in almost total seclusion.

She'd noticed slight changes in her body. Though it was still flat, her abdomen felt harder, tighter, and so did her breasts, fuller too. She was always hungry, and oh, the ache of longing for Curran was relentless. At night, erotic fabrications wove through the deep thick hours, checked only by the snoring bulky presence of Beatrice next to her. Before she fell asleep, the lover she fashioned wore Curran's face. Yet after, in the dream world, the man who pursued her so ardently never resembled her gentle golden betrothed. There he was tall and thin, his hair very black.

"Two months." Ibby sighed. "Well, at least he's willing to marry you, which is more than you deserve." Tears leaked from her eyes. "Oh, my dear, dear Lord. I don't know how we can keep this a secret. There would be no other reason for a wedding, not while we're in mourning." Her aunt sounded angry with Morrigan for the first time in her memory.

"It must be done nevertheless," Beatrice said. "We'll need to find a minister willing to marry them clandestinely." She paused. "If there were still handfasting...."

Ibby sighed. "Long and sadly dead, if it ever truly existed."

"We've allowed England to change far too many of our traditions."

"Aye." Ibby nodded. "'No One Provokes Me With Impunity,' we shout, all grand and glorious arrogance. Yet in the last fifty years we've become so anglicized we might as well all live south of Carlisle. And we're overrun with them. They pour into the Highlands like tea at tea time."

"Handfasting?" Morrigan asked.

"A mere legend, really, supposedly an old Highland custom. A trial marriage, fancifully known to last a year and a day. If the couple was satisfied with the arrangement, the marriage was recorded and became permanent. If not, they separated. But any child born from the union was legal, and considered an heir to its father's estate."

"A trial marriage…legal, but not binding?"

"In a way. If the handfasting didn't please, the woman's name and reputation wasn't damaged. She could look forward to another marriage as if nothing had ever taken place. Virginal purity was no' the be-all and end-all it is now. There was a time when Scotswomen enjoyed freer lives than you could possibly imagine. I mind my grandmam telling me it was women who taught the great Celtic heroes their fighting skills."

Morrigan stared at Ibby's plump face. "Are you teasing me, Auntie?"

"No, why would I?" Ibby lifted her chin and harrumphed. "The stories have passed from generation to generation. There must be a reason. It's said the great Cú Chulainn learned his art from Scatach, the witch, and from her sister, Queen Aife, who was known far and wide as a formidable warrior."

Could this "Eefah" be one of the women Diorbhail Sinclair had been referring to?

"Didn't you learn about Queen Boudicca at least?" Ibby settled herself more comfortably in her rocking chair. "I know it isn't proper, but I'll admit I send a prayer her way every now and then."

"Who?" Morrigan said.

She snorted her disgust. "You had the benefit of eight years of schooling, yet you've never heard of Boudicca? What *did* that man teach, anyway?"

"How to read, spell, how to work sums and some history—"

"History, yet no' a word of Boudicca?"

"No." Morrigan blushed beneath Ibby's scowl. Perhaps it would be better if her aunt remained ignorant of how much Greek history the dominie had imparted, or for that matter, the thorough study of male historical figures, from Alexander the Great to Sir William Wallace. There had also been many dry hours learning about Lord Palmerston and other statesmen, far more than what was taught about Queen Victoria.

"She rallied men and women from every corner of the land when the Romans outraged her daughters and stole her inheritance. She and her people sacked Britain, London included."

"The way I mind it," Beatrice cut in, "she failed."

"Not before she'd destroyed Roman towns across England and struck terror into her enemies. Mam told me Boudicca called upon the women in her army specially." Flushed with color, Ibby rose from her chair and raised a fist to the ceiling. "'This be a woman's resolve! As for men, they may live and be slaves.'"

Beatrice snorted. "All these years I thought you a good Christian, Isabel Maclean. Now I wonder if there isn't a liberal beneath all that fluff and lace."

Morrigan watched her paternal aunt deflate, and for an instant, she disliked Beatrice. "I wish I had learned about our women warriors," she said quickly, as

Ibby returned to her rocking chair. "They sound majestic and strong. No namby-pamby creatures with their smelling salts always nearby."

"Aye, well." Ibby wiped her nose with her handkerchief. "Maybe it's best if such traditions are forgotten. After all, women's lives have changed, and no doubt for the better. I can't imagine going off to fight a war, myself."

Beatrice gave another snort, making it clear she could not imagine that either.

They stitched without speaking for some time. "Everything seems so different from the old days," Morrigan said at last, tired of listening to the endless ticking of the mantel clock and hoping Ibby might offer more interesting historical tidbits about women's power in Scotland's distant past.

"It's the queen," Beatrice said. "She's turned us from wildcats into tabbies."

Ibby nodded. "But she means well, I think. She loves Scotland. Not like some. A trend was set when she bought Balmoral. Now all the rich *Sasannaich* want to own their bit. But it's the way they use it that vexes me. First we were cleared away like rubbish to make room for their sheep, now they're destroying the ancient forests so they can kill the deer more easily. They won't leave a twig for the poor beasts to hide under. Sometimes I fear they'll not stop until the Highlands are emptied of flora, beast, and man, and the only sound left is the cry of the lapwing."

"Auntie," Morrigan asked, "will you tell me of these clearings? What the devil happened? What was it?"

Ibby leveled a warning stare upon Morrigan. "I suspect you've enough to answer for without adding blasphemy to your list of sins," she said, emphasizing every word.

"Sorry." Morrigan dropped her gaze to her lap.

"Douglas would fly into a rage if we ever brought it up. Yet you were born in the thick of it. Here you are, expecting a child of your own, and you know nothing of your past, or what caused the loss of your mam."

"You could tell me."

"What we need to discuss," Beatrice interrupted as Ibby opened her mouth to reply, "is what to do about these wicked youngsters."

Morrigan frowned. Every time the subject came up, someone always cut it off.

But Ibby agreed. "Aye, there's more pressing matters. And just you wait until Curran Ramsay comes next to visit. Lord, how he's offended me! Laird or no', I vow I'll have a great bit of his flesh in return for what he's done."

SOOTHED, PERHAPS, BY THE WASH OF WAVES OUTSIDE HER WINDOW, OR THE proximity of the Hebrides and wild Highlands, Morrigan's dreams took on a honed, lifelike quality.

She was walking along a high, sheer cliff. A man ran up and grabbed her hand, ostensibly out of concern for her safety.

It was exhilarating, being next to such a precipitous drop. It made her heart beat fast. To fall would mean watching death come for you as you plummeted helplessly through cold, uncaring space. She turned her face upward, her gaze caught by an eagle circling, almost as though it was watching them.

Off to her right, beyond the cliff, the Atlantic stretched away to the shores of America; to her left there was nothing but peat, grass, wildflowers, and sheep.

The man didn't like not being the center of her attention. His constant need annoyed her yet also made her laugh. His grip on her hand tightened.

"I'll build you a summer house here," he said, "since you love it so much."

"I'm not a prostitute, sir. How many times must I explain that to you?"

He stopped. "You will marry me, Lilith." He frowned, boldly trying to intimidate her.

"I'm nobody. Your da—"

"Is a factor." His eyes turned ferocious. That, coupled with his black, wind-blown hair, gave him a devilish presence. "And I'm a factor's son. Shall we force his hand? He'll agree if your belly has his grandson in it."

"I'm going to marry Daniel."

After spending the day with him, she'd come to realize he wasn't the ogre many thought him to be. Though he put on an arrogant face, she had glimpsed tenderness in him. Perhaps she was the only one he'd ever shown that face to. She cared about his feelings now, and didn't want to hurt him. But that didn't mean she would betray Daniel.

Daniel was like her. She pictured herself making his porridge, digging at his side in a garden, having his babies. They could build a life. Daniel's hands were big, callused, and gentle. He had an equally big heart. She was drawn to him in ways she couldn't explain. Didn't it say something that she was still thinking of Daniel while walking along a cliff with this provocative character?

His hands weren't callused, and never would be. His fingernails were clean, his coat smart. He didn't smell of fish, or soil, or sweat, and for the last several years, he had been away at Eton. He'd only recently returned because of his father's worsening consumption.

"Your father wants better things for you than a fisherman's wean in a patched dress and fraying shawl," she said.

The cliff vanished. They were lying on a machair-covered slope looking out over the sea, caressed in breezes as soft as rabbit fur. A jewel dangled from his fingers. A necklace. Someone had died, and the pain of it was terrible. But it was time to move on.

She spoke his name—*Oo…*something. He leaned in and kissed her.

Beatrice's familiar morning shout sent the man swirling away. "Morrigan! Wake up! D'you plan to sleep the day away?"

MORRIGAN'S FINE ROMANCE ENTERED A DISMAL INTERLUDE OF PRIVATION AND difficulty. Ibby never gave her niece an unchaperoned moment with her betrothed. "I introduced you," she said to Curran more than once. "I trusted you. Now here we are. You defied my feelings and her innocence."

Morrigan began to suspect that Ibby berated him simply for the expression of guilt and chagrin he rewarded her with. She was sure the first time she caught Ibby smiling to herself as she walked away.

Her aunt would be scunnered if she knew how Morrigan had thrown herself at him, had barely given him a chance to resist. But Morrigan was confident he would never tell.

Ardent glances and the surreptitious touching of hands had to suffice. With stoic patience and unyielding good humor, Curran assured her that in the end, Ibby would lose this battle.

During one of his visits, he suggested an outing to introduce Morrigan to Kilgarry, chaperoned by the aunts, of course. They agreed, but insisted he return them in two days, as they were eager to attend Mallaig's annual Highland Games.

He hired a local fisherman and his crew to ferry them up and they set out on a bright, sweetly scented afternoon. They passed Loch Hourn and the Sandaig islands, and Curran pointed. There, towering above that riotous portion of the Sound called the Kyle Rhea, framed within a thickly wooded hill, glinted the upper storeys of his home. With the help of the fisherman's telescope, Morrigan saw crimson flags streaming from two turrets, and even the rearing silver unicorns embossed in the center. The late afternoon sun lit the reddish stones and blazed against the leaded windows in the nearer turret, exactly as Ibby had once described them. Diamonds, in a cinnabar setting.

The rocky coast of the Isle of Skye lay directly across on the other side of the Kyle Rhea. Hills clambered in an eager race to a finish line of bluish white clouds. Water reflected the land, deep blue-green fading to violet.

Dolphins vaulted alongside the boat, whistling a welcome. It was all so rich, green, and thrilling, yet without warning or reason, Morrigan's heart began to thud heavily.

"We have deer and a few wildcats. *Cait fhiadhaich,* we call them in the Gaelic." Grinning, Curran took on the bland monotone of a lecturer. "They can be quite savage. Their favorite meal seems to be their own offspring. As for the deer, it's almost time for the rut. You'll be here when it begins. They roar through the night. I find it strangely fascinating."

Morrigan was distracted by a sense that the land was shifting. She could see, but not clearly—hear, but not Curran's voice. Premonition speared her, heightening her senses, magnifying the damp scent of mountain clouds and the flutter of a kestrel's wings.

Her attention locked on two men standing at the shoreline, dressed in rough fishermen's clothing.

"Seaghan," Curran shouted. "Aodhàn!" He waved. The shorter figure waved back.

As she stared, unable to blink or turn away, a pulsating, reddish orange halo formed around the taller man, leaving her with the urge to rub her eyes. The shimmer reached out somehow, striking her in the solar plexus like a thunderbolt. Her heart skipped; cold sweat broke out on her forehead. She closed her eyes, taking several deep breaths, and then felt nauseated when she breathed in pungent smoke from someone's pipe.

Above her head, the sails clapped. Curran's cheerful voice droned on and the dolphins made their merry welcoming cries. The landscape cleared, green, fragrant, sweet, as the two men fell away to the stern. She gradually realized they must have been the same two men Curran had described at their picnic beside Castle Kennedy.

Curran put his hand on her shoulder. "You're pale. Are you seasick?"

"No." How weak she sounded. Not like the girl she often dreamed of. *Aridela*. That intrepid lass would never sound feeble.

"Come, sit down. We're almost there."

They disembarked at a wooden pier extending from a shingle beach in Glenelg Bay. Several buildings lay beyond the shore, marking the near edge of the village. A thin, long-legged young man, smoking a pipe that seemed much too large for him, leaned casually against a spotless wagonette garnished with fancy red wheels, hitched to a matched pair of bay geldings, also spotless. Tamping out his pipe, he came forward with a relieved expression, making Morrigan wonder how long he'd been waiting, and welcomed Curran in barely recognizable English.

"Kyle Ross," Curran said. "Kilgarry's gardener, and, today, her coachman."

The boy nodded, shyly red-faced.

When everyone was comfortably settled on padded leather seats so well sprung she thought she was sitting on air, Kyle sent the geldings south along the coast. Morrigan hoped they would see those two men again, but there was no sign of them. The rough, shingled track led them to an estuary crowned by an old stone building: the local Catholic Church, Curran told her. From there the road veered inward and continued on beside the river, climbing as it entered a forest. Trees loomed closer and closer, to the point where branches grated against the sides of their vehicle.

Glenelg. She was in Glenelg, where Douglas and Hannah met and fell in love. Hannah had given birth to her here. Apprehension brushed across Morrigan's arms; she was only dimly aware of Curran's intent gaze.

They came to a fork in the road. One side meandered tantalizingly away eastward, into a wooded, velvet-green glen, while the other crossed over the river via a bridge and continued south through open meadows and farmland.

"Gleann Beag lies that way," Curran told her, nodding towards the east. "It's Gaelic for the 'Little Glen.' Would you like to see it before we go on?"

She nodded, not trusting her voice to be steady. Kyle spoke to the horses and the wagonette followed the rutted track. It was so thickly wooded that for some time she couldn't see anything other than a wall of trees, but every now and then they thinned and she glimpsed steep hills, verdantly green and purple with heather, and once, a pretty waterfall. Smoke rose from the chimneys of two crofts, but they saw no one.

"What's that?" Morrigan pointed to what appeared to be the crumpled shell of a tower. The fitted stones rose twenty or thirty feet on one side, but the rest had vanished or fallen in, leaving only a circular foundation covered with weeds.

"It's called *Dùn Teilbh* hereabouts," Curran said. "It's all that's left of an ancient building of some sort. There are three of them along here. Nobody knows how old they are, or what they were built for. They could have been forts, or farms, or lookout towers. Some say the Picts, or another lost race, must have built them, long before Scotland was civilized. Every now and then men of science come and make a great study of them."

The aunts fell oddly silent. Both averted their eyes. Ibby clutched at Beatrice's forearm, the color draining from her usually flushed cheeks, her earlier gaiety gone as though she'd been doused by freezing water. Morrigan wanted to ask what was wrong, but an oppressive, sourceless fear stoppered her tongue and kept her silent.

On they drove, and after a moment arrived at the next ruin, which Curran called *Dùn Trodan*. Morrigan could no longer ignore the weighted atmosphere. She sensed it emanating not only from her aunts but also from Kyle, and, to a lesser extent, from Curran.

"Is something wrong?" She addressed Ibby, thinking her garrulous aunt most likely to give her an answer.

She was surprised and not reassured when all Ibby said was, "No, nothing, my love, but I am rather peckish. Perhaps we could go on to Kilgarry, and explore another time?"

"Of course," Curran said immediately. "Forgive me, I should have thought of that." He said something to Kyle, who turned the wagonette around. Soon they were back on the coast road, breezing along at a good pace until the open land gave way to another forest. The track forked again and Kyle took the one to the right, into a deeper wood.

Trees and undergrowth closed in, alive with birds and squirrels and one red doe, which stood its ground and observed them curiously.

Glenelg. The name alone filled Morrigan with both agitation and excitement. Magic emanated from the soil, swirled around the trees, beckoned in the flutter of leaves. She wouldn't be surprised to see a faery, and eagerly turned towards every movement and sound.

Meanwhile, the tangible world displayed a bright, colorful autumn. Blood red rowanberries competed with foliage fading from green to buttery yellow, and everywhere was the pervasive scent of fallen leaves.

Flashes of warm stone appeared ahead. They came to tall iron gates, propped open, and the rough track was replaced with a neatly shingled drive. Flanking the gates were square stone posts mounted with regal unicorn heads.

Morrigan seized Curran's forearm. Such civilized grandeur was hard to fathom in this wild, primitive place.

A central tower loomed, magnificently lit by hazy sunbeams. Newer towers, topped with capped turrets, nestled at the east and west ends. In between were ivy-covered chimneys, crow-stepped gables, and, Morrigan saw as they came closer, a half-moon staircase curving up to the door. A line of men and women were hastily assembling on the drive.

Curran stepped from the wagonette and offered his hand. He hadn't said a word to prepare her for being put on display. Blushing with embarrassment, she squeezed his fingers to let him know he'd vexed her, but he merely grinned, lifted a mocking brow, and turned to assist the aunts.

"Welcome to you, Miss Lawton." A grey-haired woman in a neat black dress and white apron bobbed a curtsy. "I am Fionna Dunbar, the housekeeper."

"I'm pleased to meet you." What should she do? Take the woman's hand? Curtsy in return? Morrigan had no idea, and chose to extend her gloved hand. Fionna took it graciously and released it swiftly. No one seemed shocked.

"This is Tess." Curran paused beside a young woman with black hair and large blue eyes, who curtsied, smiling. "Fionna's daughter. And Janet, our cook." The woman, heavy and ungraceful, performed an awkward curtsy but her smile was friendly. Morrigan hardly dared wonder if this meant that she and Beatrice would no longer be required to prepare meals.

"Violet," Curran continued, taking another step. "She and Tess are the housemaids."

"I often serve as lady's maid for Master Ramsay's guests," Violet said after she curtsied. "I'd be pleased to do the same for you."

"Th-thank you."

Fionna took over the introductions. "This is my son, Logan, the groom."

Logan's bow betrayed subtle but certain cockiness. He was fearsomely handsome, with speculative grey-green eyes and dark, dusty hair, no doubt from working in the barn. There was a distinct odor of hay and horses about him. "I saw you birthed," he said.

"Logan!" Fionna cried, flushing.

Morrigan's own cheeks grew hot as he continued to gaze at her without any visible embarrassment. She must say something, but what? How should one respond to such a statement? Logan didn't look as though he'd lived many more years than she. She could only stammer, "You...you saw my birth?"

"Aye, and you've grown up well," he said, sending a bold, appreciative glance over her and laughing at his mother's mortification.

"Mind your tongue," Curran said, his face darkening.

The lad sobered and bobbed his head. "No offense intended, m'lady," he said.

"I'm pleased to meet you all." Morrigan spoke quickly to move them past the tension.

"Come inside." Curran nodded to Fionna, which was apparently the signal to disperse. The four newcomers climbed the stone steps to a massive black oak door decorated with an intricate carving of a rearing unicorn and a bare-chested, kilted soldier brandishing a sword. Fionna opened it and stood to one side.

Morrigan touched the carving. "Why d'you have unicorns on your flags, your gateposts, and here, on your door?"

"It's the Ramsay crest," Curran said.

For the second time that day, Morrigan felt the world tilt and slide. *Have you seen our unicorn? She comes out when the moon is full and stands beneath your window.* Nicky had always known whenever she'd felt too scunnered, too tired to fight another day under Douglas Lawton's thumb. Those were the times he brought up the unicorn.

Had Nicky known? Was that his secret message? *Be patient. Your unicorn will appear.*

"This is where we'll live?" She spoke quietly, forcing Curran to bend close. "Or are ye playin' some daft game wi' me, m'lord?"

He covered her hand with his. "I've dreamed of bringing you here." Without warning, he swept her into his arms and carried her over the threshold.

"Curran!" She didn't dare glance over his shoulder, knowing the servants would be sniggering.

"We may not be married yet," he said, "but I couldn't let this occasion pass without note."

Twining her arms around his neck, she gave in to bittersweet laughter. *You knew, Nicky. You knew he would come, if I would stay strong.*

She touched the sickle scar at Curran's brow, startled to feel that tingling, slightly burning sensation, and in the dim entry, she glimpsed that same violet blue radiance around him. It dimmed as her eyes grew accustomed to the change in light.

Curran set her on a floor so polished it resembled a deep brown pool. She smelled what she could only think of as wealth: fine wax, thick carpets, expensive quiet.

Then there came a mad scuffling. Something grey and warm jumped on her.

Laughing, Morrigan scooped the pup into her arms. "Antiope! Oh, she's grown!"

Curran gave a disgusted snort and nodded at Logan, who hauled the dog away, though she whined and nipped his arm.

"Is it true, Curran?"

"What, my love?"

"That Logan saw my birth."

"He was there. He and his folk were cleared along with yours. He didn't mean to be rude. I think he's truly pleased to see you, grown up and healthy. But I want this to be a happy occasion, *a ghràidh*. Come, let me show you my home." He beckoned to Ibby and Beatrice, who had paused outside the door to speak to Fionna.

Curran took them through spacious drawing rooms, and a parlor in the east turret with big windows that caught the morning light, then a dining room that seemed capable of seating a battalion, and, set back in the southern recesses, a dim ballroom adorned with plasterwork that looked like beaten cream where the walls met high ceilings. The library, set into the west turret, dazzled her with its fully stocked bookcases and a great stone fireplace that promised warmth on the coldest winter day. The larger of two kitchens possessed a centuries-old flagstone floor and a prodigious fireplace preserved from a much earlier era. Shiny copper pots were suspended from hooks in the ceiling, next to fragrant bunches of dried herbs, onions and garlic.

The manor house even had a dungeon beneath the central keep, where the stone walls were chilly and the way in was down a twisting, narrow, slippery set of worn stone steps. Wine racks, holding dusty bottles, took up most of the large center space. Old oak doors led into other chambers, but Curran told her they'd been used long ago as prison cells, and were empty.

A curving staircase carpeted in deep burgundy led from the main floor to the second storey bedrooms. The master suite, with its attached dressing rooms and cozy sitting room, were tucked into the upper west-end turret and corridor. Fading sunlight created speckled rainbows from an intricate stained-glass window in the sitting room, and on the bedroom's south wall, a cushioned window seat built into an alcove provided a view over the gardens, the forest beyond, and a portion of the Sound as well.

Four oak posts topped with carved pinecones accented the massive bed.

She would lie here with her husband, every night for the rest of her life. She would give birth here. Morrigan stole a glance at Curran, who leaned against one of the posts, his expression making her wonder if he guessed her thoughts.

How beautiful he was, in so many ways. Truly, Curran possessed far more than endearing dimples and bewitching eyes. Here he stood, willing to share all this with her, to make her his wife, when nothing but his own sense of right and wrong compelled him.

What about her? What could she offer that would keep him enchanted after her beauty faded? Douglas had made it clear she was a burden. He'd hated her enough to try and end her life. If she couldn't determine what it was about her that was so awful, and figure out a way to rout it, would Curran someday feel the same?

Weighted by spiraling hopelessness, she turned away to trace the lead seams in the delicate stained-glass. But, inexplicably, other images formed, hesitantly at first, then growing stronger, clearer. The inner Morrigan, perhaps, pushing at her as she so often did, willing her to transcend her shortcomings.

She saw herself at Curran's side, laughing, arguing, planning Kilgarry's crops and deciding how to educate their children. She turned away from the window and studied the bed again. They would join there, in the way of a husband and wife, but the bed could mean more. It could represent intimacy, friendship, and trust. With any luck, by the time her beauty declined, something else would have taken its place, something deeper, if she worked to create it. Though she knew she hadn't yet conquered her doubts and fears, in this moment they were dispelled, like bursting soap bubbles.

"Isoke?" Ibby rested a hand on her niece's shoulder. "You're quiet. Are you well?"

She had to swallow twice before she could answer. "More than well," she said. "I'm happy, Auntie."

Curran smiled.

Chapter 15

Aodhàn Mackinnon and Seaghan MacAnaugh rose with the sun, as was their habit. After consuming their usual gruel, they set to work, Aodhàn scraping barnacles along the *Hannah*'s hull while Seaghan sat nearby, smoking his pipe and methodically mending frayed creels, nets, and lines. Long ago, the two had divided chores according to personality. Aodhàn suffered an intolerance of small detail that Seaghan thankfully didn't share.

As the sun climbed, the intermittent foreboding that had kept Aodhàn awake most of the night escalated into sensations so powerful he could no longer dismiss or ignore them. As hard as he tried, he couldn't identify what was wrong. Nothing was different, yet inside, he felt everything had changed. It wasn't dread, yet it almost felt that way. It wasn't fear, yet fear wove through it. It seemed a mixture of fear and exultation.

Standing at the brink of land often lent temporary relief, a peace of sorts. The roar of the surf calmed the insistent *need* he could never pin down. He knew Seaghan worried when he vanished, frequently for days. Yet ever since his partner had dredged him out of the vast open ocean, Aodhàn had been a slave to his compulsion. He could not expunge it, no matter how he tried.

One spot drew him more than any other: a cave scooped out by the sea, only reachable when the tide allowed, and well-disguised by a set of rugged, sharp-edged, slippery rocks. He would descend into this cave and study the pattern of waves, the play of light and cloud. Intense concentration, no food or water, and exposure to the elements left him exhausted, sometimes feverish, yet the fear of missing some revelation that might emerge from beneath the water's surface was too strong to resist. When he stood on the sand, salt-spray stinging his skin and icy water creeping over his feet, fresh hope would spark. Maybe *this* time, the maddening, disjointed images, the lost chunks of his life, would coalesce.

Giving a pointed sigh, he threw his scraper, sending a family of eider ducks flapping and squawking.

"It's more than I can bear," Seaghan called from his sunny spot.

Aodhàn scowled. "And what is that?"

"Your mood. 'Tis black as peat. Go for a walk. Have some whisky. Find a willing lass."

"I might walk a bit." Aodhàn tried to sound casual, but the tension in his voice couldn't be stifled.

"Away with you." Seaghan heaved another swath of netting across his lap. With no small measure of threat, he added, "*A-mach às mo shealladh!*"

Aodhàn headed for the mountains. He knew he would end up at the sea eventually. Yet once more he tried to pretend he didn't have to go—that his will would prove stronger than instinct.

Get out of my sight! Seaghan had said. Aodhàn didn't blame him. He wished he could get out of his own sight, more often than not.

His head throbbed, and his stomach felt as though sharp wires were tightening around it, sending gooseflesh and sweat in alternating waves over his skin.

The hills behind Glenelg ascended higher and higher, eventually culminating on the other side of Loch Duich in the Five Sisters of Kintail, the summits of which touched the clouds. He didn't plan on going that far, though, and hiked towards a glen he'd found once, a spot he loved for its beauty and solitude. It, too, claimed a cave, a small one. He had explored it, crawling deep into the earth, fascinated for some reason by the pungent, chilled aroma, and brief infuriating snatches suggesting he had been in a similar cave before, somewhere.

Clouds were building. Wind moaned through pine branches. Out on the Kyle Rhea, whitecaps frothed, and he smelled the coming storm.

Climbing relaxed him. The pressure and ache eased, though he felt his inner torment waiting, biding its time for another assault.

No path marked the way, yet he continued forward, bending under branches, scuffing through crunchy piles of fallen leaves. At length he found the familiar lichen-spotted boulder, and inspected the hollow below. It appeared the same except for a squirrel's bustling: silent, untouched, and pristine.

Then he saw her. A girl, sitting before the mouth of the cave, so well camouflaged by a dark cloak, and so motionless, that it took him a moment to be sure she was really there. Following her gaze, he saw an eagle circling. Maybe the squirrel had caught its attention.

With breathtaking grace, the eagle swooped. It passed over the squirrel, though, and stopped in a *whoosh* of outstretched wing above the girl, holding itself with a measured beat of great wings before landing on an egg-shaped rock next to her.

Cocking its head to one side, the eagle opened its beak as though it wanted to say something, if it only could.

She stood. Her brows lowered, lending her a dangerous expression that well matched the raptor.

Aodhàn blinked, again doubting his sight. Not only was the lass confronting an eagle, she was surrounded by color—fragile lavender radiance instilled with a haze of sparkling gold. He fought a strange urge to seize this color in his fists. He wanted to drink it like whisky, to keep drinking until he was drunk.

At that moment, the clouds tore open. The veil of color dissipated in the stronger yellow glare from the sun. Her uncovered hair transformed from brown to bronze, with highlights of red and gold, similar, Aodhàn thought, to the changing leaves. Scarlet suffused her cheeks. Every color of the autumn spectrum ignited in subtle flame.

What manner of human could call an eagle from the sky and face it unafraid? Maybe this female was a member of the *daoine sìth*, and would vanish into the green mound of a *sìthean*, a faery hill. He watched, clenching the boulder.

He could swear an angry swarm of mayflies had erupted at the base of his neck.

The eagle tilted its head the other direction, and the girl fell back a step. She spoke; he heard her, though she kept her voice low. "Mama?" she said. "Nicky?" Lower still, she asked, "Who *are* you?" Her voice washed like an ebb tide. He knew the sound intimately, for every night that cold, unforgiving lover called to him. He rammed his fists against his temples and squeezed his eyes shut. Some malevolent fiend was twisting a giant screw into his skull.

Squinting through a blinding net of agony, Aodhàn watched the raptor lift into the air. It flew right over him, so close he felt the displacement of air and heard the sound of wind through its feathers.

The girl watched the bird's flight then her gaze dropped. Though he knew the boulder and thick spread of pine branches disguised his presence, Aodhàn fought an urge to kneel and hide.

Hot lightning seemed to shoot between them. He gasped.

"Morrigan," a female voice called from the other side of the glen. As one, he and the lass turned towards the sound. The spell broke, and he could breathe again.

"Here," she replied.

A stout woman, dressed in black, emerged from behind the trees, her hair and face shrouded by a prim bonnet.

He'd never seen another human being in this glen, ever, in all the years he'd been coming here. Now there were two.

"This is rugged country, mind," the newcomer said. "Curran would have my heart for breakfast if you got lost up here."

"Will the faeries steal me? I could believe it. In fact, I felt someone or something watching me a moment ago. Was it a faerie, d'you think?"

"Pish. A rabbit, maybe, or a deer."

Laughing, the girl said, "This air sweeps the dust right out of my head." Wrapping her arms around herself, she spun in a pirouette, lifting her face to the sky. "I'm drunk on Glenelg's sunlight!"

"Come along now, isoke," the older woman said. She extended a hand and stopped the younger female's cavorting. "We've been gone too long."

The lass straightened her cloak and secured a bonnet over her hair. Together they strolled across the grass and vanished into the forest.

Aodhàn slumped to the ground with a weak exhalation.

He kept seeing that strange halo of lavender and gold, like a magical net wafting around her. He'd half believed she might take wing and fly away with the eagle, or, as she said, join the faeries in a toadstool ring.

That term. *Isoke.* He'd heard it somewhere. He felt his memories. He could almost grasp them.

Crisp air washed through his lungs. Layers of fallen leaves gave off the heady scent of coming winter. He looked about, feeling as though he was waking from some endless dreary nightmare.

I am alive. Alive after all.

With a dawning sense of wonder, he realized what was different. The throbbing pressure, the tightening wires, the excruciating whine of voices… were gone.

For the last night of their visit, Janet presented a special meal, beginning with fine bread and a traditional partan bree that smelled divinely of crab. She followed this with tender baked pheasant, creamed kail, fluffy tatties, cheese, and, finally, a golden sponge cake. Fresh raspberries from the east coast filled an enameled bowl, and she presented a dewy bottle of heather wine she'd made herself. Beatrice ate with a suspicious frown, but after consuming two slices of cake drenched in clotted cream and covered with fruit, a muttered, "She'll do," escaped.

Ibby rose, lifting her wineglass. "*Slàinte!*" she cried.

"Aye," the others replied, raising their glasses. "Good health!"

Curran dabbed Morrigan's lips with his napkin. "Oh, I thought you'd smeared raspberries, but your lips are just that red." Moving next to her ear, he added, "And as sweet." He took her hand and folded the band of lace at her wrist so he could kiss the birthmark, something that was becoming a habit.

"Behave yourself, sir." Ibby shattered the moment by rapping her knuckles against the tabletop. "You're not yet wed, and you've already caused...." She broke off with an anxious glance towards Janet. "Behave," she finished lamely.

Holding Morrigan's gaze, Curran murmured, "You don't know what you ask of me." He brushed a final kiss on her knuckles before releasing her.

Curran herded them onto the west terrace. An earlier rain shower had freshened the air. Bands of pastel colored cirrus clouds radiated like spider's webs, sending the peaks of the mountains on Skye into sharp black silhouette. Curran assured Morrigan every sunset was this extraordinary, since no place on earth was as blessed as the west coast of the Highlands.

Beyond a narrow stretch of tended lawn the forest encroached, hiding the rocky precipice that descended to the Sound of Sleat. Morrigan gripped the balustrade, picturing Kilgarry as a bird flying overhead would see it—a carved-out oasis surrounded on all sides by looming, ancient woodland.

Faint, directionless, making her wonder if the mountains themselves played them, came the faraway drone of bagpipes.

She turned a startled gaze to Curran and caught such a pleased expression that she knew he must have arranged it. The unseen piper's haunting music gradually faded into the blue-gold twilight.

A flock of trumpeting swans flew overhead, so low Morrigan heard their wings beating.

Her reverie was broken by a muffled sound. Feeling as though she was waking from a seductive hallucination, she glanced at Beatrice, shocked to see tears streaming over her aunt's face.

"Auntie?" She spoke low, reluctant to break the spell.

"I didn't know how I missed this place," Beatrice said, and walked quickly away, hunching her shoulders.

"Nor I," said Ibby. "How could we have allowed Randall Benedict to clear us from our land? It's good he hid himself in Edinburgh and ordered his factor to carry out the task. No doubt someone would've slit his throat had he been here, and thrown his carcass into the sea."

They stood without speaking for some time.

"It's time we were away to our beds," Ibby said finally. "We must rise early and go home." She waited, refusing like any good chaperon to leave Morrigan alone with Curran. It was silly. He'd already done the worst he could do. It wasn't like he could put another child inside her, not yet anyway.

Sighing, Morrigan followed her aunt indoors and prepared for bed, but she couldn't sleep. She kept fighting the bedclothes that tangled around her like linen nooses, and remembering that brief but meaningful look Curran had given her as she'd left.

It was easy to slink along the corridor to the master suite. Moonlight poured through the southern window, illuminating his uncovered body in white effervescence. She shrugged out of her nightgown and slipped into his bed. Instantly, he rolled over as though he'd been awake and expecting her.

He rewarded her courage in coming to him by kissing her from forehead to toes, his tongue tracing the sensitive undersides of her arms, the hollow in her throat, where the babe grew, her thighs, even the backs of her knees and heels, speaking promises of more, for years and years to come, in this bed. Morrigan began to feel something new, an escalating, dizzying need. She pulled him in, driven beyond shyness by an urgency she couldn't restrain. Their breaths became one and movement became perfect rhythm, building, like Chopin's first ballade, ascending to the climax she finally understood, beyond where she had been or knew she could be. For an unknown length of time, awareness fell away, lost in an avalanche of consummation.

Now I see, she thought when the ability to think returned. *No wonder folk forget society's rules and restrictions. No wonder.*

She wound her limbs around his and sank into almost instant sleep. The last sounds she heard were his words of love against her ear.

The tip of a dagger prodded Morrigan's throat, letting her know how easily it could slay her.

Witch! Devil's whore!

She saw her husband fighting their attackers, but what was the use? He would never overpower so many men, and she didn't want to live now her children were dead, their bodies bloody and torn, their voices forever silenced.

This is Christian land!

The blade pressed, splitting skin, spilling blood. She refused to cry out or beg for mercy. Curse them all.

Follow your spawn to the Devil.

"Morrigan…wake up. You had a nightmare, my lass."

"Aye." She was safe, surrounded by serene moonlit shadows. No one had murdered her daughters. Men hadn't forced her down and slit her throat as her husband fought to save her. She was Morrigan, Morrigan Lawton, not the name the man had shouted. *Lilith.* The terror faded. "I have many bad dreams."

Curran kissed her forehead. "When you're my wife, you'll never have another."

What she wouldn't give if that could be true. Clinging to him, she pressed a hand against her stomach. The babe grew there still.

What sort of world did it grow towards?

Chapter 16

It rained the morning of the Games, but by noon, clouds scudded on a breeze from the Sound and the sky was flooded with clear, dazzling light.

Banners and flowers decorated the shop-fronts. Revelers from every nearby village and the Knoydart peninsula crowded Mallaig's cobbled streets. Folk came from Skye, too, and the Small Isles—Eigg, Rum, Canna, and the tiniest, wee Muck. Everywhere one looked were *fèilidhean*, the kilts, and tartan sashes, silver brooches, cairngorm jewelry, and glengarry caps. Pipe music skimmed from the high meadows, and children swarmed around a Punch and Judy show.

Curran, in Ramsay tartan with the addition of a black armband for Nicky and Douglas, arrived early to escort the ladies to Mallaig's festivities. As soon as he appeared, Aunt Ibby emphatically stated for at least the tenth time that they were only going for the sake of Morrigan's health, and as they left the dress shop she admonished her niece to retain a sober demeanor in keeping with her state.

Morrigan wasn't fooled. The excitement in Ibby's eyes and her jaunty step betrayed her.

The foursome climbed towards the sound of shrilling pipes. Kilted, bearded giants tossed the massive cabar to enthusiastic shouts from bystanders. In other areas, wrestlers strained and grimaced, surrounded by red-faced men who'd placed wagers on their favorite champions. Booths adorned with ivy and heather sold food; the mouth-watering scents of roasted meat and newly baked bread hung in the air. Curran bought them butter cakes, pies oozing meat juices, and tumblers of fresh, frothy milk. Women called,

"Come sample my pastries," and there was keen competition between a few locals with their jams.

Five men, standing proud in their kilts, had entered the *pìobaireachd* contest and were, by turn, playing the ancient airs. Some distance away, a string of fiddlers, two drummers, and a man with a flute performed lively dancing music beside a large, roped-off area. Curran urged Ibby to dance with him, and she gave in after a few weak protests, dancing until she was gasping and her cheeks were scarlet. He returned her to the sidelines then grabbed Morrigan, giving her a kiss and pulling her into the ring. His complete lack of reservation struck her with envy. Could she ever abandon herself in such an uproarious fashion? Maybe, under his tutelage.

"I don't know how to dance!" she protested.

"Aye? We'll have none of that," he said, and proceeded to give her a lesson.

"Eilginn!" The voice thundered over the music. Morrigan looked up to find the biggest, thickest bearded, kilted colossus she'd ever seen, enormous hands propped on hips and a mouthful of huge teeth in a mat of shaggy brown hair.

Curran grinned. "Seaghan!" Slipping his arm around Morrigan's waist, he led her out of the ring. "Morrigan," he said, "may I present Seaghan MacAnaugh, from Glenelg."

Since she'd already heard more than once of Curran's great friendship with this man, she held out her hand with a timid smile. Seaghan gave an impressive bow and took it gingerly. It was like watching a tadpole vanish into the ocean.

"I was hoping we'd see you," Curran said. "Where's Aodhàn?"

"He didn't come." Seaghan's eyes twinkled as he gazed down into Morrigan's face. "Why in the name of all that's holy are you wasting such a grand day with this dull fellow?" Releasing a bellowing laugh, the titan slapped Curran on the shoulder.

"You're speaking to my betrothed, I'll have you know," Curran said with obvious satisfaction.

"What?" The giant swiveled. "At last! You've found yourself a lass who does no' run from the sight of you?" His grin was as huge as the rest of him, but as his eyes traveled over her, taking in her mourning garb, he looked a bit puzzled.

"I have another surprise." Curran gestured to Beatrice and Ibby, who stood nearby, watching.

Seaghan and her aunt stared at each other. "Beatrice." Seaghan's voice lowered to a barely audible rumble. "Beatrice Stewart."

"Seaghan," she replied in her usual emotionless manner.

"It's been aye long," he said. "An aye long time." Morrigan thought she heard a tremble beneath his words.

"That it has."

"What's brought you to the Upper Country?"

"My niece." She nodded towards Morrigan. "Mr. Ramsay's intended."

Again Seaghan examined Morrigan, from her black ostrich-feathered bonnet to her trim black boots.

"Niece…" he said. "Morrigan…Morrigan…*Lawton?*"

"Aye." Beatrice's face remained inscrutable but for one lifted brow.

"Douglas…Douglas and Hannah's…." His ruddy face went frighteningly pale then flushed crimson. "Hannah's wean…."

"You knew my da and mam, sir?" Morrigan asked.

He glanced at Beatrice, whose mouth curved into a brief, cold smile.

"I did," he said, still muted. "May I ask…who is it you're mourning?"

There was a pause; Ibby said hesitantly, "Douglas and Nicky. Both have slipped away from us." Her face was full of something. Sympathy? Grief?

Morrigan hardly heard what they were saying. Here stood someone who might be persuaded to *speak* of her mother, who might share those things she longed to know. It was nearly impossible to remain quiet and calm, to not burst forth with every pent-up question she'd ever had.

"You have Hannah's face," he said.

She knew that, from the daguerreotype, and nodded. "I know little about her. She died when I was born."

"Aye, and now you've lost your father *and* your brother? I'm so sorry, lass."

Ibby cut in. "You look shaky as a newborn lamb, Seaghan. Let's find ourselves a dram of *uisge-beatha*." She curled her arm under his. "Whisky has great rejuvenating properties."

"Sweet Isabel," he answered, kissing her cheek. "It's been too long. How have I not seen you in all these years?"

"I'm away to taste the jams," Beatrice said brusquely. She turned and walked off.

"Dour as ever," Seaghan said.

"Pay her no mind." Ibby preened and fluttered her lashes like a young girl. "We'll be happy and lively without her here to remind us of our sins."

"Aye," Seaghan said, laughing. "Have you been in Mallaig all this time, Isabel Lawton?"

She nodded. Morrigan thought she seemed quite giddy. Her excitement at being on Seaghan MacAnaugh's arm was woefully clear.

"It's Maclean now," Ibby said. "I was married, you know." She sobered. "Gregor died four years ago."

"Oh, I'm truly sorry," he said. "I wish I'd known you were so near. You must tell me everything, all about your life."

"And you must tell us of yours," she said, pulling at his arm. "Come away, Seaghan, for I'm thirsty!"

Half turning, he offered his free arm to Morrigan. "Would you join us, lass?"

Morrigan took his arm with one hand and Curran's with the other; the foursome left the dancing square and walked along the wide path between the food stalls.

Seaghan gave Curran a glower. "Why did you tell me naught of this?"

"I wanted to surprise you."

"That you have done. She's comely, your lass."

His eyes glinting with mischief, Curran said, "I cannot wait until she's mine at last. She's guarded so well I'm amazed I was ever able to propose."

"No' quite so well!" Ibby growled.

"Let the lad blether." Seaghan patted Ibby's hand. "After the wedding, you'll have your revenge. He'll be faced then with all the men who'll be pleased to steal her out from under his nose." He lifted an amused brow and grinned as he met Morrigan's astonished regard.

"I've taken care of that, I think," Curran said. "At least for a few months?"

Morrigan could only hope that Seaghan wouldn't notice her mortified blush, or discern the meaning of Curran's words.

Twilight brought the sword and dirk dances, bright bonfires, and uninhibited behavior from those who had enjoyed too much whisky. Kilted gentlemen tripped light-footed as ballerinas between sharp blades. Bards told ancient tales and recited poetry. Late in the night, the festivities wound down with the customary Burns:

My heart's in the Highlands, my heart is not here, my heart's in the Highlands, a-chasing the deer; a-chasing the wild deer and following the roe, my heart's in the Highlands wherever I go.

"I am pleased to meet you," Seaghan told Morrigan outside Ibby's shop. In a gallant flourish, he bent over her hand and kissed her knuckles. "And should you grow weary of yon lad," he added, cocking his chin at Curran, "Aodhàn and I will take you out sailing and show you the coast, any time you wish it."

Morrigan contemplated her newest acquaintance. Deep-etched lines marked his forehead and framed his eyes. A white scar, shaped like a turned-up horseshoe, puckered the center of one cheek. But those eyes held an irrepressible twinkle and a smile dogged his mouth. "I'd like that," she said, giving up the attempt to look solemn and returning his grin.

Merry. He was the sort who'd never be sad for long. Time spent with him would be full of laughter.

Curran appeared inordinately pleased as he looked upon them. If the rest of Glenelg's residents proved as dear as this giant, everything might just turn out.

She couldn't wait to get on with her future, to marry and move into her new home. The turrets *had* nearly punctured the clouds, hadn't they? She would be forever grateful to this handsome lad who had made it possible.

Her dream had come true. Though she hadn't done a thing to deserve it, ardent love had found her. She could almost see the incandescent luster of a unicorn in the shadows behind him.

She reached out and caressed Curran's arm, adding, "But I'll not be growing weary of my lad. Not ever."

Chapter 17

Through the use of shrewd inquiry and stealthy eavesdropping, Ibby discovered a minister on Skye with a reputation of nonjudgmental kindness towards couples who had snubbed Christian modesty. A letter was posted, and when the minister replied consenting, the couple set their wedding date for the thirteenth of September, a Friday, when the moon was waxing. There wasn't enough time to have the banns read, nor did Ibby want to draw attention to the fact that her niece was getting married while still in mourning, but before she could work herself into a new fret and fever, Curran had the necessary special license in hand, claiming it was no trouble at all.

For the first time since she'd been told about the pregnancy, Ibby relaxed. "No one on Skye will know we're in mourning," she said. "Everything'll seem proper." But then she added darkly, "It'll be a different story at Kilgarry."

Ibby said she'd not have Morrigan wearing black, no matter what. "You'll return to it after," she declared.

When Queen Victoria married she began a new tradition of wearing white, and Ibby happily embraced it. She purchased yards of white satin, tulle, chiffon, and lace, and the three, plus two ladies of Ibby's acquaintance who volunteered to help, began constructing a wedding gown. It was a lovely creation, "Fit for a princess," she said, "which is what you always have been to me and what you always will be, no matter what you do. I will no' be cheated of making it, nor of seeing you stand at the altar in it."

Work on the dress began early and continued with hardly a pause until the failing light stopped them. "I have a reputation to uphold, don't I?" Ibby shook out a swath of fabric. "And I've dreamed of this day since you were born. It's my last chance to spoil you, to make you look as beautiful as you deserve."

Morrigan's paternal aunt acquired a curious and unfamiliar thin-skinned tenacity. She reluctantly gave up the idea of fresh orange blossoms for the headdress, but was nearly as satisfied with the pink and sea green chiffon roses to be tucked beneath the tulle veil.

Beatrice and Ibby exchanged scorching words over the bodice. Ibby, surprisingly, wanted a V shape—*Because you've a fine bosom*, she said when alone with Morrigan. Beatrice demanded a modest high collar. *The chit's insulting all decency as it is. Will we slap everyone in the face with her shamelessness?*

Crossing her arms, Ibby stated, "It shall be as I wish it. If you fear for your reputation, you may return to the Low Country."

Morrigan could only shake her head and wonder where her meek aunt had gone.

Tight sleeves flared at the elbow, inset with a profusion of lace. The fitted bodice—*You can breathe* after *you're married*—was fashioned in the popular cuirass style. That, coupled with tight lacing, completely disguised the reason for the rushed wedding. *It's a good thing you're small-boned,* Ibby said as she had Morrigan turn in a circle. *Some women show right well by this time.*

The final accents were fingerless lace gloves and silk slippers—*I do pray it doesn't rain,* Ibby said, with a pleading glance at the ceiling. She brought out the pearl-drop earrings she'd worn at her wedding to Uncle Gregor, and shed a few tears as she held them to Morrigan's ears, but grief vanished as she had a vision of seed pearls sewn into the bodice of the dress.

"I'm *not* a princess, you know," Morrigan snapped one late evening. She'd sewn all day, which she detested, only to hear her efforts weren't right—she must rip everything out and start over. "We're marrying in a half-mark kirk as far from civilization as we can get. No one'll see me but you, Beatrice, and Curran. You're dressing me up like I'm marrying the king of America, and spending a *fortune* on something that will never be worn again."

"There are no kings in America," Ibby said mildly, breaking a strand of thread with her teeth. "And never have been. I'd think you would've learned that much before your father stopped your education."

Morrigan sighed, knowing her protests made no difference. The gown was the bonniest thing she'd ever seen, finer by far than the one Enid Joyce had worn to marry Kit. She would have to be carved of stone to not want to wear it. What difference did her comments make, anyway? Not caring a fig about practical matters, Ibby repeatedly said that she would rob a bank, if need be, to see her beloved niece dressed to perfection, and often reminded Morrigan that the dress would become an heirloom for her daughters.

"My niece has no business becoming your wife if she cannot provide her own dress," Ibby told Curran when he offered to cover the expense. She did allow him, however, to purchase dresses for herself and Beatrice, as was the custom.

For the first time, Morrigan observed a dollop of Douglas Lawton in his sister. Custom! Form! Tradition! became the tiresome bywords of every conversation.

For most of the week before the wedding, Curran stayed at an inn not far from Ibby's shop so he wouldn't have to ferry back and forth from Glenelg.

"Would you care to honeymoon abroad?" he asked her one evening, as they chatted on the front steps.

She shook her head. "Auntie wouldn't like it, not while we're in mourning, and I want to go to Kilgarry. Are you disappointed?"

A sideways grin, accompanied by a flash of blue as he lowered his eyelids, told Morrigan she'd given him special pleasure. "If you want to go to Kilgarry, what sort of man would I be to refuse you?" He pressed her hand to his chest and gave her a pious leer.

She pushed him, hard, then gasped as he dragged her off balance. He straightened before they sprawled off the steps and onto their faces, and caught her around the waist, drawing her close.

"Morrigan." From within the shop's dark interior, Ibby's voice cut the cool air like a flying dirk. "Mr. Ramsay. Behave."

He laughed, his exhalation warm against her ear. Her senses magnified the stroke of his fingertips on her temples; the clean scent of his shaving soap encompassed her like whisky fumes.

"Shall I behave?" He kissed the junction of her throat and shoulder; the place, he'd learned through careful experimentation, which made her pliant as butter. *"Tha thu gam chur às mo chiall."*

"What does that mean?"

"That I'm going daft for want of you."

"Mr. Ramsay!"

"Blether, blether, blether," he said, but dutifully retreated, keeping hold of her fingers. They strolled down the front steps and walked to his horse.

Twilight blurred the outlines of his face. "She can't see so well," Morrigan said. "Kiss me."

He did, until they heard the door squeak. "Morrigan? Has he gone, isoke?"

"Why does she call you that? What does it mean?"

"She doesn't know." Morrigan struggled to regain her composure, to slow her heartbeat, to still her blood. "She has dreams of us. I'm her daughter, and that's her pet name for me. We live on an island in the South Pacific, or somewhere hot. Kiss me again."

He obeyed then laughed. "You've made it damned difficult to ride."

She snickered as she understood. Served him right for what he did to her.

He swung onto the saddle, checking his restive stallion. Bending down, he grasped her hand. "It's your dreams that concern me," he said. "When I get you to Kilgarry, I'm going to have Eleanor Graeme take you in hand, not only because she's a midwife, although I'm glad she'll be there for that. She's also one of the most capable women I've ever known, a healer of the top order." He frowned. "I've had my share of queer fancies."

"Like the women and the lion?"

"That. Well, I'm not sure what that was." He paused. "One day, after we're wed, I'll share some of them, if you will."

She withdrew her hand.

"You're reluctant? You think it will change how I feel about you?"

Her spine stiffened. "How did you—"

He cupped her cheek and gave her a wry smile. "Why d'you think I won't tell mine until after we're married?" He shook his head and added, "Trust me, Morrigan. I know it's hard...."

"I do, Curran." *I love you* trembled at the tip of her tongue. But when she tried to say it, her throat went dry and the pregnancy sickness, which hadn't bothered her for several days, roiled to life again.

She watched him ride away, his vow, *We'll always be together, you and I...* surrounding her, as soft and comforting as goose down.

"I love you." She forced it out, not understanding the dread that trickled down her spine, and the disturbing sense that she was committing an unforgivable betrayal.

EVERYTHING, FROM THE FISHING BOATS IN THE HARBOR TO THE RAINBOW SHEEN IN the dew on the cobbles, took on special beauty. Morrigan was marrying a most intelligent, merry, handsome gentleman, and he had promised to take a sword to everything that tormented her, including her bad dreams. What's more, her nausea continued to improve, and she enjoyed eating again. One of Ibby's trusted volunteers, a mother of five, told her that was the way, the lightheadedness and queasiness vanished as the body grew accustomed to its new state.

Not even Ibby's near-constant concern over what would happen when everyone knew the truth could dampen this relish for life. Beatrice, on the other hand, didn't seem to worry. She'd said all she had to say about it, and now went on exactly as she had in Stranraer, quiet, dour, and busy.

Perhaps it wouldn't be so bad. This was Scotland, not England, and the Scots were far more practical than their prissy neighbors. Since she would soon be properly wed to the father of her child, all would be forgiven.

Her aunt did her best to prepare Morrigan. She even continued with Curran's initial dance lesson, teaching Morrigan the steps to the *shamit reel* and to waltz, after a fashion.

Ibby insisted on voyaging to Skye a day early so that Morrigan could rise on the morning of her wedding rested, and there would be no need to risk the crossing, the weather, or unreliable transportation. Curran arranged for lodging at a decent inn in the area. So it was that early on the twelfth of September, the wedding gown was packed into a trunk amid layers of tissue and the three women set sail for the misty isle.

Ibby's cronies came to see them off, along with their children. The crowd thickened as others joined in and the departure burgeoned into a noisy throng. Two handy young lads loaded the trunk into a wagon while others wasted many a bullet shooting in the air to mark the occasion. Ibby's female friends tossed old shoes and handfuls of grain. All assumed the banns had been called in Glenelg and that everything was proper and seemly.

As they neared the harbor where they would meet their ferry, one *Tamarisk*, owned by Captain J. Fraser, Morrigan turned a fond farewell gaze to Ibby's squat residence. After today, she would never have to sleep in that narrow bed above her aunt's dress shop, flattened between the wall and a snoring Beatrice. Why, Curran's bed was so large—

"My God!" Ibby screeched. She grabbed Morrigan's upper arm and jerked her hard. "What d'you think you're doing?"

Morrigan stared at her aunt, puzzled and frightened.

"Don't tell me you didn't know you're never to look back when you set off to marry?"

Realization flooded with a sinking sense of dread. "I forgot."

"Oh, you careless chit of a girl!" Ibby cried, but soon let it go. "There's no help for it. Perhaps fate'll be kind and forgive you. It was my fault. I should've reminded you."

Beatrice merely snorted.

The ferry's departure was delayed for some reason. Beatrice, who claimed to hate sea travel—though how a born and bred Scot could say such a thing was hard to understand—went off to the stern. Morrigan and Ibby stood on the starboard side, watching incoming fishing boats and the seals swimming in their wake, hoping for scraps.

In due course the ferry worked its way from the harbor. The noise and furor of Mallaig fell away. More and more seals became visible, basking along the rocky shore, bobbing in the water. There were even two pups, still covered in white baby fur.

"Look Auntie," Morrigan said, pointing. "The weans!"

"Now here's a bit of good luck."

"How?"

"Seals are always good luck, but here in the Highlands, you'll see it's far more than that. And they're almost revered on Skye. None but the daftest, coldest devil would kill a seal, and if he did, he'd regret it."

"They're so bonny. Who could ever want to harm them?"

"Aye, it's those eyes, making you want to cuddle them like puppies. Look at that great ugly brute, throwing sand on himself like he has no' a care in the world. And here we are, making all this racket. Hard to believe such a wee bonny creature grows up into that, isn't it? Maybe they're blessing your marriage. See? There's one clapping for you."

They laughed, but the next moment Morrigan cried out when one of the careless males, lumbering across the rocks, went right over one of the pups and crushed it.

"Oh, what a shame," Ibby said.

The pup's mouth opened in a howl as it disappeared beneath hundreds of pounds of blubber.

Morrigan slapped her hands over her ears and squeezed her eyes closed. She heard the pitiful, helpless cry, calling to its mam, and was flooded with the memory of the dream she'd had in Curran's bed, a fortnight past. A stinking crowd of drunken men holding her immobile, their knives dripping with blood.

"Sickening," Ibby exclaimed. "I don't think he even noticed what he did. Morrigan, child?"

Morrigan opened her eyes, dimly realizing she was standing portside, though she had no memory of running there.

Ibby's forehead was creased with worry. Worse, Morrigan had managed to draw the attention of Captain Fraser, who came up next to Ibby, looking almost as fashed as her aunt. He worked his cap in his gnarled hands.

"'Tis the way of beasts." The captain patted Morrigan's shoulder. "They have no sensibility. Life is 'kill or be killed.'" He smiled kindly. "Can I get you a cup of tea, lass?"

Morrigan gritted her teeth as the swift inner assault faded. She was on a ferry. Tomorrow she would be married. Though the dream sent spikes of panic through her, it was meaningless. There were no babies. It was strange, though, how her imagination could conceive such clear images out of nothing. "Thank you, no," she said, trying to steady her voice. "I apologize for causing a fuss."

The captain gave her another pat on the shoulder and went off to his duties.

Life was chancy, was that what the dream meant? What would happen when the seal mother searched for her offspring? She'd find nothing but a poor, crushed corpse.

"Folk think you unfeeling, but your heart is tender." Ibby hugged Morrigan and brushed windblown strands of hair off her niece's face. "I mind the first time you saw a cat kill a mouse, how inconsolable you were, for days and days. Pinch your cheeks. Think of that handsome lad who'll soon be yours, and the happy way things've turned out for you. And don't give a thought to that silly mistake at shore. Such things are but ancient superstition. Marriage to the Laird of Eilginn will bring you years of joy. D'you hear me? Years and years of joy."

Ibby gazed at the boat's churning wake for a moment. "Thank the Lord, you'll never have the kind of memories I do. Everyone in Glenelg was so poor. And the clearings. Folk starving, freezing. Their homes burned as they watched. I'll never forget holding Beth Dunbar, that's Fionna Dunbar's daughter, the day before she died."

"Curran's housekeeper?" Distracted by Ibby's chatter, Morrigan's heartbeat slowly returned to normal. "She had another daughter?"

"She had three weans. Tess and Logan survived. Beth did not. All of six when cold and starvation stole her away." Ibby wiped tears from her lashes. "Begging for a bite of bread. But there wasn't one to give."

Morrigan ached as she imagined her warmhearted aunt weeping over her inability to provide a crust to a dying child. It was daft to grieve over a dead seal pup when such things happened to children. She must try to be more grateful. True, her life up till now hadn't offered many pleasures, but she'd never gone hungry. She'd never been left out in the cold. Douglas had seen to that.

In a brisk, no-nonsense tone, Ibby said, "I wish I could give you advice, but don't you already know too much about what a young lady should be getting advice on?" She gave Morrigan a peppery frown before turning pensive. "Curran's a dear, though, I have to admit. It's clear he adores you. D'you realize how lucky you are? It all could've turned out quite differently."

"Aye, of course," Morrigan agreed, with an attempt at a smile.

"The babe...it is his...?"

Morrigan's heart plummeted at her aunt's obvious embarrassment and hesitant tone. "You think I...I have done...been with...with other men?"

"W-well..." Ibby stammered. "You can trust me, you know. I'd never tell a soul, love."

Morrigan could only gape, speechless with shock.

"It's your father," Ibby finally admitted. "I didn't know how mad he'd become." A tear slipped down her cheek. "Why did you never tell me? I would've taken you away. I wouldn't have let him stop me. I *should* have known. I'll never forgive myself for leaving you there."

Oh. Now Morrigan understood, and it made her sick. "How?" she asked. "How would you have done that, when you couldn't even get me away for a visit?" She gripped the rail, white-knuckled. "You think the child is...." She couldn't finish.

Ibby paused. It did seem a monstrous thing to say while impaled in bright sunlight and clean sea air. "It's...the way he attacked you. I could tell he had some mad notion that you *were* Hannah. He was enraged, yet...there was something else as well." Tears spilled over her cheeks.

Morrigan knew she had to protect Ibby. "No, Auntie, Papa never did anything like that," she said as firmly as she could. Heat rose then dissipated in her cheeks. This must be why Ibby had counseled Morrigan to hide the marks on her throat from Curran, to lie about what had happened. "I swear it. Curran's the father." Knowing she would shatter into bits if the subject wasn't changed, Morrigan stammered, "Auntie, Nicky told me when I was small Papa treated me well. Is that true?"

"Oh aye." Relief swept over Ibby's face and she nodded vigorously. "That's why I never knew...was scunnered when I saw.... D'you know why you didn't die when we were cleared? We found a goat, and Douglas fed you its milk from his finger. Goat's milk off your da's finger—that's why you're here today. And when you were older, why, he always carried you about on his shoulders. You'd laugh and laugh. You should know these things. Now Douglas is dead, I won't keep your past from you anymore. One reason I agreed to his demands was because it's a sad, sorry tale, and I didn't want you burdened."

"It's like a great dark hole full of mystery and fear. Like I did something so awful everyone has to shield me from it."

Ibby shook her head. "You were a bright blessing in the midst of horror. After you're wed and settled in at Kilgarry, I'll tell you everything. Of course," she added, "Beatrice knows more than I. There were those months they were in Ireland. She was with them. None on earth knew Douglas, or your poor mother, as well as she."

"Getting her to speak of those days is like tearing out fingernails with pincers."

"Maybe now he's gone she'll relent. Speaking of fingernails...what are we going to do about yours?"

BEHIND THEM AND BEFORE THEM WERE MOUNTAINS, MOUNTAINS EVERYWHERE.

"The Cuillin." Ibby nodded at the range straight ahead that reached for the clouds like sharp teeth seeking sweetmeats. "Bonny to look at, terrible to be lost in."

"And those?" Morrigan gestured towards the massive peaks behind them.

"The Knoydarts. That hulking brute there is Beinn Sgritheall. Your new home is on the other side, beneath The Five Sisters. Now there's a sight you'll not soon forget. You saw hardly anything when we went there before. After the child is born, you must go out riding. If Curran doesn't have the time to take you, I shall do it. I grew up there, after all. There's many a spot I can show you."

Morrigan stared at the peaks, not sure what she was hoping for. A message of reassurance? Some glimmer of welcome? They were so beautiful she couldn't turn away, yet their summits were shrouded in rainclouds, and as she looked, lightning flickered, sending branches in a hundred directions. One thick, white, wicked bolt came out of the darkest cloud, striking the ground three times, and distant thunder resonated across the water.

THE FERRY SLID AGAINST THE PIER AT ARMADAL LIKE A BABE TO ITS MOTHER'S breast. Morrigan and Ibby found Beatrice dozing on a wooden bench, her mouth hanging slack. They woke her and paid two eager lads to haul their trunk and lead them to The Hart and Wench, where Curran had arranged for rooms.

After a meal and an hour spent listening to the proprietor's garrulous tales, Morrigan and Ibby went sightseeing while Beatrice retired for a nap. They walked to the pier then north, into lush, overgrown wilderness.

Many of the locals wore little more than rags and much of the area appeared abandoned, strewn with rubble and burnt-out shells of cottages.

"Folk once believed Scotland invincible," Ibby said. "She's seen strife and slaughter, at Culloden, Phillipaugh, Glencoe, and more. Yet always there remained a steadfast belief that these mountains and burns, fed with our precious blood, would survive, no matter the assault. Aye." She mopped her tears. "D'you know what destroyed us at last? The clearings. Over a thousand years we withstood everything: the Romans, the Vikings, greedy English kings with their massacres. Oh, how they tried to bring us to heel. But in the end, it was our own who achieved the English desire. Our own kin, shipping us away and replacing us with sheep." She shook her head. "Betrayal from those we trust is the worst treachery," she said, and left Morrigan, saying she needed to be alone for a bit.

Her words replayed like a grim prediction as Morrigan watched the sunset create deep, frowning shadows on Beinn Sgritheall.

MORRIGAN WOKE FULL OF ENERGY ON HER WEDDING DAY, THOUGH SHE'D HARDLY slept. She traced the slight swell, the tautness of the flesh over her womb, which she hoped lacing would disguise. Outside her window, the sea lay calm, speckled by sunlight. "I wish you could be here, Mama," she said.

The image of Douglas's face reared before her. *Don't play the innocent.* She closed her eyes and pressed her forehead to the glass, fighting despair and a sinking sense that he could somehow still take everything from her.

Ibby burst in without bothering to knock. "We've much to do," she said by way of a good morning. "First you will eat. I don't want you fainting today. How d'you feel? Is there any sickness?"

"Hardly any," Morrigan said. "I was queasy when I woke, but it's gone now."

"I've heard that many expectant women have more energy than they know what to do with, once the first sickness is done."

"That would be grand."

Ibby threw orders like a desperate leader in the midst of heated battle. Whenever she heard the clop of a horse or the grating wheels of a carriage, she rushed to the window, but Curran still hadn't made an appearance by the time Morrigan was dressed.

"Where's our bridegroom?" Ibby wrung her hands.

"Don't worry, Auntie. No doubt he's gone straight to the kirk."

Beatrice arranged her niece's hair, rubbing each lock with silk to make it shine. She braided and coiled it with the chiffon roses, and positioned the lace veil.

Draped white satin gleamed through tulle, shocking in its contrast to the black she'd been wearing since the beginning of August. The eyes staring back at Morrigan in the borrowed looking-glass seemed brilliant as polished crystals, and huge, perhaps because her cheeks had scarcely more color than her dress. Under the veil, her hair appeared as dark as Beatrice's special molasses cake.

The world felt as though it was lurching end over end, trying to throw her off.

"Here." Beatrice dropped a rolled ribbon into Morrigan's hand. It had likely been bright blue once, but was now faded almost to grey. "It was Hannah's," she said.

"Thank you." Morrigan kissed her aunt and tucked the ribbon into her bodice over her heart.

"I've something old." Ibby dug into her case and pulled out a worn velvet bag. Untying the silk strings, she produced a delicate fan with a threadbare violet tassel. "It was your grandmam's. It's the only thing your father brought home from India besides his uniform."

Morrigan opened it. Though it was old and dull, the ribbon threaded through the slats held. She caught a hint of the warm, exotic scent Ibby called "sandalwood."

Silence fell when she descended the staircase and the men in the pub caught sight of her. One bold lad raised his ale and shouted a toast to her happiness. She'd seen enough men making toasts to know, though he spoke the Gaelic. Another nearly tipped Ibby over trying to reach Morrigan, blowing kisses and pretending he was on the verge of collapse. Aye flattering it was, but she would have enjoyed it more had her aunts not acted so annoyed.

"I must say this is not how things were done when I was a lass." Ibby put her hands on her hips. "Men didn't dare speak in such a fashion or they'd have a father's knife tickling their throats. Where has common decency gone?"

"Men are a brutish lot," Beatrice said. "If it weren't for women, the human race would still be living in caves and grunting like pigs."

Ibby whisked Morrigan away to meet Mr. and Mrs. MacDonald, the long-married couple who would walk before the newlyweds. The lad who'd toasted her insisted on coming along and playing his da's ancient fiddle. Morrigan was placed in an open carriage drawn by two lovely Clydes, and off they went, the tipsy men from the pub firing their guns, shouting, singing, and generally livening the passage. As they journeyed they drew more folk, including a few giggling girls, plus a barrel-chested grandfather with a set of pipes.

An eagle was perched on a rough stone dyke to the left of the kirk. It fluffed its wings at the ringing gun blasts and released a protesting scree, but it didn't lift off.

The carriage pulled to a halt and Morrigan's attention moved on to the structure. Though fallen into a state of disrepair, it retained its charm, nestled as it was in the lithe of two heathery hills, near the Sound and a ruin she was told had been a MacDonald stronghold in centuries past. The minister, a man with a great mass of curly hair, came out and welcomed them in rapid Gaelic, which left Morrigan blushing and mute. Ibby replied with a gesture towards her, and he immediately switched to fairly decent English. Patting her hand, he told her his name was Ruairidh Ogilvy, and he drew her to the peeling wooden doors. Morrigan turned once more before entering. The eagle had flown up and now circled above them, its wings motionless, resting, perhaps, on cushions of air.

Their impromptu entourage remained outside, sipping from flasks and listening to the piper, who played one tune after another.

The black garbed, white-collared clergyman coaxed her through the doors and off to his sitting room. "Who'll be giving away the bride?" he asked, pouring tea into sturdy china cups.

"My da and mam have both…passed on," Morrigan said.

His smile dissipated. Handing her a cup, he said, "You're too young to have suffered such a loss."

"She lost her brother as well," Ibby said. "Beatrice and I were all she had left until today."

Both the aunts regarded her expectantly. Ibby was more like a mother, but she owed Beatrice. "Could both my aunts do it?" she asked shyly.

There was a squeal and a bang. Ruairidh stood. "That'll be the bridegroom, or your admirers have knocked down the door. Don't come out. You don't want him to see your dress, which, by the way, is the grandest these old walls have ever witnessed." He left to investigate.

Morrigan's knees quivered. A wave of dizzying heat spread from forehead to toes. Pressing lace-covered hands to her breast, she fought to breathe. "I think I'm sick."

Both aunts jumped to their feet. Beatrice dipped a handkerchief in the water basin and dampened Morrigan's cheeks while Ibby fanned her.

"At least now you've some color," Beatrice said. "You were wambly as a squashed kitten before. Put your head between your knees."

"You wouldn't worry if God himself appeared, would you?"

"I'd ask why he bothers where he's not needed."

The fanning and cool water soon helped. Morrigan sat up, rubbing her forehead. "I should walk," she said, and paced from door to window.

What was she doing? This was pure daftness. Marriage, for the rest of her life, to a man she hardly knew.

Did she love him? Would they be happy? No answers presented themselves.

She saw Louis Stevenson's face, his drooping moustache and luminous eyes. *I've a notion your heart will steer you rightly.*

Oh, how she hoped he was right.

"I almost forgot." Ibby emptied her beaded reticule onto the table. "Here, Morrigan. Slip this sixpence into your shoe."

"You've been havering yourself to a froth with your superstitions since the day this began," Beatrice said. "The chit never had a swain before Curran." She turned an emotionless gaze upon her niece. One brow lifted. "Did you?"

Kit's face materialized, his eyes blazing with unspent passion, his hands gripping her shoulders like steel clamps.

Give me your promise.

Will you wait for me, Kit? Will you wait for me to grow up?

Had she broken an oath to him the day she'd seduced Curran on the moor?

Christian kissed you. Bold as could be. And you let him. The cynical expression on her aunt's face suggested she knew everything Morrigan and Kit had done, and maybe what was racing through Morrigan's brain right now, too.

A sixpence, worn in the bride's left shoe, had the power to avert any evil wishes of past suitors, unless the woman had made a vow and broken it. Then the coin lost its lucky ability. Dire consequences would befall not only the bride, but her firstborn child as well.

"Of course, only Curran, Auntie." She felt sick again.

She'd heard of cursed births, of babies with no arms, or shrieking mad, or dead, all born to women who'd broken vows to honorable gentlemen in order to wed another.

Kit's marriage to Enid must release her. They hadn't made any real promises anyway. But she couldn't ask. Ibby would swoon after the unlucky omen on the mainland. Two bad omens were more than the poor woman could be expected to bear.

Ruairidh opened the door, flourishing a bouquet of pink hollyhocks, daisies, purple and white heather, and masses of sweet clover. Morrigan buried her nose in the blooms as he said, "Your groom brought these for you, my dear, and a friend as well. A man by the name of MacAnaugh. If you prefer, he could give you away."

"That's a lovely idea," Ibby said, "and far more proper."

Beatrice folded her hands across her middle and said nothing.

"No." Morrigan shook her head. "He's no kin to me. I hardly know him. I want my aunts, if you'll allow it."

Beatrice offered one of her enigmatic smiles and Ibby beamed.

The minister nodded. "We're ready, then. Come along, bonny girl. You've lured the sun into this shabby old place."

Ibby fluffed the satin skirts and lowered the veil over Morrigan's face. Tears were already misting her eyes.

They took up their positions on either side of her.

Through a spangled haze no amount of blinking could clear, Morrigan glimpsed Seaghan standing next to Curran at the altar, his wild thicket of hair plastered down somehow, before her betrothed stole her attention as well as the remains of her composure.

She'd never seen such a grand gentleman, and gave thanks that her veil disguised her gowping like a simpleton. He observed her approach, his demeanor as calm as though he wed every week. But as she came closer, she caught a brief narrowing of his eyes, a muscle tightening in his jaw. The sickle-shaped scar stood out distinctly.

Infinite shades of blue eddied around him. As he took her hand, the colors swirled upward and turned white. A thread of energy ran from his fingers to hers, lifting the hair off her scalp. For an instant, she forgot where she was and saw only Curran, surrounded in a diffused glow.

"Who gives this bride to be married?" Ruairidh's voice was nearly lost beneath the throbbing of her blood. The aunts murmured and stepped away.

Curran placed her hand on his forearm and covered it with his. The nearness of the man who would soon be her husband left her breathless, her heart palpitating. Once, when she glanced at him, his face was overlaid with Douglas Lawton's. She blinked hard to make it disappear.

Lifting his Bible, Ruairidh recited words that managed to filter through Morrigan's anxiety.

For now we see through a glass, darkly, but then face to face. Now I know in part, but then shall I know even as also I am known.

Would she, one day, see things clearly? Her life seemed little more than a mystery of mismatched puzzle pieces, understanding a pinnacle that lay beyond reach.

The minister began a tale about how God created woman from Adam's rib while he slept, and how Eve became the mother of every living person. Morrigan liked the sound of that. It made females seem more important than she'd been led to believe.

She stole another glance at Curran. For the rest of her life he would have the final word, the power, legal and otherwise, to command her every action. He could beat her if he wished. She had dreamed of freedom, freedom to go places, do things, make her own choices, but she'd always known it was impossible, and now all hope was gone. She'd thrown away any chance of it the day she'd defied society's rules.

Even if she hadn't, there would have been some other way of binding her.

"You now surrender your individual lives in the interest of the wider, deeper life which you'll have in common." Ruairidh's voice boomed through the dim nave. "Henceforth you will be one in mind, one in heart, and one in affection."

Morrigan's lungs constricted. Was Curran only standing here because of his unborn child? Would he grow tired of her, sorry to be bound to a penniless tavern-keeper's daughter?

"I promise before God to be thy loving, faithful husband." Curran looked steadily into her eyes. "True and loyal in every condition of life, in prosperity and adversity, in sickness and in health. I promise to keep myself unto thee until death do us part." He smiled, lifted his hand, and stroked her cheek through the veil.

Scarcely hearing the minister's instruction, she stumbled through her own vows, needing his patient assistance with every sentence.

The ring, a concoction of emeralds and amethysts that prompted an amazed "ooh," was slipped onto her finger as Ruairidh said, "Forasmuch as you have consented together in holy wedlock and have pledged your undying devotion and fidelity, I do pronounce you husband and wife. What therefore, God has joined together this day, let no man separate."

After such a solemn speech, the minister's grin startled her. "You may kiss the bride," he said, "and hurry up about it, for I'll be wanting one of my own."

While she stood at a loss, Curran threw back her veil, put his hands on her waist, and pressed his lips to hers. The kiss seemed different than any other he'd given her. It was quick, easy, and possessive.

"Now you're mine," he said, eyes glinting. "Forever and ever, Mrs. Ramsay, *'s tu mo bhean is mo rùn.*"

It was Seaghan who explained. "It means you're his wife and his love." He squeezed her shoulder and kissed her cheek. "He'll never fail you."

The Discovery

Chapter 1

BACK AT THE INN, MORRIGAN AND HER AUNTS CHANGED AND REPACKED THE
wedding dress. Two lads carried the trunk to the pier, where a trim sloop, hung with garlands, waited to carry them up the Sound to Glenelg. The revelers collected seashells and danced on the pier to the piper's lively reels. The lads fired their guns and passed around the whisky. The minister was there as well, having accepted Curran's invitation to attend the wedding festivities.

Hints of winter nestled beneath a punching wind from the east. Morrigan wished she had a jacket.

Seaghan stood apart from the others, staring at a cluster of seals basking on the rocks a safe distance from the noisy merrymakers.

Morrigan approached him. "Thank you for coming, and for standing with Curran."

"It was an honor I'll never forget." His pensive expression vanished into a wide, toothy smile. "Due entirely to the beauty of the bride."

She smiled shyly.

"He's a good man, Lady Eilginn. You can trust him. Never doubt it."

"Did I seem to doubt it?" Inwardly she reeled at being addressed as "Lady." *Lady Eilginn. Me.*

"I did think your eyes might pop right out of your head." He traced her cheekbone with his index finger. "You turned as white as a prisoner facing the guillotine."

She flushed. "Truthfully, I've not known Curran very long."

"You'll never regret this day." He bent and gave her a kiss then faced the seals again as if embarrassed. "I wish I could find a lass for Aodhàn," he said. "It's what he needs, and sorely."

"The man who lives with you? Curran said you saved his life."

He nodded. "We were stuffed in the hold of the *Bristol* like herrings, hundreds of cleared folk from up and down the coast. I sneaked up on deck when nobody was looking, to get away from the stink." He absently smoothed the puckered scar on his cheek. "There was a storm. Huge waves, rain lashing us like whips. The surf was deafening, and the sailors had to rope themselves to whatever they could. I was sure we'd sink."

She shuddered. He noticed, and said heavily, "Aye, nothing makes a man feel so small as being on a plank of wood in the ocean during a storm."

Having watched many a gale work Loch Ryan into a rage, she could only nod. It must be that much worse on the open ocean, with nothing at all to break the fury of the wind.

"We'd passed the lower Hebrides when I saw him," Seaghan continued. "I figured someone from the hold had come up like me and fallen overboard. Luck saved Aodhàn, for the waves carried him closer. If they hadn't, the captain would never have agreed to a rescue. I volunteered to pick him up myself." Seaghan pursed his lips. "Maybe the bastard thought I'd drown as well and he'd have one fewer body to deal with. They put me off in a dinghy, and right away, Aodhàn was there, next to me. The boat capsized just as the men hauled us on board."

"You saved him."

"The wound in his chest alone should've killed him, but the bleeding was slow, no doubt from the cold. We emptied his lungs of water and I stitched up the cut. I've watched over him ever since. He's a good-hearted man, but I'm the only one who knows it. If he could find a decent woman, it'd cure him from his dourness. I know it would."

"What's he unhappy about? His life was saved."

"Well, lass, his life might have been saved, but his memories weren't. To this day, Aodhàn remembers little more than his name, and it was a good two months before that happened. He thinks he lived on one of the islands. He says he remembers cliffs, which made me sure it was Berneray, as we were right off those cliffs when I fished him out of the ocean, but we went there, and nobody knew him, and nothing about it seemed familiar. Of course, nine years had passed by then. He didn't want to go on looking. I don't know why. It was as though he no longer cared."

A pair of hands slipped around Morrigan's waist. Startled, she swung around to find her new husband, who shrugged out of his coat and placed it over her shoulders.

"What's Seaghan telling you?" Curran asked. "The old seal story?"

"Whisht, Curran," Seaghan said roughly.

With a derisive laugh, Curran guided her a few steps closer to the seals. Heads rose; two slipped into the water, hardly disturbing the surface. "Seals are special," he said, close to her ear. "One must never harm them, since no one knows if they are seal or human in a seal's body."

She frowned and turned to him, expecting to see the joke in his eyes.

"It's true." He nodded gravely. "Seals change form at will, *a ghràidh*. Have you never heard how maidens from the sea beguile poor human men? Offspring from those unions are not ordinary children but human and seal in one. When a man kills a seal, he never truly knows if he has killed a beast or a human…maybe a member of his own family."

"I see. And what does this have to do with the drowned man?"

"Aodhàn is Glenelg's selkie."

Morrigan stared at Seaghan. "You didn't mention *that.*"

"Stop it now, Eilginn." Seaghan grinned. "He's repeating Agnes Campbell's nonsense. She's full of selkies, devils, spirits, and ghosts. Watch out for her, or you'll end up terrified of your own shadow."

"It's not true, then?"

"Of course not. It's bloody superstitious drivel. Forgive me, lass, but if it weren't for Agnes, that rumor would've faded away years ago."

"If he could remember his past," Curran said, "he could tell everyone where he's from. That would take the wind out of Agnes's sails." He tapped Morrigan gently on the temple. "But he remembers nothing. Nothing at all other than his name."

"That's sad." It did seem quite sad, and lonely. Morrigan felt a pang of sympathy for the fellow.

"Ah, you feel sorry for him now, but when you meet him, trust me, his scowl and gruff manner will slay all your romantic notions." Curran's lips touched her ear and he drew her away from Seaghan. "Your wedding dress was lovely, did I tell you?" He held up one hand, smiling at her cry of surprise and delight. A necklace lay across his fingers, delicate gold supporting a set of emeralds, each one surrounded by diamonds. It swayed, sparkling in the glare from the setting sun. "Ibby outdid herself. But you're far more charming naked. Tonight, I'll have you in nothing but this, and your aunts be damned." He cocked a brow. "What d'you say to every night, Mrs. Ramsay?"

All the labor on that daft dress, and he dared tell her he preferred her naked. Aunt Ibby would be scunnered to hear it, and that was a fact.

Playful breezes sought to free her hair from the snood beneath her hat. "This weather's grand," she said, resting her head against Curran's shoulder.

Tendrils of warmth and poetry stole through her. She curled in closer and sighed.

"Aye," he answered, wrapping an arm around her shoulders.

She'd never heard him sound so content.
I do love him, she thought. *I will make him happy.*

Chapter 2

The sunset flared, sending glowing rays across the sky as though trying to add to the gaiety of the occasion. Morrigan discovered she had a passion for standing as near as she could get to a bowsprit, watching white veins of foam intersect the waves. She absorbed the land, sky, and swells, wishing this journey up the Sound never had to find a dock...that they could sail on to world's-end. Gusts of wind caught the ribbons on her straw hat and sent them thrashing, reminding her of the day she'd lost another cap to the sea. *The day I met Curran.* Long ago it seemed, and she quite another person.

Whitecaps sprayed. A shooting fountain signaled the presence of a whale. Its tail fin slapped the water with a great noisy crack.

Kilgarry's turrets appeared in the distance, each leaded window refracting rainbows carved of sunlight.

While Curran chatted with their skipper, Seaghan remained at her side. "The Sound is a dangerous crossing," he said, knocking ash from the bowl of his pipe and leaning on the rail. "A body has to know what he's about, or these currents will leave nothing but splinters. In the olden days, folk prayed for disaster. They needed the wood, you understand, and lost cargo could be sold."

Belying Seaghan's words, they sailed into Glenelg Bay as efficiently as a seagull to a plump mackerel.

Cool purple twilight fell across the earth, and the wash of water grew quiet.

Seaghan left them, promising to come to Kilgarry as soon as he rounded up Aodhàn Mackinnon. And, he added, he would gladly drag the lout by the scruff of his neck if he had to.

Kyle drove up with the wagonette and Morrigan relaxed into the curve of Curran's arm as he sent the geldings trotting to Kilgarry. Curran conversed with Ruairidh Ogilvy, Ibby, and Beatrice, leaving Morrigan to drink in the landscape and reflect on the day.

Several of the Skye revelers had begged to come along, and as soon as they disembarked from the boat, the lads among them raced away, fighting to be the first to reach Kilgarry. Morrigan heard their old pistols and revolvers blasting; the winner returned to meet them, bringing a bottle of whisky and a cup, his sweaty face wearing a triumphant grin.

Touching his cap, wishing her *good fortune, mistress,* Kyle led away the horses and wagonette. Kilgarry was bright with lamps in every window and Fionna curtsying in the open doorway. "Welcome," she said in a voice of respect. Many others crowded behind her, their faces smiling and inquisitive.

Curran captured her into his arms once more and carried her over the threshold. Cheers and clapping reverberated as he set her down in the entry. *No devil's work will ever bother this sonsie bride,* some female shouted.

Fionna lifted the bride's-cake and brought it down smartly on top of Morrigan's hat. The cake broke and crumbled over her shoulders and she released a surprised squeak. Everyone laughed, including Morrigan as she brushed at her shoulders and bodice, sending crumbs to the floor.

"It's a sorrow that I must perform these tasks in Mistress Therese's place," Fionna said. "I'm sure we all wish she were here to welcome her son's bride."

Some in the crowd, perhaps those who had known Curran's mother, nodded somberly.

Fionna led Morrigan to the fireplace in the nearest drawing room. With the flourish due such an occasion, she offered Kilgarry's new mistress the poker and tongs.

Ibby had taken pains to make sure Morrigan knew what to do. She scattered the logs and ash, and then built it up again, ready for lighting. When she straightened, Fionna gave her the heavy silver chatelaine full of keys.

"Lady Eilginn," the group cried, lifting their glasses. But before these eager well-wishers could surround her, Ibby seized Morrigan's forearm.

"She cannot attend her wedding cèilidh in this dress. You must be patient." Morrigan's plump aunt pulled her charge up the curved staircase.

Morrigan glanced down from the landing. The unmarried lasses from Skye and Glenelg, including Violet and Tess, were busy scooping up cake crumbs from the floor. Ibby told her it was called "Dreaming bread," and that lasses wrapped bits of it in handkerchiefs to put under their pillows, for bride's-cake had the power to bring visions of future husbands.

A white evening gown lay upon the bed in the master bedroom.

"Where did this come from?" Morrigan asked.

"I had it made," Ibby admitted. "You'll be needing several."

"You want me to change again?"

"You're no longer an innkeeper's daughter." Ibby gave her niece an exasperated glance. "You're wife to the Laird of Eilginn. Besides, you cannot dance in what you're wearing, and this is a cèilidh. You do want to dance with your husband, don't you?"

Morrigan stifled a sigh. Never in her life had she changed clothes three times in one day, but Ibby had gone to some trouble. "Thank you, Auntie," she said, and suffered herself to be undressed and have her corset retightened.

The gown was simple yet sophisticated, with lace-trimmed cap sleeves, the bodice styled in a close-fitting cuirass, and three large bows draped one after the other beneath the bustle.

A sash of Ramsay tartan was draped over her shoulder, blood red with ebony squares, pinned with a silver unicorn's head.

Once, long ago, Nicky constructed a horn out of straw, sticks and wire, and tied it to their mare's forehead. Widdie looked quite silly trying to dislodge it. Morrigan fingered the brooch, wishing her brother could be here to dance with her, tease her, and flirt with the lasses.

Violet, flushed and smiling, entered. Morrigan had noticed two of the Skye lads vying for her favor.

"Would you fetch the fabric blossoms for her hair?" Ibby asked the maid. "They're in my room on the commode."

"Aye, mistress," Violet said, and went out again.

Ibby got on her knees and fluffed the dress so the lace around the hem showed. "You'd best prepare yourself. I didn't expect to see crofters and fishermen here tonight. These are folk of deep faith, and I have no doubt they've already fathomed the truth we've tried so hard to hide. They know we're in mourning for Douglas and Nicky, and they'll see through any tale we tell. They're going to watch the changes in you, and they'll be counting their fingers."

"Now she'll see what shame feels like," Beatrice said.

"Some may judge you, child. There's no way around it. And the gossip will spread. You must do everything you can to befriend these folk, to make them see you as virtuous, as far as you're able, and do nothing from this night onward that can be deemed unworthy of the laird's wife. With any luck, you'll convince them you're a good lass, chaste but for the one mistake. What you want more than anything is to let them see how you love Curran, and didn't trick him into marrying you. They'll never forgive you if they think that's what happened."

Morrigan's high spirits drained away at this somber warning, but she was saved from having to say anything, as Violet returned, her hands overflowing with star-shaped flowers. She and Ibby dressed the bride's hair and finally, with the addition of a velvet crimson choker set off by a teardrop pearl, she was ready.

"It's a pleasure to dress you," Ibby said as she allowed her protégé a peek in the mirror. "You remind me of your mother tonight."

"Many used to say Hannah could charm the Prince of Wales himself, right away from his Alexandra," Beatrice said.

"Which isn't much of a trick from what I hear," Ibby said with a wink. "Now pious Gladstone...there would be a conquest worthy of notice." She handed Morrigan a pair of long white gloves. "Shall we?"

Morrigan ran her fingers along the edge of the neckline and stared into the looking-glass, afraid that such a display of bosom would scandalize everyone. Yet Aunt Ibby, who was a devout church-going Presbyterian, appeared perfectly at ease.

Curran was still in the entryway at the center of a cluster of men, holding a glass of whisky and laughing. As soon as he caught sight of her at the top of the stairs, he left them, propping one foot on the bottom step and holding out a hand. She inhaled and descended, placing her hand in his.

His gaze, so hotly pleased, lent her courage. He led her into the drawing room, into a spin of color, a blur of faces, and an expectant hush.

"Welcome to you, mistress." Fionna Dunbar curtsied again.

"Thank you," Morrigan said faintly.

"Morrigan, may I present Glenelg's heart and soul?" Curran swept out one arm. "My wife," he announced, moving her hand to his forearm. "Mrs. Ramsay."

The hush dissipated into applause and a flurry of voices. *Aye, she well matches you, master,* a male at the rear cried.

Morrigan gritted her teeth to stop their chattering, only to feel, in the next instant, unbearably flushed. Thankfully, Ibby had given her a fan to carry.

"Soon you'll be old friends with them all," Curran said. "But let's begin with the smoother path." He guided her straight to Ruairidh Ogilvy, who, right now, did seem like an old friend. She smiled her gratitude at Curran's discernment.

Standing before the fireplace, whisky in hand, Ruairidh was chatting with an unfamiliar man, whose pronounced grey sideburns swooped over his cheeks in curly profusion, leaving his upper lip and chin clean-shaven.

"Reverend Ogilvy," she said. "I hope you're enjoying yourself."

Ruairidh lifted his glass. "I've never in my life seen a bonnier bride, Lady Eilginn, and I'm certain I never will again." He turned to Curran. "Would you tell me the history of your portraits? These two, above the fireplace, are they your mother and father? And this extraordinary likeness of your wife.... Every eye is drawn to it there."

Kit's painting sat on an easel to the left of the fireplace. "H-How did that get here?" Morrigan managed to ask.

"Ibby and Fionna had your bride's kist brought from Mallaig." Curran frowned. His brow rose, elongating the scar.

"A masterpiece," Ruairidh said. "Who is the artist?"

Morrigan read the question in Curran's wary glance. *Aye, and why have you never shown it to me, or mentioned it?*

Making free use of her fan, Morrigan said carefully, "A lad from my hometown painted anyone he could get to hold still. He said it was good practice." She felt the heat in her cheeks. The virginal white of her gown would make them look redder. "I didn't pose for this, though. I didn't know he'd done it until...recently."

"There's something about it," the minister said. "It is you, my dear, yet different. Quite different."

"Well," she said, "he painted me as a mermaid."

Curran continued to watch her as Ruairidh laughed. Morrigan laced her fingers together.

"It's as fine as any Millais or Rossetti I've ever seen. Excuse me; I fear I'm somewhat a student of art, though I have not the means to indulge it. I did visit the Royal Academy once, long ago. Has your artist any recognition, or do we have the honor of seeing his work before anyone else? Will you tell us his name?"

"Kit...Christian...Lindsay." She paused to clear her throat, not daring to meet her husband's gaze. "I don't know what's happened to him. He married and left Stranraer some time ago."

"If this is an example of his talent, I've no doubt he'll achieve renown and riches. I'll watch and hope for other masterpieces by Christian Lindsay."

"As will we," Curran said, though he didn't sound as enthusiastic. Before Morrigan could formulate a plan to charm away his suspicion, he motioned to Fionna. She crossed to him and he spoke into her ear. With a nod, she fetched Tess; together, they carried the easel and painting out of the room.

Morrigan's heart sank. Already, he was angry. She inwardly recoiled, fearful he would denounce her before all his guests.

But he smiled at Ruairidh. "The room is crowded. I don't want it damaged." Turning to the man with the sideburns who had been quietly observing this conversation, he said, "Morrigan, allow me to introduce you to Quentin Merriwether, my friend and solicitor. Quinn, my wife, Mrs. Ramsay."

"I am so pleased to make your acquaintance, Mrs. Ramsay," he said with a polite bow.

"Thank you for coming, Mr. Merriwether." She snapped open her fan again, hoping to rid herself of this heated discomposure. She might not know much about the world, but she did know that clients made their solicitors privy to all kinds of details never shared with anyone else. She fancied the warmth of his smile did not reach his eyes. They were frighteningly keen, almost slicing her head open in an effort to uncover her secrets.

What a fool she'd been. Every eye in the room was trained upon her, every tongue forming questions. They all must wonder about her character, or lack of it.

"Quinn handles my legal affairs," Curran was saying. "His home is in London, but we see him often. I think he'd like to live here, wouldn't you, Quinn?"

"There is some truth to that," Quinn replied. Aye, he was English, but his accent wasn't overly unpleasant.

Tess and Fionna passed around ale and whisky.

"Janet will want to know how you like her recipe, mistress," Tess said.

"Only a sip," Curran replied. "I don't believe it's good for…." He stopped, blushing. Morrigan turned rigid and forcibly swallowed a horrified screech.

"It's home-brewed," he said quickly, "and potent. My wife isn't accustomed to spirits. Ah, here's Padraig." With a parting word to Ruairidh and Quinn, he pulled her away.

"Padraig Urquhart," he said. "He took over as gamekeeper when your father left Glenelg."

"What a fetching lady you've found, sir." The man bobbed his head. "And imagine, Douglas Lawton's own daughter! I mind you holding this lass when she was no bigger than a mite. Why, she's scarce grown since those days, but for her hair, which appears to have grown dearly!" His smile faded. "I was grieved to hear your father slipped away, mistress. And wee Nick. What a sorry trial for you."

"It's kind of you to remember them."

"He and I endured the troubles together. Your da near single-handed-like kept us alive, but of course you know that. He's a hero, every bit as much as Master Ramsay's father."

A young woman approached, holding an infant. Padraig drew her into the circle. "My wife, Rachel."

Padraig, a decidedly older man with white hair, rough beard, and eyes near-buried in wrinkles, had a wife whose fresh dewy skin bloomed within a frame of flaxen hair she'd plaited about her ears in a style many years out of date. Morrigan's surprise at the pairing of Rachel and Padraig was surpassed only by shock at the man's affectionate and respectful description of Douglas. Padraig's words birthed a thousand questions, but she held her tongue, not wanting to admit the Douglas he remembered was to her a complete stranger.

She couldn't help wondering, sadly, if she alone had caused the change in her father.

Rachel's costume made Morrigan uncomfortably aware that her own was far too rich for this gathering. Ibby had assumed tonight's guests would be wealthy landowners and their spouses, not simple tenants. These people had no doubt labored to clean and repair the outfits they wore in her honor. Padraig's jacket showed threadbare patches; his boot leather was cracked and weathered. Rachel's frock, a saffron-colored skirt with a tartan scarf about her shoulders to add bright color, was also mended.

One of Morrigan's old inn dresses would have worked well in this setting. It might have helped them accept her more readily.

If they knew her history, and what had caused Curran to join with her in marriage, she'd be no better in their eyes than the fallen woman of Stranraer.

Yet in his unpretentious way, Curran had invited the people closest to him —his crofters. No doubt she would one day meet the fine gentlemen and ladies of his acquaintance, but for tonight, this most important night, ordinary folk like her.

His choice of guests showed the marrow of the man she'd married.

She might not be able to change her costume, but she could at least display a willingness to be friendly. "May I hold the wean?" she asked.

Bobbing a curtsy, Rachel offered her child, saying, "Her name's Jean, m'lady."

Wee fingers curled around hers. The babe slept, her pink mouth open, skin brushed by fine, downy hair. For an instant, Morrigan forgot everything else.

"I expect you'll be making a fine mother," Rachel said.

Startled fear replaced euphoria. Morrigan stared at the sleeping infant, realizing she would soon hold her own child. *I'll never hurt it,* she swore, remembering Nicky's fears.

"You have that fierce look again," Curran whispered in her ear. Louder, he said, "This is Malcolm Campbell and his wife, Agnes. Violet is their daughter."

She quickly rearranged her expression to more properly acknowledge the red-faced couple beaming at her.

"Jean is a pretty wee thing, is she not?" Agnes said. "Poor Rachel, though. Jean's birth near killed her." Coming closer, she added, "She was breeched."

Agnes wore a red and black checked dress, and her grey-streaked hair was pulled into a simple plaited chignon. Her shiny black shoes, no doubt tucked away for special occasions, looked new and stiff. Years of exposure to wind and weather had permanently marked her plump cheeks in a rosy meshwork of broken blood vessels.

"Malcolm is Kilgarry's shepherd," Curran told her. "But more importantly, he's a grand fiddler. We never hold a cèilidh without him."

The poor man's collar looked so tight Morrigan couldn't help imagining his head popping off. His beard was freshly trimmed and he'd slicked down his grey hair. In other respects he resembled his wife, his cheeks weathered and his eyes lit by gentle kindness. The couple was exactly the same height.

Merry. He and his wife, and Padraig and Rachel, each easily identified.

All these folk appeared kind and merry. Even Curran's solicitor, who was laughing with Ruairidh, might fit into that category once she got to know him better and he realized she hadn't set out to cruelly entrap his friend.

These simple but dignified people must truly love their laird to show her such quick acceptance.

"Violet is your daughter?" she asked Agnes. "She helped me ever so much today."

"She's my joy and a blessing," the woman replied. Then Agnes asked the questions no doubt on everyone's lips.

"Master, why is your wedding feast so small? I would've thought you'd invite the entire county plus two more to such an occasion." She faced Morrigan, adding, "And why have we never met you? Violet told us Master Ramsay brought a lady to Kilgarry a fortnight ago. She called you his betrothed, but I thought she was making it up."

"I…I…."

"Where were the banns read? It's all peculiar, if you'll forgive me saying so, especially for a laird—"

"Now Agnes," Curran interrupted, "I'm not a laird, and you always see plots along with spirits and faeries. Lay the blame at my door, if you must, for I couldn't wait to marry Mrs. Ramsay. Her wishes for a grand wedding with all the formalities were swept away by my impatience. You must console her, as I will try to do."

"Och…." Agnes shook her head as Morrigan sent her husband a glance of mingled relief and awe. "'Tis unfair of you, master, to cheat your lady in such a callous manner. I *will* try to console her…though it was shabbily done. And you a gentleman raised." She clasped Morrigan's hand, clucking. "Men and their impatience. They should be taught better. Ah, well, my dear, it's done. But you have this wondrous home and the loyalty of Master Eilginn's tenants for as long as you live."

"Aye, aye." Malcolm nodded vigorously.

Agnes's blue eyes glinted. "In truth, mistress, I did know this was coming, for I saw you to Master Ramsay's left hand, a good year ago if it were a day."

Morrigan glanced at Curran. "I…hadn't met him a year ago," she admitted.

"Nonetheless." Agnes gave a careless wave. "I told Eleanor…Eleanor Graeme, who could not be here this night due to the coming of a babe…that our dear master would soon wed. And see? Here you are. The very mirror image of the woman I saw by his side."

"I don't understand…."

"She had a vision," Rachel explained. "She saw you, standing beside the master. Agnes has the Sight."

A commotion outside the drawing room caused Morrigan to look up. It was Seaghan MacAnaugh, laughing at something Fionna said as she invited him in.

Curran left her side for the first time. "You came!" he said, grinning. "What took so long? Scrubbing the fish-smell from your clothes?"

MacAnaugh fluffed the edges of his jacket. "Aye, and we swam in the bay for good measure. Your new wife cannot know the truth about us, can she?"

"No amount of poetry would keep her here; we would hear her scraiching clear back to the Lowlands."

"Aye, that's the truth!" Seaghan's voice blasted across the room. He slapped Curran on the shoulder with one great hand. "Where's the whisky?"

"Come away, you daft fools," Curran said, amidst an uproar of laughter.

He turned, almost stumbling over Morrigan, who had crept up behind him. "Look, Morrigan, Seaghan did come. I was beginning to wonder. And here, at last, is Aodhàn."

Dizziness sent a cascade of multi-colored spots spinning through Morrigan's vision, and filled her ears with a drone that overrode the clink of glasses, laughter, and conversations.

Oh, she'd die of shame if she fainted now.

Yet, through the strange physical sensations, she wanted to call out, to leap into the air.

This…is life, she thought then wondered why.

She knew those eyes, the prominent cheekbones, that fall of dark hair. *Knew* them, somehow. But the beard seemed wrong, as did the length of his hair and the rustic, ill-fitting clothes.

"Allow me to present Aodhàn Mackinnon." Curran clasped her fingers and drew her forward. He turned to the men. "Aodhàn, my wife, Mrs. Ramsay."

There was a brief pause. Aodhàn Mackinnon didn't move, but for a nearly imperceptible narrowing of his eyes.

"Well, it's done." Seaghan's voice was oddly muted. "You've come back to your birthplace, and as the laird's wife. Are you pleased, d'you think, with the way your fortune's turned out, Lady Eilginn?"

Morrigan glanced at Seaghan, blinking. "It feels like home in a way," she replied, embarrassed at the unsteadiness of her voice. "And that's true, isn't it?"

How alive her skin felt, like it might burst into flames.

In that curiously quiet voice, he said, "You have the look of your mam this night." An expression flickered through his eyes that seemed like weariness, but it was early, and the man had just arrived.

His companion stepped away. "Whisky, Seaghan?" With a nod to Curran and then, more formally, to his wife, he propelled the giant across the room.

"Morrigan?" Curran asked.

She fanned herself and drew in a deep breath, feeling the blood pulse inside her head, dark and rich. *Alive.* "It's hot in here," she admitted. "I'm...hot."

"Don't let Aodhàn vex you. He's never bothered to learn the proper form when it comes to ladies. You'll have to take him in hand." Curran's gaze veered towards the two men as they helped themselves to amber whisky. "From the moment Seaghan returned to Glenelg, lugging Aodhàn like a lost puppy, I felt I knew him. I'm younger than he by a good measure, but in some way it feels like I've watched over him forever." He laughed. "I love him like a brother, yet in some ways I hate him, sometimes so much I wish he were dead. Never have figured out why."

I felt I knew him. Aye, something about the man awakened that sense in her as well. In fact, she could swear tonight was not her first meeting with Aodhàn Mackinnon. She would have to ponder it, though it was probably nothing more than he'd traveled south and stayed at the Wren's Egg.

But Curran's other words puzzled her. "How can you love and hate him at the same time?"

"He wastes his life. He acts like he doesn't care about anything. It irritates me. But that's not it. Aodhàn's not what he appears. You know, he's had an education, though he tries to hide it. He speaks Latin and Greek. No matter how rough he acts, I have a feeling he could stroll into any London drawing room and convince the most blue-blooded lord and lady that he's one of them. Yet he remains with Seaghan in a blackhouse hardly better than a bothy, living on boiled potatoes, fish, and gruel. I think he does it deliberately; he knows he doesn't have to, but he chooses it. I often want to knock some sense into him."

Fionna appeared in the doorway then, bobbing a curtsy as she announced, "Dinner is ready."

Chapter 3

Aodhàn forced an index finger under his stiff collar and pulled, hoping to loosen the damned thing.

"God forgive me." Seaghan gazed after Curran and Morrigan as they left the drawing room behind the other guests. "It's like Hannah has stepped from the grave and this last nineteen years never passed. She used to do her hair that way. Even after we were betrothed, I'd stutter like an ignorant green lout around her. Oh aye, she knew what she did to me. She'd smile and wink. I'd gowk and wonder how she kept her eyes open—her lashes were that heavy."

"You handled it well." Aodhàn himself was reeling. He sought a last glimpse of Morrigan's head before she disappeared into the corridor. *The faery who speaks to eagles is an ordinary woman like any other.*

No. Not she, not the lass who faced an eagle without fear.

"I've never seen your Hannah," he continued, "but there's someone else Curran's wife resembles." She'd frowned at him as though he was an apparition. Her teeth had caught her lower lip. As he pictured it, he lost himself in a vivid imagining of being that lip, of feeling the warm bite as she tucked it into her mouth against her tongue.

Seaghan glared at him. "Who?"

"You. I can't pin it down though. Something about her smile."

A blooming rush of scarlet raced up Seaghan's neck and disappeared beneath his beard. He drank off his whisky and coughed. "You insult the poor lass," he said, but it was a weak joke at best. Almost immediately, he added, "There's not a speck of Douglas Lawton in her. Hannah played a deranged game and has left us to untangle the coil. Devil take the scheming of females."

In a calmer voice, he said, "I'll ponder this, especially now you've seen it too, but I don't want gossip to reach her ears."

Aodhàn scowled. "You think I'd carry tales?"

Again Seaghan flushed. "Forgive me. I'm fair muddled. Out of every lass that breathes, in Scotland, in the world, could Curran have married my own lost wean?" He set his glass down. "Why did I let myself believe so easily that Morrigan was his? I should've searched her out, just to be sure. Instead I let Douglas take her without a whimper."

"Watch yourself," Aodhàn said. "She could well be his. You're letting yourself imagine things that might not be true."

Two women came to the doorway, their brows crinkling as they blinked at the empty room. The elder held herself aloofly regal in a fancy black dress and velvet choker. The younger, in subdued grey, fanned her face.

"There's the one who could tell me," Seaghan said. "But she won't. Pure spite, that's what she's made of, the bitch."

"Which one?"

"The one in black. Hannah's sister, Beatrice. Curran told me she's lived with Douglas and Morrigan all these years. Isabel Maclean is the other. Douglas's sister."

As they watched, two more latecomers appeared behind the women. William Watson, the local Presbyterian minister, and Father Drummond, the parish priest.

Old, nagging discomfort swelled inside Aodhàn at the sight of the priest. Curse it; he'd grown weary of this itchy, bewildering urge to put entire continents between him and every Catholic. He used to blame the religion, the popery, the black robes, and incense, but now he wasn't sure. It felt like something deeper. Not knowing what it was made him want to shoot something or start a brawl.

The priest appeared frail tonight, bent more than usual. He leaned heavily on his cane. Yet his eyes perused the room with spry interest. He grinned as he clasped Ibby's hand, then Beatrice's, and asked after their health.

Seaghan inhaled deeply and left Aodhàn's side, plastering on a polite smile. "Ladies," he said, bowing. "They've all gone off to dinner. Reverend Watson? Father Drummond? If you'll come with me, I'll lead the way."

He held out his right arm for Beatrice, his left for Ibby, and led the small procession into the hall. Their voices faded away.

Aodhàn knew there was no other choice. He'd allowed Seaghan to talk him into coming, so he might as well make the best of it. It would be noticed if he never appeared in the dining room. More gossip would erupt. That was the last thing he wanted.

He tried to push out the niggling thought that he'd only see *her* again if he joined the others.

Drinking the last of the whisky, he set down the glass and stalked into the corridor.

Laughter and lively conversation came from somewhere ahead. As he followed the sound, he glanced into the open doorway of another drawing room. What he saw brought him to a halt.

Someone had painted her. The artist had seen what Aodhàn had glimpsed, that day in the clearing, and captured it on canvas.

Illuminated by lamplight, the sea-maiden's unblinking gaze rested on him almost accusingly. He stared back, fighting indecipherable emotions, until he realized he had grown physically aroused, flesh shivering, prick unraveling, elongating, searching in its selfish heedless way for satiation....

"Tha ise bòidheach." The unexpected sound of his own voice returned him from wherever it was that face had taken him. He swiveled away with a growled curse. His heart was racing; he couldn't catch his breath. She was beautiful, but this response was too overwhelming to be mere reaction to beauty. When he tried to walk, he stumbled; as much as he hated giving in to weakness, he had to lean one shoulder against the wall, close his eyes, and inhale deeply until the lightheadedness faded and his legs would once again support him.

Chapter 4

Linen napkins bloomed from wineglasses so fragile Morrigan feared they might shatter if touched. Six candelabra centerpieces scattered warm flickering light over two heavy-laden tables. Flowers exuded an intoxicating scent. Fionna opened the drapes, baring deep-set narrow windows framing on one side Kilgarry's gardens and on the other the silver-black expanse of sparkling water, set before a moonlit suggestion of Skye's craggy mountains.

The seat of honor at the table's head was given to the bride. Curran, observing old custom, made his way around, filling glasses and offering food like any good footman.

Haggis and roast venison followed a variety of soups and broths. Wine and home-brewed ale flowed. Cream-drenched puddings made a rich, unaccustomed dessert.

After the final round of cheeses, Janet presented her masterpiece, a magnificent bride's cake in fancy European tradition, three tiers, complete with glossy white frosting and pretty blossoms. She allowed several moments for dutiful admiration before removing the top two tiers and handing Morrigan a large knife.

The bottom layer was already scored into the proper number of slices; Morrigan only had to complete the cuts and scoop each bit onto a ready plate.

"Careful," Janet warned as she passed them out. "For this be no ordinary cake."

They all waited politely for Morrigan to begin. As she cut her slice, her fork encountered something hard, and her husband, a trickster's gleam in his eyes, ordered her to share what she'd received. She lifted the object on her fork, half covered in frosting, glimpsing the unmistakable shine of gold. Curran took it, polished it on his napkin, and returned it to her with a solemn bow.

It was a heavy gold Luckenbooth pendant, of the type, only finer, that was sold all over Scotland. Two entwined hearts, surrounded by a Celtic knot, with the inscription *Eternal bond of love* carved into the back.

Pretty. But why the devil was it in her cake?

"Mistress found the hearts!" Janet announced, though she seemed more satisfied than surprised. "Now, the rest of you, search out your own treasures."

The wedding guests dismembered their segments with no consideration for all the toil that had gone into the baking. Rachel Urquhart uncovered an ivory wishbone. "To grant me any wish," she cried, holding it in front of her babe, who promptly tried to stuff it in her mouth. Padraig's was a coin. "Gold to bring good fortune. I could do with some of that." Quentin Merriwether's silver bell promised a wedding, which he said he hoped meant his son, as he was already married, and Father Drummond's horseshoe foretold good luck. The somber minister, William Watson, received the blessing of a pewter thimble, but all he said was "Pagan rituals," disdainfully, and set the item aside.

"A harmless custom, in the spirit of the day." Curran's tone brooked no argument.

William shrugged.

To break the short silence, Morrigan asked Seaghan, "What is yours?"

Grinning sheepishly, he displayed a cairngorm ring, dangling at the tip of his pinkie finger, which was as far as the thing would go.

"He'll be next to marry," Janet cried. "Our Seaghan, a bachelor these many years." Her smile turned crafty. "And who might be willing, I wonder?"

Laughter inflamed the group. Fionna blushed and ducked her head.

"And you, sir?" Morrigan asked Aodhàn Mackinnon. "What was in your cake?"

Agnes Campbell pushed his shoulder, crying, "Come away, Aodhàn. Show us your charm."

He lifted a plump, heart-shaped gold locket.

Scarlet suffused Janet's round cheeks. She rushed to him and snatched the trinket, exclaiming, "Lord, I gave you the wrong slice. This was meant for the groom, Aodhàn Mackinnon, no' you. You must exchange with the master." She carried the locket to Curran, wiping it furiously on her apron.

"Never fear, Janet. A mistake easily made, easily mended." Curran gave her the ornament from his cake, a perfect rose carved from jade.

"There you are, Aodhàn," Janet said, carrying it to him. "A rose in green, to bring you true love. Wouldn't that be a miracle!"

The group examined their gifts, laughing with intoxicated abandon.

Morrigan inspected the heart Janet had returned to Curran. It possessed a minute catch that flipped the top open when pressed. Inside was a lock of her hair, bound with red string, and an inscription: *Ruth 1:16*.

"What's this?" she asked.

"Shouldn't you know?" Curran replied, his grin full of mischief. "You're giving it to me."

William Watson's gaze seemed predatory. "You don't know your Bible verses, Lady Eilginn?"

The scorn accompanying *Lady Eilginn* was so subtle Morrigan suspected she was the only one who heard it. She stilled, as frightened as a deer spotting the hunter. They must never discover, these faithful Christians, the things Douglas had said about religion. They couldn't find out she'd never read a word of their Bible.

"Don't torment the poor girl," Father Drummond cried. "D'you expect her to have memorized every chapter and verse?"

Ruairidh clasped Morrigan's hand. "Let me recite it to you," he said. "It's a sweet saying, and perfect for the occasion."

"Please," she said.

"Ruth said, 'Whither thou goest, I will go. And where thou lodgest, I will lodge. Thy people shall be my people, and thy God my God. Where thou diest, will I die, and there will I be buried. The Lord do so to me, and more also, if ought but death part thee and me.'" He squeezed her hand. "That's been a favorite of mine my whole life. It's a bonny way of professing true love, is it not?"

"Aye." She smiled at Curran. *Though a bit overdone with death.*

Curran pushed back his chair and stood. "Time for dancing," he shouted. "It isn't a proper wedding without dancing. And ale. Plenty of ale. Away to the barn!"

With a great cheer, the wedding guests rose, echoing, "Away to the barn!" Gossip and laughter bounced off the walls then into the sky as they all trooped outside.

Morrigan found herself swept on a tide of folk who shook her hand or spoke advice in her ear as she smiled and searched for Curran, who had gone missing. She wondered briefly why they weren't using Kilgarry's beautiful ballroom, but as she entered the brightly lit and decorated barn, smelling of hay and horses, she decided this was much better, especially for the present crowd. When Curran reappeared he'd changed from his formal wedding clothes into casual garb he might wear when riding on his land. He clasped her elbow and bowed elaborately, causing her to laugh and return the gesture with a deep curtsy.

The hired fiddlers began a duet, and were joined by a tin whistle and flute. One man set the beat with a hand-held drum and another played a clàrsach.

The music swept into the traditional shaimit reel and bounced off the high wooden timbers.

Curran seized Morrigan's arm and pulled her to the dancing area. Padraig, Malcolm, and Quinn stayed by the punch barrel, which held a concoction brewed from whisky, sugar, and boiling water. Violet and Tess took turns stirring it as they engaged in flirtations disguised behind insults with the lads from Skye.

For several moments she and Curran danced alone, but with the help of the whisky—she remembered it was called *uisge-beatha*—and soul-stirring music, their guests soon joined in, singing and shouting the words to the tunes as they dipped and whirled.

Morrigan's circumspect sips of punch began to add up to a drink or two. Through the wild, sweaty uproar and disjointed, reverberating sound, the image of *him* returned. The tall thin man with the black hair and bleak eyes.

She heard a faint, familiar voice, but couldn't place it.

Come to me. I've waited so long....

―――――――――――――――――――

Chapter 5

―――――――――――――――――――

AODHÀN ENTERED THE BARN AFTER EVERYONE ELSE. HE HATED DANCING, THOUGH his feet seemed to know the proper movements.

Curran and Morrigan had moved off the dance floor and were chatting with the priest and minister. Mrs. Ramsay appeared to have difficulty catching her breath—no surprise when one considered the daft folderols women bound themselves in. In this setting, there was no hint of red in her hair, only rich, dark brown that made her seem like a different woman altogether from the one he'd watched in the glen.

Father Drummond clasped Morrigan's hands, kissed her cheeks, and accepted the glass of punch Fionna offered him. The bride's aunt, Isabel, led the old man to a chair where he could watch the festivities more comfortably. He enjoyed immense popularity with Protestants and Catholics alike. His opposite was William Watson, the minister, who held himself stiff, cold, and mysterious, his collar of office as formal and unapproachable as armor. Curran spent only a moment with him before pulling his wife into the center for another dance.

Seaghan spied Aodhàn and crossed to his side. "I vow you look like a ghost," he said. "Have you had too much to drink?"

Aodhàn shook his head. "I may suffocate, thanks to this bloody necktie."

"You'll survive," Seaghan said callously. He glanced at Morrigan's aunts. "I'm going to get reacquainted. Beatrice and I were allies of a kind, once. Wish me luck." Setting his shoulders, he stalked towards the woman in black.

Aodhàn backed up until he felt the wall against his spine. Ill at ease,

206

dressed in stiff, borrowed clothing, he knew his scowl would keep most of these folk at a distance—and that was how he wanted it.

Seaghan and Beatrice whirled by. Seaghan sent his comrade a private grimace.

One of the young men from Skye cut in on Morrigan and her husband. The lass changed arms and allowed the lout to waltz her away. For a moment they twirled without incident then Aodhàn saw him draw closer—too close. No doubt he was drunk, and had lost whatever kernel of sense he'd been born with. Lowering his head, the stripling said something, his mouth curving into a leering grin. Mrs. Ramsay acquired the taut mien of a cornered rabbit and covertly tried to create more space between them. Glancing over at the barrel, Aodhàn saw the other Skye lads watching and sniggering.

Curran was dancing with young Rachel Urquhart, her babe tucked securely in the crook of his arm. He'd noticed nothing, no doubt certain in his naïve heart that all was safe in his own barn at his own wedding.

Don't ask me to do this. He is your brother, my lord.

Whose was that voice? Why did it keep invading his damaged brain? Why did it speak the same words, over and over, and only around Curran?

When next the bride waltzed by, Aodhàn tapped, harder than necessary, on the fool's shoulder. "May I?" he asked, and stole her so swiftly, the daftie was left blinking like a sheep.

Her thankful gaze sent confusing pain mingled with thrills of pleasure down his spine. It took every mote of willpower to tamp down the erection that wanted to claim her right now, here, on the polished floor, to feel her respond beneath him. He could hardly bear the thought that there might be a bit of that Skye lout in *him*.

But no. He hadn't grown hard for a woman in years…not since he'd come out of the ocean. *She* caused this craving, a need he'd thought destroyed years ago.

At least that's what he told himself.

Could she be Seaghan's daughter? Where was the nymph from the portrait tonight? Why did she seem so cursedly familiar?

MUCH LIKE THE DAY SHE'D MET CURRAN RAMSAY, MORRIGAN FELT SHE MIGHT LEAP out of her skin. She hoped this time she wouldn't make a fool of herself spouting whimsical nonsense about Greek heroes. Thank goodness, Aodhàn Mackinnon didn't resemble the dream-lover.

Her flesh tingled where his palm pressed against hers. She felt another tingling at her waist, where his other hand rested. The sensation worked its way through her body as though she were a tree, struck and consumed by a thousand-armed lightning bolt. "I doubt I've ever known anyone as tall as you, Aodhàn Mackinnon," she said, for she could think of nothing else, and she must say something. "Dancing with you fair puts a crick in my neck."

"Sorry," he said, shrugging.

His hair was long, falling past his shoulders, slightly threaded with silver. Some was pulled into an untidy knot at the back of his head. Beneath heavy brows, framed in thick black lashes, his eyes were green, like subdued light under forest cover. They seemed guarded: not suspicious in the way of Curran's solicitor, but possessing rather the look of a man who willfully refused to trust anyone.

"Seaghan told me he pulled you out of the ocean."

That odd tingling strengthened, as though his skin was suffused with crackling friction, or maybe it was a conducted charge from the Devil's spear, if this ill-tempered frown was any indication.

"It's a well-worn tale."

She tried a beguiling smile, knowing the power it held with most men and wanting to see if it would affect him. "He says you need a wife, now Curran's married."

One brow lifted, but other than that, there was no reaction.

She glanced about at the dancers. "Everything is so well managed here. There's really nothing for me to do. Perhaps I could help find you one."

At last. A short, rusty grin. "Why would you want to waste your time in such a useless manner?"

"Oh, I don't know." Something about that brief smile made her want to coax another. "My Aunt Ibby's near made a livelihood out of matchmaking. She brought Curran to Stranraer to see what she could start."

Was he grave? She had to be careful not to label him too soon. It couldn't be easy, having an entire life's memories lost in the ocean.

"It appears to have worked," he said.

"I was cross at first."

"As I've been with those who have tried it on me."

"So others have already tried. I see." She paused. "You've no wish to marry, sir?"

"I'm not a sir, a lord, or even a gentleman."

She smiled. "What shall I call you then? Mr. Mackinnon? Aodhàn?" She shook her head. "No, neither of those sounds right. Mackinnon. Aye." The name rolled so readily off her tongue she half-believed she'd said it a thousand times. She tried again, hesitantly, paying attention. "Mackinnon."

A change came over him. His eyes turned glacial. His lips tensed. She felt odd as well, half-drowned in jumbled emotion. "Could we stop?" she asked. "I'm thirsty."

Tess gave Aodhàn whisky and Morrigan sugared ale.

"I've never seen Aunt Ibby laugh so much," Morrigan said. "She's pleased with herself."

Aodhàn said nothing but glanced at the big open doors on the other side of the barn. She sensed his discomfort as though it spawned in her own stomach. Any moment he'd make an excuse and leave.

"It's so hot," she said, using her fan. "I wonder if it's cooler outside?" She strolled towards a smaller door, also open, that led to an enclosure, walled in with a dry-stone fence. Elation bloomed when he followed—she'd been half-sure he wouldn't, and she did want to continue talking to him.

Someone had decorated the space with paper lanterns and bales of hay. Candlelight through colored paper gave off a lacy glow.

The crisp September air revived her. She faced him, meaning to say something about the beauty of the night, but the words trailed off at the sight of a reddish vapor eddying around his upper body. She stared, entranced, all plans for conversation forgotten.

He returned her stare. She realized she'd lifted her hand, was reaching out to this fascinating curiosity, and lowered it, blushing. Retreating a step, she managed a smile. "So, Mackinnon," she said. "You don't want to settle down?"

His brow creased. He swirled the whisky in his glass and leaned against the wall, resting his forearm on the capstones. "There are times I feel I can scarcely breathe I'm so settled. But if you mean married, no. Any female daft enough to consider it would soon be throwing herself into the Sound to get away from me."

"You're satisfied then, with only Seaghan for company?" The mist of color disappeared when he leaned against the wall. Maybe she'd imagined it.

"Aye, well, there is his cooking. If I say it's wanting, I'm being kind."

"So, in order to eat decently, you must wed. Does Glenelg have a good selection of young ladies for you to choose from?"

"There are a few. Mostly in your house, but they've wisely never noticed me, not with two young louts right under their noses."

He must mean Violet and Tess. "Rachel Urquhart's a comely lass. What a sweet child she and Padraig have. I wonder why he waited so long to begin a family."

"He didn't. His first wife, and their son, died."

"Oh." She started to touch her stomach but stopped herself in time. "Did she die in childbirth?"

He shook his head. "A fever killed the child when he was five months old. His mother died soon after, of starvation and madness."

Morrigan stared. "Madness?"

"They were cleared in '53. Padraig wouldn't put them on the emigrant ship."

"I was born in '53."

"You were more fortunate," he said, nodding. "I heard Padraig's wife nursed you as well as her son, for as long as she could."

Morrigan swallowed three times before the lump in her throat would allow her to speak. "Aunt Ibby said my papa fed me goat's milk."

"You've gone pale." He picked up her glass from the wall and handed it to her.

She sipped. "Folk bring it up. The *clearings*, the *troubles*. But nobody will explain. My father refused to speak of it."

He paused. "This isn't the time," he said. "Not on your wedding day."

"It's so horrible?"

A brief shrug, and, "Aye."

She gazed at the forest beyond the outer paddock. "Now that I'm here, where he grew up, I intend to learn all of it."

"Why wouldn't he tell you?"

"He thought women stupid. 'Misbegotten leeches,' he liked to call us. But he has no say now. If I want to discover what happened when I was born, he cannot stop me."

"Well then, be careful...Morrigan. Knowledge could be worse than ignorance."

So he wouldn't call her *mistress*, or *Lady Eilginn*, like everyone else. Her hand released the glass and crept forward, stopping when she felt his sleeve. "Why do you say that?"

"Secrets are kept for a reason."

With disturbing certainty, she knew what it would look like if he smiled. A mesh of lines would crisscross a certain way at the outer edges of his eyes; one line would be longer than the others, beneath his left eye. There was a...a tic there, too, but only when he was angry. She saw herself touching that spot, pressing to soothe it. She was filled with the sensation that this face had long delighted her, just as she thought she knew the words he would say during the act of love.

No one can have you but me. Only me.

"I feel as if I know you," she said then stopped, embarrassed.

Another murmur rose to the surface. *You will marry me, Lilith.*

The tips of her fingers felt his sleeve shift. "Do I? From Stranraer, maybe?" she asked.

"There you are." Seaghan burst upon them, as shocking as a clap of thunder.

"Seaghan." Morrigan drew away, appalled to see how close she'd moved to Aodhàn.

"I see the lout is troubling you. Did I not give you fair warning? He could make the archangel Gabriel leap into the pit of Hell. Say the word, lass. I'll fetch my dirk and slit his throat."

"I don't think so. At least not yet." She glanced into Mackinnon's eyes. They revealed nothing now, but it didn't matter. An instant past she'd seen the same bewildered craving in them that simmered even now through her blood. She knew it as certainly as she knew a babe was forming in her womb.

Grave...merry? Graveness definitely had the upper hand. Merriment had long been stifled. He, like Louis Stevenson, defied easy categorization.

"Is there any more of that punch?" She offered Seaghan her brightest smile. "I'm as parched as an Arab in the Sahara."

Seaghan grinned. "That's why I'm here. They're all asking where you went. They want to toast you, and your lucky husband." He held out his arm. She took it, and together they walked inside, the train on her skirts rustling against the flags, soft as a whisper of warning.

Chapter 6

Morrigan peered into a froth of magically renewing sparkles. "What is it?" she asked. Before Curran could reply, Seaghan lifted his glass.

"Eilginn found a wife!" he shouted. "May he never regret it!"

There was hearty agreement and everyone drank.

Bubbles effervesced on Morrigan's tongue. It was a cold, bewitching taste, like a love potion.

Curran laughed as Morrigan held a second sip in her mouth.

"Champagne," he said. "Careful, it's tricky. It hides how strong it is, and I want you to recall your wedding for years to come."

"To the bonniest lass ever caught by the canniest of men," announced Malcolm Campbell. Fionna and Tess quickly refilled empty glasses.

Even Beatrice offered a toast. *"Tha am pòsadh coltach ri seillean-tha mil ann 's tha gath ann,"* she said, without the hint of a smile.

"Aye," cried Agnes, holding out her glass a bit unsteadily. Liquid sloshed over the rim, wetting her fingers. "True, though I'd wager that marriage to our master will offer few stings and much honey."

"It's an old proverb," Curran told Morrigan. "'Marriage is like a bee, there's honey in it and there's a sting in it.'"

"You've been warned." Morrigan grinned. "Though it's too late to run away now." She noticed that Aodhàn Mackinnon made no toast, nor did he drink to the others. He'd moved away to the big doors and turned his gaze outward, to the darkness and the murmuring forest.

She had no idea how much more time passed before Father Drummond, with plenty of assistance, climbed onto a stool and clapped for silence. "The best gift we can give this couple is to *leave*," he said, smiling rather stupidly.

"I agree," Seaghan said, "though without a doubt it's the finest cèilidh these mountains have ever seen. We'll away, and leave this couple to find their own entertainment."

Morrigan blushed at the sniggers, but Curran lifted his glass and downed the rest of his drink with zeal.

Her head buzzed and her limbs were numb. Hadn't she had only a sip, perhaps two? Yet it was a pleasant sensation. She felt quite happy.

Ibby pulled Morrigan aside through the crush of bellows, winks, and elbows pushed against ribs. "Neither Curran nor I think the traditional bedding is seemly. Not with him being the laird and these his tenants. You'll throw your stocking from the top of the stairs."

"Aye," Morrigan said. *Thank you*, she added to whatever deity had rescued her from that.

Being escorted to the marriage bed by her wedding guests, forced to endure lewd comments and suggestions, would've required more courage than she possessed.

At the staircase landing, Ibby on one side and Agnes on the other, she tossed an old worsted stocking and watched, amazed, as men and women, young and old, fought and clambered to catch it.

From the crush rose a victorious Fionna, waving the article like a battle flag.

"Ah." Agnes nodded sagely. "Fionna set her cap for Seaghan many a year ago. For him to get the ring in the cake and now this...I wager we'll attend another wedding afore yours grows comfortable." She faced Morrigan and gripped her elbow. "I'll take this moment to warn you, mistress. Be on your guard. Selkies have a way about them. Male or female, they can enchant humans...can make them do anything. Beware the selkie."

"What are you on about, Agnes Campbell?" Ibby snorted. "Is there a selkie among us tonight?"

Morrigan couldn't scoff. She remembered Curran and Seaghan telling her the seal story and warning her about Agnes. She stared at the revelers in the foyer, realizing for the first time that they'd all been gossiping about her going outside alone with Aodhàn Mackinnon. She felt her cheeks turn hot.

"Not everyone here is as he seems," was all Agnes would say, with a meaningful frown. She tromped down the stairs. Ibby, shaking her head and sighing, led Morrigan after her.

Happily tipsy, cake trinkets in hand, the guests took their leave. Malcolm Campbell and his wife gushed about the pleasant evening. Morrigan was a sweet and bonny bride, and Curran must treat her with kindness or he'd answer for it. Agnes kissed her cheeks. Malcolm bowed. One by one the others followed.

She giggled as she watched Father Drummond weave and stumble, half-supported by the sober William.

Amid a cloud of whisky fumes, Seaghan kissed Morrigan's cheek.

"You're a lucky man, Curran Ramsay," he said. "You'd best not forget it."

"It's not likely, with all of you to remind me as you seem fair inclined to do."

"And I'll continue, since you're a young man, and no doubt foolish like most young men."

"Thank you for everything," Morrigan said.

Aodhàn Mackinnon shook Curran's hand. He nodded to Morrigan. "Good night."

Not a word of congratulation or wishes for her happiness. Yet she felt closer to him than to any of those who had been so kind.

She and Curran waved until their guests disappeared into the night. The lads from Skye departed in a drunken mass of song, shouting, and shooting.

"I hope none fall overboard," Curran said as he guided Morrigan indoors.

Ruairidh and Quinn were waiting on the staircase landing. "Thank you for allowing me to have a part in your celebration," Ruairidh said, "and for giving me a bed. I'm weary, to be honest."

"Can I get you anything?" Morrigan asked.

"We've servants to tend his needs," Curran said. "Forget your days at the inn, Morrigan. That's over forever." He picked her up and swung her in a circle until, dizzy, she begged him to stop.

When he released her, she stumbled.

"Morrigan?" His smile faded into stricken concern.

"It's the drink." She sent a guilty glance up the stairs. Ruairidh had gone, but Quinn was still there, watching, his gaze as sharp as ever.

Curran wrapped her in a laughing hug. "Not one drop more."

Ibby swished in from the drawing room. "I'm half dead. It's been a long while since I've celebrated so late. Beatrice has already gone up." She kissed her niece. "Dear, sweet Morrigan. This is the happiest day of my life." Waltzing to the staircase, she caught up to Quinn, who bowed and proffered his arm. "Did you have a good time, Mr. Merriwether? Was it worthwhile coming up from London?" Together they climbed the stairs, his answer an indecipherable murmur.

"And you, Curran?" Morrigan asked. "Are you pleased?"

"I have you, don't I? And no more sharing you with your aunts, or anyone, my Morrigan."

Her name had never before seemed enchanting, an endearment in itself. She returned his laughter to hide how it affected her. "Let's go to bed. I'm about to fall asleep standing."

"Fall asleep?" He lifted a brow. "I'm sorry, m'lady?"

"Very well, my demanding husband." She ran a finger down the line of buttons on his vest. "I want to be in bed with you."

He took her hand. "Would you have a drink with me first?"

She nodded and followed him into the drawing room, where Fionna and Tess were busy collecting glasses, blowing out candles and turning down the lamps. "Finish tomorrow," Curran told them. He poured whisky and pulled Morrigan down beside him on the Brussels carpet in front of the subsiding fire.

"Remember I promised to tell you my dreams?" he asked.

"Aye." She lay on her side, propped on one elbow, and turned the Luckenbooth pendant in her hands. "Are you going to tell me now?"

He smiled, though it faded quickly. "One has plagued me for many years. I'm running up from a pit of some kind, holding a dying child. Sometimes that's all there is. Other times I run into an open place, and the child is taken from me. I wake knowing one thing. I have a choice, but I've made the wrong one. Because I don't do what I should, the child suffers, or dies."

"What is this choice?"

"To stay, or leave." Curran plucked at threads in the carpet. He frowned.

"Dreams are night's invention, you know. Mere vapor." She wound her fingers through his and smiled until she got an answering grin, but again it didn't last.

He sipped his whisky and stared into the fire. "I shout until I'm hoarse, but that other me never hears. The dream changes, where I am, where we are, our clothing. Our faces look different. Sometimes she's a child and sometimes a woman. What never changes is that I don't protect her. I don't know exactly what happens, but...it's bad. I feel it."

"What d'you think it means?"

He shrugged. "I had that dream the day we...we were together on the moor. The first time. Remember? When we fell asleep."

She frowned. She'd dreamed of *him* that day, a dream so vivid she could still recall it in detail. He'd looked different, though. Maybe it hadn't been him at all.

She saw the self-recrimination and doubt in his face, and longed to comfort him.

"Curran," she said. "Dreams are not real."

Fine words, considering how often she woke in a terrified sweat, hearing the echoing shouts of *Witch! This is Christian land!* as a man pressed a blade to her throat.

"Over the last few months it's come nearly every night," he said. "I wonder if something...something is trying to tell me I'll abandon you when you need me most."

Before she could think how to reassure him, he rose, refilled his glass, and drank off the contents.

"You'll soon be drunk at this rate," she said.

He glanced at the tumbler in his hand as though seeing it for the first time. "Did I pour another?" He shook his head and set it on the table. "Tired, I suppose." He roughed his hair. "Who painted the portrait?"

"I told you. A local artist."

"What was he to you?" Curran returned and dropped, loose-limbed, beside her.

She shrugged. "A friend of Nicky's."

Loosening his necktie, Curran said, "You blushed when Ruairidh asked about it."

"Well, it's not a proper sort of picture, is it? I look like...." She paused. She'd been about to say *my mother*. "We could store it."

Curran sat up and pulled pins from her hair, staring as it fell over her shoulders, along with silk flowers. "Every man in Stranraer must've been in love with you," he said, and leaned in to kiss her throat.

Everything he did was intoxicating. She wanted him to take off her dress and make love to her on the floor, but she didn't know how to ask. Now, oddly, when they were properly wed, she was shy, tongue-tied, fearful of what he might think of his new wife.

But he seemed to sense her fancy. He slid closer and unpinned the brooch from her sash.

No overprotective aunt would stop them, not now. They were free to share all they had waited so impatiently to experience. Memories returned of the last time, here at Kilgarry, when she had learned what lovemaking could be. She hoped that would happen again.

He turned her. "Lift your hair," he said. When she did, he unfastened the hooks down the back of her dress, one by one, kissing her as he went. The ties on her petticoat were loosened, then the laces on her corset. "Your aunt armored you well," he said, next to her ear. "But it's no match for me."

Her head spun as she faced him, as he freed her of everything but her chemise and the lacy drawers Ibby had made for the occasion. He slipped the chemise off her shoulders and lowered it to her waist. Yet he was still fully dressed.

It was mortifying. She grabbed at the undergarment and sought to cover herself.

"No," he said, stopping her. "Let me savor this."

She could hardly bear it, but she drew in a breath and gave him his way.

The ties on her drawers were stubborn. "Bloody knots," he said, and before she could help him, he'd seized the material and ripped it.

Was he vexed now? His tone cast her out of the languorous spell he'd created. Why were men so angry? She was half convinced that those who appeared friendly were hiding their true natures, simply waiting for a chance to turn violent.

Aodhàn Mackinnon's anger had seemed barely contained the whole night. He was grave, aye, but more. There was pain in his eyes. It was disquietingly similar to what she'd seen more often than not in Douglas Lawton's. Her father's rage had controlled everything for years on end, the need to avoid igniting it, or, if it was ignited, the need to hide until it passed.

His rage had frightened her, but she'd always known his anger was birthed in some kind of awful pain.

Before she'd awakened that day on the moor outside Stranraer, to warm sunlight and the weight of his head on her breast, she'd dreamed of Curran, though he'd looked different, marred with terrible scars, the worst of which was rather like the one he bore now, only much bigger, disfiguring the entire side of his face. *I will have victory,* he'd said. It had been tenderly spoken, yet threatening as well.

She placed the palm of her hand on his cheek and moved her fingers up to the scar by his eye. She felt the slight ridge of it, and a strange vein of heat.

It was gratifying how her touch instantly gentled him and drove away all hint of irritation, reminding her of the ancient princess and unicorn fable. She tucked his hair behind his ear and stroked his face, feeling newly sprouting stubble.

He drew her in, kissing her palm, her cheek, her throat, until she lay pliant and willing against him, worry vanished like shadows in bright sunlight.

She felt his heart pounding, and was deeply moved. It raced for *her.* Because of her. He wanted her. Loved her. She unbuttoned his shirt and ran her hands over his warm skin.

"Mine," he whispered, trailing his fingers over her ribs. Something in his eyes, his voice, suggested he couldn't quite believe it. He gripped her arm where it lay against his neck, and kissed her wrist. "Mine," he said again, almost indecipherably.

She closed her eyes, but that brought a fancy of dropping down an endless tunnel where she would disappear, truly *be* his, no longer herself at all.

Will I never be my own?

Wood collapsed in the fireplace, creating a small eruption of sparks. Then there was no more thought or fear. There was only the swift need to rid him of clothing, followed by the sensation of flesh, the joyous pattern of breathing, of joining and kissing, of seizing his shoulders and crying out, then succumbing to the heat of him like a candle beneath flame.

Gradually, she returned to awareness, to the crackle of wood, the rough-soft texture of the Brussels carpet, the fragrance of her perfume mingled with the sweat and weight of his body.

His voice was an ardent murmur against her ear. "You're going to wake in my bed every morning for the rest of your days."

"Loved…?" she asked.

His arms tightened. "More dearly than life."

"Forever? Will you love me forever?"

"Nothing will ever part us." He lifted his head and met her gaze. "Nothing ahead but years and years of happiness. I adore you, Morrigan." He kissed her on the mouth. "This time, I will make the right choice."

Chapter 7

Shell and pebbles crunched beneath their boots as Aodhàn and Seaghan made their way home. Traces of mist floated above the water and snagged in the branches of the nearby alders.

"Such a night brings back my trysts with Hannah." Seaghan's breath clouded in the moonlight. "We had a secret spot not too far from here."

The call of a late-flying curlew keened above their heads.

They came to the road above the coast. Here and there a star twinkled in the eastern heavens, while overhead, a plump waxing moon—good luck for the wedded couple—offered milky radiance. To the west, ominous blackness outlined a coming storm.

Aodhàn listened to the sea's husky murmur. If he could stop, if he could go into the water, maybe he would finally understand the message it tried to convey. Was he the only man who heard voices in the waves? No one else had ever mentioned such things.

He suspected the sea held his lost memories, in trust, so to speak. The secrets, the key, lay deep beneath the surface; he could retrieve them if he could find a way to hold his breath long enough.

Lightning streaked, briefly silhouetting the sharp-tipped Cuillin of Skye.

The two men slid down the scree as they descended to the bay. Lightning flashed again, and struck something on the island. Thunder cracked and wind rose, roughing the water.

"What of you, mate?" Seaghan asked. "Have you ever spent time in the arms of a lass, deep in the forest with only rabbits and deer to witness?"

"Who knows?"

Seaghan shook his head and sighed. "Maybe Curran's new wife might tempt you to give it a try?"

That got his attention. "Say what you mean."

"Do I need to tell you it was wrong to go off outside with her? You didn't hear the gossip, but I did. No doubt Curran did too. 'Hist,'" he quoted, mocking a woman's voice. "'Look at Aodhàn Mackinnon, who never bothers with the lasses, sneaking out alone with the new mistress of Kilgarry, and it her wedding night.' Oh, aye, they had a right eager time of it, damn them."

"She's the one who wanted to go outside. Should I have left her?"

"It would've been more like you. What went on out there? You both appeared far too serious for a wedding party, and for two who'd never before met."

"She was asking me of the clearings."

Seaghan's breath huffed as he took that in, and he rubbed his forehead. "Forgive me," he said. "I'm drilling you like a *Sasannach* judge. But when I went looking for you, you seemed…." He jerked his chin. "I thought you about to be improper."

"You're wrong."

The sky sparkled as lightning scattered between clouds. Thunder rumbled. Both paused, caught up by the show. Aodhàn turned his face towards the cold wind, breathing in a sweet clean smell of rain.

"This reminds me of the first time I saw you," Seaghan said. "The waves were so high I almost missed you altogether. You've never told me what happened, why you were in the sea, stabbed and half drowned."

"I cannot remember. You know that."

"Aye, well, I thought it might've come back sometime in the last nineteen years, and you neglected to let me know." He stared into the night, his face illuminated by intermittent lightning flashes. "As for me, I recall when Hannah and I were promised. We met in the forest one night. There was nothing different, nothing amiss. She was happy. In the morning she was gone, had run off with Douglas Lawton. By the time I saw her again she was his wife, and about to give birth. I wanted to throttle her."

"She smiles like you."

"Lady Eilginn?"

Aodhàn nodded.

"Do you think she's mine?"

"How can we ever know?"

"Aye, with Douglas and Hannah dead, who is left to know?" After a moment, Seaghan brought out the ring he'd received in the wedding cake. "Me, married," he said. "An ugly grizzled old man, poor as sin and set in his ways." He shook his head. "I'm going inside." He went away across the sand; Aodhàn saw a wee flare as he lit a lamp.

Waves sucked the shoreline. Aodhàn's fingers curled around the jade rose in his pocket.

A rose for true love. Wouldn't that be a miracle!

Lightning created a silvery luster on the water. It reminded him of the amazing portrait of Morrigan emerging from the ocean, clad in a gown of foam. It almost seemed she swam there now, coming in close. Her head rose above the surface, loose hair trailing, black in this light. She beckoned, her fingers long, webbed, betraying what she was. Her eyes reflected the fitful light, big and dark as a newborn seal's.

She lifted her arms above her head and retreated. She was naked, her flesh shining, her lower torso fused into a mermaid's tail. She went under and surfaced again, farther out. When she laughed, the sound of it was as cold as the ocean itself.

"Can you forget me so easily?" Her voice crooned inside his head. "Come to me, Mackinnon. My Mackinnon. Aodhàn. Come and kiss me."

Water foamed around his knees. It was so frigid it burned, but he took another step, and another.

"Aodhàn." She swam close again. Her eyes glinted with moonlight, yet shadows lurked beneath brows, below cheekbones, making her appear skeletal, and there was a dark slash across her throat. He clasped her arms and lifted her, drinking her in. She was cold, wet, and salty.

She buried her hands in his hair, drawing his face closer. Next he knew she'd pulled him over. Water bubbled around his head, the sound of wind and thunder abruptly severed. Nothing now but the voices.

His siren turned and swam away, into the deep, where the hissing water warmed and there was no more need to breathe.

Princess Aridela stared at the foreigner.

"No man will have you but me. Only me."

The lamplight revealed green eyes and hair the color of ripened barley. He was different, exotic, exciting. "I cannot regret your taking what is so sacred on Kaphtor," she said. Her own father, Damasen, had come from the mainland. Her mother had told her many times how much they loved each other.

"Regret? It is moera, our share of fortune and fate, written before the sky was formed. I am meant to love the royal princess of Crete. I alone."

Stabbing pain brought Morrigan out of the dream. She was lying on the floor in the elegant drawing room at Kilgarry, speared by nothing more evil than the horn on the silver unicorn brooch from her sash. She'd rolled over on top of it.

Curran pulled her sleepily against his chest.

"I had an unco dream." She saw him clearly, that blond hero, arrogant, exuding strength and confidence. *No man will have you but me,* he'd said. Her fantasies were insistent, as though fighting to make her understand something. Yet the message escaped her.

She'd dreamed of the warrior many times. Once or twice he'd appeared when she was awake. Who was he? Why did her brain continue to conjure him?

"No wonder," Curran said, "sleeping on the floor. Let's go up." He paused, running his cheek along hers. "I was a lout with you earlier. The way they all ate you up with their eyes tonight…you're too innocent to understand. I'm sorry." He kissed her tenderly. "It was no way to conduct myself. Tell me I didn't hurt you."

She frowned. "Ate me up with their eyes?"

"It doesn't matter. Just know that I love you…Morrigan Anna Lawton Ramsay."

They gathered the discarded clothing and climbed the stairs, holding hands, her sash trailing behind like a long wedding train.

APPREHENSION WORMED TO LIFE WHEN SEAGHAN ROSE AND SAW AODHÀN'S untouched bed.

"Eh, leave him be," he said, and boiled porridge.

But like a splinter, it gave him no peace. A deep, inner alarm clanged. *Find him,* it insisted.

He backtracked towards Kilgarry, trudging south along the coast. Sunrise was coming—the sky shimmered with promise along the hill summits. Three or four diamond-bright stars lingered in the vast expanse of cobalt, and airy clouds released insignificant veils of rain, which dissipated before reaching land. He stared at the green and purple sea awhile, watching it rush and foam. The air snapped at his cheeks.

Where had that foolish lout gone?

He came upon a group of women waulking cloth the old way, with their feet, shrinking and thickening it to make plaids, breeks, and dresses. While they labored, they sang a ribald Gaelic tune, ridiculing their men's prowess in bed. The sight of Seaghan sent them into giggles, and caused a flock of foraging sparrows to rise, making an angry protest.

He removed his glengarry. "Have any of you seen Aodhàn Mackinnon?"

"Missing again, is he?" Rachel Urquhart plucked her whimpering babe from a blanket and trilled soothing sounds.

"Well, maybe."

"Let him be," advised Agnes Campbell. "No doubt he's with the seal-folk. He'll not thank you for meddling."

"Oh, Agnes." Seaghan sent a pleading glance heavenward. "It's daft how you believe those tales. You're a grown woman."

"And you'll be a modern man of the world then, Seaghan MacAnaugh? You don't believe in selkies, who come on land in human form, or the *daoine sìth*, or *bean-nighe*, who foretell our deaths?" She made a furtive gesture with one hand against her breast. "Go on and dismiss that he was found in the sea, that he's always drawn to water, and that he has no memories. Dismiss all of that as coincidence. I will no' be so foolish."

"Agnes, for Christ's sake." Seaghan shook his head.

One of the other women snapped, "Tell us, then, Seaghan. Where is it he vanishes to?"

"I'll admit I don't know," he said with a shrug. "But that doesna make him a selkie now, does it?" Affixing his glengarry on his head, he waved and climbed down the hillside, hearing their voices rise again in song behind him.

Disturbing memories revived, of Aodhàn's sprawled body, cold and colorless on the deck of the *Bristol*. Seaghan had been surprised to feel a heartbeat. A gash across the man's chest oozed blood. Everyone thought it a knife wound.

He might live, Seaghan remembered thinking with pessimism.

Dismiss all that as coincidence. I will no' be so foolish.

Many days passed before Aodhàn regained enough strength to walk. Seaghan well minded his comrade in those days—more a bent, greenish-pale weed than a man, dark circles etched deep beneath his eyes. Silent and brooding, he stared most of the time out to sea. Only the lack of wrinkles or grey hair suggested he was young. More than once Seaghan wondered if Aodhàn hadn't meant to drown himself. He never spoke a word of gratitude, nor did his eyes ever lose their unrelenting torment.

What the devil happened to you? Seaghan had asked.

Aodhàn had frowned a long time as though concentrating, but finally admitted his memory was gone, stolen by the same ocean that even now lapped across Seaghan's boots.

He scuffed a divot in the sand and watched it fill with brown water. The rising sun spilled golden light across the hills.

Where are you, damn it? The glare off the surface of the sea forced him to squint.

He shaded his eyes with one hand. Nothing seemed out of the ordinary in this far-reaching expanse of salt water, rocks, shingle, and the occasional dead fish.

Yet...what was that? He glimpsed a huddled black speck, far along the strand, and sprinted towards it.

Aodhàn knelt so close to the water it washed over his legs. He didn't look up as Seaghan scrambled over a pile of soggy driftwood to get to him.

"Aodhàn. Aodhàn." Seaghan gripped his friend's cold, damp shoulder, but there was no response. He might as well be a thousand leagues away, leaving only the shell of his body behind.

Water ran over the man's cheeks. Seaghan couldn't tell if his face was wet from sea spray or if he'd been weeping. The suit he'd worn to the wedding cèilidh was soaked through.

Yet there was fire in his eyes. Naked emotion. Aodhàn had always looked older than his age, but now, in some unfathomable way, he appeared younger.

"What's happened?" Seaghan knelt, almost afraid to know, and watched a muscle flinch in his friend's jaw.

"My wife. She's alive."

"Christ save us all. You have a wife?"

Aodhàn rubbed his forehead. A necklace was clutched in his hand, a chain holding a round silver charm upon which was carved two crescents on either side of a dark blue stone. The first time Seaghan had seen it was the day he'd pulled Aodhàn from the ocean. It had been knotted around his forearm. Many times they'd examined it, wondering where it came from, what it meant.

"Where is she?" Seaghan asked. "Have you seen her?"

"Aye," Aodhàn said faintly.

Seaghan scanned the coastline. He saw no lass, nothing but shingle, sand, and rising hills.

Aodhàn dug into the wet sand and brought up a fistful, squeezing it between his fingers. "Every life is new for her. She doesn't remember." He gave a weak, stifled laugh then spoke something utterly indecipherable. "*Zoi mou…agapi mou. T'aste'ri mou.*"

"Bloody hell. What's that gibberish?" Seaghan tightened his grip on Aodhàn's shoulder and gave him a rough shake. "Wake up, lad!"

Aodhàn took a deep breath. "She called me 'Mackinnon' on Barra. And again last night." He turned towards Seaghan; his lips were blue. "She almost remembers. She wants to remember. But if she does…."

Practicality took over. "We must get you warm." Seaghan half-dragged Aodhàn from the water to dry sand, feeling a strange swooping sense of having done all this before. "Have you regained your memory?"

Aodhàn continued to gaze out at the water a moment more, then he actually seemed to see Seaghan, perhaps for the first time. His eyes shuttered. "Don't…don't ask me. I cannot speak of it."

No sense arguing with the damned stubborn devil now. It would keep. "Stay here. I'll just be a moment." Seaghan stumbled over his earlier footprints to fetch a blanket from the waulking women.

Agnes returned with him. "Lord have mercy, he's soaked clear through and half frozen!" She wrapped the plaid around Aodhàn, making the clucking sounds she was so fond of. "And you want us to believe there's no difference between him and other men? The differences are plain enough to those not afraid to see." Drawing the material close, she pushed wet hair off his face then pressed her hand to his cheek.

"Saint Brigit preserve and keep us from harm!" She recoiled, making the sign of the cross. Agnes had no trouble mixing pagan superstitions with Christian devotion, and would pray to anything she thought might aid her.

Seaghan's nerves, already raw, felt as though they were on the verge of explosion. "What ails you, woman?"

"Weans, crying for their mother. Brothers, split into mortal enemies. Guilt, murder, betrayal. Again and again and again."

The alarm on her face smothered Seaghan's desire to scoff. He contemplated his mysterious friend, who seemed to have retreated into a private inner world.

Gooseflesh washed uneasily across his arms.

Chapter 8

Judging by the bright slant of sunlight through deep-set windows, morning had come and gone.

Morrigan observed her sleeping husband, with his tousled hair and the countenance of an angel.

Did she love him? Would she have led him to the moor shieling and forced the issue, if he'd been an ordinary, ungolden man?

Beauty was a strange, powerful snare.

She thought of Padraig Urquhart's bent, grizzled features. He with his long ears, thinned lips, and yellowed teeth. Did those reddened, chapped hands, marred by brown spots, freely explore Rachel's tender youth? Their baby proved it.

She touched Curran's earlobe gently, so not to wake him, and tried to picture what he would look like when he was old. And what of her? Grey hair, wrinkles softening her skin, pain in her joints maybe. What would happen to this fiery passion then? If they'd seduced and wed on a foundation of beauty, then what would the passage of years do to it?

Two and a half months since Beatrice had declared Morrigan was pregnant. On no more evidence than that she lay in this bed, married. But what if Beatrice was wrong, and the nausea, nearly vanished now, had really been some illness? What if there was another reason she'd stopped having monthly courses?

Smooth bedclothes slid like cool water over her skin. How different from the scratchy sheets she'd grown up with. Everything was different. For the first time in her life she didn't have to rise at dawn and begin an endless circle, repeating the same tedious chores as the day before. By God, she and Curran could lie in bed all day if they wished—lie here touching, enjoying their flyaway, *beautiful* youth.

Last night, Curran had shown a different side. When he'd torn the ribbons at her waist, she had seen something in his eyes, and part of her had been afraid. But the wild, inner Morrigan had roused to meet him. Like two warriors, their lovemaking had been ferocious, breathless, inflamed.

Immersed in consummation, she'd briefly forgotten guilt, fear, longing, and nightmares. There had been no thoughts at all. For her, that was true beauty.

Twining her legs around his, she woke him with a kiss to his bare shoulder. He yawned, smiled, and ran a hand through his hair. *"Madainn mhath,"* he said. *"Ciamar a tha thu, a ghràidh?"*

He pulled her against him and nuzzled her throat. Before she could ask what the Gaelic words meant, a timid knock from the sitting room interrupted them.

"Come in," Curran called, drawing blankets over them.

Violet blushed as she entered. "Good day, master, mistress." She bobbed a curtsy and knelt to light the fire.

"Good morning, Violet." Morrigan suppressed the urge to jump up and help.

"Bring a tub, please, Violet." Curran kissed Morrigan's earlobe. "I'll wash your back, hmmm?"

"What time is it?" Morrigan asked, pushing at him.

"Just after midday." Violet kept her gaze averted. "Father Drummond has come to say good morning. My mother put him in the dining room with everyone else. I'll be pleased to help you dress, mistress, whenever you're ready. Bell pull's there by the window seat."

"Thank you." Lounging while a servant tended her needs. She wasn't sure if she liked it or not. It felt…odd.

After their bath, Morrigan examined the contents on the dressing table while Curran combed tangles from her hair. A heavy silver brush, a hand mirror, and a framed daguerreotype of Curran's mother lay neatly on the lace runner. Morrigan studied the delicate, expressionless face. The son had obviously inherited his mother's hair. It was bright, drawn up in a loose, heavy bun. She couldn't help but wonder what this woman would think of her new daughter-in-law.

Curran kissed the nape of her neck. "My bonny, bonny Morrigan," he said, gripping her shoulders. "Mine at last."

An unexpected and unwelcome flash of annoyance surprised her. She met his gaze in the looking-glass, stifling a rude urge to ask him if he knew the difference between her and one of his greyhounds. But he had no desire to offend. Just the opposite.

He kissed her again. "I'd hoped to show you the estate," he said. "It's best done on horseback, but—"

"I can ride."

"No, Morrigan."

She faced him. "I want to do things I'm used to doing. I've been tied up in corsets and slippers and fancy dresses, afraid of getting them dirty, afraid of saying something wrong, doing everything wrong. It sounds bonny…fresh air, seeing your land, being on a horse. Don't you have a docile mare? Please." The desire strengthened beyond all sense, as though she was soliciting a reprieve from a long prison sentence.

His regard was frowning and serious at first, then his mouth turned up on one side in a clearly sly manner. "Will you promise to keep the nag to a walk, and tell me at once if anything seems amiss?"

"I promise."

"My mother was convinced months of idle confinement worsened the pain of labor. She rode every day when she carried me, until it became uncomfortable. Then she walked every day, no matter the weather, and danced. My father told me she astounded the midwife with how easily she managed the birth. She hated how expectant women are hidden away like they've done something shameful."

"I've worked hard my whole life, Curran. I can't suddenly become a wee fragile useless thing."

"Call your maid, then," he said, "and we'll do this. I'll go down and soothe our ignored guests." He laughed. "I wonder what the minister is thinking?"

"And Beatrice." Proper Beatrice, who never allowed the slightest indecent talk or action. What must everyone think? Half the day gone, and the master and mistress still locked in their bedroom. It was no excuse that they were newlyweds, not in Scotland. Yet, strangely pleased at her small victory, she couldn't worry too much.

He yanked the bell rope as he left. Violet soon arrived with a tray of steaming dishes, a china bowl containing salted porridge, which Morrigan consumed ravenously, along with black pudding, bacon, and a pot of tea.

The maid's shyness disappeared with the master gone. "You've a fine appetite," she said. "Most ladies do seem like milksops to me. They pick at food and half the time are swooning. I do wonder if they don't lace their corsets tighter than they should."

I'm no lady, Morrigan started to say before she caught herself. "Aye, I've wondered the same thing," she said instead. "Do you know if my riding habit was brought from my aunt's? Curran wants to show me the estate."

Giggling inexplicably, Violet led her into her dressing room and flung open the doors on the wardrobe.

They were nearly overwhelmed by an explosion of color and fabric.

Morning dresses, evening gowns, tea gowns, riding habits; new clothing crowded one upon the next, and a nearby cupboard held fancy corsets and lacy underthings of every type.

Morrigan stared. "These are for me?"

"Master Curran did have it all made," Violet said, "with your aunt's help." She drew out a slim-cut forest green habit and held it up to Morrigan's body.

"This'll look grand on you, mistress. Let me help you put it on."

"No," Morrigan said regretfully. "I promised Aunt Ibby I'd go back into mourning, now the wedding's done. I don't suppose there's a black one?"

"Oh aye," Violet said. "And it's bonny as well, never fear." She pulled another swath of material out and held it up. Fine and fashionable it was, and had a matching black top hat with streamers. Morrigan thought herself rather elegant as she perused the image in the fancy Cheval glass; the female reflected back at her appeared in every respect a decent, purebred lady. She nearly laughed.

As Violet pinned the hat, the sitting room doors burst open and Curran entered, surrounded by a mad scramble of dogs, who loped and sniffed, wagged their tails, and begged for attention before being distracted by some interesting smell. Antiope leaped on Morrigan's skirts, was shooed off, and immediately jumped again.

Regal and calm, a towering deerhound watched the rest with an expression of aloof superiority.

"I hope you don't object," Curran said. "My dogs usually have the run of the house."

"Aye? And what other surprises do you intend to spring on me?"

"Wait and see." He cocked his brow and nodded. "Come away, layabed. Everyone's waiting to see how the bride has fared. They're beginning to wonder if I didn't kill you and bury your body in the garden."

"The dresses, this habit. Thank you, Curran. I never expected—"

"We must keep you happy," he replied lightly, "so you won't entertain an urge to flee."

She laughed. "Only a daftie would want to leave you."

Their guests were enjoying tea and conversation as they awaited her attendance. Ibby rose and came round the table, giving her niece a kiss before her regard turned suspicious. "Why are you wearing a habit?"

Morrigan tried to ignore the various expressions of amused indulgence, and, in Beatrice's case, disapproval. "Curran's taking me to see his land," she said. "Would any of you care to join us? Mr. Merriwether?" The bloody man was impossible to read. She couldn't tell if he was amused, annoyed, disgusted, or pleased.

"No thank you, Mrs. Ramsay," he said, setting down his cup. "Regretfully, I must set off for London."

"Nor me," Ibby said. "The two of you deserve some sort of honeymoon, so I've persuaded Beatrice to come to Mallaig and stay with me awhile."

"Alas." Ruairidh held a napkin to his lips and spoke around a mouthful of pudding. "I, too, must go. Tomorrow is Sunday, and my sermon needs attention."

"I'd love to ride with you, child," Father Drummond said. "It'll give me a chance to get to know you better."

Curran's dogs joined in the goodbyes, making the group on the pebbled drive quite noisome. Antiope bedeviled the carriage-horses' fetlocks until Curran caught sight of it. He shouted and threw a well-aimed rock, thunking her hard on the shoulder.

She yipped and crept away, head lowered, tail between her legs. "You frightened her," Morrigan said. "Call her back."

"You'd be less forgiving if she ever caused your mount to throw you," he said.

"He's right, lass," Hugh Drummond agreed. "That's a dangerous habit and must be broken."

Ibby pulled her away from the others. "Expectant women do *not* ride," she said quietly. "Didn't you hear what Curran said just now?"

"Oh, Auntie, I've never lost my seat on a horse." Morrigan kept the impatience from her voice with effort. "Curran will be there. We'll keep to a safe, boring amble."

"No. I forbid it. We must make an excuse."

Anger crept down Morrigan's spine. Her hands clamped and she took a deep breath. "I am going for a ride," she said.

"Morrigan—"

"I'm riding." Morrigan walked away, knowing her aunt wouldn't force the issue in the hearing of others.

She was right. Ibby followed and kissed her. "Goodbye, isoke," she said, dabbing at her eyes with a handkerchief. "I'm so happy. My faith in matchmaking is renewed."

"So is mine." Curran bent and kissed her cheek, which made her flush with pleasure.

"The both of you are too stubborn to bear, but I suppose that's why you fit each other so well. Will you watch over my niece, sir?"

"With my life."

"Then I'll have no fears." She allowed Curran to help her into the carriage.

"I'll return in a fortnight," Beatrice said.

"Don't go unless you want to," Morrigan said as she kissed her aunt.

"Had you traveled to the Continent, I could've put the household to rights in your absence."

"Is there something wrong with it?"

"They're on their best behavior. Once you're complacent, they'll no doubt grow shiftless and laggard."

"Thank God you'll be here to watch them." A devilish glint lit Curran's eyes.

"You don't know the servant class as I do, Curran Ramsay," Beatrice said coldly.

Ruairidh, sitting up front with Kyle, broke in. "I hope I see you again."

"Please, our home is yours," Curran said. "Thank you for all you've done." He shook hands with Ruairidh, then with Quinn.

"Bring Lady Eilginn to London," Quinn said as Kyle flicked the reins. "We'll take her to the opera and show her the sights."

The carriage wheels crunched across the drive. Ibby waved her handkerchief until they passed through the iron gates and disappeared into the forest.

"Shall we have that ride?" Morrigan asked.

"If you think Logan can saddle the horses," Curran said. "If he isn't too laggard—?"

"Don't take me to task over what Beatrice says!"

Father Drummond laughed. "The two of you are at the beginning of a long, bonny adventure. And so it comes full circle."

"What do you mean, Father?"

"Why, that West Highland blood flows in your veins, lass, and you've come home at last where you belong. This is where you were born. I believe it called to you these many years, though you may not have known it for what it was." He paused. "The Highlands never relinquish a soul."

The barn, stables, and carriage house were situated beyond a gate at the far end of a graveled path. Rowan branches, heavy with scarlet berries, met overhead, tangling into a ceiling, and Scots pine sent the breeze sighing mournfully.

As they approached the cobbled courtyard, Logan led a chestnut stallion from the stable. The beast tossed his wheat-colored mane and lifted his head, nostrils dilating as he sniffed the air.

"Augustus," Morrigan said fondly, having become acquainted with him during Curran's time in Mallaig.

"How has his leg healed?" Father Drummond asked.

"It's fine now," Curran said. "We tried a new tincture. It reeks, but it cured the infection."

Morrigan sighed. "I wonder how Leo fares, and Widdie, and Cloud, and the foal? I wonder if Sir MacAndrew is caring for them properly?"

"We'll ride over to see them one day. Would you like that? In the meantime, I hope you can get some use out of this." He nodded to Logan, who disappeared into the stables, leaving Curran to hold Augustus's reins.

Logan soon reappeared, leading a slender mare. Her russet coat, black mane and tail almost shimmered in the variegated sunlight. A long white star swooped between dark, intelligent eyes.

"Do you like her?" Curran asked.

"Well, will you look at this?" Father Drummond cried.

Morrigan touched the velvety nose, but the mare shied, snorting. Undaunted, Morrigan brought out a carrot she'd slipped into her pocket earlier.

The mare sniffed it, nickered as if to say *thank you*, and took it in her teeth.

"Her name is *Stoirmeil*. That means Stormy in the Gaelic, though she's Arab," Curran said. "I know better than to give you a gentle nag. But let's not share that bit of information with your aunt."

"Are you stormy?" she asked. Stoirmeil obligingly nodded.

Morrigan kissed Curran's cheek. "I love her, Curran. You're spoiling me."

"I've only begun," he replied. "I'd do anything to cause you to smile that way."

Blushing, she turned to the priest. "Can you ride, Father? We could take the gig if you'd be more comfortable." From beneath her lashes she gave the mare a longing glance.

"No, lass," he said. "I'll curl up and die when I can no longer ride."

Logan bent over, cupping Morrigan's boot in his hands, and swung her onto the sidesaddle, then returned to the barn for two more horses, one for Father Drummond and one for himself.

The four left the courtyard, following an overgrown track, and soon had climbed onto the road leading towards Glenelg.

Curran and the priest chatted as they rode, about the state of the wool market, and how much of the Highland forests were being cut away to suit English hunters.

Hugh Drummond sat his horse well for an old man who suffered joint pain. Though Morrigan knew little of religion, she recognized an air of authority mixed with a generous helping of kindness. She had always pictured clergy berating from behind high, forbidding pulpits. Never would she have imagined she might see one in a loose-fitting sark, breeks, and old leather boots, looking much like an aging crofter. Douglas had ridiculed Catholics, the same as Presbyterians. There had been no difference save for the particular disgust he'd voiced for Catholic popery.

They crossed the bridge over a glistening river, and followed its course into Gleann Beag. Hills rose on either side of the glen, which wound away to the east like a discarded emerald hair ribbon. The riding party passed the waterfall, and the ancient ruin, Dùn Teilbh, then further on its companions, Dùn Trodan and Caisteal Chonil.

"I wonder who gave these their names?" Morrigan asked.

"I'm not sure anyone knows," Hugh said, "but I suspect the Picts."

The track decomposed into deep, grassy ruts. The landscape opened up as they achieved the summit of a hill; mountains piled before them, purple with heather. Crisp and cool, the breeze was redolent with pinesap and clover.

Glenelg and the sparkling Sound lay behind them, and before them towered the Five Sisters, lined up so majestically it nearly stole Morrigan's ability to breathe. To the south, Beinn Sgritheall was somehow comforting in its implacability, as though assuring her; *here I am, still looking over you.*

Curran led them back towards the Sound along a narrow track hemmed in by brush and forest. He showed no hesitation—clearly he'd grown up here, and knew each hill and glen, all the lochs and everything in between. In time they came to the main village road, where they passed a blacksmith's, a general store, and a mill. Beyond, squatting in the shadow of a hill, were the massive ruined barracks, built for soldiers in the last century. They started southwards, the bay on their right, and passed Glenelg's Kirk, where William Watson delivered his sermons.

But she was given only a moment to fret about the minister's obvious dislike.

"Father Drummond is a fine vet," Curran told her. "A man of many talents."

"Are you, Father?"

"We're jacks-of-all-trades, these days." Hugh gave a shrug. "So many of the folk have gone. Those who remain must muck in together or we'd not last a year. Your husband helps most, of course. He compares in certain ways to the old clan chieftains, those who carried the responsibility of their brethren from birth to death, and in return enjoyed vast power. Let's say a clan member's wife died. If he wanted to remarry, he'd have to address himself to his chief for permission, and the chief himself picked the woman. Aye. No doubt many drams of whisky were needed to dull the bitterness of that. Clan members had no choice in time of war, either. Their chief held the power of life and death over his tenants, from infant to old man."

"But Curran, he's not like that, is he?"

"Oh, no, my dear. Those days are long gone with Culloden. But Curran, and his father before him, earned the respect and loyalty of the few who were left here, on their own merit, not because of their name or birth. It's why they call him *Eilginn.* He is their chosen honorary laird, over every speck of land between Àrnasdal to Loch Alsh, and east to Loch Duich. There's nothing they wouldn't sacrifice for him, and for you. They'd die for you if the need arose."

"I hope it never comes to that."

"It's true, mistress," Logan said.

Hearing it from him moved her deeply.

"You'll see, once you've lived here awhile." Hugh nodded. "These people, and the land, are not what you knew in the Low Country. Modern days have not yet come to Glenelg. Here folk are knitted to each other like wool in a scarf. They've had to be, for many reasons. Loyalty has meaning. Yet, I avow Glenelg is a special case."

"How so?"

Hugh glanced after Curran, who had spurred his horse forward to speak to a middle-aged woman digging in a potato patch. The woman straightened, smiling, and rested her hand on the laird's knee. The others pulled their mounts up to wait for him.

"Most wealthy Lowlanders came here for one reason," Hugh said. "Sheep. They saw the chance for profit and seized it. Much to their shame, many Highland lairds collaborated with them. In the old days that would never have happened, but poverty, and loss after loss changes things. Lairds had grown as poor as their crofters. After Culloden, everyone suffered persecution. Loyalty and duty died on that field, brought by wholesale slaughter and the rape of women and children. No surprise that history calls Cumberland 'The Butcher.'"

She had learned of Cumberland at school, but said nothing.

He paused, exhaling. "Many of our lairds aped England's aristocracy, and for that, they required gold. These crofts brought hardly a pittance, and when the potatoes rotted, they cost. Brocade and lace remained out of reach, until the landowners formed a plan." A frown tightened the priest's lips. "Randall Benedict sold Thomas Ramsay this estate on which to graze the Cheviot, and swore he'd already cleared the villages and people who lived here. Thomas purchased the land sight unseen, wanting a part in the profits. But when he brought his wife and son to Kilgarry that winter of 1854, he found rather more than he'd expected."

"Us," Logan said. "Those who refused to board Randall Benedict's bloody ship. We'd survived two months in the forest. He'd burned anything we could use for shelter."

Morrigan shrank from the terrible expression of hatred and bitterness on Logan's handsome face.

"Logan was only eight," Hugh told her. "Forced into manhood before his time."

The young groom's lip curled. He spat on the ground.

"I wasn't much help," Hugh said. "Of course I wrote to Randall Benedict in Edinburgh, again and again, but he never replied. We received a pittance now and then from the Parochial Board, but the Destitution Board refused our requests since the tenants were offered paid passage to Nova Scotia. Many days those folk survived on rotted potatoes and dulse they scraped from the rocks. Sometimes they tried to dig tunnels in the earth, but the ground was frozen. In the beginning, they sought shelter in the old barracks, but when Randall Benedict heard of it, he sent his men to roust them out, and then kept it guarded. They ended up in the Pictish ruins in Gleann Beag."

He blinked the tears from his eyes unashamedly. "Forgive me, lass, for dredging up this awful history the day after your wedding. I don't know why I've done so."

"No." She worked to keep her voice neutral as thunder reverberated from a fast-approaching cloudbank. "I want to know. My kin were part of what you're telling me?"

"Aye." His white brows rose. "Your da, both your aunts, your dear mam, your grandmam—"

"My father wouldn't allow anyone to speak of it. I know almost nothing," Morrigan said earnestly.

Hugh paused. She saw him absorbing this information. Out of respect for Douglas, he'd no doubt find a way to dodge the subject, like everyone always did.

But Logan walked his mount closer to her. In a clipped voice, he said, "When Thomas Ramsay came to Kilgarry, mistress, he went out exploring and found the last of us. Seventeen were left to die that day in November when we were cleared. Ten lived to tell the tale, partly due to your father. He labored with the Devil's own stubbornness to keep us alive. I was afraid of him before we were cleared. But by the time Thomas Ramsay saved us, in February, I knew him better. Your da gave me his boots so my feet wouldn't freeze."

Morrigan couldn't meet the groom's intense, long-lashed gaze. The old, suffocating obstruction lodged in her throat. Harsh, glittering light off the waves in Glenelg Bay made her head throb and created strange coronas. Humming filled her ears. For the first time in a long while, she feared she might swoon.

"Your mam gave birth on the ground, in the forest," Logan was saying. "The midwife had boarded the emigrant ship, so all she had for help were your aunts and your grandmam. There was a storm that day, and for many days after."

She'd always known her mother died giving birth to her. But no one had told her that Hannah hadn't had a midwife, or a bed to lie in, or a roof, and no walls but what the trees offered. Some part of her may have known, but with the help of an incomplete story, she'd managed to lie to herself all these years, to paint a less gruesome picture.

A chasm dropped away before her. She felt herself tumbling, her head no longer attached to her body.

Curran returned. "Morrigan, come and meet Eleanor—"

"Wait, Curran." Hugh held up his hand.

Their voices echoed. The chasm yawned. The ground tilted.

As clearly as if it were happening before her eyes, she saw great white walls and crimson colonnades buckling, choking pillars of dust ascending, along with terrified screams as once-solid earth roiled into a tidal wave and the sky exploded in fire and ash.

Stoirmeil reared, caught the bit in her teeth, and vaulted forward. Lost in the vision, unprepared for her horse's abrupt leap, Morrigan tipped and fell.

The back of her head collided with the ground. Constellations of stars exploded, followed by thick blackness; pain sheared through her ankle, culminating in a blinding fire that was centered in her womb.

The babe.

She heard a cry, and the shout of a man, before everything faded into nothing.

Chapter 9

MORRIGAN LAY WITHOUT MOVING, KEEPING HER EYES CLOSED. HER ANKLE AND head throbbed in unison. She wasn't sure what had awakened her, but thought it might have been Curran's voice, gravely with unfamiliar anger.

She had fallen off the horse. After being so curt with Aunt Ibby, after saying *I've never lost my seat,* she had, and when it could do the most harm.

A female spoke. "Calm yourself, Master Curran. Panic will do no good. Let me see what's what."

"Curse that dog." Aye, Curran definitely sounded angry. Morrigan sighed and opened her eyes. She was in a dim, echoing, rather chilly place, lying on something hard. A strange woman was folding her skirts up above her knees, exposing her. With the skirts out of the way, she lifted Morrigan's legs at the knees.

Morrigan jerked upright, crying out, but as she met the woman's gaze, she careened into a sense of recognition so potent that her agitation was completely quelled.

A greenish shimmer surrounded the woman's face. She frowned at Morrigan, then, "Welcome," she said, and smiled, her expression transforming to genuine pleasure.

"Morrigan." Curran came forward and clasped her hand, breaking the spell.

"What is she doing?"

"Don't worry." He kissed her forehead. "This is Eleanor Graeme, the midwife."

"May I examine you, mistress?" the woman asked.

Morrigan received the reassurance of Curran's nod. "Aye."

"Lie down, please."

Morrigan was glad to obey, as sitting up so quickly had awakened an intense wash of dizziness. The midwife bent to her task, leaving Morrigan to clench her teeth and grip Curran's hand. "When you fell," she said soothingly, "you hit your head and one of the horse's hooves struck your ankle. I fear it's swollen, but it isn't broken." She paused before adding, reluctantly, "And you're bleeding a bit from your womb."

"Bleeding?" Morrigan tried again to rise but Curran prevented it. *Oh, Aunt Ibby. You were right. I'm losing my baby.*

Eleanor withdrew her hand and washed in a basin held by Rachel Urquhart. "Aye," she said, "but I feel no contractions, and it's not uncommon to have a bit of bleeding the first few months. You mustn't sit up though. You've had a shock. D'you feel any cramping?"

"No." Morrigan placed her hands on her stomach, concentrating. "I'm just dizzy." She looked up at Curran. "What happened?"

"It's my fault." Rage dug grooves alongside his mouth. "The damned dog bit Stoirmeil on the leg. That's why she bolted."

"Antiope did it?"

"Father Drummond said I couldn't shoot her without your permission."

"No!" She bolted upright again. The dizziness swirled, coming dangerously close to vertigo.

"I see he was right."

"Promise me, Curran. She didn't know."

"Lie back Morrigan, please, darling."

She did, reluctantly, and regarded the midwife as she dried her hands. "Do I…know you?"

Eleanor nodded. "You seem familiar to me, as well. I grew up in Edinburgh, mistress, lived my whole life there until your husband convinced me to come here. Could it have been in the city?"

"I've never been to Edinburgh," Morrigan said.

Rachel Urquhart dipped another cloth in the water and laid it gently over Morrigan's injured ankle. Agnes Campbell peered over Eleanor's shoulder, clucking her sympathy. Morrigan had a feeling Agnes would always be nearby when anything out of the ordinary happened.

She closed her eyes, afraid she was going to vomit.

"Master Curran," Eleanor said, "I want you to take your wife home in a wagon. She's to have bed rest, without relations, if you'll excuse my bluntness, and no more riding until after the child is born. None at all, for any reason. It shouldn't have happened to begin with, since, as you say, she's near three months gone." She paused, still frowning. "I think you'd best put off the kirking."

"Oh, that's a shame," Agnes cried.

"The kir-kirking?" Opening her eyes, Morrigan regarded Curran fearfully. *What now?*

He waved his hand in dismissal. "A church custom. It's supposed to bring happiness and good luck to the newlyweds."

"It's more than that, Master Ramsay," Agnes said sternly. "Dire consequences follow those who have no kirking to bless the marriage in the eyes of the parish."

"Not another bad omen," Morrigan said. "We have to go."

Curran tightened his grip on her hand. "I won't risk it. We'll put it off a week. It's not important."

"No. Promise me, Curran, promise you'll take me to this kirking, for the wean's sake…for the wean."

He shook his head stubbornly. She tried to construct a better argument, but Eleanor interrupted.

"We'll see how you do the rest of this day," she said. "Let's get you home, mistress, and into bed. I'll fetch my herbs and bring them round."

Morrigan glanced at Curran, at the disappointment and anger on his face, and wondered if he blamed her for this. "I swear there's no pain but for my head and ankle," she said. "Everything where the babe is feels fine."

His expression remained angry, but he nodded.

Logan was sent off to find a wagon they could borrow. Eleanor rearranged Morrigan's skirts and Curran gathered her up. Over his shoulder, Morrigan saw a leaded glass window. They must be in William Watson's church. As usual, thinking of him made her nervous and embarrassed. Was he hovering nearby? She hoped not.

"Our secret is no longer secret," she whispered.

He warmed a little. A smile twitched at the corner of his mouth. "As long as our baby is well, I don't care. Do you?"

She pushed away the memory of the minister's wintry gaze at the wedding cèilidh. No doubt he'd suspected from the first. "No."

Outside the kirk, great old yews threw cool shadows. Gravestones poked through the grass, some neat, some slanted and overgrown with lichen. As Curran carried her towards the gate, the etching in one stone startled a gasp from her.

"What?" Curran said anxiously. "Is there pain?"

Through a suddenly pounding heartbeat, Morrigan said, "That grave…."

"Aye, it's your mam's." Father Drummond opened the gate and approached. "I was going to tell you, before you were thrown."

"You can see it later," Curran said. "We must get you home." He shifted her in his arms.

"She'll never rest if you don't let her see it now," Eleanor said.

Sighing, Curran carried her to the grave and put her on her feet, supporting her on her injured side. But she wanted to be closer. With his help she dropped to her knees and touched the carved letters. *Hannah Stewart*, it said, and below that, *Beloved, 1833-1853*.

"This gravestone," she said. "These flowers. Who…?"

"Seaghan." Tears brimmed in Agnes's eyes. "He carved the stone, and every week he brings flowers. He never forgets."

Rachel nodded, tears collecting in her eyes as well.

Morrigan stared. *Beloved.*

Hugh squatted on the other side of the headstone. "You resemble your mother, my dear." He turned away, blinking, his forehead creasing as he gazed over the quiet graveyard.

"Come now, we must get you home," Curran said.

Hugh remained where he was, one hand resting on the stone. He stared down at the grave as Curran carried Morrigan under the yew and through the gate, where Logan waited with horses and a wagon.

She tried to picture the priest in those days before the clearings. Perhaps he'd been handsome, with those long lashes and that thick head of hair. She wondered what color it had been when he was young. What was that, in his face? Grief? Regret?

Pewter clouds covered the sun. A flash of lightning rent the air, followed by an ominous rumble.

"The devil take this day," Curran growled as he wrapped her in a plaid.

Eleanor climbed into the wagon and cushioned Morrigan's head in her lap.

Before they got halfway to Kilgarry, the wind picked up and it started pouring, but the thick plaid kept out the worst.

Fionna, Tess, and Violet came at a run when they saw the wagon. Tess rebuilt the fire in the master bedroom while Violet helped Morrigan change into a nightgown.

At last she lay in warm comfort. Curran went off to his dressing room and changed into dry clothes. When he returned, she held out her hand to coax him onto the bed beside her. "Are you vexed with me?"

"Don't be daft."

"I shouldn't have insisted on riding."

"I'm responsible for this, not you. Not just riding but all of it. I took advantage of you. If you're hurt, it's me that's to blame."

Had he taken advantage of her? It seemed she'd tried her best to lure him into doing what he'd done that day.

Driven by guilt, she touched his mouth and pressed forward for a kiss, drawing him closer.

His kiss was cool, the sort of peck he might give his sister or mother, and almost immediately he pushed her away, but at that moment, Eleanor came in, carrying a tray. Brows lowered, she set the tray down with a sharp clatter.

"Were you not listening?" Glaring at them, she put her hands on her aproned hips.

Curran rose from the bed with alacrity, his face flushed, a guilty stallion.

"I know you're newly wed, but do you not care about your wife? What of the health of your child? Shall I ban you from her presence altogether? Don't think I won't."

"I wasn't…we didn't…."

Morrigan grabbed his hand, but the midwife's expression, so stern, brought up the old terror she'd felt around Douglas, and she couldn't form a single word of defense.

"Away with you, Master Curran. I want her calm and quiet. Strong emotions are not good for her, nor for the babe."

Suitably chagrined, he inclined his head, sent Morrigan an apologetic glance, and left.

Eleanor perched on the bed and held out a spoonful of steaming liquid.

"What is it?" Morrigan asked. She had to admit it smelled good.

"Barley broth blended with honey. For strength. When you finish, I want you to drink this tea. Chamomile with red raspberry leaves. It's good for soothing contractions, and helps control the flow of blood."

"This broth is delicious."

Eleanor placed her hand on Morrigan's forehead. "Are you still dizzy?"

"It's better. My neck is stiff."

"It may get worse over the next few days. Try not to turn your head sharply, and be careful getting out of bed."

Eleanor watched her until she was finished, then removed the dishes and smoothed the blankets. "You're an excitable woman, I think. In a stew about things most of the time. But I'll warn you not to tease your husband. Do you want him roused when you cannot be with him? What if he chooses to console himself with someone else?" She added, "Do you think there would be none willing? Curran Ramsay could have most any female he fancied."

"You're outspoken." Morrigan's cheeks burned. Her head renewed its pounding, sending out repeated hammer blows of pain.

"I have better things to do than play coy. You're aye young, and maybe such things are like a game to you, but I assure you, to men these are not light matters." Eleanor's scrutiny remained cold for a moment, but gradually her expression gentled. "You don't even know that, do you?" She stared at Morrigan a moment more before she added, "You've much growing up to do, I think."

Morrigan wanted to shout at her, tell her to mind her own affairs. But the way the woman could turn from understanding to steel-like judgment stopped her.

The midwife picked up the tray and straightened. "I'll come again this gloaming," she said, "and I'll decide then if you can go to church tomorrow." At the outer door she paused. "Have no fear, mistress," she said. "I do believe you'll recover."

"Thank you," Morrigan managed.

The mantel clock ticked. Kilgarry felt like a mausoleum.

Eleanor had been gone about twenty minutes when Curran reappeared. He crept into the bedroom, saw Morrigan was awake, and said, "Is it safe?"

She laughed. "Come away, Mr. Ramsay. Lie here with me. I swear to behave."

He draped himself across the foot of the bed. "Eleanor's tongue's as sharp as a cutlass."

"And I received a bloodletting. I'm no' to tease you, for fear you'll soothe yourself with some other female. There's thousands willing, supposedly."

"Is that so?" He threaded his fingers through hers. "I'd sooner cut off my own bollocks—"

"*Curran.*"

He laughed. "You need anything, *a ghràidh?*"

Her succinctly phrased answer sparked an appreciative laugh. He crawled over the blankets to lie by her side, and they spent a good half-hour kissing until Tess brought more of Eleanor's herb tea.

"All my life I've had dreams of a man," Morrigan told him after she left.

"Oh?" Curran's left brow rose, accentuating the crescent scar.

"I'm telling you because I think it was *you.*" She set her cup and saucer on the table. "You wanted to know my dreams, didn't you? You were a statue."

"A statue."

"Stop interrupting. A marble statue. But you came to life." The memory returned; she'd dreamed it so many times it never completely faded. It puzzled her, because in the first part, the statue had Curran's eyes, though his hair was long and dark. Then he changed. He became the blond male she'd long ago named *Theseus.*

"Morrigan? Aren't you going to tell me after all?"

She returned to the moment. "I've always called the statue 'Theseus,' after the Greek stories."

"Ah…. That's what you called me when we met."

"In many ways, you resemble him."

"And you…" He bent and kissed her, "could easily bring a statue to life."

After a moment, he said, "What of the dreams that frighten you? Will you tell me those?"

She hesitated. But why not? Perhaps speaking of them would break their somber spell.

"A crowd of men is all around me. They say I'm a witch...."

He didn't laugh or smile. Didn't even blink. But his brows did lower slightly.

"I'm not this evil thing they're calling me. I've done none of what they're accusing me of."

She heard the rising defensive note in her voice, and her hands clenched.

Curran brushed strands of hair from her forehead. "Dreams are vapors of the night. You told me that."

"Aye."

"Is that what frightens you, being named a witch?"

How could she say it? She almost feared describing it might make it real.

"The wean...."

Morrigan shook her head. "I'm fine." She picked up the teacup and held it in her lap, running the tip of her finger around the rim. "The dream feels like it's in Scotland. Someone calls it...Barra."

"Barra is an island. It's part of the Hebrides."

"Truly?" She hadn't known that. The dominie hadn't been too interested in geography.

He frowned. "Barra," he said. "Barra."

"Curran?"

"I think I've dreamed of it as well," he said in an oddly contained voice.

They stared at each other.

"Tell me the rest," he said. "Why do they call you a witch?"

"It gives them the excuse they need, so they can do what they want—"

"I'm sorry, *a ghaoil.*"

She sighed again, ashamed of raising her voice. Plucking one of his hands from her shoulder, she wove their fingers together and pressed her palm against his. Warm tingling traveled up her arm, like sunlight in her blood.

"I've a husband and two wee daughters." She frowned. "No, three, I think. Men break down the door and fill my house. My children are screaming."

Curran rubbed his cheek against her forehead. "Stop," he said. "I don't like to see you so upset."

"I have to say it." The words would suffocate her now if she didn't speak. "They're begging me to save them." She pressed her hands over her ears. "But I...can't."

"Morrigan, it's horrendous. No wonder...."

She needed a deep breath to continue. "They kill my daughter. I try to force the blood back into her, but it keeps coming out between my fingers. I'm dragged from my baby. I feel the blade. I see my blood. Then...there's nothing. I wake up."

Curran leaned across her to set her cup on the table. He gathered her against him, tucking her head in the hollow below his chin.

"Why would I dream such things?" Morrigan asked. A shudder formed, small at first, then migrating outward. Speaking the nightmare seemed to make it so much more sinister.

"I don't know."

She listened to his pulse beat. Her muscles relaxed and the headache retreated. A deep inhale cleansed most of the tension, and she could think clearly again. It did feel better, now the words had escaped, like the draining of an infection. She closed her eyes.

"You've had this nightmare your whole life?" Curran asked.

Nestled against his throat, she felt the reassuring vibration of his voice. "As long as I can remember."

"You know what I'd like to do? Replace your nightmares with other dreams. We can do it." He spoke gently, and kept up a slow, circular stroking on her temple. "Are you listening?" He pressed one of her hands against her stomach and placed his own over it. "Our son or daughter is growing inside you. If our child's a girl, she'll look like you, and we'll spoil her so much no one will ever want to marry her, and she'll always stay with us. We'll grow old here at Kilgarry. We'll be a noisy horde. Our sons will treat their sisters like princesses, and will put any suitors to the sword. We'll have picnics by the sea. You're going to get fat, because I'm going to feed you cheese, and scones with cream and jam, every day."

Morrigan turned her face up, smiling.

"When you smile like that," he said, "you cast a spell over me. Your smiles are magical, my Morrigan. Right now they're rare, but I want to see that smile every day, all the time. I love how it reaches into my chest and squeezes my heart."

Embarrassed, she hid her face again, longing to believe him but afraid. It was hard to believe. Hard to feel both yearning and fear at once.

He laughed and patted her cheek, and she felt he understood.

The patient brush of his fingers calmed her, so that she saw them picnicking at the seaside, surrounded by a rowdy gaggle of sticky-fingered weans, and she was plump, with a double chin and dimpled thighs.

He continued to describe their future and she tried to stay awake, not wanting to miss one word. *All my life,* she heard him say, *I've lived with a feeling that I'm missing something, something I could never stop searching for. It vanished that day on the moor, and I've never felt it since. Not once.*

His voice drew her deeper. She couldn't keep up thinking or wondering about anything.

She sank into green waves. Feeling playful, she threw handfuls of water into sprays as glittery as diamonds. Her clothes vanished; her hair streamed loose. A porpoise chittered at her, then a seal appeared. It nosed her, round and round, until she was breathless from giggling, before its flippers vanished and she was clasped against a man's bare chest. He held her close, his hand pressed against the back of her head so she couldn't see his face as he kissed her shoulder then the sensitive place behind her ear. *Save me, Aridela,* she heard. *Open your heart.* Yet with astonishing violence, the figure blurred, alchemized. Now his grip was brutal; his hand smashed over her mouth. *You didn't want me to die,* she heard. *You were happy for me to trick you, as long as you didn't get blamed.* Pain speared her neck and she screamed.

The ocean swept away. Morrigan rushed through a cold black tunnel.

"It's a dream, Morrigan. A dream. I'm here." Curran's clasped her upper arms.

"It didn't work."

"It will," he said. "I will make it work."

Agnes's warning returned. *Selkies have a way about them. Male or female, they can enchant humans, can make them do anything. Beware the selkie.*

She sent out a desperate prayer. *Mama, what's happening to me? I need you.*

But now, because of Logan, the only picture she could form of her mother was of her lying in bloody snow, screaming, helpless, and suffering as Morrigan ripped her apart to be born.

Chapter 10

Eleanor gave Morrigan permission to attend the kirking, as long as she returned home straight after and did nothing strenuous.

Morrigan sat in a pew near the front, reveling in her triumph and looking about with great interest until William Watson began his sermon. For nearly an hour, he spoke about the sanctity of virgins, the imperative that a man's chosen come to him not only innocent, but also ignorant of life's baser aspects, for, as he claimed, female purity was the glue that held civilizations together. If men had to spend their days wondering what their wives were up to, or who had fathered the children they bore, that glue would disintegrate, and society would crumble into violent anarchy.

She soon felt as humiliated as he no doubt intended, convinced she was little more than spoiled fruit that ought to be tossed out. Then came teeth-clenching fury. He managed to speak the entire sermon without saying one word about male purity. Curran sat beside her, his hand resting calmly upon hers. And why not? He wasn't being attacked. Though they'd never discussed his past with women, Morrigan reckoned her husband was not as innocent as she had been.

There was something else to notice and ponder: a fresh bunch of daisies on Hannah's grave. What had Morrigan's mother meant to Seaghan MacAnaugh, the gigantic man with the tender heart? He still thought of her, after so long. Morrigan wanted to ask, but feared being hurtful or rude. Maybe when she knew him better.

After the service, as the congregation formed a corridor beneath the yews for the laird and his wife to pass through, Curran squeezed Morrigan's hand, leaned close, and said, "His balls withered away years ago since no woman will have him. He says those things because at night in his lonely bed, he wishes he was me."

Which made her smile and utterly routed the suggestion that she was something foul or sinister.

Morrigan's fine new station was snatched away as though it had been mere fantasy. Even Tess and Violet ordered her about. Eleanor insisted she not get out of bed except to use the chamber pot, but when left alone, Morrigan defied every command. Wrapped in a tartan shawl, she limped to the window seat and gazed out across Kilgarry's gardens and beyond, to rolling wooded hills. Sometimes she managed to get the window open, and was able to breathe the enticing aroma of sea and forest. Spellbound by beauty and her tendency to daydream, she'd forget to keep up her guard, and was all too often startled by a hand clapping upon her shoulder, and orders to return to her stuffed-feather prison, usually with stern lectures on obedience.

By Tuesday, her healthy body, so used to activity and toil, rebelled. Aches gnawed at her spine. Her limbs stiffened. Bruises manifested and patience splintered.

"Tell me more about this kirking," she asked Curran as he squatted on the floor beside the bed, massaging her ankle in a salt-water bath. It had turned ten different shades of purple by now, and was still swollen.

"Lower, Morrigan. Put it all the way in the water." When she did, he said, "It's an old custom. Every newly married couple is kirked. Like Agnes said, it blesses the marriage in the eyes of the parish. If there happens to be more than one wedding in the same week, which is as rare as a drought these days, the couples vie to be first to reach home after the sermon. It's said the first couple home will enjoy a long, happy life while bad luck and misfortune dooms the losers." He dipped his hands in the water and rubbed her ankle before grinning at her again. Sunlight, snaking through the east window, lit his face and filled his eyes with indigo sparkles. "There weren't any other weddings, so calm your superstitions. I don't know why I let you talk us into such needless risk. I'll admit my crofters would've been disappointed if we hadn't gone, and those who believe in omens and evil eyes…like Agnes…would've made dire predictions. But be careful, Morrigan. Agnes will have you seeing ghosts on the staircase if you give her half a chance."

Morrigan dismissed his warning. The consequences might be dire even without Agnes to predict them. She'd looked back at Aunt Ibby's shop as she ferried off to be married, and some might believe she'd broken a vow to Kit.

In all her life she'd never fallen off a horse. That it happened the day after her wedding, with a child in her womb, had to be a sign.

FATHER DRUMMOND VISITED ON WEDNESDAY. CURRAN ASSISTED HIM INTO AN armchair beside the bed while Violet bolstered Morrigan with pillows and brought the tea tray.

Though near-crippling joint pain plagued the poor man, a smile flickered about his lips, waiting for the slightest cause to turn full-blown. She decided he was merry, a blithe, caring gentleman with an inexhaustible sense of humor.

He asked after her injuries, and expressed his happiness that the bump on her head hardly hurt anymore and the swelling in the ankle was receding.

"I do hope you're strong by Michaelmas, my dear," he said. "Folk come from near and far to attend our festivities. It would be awful if you missed it."

"I'm going to win the *oda*." Curran moved his chair closer to the bed and rested one arm on the quilt. "I've found the perfect hiding place for Brutus and Glendessary."

Hugh slapped his black-clad thigh and guffawed. "His finest Clydes are forever being stolen from him," he told Morrigan. "He's left with Thorough-breds, and sometimes, as an added insult, a swaybacked nag or two. Your husband's never won the Michaelmas race, and he with the most highly prized horseflesh in three counties."

Puzzled by this talk of theft coupled with laughter, Morrigan asked, "Who steals his horses?"

"I'm sure it was Logan last year." Curran shrugged. "Though he still denies it."

"Why would anyone do that? And why Clydes? Wouldn't your Thorough-breds fetch more silver?"

"Not around here." Hugh nodded at an offer of more tea. "Only Clydes run the oda. Tradition, you see. They're stolen because there's glory in lifting your neighbor's steeds the night before Michaelmas. They're returned after, of course." He scratched his nose with the tip of his pinkie finger. "Curran's beasts do often win, yet he's never the one riding them."

The way the priest's eyes twinkled made her want to smile. Morrigan dropped a smallish lump of sugar into his cup. "Doesn't seem like they'd be good runners. More, Father?"

"Aye, lass, give me another. I've a sweet tooth. The race is short, along the beach. Clydes can run. They love to run."

"I mind how Leo used to race round the paddock." She sighed, remem-bering the huge and gentle animal. "I've never heard of the oda, or stealing horses for Michaelmas. I'm afraid I'll shame Curran."

Her husband laughed. "Of course you won't, silly wench."

"Never concern yourself about such things, lass." Hugh stirred his milky sweet brew, the spoon grating over sugar in the bottom of the cup. "Your husband and I will make you so familiar with our traditions you'll feel you were born here. Oh...." He broke into an unselfconscious bellow of laughter.

"You were! Though…" his smile faded, "the circumstances…." He shook his head, refusing to succumb to distress. "Things did turn out well in the end."

"Aye, Father," she said, frowning at her tea. *But the cost was high.*

"Michaelmas is held on the twenty-ninth of September to celebrate the harvest."

"Aye, it's the same at home…I mean Stranraer."

"Everyone attends hereabouts, from grandmams to suckling babes. It's something we look forward to during the growing season. Along with giving Christian thanks, we feast, dance, and race. This year will be especially happy. The harvest was good, and you're here. It's a miracle. One of our own restored to us. There's much to celebrate."

Curran perched on the edge of the bed, crossing his legs and knitting his fingers through hers. "Next Sunday is Carrot Sunday. All the women come together and dig for wild carrots. Then they bake *strùans*…a holiday bannock. Men slaughter lambs for the feast and steal horses. On Saint Michael's Day, we attend church, show honor to our ancestors, and feast. We hold the carrot giving and the oda. There are other sports as well, much like the Highland games, and the normal mischief and drinking."

"Mischief?" Morrigan said, lifting a brow.

Hugh's lips twitched. "It's traditional to ask your true love to become your wife on the night of Saint Michael's. Sometimes there's the sort of revelry we clergy frown upon." He attempted to appear disapproving, but his infectious grin triumphed. "One man watches the crops and circles the town, guarding it from evil spirits. These customs come from a time long ago, when folk believed in gods and witches. Few understand nowadays the old meanings behind what they do. They perform the rites because they grew up seeing them done. I doubt there's many left who could tell you Saint Michael used to be the god Michael, once upon a time."

Morrigan shifted to ease an ache in her hip. "How did he become a saint?"

"It's the same with Brigit, who used to be *Brigentis*, goddess of wisdom and poetry, long before she became Christ's foster mother and a saint. Changing their designations made the new religion easier to stomach, centuries ago when Columba converted pagan Scotsmen to Christ. That way, there was no need for folk to abandon their gods and goddesses. They merely addressed them differently."

"So…they were tricked?"

"Aye, well," Hugh said, shrugging, "what does it hurt in the end, when folk are saved to go to Heaven when they die? After time, when memories of the old beliefs faded, the new and more proper Christian order took over."

"But which one is true, then?" Her breathing shortened in warning. She knew instinctively she was leveling a challenge towards a man far more powerful than she would ever be.

"Morrigan." Curran frowned.

Not only had she cast doubt upon the priest and his beliefs, she'd embarrassed her husband. When would she learn to keep quiet, especially on subjects about which she knew nothing? "Pardon me, Father," she began, but Hugh lifted a hand.

"Please don't chastise her. It's truly like her mother is sitting here in front of us. Hannah questioned everything as well. I miss her. I miss her still." His voice was so muted Morrigan barely heard him. "Hannah Stewart sparked life in all who knew her."

When Hugh looked up, Morrigan glimpsed tears in his eyes. He blinked them away, smiled, and said, "Your own name comes from the Celtic wargoddess."

"I'm named after my grandmam I think, Father."

His smile widened. "Yet before your grandmam, child, there was the Goddess Morrígan, or some call her *Morrígu*, the great queen of the Irish *Tuath Dé*. It's said she visited battlefields as a raven, and cast spells from dead men's blood. Why, I remember reading in an old Church tome on ancient myth that the Morrígan and the Greek goddess of wisdom, Athene, were sisters."

A thrill ran through her. "I'm named for a goddess?" Of all the Immortals of Greece, Athene was her favorite.

"Look what you've done, Father," Curran said, laughing. "There'll be no telling her anything now."

Eleanor came in, shielding a cup from drafts. "Hand this to your wife, please," she said, giving the cup to Curran, who passed it to Morrigan. "It's a new mixture I've brewed, to assist in calming the womb."

Morrigan thanked her and sipped the tea as Curran said, "I've heard The Morrígan called Queen of Nightmares." He pulled up another chair for Eleanor.

"She sounds bauld and ferlie," Morrigan said.

"Aye, that describes her well, bold and wondrous." Hugh nodded his agreement. "Morrígu appeared in many forms, as a beautiful woman, a terrifying hag, a raven. Once, when the hero Cú Chulainn insulted the Morrígan, she vowed to appear when next he fought and wrap round his feet as a serpent, trapping him for his enemy. She was goddess of prosperity as well as death. Her nature was threefold, like our Holy Trinity. Have you ever heard the old Celtic lore about the Trinity?"

"No," Morrigan said.

"Legend claims that long, long ago, the Trinity was feminine. Mother, Daughter, and Crone."

It struck her that Hugh Drummond was very much like Louis Stevenson— tolerant and eager for knowledge, unafraid of where it might lead. "How do *you* know these things, Father?" she asked.

The pink in Hugh's cheeks brightened and he grinned sheepishly. "I confess the old religions fascinate me. There's no harm in studying them on a blustery winter's night. It doesn't surprise me though that you're ignorant of your Celtic heritage. My brother, Oswold—he has a parish in Dumfriesshire—often laments the fact that Lowlanders are an over pious lot, dwelling on suffering and damnation over everything else faith can offer."

"There were festivals and celebrations in Stranraer," Morrigan said, "but I was never allowed to go. Papa called them rubbish."

Curran sighed. "She was buried under endless labor when I met her, Father, far too much for one slip of a girl, but Douglas used her like a—"

"Curran...." Morrigan couldn't bear anyone knowing the truth, not even her husband's incomplete version. She'd die rather than have folk stare at her with curiosity or worse, pity.

He stopped, though his eyes darkened and his jaw tightened. He turned towards the priest. "I'm going to bring a physician to look at her. I know someone, a brilliant doctor. He treated my aunt."

"But why?" Hugh frowned as he glanced from one to the other. "Because of this fall? Is it the ankle, lass? The babe?"

"Your wife is healing nicely." Eleanor gave Curran a challenging glare.

"She's been having...bad dreams. I want to find a way to stop them, and this man knows about such things."

With the barest pause, Eleanor said, "She needs no fancy medical man, Master Ramsay. I can take care of her without interference. I wager I already know more about your wife than any city doctor could learn in a year."

Morrigan half-expected Curran to reprimand the woman, but he merely smiled and said, "Perhaps. We'll talk about it."

"Eh, well," Hugh said, "I've heard of many unexplainable things happening to expectant women. Some do believe the odd dreams that come to a mother-to-be are memories of the unborn child's previous life...not that I give credence to such fantasies. I am sorry to hear you're not resting well." Finishing the last of his tea, he said, "I'd best make my way to the rectory, or they'll be sending out search parties," and clasped her hand after completing the difficult chore of standing. "Visit me when you're better," he added, and allowed Curran to help him out and down the stairs.

"Goodbye, Father," she called. What a dear man. Little doubt remained that he meant to be her friend, unlike William Watson.

Eleanor plumped Morrigan's pillow and laid a hand briefly on her forehead. "Father Drummond likes you," she said. "Now tell me about these dreams."

Morrigan began reluctantly, but Eleanor's intent interest and ability to listen without interruption soon loosened her tongue. She poured it all out, her fear, her suspicion that the people she saw in the dreams were real, the vividness of the experiences, and most especially the violence they contained. *Could they be her child's memories?* She placed a hand on her stomach, aware of the strange connection between herself and another human, in a way she'd never known could exist.

"You certainly need no proud physician coming in here and talking down his nose at you," Eleanor said. "I'll insist the master delay that plan until I've had a chance to work with you."

"D'you think we can get rid of them?"

"I don't know," Eleanor said. "Let me ponder it." She drew the blankets up, for the day was chilled and stormy. "Are you certain you truly want to?"

Morrigan started to say *of course,* but couldn't. The dreams were always there, weaving through her, as much a part of her as her blood and skin. Now that she considered it, she wasn't sure she could survive losing them. Would she even know herself?

With a discerning glance, Eleanor said, "There's nothing like an afternoon nap on a rainy day. It's good for you, and for the bairn. I'll come again tomorrow. I think I can roust up an herbal that may help you sleep better, at least."

"You seem to have remedies for everything, Mrs. Graeme."

"Mrs. Graeme? I won't have you calling me anything but Eleanor, mistress. Aye, I have many remedies and potions."

"Have you something like dreaming bread, that will show the future?"

"Aye." A smile flitted across Eleanor's lips. "That's a popular herbal, that and love concoctions."

"You have those, too?"

"Why d'you sound so interested?" Eleanor's gaze sharpened. "It's obvious you possess the full love of your husband."

"Oh, I know." *But keeping it could be harder,* she didn't say. "What of the past? Is there a drink for that?"

Eleanor paused. "There are brews that help with seeing the past," she said. "The problem comes when things are seen that shouldn't be."

After Eleanor left, Morrigan lay propped upon her pillows, watching the fire burn.

Soon Curran returned. Many hours they spent threading their fingers together, talking, or reading. She learned more of her husband than she had ever known before they married.

All this talk of dreams started her thinking about them. There was that one of the seal turning into a man. Though she hadn't seen a face, she couldn't help but associate it with Aodhàn Mackinnon, after so much gossip about him being a selkie. The man had certainly captured her imagination. But why? He hadn't been welcoming, not like Father Drummond, or the crofters. He hadn't even joined in the toasts. And he was *old.* She didn't know how old, but the lines across his forehead and the grey in his hair revealed the truth well enough.

She'd told herself for years she loved Kit. Then Curran's smile had liquefied her good sense into a puddle. Now it was Aodhàn Mackinnon. He'd seemed both angry and entranced at the wedding cèilidh. The man lacked any trace of Curran's charm, and he didn't possess two coins to rub together. Yet she kept thinking of him.

Perhaps she was what Douglas had called her when he'd caught her telling Kit goodbye. A whore.

Kilgarry's library provided welcome distractions. Morrigan's tastes varied from *Jane Eyre* to Robert Burns, from *The Iliad* to the works of Allan Ramsay, her kinsman by marriage.

Curran rose early on Friday and dressed in the half-light of daybreak. "I'm going out with the crofters," he said, buttoning his sark. "There are drainage problems, as usual, in one of the oat fields."

She tried not to admire her husband, those highly polished boots, the close-fitting kidskin breeks, or the width of his shoulders under a pristine white cotton sark. She'd like for him to come back to bed, but Eleanor had forbidden intimacies, and Eleanor Graeme unnerved her.

"I'll bring you some Michaelmas daisies." He bent to kiss her, snaring her in a heady mixture of shaving soap and autumn air.

Her fingertips traced up the front of his thigh, but he didn't notice. If he was this disinterested now, how would it be when the babe puffed her out like a whale? She tangled her fingers in his hair and bit his lower lip none too gently.

He jerked away. "Why the bloody hell did you do that?"

"You kiss me like I'm eighty years old." Morrigan glared at him.

He said nothing for a moment, merely frowned, his jaw clenching. "You think it's so easy for me? Do you think I don't want you, every second, every day? I could tear that gown from you and have you, four, five…a hundred times. Still I'd want more."

"And yet you cannot kiss me like a proper husband."

He bent, growling, "Devil take all women!" He seized her shoulders and gave her the kiss she wanted.

She forgot her petulance. He did want her. Thank God, he did still, but he extricated himself from her embrace and stepped away, leaving her confused, slow to realize she'd been abandoned.

"Are you pleased?" His hair fell over his eyes and he pushed at it impatiently.

"I didn't mean to vex you," she said. "I just…I miss you. And—"

"If I do what you so plainly want," he said, "you could lose the baby."

"And you'll have wed me for nothing, is that what you're trying to say?"

He snapped up his jacket and stalked from the room without another word.

"Go on," she cried. "Go and enjoy yourself. Don't come back unless you want to!"

Fury left her breathless. She picked up a beautiful—and no doubt expensive—vase that had traveled clear from India, and almost threw it. Almost. Instead she managed to set it carefully on the floor by the bed.

She must control her anger. It could hurt the child. She had to hold onto sanity, eradicate the insidious red tinge bubbling through the walls and sheeting the glass at the window.

Fisting her hands, she worked to slow her breathing and calm her heartbeat, and had only begun to succeed when there was a knock and Violet entered. "Seaghan MacAnaugh's come to see you, mistress," she said.

Morrigan nodded, and Violet quickly helped make her presentable. The maid escorted Seaghan in, then retired to the sitting room with a basket of mending.

He held an enormous bunch of amethyst-colored daisies in one hand, which he presented with a fancy bow. Morrigan thanked him and spread them over the bed, hoping he wouldn't notice the tremble that hadn't yet left her fingers. The scent of moss, rain, and rich loamy earth filled the room. Smells of freedom. She inhaled wistfully.

"I couldn't believe when I heard what happened." His voice, even gentled, still rumbled like a train engine. "And the day after your wedding. What a shame."

"The wean's still here, so I'm counting my blessings, and looking forward to Eleanor allowing me out of this room." Morrigan pasted on a faint smile and tried to pretend she had no emotions at all, like a true lady. How did they do it? No one had ever shared the secret with her.

"She has a magical ability to heal. You must do as she says."

Heightened color crept up his neck and into his face; his gaze faltered. The topic of pregnancy and bedridden females, no doubt, or was it something else, perhaps the fact that this child was conceived before the wedding?

"True," she said. "I suppose keeping the babe healthy is worth any amount of boredom."

"She learned real medicine from her brother in Edinburgh. Then she spent a year with several old Highland wisewomen, learning their secrets. Folk come from all over, even the islands, to be treated by her. I don't know what your husband did to get her here, but we're all thankful for it."

"She did say that if I improve enough, I could go out on Saint Michael's Day."

"That'd be grand. Are you familiar with our Michael's Day customs, Mrs. Ramsay?"

"Curran's told me a bit. Why are you calling me 'Mrs. Ramsay'? You were never so formal before."

He smiled, clearly pleased. "Now you're wife to the laird, you know, a grand lady. But you're right. We've gone beyond such formalities, and I'm glad of it."

"As am I."

"If you're no' on your feet by Sunday, I'd be pleased to collect carrots for you."

"Mistress." Violet craned to survey them from the sitting room. "Tess and I are going to do it. We've already discussed it." She slapped a hand over her mouth yet several giggles escaped, turning Seaghan's face thunderous and sending him into nervous shifting, which in turn caused the chair he sat in to creak painfully.

"Thank you, Seaghan," Morrigan said. "Fionna told me the carrot-gathering is a woman's custom. I wouldn't want to trouble you with it. Lasses give them to their sweethearts on Saint Michael's Day?"

He shrugged. "Aye, they do, and I'd be pleased to help you any way I can."

From the other room came more half-muffled giggling and Violet gasped, "I can see you, MacAnaugh, gathering carrots in the forest with your wee knife. Oh, what a picture it makes!"

Seaghan shook his head like an aggravated bull. "Well try not to choke on it," he said, and changed the subject. "Has Curran told you of his name, what it means?"

"No. What does it mean?"

"*Curran* is carrot in the Gaelic. Agnes says the Sight told his da to name him so because every lass in the Highlands would want to give him her Michaelmas carrots. Your husband endures many a jest this time of year."

"Every lass in the Highlands?"

Seaghan blinked, looked guilty, and clumsily backtracked. "In years past, of course. A few hearts are broken, I'd wager, now he's so happily married."

"Are they?" Morrigan wondered if any of those ladies would offer him comfort while she lay in this cursed bed, unable to give him more than kisses, which he didn't want.

"You're bonnier than the best of them put together," Seaghan added, and he sounded sincere. "Curran was canny. He chose well."

She gave him a wry smile. "Thank you, Seaghan."

Another reference to beauty, the gilded invitation that won her this coveted position. Seaghan appeared to believe no more than that was required for her to be Curran's perfect mate...or any man's.

It was disquieting to think that if she'd been plain, she might beg for farthings in Stranraer's gutters as her belly rounded. None of the Glenelg folk would ever know of her. But because of beauty, she slept on fine sheets. She was served, cosseted, and spoiled.

"Aodhàn's had an accident." Seaghan's words jolted her out of her dark thoughts. "A good wetting in the sea."

Shock ran through her, then surprise at the breadth of her anxiety. "Was he hurt?"

"He'll live."

"What happened?"

"Lass, if I knew, I'd have the man's secrets cracked." He paused. "One thing came out of it though. His lost memories. The sea stole them long ago, and it appears the sea has finally given them back. Yet still he won't tell me how he came to be drowning in the ocean that day, nineteen years ago. In my opinion, it's his damned—pardon me—closed-mouthed secrecy that keeps the gossip alive and thriving. That and his habit of spewing words in foul languages nobody understands, his refusal to choose a faith or attend a church, and his bloody habit of vanishing for days. As you know, Agnes claims he returns to the sea to visit his selkie kin." He rolled his eyes; his sigh was patently long-suffering.

After nineteen long years, Aodhàn Mackinnon's memories were restored. It seemed momentous. Morrigan wondered if she would ever know him well enough to ask for his history. "I had a dream about a selkie," she said.

"Did you?" His smile was indulgent. "Did it change into a man, or a woman?"

"Oh…it was just swimming." She could never tell him or anyone how this selkie, once it transformed, had pressed against her, had kissed her, or how she had allowed it and wished for more.

"To Agnes, it's as clear and constant as the Five Sisters. He was found in the ocean, wounded, his memories washed away. Ever since, he disappears without warning, and when he reappears, he smells as though he's been dunked in the Sound. Agnes needs no more than that."

"I'll admit she warned me about him at the wedding cèilidh."

He snorted rudely. "Did I not tell you as much? But he does spend a good amount of time on the coast. I can well believe he'll be a sea serpent's breakfast one of these days. Which reminds me. We had a serpent sighting last month."

"Aye?"

"William Watson and his cousin from Aberdeen borrowed Curran's skiff, the *Endeavor*. It was a fine August day, no wind to speak of. They both saw the beast rise from the water, then up came its humps, one after the other…six of them. They saw it again the next day, and said it had a ruff of scales round its neck. Ferrymen on both sides of the Kyle Rhea swore they saw it too."

"We can never know what is down there, can we? There could be vast worlds, completely hidden from us." She was thinking of Curran, of how he'd entered an underwater castle, fought a lion, loved a woman, and saved the earth. Now it seemed Aodhàn Mackinnon had a connection to water as well. Veering off this dangerous path, she asked, "Have you ever seen a sea serpent?"

He shrugged. "I've seen many things I don't much care to speak of, on dry land anyway. One of these days, I'll tell you some tales."

"If I'm ever allowed out of this bed."

The lines in his face softened. "I can see you hate to be confined. I'd feel the same, were it me. I'd be a devil, no doubt about it. I wish there was something I could do."

"You're doing it, Seaghan. Entertaining me. I'm grateful."

There came a great pounding on the stairs then, and Curran burst in, surprising them both. "Morrigan," he said, crossing to the bed in three big steps. He reached out and grabbed her, pulling her into an embrace. "I'm sorry. I'm so sorry. Forgive me, Morrigan. Will you forgive me?"

She couldn't help laughing as he kissed her, over and over again, on her cheeks, her eyelids, and her mouth, paying no attention to Seaghan at all.

"Poor lass," he said between kisses. "I was selfish and cruel. Come now. I'm taking you to the garden. It's a bonny, bonny day, and I don't care what Eleanor says."

He scooped her into his arms while Seaghan laughed and so did Violet, and carried her down the stairs, out of Kilgarry, and off to a shady spot beneath an old oak. Filled with equal measures of delight and embarrassment, she giggled at the sight of Kyle and Logan placing a red velvet fainting couch beneath the branches. Curran ensconced her gently upon it as the lads went off and she protested weakly that she was not dying, and this was all too much.

Happiness flooded her as Seaghan threw himself down in the grass beside the cobbled path and Curran perched at the foot of the couch, resting his arm along the back support. She felt cocooned in affection. It was new, this feeling, and addictive.

"What did you do?" Seaghan asked Curran with a suspicious grin.

"Nothing, nothing," Morrigan said before Curran could reply. "He's weary of this bed rest, as I am." Seaghan didn't have to know what else Eleanor had forbidden, or the trouble it had caused.

"We men have it easy," Curran said. "I'm beginning to understand what a spoiled lot we are."

Morrigan fluffed her skirts. "Why didn't Mackinnon come with you?" she asked Seaghan.

"It isn't easy coaxing Aodhàn into the big house. But he sends his best wishes."

Morrigan rubbed her arms; though she wore long sleeves and the day was warm, an unaccountable rash of goosebumps flared. "I'd like to get to know him better." She had no idea what she would say to the man if she ever saw him again, but there was no denying this chafing urge. She glanced at her husband. "Curran thinks so highly of you both."

Violet brought a teacup into the garden. "Your herb drink, mistress."

Seaghan rose and clasped her hand. "Take care of yourself, lass. Next time I visit, I'll bring Aodhàn, even if I have to drag him by the ankles."

"I'll see you off." Curran rose and kissed Morrigan before following Seaghan.

Gloominess and irritation revived as soon as she was left alone. She wanted to ride her beautiful mare, and admire the mountains surrounding her new home. She wanted to visit Glenelg's crofts and show the women that she was no different than they. Instead she was held prisoner to a bed, like an old, sick woman.

Soothed by the lonely *cour-lee, cour-lee* of a whaup foraging by the pond, she closed her eyes.

She remembered that mist of color she'd glimpsed around Aodhàn Mackinnon, and the sensation of being shocked when their hands touched. She'd been sure at the time that he'd felt it too, but now she doubted her memory, since he couldn't be bothered to visit.

Only the curlew's faint cry broke the quiet of the afternoon. Drifting deeper, she saw the hidden green world far beneath the surface of the sea. There were the iridescent turrets; rippling banners invited her into the castle on the ocean floor.

Now that she'd found it, she, too, would meet Curran's lion, and the beautiful ladies. Maybe she could help him in his quest.

An enormous moon grinned like a fat old woman, the color and texture of yellowed heirloom lace. It sank lazily into the water, spreading outward in an ever-expanding froth of white.

She headed towards the castle gates but there was the seal, barking, cutting her off as it transformed into a man. "You've come at last," he said, pulling her down. He seemed to want to drink her in, the way he held her so tightly and kissed her so deeply.

The castle was forgotten. The water lost its greenish hue and darkened to black as the moon set. Morrigan floated to the surface. She woke, startled from sleep, and sat upright.

Curran was there, legs stretched out on the grass, his back against the couch. He must have returned while she slept and dozed off as well, but her movement woke him. He blinked, rubbed his eyes, and yawned.

The curlew keened sadly. Morrigan glanced around the garden, feeling the seal's presence. Words from the dream turned to dust as she tried to recapture them, leaving only gauzy images of pale light beneath warm ocean waves.

Wiping perspiration from her forehead, Morrigan leaped from the couch.

"Morrigan?" Curran stood too, frowning.

She limped to the old iron gate in the stone wall and looked out at the forest through the bars. No one was there. Perhaps all this rest and boredom had unhinged her.

Curran came up and put his arms around her waist. "What is it, darling?" She turned and nestled against him, drawing in an essence of trust and safety.

But she couldn't let go of the dream. "Nothing," she said. "I woke and didn't know where I was."

Extricating herself from his embrace, she left the wall and walked to the pond. She sat at its edge and regarded her reflection in the surface of the water. Her hair had loosened from its clasp. There were shadows beneath her eyes.

Yet she felt the flush rise like a flame through her cheeks. The pale, tired girl vanished, replaced by that radiant creature no one else knew, the hidden Morrigan, born from secrets, madness, and rage.

A wicked, unfathomable smile curved the reflection's lips as her husband dropped onto the grass beside her and kissed her temple.

Chapter 11

GAILY OUTFITTED IN THEIR MOST COLORFUL DRESSES AND BRIGHT PLAID SHAWLS, the women of Glenelg gathered for the traditional digging of carrots on *Dòmhnach Curran*, Carrot Sunday.

"You may go," Eleanor told Morrigan, "if you promise not to overdo things. Here." She held out a bag, embroidered with green holly leaves and dainty red berries. "Use my *crioslachan* to keep any booty you find." With a wink, she added, "Though somehow I doubt carrots will ever be needed to make you fertile."

"Thank you," Morrigan said. One moment frowning and stern, the next blithe and generous, Eleanor was a contradiction, and always, there was that odd sense of familiarity and instinctive trust.

"Hang it here, on your belt," the midwife instructed as they made their way to the forest.

Laughter and chattering echoed, though most was spoken in the Gaelic Morrigan couldn't understand.

"Would you care to learn some?" Agnes Campbell asked.

"Aye," Morrigan said. "Teach me 'boy' and 'girl,' for when my child comes."

"*Gille* is a boy," Agnes said, "And *caileag* is girl. But you might as well forget the Gaelic for boy, my lady. You're going to have a wee daughter, a *nighean*."

Rachel approached Morrigan from the other side. "You and your husband are still on a honeymoon," she said. "We call that *mìos nam pòg*. The month of kisses."

"Mus name pock," Morrigan dutifully repeated.

The women laughed at her. *"Mees nim pawk,"* Rachel said. "Gaelic is a language born from the sea. Let it flow."

Her companions gaped and smirked when Morrigan unearthed three monstrously deformed carrots the moment she pushed her fork into the soil.

Three! What good fortune for the laird and his lady, they all exclaimed.

Tess told her that such contortions were a powerful sign of fertility, and to find three so quickly, well, mistress must indeed be fertile. The poor lass stood blushing, shifting from foot to foot.

Morrigan blushed too. No doubt she'd been the subject of gossip from the moment Curran had announced he was taking a wife, and the question of why he'd done it in such haste had been clearly answered, thanks to her fall and William Watson's revealing sermon. Though she was two years younger than Tess, she was pregnant, and had ended up that way without the legal and moral benefit of marriage.

Soon Tess pulled her own forked carrot from the ground, which drew Violet and a hopeful Rachel to the same spot. Agnes, Eleanor, and the others dispersed, saying the last thing they wanted were more weans, and they'd prefer nice, uniform carrots.

It seemed they'd barely begun when Eleanor ordered Morrigan to rest on a blanket near Tess, who went on digging for them both.

"Have you a sweetheart to give your carrots to?" Morrigan asked the girl.

"Maybe. I fear he sees me as no more than a sister."

Eleanor brought Morrigan a tumbler of cold water from one of the burns and sat beside her, wiping her damp forehead with a handkerchief.

"Have you ever been married?" Morrigan asked.

"Me?" the woman replied. "Hardly."

"Did you never find anyone to love?"

The midwife made a phlegmy sound of disgust. "I did indeed."

"What happened?"

She shrugged. "I wanted to keep things as they were. That isn't the way it's done though, is it? He wanted me in his bed every night, bearing one babe after another, making him breakfast and dinner."

"How else is there?"

"You're aye young, mistress. I have no desire to sour you on wedded bliss."

"Please, Mrs.—Eleanor, tell me. How did you want things?"

"I wanted to spend time with him, aye, but I've a life of my own, and didn't wish to relinquish it in favor of serving his needs from dawn to dusk."

"Would he not have allowed you to be a midwife?"

Eleanor shook her head. "Can you hear what you're saying, mistress? Aye, he said he'd give me the freedom I required. And I pointed out that if marriage meant he suddenly had the power to take it, or give it, then it was already lost."

"Oh." Morrigan tried to sort through that.

Eleanor tucked a few strands of escaped hair back under her kerchief. "Someday you'll understand, though wed to the handsome, whisky-voiced laird, maybe not."

She leaned forward, her eyes narrowing. Morrigan stiffened, wondering if she'd done something wrong. "Men never cease praising us," she said. "They go on and on about how important we are. But if they really believed that, there would be no laws forbidding women all that men have, and enjoy. Education, Parliament, fields of science. I could be a physician." She shook her dirt-crusted index finger in Morrigan's face. "Watch out when men start to praise you. It's their means of keeping you willingly in fancy gilt cages."

She laughed, but it was not a happy sound.

Morrigan nodded. She wasn't sure when she'd ever felt quite so unclear, but Eleanor's lecture did make her recollect all that Curran had given her: the emerald and diamond necklace, the wardrobe full of clothing. Stoirmeil. Were they innocent gifts, or bribes, artfully designed for some murky purpose?

Gloaming settled over the hills, bringing cooler air and a mist. The women returned to Kilgarry so Tess, the oldest daughter living in the house, could bake the Michael strùan.

Cereal meal, eggs, and butter were whipped with the richest cream. The oven was cleaned out and restocked with sacred wood: bramble, oak, and rowan.

Every detail here had importance. Every act, specific meaning. No wonder Ibby caviled about tradition during the wedding preparations. These High-landers lived close to the earth and seasons. Closer, Morrigan would wager, to those old gods and goddesses than Father Drummond might care to admit.

While the cake cooled, the women drank tea and admired Tess's culinary skills.

"We'll carry it with us to Mass," Fionna said. "Father Drummond will bless it. Master Curran always attends our Saint Michael's Day Mass, though he was raised in the Kirk. It's but one of his many courtesies."

"Glenelg changes little," Beatrice said, "no matter what landowners do." She stared around the huge kitchen. "I mind Father Drummond blessing our own strùan."

"You were Catholic?" Morrigan asked. She'd never before considered Beat-rice and religion in any way connected.

"Not after the clearings," she replied in her usual emotionless manner. "Not Catholic or anything else."

After a short silence, Fionna said, "I didn't lose my faith. I know John and Beth are waiting in Heaven to be reunited with Tess and me. If I couldn't believe that...." Her lips trembled. "Without religion, what is there to comfort you when a child dies? What is there to keep you from going mad?"

Tess pressed her cheek to her mother's and squeezed her shoulders.

"John?" Morrigan asked.

"My husband. Beth was my daughter." Fionna stroked Tess's hair. "It was almost too late for Tess as well the day Thomas Ramsay found us. There he stood in his fine clothes. I thought we were about to be persecuted again, maybe chased out of the ruins. I tried to stop him when he picked Tess up, but I was too weak. Every one of us alive today is here because of him. I would've done anything for him and will for his son until my last breath. God made Thomas Ramsay his angel of mercy."

Morrigan remembered Aunt Ibby telling her about Beth, the child who had starved to death. The heathen lass inside her spoke. *If God had brought him a day or two earlier, Beth might've lived, too.* Not content to stop there, she added, *What if God had prevented Randall Benedict from clearing his tenants? Nobody would've starved or frozen that winter. Hannah might still be with you. You might have your mother.*

Kyle and Logan brought in a freshly slaughtered lamb, their clothes redolent with the tangy scent of autumn.

Tess blushed and knotted her fingers together. Shy embarrassment shouted her secret, though no one but Morrigan appeared to notice.

Since Logan was her brother, Kyle MacPhee of the curling brown hair and bright intelligent eyes must be the male for whom Tess had gathered carrots. Morrigan leaned down to scratch Antiope's ears and wondered how she could assist the romance. No doubt Kyle was oblivious, as Tess had implied. Perhaps Logan could help, but she'd have to be careful with that, as brothers could bedevil a lass half out of her senses.

Teasing had been Nicky's special genius. He'd used it liberally, his intent, she suspected, to get her spine up and keep her from sinking into lassitude or self-pity.

Beatrice ordered her niece to bed early. It didn't matter that Morrigan was now formally known as "Lady Eilginn," or that she was a married woman, or expecting a child. Had High and Mighty Miss forgotten she'd nearly lost her unborn babe? Was it too much trouble to err on the side of caution?

No doubt the other women would stay up late. They'd roast the lamb and celebrate while the men drank whisky and guarded Curran's stallions.

She fell asleep at last to dream of Kyle and Logan stumbling drunkenly through Glenelg, terrifying evil spirits with their off-key singing.

CURRAN WOKE MORRIGAN IN THE HALF-LIGHT OF DAWN, SO THEY COULD DRESS and attend Father Drummond's Mass. She'd never seen the coastal landscape this early. Crimson light fought with stark shadows, creating an illusion of skeletal grinning mouths and enormous black eye sockets in the craggy mountains over on Skye.

It was the first time Morrigan had ever been inside a Catholic church. She listened to the Latin and watched folk cross themselves as they drank the wine and consumed the host. Incense stung her nose and candlelight flared. These were ancient, sacred traditions, going clear back to the Christ himself, so Agnes said. Morrigan couldn't understand why it caused her palms, encased in fine black leather, to break out in a sweat.

Curran took her to the Protestant service in Glenelg as well, for the laird didn't like to play favorites. Morrigan could almost hear Douglas Lawton's disgusted snort at all this church-going. After the services there was the noisy and satisfying Michaelmas feast, followed by wrapping up leftovers for the poor. "Master Curran never forgets those who struggle," Fionna told Morrigan. "He wants none to go hungry."

At last the time came to loosen tight collars and begin what everyone had most anticipated—the seaside festivities. An impressive crowd from several parishes congregated in preparation for the oda at the long stretch of beach hugging the Kyle Rhea.

"Pardon me, Morrigan," Curran said. "I want to see...." He disappeared into the throng without finishing his sentence, shouting for Malcolm and Padraig.

Morrigan watched Tess offer her carrots to Kyle. With a stiff, formal bow, he accepted them and handed her something in return. Morrigan couldn't see what it was, but Tess smiled and appeared pleased. Not far away, Agnes Campbell kissed her husband's cheek. He put his arm around her shoulders and said something that made her giggle.

It felt as though every lass had found her lad as Morrigan lost hers. Curran's new wife, foolish woman, stood alone in the midst of couples. There was Seaghan, grasping Fionna's bunch of carrots. Aye, Fionna, blushing like a virgin.

Morrigan retreated, embarrassed and jealous as she wondered if he had gone to meet another girl. Intending to duck away until all this mooning was done, she turned, and almost ran into Aodhàn Mackinnon.

She stared up into his face, mortified to be caught so blatantly deserted, and somehow that it was by him made it worse. He returned her stare, one brow lifted.

Without thinking, she held up a carrot.

It hung there, suspended by lacy greenery from her fingers, one of the most warped of those she'd unearthed, she saw with dismay. Sunlight glittered against the stones in her wedding band. Deep within, she floundered. *What am I doing?* She only knew that she'd pictured Mackinnon more than once the day she dug up the bloody things, and had imagined giving him one.

The slightest hint of a smile lifted one side of his mouth. He reached out, fingers brushing hers, and accepted her offering.

"Morrigan." Curran appeared from behind and swept her into a hug, lifting her off her feet. "Someone's managed to steal my Glendessary, but I still have Brutus. I'm going to win this race for you, I swear it." He kissed her soundly and dragged her away, giving her companion a careless, laughing nod.

Morrigan glanced back once as she trailed behind her husband. Aodhàn's hand rested over his jacket pocket, where he'd tucked her gift.

She handed her remaining carrots to Curran, trying to ignore the skittering of her heart.

"Thank you, my love," he said, but she saw his competitive nature had already returned to the race, leaving nary a thought for her or silly vegetables. What had it all been for, anyway?

She thought of Eleanor's grievance on Carrot Sunday, and for a fleeting instant, saw clearly to its heart. If females directed their own lives as men did, would they still choose the same things? Would it cause change so profound the world would fracture, as William Watson claimed?

Contestants rode the oda bareback and barefoot, using bridles woven from dried bent grass. The men spurred with their heels and used whips of seaweed. Curran, eagerness manifested in his hot-bright eyes and flushed cheeks, leaped upon his glossy bay, Brutus. Pressing his thighs against the stallion's shoulders and grabbing handfuls of mane, he became as near to a Greek centaur as Morrigan could ever wish to see.

Looking at him, she couldn't imagine making any other choice. This golden hero, shining like the sun upon a snorting, magnificent, dark as sin behemoth, was hers—hers to sleep with, wake up with, grow old with.

Then mighty Glendessary thudded onto the scene, bringing with him ripples of laughter. Astride his broad back, displaying an enigmatic smile, sat Aodhàn Mackinnon.

"Damn you," Curran shouted. "*You* stole him, Aodhàn!" He turned his face to the sky and laughed as if he couldn't be more pleased.

The man's gaze met Morrigan's for a long moment then traveled down, clear to her boots and up again. At that moment, Padraig Urquhart slapped Brutus's rump, eliciting a startled rear. Curran put his attention on staying astride and calming his steed, giving Morrigan the time she needed to dismiss the promise she fancied she'd seen in Mackinnon's eyes.

No one else appeared to have noticed anything amiss. Aodhàn's expression had only seemed, for an instant, lascivious.

His regard remained steady; a slight smile implied her thoughts held no secrets.

Glendessary pawed the sand and tossed his mane, eager to run. Just before swinging the horse around, Aodhàn nodded and mouthed something. It looked like *My jo.*

Had the world turned inside out? Had this dour, sullen man—for surely he was that, though intriguing—transformed into one who smiled, who flirted with his expression, and followed that up with suggestive endearments?

Then she remembered what Seaghan had told her. *One thing came out of it. His lost memories. The sea stole them long ago, and it appears the sea has finally given them back.*

That's what was different. No wonder he appeared lighter, as unfettered as an eagle.

This Aodhàn might require an entirely new designation.

Morrigan tore her gaze from the fisherman and rested it on her husband. But as Aodhàn had pulled his mount next to Curran's, she couldn't help comparing the two: Curran like sunfire on a fine June morning, Aodhàn dark and cool as a mist-shrouded October night.

The massive Clydesdales, prized by crofters above any other creature on earth, milled at the starting line. One gigantic hoof could kill with a single blow, yet the majority of the great beasts stood quiet and docile, muscles rippling beneath the knees of their jockeys. The scent of fresh dung permeated the air.

Kyle, astride a monstrous brute, leaned down to speak to Tess. Next to him, Logan's sideways grin settled on Violet. Seaghan's mount bared his teeth and swished his long tail.

"Where did that sorry beast come from?" Curran asked.

"I'd advise you not to ask such questions, Curran Ramsay." Seaghan winked at Morrigan. "Now don't tire yourself, Lady Eilginn. Sit you down in the bent where you can be properly impressed by our manly exploits."

Seaghan's rebellious steed broke loose from the starting line and Brutus bit Glendessary's shoulder as Morrigan dutifully moved to the side and sat in the grass.

Father Drummond pointed a revolver into the sky. When it discharged, the crowd surged forward like a roaring wave. Morrigan leaped to her feet.

Seaghan pulled in front but soon lost his advantage when his mount stopped to rear and thrash. Brutus and Glendessary swept past on either side, Curran's golden hair blowing wildly behind him, Aodhàn's longer, giving off a sheen like raven-feathers. White sarks billowed. Legs fused to horseflesh. In unison, the two settled into their stallions' manes and drew ahead of the rest.

"It'll be your husband or Aodhàn Mackinnon!" Rachel bounced her daughter so hard the babe wailed in protest.

Morrigan clenched and unclenched her hands. Her injured ankle throbbed, but the worst was her heart, scuttling with such mad strength it made her light-headed.

The riders veered at the far end, hardly more than sand clouds and smudges, and began the return. Glendessary and Brutus continued, neck to neck.

"Aodhàn has it," William Watson announced.

"No, the master must win!" someone else shouted. "He's the newlywed and in most need of good luck!"

Morrigan ignored the malicious tittering as a salvo of disconnected phrases erupted from the depths of her subconscious.

You are the skin covering the heart of the apple.

You are the spear of lightning after his roar of thunder.

You are the ocean battering his cliffs.

Sun and moon. Mountain and sea. Good and evil, woven together, joined yet separated, one unable to exist without the other.

Aodhàn Mackinnon and Curran Ramsay. Two halves of a whole, like a rope spitefully unraveled. More than friends, more than enemies, more than could be explained.

Pounding hooves threw sand in skyrocketing fountains. The bystanders fell silent. Could they sense, as she did, that this race had unspoken yet immeasurable significance?

Curran, crouched low against Brutus's neck, whipped furiously with his seaweed. Aodhàn gripped Glendessary's mane. He rode with his mouth near the Clyde's ear as though he was whispering to him.

Two women held a red streamer across the sand to mark the finish line.

"Oh, come away, come away," Morrigan whispered.

Brutus leaped and snagged it. A unanimous deafening shout rose as Curran straightened. Wind had flayed his sark, baring a sweaty chest and abdomen dusted with sand. Lifting the ribbon, he searched the crowd, and when he spotted Morrigan, kicked his horse towards her.

She touched his foot. Grinning, he reached down, caught her, and swept her up, sitting her before him as though she weighed no more than a midge. Amid shouts and folk cramming ever closer, he seized her face and pressed upon her a long, heated, suffocating kiss. She felt half-affronted at being treated like plunder, but excitement ran so bright and joyous across his features that she stifled her protest and laughed with him. Anyway, the crowd was cheering as though the laird had single-handedly defeated an entire English army.

Brutus pranced and preened, not at all afraid of being hemmed in so closely. Morrigan glanced to the finish line, where Aodhàn Mackinnon sat astride Glendessary. As though he'd been waiting for her to seek him out, he nodded, lifting a brow like he'd fulfilled his end of an unspoken pact.

Had she really seen him jerk on Glendessary's mane seconds before the end? But why would he do that?

Next came the women's race on horses of every make and description. Morrigan longed to participate, but her stern midwife would never countenance such a thing. Utterly astonished, she watched her ladies' maid, Violet, mount Stoirmeil, the flighty Arab mare Morrigan had ridden but once. Who had stolen her? The answer was revealed in Logan's swelling pride, the way crusty old Padraig Urquhart slapped him on the shoulders, and the glee with which Kyle was laughing.

Violet won of course. The young woman Morrigan had judged acutely shy looked triumphant and uncommonly beautiful. Her dark brown hair spilled over Stoirmeil's russet flanks and her cheeks bloomed with color. Not only were her feet bare, but her ankles and fine white calves, yet no one appeared shocked. Malcolm led her, astride Stoirmeil, to the pine-draped Michaelmas barn, and escorted her onto a platform, handing her over to Curran. The jubilant pair raised clasped hands, sparking a resounding cheer which no doubt terrorized every bird for five miles.

Tess, known throughout the parish for her sweet, lilting voice, stepped forward to sing. She stood between the victorious pair, giving voice to a mournful lament while Malcolm accompanied on his fiddle.

I search the far distance for my sailor-lad,
I sing to the spindrift of the love we once had.
I long for the day when thy fortunes bring thee,
Back to these heartsick mountains, searching for me.

The listeners swayed. Seaghan put his arm around Fionna's shoulders.

I mind when you warmed me so bonny and bold.
Now the wind shakes this high hill, so empty and cold.
I search the green ocean but it laughs at me.
Your love is your tall ship and my love is thee.

Fionna wiped tears from her cheeks. After a moment of silence, Seaghan raised his tankard, blinking away his own tears, and cried, "No lass'll weep over any lad this night. Come away! To the dance!"

Regal as Peers of the Realm, Curran and Violet promenaded around the barn. They shared a goblet of wine and began the dancing with the traditional *Cailleach an Dùdain*.

Gossip eddied. Morrigan caught many surreptitious glances thrown her way when Violet seized Curran's face and kissed him on the mouth. And did he protest? No indeed. His hands circled Violet's waist and he returned the kiss with enthusiasm.

Fiddle-music filled the air and whisky made the rounds. Tess draped a daisy garland around Curran's neck as tipsy singing echoed off the high eaves. He lifted his tumbler and shouted something in Gaelic. Countless toasts ensued.

It would seem this horse race was the most daring act ever performed. Fawning women, young and old, mobbed Morrigan's husband.

"I believe he's forgotten the blackening we gave him the night before your wedding. You should've seen him frantically scrubbing himself clean."

She didn't turn to see who spoke into her ear, but warmth expanded through her chest, where a moment before cold jealousy had reigned. "What did you use?"

"Soot, eggs, and dirt. And feathers. A right good number of feathers. Now look at him. He's aye proud of himself."

Morrigan glanced at Violet, whose fingers clutched Curran's forearm tightly. "It appears I've been replaced anyway."

"Men are fickle creatures. Generally not worth a woman's trouble."

Aodhàn offered his arm like a practiced gallant. She placed her hand upon his wrist lightly—no mad clutching for *her*—and followed him from the barn, wondering if he'd planned this all along.

The cool air was refreshing after the close heat of packed bodies. Others had abandoned the barn as well. There was almost as much talking, laughing, drinking, and flirting here as inside.

Malcolm Campbell lifted his whisky as they passed. "Mistress," he said. "'Tis a braw night. I'm pleased Eleanor allowed you to come."

"You're missing your daughter's glory, Malcolm."

He shrugged. "We do it every year, and I've seen any number of winning couples. Does no' mean they won't boak later and feel quite sorry for themselves...beg pardon for my crudeness."

His conciliatory tone stung her pride even as she snickered at the image of her husband and Violet vomiting into the bushes. Had her jealousy been so plain? "My only regret is that I couldn't take part. Had I been riding Stoirmeil, I would've won."

"I've no doubt of that," he returned, with an approving smile.

Morrigan and her escort strolled to a flat-topped boulder at the water's edge. He gave her a hand up and she arranged her skirts. The seat brought her level with his face; she could, for the first time, observe him straight on, like an equal.

Away in the hills, bagpipers played. The sound floated so faintly she almost thought it her imagination.

For a moment, everything…her new life, Kilgarry, Curran, and most especially Mackinnon…seemed no more solid than a cloud.

She used conversation to keep hold of reality. "You stole Curran's horse."

"Aye." His self-deprecatory nod didn't fool her. "Though I still lost. You're getting most of the accolades."

"Why?"

"He made more of an effort to win than he ever has before."

"Have you stolen one of his horses before?"

Light spilling from the doorways betrayed the flash in his eyes and the smile playing at the corners of his lips, but he didn't answer.

She wrapped her arms round her knees and listened. "I can almost hear voices in the sea tonight."

"Oh aye, it speaks. Try getting it to stop."

"I've had dreams of the sea since I came here." She met his gaze. "I can swim without being cold, and I don't need to breathe."

His regard grew more intent, but he said nothing.

"There are porpoises. Seals."

He remained still but for the slightest narrowing of his eyes. No doubt she saw more in his expression than was really there, thanks to Agnes and the dreams.

Seaghan had once mentioned that Aodhàn Mackinnon spent days staring at the ocean, hidden in some secluded place. Perhaps he, like the lass in the song, longed for a lost love. What if he'd been married? He might have children. Now that he remembered all that had been lost, would he leave and go searching for his past? The idea that he might left her uncomfortably anxious.

How could she be angry with Curran for anything he did when she entertained decidedly unforgivable ideas and fantasies about one of his closest friends? She wished Aodhàn would call her *my jo* again. She wished he would place his palm against her cheek, so she could see if his touch still made her flesh tingle, like two wool blankets being rubbed together. She could almost imagine his fingers resting on her temples and combing through her hair, and it carried a familiar feel, like an oft-repeated thing.

"The sea will bewitch you," he said.

She started. "In the dream, that's what I want."

"Once she has you, she never releases you." A frown deepened the lines between his brows. "The sea claims final possession."

"And leaves nothing behind." She had no idea where those words came from. Searching for equilibrium, Morrigan placed both hands on the rock, closing her eyes and drawing in a deep breath of cool air to clear her head. "In the dream, I didn't want to be released. I wanted to drown."

"She will take all of you without remorse."

His flat, bitter tone brought Morrigan's eyes open. He'd edged closer. Was he still speaking of the sea?

"What's your purpose?" he asked. "Are you trying to make a fool of Curran?"

"Why…why do you say that?" she managed.

"Maybe it's me you want to make a fool of."

"I don't want to make a fool of anyone."

"Ah, so you're already spoiled, and bored with your lot. Or a silly wean, ruled by selfish ignorance."

She exhaled, incensed. "I am searching my way through life. I am not 'spoiled,' or 'bored,' or a 'silly wean.' I am *Morrigan*—Morrigan Lawton Ramsay. What of you? What is *your* purpose?"

"Mine? To follow. To fight. To die, and do it all again. To be God's pawn."

"Pawn? How? How can you die and 'do it all again'?"

His gaze wavered then he glanced towards the water, shrugging. "I've had too much whisky."

Morrigan knew she should let the subject die, but she heard herself say, "I picture God with the face of my father, which is daft because Papa hated God. God was to blame when he and Nicky nearly starved and my mam died, so Papa renounced God. In retaliation God took Nicky… the child he loved. I often imagine God snapping his fingers and laughing as he brought death to both of them. My father was arrogant, and he paid the price."

She wanted to discover where this pain led, and instinct told her Mackinnon might be the only man in Glenelg who wouldn't be offended. "This morning, Father Drummond talked of Paradise. He said Adam and Eve lived there, content, until God planted the Tree of Life in their midst." She hesitated. "Why did he put it there, tell them not to touch it, then send the serpent to lure them? And of course it had to be the female who gave in to temptation. We've never been forgiven for that, and never will be."

"Some say the Devil tempted her because of her strength." Aodhàn's eyes reflected sparks from the nearby bonfire. "He knew if he could sway her, Adam would follow. Adam was easy."

She examined the idea, not sure if this was a compliment or another attack. "Was it a gamble, then? The Almighty and the Devil, wagering how long it would take humans to commit the first sin? If so the Devil won, didn't he, because Father Drummond says he was made king over us."

Futility descended like a shroud over her earlier exuberance. A moment ago, emotions had burgeoned, clear and fire-bright, insisting on a voice. Now everything seemed murky, out of reach. "If there is a God," she said, feeling her way, "he must want us to suffer, to know only failure and sorrow. If he hadn't given us to the Devil, there would've been no need for his son to be crucified. We'd not know the meaning of sin."

A midge landed on Aodhàn's cheekbone—she brushed it away since he didn't seem to notice. His prominent bones, coupled with the shadows, lent him a subtle predatory air. "So we have to refuse to be his pawns. That's our revenge. I think I know why it's such a sin to take your own life. God is furious, isn't he, when we spoil his game by making our own choices?"

"Stop it."

He sounded angry. She must have been wrong about him. Now she wondered, stiffening with a feathered edge of dismay, if he would tell William Watson of her blasphemy.

"Don't let anyone hear you say such things," he said. "They won't forgive or forget it. When will you learn to think before you speak?"

"What?"

He blinked and turned his face away. "The world has worshipped many things. Gods, goddesses, love, money, land. Since the beginning we've blamed our idols for all that displeases us. Everything from wars, plagues, bad harvests, to a poor gambling hand. It's the way of cowards, to blame something or someone else for what we do." An expression flitted across his features, too hard to define in this indistinct light. "And we have done things, things beyond redemption."

She recognized the self-hatred in his voice. She'd spoken the same way, echoing Papa, whipping herself for stupidity, laziness, and greed.

Deep inside, the wild, secret Morrigan roused and took notice.

"Once," he said, "all I cared about was glory, fame, praise. *Kleos,* the Greeks call it. I would've done anything…did anything in bondage to it." He stopped. When he continued, his voice had grown faint. "I've paid such a price. And so have those around me." His jaw clenched, and clenched again.

The wash of water intensified as the wind caused a surge of ripples to caress the shore. It felt like a language she'd once understood. "Mackinnon?" she asked.

He returned then, to the night and the boulder by the sea. "If we were brave enough to admit who's truly responsible for our actions, everything might change. The world might change. But it's too hard. We're too weak. I ask your pardon. You're not a wean or a spoiled wife. You're Morrigan Lawton Ramsay, searching out her way."

Even as she started to smile, basking in the still-unfamiliar sensation of warm acceptance, he leaned forward and kissed her, at first gently, yet there was a tremble to his lips. His hands descended upon her shoulders and he gripped them, hard, then harder.

He lifted his head. His eyes were wide. She saw passion and longing, aye, but worse things too. Suffering. Regret. Horror. All swept past so swiftly she couldn't be certain of anything, and didn't know what to do.

His hands were shaking. Instinctively, she lifted her own and pressed them over his in an effort to lend him calm if she could.

He closed his eyes. "For as long as…as…." He drew in a choked breath. Pulling his hands free, he retreated.

The man was confounding. He was meanly dressed, his hair coarsely cut, his beard untrimmed, but the way he talked was every bit as educated as Curran. Hadn't he spoken Greek earlier? Most disturbing of all was how familiar everything about this man seemed, and when she'd rested her hands over his, she had again felt that subtle tingling.

She longed to comfort him. But an inner voice shouted a warning, dragging her attention away.

Silhouetted against the buttery light from the barn stood two figures. The glow made a halo of Curran's hair. Next to him, Violet resembled a willowy tree-faery.

They approached. Moonlight reflected off the scar beside her husband's left eye. Morrigan couldn't stop staring, as it almost seemed to pulsate.

"What d'you think you're doing, Aodhàn?" Curran's voice was on the rougher side of courteous.

"Handing out Michaelmas kisses to all the bonny lasses," Mackinnon said easily.

Violet regarded Morrigan, then Mackinnon, with trepidation. "Oh, there's Da," she said, and melted into the night.

There was a tense moment or two more before Curran said, "Come, Morrigan, let's get you home. In your condition, you need rest."

She slid off the boulder and smoothed her skirts, mortified that he'd brought up her pregnancy. "Good night, Mackinnon," she said. "Happy Saint Michael's Day."

Aodhàn inclined his head. His face now wore the usual impenetrable veil. But for that brief moment, she'd never have guessed what seethed behind it.

What had he been about to say? Why had a kiss made him lose his implacable control?

Curran escorted her to the gig, his grip firm on her arm. After assisting her onto the seat, he lit a cigar and threw the match away with alarming force. He climbed up and flicked the reins. The horse trotted from the gathering, leaving behind singing, bagpipes, fiddles, and many who would suffer splitting heads come morning. There might even be a new pregnancy or two.

A silent, watchful Highland night soon fell around them, broken only by regular hoof beats. The cool air was scented with pine and cigar smoke. Morrigan drew her shawl closer.

"Are you going to tell me?" he asked.

"What?"

"Why it is every time you and Aodhàn Mackinnon get a glimpse of each other, you run off and hide. Did he kiss you on our wedding day too, when you went outside with him?"

"Of course not. And we weren't hiding. I asked Mackinnon to take me outside, if you want to know. I was sick of watching you and Violet. You had plenty of kisses for her, and anyone else who wanted one."

He hauled on the reins, making the horse snort and stamp. "It's the custom to have the winners share the wine and dance the Cailleach an Dùdain. It means nothing."

"Maybe it's our marriage that means nothing." What she said next surprised her. "The days when I had to endure whatever was done to me are past."

Curran faced her as the horse came to a confused stop. "It's one thing to kiss someone in a barn full of folk, as part of custom, and another to go off into the night and do it."

"We were hardly alone. Malcolm was there, for one. And don't you want me to be friendly with the folk you've telling me about since July?"

"Friendly, yes. Letting men fondle you like a slut? No."

A slut! Branded again, now by her husband, and they'd only been married a fortnight.

Later, when she tried to recall slapping him, she couldn't. Yet she remembered her palm burning, and his head jerking to one side.

He rose, towering over her. "You're a wife now," he shouted, "and you'll conduct yourself like one. No more going off to the moor and charming a man out of his good sense!"

Without blinking, she wrenched the reins out of his hands and snapped them against the horse's rump, causing it to leap forward.

Curran was thrown, cursing, over the side of the carriage.

Morrigan sent the horse flying, leaving her husband sprawled out dead for all she cared.

Chapter 12

FIONNA POLITELY STIFLED HER YAWNS AS SHE LISTENED TO AGNES RAMBLE.

"I know," Agnes said, partly to her, partly to Seaghan. "The lass is with child. No doubt you think that's why he wed her." Holding out her glass, she shook it in Fionna's face, sloshing whisky. "But you didn't see his face when she fell off that horse. Near daft he was with fear, and fury at that poor dog. He loves her. Malcolm used to have that same fire in his eyes." With a heartfelt sigh, she added, "Marriage ruins the finest romances."

Seaghan's cheeks turned bright as holly berries as he glanced at Fionna. She wanted to say, *Don't heed Agnes. She's drunk.*

"You know, don't you?" Agnes grabbed Fionna's arm, shaking it for emphasis. "John made three weans on you. Was your life ever again what it had been? Once you have weans, that's when your fine glorious love flees like a noonday shadow."

Fionna did mind how their first, Logan, changed things. John loved having a son, but the couple never again enjoyed an uninterrupted moment.

What did that matter now? Her surviving children were grown. Why shouldn't she and some braw strapping man enjoy this time of freedom? She regarded Seaghan, reveling in the slight quiver that crept through her knees. One of his hands could near span her waist; they were that big. When she stood next to him, she felt flighty as an untried girl.

It was long past time for him to relinquish his attachment to Hannah. She hadn't deserved Seaghan's devotion, Morrigan's mother or not.

Tess joined the group. "You'll never believe it," she said. "Master Curran caught his new bride kissing Aodhàn Mackinnon."

"Saint Brigit save us." Agnes made the sign of the cross on her breast. "That selkie has thrown a spell over her."

Fionna peeked at Seaghan. She hoped her expression didn't betray the question she couldn't help but think.

Was Morrigan more like Hannah than anyone might care to admit?

"Excuse me," Seaghan said, and left them.

HE FOUND AODHÀN EVENTUALLY, STARING OUT AT THE SEA.

"Is it my daughter you think you can amuse yourself with after these many years alone?" He felt as though someone had set off Chinese firecrackers in his gut.

Aodhàn didn't respond. He didn't move.

"What of Curran? What's he ever done, to make you want to treat him this way?" Seaghan's breath came hard. The pattern of his heartbeats raced then grew lumbering and heavy. The two had seldom disagreed about anything. "Well?"

"There comes a time," Aodhàn said at last, "when a woman is neither daughter to some man nor wife to another. You cannot jam her into a box to fit your idea of what she should be. You'll lose her if you try."

"I'm not fashed for myself!" Seaghan slashed the air in a fury of impatience. "Don't you realize Curran could throw her out of Kilgarry and keep the child? Few would blame him."

Aodhàn turned finally and met his old comrade's narrowed gaze. "I'll try to stay away from her. If you want, I'll apologize. But I tell you, there's been no life in me until she came." As he spoke those words, his free hand balled into a fist and the knuckles of the other whitened around the whisky glass. "I might as well have been dead."

Seaghan's anger subsided as he pictured the exultation on Aodhàn's face the morning after the wedding. He'd been transformed. "What of your wife? You haven't mentioned her since that day by the sea. Does she exist? If so, you have no right to call yourself a dead man without Morrigan. Your duty is to that woman, whoever she is, and wherever she may be."

Aodhàn stared at Seaghan then laughed. It was a choked sound, escaping from his throat like it burned. "Aye," he managed at last.

"You find this amusing?" Seaghan's ire reignited. "God knows I loved Hannah Stewart. But after she ran off with Douglas, I wouldn't let myself be her plaything. I told you she came to me once, days before the clearings. She begged me to take her away, and swore her unborn child was mine. I didn't believe her. I thought she was sorry for the match she'd made. I see now that maybe I was wrong. I have to live with the fact that my *pride* may have kept me from my own child all these years. Damn it, I don't begrudge you happiness. You've had little enough. Many times I've thought you deserved better. But if you think you can steal the laird's wife from him, I'll fight you with everything I've got. D'you hear me? I won't see her harmed."

Aodhàn drank off his whisky and threw the glass into the sea, where it made a barely audible *plunk* before sinking. He stood there, saying nothing, giving no promises.

"I see I'll get nowhere with you. You have to live with yourself, but mark me, Aodhàn. I'll do whatever I must to protect my daughter."

"If she is your daughter."

Seaghan, gritting his teeth and releasing a feral growl, strode away into the black night.

Lost in a sticky jumble of anger, despair, and betrayal, Morrigan gave no attention to where the horse was taking her.

She'd not thought Curran capable of speaking such things. There could be more secrets, worse surprises. Like the unrestrained girl who lived inside her, he might have other personalities. For the first time, she feared the possibility of a Douglas inside him. Had she seen a glimpse tonight?

Gradually she realized she had no idea where she was. She couldn't recall what direction she'd gone after leaving Curran. Night drew a black, impenetrable cape over the world, preventing her from seeing if the road continued before her. She pulled the horse up and pounded her fist against the leather seat. How dare he reproach her after the way he'd acted? He'd insulted her and issued orders like she was his property, the same as one of his dogs. Yet in the eyes of the world a wife was nothing more.

Cold air crept beneath her tartan shawl. She jumped out of the gig and paced, rubbing her arms. Wind fanned through pine branches and an owl hooted; she sensed it watching her.

It's what he deserves, for his child and me to die in this wilderness. Won't he wish then he could say he's sorry?

Surely Kilgarry was close. Curran must have been heading for home.

She peered into darkness that felt alive with watchful eyes and unidentifiable sound. The horse shook its head, jingling the harness.

The hair on Morrigan's neck lifted; at the same instant, the horse shied and reared.

"Whoa, dearest, softly now." She stroked its muzzle, but rather than calming, it snorted, jerked, and leaped forward. She had to jump to avoid being struck by the gig.

"Stop," she cried. She started after the wayward creature but tripped on the hem of her dress and plunged face-first onto pebbles and dirt. As she picked herself up and brushed off her hands, the rattle and grate of wheels and thud of hooves faded into the night until all was again silence.

"He won't run forever," she reassured herself. "If I follow this road, I'm sure to come across the bloody beast." Afraid to look behind her, of what may have startled the horse, she took one hesitant step then another, but there were too many pebbles, and every time her shoe landed on one, it made a scratching sound.

Agnes Campbell had made it her business on Carrot Sunday to explain things she'd been sure Curran's wife needed to know.

"Never go out in a mist," she'd said. "Mountain mists can be thicker than the blackest night. You think I'm exaggerating? Heed me, mistress. Folk have walked right over the edge of cliffs. If a mist comes when you're out, don't try to find your way home. It's better to sit and wait for things to clear."

What of Agnes's other warnings? The harder Morrigan tried to banish them, the louder they spoke…ravings about the *glaistig*, a frightful grey creature, and the *ùruisg*, part goat, part human with tangled hair and protruding eyes.

A bleak, keening wail sent Morrigan's heartbeat into sickening palpitations. Darkness pressed against her.

"Watch out for the bean-nighe," Agnes had said. "She lives in burns and rivers, washing death shrouds. You'll hear her coming, for she sings a dirge."

Maybe, if she remained very still, nothing could find her.

The owl gave another hoot. Something hummed past her ear. "Get on," she said derisively. "Don't be a gawpus." Grabbing up her skirts to keep from tripping again, she walked. "Be a creature of the night," she said, remembering how she'd played such games as a child. "You're a fox. You've sharp eyes and ears. There's nothing can take you by surprise."

A squeak and the quick scuttle of some invisible creature, not five steps ahead, decimated her weak courage. She had to breathe deeply and draw resolve around her like a cloak before she could continue.

Agnes had warned her a second time about selkies, how they possessed the power to beguile humans into the ocean to drown. That was why, Agnes said severely, she never, ever looked Aodhàn Mackinnon in the eyes. She'd given Morrigan a stare so piercing Morrigan had recalled her selkie dream and felt quite guilty.

But the man in the dream had held her face against his throat, preventing her from looking into his eyes.

These disturbing thoughts were interrupted by a small, square illumination bobbing beneath the trees to the left, making the branches above jerk and writhe like living arms. Growing steadily clearer came the sound of a female, singing.

The bean-nighe *washes death shrouds. You'll hear her coming, for she sings a dirge.*

Morrigan fought to stifle the shriek building rapidly in her throat.

A figure emerged from behind the pines and stepped onto the road. The lantern she held in one hand threw feeble light across her face but left her eyes in shadow. She stopped. Those black eye sockets stared at Morrigan. After a moment she raised the lantern higher and took a step closer. "It's you."

Impaled by the light like an insect in a collector's scrapbook, Morrigan could only gape.

Then, astoundingly, the woman addressed her by name. "You never used to fear me, Morrigan Lawton."

"You...you know me?"

"What are you doing here, in the night, and so far from your home?"

"I'm lost."

The figure gestured. "Come away then," she said, and returned to her path beneath the trees.

Morrigan stared down the depthless, yawning tunnel that had swallowed her horse and gig. What else could she do? She didn't want to be alone out here.

The wind sighed and whispered.

They walked for a long time. Morrigan stumbled over hidden stones and into unexpected holes. Her injured ankle, much improved over the last fortnight, began to throb and swell. Before long she was limping and trying not to groan. At last the trees thinned into a clearing. She glimpsed a squat dark mass —a bothy. Her guide approached the door, pushed it open, and vanished inside. After a moment of unease, Morrigan followed.

A small fire burned in a crude round hearth. Some smoke escaped through a hole in the roof, but the room was uncomfortably acrid. "Warm yourself," the woman said, picking up a ladle from the floor. She spooned steaming liquid from a cauldron over the fire into an earthenware mug.

Morrigan sat down, glad to rest her ankle, and tried to study her odd savior without being obvious. Twigs and bits of leaves were stuck in a snarled braid. The woman's face was gaunt, dirty, her shapeless gown worn clear through in places. Creases around her mouth and the one laid deep between her brows made her look old, though dirt and want could give a deceptively aged appearance. She was skinny too, flat-chested, bony-wristed, as though she hadn't had enough to eat in a long while. Her hands, working the fire to renewed life, were rough and chapped, black under broken nails. Perhaps if she were bathed, her hair combed, she might pass for a decent crofter's wife.

"My horse ran away." Could this creature be one of Agnes's monsters in disguise? According to her, they all had the ability to hide behind illusion.

The woman came around the fire and held out the cup. Morrigan took it—it was nicely warm to the touch—and looked up to say *thank you*, but a shock of delayed recognition stopped her.

For what seemed an endless interlude she stared at that broad forehead, so fine but for the raised, angry red scar in the center, spoiling what could have been the woman's best feature. "Diorbhail," she said on a gasp. "Diorbhail Sinclair."

For one confused moment, she thought Curran, Kilgarry, Glenelg, and her new life had been but a dream, and she was still in Stranraer, staring into the poor, misused face of the local whore. It was intensified by the appearance of that same sheen of light, brighter than it had been the first time she'd seen it at Stranraer's train station.

"Aye." Diorbhail nodded.

"How can it be you? How in God's name can you be here?"

"Well, God had nowt to do with it," Diorbhail replied. "If he had his way, I'd no doubt be dead."

"How did you *get* here?"

"I walked to Mallaig. From there I came by boat."

"You walked? From Stranraer?" Morrigan looked into each corner, expecting to see a small, pinched face. "Where's your daughter?"

Diorbhail turned towards her hearth fire, sighing. "I saw you limping, Miss Lawton. The brew I've given you will deaden the pain."

"It's Ramsay now," Morrigan said faintly. "Morrigan Ramsay." She lifted the cup. The liquid inside was thick, with a mild, earthy smell. She sipped warily. It seemed rather like a stew, with small chunks of vegetables or what-not. It burned her throat and sent soothing warmth through her limbs. "Thank you," she said, draining the cup. She hadn't realized how hungry and thirsty she was.

"Will you show me your ankle?"

Morrigan stretched out her leg. Diorbhail removed her shoe and stocking, revealing an ankle swollen to twice its normal size, and angry purple bruising. The calf was swollen too, halfway to the knee.

"I dreamed of you every night," Diorbhail said as she gently massaged it. "I left Stranraer and walked to Mallaig, wanting to find you, but by the time I arrived, you were gone from there as well. A lady who knows your aunt told me you had come here. I could no' pay for sea passage, so I was going to walk, but she said I'd die for sure, and talked her husband into bringing me on his fishing boat. I've been here, waiting, not knowing how to approach you." She refilled the cup and handed it to Morrigan, then ripped a length of cloth from the bottom of her ragged petticoat and went outside. When she returned, the cloth was sopping wet with icy cold water. She wrapped it around Morrigan's ankle, bringing immediate relief.

Morrigan wanted to ask more questions, but her tongue felt thickened and numb. Her ears were ringing. The pain in her ankle had somehow diminished to a faint annoyance, and she became aware that her anxiety was also gone.

"I've given you the mushroom," Diorbhail said, "to help you remember what you've forgotten. It should be working by now."

"Mushroom?" Morrigan's voice sounded different—faint and tinny, with a slight echo. Diorbhail's face wavered like it was underwater.

"That's the last of it. Every day I've searched, but I can't find any more. I was going to have the rest of it myself tonight. I hoped it would show me a way to speak to you."

"Where...where is your daughter?" Morrigan had to know the answer to this, at least.

Diorbhail's jaw clenched; her face sagged. Morrigan felt, with sharpened sensitivity, the pain radiating off the woman, and wished she could withdraw the question. Again, Diorbhail gave no answer. She stood and clasped Morrigan's hands, pulling her to her feet. Morrigan stumbled and nearly fell. She was shocked to hear herself giggle, the sound seeming to bounce around the inside of her skull. Diorbhail's body rippled and the twigs in her hair undulated. For an instant, Morrigan thought she saw yellow eyes and darting forked tongues.

Maybe Diorbhail was a snake woman, a Medusa. But with those eyes gazing into hers, unblinking, possessing a hot, unworldly spark that seized her and snapped her to attention, wouldn't she already be turned to stone?

Diorbhail led her to a narrow pallet. "You can sleep here."

The sweet aromas of straw, clover, and heather rose around Morrigan as she sat down. "Thank you for helping me," she said.

There was a soft hissing sound as Diorbhail leaned closer and kissed her. The kiss sparked tremors of unease, yet also a strange familiarity. Morrigan tried to push the woman away, but the drink had sapped her strength, making her effort no more powerful than a babe's. She caught a new scent, one that carried her backward in time to lost hours hiding in the forest or on the slope by Loch Ryan. She inhaled. Diorbhail smelled like old books.

"It's been so long," her rescuer said, her brow furrowed, a gleam of tears in her eyes. She withdrew, resting on her heels briefly before becoming practical again.

She unknotted and removed Morrigan's shawl and velvet jacket, and unbuttoned her blouse, lending assistance as Morrigan slipped off the blouse and camisole. The corset was unlaced and placed to the side.

"There was mushroom in that drink?" Morrigan asked as she lay down. The air was cold on her bare arms, bringing out gooseflesh.

"Aye. It has many names." Diorbhail tucked the shawl around Morrigan's shoulders. "My mam was a healer; she taught me the properties of herbs and plants before she died. She called it 'the prince of flowers.' It's a potion from ancient times. I've seen that these aids have made you ill in the past, but I swear the mushroom won't hurt you or the babe you carry. My mam gave it to expectant women who were overly feared of labor and birth."

Morrigan giggled again at the thought of a lowly mushroom making her feel so strange. Diorbhail giggled too. They laughed helplessly, as though tickled by invisible fingers.

Some time later, a voice she thought was Diorbhail's startled her awake, but her companion had her back propped against an old rocking chair a little distance away, and appeared to be asleep.

She must have been dreaming. She'd been sitting beside Diorbhail in some cavernous place of uncertain light and dripping water. She knew the woman was Diorbhail, though she looked nothing like the woman by the fire. The figure in the dream had cascades of white hair and skin as flawless as marble. Her arms were muscled like a warrior's.

Tell me what it's like, when a man and woman join, Morrigan had asked. *If the god comes, I want to know what to expect.*

The dream-Diorbhail stroked an enormous stalagmite. *See this? It is the manhood of Velchanos, buried here in Athene's womb. As it is for Athene, so it is for women and men.*

The muffled crackle of wood in the hearth fire, gently undulating shadows, and peaceful silence soon sent her back to sleep. When next she woke, Diorbhail was sitting beside her, weeping silently.

Morrigan sat up and placed her palm on Diorbhail's cheek. She *knew* this woman. Trusted her. Loved her even. Somehow, Diorbhail was dearer than anyone she'd ever known, and had been, for longer than could be fathomed.

"Since the first time I saw you in Stranraer," Diorbhail said, "I've known there's something that connects us. I took the mushroom, and that's when I saw your colors, gold and purple, all around you like a cloud. The mushroom gives us power to see things that cannot usually be seen."

"What is this mushroom?"

"It's as close to magic as we can get. It shows us things that cannot be seen in the light of day. I saw myself with you. We were close, closer than sisters, somewhere…a different place, a different time. You trusted me. You need to trust me again, Morrigan Lawton. The mushroom showed me. You're the one to choose the path for the future, for all the world."

"Choose the path for the world?" Morrigan bit off a cynical laugh and shook her head. "That's pure daftness. Women like me can't do anything other than vex men. I'm rather good at that. My father and my husband have made my failings quite clear."

"You must reject those lies and follow the truth. Well do I know how hard it will be, and how easy for you to say you cannot, because of this or that reason. You have to stand up though you feel weighted down, buried under all the words they use to keep you from trying."

Diorbhail stroked the side of Morrigan's head tenderly. "I've seen other things, things I could no' understand, but I'll tell you anyway. Like I said, I've been here, hiding, trying to find a way to approach you when no one else was around." She looked away, blinking several times. "I fear folk. I could no' make myself come to you in the open."

"I understand," Morrigan said. After what the woman had endured, it was no wonder.

"I hid in the woods. I stole food. I found this place and stayed. I've been watching you, and the village, and listening...."

"Go on."

"That's how I knew you're carrying a child. Folk speak of it. It's no' like it was for me in Stranraer, though. They like you. They're pleased the laird has wed. But there's something else. A man...a fisherman. At least that's what he wants folk to think. I heard him called Aodhàn."

"Mackinnon. Aodhàn Mackinnon."

"Aye."

Hearing his name brought images of the anguish on his face, of the kiss that had prompted everything leading to this moment. "What about him?"

"I saw colors around him, too. He's special in some way, but no' the same as you. I felt sick when I saw him. I cannot explain why, but I fear him. He is not what he seems."

"What colors did you see?" Morrigan remembered her wedding cèilidh and what she'd glimpsed, but waited, her breath catching, to hear what Diorbhail would say.

"Red, orange. Dark brown. He frightens me. I think he's...connected to you, as I am. I felt the force of him. It was like thunder." Her gaze upon Morrigan was penetrating.

Morrigan resisted an urge to defend Mackinnon and asked instead, "Have you seen colors around anyone else?"

"Aye." Diorbhail smiled for the first time, a smile that made her look younger. "Around Master Ramsay. He carried you into a garden and put you on a red couch. There was another man there too, and you were all laughing."

"Seaghan MacAnaugh," Morrigan said. "Aye."

Diorbhail nodded. "I was watching from the forest. I could barely tell what colors were yours and what were your husband's. They mixed together, maybe because he was carrying you. There was blue, and purple, and gold, and white. Every shade of purple you can imagine."

"Did he make you feel sick and afraid?"

"No." Diorbhail shook her head emphatically. "No." She opened her mouth as if to say something else, then looked away to the hearth, her hands clenching. "But I did feel badly about what the other one did. Aodhàn Mackinnon."

"I don't understand."

"Him kissing you. It was wrong."

"What? You're leaping about like a snagged fish. You mean before I came here tonight?"

Diorbhail blinked. Her brows rose. "I mean in the garden that day."

"Mackinnon wasn't there."

"Aye, he was. He kissed you."

"You'd best tell me exactly what you saw."

"Aodhàn Mackinnon came in through the forest gate when you were alone. He knelt beside you; he stared at you a long time, then he bent over you, full of nerve, and kissed you on the mouth."

Morrigan concentrated, trying to recall that day. She'd fallen asleep after Curran and Seaghan left her. She'd dreamed of swimming in the sea, of the seal thwarting her efforts to reach the castle. The seal had drawn her under the surface. She knew she would drown, yet she didn't care. She accepted it. The dream man had kissed her.

She'd awakened in the garden, feeling corrupt and full of fire.

"Are you saying Mackinnon was in the garden with me?"

"Aye. He kissed you, and you didn't seem bothered by it."

"I didn't know. I was asleep. I've had trouble sleeping; I suppose I was exhausted."

Diorbhail frowned. "Doing that was an evil thing. Did you say he kissed you again? Right before you came here?"

Morrigan was reeling. "No...no. I didn't understand." She wasn't sure why she denied it. Why protect him, if what Diorbhail said was true?

Diorbhail's gaze was wary and suspicious. "He's a trickster, that one," she said, low. "I wanted to do something, but I was afraid, and like I said, you didn't seem bothered. I was going to throw a rock at him, but I feared I'd hit you. He stood up and looked down at you, and then he left. Your husband returned a moment after. Aodhàn Mackinnon must've seen him coming."

Morrigan turned towards the fire and imagined Mackinnon bending over her while she was asleep, stealing kisses, in the very shadow of Kilgarry. She touched her lips, realizing she wasn't horrified, or angry, or shocked, though she should be. No, this reaction was something else altogether. She wondered if Diorbhail's mushroomy brew caused this, because what Mackinnon had done was terribly wrong. If what Diorbhail said was true, Mackinnon had come into the garden, set upon her while she was unaware, and left before Curran returned. How...how *bold*.

Her thoughts were fuzzy. Tomorrow she would examine what Diorbhail had told her and make sense of it. "I'm so tired," she said, and lay down again, closing her eyes and turning to face the wall. "My head aches."

Diorbhail murmured something soothing and the bothy fell silent again but for the gentle, intermittent crackle of the dying fire.

Morrigan drifted in and out of sleep, startling at times, languid at others. Once when she woke a cloud of white mist was coming through the window, seeping to the floor and expanding, filled with delicate tinkling laughter reminiscent of tiny silver Christmas bells. The mist thickened, obscuring everything beyond it.

Agnes's warning about West Highland fogs returned. She'd said they could be perilous, but nothing about how they might lie upon one like a ghostly lover.

Hands caressed Morrigan's arms and shoulders. A face formed, one she had seen before. His eyes were Curran's, seductive and darkest blue, like the heavens succumbing to night.

I will have victory, Aridela. She heard the voice in the mist, like a whisper running across the surface of still, cold water.

Longing swept through her, so terrible she woke and sat upright with a groan.

"You're safe." Diorbhail laid a hand upon her forearm. "I am watching over you."

"I have such dreams," Morrigan said. "They tear at me."

"Your power comes from your birth in this forest," Diorbhail said. "The mountain is part of you and you part of this mountain, the flesh of *Sgurr Mhic Bharraich*. Your mam's death blood bound your roots deep into caves and all the buried, fertile places."

Her voice diffused into a quiet thrum. "Against the mountain, the seal is powerless. Who is the mountain? Who is the seal? Faces and hair will change; clothing and station can change. You will have to see beyond the surface or you'll be forever tricked. See beyond, and no face can ever fool you."

Consoled and intrigued, Morrigan lay down and closed her eyes. As she let herself float away, she thought she heard Diorbhail again.

We're all of us gathering, and no' for the first time. We can make something happen, if we open our eyes and truly see. We can bring the Lady home. That's what we're meant to do.

SUNLIGHT POURED THROUGH THE WINDOW THAT LAST NIGHT HAD BROUGHT VISIONS in mist.

I must go home. Curran will be...fashed.

But Diorbhail's bothy possessed a spell, a spell of holding, while contrarily granting a sense of freedom.

Perhaps, like the faery realm, a mystical barrier hid it from the real world, and while she was here, time outside would not pass. Curran wouldn't worry, or even know she was gone.

In this old, rotting place, she felt as though she could live that life she had once described to him. She would ride her stallion, swim naked in lochs, and make her own choices.

Something else held her. For the first time, she felt as if another human being understood her completely. Odd, that this should come from poor, fallen Diorbhail Sinclair.

Diorbhail brought her a sturdy stick with a forked end. Morrigan limped about with it, collecting wood, hauling water, and carrying eggs provided by the stolen hen. The habit of working came back as if no time had passed and she was still running to the demands of her father's inn.

When the sun passed the midday mark, they sat beside the burn and dipped their feet in cold water.

The things Diorbhail said lit a wild, livening pleasure deep inside, where the babe grew, almost as though it, too, listened. The woman had never been inside a school, yet she possessed surprising intelligence, and the courage to say what Morrigan had only thought.

"The mushroom has shown me many things," Diorbhail said. "That you were born to bring great change."

Morrigan believed everything Diorbhail said...everything except that *she* had the power to change anything.

As they talked, Morrigan became aware of an eagle perched in a nearby tree. It was still and quiet, canting its head one way then the other as it watched them.

"Would you look at that," she said, low.

"I saw it." Raising her voice, Diorbhail spoke to the bird. "Am I pleasing you?"

Morrigan sucked in a breath when the bird fluffed its wings, opened its beak, and replied with an eagle's typical weak screeing. "Does it understand us?"

"The Lady's eyes and ears are watching you."

"What? An eagle!"

"A deity can take any form, or she can send one of her maids. You are not alone, Morrigan Ramsay."

Warmth crept through Morrigan as she watched the bird. She remembered the eagle on her wedding day. Could it be true?

When twilight fell, she reclined in the splintery rocking chair Diorbhail had salvaged from the midden heap, and listened to more revelations.

"The mushroom showed me another time and place," Diorbhail said. "In that land, woman could make herself pregnant. She chose it and caused it to happen. She used the north wind, or fertile water. Water is the beginning and the end of all things, and woman is water's guardian."

Morrigan closed her eyes and rested her head against the back of the rocker. Now it made sense, the love she'd always felt for the ocean. The pull it exerted on her.

"Who is this 'lady'? I heard you say something last night, too. Something about bringing a lady home."

Diorbhail smiled. "I thought you were asleep. She is the Lady of Many Names. The Great Goddess, who even now has her eye on us all."

"Oh, Diorbhail. That's wishful thinking. A dream."

"It's you who've been dreaming, m'lady."

"You must mean God. You're speaking of God."

Diorbhail's mouth tilted up. "So you believe in that one, then?"

"I...I don't know. I suppose you're saying if one exists, why not another." Morrigan shrugged. "You're right."

"I believe in She who plants every seedling, who stretches out her hand...." Here Diorbhail stretched out hers, palm down.... "And brings the rain. I believe in She who men face when they die. She was the one we all worshipped first. She made everything we see around us. She has been here from the beginning. This God of yours is a mewling wean compared to her. He was created from men's fear of her, from their desire for power and their need to rule over women."

Morrigan started to scoff, but stopped and considered. She didn't have to pretend, not with Diorbhail. "I knew it," she said. "I knew there was another."

"She lives," Diorbhail said, "though She is quiet now. Watching. Waiting."

"How do you know all this? Why do you see so many more things than I ever have, if I am supposedly the special one?"

Diorbhail didn't answer for a moment, and seemed to ponder. "I think it's because I've been alone. Except for my child, no one ever spoke to me. All I ever had were my own thoughts, and the mushroom. You were busy every day, and you seldom had a chance to be on your own. Maybe she tried to get your attention but you couldn't hear."

"When I ran away from my chores to the forest, or the moor, or the edge of Loch Ryan, I did have...thoughts. I saw things. When I was alone, and quiet." Morrigan tapped the arm of the rocking chair. "You listened. You paid attention, and I didn't, or when I did, I denied it, or told myself it was a dream, or I was hearing things, seeing things that weren't there."

"I wish I had more of the mushroom. Maybe it's for the best though, since it does make you ill."

"Why do you say that? It didn't make me ill last night. I feel better than I have in a long while. Tell me…what else has the mushroom shown you?'

"I saw that it would help you mind what you've forgotten." Diorbhail's head leaned to one side and she frowned. "Have you had more dreams since you came to Glenelg? Does it feel as though this place is making you dream?"

"Aye. Strange, strong, *loud* dreams. Frightening, sometimes. Sometimes magical and inviting."

"My dreams are loud here, too. My skin feels like it's had too much whisky. I'm itchy and tingly all over."

"Aye." Morrigan nodded. "Aye."

"One day, we women will rise again. Our Mother, Lady of us all, will step from her cave. She will open our hearts and we will have thousands upon thousands of years of joy, not just men, and not just women, but all of us, together."

"When will it happen?" Morrigan asked, enthralled, wanting it to come now.

Diorbhail smiled. "When you bring it."

EARLY IN THE MORNING, BEFORE THE SUN HAD FULLY RISEN, THE DOOR TO THE bothy crashed open, waking both women. A whirling fiend rushed in, spouting curses and leveling a stout cudgel.

Morrigan rose, using Diorbhail's shoulder as a crutch, rubbing her eyes as she recognized who had found them. Eleanor Graeme.

Fright subsided into relief. Eleanor would unwind these ropes of lassitude. She would crush whatever it was that had put Curran and her life as Lady Eilginn far away in a distant, foggy place that no longer mattered.

"What is going on here?" Eleanor's glare would have cowed anyone. Not surprisingly, shy Diorbhail cringed. "What d'you think you're doing to Master Curran's wife, you cursed bogle?"

She lifted her stick, and Morrigan quickly stepped between them. "She saved my life. Stop shouting and brandishing that thing."

"D'you realize Master Curran is half out of his wits?" Eleanor's voice was quietly dangerous, in a way that reminded Morrigan of Douglas.

"I could hardly walk yesterday. My ankle's swollen. Diorbhail was going to take me home today or tomorrow. As soon as I was better."

"Could you not send word? Could this…*woman*…not walk down for you to let us all know?"

Morrigan and Diorbhail glanced at each other. Morrigan saw the same truth in Diorbhail's eyes. Neither had wanted this time to end. Neither dared admit it.

"Let me see." Eleanor gestured impatiently as she propped her cudgel by the door.

Morrigan sat in the rocking chair and Eleanor knelt to inspect it. "It is swollen," she admitted reluctantly. "I can see it would have hurt to walk down this hill. But you—" she sent a venomous stare towards Diorbhail, "should have. Now I will take you." She stood. "You can lean on me and we'll go slowly. No doubt we'll soon come across other searchers. They're everywhere."

"Can she no' wait one more day?" Diorbhail asked, her voice halting.

"No, she cannot! You'll be lucky if the master doesn't put you up on charges of kidnapping."

"I...I...kidnapping?"

"She did nothing of the sort!" Morrigan jumped up, forgetting her injury until the stab of pain reminded her. She quickly took her weight off that foot, hissing. "Would you have wanted her to leave me in the forest? I lost my horse and the gig. I was alone. She brought me here. She fed me. She's taken care of me!"

After a pause, Eleanor said, "Well," in a calmer voice. "That's as may be, but now we need to get you to Kilgarry." She slung Morrigan's left arm over her shoulder. "Don't be afraid to lean on me. I'm strong."

Morrigan tried to look back at Diorbhail as Eleanor propelled her towards the door.

"Wait!" Diorbhail cried, as Eleanor turned sideways to get them through the narrow doorway, careful to avoid protruding nails. "Wait. I've seen you."

"Aye?" Eleanor said, shrugging. "I have lived here many years. So what?"

"No, no, I saw you...in a vision."

Eleanor's frown was ominous. "What do you mean?"

"Your colors.... Light and dark green, a healer's colors. You're part of us. You...and me...and her. We're supposed to be together. You and I. We're to help her. D'you no' sense it?"

Morrigan half-expected Eleanor to explode or send ridicule slicing like knife blades, but she did neither. Glancing at Morrigan, she said, "I saw color around you in the kirk, the day you fell off your horse. I felt I knew you. It was...an unco thing." As Diorbhail took a timid step closer, she added, "I have to admit you seem familiar as well."

"I have seen myself holding you," Diorbhail said. "Trying to give you comfort at a bad time."

Eleanor nodded. "I see you with hair the color of seashells, and you smell of juniper. There's color around you right now. It's white. Like a cloud."

Morrigan gowked, shocked into speechlessness at this turn.

"Wait one more day," Diorbhail pleaded. "Stay with us. Share your knowledge."

Eleanor's mouth tensed. "I would not feel right about it. Sitting here while everyone searches for her."

"Just one day?" Morrigan asked. "I…I'm not ready to go back."

No one said anything for a minute or two. At last Eleanor shrugged. "Let us in, then," she said, and helped Morrigan return to the rocking chair.

"Eleanor," Morrigan said. "This is Diorbhail Sinclair. She's no stranger. I knew her in Stranraer. She walked most of the way here to find me."

"She walked from the Low Country?"

"Aye."

Eleanor regarded Diorbhail, her brows lifted. "Well, well," she said and nodded, as if reluctantly impressed.

THEY PASSED AROUND WARM BARLEY TEA IN THE SINGLE WOODEN MUG DIORBHAIL had found in the rubbish heap outside the bothy.

"I couldn't sleep for thinking about you," Eleanor told them. "You were who knows where, and quickened with child. Then I remembered this old bothy, how it was so remote not even Randall Benedict's mercenaries found it when they cleared Glenelg. A woman named Clara lived here. Mad Clara, she was called. She could hardly speak the Gaelic, much less English. I started to wonder if you could've found this place, and if you were hurt, you might have used it for shelter. I decided to come and have a look."

"The Lady was guiding you to us," Diorbhail said. "You're part of us. She wants us to be together. She kept you from saying anything or bringing anyone with you."

Eleanor shrugged, but she didn't deny it so that was something.

"Tell me your story," Morrigan asked Diorbhail. "I've often wondered about you and wanted to know."

Diorbhail chewed her lip for a few seconds. "I was born near a village called Durness, on the northern coast," she said. "My mam was the healer. I don't remember my da at all—he was a fisherman, and died in a storm when I was a babe. In those days, my mam had to be aye careful, for the Christians watched her, hoping she would make a mistake they could hang or burn her for. They didn't seem to care they'd be left without anyone who knew how to keep their cuts from festering, or what to do for flux."

Eleanor snorted her understanding.

"She died," Diorbhail said, "and I was on my own. My tale is an old one. I fell in love. He was handsome, and being with him made me happy. He talked me into lying with him, and when I realized I was going to have a child, I told him." She laughed without humor. "You've never seen a lad change so fast. Now I was a slut, and who knew how many I'd spread my legs for. I thought he loved me, and I was a fool. When I could no longer hide it, the Kirk cast me out. He was right there among the rest, throwing rocks. I made my way south, and eventually landed in Stranraer. My child was born by then. I gave birth to her in the ruins of a byre near Kilmarnock. I tried to say I was a widow but I suppose I've ne're been so good at lying. It worked for a while, until a man who knew my history came through. I wouldn't leave again, though, and... there was you. I could no' leave you, Morrigan Lawton."

"So you stayed, though I never spoke to you."

"I knew that would change one day."

"I hate him for hurting you," Morrigan said.

Diorbhail shook her head. "He does no' matter. I knew what I did with him was wrong, and no' because it went against what the Kirk demanded. I felt it in here." She struck her chest. "I knew it because my heart told me he wasn't for me. He wasn't the one I was meant to be with. I think we all have this understanding inside us. We get impatient with the waiting, the no' knowing when or if the right one will come, so we ignore it, to our sorrow."

"That's how I felt with Kit." Morrigan sat up straight in the old rocker. "At first I wanted to be with him, but then...I cannot describe it. It was like I would suffocate if he didn't stop, if I didn't get away from him."

"I wish I'd listened to the warnings in my own heart," Diorbhail said. "But then I would no' have had my child. And I might never have come to Stranraer. I might never have found you."

"And if I hadn't listened, I might have been forced to go to America with Kit, instead of here, with Curran."

Morrigan saw how events had shaped the future. If she'd gone to America with Kit, she never would have met Eleanor, or Seaghan...or Mackinnon. Diorbhail would not have been able to follow. Morrigan glanced at Eleanor half-fearfully, realizing she'd all but confessed to lying with another man besides Curran, but the midwife was merely listening, no judgment or shock on her face.

Eleanor spoke musingly as she stared at the fire. "Women are punished for knowing how to heal. For being creative, for having opinions. For wanting to be educated. They're punished for defending their own. They're punished for how they look, or how they don't look. But most of all, women are punished for giving love. The men who talk them into the giving aren't punished, nor are most of the men who take what they want by force. I pray that one day all women see and understand what's been done. Only then will anything change."

Morrigan chalked up this blasphemy to the strange freedom the bothy inspired.

Leaning forward, she clasped Diorbhail's hand. "Will you tell us," she asked, "why your daughter is not with you?"

Diorbhail shrank into herself. "She was trampled by a horse," she said at last, very quietly.

"Diorbhail." Morrigan could have cut out her tongue for not leaving it alone.

"It was done deliberately," Diorbhail said. "Louts who had long taunted me. They used a horse to crush her like a china cup, and laughed. Nobody cared. None but me."

Morrigan knelt in front of her. Eleanor stood, and in her logical, dispassionate way, proceeded to make more barley tea. She gave the mug to Diorbhail, briefly clasping her shoulder.

"What was her name?" Morrigan asked.

"Alecto. It came to me in a dream two days before she was born. I had never heard of it. I don't know where it came from or what it means."

"I do," Morrigan said, tightening her grip on Diorbhail's hand. "It's Greek. It belongs to one of the Erinyes. There are three of them. They're sisters. Tisiphone, Megaera, and Alecto."

"I thought it sounded grand, but I shouldn't've named her that, because it brought her nothing but torment." Diorbhail rubbed her eyes wearily. "I wanted to die," she said. "I walked into the ocean. The eagle stopped me. I kept seeing you, hearing your voice. You're the reason I still live. Because I couldn't save my child, but I will try to help save yours."

DIORBHAIL WAS UNSURPRISED BY THE VIOLENCE OF MORRIGAN'S DREAMS. "THEY show you what you need to remember. A witch, the men called you. And it's true. A witch you were."

Morrigan stiffened. "I wasn't!"

"To them, you were something to fear. There was something about you the dream didn't show. It's no' important why they thought what they did. Don't you see? No matter how strong or wise a man is, no matter how much power he wields over others, he loses it all, his strength and his pride, in his need for the woman. He hates the way he's drawn to her. For some men, she becomes a witch. A devil."

"A temptress," Eleanor said.

Diorbhail nodded. "That's why those kind of men rape. It's why they kill. 'Tis their way to defeat what they fear. It's how they tell themselves they have no longing, no weakness, and that it's not their fault. There are more of those men than you might realize, mistress. Some slaughter every last speck of tenderness they were born with. They no longer feel guilt, no matter what they do. They crave the pain they cause. We're leaping towards a world where that is common. Someday, if that world comes, women will be the same as cattle or sheep, and there will be no succor anywhere."

Eleanor nodded. "Aye," she said. "The more we accept the cages fashioned for us now, the easier it will be for that to happen."

"They blame us for their own weakness," Morrigan said, pondering it.

"There are men who rise beyond what they are taught, but many cannot… so woman is bound at the bottom of the sea, always looking up, never able to rise. It's easier, you ken, to think of her as a witch who uses her body to trick and deceive. When all, men, women, and children, accept that a woman is evil, a whore in the making, then confining her is necessary, 'for her own good.' Guilt is smoothed over, and their fear ebbs."

Eleanor said, "I have two brothers. One is a surgeon, the other a priest. They are vastly different, and both have taught me many valuable lessons. My brother the priest liked to make me sit on a stool for hours, memorizing texts proclaiming the evil of women, how we single-handedly introduced sin into the world. The early Catholic leaders taught that women are paths to the Devil, created only to kneel, serve, and submit. One called us accidents, misbegotten men, made through illness or ill wind. They blame the crucifixion itself on women. Their fear and hatred is clear for those who look, who are not afraid to believe. My brother took it to heart. He liked to whip me until I bled, and force me to ask his forgiveness for the sins of the female. My other brother finally took me away. He and your husband knew each other, and eventually, I came here."

"But…it isn't fair. We've done nothing." Morrigan inwardly derided herself for complaining about fair play. She'd known better than to believe the world was fair before she turned five.

"It's their fear," Eleanor said. "Fear they cannot purge, though they would laugh and deny it to hell and back if confronted."

They were quiet for a while, watching the fire, then Eleanor said, "When a woman turns evil, it's almost always because of what was done to her by her father or some other man. More often than not that's true for men, as well. Generations upon generations, passing along hatred, bitterness, torture." She paused again, her brows lowered in thought. "When my brother was teaching me his craft in Edinburgh, we treated many who had been misused as children. I saw that such women, as they get older, are loath to harm anyone or anything, but the opposite is true for men. I saw it again and again. Men who are mistreated when young will do the same to others, even to their own children, though they remember with hatred what was done to them."

Morrigan had longed to hear someone say the things she had privately thought and felt so guilty over. Yet it made her apprehensive, off-balance, like the air was being released from the world and the ground was slowly collapsing.

Did it mean she was not those things Douglas had always called her? That she was not lazy, or useless? Not a hoor?

"Men have so much, but it's never enough," Eleanor said. "They try to steal women's magic, through force or trickery, ridicule, humiliation. As Diorbhail says, if they succeed, then I can only hope those I care about are dead. If that time comes, there will be no more pretense, no words wreathed in praise. I've long sensed it coming, and despaired."

"Does Curran know you feel this way?" Morrigan asked.

Eleanor shrugged. "What business is it of his what I think? All he needs from me is to bring a healthy child into the world. I've known since I first watched my father kick my mother as he would a dog, that I would never trust a man. Now that you've told me about the argument you had with the master, and how you ended up here, I'm not so sure I have much use for him any longer."

"He was…provoked."

Eleanor smiled slightly. "I heard what provoked him."

Morrigan looked away, blushing.

"One of the reasons my father beat my mother was because of the things she taught me, things like what we've been saying. My da vowed he would kick good Christian obedience into her. He killed her finally then abandoned us, for which I was thankful. Fortunately for me, my brother the surgeon didn't turn out like him. He was my savior."

As Eleanor poured more tea, Diorbhail mused. "When a woman loves a man, she shows him everything he can be, and everything he's not."

"Everything and nothing," said Eleanor, stooping to slide a few sticks onto the fire. "The heaving abyss from which he came, and to which he travels all the days of his life."

"She is the terrible face of the Goddess," Diorbhail said, watching Eleanor intently, "of the judgment awaiting him. She is the sun, and she is shadow."

"Shadow?" Morrigan rocked faster. "D'you mind, Diorbhail, when you said shadows hold lessons for us?" The rocker creaked dangerously as she grew more excited. "You told me my shadow was long, that it would devour me if I wasn't careful."

Diorbhail took the mug from Eleanor. "Of course I mind it," she said, grimacing at the tea's bitterness. "She it was who put the words in my mouth."

"Diorbhail called me an avatar," Morrigan told Eleanor.

Eleanor shrugged. "What is that?"

"A friend of Nicky's told me it's a god who comes to earth and lives like a human." Morrigan turned to Diorbhail. "Shouldn't this goddess of yours have made me a queen, or someone with power? How does she expect me to do all these great things? I'm nothing, nobody, penniless, and a woman. Without Curran, I couldn't even feed myself."

Eleanor glanced at Diorbhail then lowered her gaze to the cup as Diorbhail passed it to her. "I don't mean to insult you, but how did *you* know what it meant?"

"I was told what to say. I didn't know the meaning of the word. I barely remember speaking to her. I had taken the mushroom. It's a rare, special mushroom that gives visions, knowledge. My mam taught me how to use it. That's how I saw you, Eleanor Graeme."

"Witch's cap, you mean?"

"Some call it that. I brought what I had with me, and gave it to Mistress Ramsay night before last. I've searched the fields, but I can't find any more."

"I have some."

Both Morrigan and Diorbhail stared at Eleanor, who nodded. "I collect witch's cap every year. I've told no one hereabouts what it can do, but I've used it myself more than once, and I've seen things. Strange things."

"We should take it together," Diorbhail said eagerly. "It will strengthen us threefold. Oh, aye! Taking it together will show us things we could never see on our own."

"I don't know what you mean by that," Eleanor said. "And I'm not so certain it'd be good for Mistress Ramsay."

"Don't you see?" Diorbhail rose, rubbing her arms as she paced. "Mistress sees bits of things. She hears half-spoken sentences, morsels only. What you call 'witch's cap' can help return what's been lost. We'll see clearly if we do this together. I'm sure of it. You know as well as I that her dreams are memories. She'll never have complete understanding unless she sees truly."

"Wait," Morrigan said. "My dreams are memories?"

Diorbhail poked at the fire with a sooty stick. "I think when you sleep, the lives you've lived before come back. The dreams try to help you remember, so that you don't repeat the same mistakes."

"Are you saying I was murdered? Actually murdered?"

Diorbhail shrugged. "Maybe. Probably."

Morrigan thought about that for a moment while her insides lurched. "Father Drummond visited me after I hurt my ankle. He said some believe that expectant women's dreams are the baby's memories of its past lives."

"No!" Diorbhail spoke fiercely. "Never listen to priests."

Eleanor agreed, somewhat reluctantly, to go down and retrieve her stockpile of witch's cap as soon as there was light enough to see her way.

"Did you know I would be in the forest?" Morrigan asked Diorbhail. "Everything you've said...did it all come from this mushroom? Did you ever go to school? I did, but I never learned these things."

"Many questions." Diorbhail grinned, displaying the hole where a tooth had gone missing or been knocked out. "They'll give you no rest now. They'll pull you to your fate." Her grin faded. "Schools are run by men. D'you think men are going to teach you about your power? No, *a ghràidh*, they'll teach you the opposite, how you cannot survive without them, how you must obey them for your own good, how they have to guide your life for you, how you are silly and weak, and must follow their version of right and wrong. How their god gave them control over you, and you must submit if you want to go to their heaven, where, no doubt, you'll be serving and submitting for eternity." Going off to one corner of the bothy, she retrieved a small container and shook out a handful of brittle green leaves. "There are other methods of Sight. Some use this leaf, or venom from snakes. Both are too dangerous for you. Some only have to listen. I listen to the voices in the wind and I can see what the water shows. Fire sometimes speaks to me. I've forged my power for many years. I will try to teach you how to do these things as well, mistress."

"What else have you seen?"

"Mostly things meant for me. Now you need to learn your fate. If we're lucky, you'll see who means you harm and who will help you on this long journey. Do you feel the Lady? She whets us against her mighty grindstone!"

Eleanor left in the translucent light of predawn, promising to return as soon as she could. She added acerbically that they could use the witch's cap once; then Morrigan must go home.

But the gloaming was deep before she returned. It was little wonder no one had found them yet, if Morrigan had managed to stray so far.

"Glenelg is in uproar," Eleanor said as she came in. "Mistress Ramsay must come with me now, before anything worse happens." She sighed. "I cannot believe I allowed you to talk me into such a foolish and cruel delay." She gestured in her indomitable fashion. "Come now, let us not put your husband through any more agony. There are those telling him you've fallen into the sea and drowned! What he said was wrong, but you've punished him enough, don't you think?"

Morrigan could hardly argue. "I miss him." Only after saying it did she realize she'd spoken out loud, and that it was true, despite the memory of that awful thing he'd said. "I want to go home." Diorbhail's stricken expression filled her with guilt and confusion. "You knew I couldn't stay much longer."

Diorbhail blinked and looked away, then she clenched her hands. "Why d'you think about that place? That *Kilgarry?*"

"What of Curran?" Morrigan asked gently. "What of his child?"

"She's *your* wean. It's *your* belly she grows in."

Morrigan took a step closer. "I've always believed that my thoughts were evil; that *I* was evil. But you, and Eleanor, and this place, have changed me. I can hardly understand it all yet, but I know I won't ever go back to what I used to be." She drew in a deep breath and let it out slowly. "Even though we see the truth, we cannot change the way things are. What you want is impossible. The world belongs to men, and they will never give it up, no matter what we think or feel."

Diorbhail frowned. She opened her mouth but Morrigan stopped her. "It's a fantasy," she said quietly. "They'll never give up their power."

"*You're* changing," Diorbhail said, so low her voice was nearly drowned by a thrush's singing outside.

"I'm but one small person. I cannot cause the entire world to be different than it is."

Eleanor waited, her arms crossed, looking from one to the other.

"He'll never stop searching for me," Morrigan said. "I don't want to give birth here, in the dirt."

Diorbhail looked sad and defeated. The idea of walking off and leaving her was intolerable. "Come with me." Morrigan held out her hand.

"I'd no' be welcome. I'm naught but a hoor in the eyes of the world."

"You will come with me," Morrigan said. "We won't tell anyone of your past. You'll simply be the woman who saved me when I was lost."

Morrigan kept her hand outstretched. Hesitantly, Diorbhail came forward and took it. Morrigan smiled and they began their trek down the mountain.

MORRIGAN'S ANKLE FELT ALMOST NORMAL AFTER THREE DAYS OF REST AND MANY cold compresses. Eleanor and Diorbhail took turns serving as support. Eleanor had cannily thought to bring two candles. Diorbhail put one inside her cracked lantern, so they wouldn't have to make their way in complete darkness.

Morrigan looked back, this time deliberately. Water from an earlier shower still dripped from the thatch. She fancied the lonely bothy was weeping. Part of her wanted to greet too. Her adventure was over. Her moment of imaginary freedom. She knew she must go home, but this broken wee place would always be a cherished memory.

With Eleanor and Diorbhail beside her, Morrigan wasn't afraid of the dark or any supernatural beasties hidden beyond the glimmer of their lamp. In fact, she told her companions of Agnes Campbell's warnings—all but the one about selkies—and they laughed as they walked.

But the downhill foray soon began to pall. "It could be worse," Eleanor said. "At least we've this road, foul though it is. Did I tell you, mistress, that the horse and gig were found the day after you went missing? Not anywhere near here, though. They were on the other side of this mountain."

"Curran...poor Curran."

"Aye, mistress. I had naught to do but think as I walked all that way, and it ate at me, what he's going through. We're not to the days when men have no care for us, not yet, and I think I have an idea of his suffering. That's why I insisted we go, and not wait for daylight."

They came to a fast-flowing burn. The cold water felt delicious upon Morrigan's ankle, but the rocks were moss covered and slick. Eleanor lost her footing and fell, but she rose laughing, proclaiming that her dowp was padded enough to soften the blow. All three giggled as they helped each other clamber up the bank on the far side.

"What's this?"

Morrigan nearly jumped out of her skin and almost slid back into the water at the sound of a man's voice.

Eleanor and Diorbhail moved in close on either side of Kilgarry's mistress; Diorbhail raised her lantern.

He stood beneath the branches of a holly oak, a shotgun slung over his shoulder. For the briefest instant, Morrigan thought she was looking at a younger version of her father. She gasped, caught in a rush of dizziness.

But it was Aodhàn Mackinnon, not the ghost of Douglas Lawton. He propped his shotgun against the tree trunk and came forward swiftly. "Morrigan," he said, his voice unguardedly relieved.

"Aye, she's been found," Eleanor said. "But how d'you come to be here, in the middle of the night, so far from home?"

"You think that matters to me?" He sent Eleanor a cold glance before returning his attention to Morrigan. "Everything closer has already been searched twice over."

He frowned at her. "Are you hurt?"

"My ankle's a bit worse for wear." She tried to make light of it but was moved to her core that he would be out combing the land for her so late. His face was drawn and tired.

"Here." Without any warning, he plucked her off the ground. "Put your arms round my neck," he said, and cradled her, one arm supporting her back and the other holding her behind the knees.

"I'm too heavy," she protested, in an attempt to cover her embarrassment and something else, an inner thrill she knew was wrong.

He merely nodded at his gun. "Fetch that, would you?" he said, glancing for the first time at shy, silent Diorbhail. Only Morrigan saw the sudden intensity of his gaze then the bitter loathing that passed across his face. His arms tightened. Puzzled and nervous, she looked at Diorbhail, but saw nothing amiss. Diorbhail had her head lowered and was scurrying to get the gun.

"You're light as a midge," he said. While she'd been staring after Diorbhail, he'd turned to her again. Diorbhail's lantern was some distance away; she was surely wrong about what she thought she'd seen. There was nothing of anger or hatred on his face now. What she saw was something else entirely. He was so close she felt the heat off his skin, and his gaze dropped to her mouth. She waited, her heart pounding so dreadfully she was sure he could feel it.

But he drew in a deep breath and began to walk, instructing Diorbhail to hold the lamp higher so he could see his way.

Her faithless brain recreated the boulder by the sea, the kiss, and how, for an instant before Curran appeared, she had wanted to open herself to him.

Under the disguise of darkness, it seemed only natural to rest her cheek on his shoulder, close her eyes, and give herself over to his competent strides.

<h1 style="text-align:center">Chapter 13</h1>

MORRIGAN SAT UP IN BED AND STARED. THE ROOM WAS FAMILIAR, YET FOR SOME reason it seemed she hadn't been here, or seen it, in ages. She drew the soft, sweet-smelling covers up to her throat. They seemed wrong as well, far finer than what she knew.

Curran entered. When he saw her, he broke into a wide smile and came over to sit on the bed beside her.

"Curran," she said. Her voice sounded hoarse. "I feel like I've been asleep for a month."

He gathered her to his chest and pressed her face to his throat. "Morrigan, thank God."

Feared to her core by the strange catch in his voice, she pulled away. His lashes were wet. "What's happened?"

"I swear I'm never letting you out of my sight again."

The wean. Nothing else would bring tears to Curran's eyes. But when she touched her stomach, it felt the same, harder, slightly rounded.

Eleanor came in with a teacup. She approached the other side of the bed and sat on the edge. "I was hoping you'd be awake by now," she said. "Would you drink this, please?" She held out the cup to Morrigan.

It was filled with steaming yellow liquid. "Tell me what it is, first," Morrigan said, smiling at the older woman.

"Cinnamon oil, lemon, and honey, mixed with chamomile," Eleanor said.

Morrigan's memories returned as she took the cup from the healer's chapped hands. The bothy. Diorbhail and Eleanor. Sleeping on straw and crushed wildflowers...and Mackinnon carrying her, league after tireless league, until they stumbled across Curran and Seaghan. Mackinnon had handed her off to her husband and swiftly vanished without saying goodbye.

"Drink it, please, darling." Curran said.

She sipped. Honey sweetened the cinnamon's bite.

"I'm so glad and grateful to Eleanor for thinking of that old ruin and going there to look for you. Who knows how long it would have been otherwise?"

"Aye." Eleanor threw a narrowed glance at Morrigan. "I told him how I thought of the bothy two days ago and walked up."

Morrigan nodded. It was only a small lie, after all. "Am I sick? My ears are stuffy."

"I don't think so, *a nighean*," Curran said, "but you slept through a night, a day, another night, and half of today." He glanced at Eleanor. "I'll make sure she drinks it."

Eleanor nodded and left, but as she opened the outer door, Antiope squeezed past her and rushed in. She leaped, splaying her long graceful legs on the bed and cocking her ears, which created a worried pucker between her eyes.

"Lassie-wean." The presence of her dog brought a sense of calm, a return to comfort and safety. She realized she was happy to be home. It was daft to feel pangs of sorrow for that rotted, leaking hovel.

The dog tried to lick her mistress's cheeks.

"Get down, ye cursed beast," Curran said impatiently.

Her expression was wretched, but Curran pushed her away. She curled onto the floor, gazing from one to the other.

"Tell me what happened," Curran said. "I cannot wait any longer."

"D'you know how handsome you were on Saint Michael's Day?" She ran her index finger along his jaw. "Like a centaur, joined with your horse. That's exactly what you looked like."

He laughed and wrapped his arms around her, so tightly she finally had to protest that she couldn't breathe. He kissed her lips, eyelids, ears, and cheeks.

"But you and Violet." She frowned. "I didn't like that. I wanted to make you jealous."

Amusement flashed in his dark blue eyes.

She remembered whipping the horse, knocking Curran clear out of the gig. There was a scabbed-over cut on his cheekbone, and a bruise fanning out around it. "Oh, my temper," she said, horrified. "It's like a great fire. Sometimes it consumes me." She hesitated, searching for the words. "I lose control. I see what I do but I can't stop. Like when I bit you." she touched his lip. "I'm so sorry. I'm sorry for many things. Somehow I think the anger is really towards...myself."

He gripped her shoulders. "That night, I would've deserved it if you'd whipped me. When I saw Aodhàn kiss you...." He paused. "I lost all sense and reason. I'm the one who should apologize, and I do. For everything, especially what I said. I was so afraid those were my last words to you."

"So you were jealous?" She lifted a brow and slanted a teasing smile at him.

"Aye." His tone brought Antiope's head and ears sharply up. "You damnable woman, I was tortured by jealousy, as you wanted, but that's no excuse."

"I regret what I did, too, Curran. Let's just forgive each other."

He nodded and kissed her. "Tell me about this woman you were with. Where do you know her from?"

"She lived in Stranraer. I didn't really know her. My da hated her. Beatrice told me never to speak to her. Diorbhail was the 'fallen woman,' an outcast. That scar on her forehead? It's from a rock. She had a wee daughter, but she's dead. She was murdered."

Curran's brows lowered.

"She walked to Mallaig searching for me, but I'd already come here. She meant to come here on foot, can you believe it? I wonder if she would have survived crossing the mountains."

"I doubt it," Curran said.

"A fisherman brought her up on his boat."

"Why did she hide? Why did she want to see you?"

"She's afraid. She's been so badly treated. She said she'd dreamed of me. That's all I know. Promise not to repeat anything I've told you. I swore to her no one would ever know her past, and she must stay here, with us. She has no one in the world, Curran."

"Of course," he said, so quickly and honestly that she had to kiss him for not hesitating, or having to think about it.

"Where is she?" Morrigan asked.

"Fionna put her in a room and is taking her meals. I haven't seen her since you were found."

"She won't come down alone. She's far too shy. I'll have to go and get her. Oh, I want to see Stoirmeil. I want to play with Antiope and sit in the garden."

"Your ankle...."

She uncovered it and angled it in different directions. "It doesn't seem so bad. I hardly had to take a step on my own the whole way down."

"Aye, well." Curran's eyes darkened. It unsettled her, though she wasn't sure why. "Drink your tea then, and we'll do everything you want. Sometimes I think you would've been happier living in a shieling so you could always be one step from the outdoors."

"Maybe."

He rang for Violet, kissed her, and went off, calling to Antiope to follow.

Fionna found Diorbhail a dress that didn't need many alterations. Morrigan made her eat as much porridge as her shrunken stomach could hold, then she was coaxed outside to relax in garden chairs under the beautiful old oak.

"Are you certain you want me to stay here?" Diorbhail asked doubtfully.

"Aye, Diorbhail." Morrigan threw a handful of crumbs for the ducks. "Look, there's Curran. Now don't be afraid. He won't bite."

Curran approached, smiling. He leaned down to kiss her then gave his attention to Diorbhail.

"This is Mrs. Sinclair," Morrigan said. "Diorbhail, my husband, Mr. Ramsay."

He bent over Diorbhail's hand, which made her eyes widen and her cheeks flush. Seeing this, he knelt. "Our home is yours for as long as you wish it," he said. Morrigan had seldom heard him sound so gentle.

Diorbhail stared at Curran. Then she did something that left Morrigan gaping. She placed her fingers on the side of his head and stroked his hair. Tears filled her eyes, but only one fell down her cheek.

Curran didn't appear shocked or annoyed. He returned her gaze. Gradually, his brows lowered into a puzzled frown. He brought his hand up to hers and clasped her wrist. "Have we...met?"

"I've seen you." Diorbhail's voice was nearly too subdued to hear.

"In Stranraer?"

"No. Not there."

Curran was obviously bewildered yet fascinated. "You seem so familiar," he said. "Does the word *Xanthe* mean anything to you?"

"Aye," she said, after a long pause. "But I know not why."

"I don't know either," he said.

As if waking from a dream, Diorbhail blinked and turned to Morrigan. Her face acquired a mortified expression. Her eyes begged forgiveness.

Morrigan seized her free hand. "Is this how you felt when you saw Eleanor?"

"Aye," Diorbhail said. "But...more."

"He's part of us, then?"

"I think so." Diorbhail was visibly trembling. "We're connected, all of us, somehow."

"What's she saying?" Curran asked, but he didn't look at Morrigan. He seemed unable to tear his gaze from Diorbhail's face.

"What do you see when you look at him, Diorbhail?"

She blushed and dropped her gaze to the ground.

"That's all right." Morrigan squeezed her hand. "You don't need to speak of it."

Curran released Diorbhail's wrist and stood. "Here's your bloody dog," he said, as Kyle opened the gate and Antiope raced to them. She ran first to Morrigan, shoving her snout into her mistress's hand, then thoroughly welcomed Diorbhail until she had the woman giggling, then she ran off to smell things and bark at the ducks.

"May I spend the day with you?" Curran asked humbly.

Morrigan laughed. "We'd be aye disappointed if you didn't," she said, tapping his forearm with her fan.

Seaghan came through the gate just then. He stood there, kneading his glengarry.

"Why won't he come over?" Curran gestured, but Seaghan merely shook his head.

"What's wrong with him?" Morrigan asked.

"I don't know. Let me see what he wants. Forgive me, ladies."

Morrigan watched him walk away, admiring those buckskin breeks that fit him like a second skin. She really must talk to Eleanor about reversing her decree that there be no relations until the babe was born. It would be hellish to wait so long.

"See?" she said, fanning herself. "He's no' so bad."

"No." Diorbhail kept her gaze locked on the pool. "He isn't."

Morrigan wanted to ask Diorbhail what had so moved her, but the woman appeared a bit shaky still. "Come," she said, "we'll promenade like grand nobles."

She rose, pulling Diorbhail up beside her. Arm in arm, they strolled around the pool. "Would you allow Violet to arrange your hair? She's quite good."

"I'll never be a lady. That's no' why I came here," Diorbhail said angrily.

"I'm not trying to make you into anything. I only want to get the tangles out of your hair. I swear there's a bird's nest in there. I want your life to be better, and I'm going to make it happen. I'm no' a lady either, you know. All my life I've been a chambermaid, a dishwasher, a laundress, a drudge. Oh, and Papa's whipping post. I dread the day I have to meet Curran's highborn friends and business associates."

Diorbhail's anger vanished. "I'll do whatever I can to help you." She cupped Morrigan's cheeks in her hands. "I love you," she said, her voice shaky. "I'd die for you. Never think otherwise."

Morrigan pressed her cheek against this odd woman's. "I wish I'd had the courage in Stranraer to stand up for you. But I was too afraid."

"It'll come. I know it."

She wasn't ready to say it out loud yet, but with such an ardent supporter, Morrigan felt it too.

Curran returned, leaving Seaghan at the gate. "Aodhàn's gone off some-where. Seaghan never seems able to accustom himself to it. He fashes like a wee lad who's lost his puppy. I keep telling him the moody bugger just likes to be alone. I'll help him look for an hour or so, then we'll have a picnic."

Morrigan fought to hide a flood of dismay, especially when she sensed Diorbhail's eyes boring into her. But Curran's dismissive attitude calmed her somewhat.

"I hope you find him," she said, keeping her tone restrained. "He seemed so tired, and he carried me all that way. You'd think he'd only want to sleep." She rested a hand on Curran's forearm. "I understand why Seaghan is worried. It doesn't seem right."

"He's inconsiderate, and always has been." He covered Morrigan's hand with his own then offered a bow. "Ladies, I promise to return as soon as I can."

This time, as he walked away, Morrigan could only feel disquiet.

Chapter 14

Most of the ruin was obscured in early morning shadows.

The land upon which Bishop House had once stood was the highest point of the hill east of the village of Castlebay, which the Gaelic-speaking locals called *Bàgh a' Chaisteil,* on the isle of Barra, or *Barraigh.* It was a craggy hill, lacking a single tree or bush to disguise him. If Aodhàn had come up here in daylight, he would've risked being seen by the villagers below, and that would seriously compromise his plans.

Cold wind buffeted him as he walked around the foundation. Many of the stones that had made up his stately multi-storied home were gone, filched, no doubt, to be used elsewhere, maybe by the same men who burned it after murdering Lilith and their children.

Lilith. You're alive again, in the body of Morrigan Ramsay.

He recalled coming here from Edinburgh just before his thirteenth birthday, how the empty rooms echoed and the newly hired servants giggled as they went about making Bishop House habitable for the new factor and his son. Colonel Gordon of Cluny had purchased Barra, but had no desire to live here, or even see it. Aodhàn's father had been hired to relocate in his stead and make the island profitable.

Here, on this remote speck of land Aodhàn was dragged to against his angry young will, he had found Aridela.

The instant he yanked her from the hidden passage in the wall and looked into her frightened face, all his other lives resurfaced.

The return of the memories was an agonizing process. He likened the sensations to having his skull split open, his brain ripped out. The past came in a crippling barrage, image after image, screams, faces, words rushing past, dissolving into other words, his own bitter betrayals reforming in unbearable clarity. And always in the background, the murderous rumble of the earth-shaking and searing ash-filled air.

His brain would gradually acclimate and he would begin all over, wooing her, loving her, vowing *this time* he would win. There was never any other choice for Chrysaleon of Mycenae.

What was Athene's cursed plan, anyway? He hoped he was thwarting it, but he knew he might be doing exactly what she wanted.

He might be…but he doubted it, for in every life she was fainter. Weaker. More distant. He'd long ago convinced himself she was losing.

Aodhàn's teeth ground together. His fists clenched, unclenched, clenched again.

I will have blood.

The morning after Morrigan's wedding, after Seaghan found him at the edge of the bay, he'd gone to Kilgarry. He'd stood outside the iron gates. It was everything he could do to stop himself from forcing his way through the front door and dragging her off like a modern Genghis Khan.

But that would only get him shot.

A gold and crimson band burst above the eastern horizon, throwing the mainland into silhouette. Looking down, he saw the shadow of the medieval castle on its island in the bay. If any early riser were to glance up at this hill, they might see him, but he'd be little more than a ghostly outline. His mouth lifted in a snarl at the idea, before he turned and hiked down the far side, wondering if Lilith's mother was still alive.

The sight of her long dead son-in-law caused Faith to collapse, or start to. Aodhàn caught her, put her in a chair, and fixed her tea as she regained her normal impassive calm.

When he set the teacup in front of her, she grabbed his hand and held it to her cheek. She wasn't an affectionate woman, so he assumed it was a method of determining if he was real or spectre. "Aye," she said, in confirmation. "It is you. You're alive."

"I'm no ghost."

"Well then, where have you been?"

"The mainland."

She was good with English, having been a schoolteacher, but she switched to her native Gaelic, perhaps out of shock. "Why have you come now?"

Aodhàn sat next to her, his direct gaze brooking no nonsense. "Where is my money?"

She seemed unsurprised. "The Church took it, long ago."

As he'd suspected, but it still made him so angry he had to breathe deeply or he'd pick up the rickety table and throw it across the room.

"I petitioned them for assistance, and they dole out a wee sum every few months. Greyson Fullerton also receives a few pence. They keep the bulk for themselves of course, the bastards."

"Greyson. He's alive?"

"After a fashion. He lives south of Earsaraidh. I cook for him now and then, do his washing."

Aodhàn could hardly believe his luck. His loyal slave, Alexiare, still alive. He must be in his sixties. The old man would have done whatever he could to preserve his master's wealth and keep the priceless treasures safe. This was more than he could have hoped for, and he began to feel less enraged.

"Romy lived as well," Faith said.

"She did?" Wee Romy had escaped gypsy captors and had been found by Evie and Claire, starving and lost, in the Black Forest. Lilith had insisted they bring her home to Barra, and the waif became their third daughter. "Where is she?"

"Returned to her homeland. Some outlandish place. The Church wrote to someone, and her kin were found."

So she was, in essence, gone as well. The hope that leaped within at the news of her survival plummeted again.

While he sat there, immersed in his black thoughts, Lilith's mother rose. She crossed to a chest and brought out something wrapped in cloth, which she placed in Aodhàn's hand. He unwrapped it, gritting his teeth and blinking at the burn of tears against the back of his eyelids.

Lilith's wedding band.

The band had no fancy gems, like the one Curran had given Morrigan, only a phrase etched into the gold. *Gaol mo chridhe.* Love of my heart.

"I don't know who took it from her finger," Faith said, her voice low but harsh. "It was left outside my door three mornings after the murders."

He nodded, unable to speak. He put the ring in his vest pocket.

"So what do you want from me, Aodhàn Mackinnon?"

"The men who killed Lilith. Where are they?"

"Are you just now caring about that? I would've thought, if you weren't dead, you would have taken your vengeance long ago."

"Well, I didn't, old woman. I couldn't. I came the moment I could."

Her eyes narrowed. "Have you been in prison?"

"In many ways."

"They said they killed you. They threatened to kill me too, for giving birth to Lilith. I've had to say and do things that near made me puke, to save myself. Sometimes I've wondered why I bothered."

He was surprised to see tears build in her eyes. "I loved her, and her weans," she said. "Evie, who never stopped chattering, and Claire, so solemn and kind, and Romy. She never lost that foreign air."

Again, he was forced to grit his teeth. "Are the men still here, Faith?"

"All but Owen Anderson. They don't look me in the eye. Never. If they see me, they go away fast."

"Owen Anderson. Who is that?"

"The one who got them drunk and inflamed. He sent those men to your house that night. You didn't know that?"

"No." Frustration brought Aodhàn out of his chair. He paced, scraping at his cheekbones, trying to contain the flooding need to kill. "I mind no Owen Anderson."

"The rest were naught but his boot-lickers. He's the one truly to blame, though I'd like to see every one of them rot in hell."

"Where is this man?"

"No one has seen him since. Some say he was never here, that the men who did it invented him, trying to shift the blame and appease their guilt."

Aodhàn remembered a bag being shoved over his head. It stank, but still he'd caught a whiff of something else…of ashes, the smell of…of *Harpalycus!* And that crooning voice, before he was knifed and thrown over the side of the boat. *My father could not save you this time, could he?*

Fury roared through his body. He'd believed Harpalycus dead the last six hundred years. His specially chosen band of trusted knights had sworn they'd found the inquisitor, Heinrich Baten, and his assistant, on the road between Wiesbaden and Mainz. They claimed they'd lanced Baten through the chest.

They'd either lied or Harpalycus had found a way to survive. He was nothing if not inventive.

Harpalycus had done one other thing that should have made it clear who he was. He'd wrapped the necklace around Aodhàn's forearm. The bastard must have ripped it off of Lilith after his lackeys slaughtered her. He would have delighted in the thought that it would be lost at the bottom of the ocean, wrapped around Aodhàn's skeleton.

It all made sense at last. Owen Anderson was Harpalycus. Rather than kill his enemy outright, he'd played one of his cruel games. Then he'd gone, of course. Nothing left on Barraigh to entertain him.

A creeping chill ran over Aodhàn's flesh. If Harpalycus lived, he would be drawn to them, especially now that he, Aridela, and Menoetius were alive and reunited. That meant Harpalycus would be near, or on his way.

Chrysaleon had never learned Harpalycus's secret for sensing and finding them. But find them he did, and it always meant chaos and death.

I must be vigilant. I cannot risk being caught unaware again.

Sometimes it felt like the prince of Tiryns always won. He did have an advantage, with that cursed trick of being able to enter the body of a stranger and take it over, along with the ability to find the triad, no matter where they were in the world. Chrysaleon would have killed Harpalycus long, long ago if he could manage either of those things, but he couldn't. He never knew where Harpalycus was or what body he inhabited, not unless the bastard came close enough to smell.

Harpalycus's ancient threat taunted him. *You and your entire House will perish. The world will forget there ever was a Mycenae.*

It was true. Who knew, anymore, of Mycenae? Only the crustiest historians.

He couldn't think about that now. He'd go mad. Somewhere, some time, Aodhàn would have the opportunity to make Harpalycus pay for all he'd done.

The others would pay now. They'd best begin making their final confessions.

Chapter 15

It became a common thing to see Morrigan, Eleanor, and Diorbhail together. Janet began calling them "the cronies." Curran looked on indulgently, so it was easy for the trio to find ways to be alone, especially after Eleanor reassured Curran that fresh air and exercise were of utmost value to his wife's health and the health of the growing baby. The weather was their accomplice, as sunny warmth went on and on, with few exceptions, deep into October.

Eleanor brought a jar of what she called "witch's cap." Hers was dried, and had little smell or taste.

"I've never heard of miscarriages with this," she said, "but I want to be careful. Here, m'lady." She gave Morrigan an amount no bigger than the end of her pinkie finger.

Diorbhail and Eleanor took the same small pinch and they all waited, but after an hour nothing had happened other than a tendency to giggle on Morrigan's part.

"You need more than that," Diorbhail said. "I could have told you."

"I don't want to take chances with the laird's first child."

"Might as well do nothing as take too little."

"I learned my trade in Edinburgh, from trained medical men. Where did you learn yours?"

"I know when something's not working. And I wager your city doctors know less than you or me about mushrooms. My mam gave this to women heavy with child. It soothed their fears and never did any harm."

"We'll try again tomorrow," Morrigan said.

Deep in the night, Diorbhail sneaked, quiet as a beetle, into the laird's bedroom and woke the laird's wife. Motioning, she pulled Morrigan into the sitting room, where she whispered, "The moon is full. Come outside."

With a glance to make sure Curran hadn't awakened, Morrigan went with her, not bothering with anything but a robe and slippers.

The night was briskly, invigoratingly cold. Diorbhail led her to a barrel in the stable courtyard. It was sliced to about a quarter of its original height and filled with water for the horses.

"You can see things in water, especially with the help of the moon," Diorbhail said. "Look. See what you can see. The truth of things." She ducked her hand in and stirred the water.

Morrigan knelt and waited for the ripples to still. Moonlight leaped, but as the surface smoothed, the bright circle acquired an indistinct face then a woman's body.

Spinning day, spinning night, Diorbhail sang, soft and low.
Goddess alone has the sight,
Of fate we cannot comprehend,
Mother, daughter, sister, friend.

The woman had hair the same shade as the moonlight—creamy, waving tresses that fell to the middle of her thighs. "It's you, Diorbhail," Morrigan said. "But you're younger, and your hair is white. You have a sword and a bow." As she contemplated the water, the warrior lifted her bow and strung an arrow.

"Can you picture her name?"

Morrigan concentrated. "Se…Selena? No, Selene. I saw her before, at the bothy. You were asleep, I think. I might have been as well."

"Women have long proven themselves valuable as warriors," Diorbhail said, "though that knowledge has been wiped out. They can be swift and merciless, but slaughter does no' give them pleasure, unless they've been perverted by earthly misuse. They know the sanctity of life because it grows within them."

"When I'm with you, I feel powerful," Morrigan said. "I have worth. Until you came, I never felt that way. I was like a pebble in the ocean, at the mercy of the waves." She struck her chest with her fist. "No one is going to take that away from me now. I won't let it happen."

Diorbhail nodded. "You're learning." She tipped her head to the side. "The woman you saw in the water…."

"Aye?"

"That *was* me, long ago, in another life. Even then, I was with you. I think we always will be together in some form."

"Truly?"

"I've seen myself in that body many times." She stirred the water again. "Look again. Maybe you'll see someone else."

Morrigan stared at the water, hardly daring to blink. Gradually another figure materialized. This one was eerily beautiful. Her long hair was done up in elaborate twists and knots; there was an upturned crescent shape painted or tattooed in the center of her forehead.

"I see someone," she said. "Another woman."

"Describe her."

"She seems commanding. Proud. There's a mark on her forehead like the moon, when it's waxing or waning. I've never seen a woman so beautiful."

"Picture her name."

Eventually, after several tries, she got what felt right. "The-meest-ee."

"Does she seem familiar?"

"Aye."

"She's your grand physician. Eleanor."

They giggled. "Oh, my, she's changed," Morrigan said. "Does she know?"

Diorbhail shrugged. "She's said nothing to me."

"Let's show her."

Diorbhail nodded. "Soon."

"Who else can I see?"

"Who d'you wish to see?"

"Curran!"

Diorbhail stirred the water and waited, now silent and subdued.

Morrigan stared at the surface, excited, anticipating her handsome husband in some equally handsome "other" version.

The ripples calmed and stilled.

Gradually, Morrigan saw a man in the silvery light. His eyes and brows were shaped like Curran's. But his hair was dark and very long, and that horrible scar tore through his cheek, ruining any chance of him being described as comely.

The man in the mist! At the bothy! She remembered dreaming of that same man the day she and Curran spent the afternoon on the moor outside Stranraer.

The figure in the water wasn't alone. He was holding a woman's hand, gazing into her face, and she into his. Morrigan drew in a breath. The woman was the warrior, Selene, and she was heavily pregnant.

Morrigan looked up from the water at Diorbhail. She said nothing. She didn't need to.

Papal inquisitors were adept at preventing death. Corpses could not make confessions.

The pulley creaked as it turned, drawing the rope taut. "Don't," Morrigan cried. "Please, please, stop…."

"But pain is the road to redemption. How do you do it, Caparina? Even bleeding and filthy, your bones broken, you tempt me like the seductress you are. Perhaps it is true, what my superiors claim, that women are the Devil's creatures, and you are trying to trick me into releasing you. But I will not, do you understand? I'll let every one of these men have you, and the soldiers in the courtyard, unless you give us your confession."

The little man in the rafters worked the pulley's handle. Rope ground over the wheel, lifting her into the air. Morrigan's shoulder sockets were already dislocated. She'd give anything to escape this agony, but only death would grant release, and the inquisitors wouldn't allow that.

Even if she confessed to the crimes they accused her of, she wouldn't be pardoned. Still, she might confess anyway, if for no other reason than to end the torture. If they had their confession, they would let her die. The pain would end.

But then, what would stand between these monsters and her daughter? Nothing.

"Your own weak nature makes you subject. Do you confess your weakness? Or shall I demonstrate it?"

"I've done nothing. Nothing." Then she could no longer stifle her screams.

Eleanor's face was ashen. "I have never witnessed anything like that in all my fifty-two years," she said. "Never. How do you feel?"

"I'm not sure." Morrigan coughed. "What happened?" Her throat felt raw and sore. Eleanor looked fearful and exhausted, as if she'd done battle with one of Agnes's glaistigs.

Diorbhail helped Morrigan sit up, and wrapped a blanket around her shoulders.

They were in the cave Morrigan had found at the end of August, when she, Ibby, and Beatrice had come to Kilgarry the first time. She'd remembered it, and suggested it might be a good place to experiment with the mushroom, as it was so remote there was hardly any chance of being discovered or spied on.

She coughed again. Diorbhail found a curved piece of bark on the ground, filled it with water from the nearby burn, and carried it to Morrigan, who drank gratefully. "I don't remember lying down," she said. "When did I do that? My throat hurts."

"I am not surprised," Eleanor said grimly.

"You've been screaming," Diorbhail said. "You had a vision. Can you recall it? Tell us before it fades."

"Why was I screaming?"

"Well, because you—"

"Don't," Eleanor interrupted. "Let her tell us if she can."

Diorbhail nodded and turned an expectant gaze upon Morrigan, as did Eleanor.

Morrigan closed her eyes, knowing she'd never mind a thing with those two staring at her like basilisks. She delved within and conjured a name—Klaus Berthold—which threw her headlong into the dream, or vision, or whatever it was, though as she watched it play out in memory, part of her knew it was more.

"Everyone has foreign-sounding names and strange clothing, but for the priests. They wear robes like Father Drummond's." Perspiration beaded on her forehead as she added, "I see stained-glass windows. We must be in a church. There's a priest. He points at me and says something...." She sought to remember. "Caparina Naske. I think it's my name. He accuses me of witchcraft, and... and something he calls 'heresy.'" She lifted her hands. "I don't know what that is."

"If you'd been raised Catholic you would," Eleanor said. "Heresy is when a Catholic dares question Church teachings. A heretic is someone who denies Church authority."

Diorbhail clutched at Eleanor's forearm. "You see what this means? She heard a word in vision she doesn't even know!"

"I'm aware," Eleanor said. "Let her continue."

"He says I've cast spells on...on.... He looks at the end of the chamber, and I look too. There's a man, on a throne. He's...let me think. I had his name a moment ago."

"Klaus Berthold," Diorbhail said.

"Wheesht!" Eleanor said impatiently. "Let *her* tell it."

"She's right." Morrigan eyed Diorbhail suspiciously. "That name is right. Klaus Berthold. My lover."

"Lover...?" Eleanor repeated.

"His hands are shaking. He's sick with fear." Morrigan delved into what she'd seen, and came up with another name. "The priest, Heinrich Baten, tells me I must confess my crimes. If I refuse, I will be purified."

"Good, that's good," Eleanor said. "Go on."

"Everyone wants to see what my lover will do. They're all listening, hoping for some excitement."

Morrigan's memories were clarifying. She heard doves cooing in the rafters. She remembered her lover, Klaus, speaking against her throat before she'd been arrested. *Nina, my love.*

"Klaus can stop this with a single word. Yet he says nothing. He motions to one of his attendants, who holds up a basin for him to vomit in.

"If I confess, Klaus will be punished. That is Heinrich Baten's real goal, to have Klaus at his mercy. Klaus is important. If it's known that he's taken up with a woman, it'll be the end of him. Heinrich Baten is famed for burning folk alive. No one is safe. Not even Klaus.

"There's no saving me unless Klaus orders Heinrich Baten to stop the interrogation. But he doesn't. I'm taken to the dungeons. I'm hung from the ceiling by the arms and dropped until my shoulders are broken. I'm stretched with ropes. They stick things inside me that rip me apart. Heinrich Baten watches. He enjoys it. He strokes my hair as I scream."

Morrigan opened her eyes, shocked out of her recollections by Eleanor grabbing her upper arms. She realized she was shaking, gasping as though there wasn't enough air in the cave. She felt dizzy, and was grateful when Eleanor shoved her head between her knees, as it quickly eased the sensation of the cave spinning and bouncing.

Taking a deep breath, she lifted her head and wiped sweat from her face with the edge of her cloak. Diorbhail gave her more water. She was uncommonly thirsty, and drank it all.

"That's it, then," said Eleanor after Morrigan's breathing calmed. "No more witch's cap for you, m'lady, no' as long as you're carrying a babe in your womb. I can only hope this once was not enough to do harm."

"Wait," Diorbhail cried. "She's seeing the past. That was no mere dream. Her voice changed. She was there as it happened! She spoke words she doesn't know!"

"I understand, aye," Eleanor said darkly. "And I will do whatever I can to keep it from happening again. My first obligation is to her health, and the babe's. No more witch's cap."

The memories retreated and Morrigan's physical reactions subsided. Emotion took over. Agony from the betrayal. She'd truly believed Klaus loved her. And what about…about….

"Rosabel."

"There's more?" Diorbhail rubbed Morrigan's hand.

"I'm lying on filthy straw," Morrigan said. "It's cold, and there's blood all over me. The guard feeds me and gives me water. He puts a blanket over me. He promises to protect my baby, to raise her like his own child. He says he'll tell her how brave her mother was. That makes me angry. I order him to tell her how stupid I was, so she won't make the same mistakes. 'Bocho,' I call him, but that's not really his name. He tries to be strong, but he's weeping. We can't hold each other because of my broken bones. He can only touch the palm of my hand."

She looked up, distracted by a sound. Both Eleanor and Diorbhail were staring at her, and both were weeping. At first Morrigan couldn't remember what she'd said, but gradually she was able to picture the child, Rosabel, a brown-haired, scarlet-cheeked, green-eyed baby who loved to laugh.

Klaus Berthold's child.

"Hell is what Earth becomes without her mother," Diorbhail said.

Chapter 16

Aodhàn killed the first of his targets two nights after arriving on Barra. It wasn't planned, but he happened across Peter Bateson, stumbling along half-drunk, his hair gone grey and sparse, his once-flat stomach deteriorated to the paunch of a man who drank too much. It was late, and dark; there was no one about. It was like a ready-wrapped gift. Aodhàn threw him to the ground and pointed a dirk at his face.

"It's *you!*" Peter cringed. "I...I'm sorry, m'lord. Not a day has gone by where I don't wish I...I hadn't—"

"Where is Owen Anderson?"

Peter shook his head. "No one's seen him since that night."

"How did he make you attack us?"

Aodhàn watched the man's eyes light; he was grabbing at this slender hope, hope that the enraged brute threatening him with a knife didn't really blame him, but another who was long gone. "He plied us with whisky. Told us you and your wife...her especially...worshipped the Devil. He told us you were doing cursed things to your children, and that your evil was damning us all. He said you were the reason the potatoes were rotted! We were fooled by his lies, m'lord, all of us."

At that point Aodhàn punched him, savoring the moment while Peter lay gasping and retching. He took his time ripping out his victim's throat, in memory of Lilith.

He left the body there, sprawled and bloody, on the main path out of Castlebay, as a message to the others that he was coming. Then he went off to find Greyson Fullerton.

IT WAS A BATTERED BOTHY, NEAR THE SEA BUT FAR FROM ANY VILLAGE.

Aodhàn stood looking at it for several moments. He didn't really think Faith would betray him, but he had to be careful.

When he was quite young, long before he and his father moved to Barra, an Englishman had been hired to tutor him. It made little sense, as his father disliked the English on principle. Aodhàn had stared at Greyson Fullerton, wondering how this one had managed to slip past Kenneth Mackinnon's guard. He also knew, even then, before the restoration of his memories, that this man was no stranger, though he couldn't remember ever being introduced to him.

Later, when they were alone, his father confessed the man had been hounding him for weeks, plying him with references and recommendations. Kenneth had finally decided on a trial period. Greyson was indeed well-educated. There was little doubt he would ably prepare Kenneth's son for Eton and Oxford.

As for Aodhàn, he knew within hours that he needed Greyson in some unfathomable way. He didn't understand then, and, as it turned out, neither did Greyson. That didn't happen until after they moved to Barra, and Aodhàn met Lilith.

With the return of buried memories came recognition. His English tutor was Alexiare, the old slave.

Aodhàn knew what to do. He'd revived Alexiare's memories three times by then, in other lives. He procured the mushroom from a wisewoman on the northern edge of the island, took Greyson into the hills where they wouldn't be disturbed, and made him eat it. As usual, the man became violently ill, but after he'd vomited and proclaimed he was dying, he began to recover and remember. Within two hours, he was bowing, scraping, and calling Aodhàn "my lord."

They had compared histories and determined that neither had lived without the other since their last excursion, six hundred years ago, during the German Inquisition.

Greyson told Aodhàn his story. "I was a Londoner, and I had good prospects. My future was planned. Then it happened. The compulsion. I had to come to Edinburgh. I didn't know why, but it was either obey or go mad. Once there, I had to search again, but for what, I didn't know. It wasn't until I was introduced to your father at his club that I began to feel I was getting close. One day I met him in Holyrood Park, and saw you playing there at his feet. I knew I had to find a way to attach myself to your father, and you. But my lord, I still didn't know why. Not until now." He'd pondered awhile, then he'd said, "Why does she keep bringing us together, my lord? She *wants* us to find each other. She makes it happen. But she knows my loyalty is to you. Surely she knows by now that I will always do my best to help *you*, which means I will always do my best to defeat *her*."

"You've said it yourself, more than once," Aodhàn replied. "Because of the curse."

Selene's curse.

It ran through Aodhàn's thoughts as he stood above the silent, moldering bothy, preparing to go down and see his old slave.

You and your master will wander. Glimpses of joy will be ripped from you. You will follow and follow, without end.

Those ancient words sent waves of exhaustion through him. How many more times? How long could he keep fighting? What would appease her?

The one thing he would never give.

He ran down the slope to the bothy door and knocked. There was no response, but he heard shuffling, so he opened the door. It was dark inside, the shutters closed. There was a distinct smell of rotted food, unwashed human, and shit.

"Greyson?"

He discerned a shape, a shadow, hunched in front of the hearth. "Greyson?" he repeated. "It's Aodhàn."

The shape moved, uncurled, and rose. "M-m-master?"

"Aye, 'tis me." The stench was overwhelming. Aodhàn strode to both windows and threw open the shutters to let in the sea wind.

"Ah, no. Not him. It's not him…not him. He's dead. Dead until next time. They're all dead. Why haven't I died? I won't be able to find them."

"I'm not dead." Aodhàn stepped closer. He reached out and seized Greyson's hand. "See? I'm real. Alive. It's me, here in the flesh, and I've many questions."

Why was Greyson so dirty? Why did he live in such squalor? "Come outside," he said, wanting to escape the oppressive atmosphere. "Walk with me."

Palsy had set into Greyson's limbs. His hands shook, as did his uneven gait. He was bent. This was not the proper English servant Aodhàn remembered, who had always taken pride in his appearance. Moreover, he kept mumbling. Aodhàn pushed away the thought that he was to blame for this.

He led his one-time manservant towards the sea, not particularly concerned about anyone seeing them in such an isolated place.

"I killed Daniel," Greyson said. "The master told me to. He knew I'd be punished for it." He giggled. "He didn't care. Lilith married the master. She wouldn't have though, would she, if I hadn't killed Daniel? She wouldn't have if she'd known what we did to Daniel."

"Stop talking about it!" What the *hell*. Who else had Greyson been telling their secrets to? "You're not to ever repeat those things, d'you hear me?"

Greyson's face sagged. "I do what I'm told." He began to weep. "I obey. Nothing to be ashamed of."

They came to a large rock. Aodhàn helped Greyson sit, since he looked as though he might collapse.

Greyson continued to mutter and scratch his scalp. He stared at a dead starfish, though before him lay a magnificent sea full of color, movement, and life.

Daylight was not kind. Greyson's eyes were red, watery, and had a greenish pus-like substance crusted in the corners. He was unshaven, his beard thin and scraggly; the scant hair that remained on his head was greasy and lank, and no doubt full of lice. He resembled the aged slave from Crete more than a little.

What had happened here? Was it because Greyson had been drifting too long with no purpose? Maybe he should dose the old man with the mushroom again.

The very first time they had all been dragged out of death, it was Alexiare's own mother who suggested the mushroom. It worked, and had resurrected Chrysaleon's staunchest, most loyal supporter in every life since.

Maybe another dose would clear out this insanity and restore the sharp-witted companion he needed.

But he had none of that special mushroom, and didn't know where to get any.

Watching Greyson's face for a reaction, he asked, "Do you remember the night we were attacked? The men who burned Bishop House? How did you get away? Faith says Romy is alive, too. Do you know where she is?"

Greyson stared at the starfish, mumbling. Aodhàn heard "Kaphtor," and "Selene's curse," but other than that, understood hardly anything.

Aodhàn leaned over Greyson and grabbed the front of his stinking, blackened sark. "What's happened to you?" he shouted, shaking him.

"Leave her alone," Greyson said. "Don't bring her into your curse. Leave her…leave her alone."

"I wouldn't harm her. She's my child, as much as Evie and Claire."

"She escaped you." Greyson blinked and squinted as though the sunlight hurt his eyes.

For one brief moment, comprehension and recognition flickered across his face. "You ordered me to kill Daniel," he said. "So I did. He's one of *hers*. The triad. As much as you. Maybe more. Cannot…cannot kill them, not without a reckoning. I burn. I burn inside. It never stops. Every day, every night, I burn. For what you made me do."

He swept a grimy palm across his eyes, wiping away tears. "Let me go. You're here again. You can pay her reckoning. You."

"You're not going anywhere," Aodhàn said. "I still need you, Greyson."

Greyson shook his head; the clarity vanished. "No, no more. I cannot hide it. The things he does to her. If she ever finds out she'll use that knife on him. She'll slice his heart from his chest and for-force him to watch it stop beating." Bending, he picked up the rotted starfish and put it in his sark. "I'll be alone, no one to follow, no one to love. The Lady is cruel. Everyone is dead. They've all been reborn and I've been left behind. I don't know anyone anymore. What will he do without me? What will he do to her next time?"

"I'm right here, old man. I need your help. Wake up!"

It was no use. Growling a curse, Aodhàn left him. All he could do was search the hovel, though he realized others had probably already done so. If Greyson had saved anything the night of the fire, no doubt someone had stolen it long ago. But they would have searched for ordinary valuables like gold or jewels. What he hoped to find was different, and might have been overlooked.

He entered the blackhouse. It was still dim, though he'd thrown open the shutters. He lit two candles and began his search, disgusted by the piles of dried excrement, the swarming maggots, the decomposing rat. He went along the walls, inspecting every stone.

At last, on the wall facing the sea, next to the window, he pushed against a stone and it grated. He knelt and worked it loose.

Everything was forgotten: his frustration, his rage, Lilith, those cursed men who continued to live while she and their children turned to dust.

He laughed out loud as he withdrew the familiar silver coffer and opened it, not allowing himself to contemplate the possibility of its contents being gone.

Alexiare must have replaced the old cloth with this soft, cushioning velvet when he still had his wits. He pulled it away impatiently. The knife was a beautiful work of art, the ivory hilt depicting Athene in flowing robes, an owl perched upon her shoulder, the blade itself fashioned of glossy black obsidian. It would draw blood, no matter how lightly he ran the edge across his flesh.

Thank God none of those drunken louts had found this! They wouldn't have known what it was. It might've been damaged, destroyed, sold for a pound, lost forever.

He held it to the light. It was flawless, as it had been three millennia ago on Crete, when Aridela used it to slay Harpalycus the Butcher.

Or so they thought. They couldn't have been more wrong.

He started to replace the weapon in its casket but paused as he noticed something else glinting in the velvet. It was a miniature portrait of Lilith, painted by a master artist in Freiburg. Lilith hadn't wanted her portrait painted. It had been a fierce battle between them. He picked it up. Her dark eyes gazed at him, solemn, mysterious. For one agonizing instant he was thrown backward in time, and clenched his jaw to keep his emotion in check. He touched the edge of her cheek. Then, swallowing hard, he put it in his pocket and carried the knife outside. "Alexiare," he called. "You're in my good graces again." He went around the side of the bothy, but the old man wasn't on the rock. One set of dragging footprints led towards the sea and vanished at the water's edge.

A scrap of paper lay next to the water, weighted down by the rotted starfish. Aodhàn picked it up, grimacing at the stink, and unfolded it.

One line, in shaky script.

It is sorcery beyond our understanding.

Aodhàn searched for over a mile in both directions, but there was no sign of Greyson Fullerton.

As he turned the knife in his hands, watching it glitter, he decided to take it to Glenelg. But what then? It wasn't something he could set on a shelf in Seaghan's blackhouse.

He would bury it. He'd done that once before, long ago, in the underground warren of tunnels at Cape Wrath. It had been a good choice. The knife remained, dry, safe, and hidden for thirteen hundred years, until he retrieved it one summer when he was on holiday from Eton.

He alone would know where it was. If he were to die, it would remain undisturbed, waiting for him to dig it up in some future life.

This knife was dangerous. He knew instinctively that when Aridela used it against Harpalycus it acquired powerful magic. What else could explain how it managed to come, unscathed, through so many thousands of years, or how the slightest cut from the blade putrefied flesh and almost always caused death? No one knew its intended purpose, but every instinct warned him to keep it close and secret.

He gazed out at the water and lifted the knife in triumphant homage to his slave's endless loyalty. "Rest well," he said softly, "until next time, old man." He patted his pocket, feeling the hard edge of the portrait. "You kept what was most precious safe, and I thank you."

Chapter 17

Winter set in at Kilgarry, and still Aodhàn Mackinnon did not come home.

Morrigan could tell by the shadows in Seaghan's eyes, his failure to smile except in a tight, unnatural way, that he suspected his old comrade had come to a solitary and unknown end.

Morrigan refused to consider that possibility. But Curran told her he'd never been gone so long; usually no more than two or three days at most.

She secretly set her birthday as the day he would turn up. He would burst into Kilgarry with a small gift, perhaps something he'd made.

She woke on her birthday to a fresh blanket of snow and the wean's quickening. "Curran, Curran!" She shook him. "I *feel* something." Eleanor had warned her what would happen so she wouldn't be frightened. Still, it was a queer sensation, a fluttering, like a sparrow was flapping its wings inside her. She didn't know whether to worry or laugh.

Curran placed his hand on her stomach. When the movement came, the poke of a foot too small to comprehend, his smile stretched into a huge grin, like a lad who had caught his first trout. "It's kicking," he shouted. "The babe's kicking!" He brought Morrigan in, tucking her face against his whiskery throat, enclosing her in a protective cocoon. She closed her eyes as he massaged the small of her back with strong fingers, soothing the tightness and ache. One hand slid around to her stomach and he caressed the fullness there, murmuring about *our bairn, our wean, an aye fond memory of that day on the windy moor.*

Ibby had come the previous day. She gave Morrigan a dress she'd sewn for the final months of pregnancy. Curran gave her a necklace of matched pearls, and Janet made confections rich with butter, cream, and cheese.

But there was no Mackinnon. Morrigan kept her disappointment hidden and called herself a daftie for conceiving such a fantasy then expecting it to actually happen.

Night fell, cold and clear, offering its own gift of twinkling stars and a display of the Northern Lights, which Curran told her was rare. They all went outside to admire the phenomenon, bundled up in wool and fur. Secretly, while the others exclaimed at the changing colors hanging in the heavens like vast curtains, Morrigan regarded the iron gates. The night was magical enough to believe that at any second, Mackinnon's tall figure would come striding through them.

They trooped inside for hot cider. Soon after, the front bell was pulled and Morrigan's heart leaped. It was everything she could do to continue to sit by the fire, sipping her drink.

Seaghan came in, wishing her a happy birthday. Morrigan waited, but no one followed. There remained that slight frown between his eyes, the shadow that spoke of grief he tried to hide. She clasped his hand longer than necessary, to let him know she understood.

Curran entertained them by relating the tale of the race between the two tea clippers, *Cutty Sark* and *Thermopylae*, which had begun in June and finished in mid October. "When they left Shanghai," he said, "loaded with cargo, the two captains decided to try and outdo each other. *Cutty Sark* was ahead off Algoa Bay when a storm severed her rudder."

Morrigan nodded, only half-listening.

"Captain Moodie could've made Cape Town, but instead he trusted the repairs to *Cutty Sark's* carpenter, a Scot named Henderson, who rigged a makeshift rudder that brought them home a mere week behind *Thermopylae*. A miracle, don't you think, considering?"

How his face lit up when he spoke of his boats, sails, and sailing gewgaws. "I mind the day you first told me of that race," she said, and blushed, for that was the day they'd started this child who had changed both their lives so drastically. "Nicky was going to write about it for his newspaper."

He gripped her hand, his eyes darkening in sympathy.

She excused herself, saying she was tired. Seaghan followed her into the hall. "Did Aodhàn say anything to you?" he asked. "Anything that would give a clue where he's gone, or why?"

"No," she said. "I would've told you." Mackinnon hadn't spoken after he'd picked her up at the burn. He'd probably been trying to conserve his strength.

"What is happening in our village? First you go missing, and the moment you're found, he vanishes."

She reached up on tiptoe and kissed his cheek.

"I almost feel you're the only one I can speak to about it," he said. "I feel you understand."

"I do," she said.

He hugged her, sent her on her way, and rejoined Curran in the drawing room.

Morrigan felt unsettled, and doubted she'd be able to sleep. Violet helped her into her nightgown, brushed her hair, plaited it, and went off yawning, leaving Morrigan to blow out the lamp and sit on the window seat, looking out at the night. Gradually, her eyes grew accustomed to the dark and she saw the figure, straight and still like a statue beneath her window.

She rose onto her knees and pressed her hands to the glass.

He didn't move, wave, or give any indication he saw her. Yet she felt his gaze. Her hand fumbled for the brass lever. It turned easily enough, but the window was stuck; dampness had swollen the wood. Using both hands, she pushed and pounded on it, groaning her frustration. Finally, it released and with a protesting scrape, swung open. She leaned out into a downy torrent of snow knocked loose from the casement.

"Mackinnon," she whispered. But there was nothing there. Had she imagined it, that shadowy human form?

She stared into the night for some time, until she was shivering and ready to admit her eyes had played a cruel trick. She pulled the window closed and went to bed.

MORRIGAN WAS AWAKENED BY A MALE VOICE REVERBERATING FROM THE SITTING room. Curran, she noticed, was gone already. He always rose early and left quietly.

"Let me see her," she heard, and while Violet tried ineffectively to stop him, Seaghan bounded into the bedroom. "Wake up, m'lady!" he cried. "You're wasting this bonny day!"

The shadows were gone from his eyes, the frown as well. He was laughing, his face touched by sunlight through the south window, the one she'd wrestled with the night before. She sat up, pulling her nightgown around her throat, and smoothed her hair, embarrassed to be seen by a man in such a state, but he didn't appear to notice a thing, or care one whit about his impropriety.

"He's back!" Without waiting for an invitation, Seaghan pulled one of the chairs from the fireplace over to her bed. "D'you hear? He's alive!"

"It's all right, Violet," Morrigan said to the flustered maid. "Maybe fetch us some tea?"

Violet bobbed a curtsy and left, grousing about the crudeness of fishermen.

The moment she'd gone, Morrigan stretched out her hand and Seaghan grabbed it, squashing it between his. "Mackinnon, I suppose you mean," she said.

"And he's sent you something for your birthday." Seaghan pulled a wee box from his coat pocket and gave it to her.

It appeared to be handmade, of exquisitely carved and polished driftwood. The top had a beautiful Celtic design of knots and two herons, their long necks intertwined.

For some reason she wanted to be alone when she opened it, so she set it on the table beside the bed. "Tell me everything. When did he come back? What did he say? Why isn't he here with you? Where the devil has he been?"

Aodhàn did not visit, so Morrigan had to take Seaghan's word that he'd returned. All Seaghan could say was that it was anyone's guess where the man had been or what he'd been doing. "Aodhàn Mackinnon is a close-mouthed bloody fool, who'd as lief have iron shavings stuck through his gums than reveal anything about himself," he added caustically.

Hiding her impatience, she had waited for Seaghan to leave before opening the box. Nestled in a padding of black velvet was a ring. It looked like a wedding band, made to fit a small finger. When she picked it up she saw an etching on the inside. She knew the word *gaol* meant "love," and *mo* meant "my," but she wasn't sure about *chridhe*, though she felt she had seen the word before. The ring itself seemed hauntingly familiar. One thing was certain: Curran would be rightfully furious if he saw it. She told no one of the gift and hid it behind her dressing table.

Eleanor insisted Morrigan rest every afternoon, and took those opportunities to massage comfrey and lavender salve into her skin, to feed her strengthening herbs, and ply her with simmered quince tea, parsley, and watercress. She still approved of the mistress taking walks every day, so the three cronies were often seen together, laughing as they danced in the snow.

Diorbhail looked much nicer these days. Violet had cut the snarls from her hair and had added a fringe that disguised the scar on her forehead. It now curled about her face in a most attractive way. Moreover, she was cleaner than she probably had been in years. She'd put on a little flesh, and lost much of that fearful, shy demeanor.

They went back to the clearing with the cave, but it had lost its appeal. The low, cavernous opening made Morrigan want to run away, but she was embarrassed of such feelings, and kept them to herself. Anyway, with the onset of winter, the inside was clammy and unpleasant.

"I've seen something," Diorbhail announced as they circled the clearing, arm-in-arm. "In vision."

"You've taken more mushroom?" Morrigan asked.

Both Eleanor and Diorbhail looked a bit sheepish before confessing they both had done so.

"Without me?" Morrigan asked, stung.

"It wasn't like that," Eleanor said. "You and the babe are healthy, and I want to keep you that way. You've no business taking something that could cause harm, and if you ask me, the last time did cause harm. Such strong emotions are not good for an expectant woman."

"Well," Morrigan said, "you'd best tell me what you saw."

"A knife," Diorbhail said, frowning. "With a blade of glass. You were holding it."

"Hmm. A blade of glass, you say? That doesn't sound very practical."

"I don't know what it means," Diorbhail said, "but it's important. We must find it."

"Did the vision tell you where it is?"

"No."

Giving a sharp sigh, Morrigan turned to Eleanor. "And I suppose you've seen amazing things as well?"

"I did see something I can hardly explain," Eleanor said, "something that may or may not be important. But I will not share it with you when you're in such a mood."

"I never thought you would keep secrets from me."

"It's because we knew you would be like this. I assume you care about having a healthy child?"

This was something Eleanor could always use to control her. "You know I do."

"Diorbhail and I thought we could see things that might help you without putting you or the bairn at risk."

"There's something else," Diorbhail said. "That man...the one who carried you from the bothy...."

"Aodhàn Mackinnon."

"I don't trust him." Diorbhail's face turned alternately pale then crimson.

"You still feel that way? What's he done, besides help search for me when I was missing, and carry me so I wouldn't strain my ankle?"

"It's a feeling." Diorbhail placed her fist on her chest. "Though he seems to want the best for you, I don't think he does. No' really. There's something driving him...it came off him in waves that night. If you're no' careful, he may well do something to you that cannot be remedied."

"He's lonely," Morrigan said. "You don't know him...." She stopped herself from adding, *like I do.*

Eleanor folded her arms across her chest and frowned as she regarded

Diorbhail. "Could it be you've been influenced by Agnes Campbell? She has long distrusted Aodhàn."

"Agnes Campbell?" Diorbhail shook her head. "I don't know who that is. The color I see round him is not bright and clear, but dark. I felt anger in him. Colors do no' lie."

Sighing deeply, Eleanor said, "In all honesty, I've never quite trusted him either. There's something about him, Mistress Ramsay, and I probably know him better than you do."

No you don't! Morrigan wanted to scream. But that would only cause more questions, and more speculative stares when she refused to answer.

"Watch yourself," Eleanor said. "That's all we ask. Diorbhail and I care about you."

"Do you?" Morrigan turned a baleful stare on Diorbhail. "You think I've forgotten what we saw in the water that night? Tell me the truth. Is there something between you and my husband, something you haven't told me?"

Diorbhail flushed. When she spoke, her voice trembled. "I would never harm you. That wasn't Master Ramsay you saw. I think it was another life, a life long gone. He loves *you*. You alone."

"What in the name of God...." Eleanor looked from one to the other. "Water?"

"Diorbhail showed me how to see things in water," Morrigan said tightly. "I expect she didn't realize just how much I would see."

Eleanor's brows rose, creating deep creases in her forehead. She waited, but her expression was impatient.

"I saw a man in the water. I saw Diorbhail. They looked different, but I recognized them. They were lovers. Diorbhail was pregnant. The man was Curran."

"That seems a fanciful conclusion. You saw images, in *water,* and now Diorbhail is making a play for Master Ramsay? Truly?"

Morrigan felt the absurdity even before Eleanor snorted in her usual eloquent way. She knew she was right, though. The figures she'd seen were Diorbhail and Curran.

"You're being unfair." Eleanor grabbed Morrigan's upper arm and shook her.

Anguish emanated from Diorbhail's face.

"Maybe." Morrigan rubbed her temples. "You're the ones who believe all this. You're the ones who see things and have visions. Now that I've seen something, you want to ridicule me."

"You did see something." Diorbhail met Eleanor's gaze. "She did. But it was another time, and they weren't us. It's different now."

"You're both wrong about Mackinnon," Morrigan said.

Eleanor said nothing for a moment then she sighed. "About the mushroom. I would be willing to try something else."

"What?"

"My brother calls it *monoideism*. He learned it from the surgeon who developed the method."

"Surgeon.... You want to cut me open?"

"No, no. Another name for it is hypnotism. It's not surgery, mistress. You relax and concentrate on an object I will choose for you. You allow yourself to open, or as Diorbhail would say, 'to remember.' You don't drink or eat anything, so there's no danger to the babe."

"That sounds like what Diorbhail and I did. She had me look into the water and think about what I wanted to see. I saw her, and you. I saw her and..." she sent another narrowed glance towards Diorbhail, noting her flush. "Let's do it now."

"Half the day is gone, and you should rest. Tomorrow is soon enough. Oh, and did you do this water experiment without *me?*"

Morrigan's teeth clenched, but Eleanor, after lifting her brows, smiled, and all was forgiven.

Later, when she was tucked into bed for her afternoon nap, Eleanor said, "I want you to practice the hypnotism after I leave. While you're resting, concentrate on...this swirl here, at the top of your looking-glass." She reached up and put her hand on the flourish at the upper corner of the mirror. "Try to let go of thoughts and concerns. Practice will make it come more easily, and it will be more effective."

Morrigan nodded.

"It's not as simple as it sounds. But if you master it, it will help you in many ways, for instance, when you go into labor. I've improved my joint pain using this, and I've also used it to bring sleep."

"I've had trouble sleeping," Morrigan said. "I'll do my best."

"Another thing. I don't like you being cruel to Diorbhail. D'you comprehend how fragile that woman is?"

"I know. I didn't mean it. I'll apologize. But Mackinnon's been good to me."

Eleanor's gaze narrowed and one brow lifted, but she said nothing else.

After she left, Morrigan tried to do as she'd been bid, but it was hard. The more she worked at not thinking, the more her thoughts clamored for attention. Finally, since she kept picturing it no matter how hard she tried not to, she got up and retrieved the ring Mackinnon had given her, and slipped it onto her middle finger.

Only then, as she stared at the circular flourish, keeping her eyes half-closed, did she succeed in losing cohesion and sliding away.

They don't understand, was the last thing she remembered thinking.

Mackinnon led the woman up the hill blindfolded, stopping her before the newly finished cottage.

"Here." He removed the blindfold and handed her a champagne bottle.

"What's this for?"

"Christen it," he said into her ear.

She laughed and approached the corner.

"Swing it hard," he advised.

The wind blew champagne all over her dress, her gloves, and her face. Some splashed where it was meant to go, onto the fieldstone wall.

Mackinnon remained where he was, arms crossed, looking quite satisfied.

"I'm all wet and sticky!" she cried.

"Now name it," he said. "Name our Mingulay home."

She crossed to him and smeared champagne on his face. "*Taigh na Gaoithe,*" she said, before kissing him.

Morrigan woke with a gasp, her gaze immediately meeting Diorbhail's. The woman was sitting in the armchair by the fire, watching her.

Aodhàn Mackinnon! With no creases in his forehead, not one grey strand in that black windblown hair, and an expression of relaxed happiness on his face.

"How long have you been there?" she asked, thinking Diorbhail's stare seemed too discerning.

"Half an hour," Diorbhail said. "I came to tell you again that what you saw in the barrel was nothing to do with here and now. You were restless, so I stayed in case you needed anything."

"Oh." Morrigan hoped she hadn't talked in her sleep. "I was dreaming." She searched Diorbhail's features, looking for anger or shock, but Diorbhail rose and went to the washbasin. She poured a cup of water and brought it to Morrigan, then said, "I'll go and help Janet in the kitchen, if you need nothing."

"No, I'm fine," Morrigan said. "Thank you. Thank you for sitting with me. And I'm sorry about the way I acted. I've been out of sorts."

Diorbhail inclined her head and turned to go, but before she reached the door, Morrigan stopped her. "Have you heard of...do you know...what is...Mingulay?"

Chapter 18

DIORBHAIL TIPTOED PAST THE DRAWING ROOM WHERE MORRIGAN WAS PLAYING some exquisite piece on the piano. She glimpsed Curran reading a newspaper, and Fionna setting down the tea tray.

Diorbhail knew she wasn't wrong about Aodhàn Mackinnon. He was dangerous, though from the way Morrigan reacted when confronted by this, it was clear he'd already done much to worm himself into her trust. That night he'd carried Morrigan from the bothy, his malevolence had struck at Diorbhail's senses as though it was written in fire on the ground. She'd caught him staring at her with an expression she could only describe as hatred. A warning response had awakened, and had not abated with time.

Twice since the man reappeared from wherever he'd been for two months, Diorbhail had clandestinely followed him. The second time, she'd caught him hiding something along the river in Gleann Beag, and putting some effort into being secretive about it.

She went outside, closing the great oak door quietly behind her, and bundled up in her heavy wool shawl, the one Morrigan had given her as an early Christmas present. A few stars glimmered as she set out, determined to follow the path shown to her, and see what she would see.

BY THE TIME DIORBHAIL REACHED HER DESTINATION, HER HANDS AND CHEEKS WERE numb and it was snowing again. She made her way along the north side of the river to a dense thicket of stunted trees on a steep slope leading down to the water.

Aodhàn had stood a long time, looking around to make sure he was alone before he ducked and vanished into the copse. When he emerged, he no longer had the container he'd been carrying. He must have left it in there.

As Diorbhail approached, she saw a vaporous, nearly transparent red mist issuing from the ground within the stand. She forced her way in, pulling away twigs and branches, thankful for her long wool sleeves. In the center was a cleared space. The light made a faint halo around a large rock, which she dragged to the side. An opening was revealed, like a badger hole, though larger, leading into the earth. After reaching in as far as she could and finding nothing, she realized with dismay that she would have to crawl into the hole if she wanted to find what Aodhàn had hidden.

She draped her shawl over the nearest branches and forced herself to enter quickly, before she could think too much and dissuade herself.

It was a claustrophobic, muddy tunnel, only slightly wider than she, and pitch black. She inched along, cold, wet, and afraid. The heavy weight of the earth pressed on her. At least there was no sign or smell of habitation.

When she'd gone some distance and the tunnel squeezed around her, she saw again the red glow and her knuckles struck something hard. She backed out, bringing it with her, until she resurfaced at last and could stand, gratefully sucking in deep breaths of fresh air.

She was a mess, covered in mud, but she hardly noticed as she opened the metal casket Aodhàn Mackinnon had been carrying. Amid a wash of reddish colored light, luxuriant velvet protected the knife she'd seen in visions, the knife she knew was profoundly important. The visions had made that clear, though they left too many things out, as usual. She had seen an unknown man lifting the knife, and she sensed this blade might one day be not only important but holy…if it fulfilled its destined purpose. If thwarted, something else would happen. It would be handed down from generation to generation, and there would be many legends attached to it, legends twined with dread.

Diorbhail had suffered through glimpses of carnage and cruelty so horrific she couldn't help veering away from the memories, though she knew she must face them someday, if she was to help guide the future.

She started to run to Kilgarry, to show Morrigan what she'd found. But she soon reconsidered. Her steps slowed.

Telling Morrigan she had followed Aodhàn Mackinnon, that it was he who buried this knife, would cause another rift. She couldn't risk Morrigan severing their friendship, not when she knew that a day was coming when everything, perhaps even Morrigan's life, might depend on her.

Chapter 19

Snow blanketed the land and weighted down the spruce boughs. Arctic gales blew. The Aurora appeared again, blazing blue, green, and purple fire.

Morrigan posed before the beveled looking-glass and admired her rounding stomach. "*A nighean,*" she said experimentally. "With Curran's blue eyes." But alongside every happy thought came the secret fear she shared with no one, that the babe would be deformed, sick, or dead.

Stop it, she told herself. Since her sojourn at the bothy with Diorbhail and Eleanor, Morrigan had paid more attention to what she was thinking. Believing herself unworthy was the way things had always been. Changing would take much practice.

In this, perhaps the wild, inner Morrigan could help. She had always seen things more clearly. She was the voice of freedom and acceptance.

When Morrigan came across Agnes Campbell having a cup of tea with Janet in Kilgarry's kitchen, she used the opportunity to forage for more details about her birth.

"I'm not the best person to ask," Agnes said, "but I'll tell you what I can. Malcolm and I arrived in 1856. We'd come from Orkney, seeking a better life. Malcolm thought he could find work in Fort William, but our Violet chose to be born here. While I recovered, Malcolm met Master Thomas. Three years had passed since the clearings. There was still rubble everywhere. The new kirk was going up right over where the old one used to be. It's a miracle those ancient yews weren't destroyed in the burning. I thought Glenelg a cursed spot and couldn't wait to leave, till my husband introduced me to the laird."

Morrigan splashed a dab of milk into her cup, added tea, and stirred it absently. "I've heard many fine things about Curran's father."

"He put a mighty effort towards righting the wrongs that were done here. He gave us land to croft, land of our own to pass to our children."

"Mr. Ramsay *gave* you land?"

"Aye, mistress. A more generous man was never formed by God." Agnes tucked a spoonful of fruit compote into her mouth and closed her eyes, adding, "Your Janet's a miracle, that she is."

Janet beamed and blushed before she left them, saying she had chores to finish.

"Aodhàn Mackinnon said Padraig's wife nursed me before she died."

"That's what I heard, as well. I might not be speaking to you now, were it not for Wynda Urquhart. I mind when I first met poor Padraig. Their five-month-old son died too, Saint Brigit bless him. Padraig was miserable." She blew on her tea, saying she preferred it almost cool. "But Master Thomas helped," she continued. "He made Padraig his gamekeeper and he hired Malcolm to be one of his shepherds. Most Lowlanders brought their own shepherds, but not Master Thomas. No, he returned dignity to every Highlander within his reach. He understood us like he'd been born here."

"I wish I could've known him."

"His son is his doppelganger. You're a fortunate woman, if you'll forgive me saying so."

"Aye, it's true."

Looking at Agnes's weather-roughened cheeks and neatly plaited hair, Morrigan wondered what would have happened if the clearings hadn't destroyed Glenelg. Though she possessed fine clothes, a grand home, and a wondrous husband, an instant of unaccountable regret flashed. Had she grown up here, she might've married Logan…Kyle…or some other lad she'd never know because he'd been sent in exile to Nova Scotia. Instead of being awakened by Violet, perhaps she would have risen without help, lit the fire, and boiled gruel. Her husband would have labored dawn to dark and come home smelling of dirt, sweat, fresh air, and horses. His rough hands would've held her, his sweet mouth offered love. Why, she could almost see herself ruffling his messy ginger hair, and hear his words.

Can I trust you? You're not like other girls. You do what you want, what moves your wild heart.

It was strange that she would sit in Kilgarry's kitchen and construct such a vivid fictitious life. Odder still was the longing and grief that followed.

Agnes, unaware how far her audience had mentally wandered, went on with her tale. "The land hereabouts is best suited to grazing sheep and cattle, but we ploughed every bit we could. We provided honest labor to support ourselves and this land." Her expression sobered as she added, "'Twas a sad day when the lung fever stole him from us." Then she frowned at Morrigan. "So...it was Aodhàn Mackinnon who found you, who brought you down off the mountain, was it?"

"Aye." Morrigan's face grew hot at this unexpected turn.

Agnes's gaze sharpened. "And he vanished that night, and wasn't seen for two full months after."

"I had naught to do with that...."

One of Agnes's wiry brows lifted. "Of course not," she said. "I wasn't suggesting you did. I do wonder what sent him fleeing. He's never gone away for so long."

Morrigan spluttered. "We hardly spoke."

"Mistress, I know you didn't cause him to run away. He rejoined his seal kin; it's what he does. What I worry about is you, to be honest. I believe Aodhàn has cast a glamour upon you, m'lady. Did you look into his eyes at all? I'll see what sort of protection spell I can work up, otherwise, well, who knows what might happen?" Agnes glanced into the rafters, blushing. "Perhaps I shouldn't have said anything about this."

Agnes's obvious discomfiture conjured the way Mackinnon had stared into her eyes the night he'd carried her off the mountain, and before that, the raw passion on his face at the Saint Michael's festival, the way he'd kissed her, as though she was his long lost love. He'd held her gaze then as well, giving her a glimpse of his soul.

At least this good woman couldn't see how reliving that kiss made Morrigan's whole body ache for another, no matter how hard she tried to stifle it.

Padraig Urquhart said the last time it had been this cold was the year they'd been cleared. Folk gathered at the Michaelmas barn for robust dancing to while away the bitter nights of the new year. Malcolm played the fiddle. Seaghan, their *seanchaidh,* or taleteller, retold the ancient adventures of Conn of the Hundred Battles, of Fionn MacCumhaill, Cú Chulainn, and other Celtic heroes, and added a few stories of the Goddess Morrígan in honor of Kilgarry's new lady.

Glenelg's women prepared for *Là Fèill Bhrìghde,* Saint Brigit's Feast Day, which fell on the first of February. Morrigan and Beatrice had begun a habit of rocking away the evenings in Morrigan's cozy turret sitting room, sewing blankets and baby clothes. Neither knew the local tradition, so Morrigan asked Fionna about it when she brought tea.

"It once was a grand celebration," Fionna said. "Over five hundred folk called Glenelg their home when I was a girl. Not like now. They're away to

Nova Scotia…dead…or getting old, like me." Her hands faltered over the teapot.

Beatrice nodded her agreement.

Morrigan wound yarn into a bright blue ball and marveled how the clearings still affected everyone, like it had happened only a year ago rather than nineteen. The event draped like a permanent shroud over the entire coast. Mentioning the word *clearings* always brought pensive expressions and uncomfortable silence.

Fionna recovered and began pouring. "We decorated corn dollies with shells and grass and feathers. We put on our bonniest white dresses and collected gifts from the whole parish. By the by, our lads would come, bow their heads, and ask permission to enter the special Bride's house. We made fun of them and forced them to wait until they turned blue. Women have the upper hand one night of the year, and that's Saint Brigit's."

Morrigan was reminded of something Diorbhail said at the bothy. *I believe in She who men face when they die. She was the one we all worshipped first. She made everything we see around us. She has been here from the beginning.*

"Are you cold?" Beatrice asked.

"No."

"I clearly saw you shiver just now."

"Maybe someone stepped on my grave."

If that world comes, women will be the same as cattle or sheep, and there will be no succor anywhere.

Fionna continued her description as she covered the teapot with a towel. "Dancing lasted the whole night. We've kept up the tradition, though it's a sad, shallow imitation of what it used to be." Nodding towards Beatrice, she added, "As the oldest woman in the house, it will be up to Miss Stewart to make the Bride's wand and bed of straw. She'll douse the fire and smoor the ashes. If our fortune's to be good in the coming year, Saint Brigit will mark the ashes with her wand while we sleep."

She picked up the tea tray. "I do wish you could have seen how things were in the old days, mistress. Can I fetch anything else for the two of you?"

Morrigan and Beatrice told her they needed nothing, and Fionna left.

"Aunt Ibby says I can't go out now." Morrigan sighed. "Will I ever be through this, and free again? It seems I've carried this babe inside me forever."

Beatrice tisked as she worked a bit of saffron thread through the eye of her needle. "This is the freest you'll be the rest of your life. Once a wean scraiches its way into the world, you'll learn how thoroughly a mother can be tied down."

"But we'll have a nanny," Morrigan reminded her.

"Aye, you've come up in the world, haven't you? The high and mighty miss."

"Curran says it's the common way among folk who can afford it."

Beatrice scanned the sitting room, her gaze lingering on the mahogany mantelpiece. "Times there are this richness fair scunners me," she said. "I find myself wishing I still lived in a *taigh-tughaidh*, like we did before you were born. Hannah and I shared it with Douglas, his mother, Ibby, and Nicky. The life was simple. Most would think us daft to prefer that to how we were raised, and aye, Hannah hated it. But I took to it. I'll never forget the smell of autumn, or cutting the peat and bringing it in on a pony."

"Tie-toouh?"

"The Gaelic for a thatched house. You should put more effort into learning the language spoken hereabouts."

"You'd prefer such a life to this?"

"There's much I'd suffer rather than be indebted to a miserly landlord for every rag on my back." With a growl of disgust, Beatrice thrust her needle through the cloth. "The night's grown thick to be sewing, and my eyes hurt."

Morrigan scowled. Was that what the woman thought of Curran? And after everything he'd done for her.

When Tess brought coal in the morning, she told Morrigan that in the High-lands, Saint Brigit was sacred to expectant women. "When you go into labor, Eleanor will call upon her to give you an easy delivery."

The maid blushed as she glanced at her mistress's ever-expanding abdomen. It made Morrigan feel old, and she wasn't even twenty.

All this because of an afternoon's impulsive passion on the moor above Stranraer. It was hard now to remember the excitement and ardor of that day, but at least she and Curran had been closer lately. They did other things at night in the big feather bed, things that wouldn't jeopardize the baby. Still, she longed for the day when....

She caught herself. Her thoughts had strayed to Aodhàn Mackinnon again. She tried to quash these fancies, but they had a way of sneaking in when her guard was down. Her wayward imaginings made him cold and reserved with everyone except her. With her he was fever-hot yet sweet as well, even teasing. It didn't seem to matter how often or how sternly she told herself such fabrica-tions had little to do with real life. Some secret part of her, suppressed when she was awake, obviously wanted to be that important to Mackinnon.

Dreams were strange, the way they seemed so lifelike. They affected her mood, sometimes for days. She often pondered the dream Curran had shared with her. He had jumped into a mountain tarn and had encountered an under-water castle. He'd fought a lion, and the two merged. They had loved the woman and freed her from the oak tree. Through this merging and loving, the whole world was redeemed and forgiven.

CURRAN OFFERED KILGARRY FOR THE HOLIDAY FEAST, OSTENSIBLY SO MORRIGAN could participate.

On Saint Brigit's eve, Tess and Violet donned white dresses and unbound their hair. They collected Bride gifts from every home in Glenelg and ran laughing into Kilgarry, their arms overflowing with all manner of things from cakes and cheeses to herbs, painted shells, and bright wooden beads.

Bitter cold fired their cheeks with scarlet. Frost sparkled against their cloaks. They danced about the kitchen, giggling and singing, their exuberance heating the room. These were the only two never-wed virgin lasses in the township, and this was their special night.

Beatrice and Eleanor fit into the unmarried category as well, but no one had courage enough to ask if either were still virgin, and both snorted at the idea of collecting gifts with Tess and Violet.

Morrigan succumbed to unwelcome envy. Tess Dunbar and Violet Campbell possessed waists so small a man's two hands could span them. Morrigan glared at the doorway as she pictured her husband, banished right now because he was male, a virile male who had taken her chastity and impregnated her in one afternoon. *How Zeus-like of him.*

The baby rolled heavily, and the middle fingers on her right hand tingled. She didn't know if the two events were related, but they always happened together.

Tess and Violet draped their arms around each other's shoulders and examined the gifts they'd collected as they sipped Janet's special recipe, a richly churned flip made of cream, eggs, brandy, and spices.

These were free, pure, innocent lasses, the very standard of the wild, sweet Highlands. It didn't matter if Tess was two years older than Morrigan. She appeared younger because she was untouched. Unspoiled. What every man most longed for.

And Violet. Not quite seventeen, with shining russet hair and eyes so blue they rivaled Curran's. Never had Morrigan forgotten the way her maid had bolted her fingers onto Curran's arm at Michaelmas, or the pride in her upturned face. Beside her, Morrigan felt massive and ugly.

Stop, stop. She was catching these mental attacks and halting them more quickly. Now she heard her father's voice in the rebukes instead of her own.

Why were females so often cruel to each other? Why did they choose hostility over friendship towards those who could and should be perfect allies?

Morrigan pressed her palm against a gnawing ache in the small of her back.

Perhaps because their futures were created through plotting, planning, and battling, not only for themselves, but also for the children they bore. Without the support of men, they would likely die, or at least never escape poverty and want. Men had fashioned the world thus.

Though Morrigan had attained one of the highest pinnacles a woman could hope for, the fight wasn't finished. Younger women would always beckon to lustful male instincts. Even in the wilds of Scotland, men were in some ways like Turkish pashas, spoiled, cosseted, taking for granted the fact that beautiful females would compete for their favors.

Women were scavengers. Or perhaps a better comparison would be urchins, like Diorbhail's poor murdered daughter, fighting for tossed bread crusts. A bigger crust meant longer life.

The doorbell scattered her thoughts. Glenelg's gentlemen were clumped up and down the front steps, their caps dutifully, humbly, removed.

She regarded them from behind Tess and Violet.

"May we come in and honor Saint Brigit?" Logan asked politely.

"You could if you were worthy, but sadly, you're not." Tess stifled giggles behind one hand. "And you stink."

"Poor frozen starvelings," Violet cried, "are your privates as shriveled as your faces?"

Tess squealed and gave her companion a shocked blow on the shoulder then both fell into paroxysms of laughter.

"Is this the best we have to choose from?" Tess propped hands on hips. "This pathetic lot? Where is our brave William Wallace, our bonny Prince Charlie?"

"What's become of the Highlands?" Violet gave an exaggerated sigh.

Logan turned his cap in his hands. The look he sent the lass promised future retribution, but he kept his mouth shut, as he must at Saint Brigit's.

"Oh, let them in," Janet said from behind Morrigan. "They're blue as Picts."

Curran passed Morrigan with only the briefest winter-chilled kiss. He was far too involved in discussing the merits of breeding his Augustus with delicate Stoirmeil to bother with his pregnant wife.

Seaghan entered, spilling snow from his boots, and right behind him, Father Drummond. The crowd dwindled. Frustration and hope melted into relief. Aye, she longed to see Aodhàn Mackinnon, but he'd never wish to kiss her again, would he, if he saw her, looking as awkward as a bull seal?

Beatrice closed the great oak doors and Glenelg's residents crowded through the corridor to honor Saint Brigit and enjoy their cèilidh.

Malcolm displayed in full measure his musical energy. There was dancing, drinking, and the consumption of delicacies Janet had labored over for days.

"You don't look well," Beatrice said. She glanced towards the dance floor. "I don't see Violet. Shall I fetch that pet whore who hardly ever leaves your side and have her help you get into your nightclothes?"

"Don't call her that. I promised no one here would ever know her past."

"I'll say and do what I please, you wee, haughty besom, and there's one thing I'm certain of. Douglas would not want Stranraer's famed slut filling his daughter's head with her sinful ideas." Beatrice huffed. "You may now be a laird's wife, but taking in this whore and treating her like she's decent proves you're still the same glaikit wench you've always been."

Hearing the slurs Douglas used to shout at her was almost more than Morrigan could take. She set down the crystal glass she'd been holding so hard the stem snapped as it struck the table. Wine spilled over the lace runner.

"Go to bed," Beatrice ordered, one slightly lifted brow the only indication she knew she'd annoyed her niece.

"I can't do that."

"No one'll care. You shouldn't be here anyway. It's indecent if you ask me."

Of course no one would care. Doubtless no one would notice.

When Curran finished his turn about the floor with Fionna, Morrigan approached him.

"Beatrice has ordered me to bed."

"Is something wrong? I want to dance with you."

She shook her head. "She thinks I need rest. I confess I am tired, and out of humor."

"I'll go with you." He scooped his coat from a chair.

"You can't leave too. That would be rude."

"No arguments, Morrigan, I'm going with you." He beckoned to Fionna.

"One of us has to be here," she said. "If you won't let me go, then I'll stay."

He hesitated.

"Aye, Master Curran?" Fionna asked.

"For God's sakes," Morrigan said. "I'm just going upstairs. Am I so helpless as that?"

He glanced around the room. "Well...."

"I'm too gloomy to dance anyway. You dance for me." *With Violet, no doubt.*

"Very well," he said. "I'll check on you in an hour or so. If you're asleep, I won't wake you. If you're not, I'll keep you company."

He kissed her cheek. Already his attention seemed diverted, and she felt about as interesting as a housefly. Had he not done this, turned her into this ponderous thing? A compassionate husband wouldn't let his wife dissuade him. He would insist on attending her.

As she left the room, her imagination transformed the crofters from happy, half-drunk neighbors and companions into sucking, purple leeches. They had to have their feasts and celebrations, always at the Laird of Eilginn's expense.

This was a foul mood she'd dropped into. It was Beatrice's fault, with her vicious comments. And mental lectures on her good fortune seemed to have an adverse effect tonight. Eleanor had warned that expectant women often wept for no reason, and for some, the doldrums grew far worse—sometimes deadly —after the child arrived.

Candlelight cast leaping shadows that waltzed with her to the round front vestibule, where traces of snow and muddy boot prints marred the expensive wood floor.

She started up the stairs. Tomorrow she'd be better. Maybe she was simply more tired than she realized.

"Lady Eilginn."

She turned. "Mac-Mackinnon." Humming filled her eardrums. *Damn. Damn and blast.*

He stepped out from the doorway of the drawing room opposite the staircase, looking up at her. "I hope you're in good health?"

"Aye, thank you. I thought you weren't coming. Why were you in there?" She descended the stairs and crossed the floor to stand in front of him. She had to tilt her head to meet his gaze.

"I was late, and not sure where to go." He held up his hand with a faint smile. "I thought I'd take advantage, and have one of Curran's cigars."

He couldn't have been inside for long. His hair was still dampened by snowfall, and more snow glittered on his wool-covered shoulders.

Heat gathered in her solar plexus and crawled upward into her cheeks. "They're in the ballroom," she said. In confirmation, fiddle music and faint shouts of laughter drifted down the hall.

Before she could lose her nerve, she blurted, "D'you realize I've not seen you once since you carried me off the mountain?"

"It seemed best. Seaghan has kept me informed."

Wishing she had her fan, she forced herself to go on. "I wanted to thank you for what you did that night."

"It was nothing."

She stared at him and he shrugged. "After the trouble between you and your husband, because of me, I promised Seaghan I'd keep out of the way."

She couldn't stop clenching and unclenching her hands, and tucked them behind her back to hide it. Anger coursed through her. He cared so little he didn't even protest being told to stay away. "Well, Beatrice has ordered me upstairs, so I suppose you won't have to see me tonight, either."

So unblinkingly intent was his gaze that she feared he saw more than she wanted. "Morrigan...."

She sucked in a breath as she thought of Agnes. "Sometimes I-I think you hate me," she stammered.

"Didn't you receive...my gift? Seaghan said he gave it to you."

"I did. I wanted to thank you for that, too. Where did it come from? What do those words mean?"

He scanned her as he had at the oda. "I hoped you might remember."

"Remember *what*?"

He gripped her shoulder, drawing her close before he glanced down. For one stifled moment he regarded the ample evidence of another man's ownership.

"You should go to bed." He retreated a step or two, holding himself as rigid as a coat stand.

Her breath caught in her throat. With a tightly spoken, "Goodnight, then," she turned sharply and climbed the stairs. When she came to her sitting room she slammed the door and leaned against it.

She felt like a dragon, consumed in its own fiery breath. The girl underneath, the one trained by Douglas Lawton's harsh lessons, cringed.

This would not do. She'd been cross for days, and sleep had long been elusive. She entered the bedroom, pulling off her shawl and gloves, dropping them carelessly on the wing chair by the fireplace.

Why had Mackinnon seemed so angry, like she had played him false?

As she pondered she stared at the fire, then at her reflection in the looking-glass over the dressing table. Her gaze rose to the flourishes at the upper corners. Eleanor had encouraged her to use the trick she called hypnotism whenever she couldn't sleep or her lower back ached. Perhaps she should try it now.

She undressed and donned her winter nightgown, laughing at the clumsiness of her fingers. It had only been six months since she'd had no maid to dress her, but she seemed to have forgotten how to manage on her own.

There was a warming pan near the fire. She ran it between the sheets and tucked herself in. The flourishes on the mirror were in shadow, barely visible, but she stared at them anyway. Gradually, her thoughts eased and the tenseness abated. The flourish grew larger and began rotating. Everything else faded, leaving nothing but a wheeling spiral.

WHISPERING VOICES CREPT OVER THE FLOORBOARDS, ACCOMPANIED BY FLASHES OF white light and stark black shadows. Agony stabbed behind her eyes, heralding the rage, and its close companion, terror; terror that her loss of control would annihilate the world.

Her head lurched as though someone had plucked it off her shoulders and thrown it through empty space. She felt it soaring. The voices escalated. They sounded almost demented, but she couldn't make out any words.

She was in a high-ceilinged room. A one-eyed, stubble-faced man plucked her four-year-old daughter right off the floor as she was running to her mother, her arms outstretched.

Evie! Morrigan screamed, but she was being held by two other men, who laughed at her struggles.

The one who had grabbed Evie threw the child against the stone hearth. Her wails stopped and she lay motionless.

Morrigan's awareness compressed. She was so dizzy. Worse than dizzy. This was the sickening spin of vertigo.

Mama, Mama! Claire's shrieks echoed into a vast black emptiness.

Morrigan opened her eyes. She didn't see Kilgarry's cozy master bedroom. Only Claire's terrified face, begging her mam to save her.

A pair of sewing scissors lay on the table between the high-backed wing chairs. Morrigan snatched them up and brandished them. Firelight leaped along sharp edges.

She would murder these men, every one of them. She would save Claire and Romy, and her husband too. She lifted her weapon and stabbed, again and again, until blood and froth enveloped her. She moved from one brute to the next, smelling the whisky that gave them courage, and their unwashed bodies.

You've cursed us all with your sin.

Clouds of golden light suffused the room, blinding her. As it faded, Morrigan stared, uncomprehending, at what she held. In her arms lay the remnants of a doll, one Curran had ordered from an exclusive Parisian shop and had shipped over for the baby. Its body was torn. It bled stuffing. The porcelain head with its glass eyes and pink painted lips hung by threads.

Snowstorms of goose down floated in the air from a mangled pillow.

She blinked, trying to clear her vision. Her throat was burning. She gasped desperately, trying to soothe the anxiety that lifted gooseflesh and tensed her muscles. She couldn't remember getting out of bed. She couldn't remember any of this.

A pair of strong arms forced hers to her sides. The doll and scissors fell.

Thank God, someone had caught her. The rampage would be stopped. She leaned against the solid form behind her and closed her eyes. Her murderous rage dissipated, leaving her trembling and utterly exhausted.

It had been childish to hope this new life would halt the horrors that lived inside her. Primordial Glenelg had unleashed their full power. Hypnotism might be helpful to some, but it was like gunpowder for Morrigan.

"Lie down." The man's voice was familiar, the voice she needed at that moment beyond all others. He helped her onto the bed, brushing at feathers, tucking the covers around her.

She felt heavy, so heavy. "Look what I've done to the doll. Curran bought it for the baby."

"He can get another." Mackinnon stroked her cheek.

"Why are you here?"

"I heard you scream. I was sitting on the staircase, smoking."

"You should go. Curran must've heard as well. He'll come. If he finds you here—"

"I barely heard you. None of them could have, not with the music. I won't leave you; you're shaking. Here...." He rose and moved to the washstand, pouring water into the basin and dipping in a towel. He wrung it out, brought it back, and placed it gently on her forehead.

"That feels good," she said. "My head aches like it's going to burst."

He dabbed at her temples and cheeks. He wet the towel with more cold water and stroked her face again.

"I can't run from my madness anymore," Morrigan said. "What might I do next? I felt such joy in the killing of those men...."

"There are no men. Nothing'll harm you. I'm here."

"But, oh, Mackinnon, it felt so real. They murdered my babies...." Hysteria started to rise again.

"Shhh." She saw his lips tense, his nostrils flare. "You don't have any babies. Not yet. You didn't kill anyone, *m' eudail.*"

It felt so good to let her eyes close beneath the impersonal comfort of the wet cloth. She was almost asleep when he spoke; she smelled the cold Highland night clinging to his skin as he leaned close.

"Someday we'll be with them again," he said. "The Greeks have a word. *Lethe.* Oblivion. Let me tell you about the river of forgetfulness."

"Aye," she said, or she thought she did. She wasn't sure.

"Five rivers pour into the Underworld. Acheron, the river of sorrow, Phlegethon, the river of fire, Styx, the river of hate, Cocytus, the river of lamentation, and Lethe, the river of forgetfulness. We must have our memories wiped clean by Lethe before we can be born again."

"You know many things, Mackinnon."

"So do you. It's all there, beneath the surface."

"Tell me a story. Be *Lethe.* Make me forget."

Placing the towel on the bedside table, he cupped her face in his hands. Firelight reflected in his eyes, and he smiled. "Like the night that Evie...."

He stopped, frowning.

"Go on. Who is Evie?" Hadn't she said that name in her rage? It was attached to a small child, wasn't it, the murdered child? And there had been two others. Claire and Romy. But the interlude of blood-soaked rage was growing blurry now, fading away.

She felt she was teetering on a precipice, seconds away from learning something she longed to know. Something about his face...the *knowing* in it, promised her life would never be the same. "Tell me."

He'd been stroking her cheeks with his thumbs. They stilled and rested against her skin, warm and reassuring, but she felt a slight tremble. His eyes acquired a faraway look.

"Mackinnon?" She put her hand over his wrist.

His eyes cleared. "Once upon a time," he said, "a beautiful, wise, and powerful queen was much revered by her people. The gods grew jealous, as petty gods always do. They forced her to live endless lives, each one worse than the last, until she was bent beneath the suffering, and could no longer remember her power or her glory."

A faery tale. Morrigan loved faery tales.

"Her lover found a way to follow her through the centuries. He tried to protect her from the gods, but they were too strong. In every life the two were ripped apart and punished, over and over.

"At last the queen's lover discovered a place the gods could not see. The couple married and had a child. A daughter."

"A love story...."

He smiled. "After a few years, the queen quickened again. When it came time for the child to be born, she labored through the night, and as the morning sun rose over the hills, they had themselves another baby girl. Their oldest daughter was pleased, for she wanted no pesky brothers."

"Brown eyes and curly brown hair," Morrigan murmured. "As fine as spider webs. It tangles, oh, how it tangles when she sleeps."

Mackinnon's jaw clenched, but after a moment he went on, his voice breaking at first, then steadying. "The older daughter thought the baby was hurt, because of the blood. Her father told her not to worry, that the babe would soon be clean, and to give her mama a kiss, because she'd labored hard to bring this wee sister into the world."

Morrigan sighed and curled her hand against her cheek. "A happy ending. Thank you, Mackinnon."

The rage was gone and so was the headache, under the cool damp towel and Mackinnon's gentle massage. Drowsily peaceful, she envisioned the couple who lived beneath a magical obscuring cloud that allowed them to snatch joy in defiance of ruthless gods.

She saw the man brush his fingertips up and down his lover's arm as she ladled soup into bowls for the children. She imagined him reading to her while she rocked and nursed the babe. She pictured the lovers on their impossibly high cliffs, the ones she had seen before, and knew this was their special place, where they renewed the spells that kept them hidden, and where they conceived their weans.

"I should have tried harder to find you," he whispered. "If I'd found you first...."

She sighed. She never would have guessed such rough hands as Mackinnon's could be so tender.

"*Lethe* is what I long for." His voice was sad. "Oblivion. It's the one thing I am forever denied."

"You don't hate me at all, do you?" she asked.

Benevolent, happy dreams teased now, coming closer. The breezes were brisk and salty. There was a continuous roar as the ocean battered the rocks below. Mackinnon was already here, waiting for her. This was their place, these high cliffs, above the sound and fury of the sea, with the lonely cry of gulls, and an eagle soaring overhead.

Never.

Chapter 20

ALAS, NO ONE COULD PRETEND THE MARKS OF SAINT BRIGIT'S WAND HAD BLESSED the house.

Memories of the night dissolved into confusing fragments. Morrigan was unsure what had happened, and wondered if it had all been a dream. She didn't feel daft when she woke, or violent, only tired and ashamed.

She dawdled over breakfast, stroking her stomach. Bonny, bonny babe. This child had done more to make her feel worthwhile than anything else in her whole life.

Had Mackinnon come to her bedroom? Had he spent hours perched on the edge of the bed, brushing her temples, telling stories?

Curran had promised to check on her. If Mackinnon had truly been there, Curran would've shot him. But she couldn't recall seeing Curran. Maybe he hadn't ever come up to bed.

It had been months since she'd seen Mackinnon, and it wouldn't surprise her if months more passed before she saw him again. Last night might have been her only opportunity to ask about Diorbhail's claim that he'd come into Kilgarry's garden when she was asleep and kissed her. But what if Diorbhail had misunderstood, and he hadn't done such a thing, had not even entertained the idea? It would be too humiliating.

"How was the evening?" she asked when Curran returned from his early-morning errands.

"Oh, lass, it was boring without you." He kissed the top of her head.

"When did you come to bed?"

"It was late. I didn't wake you, did I?"

"No."

There was no sign of feathers or the ruined doll. Their absence made it easy to convince herself she'd dreamed the whole thing.

Douglas and Nick Lawton had been dead six months. Morrigan pictured her father's glowering face and Nicky's, so rakish, his hair always a mess. Now he was nothing but rotted flesh and bone in a horrid box. But this baby brought hope. New life. It was an endless circle, life, death, and constant renewal. She'd seen the truth of it from the flourishes on her mirror to the pattern of the seasons to the full moon and her own body. Everything was a circle.

Morrigan seldom felt the babe kick now.

Two more months to go, and she would enter an unfamiliar land behind closed doors where women screamed and blood flowed. Hannah Lawton died having her. Soon, Morrigan would risk her life in the same way.

Eleanor tried to determine whether the babe lay breeched or headfirst.

"Is she healthy?" Morrigan asked.

"Aye, of course." Eleanor hardly paid attention. "But not yet turned," she added. "And don't you be setting your heart on a girl. There's no way of knowing beforehand, no matter what anyone says."

Such was Morrigan's trust in Eleanor by now, and so troubled did she feel every time she thought of Saint Brigit's Eve, that she confided about her rages and the fainting. "D'you have a tonic or tea for that?" she asked, hoping her smile would hide her anxiety.

"Do you see flashes of light?" Eleanor asked.

"Aye, and I get the most awful headaches."

"How long has this been going on?"

Morrigan had to ponder. "A long time. I was about twelve or thirteen, I think, when it started."

Eleanor listened to Morrigan's heart with a narrow wooden contraption. When she straightened, she was shaking her head.

"Well?" Morrigan asked.

"I hear nothing untoward. Usually, what you describe is caused by a problem in the heart, though from what you say, the swooning is connected to strong emotion."

"One never happens without the other."

"I have seen this before, in Edinburgh. My brother called it *syncope*, a fancy Latin term for fainting spells. Have you ever had an injury to your head?"

Morrigan thought back to Douglas's thrashings, the times he'd struck her in the face or cuffed the side of her head hard enough to make her ears ring. Come to think of it, the fainting, rages, and headaches had started about the same time as her father's beatings. When she left school, at thirteen.

Eleanor's brows lifted at Morrigan's flush and downcast gaze. "Ah," she said, and frowned.

Morrigan couldn't make herself say the words. She tried, but her voice wouldn't work. She picked at the coverlet.

"I'll write my brother," Eleanor said, "and ask him about it."

Morrigan nodded.

"I did find out something else that might interest you."

"Aye?"

"It's about what you saw, the last time we gave you the witch's cap. Apparently, the things you described actually happened. I was curious, so I spoke to Father Drummond, and he wrote a few letters. Seems there was an Inquisition, many centuries ago, in what is now the German Empire. Those names you spoke did sound like they came from that area."

Morrigan had tried to banish the memory over the last four months. Sometimes she didn't think of it for days or weeks. Sometimes it flooded in with horrible clarity, leaving her cold and shaking.

"It's interesting to me how you knew that," Eleanor said, without inflection.

"I didn't."

Eleanor perused Morrigan. At last, with a sigh, she said, "Heinrich Baten lived, mistress. So did Klaus Berthold. He was the Archbishop of Cologne. Heinrich Baten was an inquisitor, given special powers by the pope to stamp out heresy."

"I don't know what an inquisitor is. Or an Inquisition, or an archbishop. I only know heresy because you explained it."

Eleanor's brows lifted. "And yet, when you related your dream, you did so without hesitation, without stumbling or doubt."

"What about...Caparina Naske?"

"He couldn't find anything on her."

She paused for a long time. Morrigan's nerves twined and stretched.

"According to the priest who searched the history at Father Drummond's request, Heinrich Baten was ambushed and murdered in suspected retaliation for all those he had burned at the stake."

"You told Father Drummond about my dream?"

"I did not involve you, and never spoke your name."

"What does this mean?" Morrigan rubbed her temples. The dizziness was returning.

"I really don't know." Eleanor rose from the bed and fluffed Morrigan's pillow. "It's odd. Because I've discovered that at least some of those you mentioned are folk who really lived, I feel I must regard everything you say when you're not yourself as possibly real."

"Do you remember that night last autumn, when Diorbhail and I looked into the water?"

"Aye, you were quite upset as I remember."

"I saw you in the water that night, Eleanor."

"Did you?"

"You had a mark on your forehead."

"I know what you saw. I have seen her as well. She seems a tortured soul, and I have long tried to delve into her story. I have...seen and heard things I am not ready to share." Eleanor pursed her lips and frowned.

Curran came in then and Eleanor took her leave.

He brushed Morrigan's hair with soothing strokes, and rested his hand on her stomach for long stretches, not wanting to miss any kicking that might come along.

"You love me still?" she asked.

"Of course I do. More than ever."

"I might die."

He gathered her close. "We're going to have ten bonny, brave, fair and reckless weans, and you'll be fine. You're feared because it's your first, and I don't blame you. I imagine all new mothers feel the same."

Ten babies! Easy for him to be brave. It wasn't him who would go through it. His part ended with the pleasure.

"I wish we could love each other again," she said.

"I can wait," he returned, trailing kisses down her neck and across her shoulder. "If I can touch you, it's enough."

Caught in an unusual period of boundless energy, she insisted on decorating the nursery and asked Curran how they would go about finding a suitable nanny, with Glenelg cut off by mountains and snow from the rest of Scotland.

"Well," said Curran, "what about Diorbhail? She was a mother."

Morrigan stared at him. "Why didn't I think of that? She's perfect, if she'll do it. Thank you, thank you, Curran." How different he was from Douglas and Beatrice and their petty contempt. "I'll ask her. I'll have to be tactful, since she's still grieving her own child, but I think she'll do it. It'll help her."

Diorbhail was moved into a bigger, snugger bedroom next to the nursery.

"Could we travel after the baby's born?" she asked Curran that night. Untying her robe, she added, "I want her to know the world."

"Why are you so sure you're having a wee lass?"

"I see her. She has your eyes. I want to name her Olivia. Olivia Therese, for your mother."

"I hope you're right." He reached around from behind and stroked the sides of her stomach.

She leaned against him, resting her cheek against his throat. All day she'd suffered cramping and odd pains, but his warm hands soothed it all away. "I want," she said. "I want...." How braw he always smelled, like storm clouds mixed with fallen leaves. It had become for her the scent of pleasure, contentment, and safety.

"Tell me." He walked with her to the bed and joined her under the blankets.

"Morrigan...?" Beatrice opened the outer door and entered, looking at a tangled knot of thread she was holding. Not until she'd passed through the sitting room and stood at the bedroom door did she look up. Her brows lifted.

"Michty me." She wheeled, deliberately stomping, releasing a string of Gaelic. "*Chan fhaca mi a leithid....*" She shut the door behind her with a solid judgmental thunk.

"Why can't folk knock?" Curran scowled. "Don't they know what a closed door means?"

"What did she say?"

"That she's never seen the like." He rolled his eyes.

His surly expression sent Morrigan into a giggling fit. He began tickling her.

"Stop it, *stop.*"

His hands left off tickling and returned to stroking.

"Love me."

"We can't." He kissed her, long and slow, leaving her breathless.

"Please, Curran, we'll be careful. I want you." She pressed against him.

"A saint couldn't resist you," he said, arranging himself behind her.

"Ah, that's grand." She closed her eyes.

"This is dangerous." But his voice held no conviction.

Her strong-willed husband, the powerful man accustomed to having his own way, lay completely helpless in her thrall. She smiled.

A witch, they called you. And a witch you were.

Night had grown old when she woke to a flow of liquid drenching her legs and the bedclothes. "Oh," she gasped.

Curran rolled over. "What?" he asked, sleepy and indistinct.

"My water." The midwife had warned her.

Leaping from bed, he jerked on the breeks he'd left crumpled on the floor. "I'll get Eleanor."

It seemed then that Morrigan heard shrieks of laughter outside the window, and fingernails scratching the glass. Dwarves and faeries—they would break the glass as soon as Curran left. They would steal her babe and leave a changeling. "No!" She clutched his arm. "Don't leave me."

"Let me call Fionna then," he said half-impatiently.

Curran told his housekeeper to send Logan for the midwife. "Tell him to use the fastest horses," he said.

Fionna peered past the master, but bobbed a curtsy and promised to hurry. "D'you want the minister as well?"

Morrigan's abdomen contracted in a furious, insistent, breathless push. She tried to answer but could only gasp. Thankfully, Curran knew her thoughts. "No," he said firmly. "We don't need him."

The contraction released its grip, allowing her to breathe again. "The bed's wet."

"I'll get someone." Curran rang the bell. "Don't move, Morrigan."

Fright paled Tess's face as she brought armfuls of clean linen. Curran helped Morrigan out of bed and into the wing chair. Avoiding Morrigan's eyes, Tess swiftly remade the bed and helped her into dry nightclothes.

Nearly an hour later, Eleanor rushed in, still unraveling her cloak from her shoulders. Half-melted snowflakes showered to the floor. "Aye, and is it your time, then?" she cried. "Lie you down, mistress, and let's bring you a baby."

The pains were coming fast now, scarcely giving Morrigan a chance to breathe. She lay on the bed, clumping handfuls of the blanket in her fists.

"Well?" Curran asked.

"What are you doing here?" Eleanor replied. "You must leave. I'll have no men underfoot."

"But what of Morrigan?"

"I'm here now. Time to give way to what you cannot control." Eleanor pushed him into the sitting room, chanting as she returned,

Bride, Bride, come in,
Thy welcome is truly made,
Give thou relief to the woman,
And the conception to the Trinity.

She washed her hands in the basin. "The babe's turned," she said. "Don't hold your breath. Breathe deep."

"She—isn't—breeched? That's good—but—I'm only seven months!"

Eleanor nodded and frowned. "Aye, 'tis early, but don't you fear, mistress. I'll bring you through, both of you."

Diorbhail came in. Morrigan beckoned to her and took her hands. "I'm afraid," she said. "But you gave birth alone in a byre. Teach me how to be strong like you."

Before Diorbhail could say anything, a horrific contraction splintered Morrigan from throat to knees, and shoved her body beneath the wheels of a roaring train. She opened her mouth and screamed.

CURRAN FROZE. HE HEARD ELEANOR'S INDISTINCT, REASSURING VOICE. TESS RAN past with hot water and a pile of cloths. Violet dallied by the door until Fionna ordered her sharply to be about her business.

Beatrice offered him a frown that seemed to say, *See what you've done?* His own wild imagining added, *Rutting goat!*

Two months early. Two months. Few babies lived who came this early. Many women died as well when they went into labor so long before the proper time.

Had he caused this, tonight, when he, when they'd…no, no, it was too frightening to contemplate.

The sound of Morrigan groaning came out of the bedroom. He couldn't take this, couldn't stand here, doing nothing. It was his fault she was suffering. His alone.

He poured a large helping of whisky and drank it in one bitter gulp, then stiffened as the room around him grew hazy. A memory of the old dream returned, the one he'd had so many times, where he was carrying a bleeding child with enormous black eyes. He saw himself running into a large open space, calling for help. A crowd of hostile, shouting people tore the child from him.

The memory swirled away. He looked down. The empty glass had fallen from his numbed fingers, and was rolling on the carpet.

He heard Diorbhail sobbing. Eleanor spoke firmly, confidently.

"Give me the chance to protect you," he said. "Live, Morrigan. Live."

Chapter 21

She's so tiny. How can she be alive?

Morrigan slipped in and out of consciousness, retaining no more than glimpses when she woke lucid and free of agony.

Fetch the minister. She must be baptized.

Our daughter is here, my darling. Will you wake up and see her?

Sweet Jesus, she's no bigger than a carving knife. I can see her blood vessels.

She's like a faery child. A toy.

Padraig has made a coffin.

Taigh gun chù, gun chat, gun leanabh beag; taigh gun ghean, gun ghàire.

Morrigan opened her eyes in time to see Eleanor wearily place three drops of water on the newborn's forehead and a spoonful of earth and whisky in her mouth as she spoke the necessary words.

She thought she remembered seeing Diorbhail and Eleanor hold a basket above a cluster of burning candles. *I'll cover it with iron tongs,* Diorbhail promised, and Morrigan remembered her saying that would keep away mischief-inclined faeries.

She longed to hold her baby. She cried out for her, and was told she could not, not until the fever broke.

"Livvy." She tried to say the babe's name, though sometimes it seemed she lost the name and called her *Evie,* and sometimes fancied her newborn growing older, old enough to walk and talk—talk too much, sometimes.

It seemed as though Curran sat beside her and kissed her hand as he described all they would do when she was well. There was something about holding the grandest celebration Kilgarry had ever seen, and names she'd never heard before. Sir George Napier and his wife Mhairi, Oscar Colquhoun's family from neighboring Knoydart, Hamish Macgregor, his wife Elspeth, and Curran's shipping partners, Marcus and Thomas. She would enjoy the Donaghues the most. His friendship with Richard Donaghue was long-standing, since his days at Edinburgh Academy. Richard had gone off to London after they'd graduated. There he'd met and married an English woman four years older than he, which would make her eleven years older than Morrigan, but that mustn't frighten her. Curran was quite certain she and Lily would get on famously, for they had the same wildness of spirit.

When he saw she was listening, he recounted other stories and interesting news of the day, his tales often revolving around the sea and ships. He described the mysterious disappearance of every passenger aboard the *Mary Celeste*, a ship found empty and adrift last November. Since the tender was missing along with her people, many continued to hope they still lived, perhaps stranded on a hidden island, but so far, nothing had been found.

Where do you think they've gone? he asked, and she wondered about the underwater castle, but wasn't sure if she suggested it or not. Another name floated through her thoughts.

Inis Tearmann.

She wanted to ask him if they might have gone there, but she didn't know what Inis Tearmann was.

He went on trying to get her to talk. *Do you want to travel when you're well? We can go wherever you wish. Paris? America? Where d'you want to go,* a ghràidh?

Later, she thought she might have said *Mingulay*, but that could have been a dream.

She remembered thinking how awful he looked, exhausted, unshaven, his eyes red, the skin dark underneath like they were bruised. She felt sorry for him and tried to smile, then it seemed there was an interlude of cramping and screaming, of voices and faces she didn't recognize, and someone talking again about *the coffin.*

Other times there was nothing but drifting silence.

Once she woke to Eleanor, sitting on the bed next to her. *I'll tell you what I saw now,* she said as she placed a wet cloth on Morrigan's hot forehead. *When I chewed the mushroom, d'you mind? When you were vexed with us for doing it without you. That woman in the water, the one with the mark on her forehead? Her name is Themiste, and she has spoken to me many times. She told me that you are meant to live seven lives, and this is the sixth. Mistress, there is only one more for you after this one. If my visions are true, we're almost at the end, and I vow I'll be there, to help you however I can. Diorbhail too, she'll always be with you, child. You'll never be alone. But I don't think now is the time for you to leave this life, this 'labyrinth,' Themiste called it. It doesn't feel right. Please, m'lady, get well, so you can do whatever it is you're here to do.*

Morrigan wanted to say *I'm trying,* but she was never sure if she actually did. She pictured her baby lying in the crook of her arm, warm and content. *You need me, don't you,* she imagined herself saying. Her daughter nodded and gripped her mother's finger. *You're the only one who's ever needed me. I need you, too. I'll protect you. No one will ever hurt you.*

Nicky's voice echoed. *I felt it in me, the violence. It strangled me sometimes. You fight it too, I know.*

She remembered crying out her denials, her desperate vow to never harm her child as someone held her down and spoke soothing words.

Wasn't that Rachel Urquhart in the rocking chair? She held an unbelievably small figure to her breast, a mewling being hardly bigger than a bird.

Even Fionna came and sat beside her, speaking gently as she urged the mistress to take a bite of Janet's special gruel. *Truth is, mistress,* she said, *I'm concerned over your husband. Oh, he's not sick, dear, don't think that. I believe it's more an illness of the spirit.*

Fionna set aside the bowl and dabbed at Morrigan's lips with a napkin. *I came upon him in the garden. He was in a rage. Smashing his fists against the wall. I tried to make him stop. I've never seen him so angry. He said this is what he always does. He makes things worse for you.*

After a frowning pause, she said, *I shouldn't have repeated this. He'll be fine if you'll get well. Another bite, please? These are fine Scottish oats, madam, what'll put a bloom in your cheeks. Poor Master Curran's near out of his senses, and none of us have had a moment's peace for worry over you.*

Morrigan worried over Curran too, yet at the same time, part of her seemed to want him to suffer. It was like she wanted him to be punished for something, but she didn't know what. It made no sense. He was the perfect husband, unrivaled in every way. He'd married her, though she was an innkeeper's daughter with no rank or title, not a penny to her name, and never once had he thrown that in her face. She had a strange conviction that he had left her when she most needed him, and that's why she was vexed…but he hadn't done that. It was puzzling.

One good thing about dying. She wouldn't have to think anymore.

She thought she saw Seaghan's face once. *Come, get well,* he said. *Aodhàn and I want to take you out on the boat.*

Then there was Diorbhail.

Morrigan couldn't weep, Douglas had beaten that ability out of her long ago, but Diorbhail could. Diorbhail rested her cheek on Morrigan's chest and wept the tears Morrigan could not shed. Diorbhail spoke the words Morrigan had always been too afraid to speak. Diorbhail called to the wild, inner Morrigan—called to her to come out and bring her witch-fire, for mistress needed its magic and heat to cauterize her wounds.

Morrigan felt the tumultuous lass rise up at Diorbhail's call with an answering shout. *Selene! Oh, how I've missed you!*

Seaghan listened to the wind whistle against the casements. He cleaned the dishes, sat before the blue peat fire, and tried to prepare himself to say goodbye to the lass, lost for nineteen years, who might well be his daughter.

In the morning he woke, cramped and sore from restless sleep in the hard chair.

Aodhàn's bed lay untouched, as it had every night since Morrigan went into labor.

He stirred the fire to life and stepped outside, scanning the surrounding hills. Though he saw no sign of Aodhàn, he did spot a black brougham barreling along the snow-packed track from the direction of Kilgarry, and recognized it as the one used by the physician Curran had brought from Fort William. Seaghan waved to the driver and stumbled through the snow to its side.

"Have you seen Lady Eilginn?"

"It's a miracle," the man said. "She's awake and eating. Claims she's starving. I believe she'll recover after all."

"This be f-fine news indeed, sir." Not dead. Not the statement he'd braced himself to hear.

The driver whipped the horse. Seaghan stared as it bowled away.

He slogged to Kilgarry and was welcomed before he pulled the bell by an exuberant Fionna, who had spotted him through the window.

"Mistress is better!" she cried.

"Can I go up?"

She nodded and he tore up the staircase two steps at a time, bursting without preamble into her sitting room.

"Seaghan." Curran welcomed him with a grin. From the bedroom came the sound of feminine laughter and chatter where before there had been nothing but feverish moaning or the silence of death.

"Let me see...her." Seaghan pushed past, barely stopping himself from saying, *my daughter.*

Morrigan was trying on earrings and admiring them in a silver-edged hand mirror. Her hair, loose and freshly brushed, damp from washing, flowed onto the white coverlet like a shining chocolate waterfall.

Ah, she was thin and pale, but those big doe eyes held newborn sparkles, and the smudges underneath were already fading.

Eleanor sat beside the bed, holding an open book. She looked up as Seaghan came in, and winked. The woman appeared as satisfied as a well-fed cat.

"Seaghan." Morrigan smiled and held out her hand. "Tell me. What do you think of these earrings? They belonged to Curran's mother."

He gaped.

Curran slapped him between the shoulders. "He thinks his eyes are deceiving him. Yesterday he couldn't get a word out of you."

"I'm weary of being ill," she said. "And no one—*no one*—will force me to stay in bed. I've had quite enough of that."

"You'll do what the doctor has advised," said Eleanor with comfortable authority, "that's what, m'lady."

Morrigan shook her head; her hair rippled and her nostrils dilated, vividly reminiscent of her defiant Arab mare.

"Where's the baby?" Seaghan asked.

"Diorbhail has her," Morrigan said, scowling. "They all seem to think she's tiring me."

"Impatient chit." Eleanor laughed. "Give yourself a moment to recover!"

Soon after, Eleanor intimated that her patient should not be overexcited, so Seaghan, after clasping the lass's hand and drinking in the sight of her, obediently took his leave. He ground his cap down on his head and trudged through piled, crunching snow. Enormous flakes landed on his coat, each offering its own unique pattern of beautiful lace.

He gazed at the sea as it thundered, pewter and ice, leaden green. Sometimes he was amazed anything could survive in such harsh surroundings.

Smoke rose from the chimney. Aodhàn must've returned. He ran, throwing open the door to find his comrade sitting in the chair by the fire, his legs outstretched to the warmth and a cup of tea on his lap.

"Where have you been?" Seaghan demanded. "I thought you frozen solid somewhere." He tore off his coat, hat, and scarf, shaking snow on the floor.

"Nowhere in particular. Come warm yourself. Have you been to see the lass?"

Seaghan choked and sputtered as he tried to swallow tea and speak at the same time. "She's better. The doctor called it a miracle. It's true. I saw for myself."

"Good." Aodhàn appeared pleased but not surprised.

"What have you done?" Suspicion lifted Seaghan's brow.

Aodhàn's answer was low. "Probably nothing. There are things beyond our ken. Things we can't sort or explain." His gaze lifted. "No doubt Eleanor saved her. She's a good midwife. But I had to do something, so I walked. Now Morrigan is better. That's all that matters."

"Aye, that's what matters." Seaghan held Aodhàn's gaze. "She has another chance, and I'll do whatever I can to help her take it. No matter the cost."

"You had a lass, just as you predicted." Curran lay next to Morrigan and perused his daughter as if he was slightly afraid of her. He ran one finger over her diminutive fist. "Do I sound sure of myself?"

"As always," Morrigan said.

"I was a *bit* fashed." He kissed the baby then Morrigan on their foreheads, tender kisses with hints of relief. "To be honest about it."

Morrigan hadn't realized how frail the child would be. Why, she couldn't even hold up her own head, and she was so infinitesimal, like the most fragile of dolls. It was disquieting.

"Rachel's been nursing her," Eleanor said. "She's willing to go on doing so, if you'd like."

"Can I? Is it…is it possible?"

"Oh, I think so," Eleanor said, grinning her approval. "I think your milk will come if you work at it."

With the help of Diorbhail's advice gleaned from her own premature child, the mother guided the wee hungry mouth to her breast. "Livvy," she murmured.

She searched for signs of deformity or illness and found miniature perfection. But the baby was so frighteningly small, her skin translucent. Sometimes her lips and fingers turned blue and she was still so wrinkled. The danger wasn't over.

They'd kept Olivia wrapped in clouds of wool, near the fire, for such a wee babe could hardly be expected to generate any heat of her own. For the mother's sake, they performed the protection spell again, placing Olivia in the specially prepared basket, filled with freshly baked bread, chunks of cheese, and folds of clean linen. They held her above three lit candles. Then they shared the bread and cheese, which promised good health in the coming year. A sense of continuity, of belonging, made Morrigan's spirit soar as she joined in the old Highland ritual.

Time ceased to matter as mother and daughter cuddled, day after day, in the great bed. Warm nape, milky breath, and satin skin. Delicate heartbeat and the clutch of toy fingers. If they could remain here in the bed together, Morrigan thought she would be content until the day she died.

No one had prepared her for this losing of herself. Her entire substance… bones, skin, blood, and heart, clear down to her intangible soul—all now belonged to Olivia Therese Ramsay.

"Be strong, Livvy," she said, again and again.

Was this the elusive love she'd always desired? No. Somehow she knew this was more. Love was for men and women, for misty sunrises and Chopin. This was consummation. Deliverance. Every feeling she had ever experienced was barren counterfeit.

She kissed each perfect toe, laughing at how they lifted and stretched. Men couldn't do this, could they? Of course she should be sorry for them. They couldn't begin to comprehend what happened to women through the growth and emergence of their children, but they knew—*they knew*—it was wondrous. It was the most powerful thing on earth. Maybe that was why they made such a business of shackling females. Now she saw it for what it was, a pathetic dominance born from envy.

Woman was man's only pipeline to this joy, to this exquisite love for one's own offspring. That's why they fought it, ridiculed it, and pretended it didn't exist.

They fear we'll win back our power.

Diorbhail had said that, long ago in Stranraer, to a Morrigan who no longer existed, a child throwing her fists at life as though it were glass she could shatter.

She finally understood not only the words, but also the rage that had glittered from Diorbhail's eyes.

Thinking of what Diorbhail had suffered, *still* suffered, made her tremble with an answering swell of fury. She wanted to find the bastards who had thrown rocks at her. She wanted to bring an army, an army of females, like Queen Boudicca's, and send Diorbhail's tormenters fleeing in terror. She envisioned finding the boy who had run down Diorbhail's child with a horse, and doing the same to him.

Unless a woman was properly married when she bore a child, she was outcast, turned into a whore—that ugly word branding women who gave men what they most desired. The innocent child was condemned along with her, of course. Yet men suffered no ill effects whatsoever when the seed they carelessly planted grew fertile. Males enjoyed unspoken freedom to experience and enjoy however many women they could, and move on to the next.

When would it change?

Never, if men had their way.

ELEANOR URGED VARIOUS HEALTHFUL CONCOCTIONS UPON MORRIGAN AND ordered her to remain in bed. "I'll delay it as long as possible, but you'll have to be kirked again, like you were when you married. This time, it will cleanse you. Until the kirking, whatever you touch is tainted."

"Tainted? How? Will I hurt Olivia?"

Eleanor snapped open a napkin and tucked it into Morrigan's neckline. Balancing a bowl on her lap, the midwife scooped broth into a spoon and held it to the mistress's lips. "No. You misunderstand. A new mother is unclean in God's eyes until purified by prayer or other customs. She's to stay in bed and touch nothing until her kirking. She can do neither work, nor cooking, nor visiting. We Catholics have an entire ceremony for it, but you'll only have to go and walk round the kirk with the other women of Glenelg, then attend the regular service."

Morrigan snorted. Eleanor tried to maintain a sober demeanor but when Morrigan began to laugh so did she. They laughed until tears ran from Eleanor's eyes and Morrigan was looking down her nose, saying pompously, "Females are unclean," in a fair imitation of William Watson.

Olivia's fist closed around her mother's index finger.

Unclean, for bringing this marvel into the world? Aye, indeed, the envy was clear to see.

"I think I was wrong about Aodhàn Mackinnon," Eleanor said as she wiped away her tears.

"Why?"

"He's walked deiseal around Kilgarry every night since you went into labor. I saw his face in the light of the brand he carried. He honors the old ways, from before Christianity."

At Morrigan's bemused expression, Eleanor said, "If a man walks round a property in the same direction as the sun, holding a lit brand in his right hand, it casts protection over all inside. Doing it after a woman gives birth protects both her and her newborn from faeries and evil spirits. Someone should tell Agnes and Diorbhail about this. It might make them look more kindly on the man. Anyway, it's thanks to him that I don't fear putting off your cleansing and Olivia's baptism."

The image of Mackinnon walking round and round Kilgarry in the dark, in the bitter cold of February, simply to provide her and her child with supernatural protection, moved Morrigan profoundly. Several times she dreamed of watching him from her window seat, of him turning up his face to hers as he passed beneath the window, his gaunt cheekbones thrown into relief by the flaming brand.

During one of the few afternoons she was left alone she extracted the ring from its hiding place.

Why did this trinket seem so familiar? *Gaol mo chridhe.* She wished she could ask someone what *chridhe* meant, but no one would tell her without asking why she wanted to know.

"Morrigan. You're up."

She nearly squeaked. Her fist closed around the ring and swept it behind her as Curran came in.

"What?" he asked, taking in her expression. "It's only me." He grinned. "Did I catch you looking at a naughty book?"

"No, but I would appreciate something to read. That is, if you think my touch won't pollute it."

The weather finally relented, allowing Ibby to come from Mallaig. She was inconsolable at having missed the birth, though Curran told Morrigan he was glad. "It was harrowing," he said, "and I'm not quite sure her constitution would have survived it."

Morrigan remained cloistered until March was waning. By then, she was so sick of being cooped up that even the idea of the kirking wasn't enough to keep her hidden any longer. Leaving Olivia in Diorbhail's care, she went off to Glenelg and walked around the church as Eleanor and the other village women watched, then downed the dram of whisky they handed her, and magically, she was cleansed.

The pews were crowded. This time, William Watson said nothing suggesting disdain for Kilgarry's mistress. Afterwards, Morrigan was admired and exclaimed over, praised for the way she'd fought off death's embrace. Childbearing was a chancy thing. To see recovery gave everyone cause enough to celebrate, though there remained a pall of anxiety over wee, frail Olivia.

Rachel confided that Padraig had made a coffin shortly after Olivia entered the world—that's how certain they all were she would expire. She shed a few tears over the poor babe, weightless as a feather, and so weak she could hardly manage to make a sound. But now, Rachel said with assurance, she no longer feared. Olivia would survive.

Diorbhail had said the same thing. But it was Eleanor's promise Morrigan most wanted.

Seaghan's grin revealed how pleased he was that she'd overcome the dangers of childbirth. "I see Mackinnon didn't come," she said, when Curran's attention was elsewhere.

He shook his head with a rueful grimace. "But he promised to attend Olivia's baptism, and he's no' one to break his word."

Curran returned to Morrigan's side, laughing at some quip made by Malcolm Campbell. "Come to dinner tonight," he said to Seaghan. "And bring that moody recluse who lives with you. I feel like celebrating, and Morrigan's been shut in with only Eleanor, Diorbhail, and me. She seems to appreciate the both of you, though I cannot fathom why."

"If you let us bring the main course," Seaghan insisted, and they shook hands on it.

CURRAN GLIMPSED NO ANIMOSITY IN THE FISHERMAN'S FACE OR TONE AS Mackinnon said, "To Glenelg's newest father," and touched his glass to Curran's before sipping his whisky. Still, he couldn't quite vanquish an interlacing of anger and bewilderment. The man had helped Morrigan, but....

He discreetly studied his wife, searching for any betraying gestures between her and this tall, quiet man he'd always considered a spiritual brother, though he didn't know why.

Morrigan left the piano and joined the men who stood chatting before the fire. Dimples appeared when she smiled. There was a beautiful blush of color in her cheeks, showing how far she'd come in her quest to regain her health after that terrifying fortnight when he'd nearly lost her.

Placing a hand on Seaghan's forearm, her fingers caressed, perhaps unconsciously, as she described Olivia's angelic expression while sleeping that afternoon. Then she blushed and apologized for being one of those tiresome, obsessed mothers.

"You've truly returned to us," Seaghan said, voicing Curran's own thoughts. "You're the picture and pinnacle of health." He covered her hand with his own. "When I mind how sick you were, and I look at you now, I can hardly credit my own eyes. You're bonny, Morrigan. Bonny as a West Highland sunset. You've become a *bean-uasal*, a true Highland lady."

She blushed again, ill at ease as usual when receiving compliments. "Come and sit," she said. She and Curran settled on the loveseat, while their guests took the matching armchairs.

Curran rested his arm along the back of the loveseat behind Morrigan. When she smiled at him, he ran a finger over her cheek.

He stole a glance at Aodhàn, but the man was staring at Morrigan's portrait on its easel by the fireplace. Curran inwardly cursed, having completely forgotten about that when he'd brought them in here, thinking only that this was one of Kilgarry's warmest rooms.

Yet, as the laughter and conversation continued, Morrigan paid scant attention to Aodhàn. No more than she paid Seaghan, and every bit as inoffensive.

Maybe she *had* only been trying to make him jealous at Michaelmas. Damn her, she'd succeeded, and he was ashamed of his weakness.

Seaghan though, was puzzling. His voice audibly gentled when he addressed her. His eyes revealed the pride of a father or husband. Curran observed the phenomenon as Morrigan began telling a story. All three men watched her, never interrupting, as though whatever she said was the height of wit and wisdom. Aodhàn kept his features guarded, but Seaghan's lay guilelessly unmasked. He was obviously, openly, happily enraptured.

Curran caught himself wondering if Seaghan could be his true rival, and almost laughed. He feared her affections straying like a rutting stag whose favorite doe was in season.

"Aunt Ibby and I went exploring the first time Curran brought me to see Kilgarry," Morrigan was saying. "She got tired and wanted to rest, and I left her. The hills were covered in mist. I felt I was walking in another world. It was completely quiet; there wasn't even any birdsong. In Stranraer it was never quiet. There were always folk about, carriages, ships coming and going, and the train. In a way, the silence was frightening. It made me feel someone was watching." She paused. "Then I heard something. You'll think me daft, that's why I've never told anyone." Giving them each a challenging glare, she said, "Bagpipes. It was the saddest sound. And I heard a woman singing."

"Could you make out the words?" Seaghan asked.

Curran propped his cheek against his palm, captivated by her voice, the lash-shadows, the habitual restless gestures she made with her hands, and her mobile expressions.

She nodded. "'*What did it mean when I lost the soft hills?*'" she said. "'*Time melts into mine, jewels and ancient forgiveness.*' There was more, but the wind blew it away, and as I mind it now, it seemed she sang in the Gaelic, yet somehow I understood."

"The woman of the hills," Seaghan said quietly. "She sings for those who can never come home. She sings for all that is lost." His head drooped as though he was beyond weary.

"The woman of the hills?" Morrigan frowned. "I tell you, the song was familiar, so familiar, as if I'd known it all my life."

"Of course it was." Seaghan lifted his head and gazed at her. "It's in your blood, as it is in ours." He cocked his chin towards Aodhàn.

For a long moment the silence was only broken by the crackle of pine boughs in the fireplace. Aodhàn stood and strode to the far window.

"Aodhàn?" Curran asked.

"Curse *na Sasannaich*. Curse the Lowland Scots and all who conspired." Mackinnon's voice was rough, almost breaking. "They destroyed us and called it progress. Highland children died for want of a taste of milk while Southerners burst their guts on meat paid for with our blood and the blood of our children."

The ensuing silence didn't last long. "Meanwhile, the queen fancies us a land of enchantment," Seaghan said. "She imagines the Highlands filled with brave men and bright tartan plaids, all happy and singing ballads. *Charming*, the English cry. *Romantic*. None have a notion of the rage that has bled into our soil. If they'd heard such a sound in the hills, they'd no doubt scraich in terror and leap upon the first train home. It's a sad thing, and you're too young to understand what's been done, lass. Besides, your father raised you in the south. It'd be a wonder, I suppose, if you weren't poisoned to us. But maybe you are. You wed the son of one of those men who had visions of wool smearing our hills."

In unison, Curran said, "Are you saying my father hurt Glenelg?" as Morrigan said, "I'm of peasant stock!"

Shock, anger, and unexpected pain flared through Curran's nerves.

Seaghan had been frowning at Morrigan. Now he faced his host. "He wanted profit, didn't he? Because of rich men wanting to be richer, our folk were swept out like rubbish to make room for sheep. Your life is one of comfort and plenty because of his investment. This land you love—how many Scotsmen live on in other countries, never to see their own again? Scotsmen whose kin lived here, on this land, for generations, gone forever because Randall Benedict wanted to sell and Thomas Ramsay wished to buy. How many weans grow up on tales of Scotland without a hope of seeing what inspired the writers?"

Curran jumped to his feet.

Morrigan rose too, and seized his arm. "No."

Seaghan stared blankly, his eyes glittering with fury.

Aodhàn left the window to stand beside Kilgarry's laird. "Curran nor his father can be blamed for what happened here, Seaghan, you know that. 'Tis over and done years ago. But ghosts will haunt the hills for a long time yet. If you're frightened by it, Lady Eilginn, you'd best leave exploring to others no' so fey."

Her gaze, anxious as it journeyed from her husband to Seaghan, softened for an instant as it met Aodhàn's. Curran felt himself go cold then hot.

"I wasn't frightened," she said. "Sad, aye, and sorry."

Seaghan stood, rubbing his forehead. "Forgive me. I didn't mean what I said. Sometimes the anger in me comes out all over the place. It's Randall Benedict I blame. Aodhàn's right. If your father hadn't bought the land, someone else would have. And what that could've meant, to Morrigan especially, I cannot bear to think. Thank God it was Thomas Ramsay. I mean that. Thank God."

Curran's hands relaxed. He turned away, thinking not of his father or the clearings, but of her, the woman he'd wed. Had she ever looked at him the way she'd looked at Aodhàn a moment ago? He scowled at her portrait by the fireplace. Whenever he contemplated this work by Christian Lindsay, he didn't see Morrigan as much as the faceless artist. Sometimes he fancied he glimpsed the man within the brush strokes, desperate, unable to show love in any other way than this, his painting. A man who tried to erase the force of his emotion by imprisoning the woman in canvas and paint.

But no one could imprison Morrigan. The authority Curran attempted was laughable. Somehow she eluded everything, the expectations and rules, the requirements. She escaped him while living in his home, sleeping in his bed, even giving birth to his child.

upstairs to check on Olivia.

"I forgot my hat," Seaghan said. "Go ahead, Aodhàn, I'll catch up."

Aodhàn nodded and descended the steps. "Good night, Ramsay," he threw back. "Thank you for the fine meal and finer whisky." Cold winter darkness quickly engulfed him.

"Are you still vexed with me?" Seaghan asked as he and Curran went inside.

"Of course not," Curran said, wishing the conversation had never taken place.

"Then give me a moment, for I've decided there's something you should know."

Puzzled, Curran took him into the study and closed the door. "Have a seat," he said, gesturing, and offered a cigar as well.

"No, Curran. I need to catch Aodhàn before he suspects I was after more than my cap."

Curran began to feel uneasy.

"It's about something that happened the morning after your wedding. Aodhàn disappeared and I went searching for him. I found him by the water. He was…peculiar. Rambling. Almost like he was drunk."

"Isn't that the day he remembered his past?"

"Aye."

"Well, recalling nineteen years all at once couldn't be easy. And isn't he usually a bit off after these vanishing episodes?"

"Not…like this. It was unnatural. I've never told anyone what he said at the edge of the sea that morning, but I'm going to tell you now. He's married. His wife is alive, or was, on Barra, if I understood him. Apparently she used to call him 'Mackinnon,' like Morrigan does. Maybe that's what made him remember. I don't know, damn it! But then…what he did at Michaelmas…I have never betrayed a confidence, but this seemed like something you had a right to know. As usual, I can get nothing more out of him. I'm surprised he said as much as he did. It shows how affected he was. I almost wonder if, those two months Aodhàn disappeared again, he didn't go to Barra, searching for his wife. If so, he must no' have found her, or why would he come back?"

"Why indeed?" Curran wondered if the jealousy he'd felt all evening had been so easy to see.

"It has been a long time. Maybe she died or is gone."

Aodhàn Mackinnon…married. He would have to mull over this startling information, and decide how to use it. Curran smiled and shook Seaghan's hand. "Thank you for telling me," he said. "I know it wasn't easy."

Another hour passed before Curran remembered how Morrigan had once described a dream she said came often to her, a dream in which she was married…and lived on Barra.

Chapter 22

Mackinnon kept his distance from Morrigan at the Beltain feast on the first of May. When she tried to reach him to say good evening, he'd vanished into the crowd.

Padraig Urquhart received the blackened cake and leaped over the fire while Father Drummond explained that in the old pagan days, the person who drew the black portion of cake was sacrificed—aye, murdered, he clarified at the sight of her shock. Sacred human blood was believed to preserve the fruited harvest. Nowadays, since everyone was civilized, the chosen merely jumped over flames to ensure good fortune and healthy crops.

Rachel Urquhart held Jean on her hip. Her free hand rested on her belly, where another babe was beginning to show.

Morrigan wondered if Padraig's wife ever had inexplicable nightmares, questioned where she belonged in the world, or longed for things she could never attain. Judging from her relaxed smile, Morrigan thought not.

Agnes and Fionna were chatting and laughing. Curran, holding a cup, nodded at something Seaghan was saying. Kyle and Logan were eating ravenously and flirting with two lasses Morrigan had never seen before.

Morrigan felt as out-of-place as an otter up a tree. Why was she so different? Why did she feel, more often than not, that she was spinning end over end through a dark, barbed landscape, that any moment she might shriek and throw herself from a cliff?

This was not more of her father's ingrained hatred. No, this was a scratching sort of sensation like she had forgotten to do something important or ignored an obligation, and there would be terrible consequences.

Then Diorbhail and Eleanor appeared, one on either side. Eleanor put her hand on Morrigan's shoulder as Morrigan took the baby from Diorbhail. The twining echo faded, and the world again settled into sense.

It was a fine, fresh morning, the kind of morning, Seaghan liked to claim, only possible here, at the foot of the Five Sisters.

All of Kilgarry but for shy Diorbhail had turned out to mark the arrival of Quentin Merriwether, Curran's solicitor, who was making the long journey from London to attend Olivia's baptism. The child herself was on hand, securely ensconced in Fionna's arms.

"I'm not sure Mr. Merriwether approves of me," Morrigan said quietly to her husband, who squeezed her hand and grinned.

"That's his way," he said, also low. "He's reserved. Part of his English personality, and in a solicitor, I prefer that to a gasbag."

"This other man. What's his name again? Where was it you met him?"

"Patrick Hawley. I met him in Liverpool, when Quinn and I were there last July, remember? When I lost a ship. He's one of Quinn's wealthier clients. A factory owner. I suppose that's why Quinn is going out of his way to accommodate him."

"And now he wants a bit of Scotland."

"Aye. He plans to travel around the Highlands, looking for likely property. I don't think we'll see much of him."

"Patrick Hawley...."

Curran laughed. "You're not going to fall down the stairs or spill tea on him. You're an exquisitely intriguing woman, and every man is jealous of me. It'll be no different with Patrick Hawley."

Kyle drove through the gates with the two gentlemen, and pulled up beside the steps.

"How delightful to see you again, Lady Eilginn." Quentin bent over Morrigan's extended hand and gave it a brief, cool kiss. "And what a happy occasion. I am so pleased to hear your daughter is gaining strength. Oh yes, Mr. Ramsay has kept me apprised. It's an honor to be asked to her christening." Gesturing to his companion, he said, "May I present Mr. Hawley?"

Morrigan had already become aware of Patrick Hawley in the way one becomes aware of the unwanted attention of a wasp. She felt him staring at her in a most uncouth fashion; when she met his gaze she was overwhelmed by a swarming hum inside her head, and a desire to pick up her skirts and run. Somehow, she managed to smile, though she feared it was more a shaky, unattractive caricature.

"A pleasure, Lady Eilginn." Mr. Hawley's cool English accent returned unpleasant recollections of arrogant, ill-mannered guests at the Wren's Egg.

Where Quinn was short and ruddy, with thick, wavy hair the color of steel and a proud set of bushy sideburns, Patrick Hawley was tall, with receding strawberry blond hair and shallow blue eyes. They almost lacked color altogether. Pinkish freckles dotted his nose. His cheeks were hollow and his lips stretched in a flat, narrow line. He resembled a skeleton covered by a thin layer of ivory flesh.

Grave. Cold as a jellyfish, Morrigan thought. She realized she hadn't extended her hand. Nor could she, though she had for Quinn. It didn't matter if this man thought her rude. She couldn't do it, and was glad for the unspoken rule that a gentleman could not induce a lady into such intimacies.

He bowed, all propriety and courtesy, but as Curran drew Quinn's attention to Olivia, his gaze traveled over her in a most improper way, as though he was trying to see through her gown.

Morrigan snapped open her fan, hoping to cool the discomposure that intensified with every penetrating movement of this man's eyes.

"Have you burned yourself, Lady Eilginn?" Frowning in a fair imitation of alarm, he reached out, quick as an adder, and seized her wrist, exposing her birthmark.

She snatched her hand away, thinking she detected a smirk on the man's face. "No, thank you for your concern, Mr. Hawley," she said, holding onto courtesy with all her might.

Quinn and Curran rescued her. "Come inside," Curran said, after shaking Patrick Hawley's hand. To Fionna, he added, "We'll have tea in the east drawing room."

Both Curran and Quinn seemed perfectly at ease. Unfortunately, Mr. Hawley offered his arm before Curran; she had little choice but to take it and allow him to escort her. A pervasive smell hung about him. It was acrid, like stirring up a cloud of ashes in the fireplace, making one want to sneeze. She tried to hide both dizziness and queasiness, and wondered if she had imagined that sardonic smile.

"Where do you intend to search, Mr. Hawley?" Curran asked when they were seated.

"Oh, north I think, mostly in Ross Shire, and I might go down around Inverness. I do appreciate you offering Kilgarry as my base, Mr. Ramsay. It is kind of you. Do you know of any available properties hereabouts?"

Their conversation turned into a meaningless hum as Morrigan sipped her tea, smiled now and then, and waited for the moment she could make her excuses and go upstairs.

Curran stared out his study window and smoked without tasting the cigar. He barely heard Quinn's voice, and blinked only when his solicitor came around the desk and blocked his view.

"You've been damnably distracted since we arrived," Quinn said. "I've been trying to talk to you for a solid minute."

"Sorry." Curran half rose and motioned Quinn to one of the wing chairs. He opened his cigar box and Quinn took one.

"Has something happened? Are you worried about Olivia?"

"No, not anymore," Curran said. "They've both pulled through, no thanks to me."

"What do you mean?" Quinn, who often used his piercing gaze to quell miscreants or confound liars, now leveled it upon Curran.

Curran shrugged. It wasn't like he could tell anyone his uncontrollable need for sex was the cause of Morrigan's early labor. He poured his old friend a dollop of port and changed the subject. "I've been told something that's disturbed me," he said. Though he hadn't planned to ever share with anyone what he considered humiliating, he found himself relating what happened at Michaelmas, how different Aodhàn seemed around Morrigan, and lastly, what Seaghan had told him in March. He stopped short of describing the soft look his wife had given Aodhàn that night, fearing he might choke on the words.

Quinn sat and smoked without interrupting, his face unreadable.

Damn it, Curran thought. *I've given him the perfect opening to blame Morrigan, to question her innocence, her motives. I swear if he so much as—*

"I've found these instinctive reactions are usually accurate," Quinn said. "You should trust the worry you feel, though there isn't any real evidence of wrongdoing…yet. You say this man has a *living* wife, on Barra was it?"

"Seaghan wasn't sure, but that's what Aodhàn said."

"I wonder how he knows she's alive, if he's been here all these years, and why he hasn't returned to her."

"I wondered that, too. He did disappear for almost two months before Christmas. Maybe he went there. Maybe he found out she's dead."

"Or married to someone else. It should be fairly easy to discover. Why don't I sail over to Barra and investigate? It wouldn't take long. I've always thought it rather odd, his loss of memory. He could be anyone, anything. A criminal. A lord. Don't I remember you telling me he'd been stabbed when Seaghan found him in the sea?"

"Aye, well, Seaghan thought it was a knife wound. Who knows? Aodhàn never said."

"That's another thing. Why is he so secretive?" Quinn swirled the liquor in his glass.

Curran had always accepted Aodhàn's quirks, but Quinn's questions made him wonder. Why *was* he so secretive? "I don't know."

"Shall I go to Barra? No one will know you're involved. Let me see what I can ferret out."

The idea made Curran not only uncomfortable, but ashamed. It seemed slightly reprehensible. After what he'd done to Morrigan, to wee, sweet Olivia, he'd tried to be more thoughtful in his decisions. "I'm not sure that's necessary."

With a shrug, Quinn said, "If we can find this woman, and make the facts known, it could ease your concern and arrest any problem before it goes too far."

"Let me think about it," was all Quinn could get that day from the Laird of Eilginn.

Chapter 23

Olivia's baptism brought out all of Glenelg. Father Drummond grinned irrepressibly as he chatted with Aunt Ibby, his hands resting on the handle of his cane.

Tradition demanded the father hold the newborn at the baptismal basin.

The minister touched Olivia's forehead with sanctified water in the name of the Father, Son, and Holy Ghost. Olivia, who had lost much of her original red, pinched look, gave an astonished, unhappy wail. Curran handed her to Morrigan and she instantly quieted, rooting at her mother's breast. Disapproval narrowed William Watson's eyes, but Morrigan no longer cared a fig and hoped he could read that in her expression. Puffed-up fool. Olivia knew what idiocy this ceremony was—man's invention, nothing to do with her.

These were evil, blasphemous thoughts. Morrigan glanced towards the kirk's dim ceiling, half-fearful an angry patriarchal Creator might strike her dead. Curran and Mackinnon, both fine men, and many others, had labored tirelessly to find her when she'd gone missing at Michaelmas. Yet since Olivia's birth, she seemed to see everything through an angry red veil. Why weren't women honored for their qualities as men were? Why were they refused the same prospects? Was this to be her daughter's fate as well?

Murmurs of approval rose from the pews. Women nodded, pleased to see Olivia cry. "A wean who does not shed tears at its christening is in danger of dying young," Fionna had told Morrigan the day before. "Everyone'll be listening for it. Some parents secretly pinch the child's foot."

After the service, much was made of Olivia. Each person pressed a coin into her miniature fist. Some she clutched and some she dropped, leaving confusion about whether she'd grow up to be frugal or a spendthrift.

Seaghan acted the part of a proud grandparent. Though his pleasure was infectious, his comrade Aodhàn managed to remain guarded, and stood at the periphery of the group. Wouldn't that always be his way? Grave, grave man. One of the gravest she'd ever met, yet she was convinced that deep inside, he longed to be merry.

She glanced at Diorbhail, sitting in her shy, unobtrusive way at the rear of the kirk. Diorbhail claimed that Mackinnon couldn't be trusted. But it was the rest of what she'd said that most worried Morrigan, the part about him being driven by some inner turmoil, and the possibility that he might do something harmful, who knew what?

Morrigan returned her gaze to Mackinnon. He wasn't smiling, and showed no pleasure in the ceremony.

No! It could not be. Diorbhail's suspicions had no weight. She herself had said it was no more than a feeling. Many distrusted Aodhàn, but Morrigan knew it was simply his natural reserve and somber attitude that made one think he was capable of grim things. She would never forget how he'd comforted her when she'd brandished a pair of scissors like a weapon. Why, any other person who'd come across her that night would have gone right to Curran and advised him to have his wife committed. Not Mackinnon.

Dark thoughts fled as Seaghan wrapped his enormous hands awkwardly around Olivia. Morrigan giggled. Eleanor had only recently decided the infant was strong enough to be handled by others, so this was the first time any outsider had been allowed to touch her.

"She's bonny," he said, his eyes twinkling, "and so like you, lass."

Everyone compared Olivia to her mother, though her fine hair was as blonde as her father's. In some exasperation, Curran said, "You'd think I had nothing to do with this child at all."

Morrigan moved closer until she stood within the protective circle of his arm. Though it was quite improper, especially in a sacred setting, she turned her head up and kissed the corner of his mouth.

Almost involuntarily, she glanced at Aodhàn. His nostrils were flared, his eyes narrowed. It was a brief reaction, easily missed if one wasn't watching.

Morrigan stifled an urge to smile, but as her gaze veered to Aodhàn's left, she saw that someone else *had* been watching. Quinn. His canny gaze missed nothing, short though the exchange was.

Heat rose through her cheeks. *Damn* her inability to control these blushes. He wouldn't miss that, either, and would take it as a sign of guilt.

Hugh Drummond interrupted her turmoil. "You've done a grand thing, Mistress Ramsay." He kissed her. "I'm proud of you."

Curran sighed in mock exasperation, eliciting laughter.

"Are you wanting credit for your labor?" Beatrice asked. "Let's all applaud the master because he had a moment's pleasure one day many months ago. She's the one carried the life in her belly month after month and gave birth in pain and suffering. And who is it what teaches the child from birth to the moment it leaves home to make its own way? I've heard tell a rooster crows, but it's the hen that lays the egg. Which one contributes more to the future of chickens?"

The women cried *aye, she's right,* and *Beatrice sees the truth of things.*

"Menfolk do think themselves aye extraordinary for their wee bit," Rachel Urquhart ventured.

A flushing Padraig jerked his wife's arm and hissed into her ear.

Morrigan regarded the females surrounding her, half-shocked, half-pleased. In some ways, women were wound into a tight-knit, impenetrable circle. Perhaps, at least when it concerned children, females could be allies. She had a feeling that if she were to voice the unholy thoughts she'd had while lying in bed with this small miracle, they would nod in understanding, but only if no men were present, or anyone who would betray them.

"I see I'll receive no respect here," Curran said in good-natured surrender, though Morrigan didn't miss the annoyance that hardened his jaw. Cradling Olivia, he crooned, "You love me, though, don't you, my wee lass?"

"Is she truly healthy?" Agnes asked. "I've ne'er seen a babe so tiny."

"This child is as healthy as poppies in a cornfield," Eleanor retorted, taking offense.

Morrigan thought the midwife's words strange and ill fated. They reminded her of the bothy, of the strange, visionary mushroom, and of Diorbhail's murdered daughter.

They used a horse to crush her like a china cup, and laughed. Nobody cared. None but me.

She fought against it, but the cloudy memory sent a trickle of ice down her spine, where it joined the one formed by Quinn Merriwether's penetrating stare.

OLIVIA FASCINATED THE DOGS. THEIR EARS PERKED WHENEVER SHE MADE A SOUND. They paced, stiff-legged, tails wagging, trying to get a look at her, so Morrigan sat on the floor, the baby on her lap, to let them get to know her better. Antiope adopted a position beneath the cradle, steadfast and alert, often growling at the approach of anyone other than Morrigan, Diorbhail, or Curran.

"I want to ride," Morrigan told Curran, three days after the baptism, after Quinn, thankfully, had returned to London. "But for the kirking, I haven't been outside these walls in ages. I crave wind and sunlight and the feel of a horse."

An additional impetus was that Patrick Hawley had taken himself away to continue his search for land. The absence of both the oily Hawley and the judgmental Quinn lightened her mood considerably.

"Has it been long enough?"

"Aye, more than enough." She came around the table and leaned down, running her hand over the knot of his tie then up, flicking his earlobe. "After I ride Stoirmeil, I'm going to come home and ride you, my fine stallion."

Curran started; his tea splashed, staining his crisp white shirt. He reached for a napkin with the admonition, "Has no one ever taught you that ladies mustn't say such things?"

Half sitting on the edge of the table, she gave a careless, one-shouldered shrug. "No, since that lesson would require speaking of subjects that are supposed to make us swoon. Do you want me to behave like other ladies?"

The corners of his mouth turned up. He rose and deliberately pulled a lock of her hair free of its restraining pins. "I wouldn't go that far."

Ibby entered the dining room as Morrigan scolded him for disheveling her hair.

"Would you ride with me today, Auntie?" she asked.

"Certainly." Ibby eyed the sideboard. "Are you sure you're ready?"

"Don't caution her." Curran finished what remained of his tea. "She's set on it."

"Well, then, there'd be no use in trying." Ibby piled fluffy yellow eggs on her plate. "I see you're learning, Curran Ramsay. You've married a woman with a particularly stubborn backbone." Her gaze turned quizzical. "Do you realize you've spilled tea on yourself?"

They left Olivia yawning her way into a nap after receiving a belly-full of milk.

"Come, isoke." Ibby drew on her gloves. "Or we'll miss this glorious weather. It'll turn chilly later, and no doubt rain."

"Could I speak to you about the cough Olivia had the other day?" Diorbhail asked. "It'll only take a moment."

Morrigan knew that look in the woman's eye. "Of course," she said, and sent Ibby off to the stables.

"Well?" she asked when they were alone.

"I've been wanting to show you something." Diorbhail got on her knees and withdrew a bundle from under the wardrobe. She unwrapped it carefully.

The curved black blade reflected sunlight from the window in an ominous glitter. Morrigan stared, enthralled by its deadly beauty.

"D'you mind when I told you I'd had a vision of a knife?" Diorbhail asked.

"When you and Eleanor used the witch's cap."

"This is the knife I saw."

"You found it? How? Where?"

"I saw light coming out of the ground. It was down in the earth, by the river." She paused before adding, "I feel the age of it. It's older than we can comprehend. I've been thinking that I was led to it for you. It's meant for you, somehow. You'll know when and how to use it."

She handed it to Morrigan. The hilt was carved in the shape of a woman, an owl perched on her shoulder, and was exquisitely detailed, down to the woman's grave, resolved expression.

"D'you mean to tell me you saw this knife in a dream, and then found that knife *here*, in Glenelg? Where did it come from? How did it get there? Whose is it?"

"I...I don't know any of those things. I feel it was brought from far away, but that's only a feeling."

"Tell me everything you saw when you took the witch's cap."

"The two of us were fighting side by side. This was a long time ago, before rifles or cannons. There were only swords and knives, spears and shields. You were using this knife."

Diorbhail's anguish was clear to see, but Morrigan didn't know how to comfort her. She didn't know what to say.

"Terror clings to this blade," Diorbhail said, low. "Terror and hate. But its shape, the shape of the waxing moon, gives it sanctity. You wax, too. You're growing. Changing. Maybe the Lady led me to it so I could give it to you. I think you're supposed to have it. Keep it secret and safe; make it a part of you. When I first brought it out of the ground and held it, I had a sense that if it's used as she wants, we'll find peace and the wound in the world will heal. But I also saw that it could be perverted, used for evil. If that happens, there will be much suffering."

Morrigan's limbs trembled like she hadn't eaten in too long. Deep inside, a picture formed. She saw the blade rip out a man's throat, and heard a woman's voice. *I will feed your carcass to the sea!* The image was brief, but the horror lingered. "'Used as she wants....' What if I use it the wrong way? What if I can't use it, or I refuse?"

"Then something that needs to happen won't," Diorbhail said. "I wish I had better Sight." She clasped Morrigan's elbow. "I can only tell you that this blade has power, and in the proper hands, it can right an ancient wrong. I believe those hands are yours."

An exhausting weight descended. Diorbhail asked much of her, yet her visions left more questions than answers, and made the right choice seem chancy, even unobtainable. Morrigan wanted to shout, *Why do I have to be the one? Why can't you tell me what I must do!*

"Don't be afraid." Diorbhail rightly discerned Morrigan's expression. "Somehow, you'll be shown what you need to see. And I promise, I will keep searching, trying to find out more."

Morrigan took the knife to her bedroom, meaning to hide it in her wardrobe, but she paused. She stared at the blade then slipped it into the pocket of her riding habit. The thing made her feel sick and strong at the same time, and seemed to demand she keep it close.

Logan had their mounts saddled and ready.

"I could show you where your father and I were born," Ibby said as they cantered through the gate.

Stoirmeil whinnied and tossed her head, making Morrigan realize she'd jerked the reins. She patted the mare's neck in apology. "I'd like that."

They traveled north, stopping to speak when they passed Agnes and Rachel, and farther on, Malcolm.

Beyond Glenelg, at the summit of a steep grassy hill, they paused to admire the village nestled against the bay. Hills rolled behind the township, gradually growing steeper, cutting off the area from the rest of Scotland. To the southwest glittered the Sound of Sleat and beyond, Skye's blue-violet mountains. Below lay the straits of Kyle Rhea where, she'd been told, a sea serpent had boldly reared its head.

"What a pretty spot," Morrigan said.

"Aye," Ibby agreed. "And a perfect day. How d'you feel? Are you hurting?"

"Not a bit," Morrigan assured her, though the tough leather sidesaddle did seem more abrasive than it had before she'd been banned from riding. "It's been three months."

It had either rained or snowed almost every day for a month, but now, at last, there was a shining sun and warmth. The earth smelled and looked scrubbed, reborn. She reveled in the fresh air, drawing it deeply into her lungs. Nothing would induce her to spend another day indoors.

Away in the distance, someone cursed his horse as he broke ground, and out on the water, a skaffie trolled, slow and lazy. Sheep bleated across the hillsides, and nearer, a shaggy Highland bull observed the two riders in an aloofly disinterested manner.

"Come away then," Ibby said. "You can see what remains of our *taigh-tughaidh.*"

In the lee below the summit of the hill, Morrigan made out stones, now covered with moss and lichen, spread in a blurry rectangle. Ibby led her through long, lush grass and hardy wildflowers to a flat area containing a few stunted pines, giving way to dirt and scree on the slope leading to the water.

"Padraig Urquhart and his family lived there, beneath that burned stump," Ibby said. "It used to be a great old ash tree." She dismounted, letting the reins drag, and walked to the mounds of stone. "This was our home."

Morrigan remained on Stoirmeil; her hands tightened around the reins as disquiet crept through her.

"We lived here together after my da—your grandfather—abandoned us. Mam, Douglas, and me. Later, after he came home from India, Douglas became Randall Benedict's gamekeeper and went off to his own home with Neala. After she died, he married your mother and took her away to Ireland. They returned a fortnight before the clearings. She didn't like sharing space with the kye and the goat, and it was crowded, so he started building a byre, over there." Her voice trembled as she added, "It wasn't quite finished when the soldiers came. They burned it as well as the cottage, after they saw we'd not get on their ship. They didn't want us using it for shelter."

Morrigan slipped off her horse. "It's hard to believe that your home, everyone's homes, were burned, and you were all left to die." The toe of her boot grated against one of the stones.

Because of rich men wanting to be richer, our folk were swept out like rubbish, Seaghan had said. After all these years, he'd still shaken with rage.

"Randall Benedict paid to have us shipped to Nova Scotia. If we refused his offer, well," Ibby shrugged, "he'd done everything he could, hadn't he?" She squinted at the glittering water. "He wasn't a man of the land. He couldn't understand how we felt, how the legends nurtured and sustained us. He had no idea what it meant to grow up on the same land as our grandfolk and their grandfolk. Land they fought to protect clear back to Culloden and further, back to Scotland's beginnings." She paused. "We knew every stone. The course of every burn. All the secret spots where the red fish leap. We knew each tree and bush, where the rabbit holes were. How could we leave those things? How could they ask it? Better to die of starvation in our own hills, with the scent of home in our noses."

How many Scotsmen live on in other countries, never to see their own again?

Sorry now that she'd agreed to come to this place that dredged up so many awful memories, Morrigan put her arm around Ibby's shoulders, hoping to comfort her.

Ibby wiped away tears with an impatient swipe. "Douglas was poisoned to it afterwards. Once he told me he heard the screaming, the sound of burning, every day and night. That's why he left, moved you and Nicky to Stranraer. Gregor fetched me away to Mallaig. I never stopped missing my home, though. I think in the end, it was the same for your father."

She stepped over a disrupted pile of stones. "Nicky played here. Dear lad. Mam and I tried to make up to him for the loss of his mother. Hannah treated him well, too. But we never could make him understand why Neala wouldn't come home. He couldn't understand death left her no choice."

Nicky, I know. My heart knows. As blithe and carefree as you seemed, you weren't. An ocean of hurt lived inside you.

"My God." Ibby knelt and pulled at some grass. Whatever she worked for gave her difficulty. She had to dig, but in the end the ground yielded its treasure. She held it out, a waterlogged, moldy hunk of wood. "This was your brother's. I *remember* it."

It was a carved wooden boat. There was still the broken-off stump of a mast, and a bit of twine that probably had fastened a scrap of cloth for a sail. He'd watched it bob on the water, maybe at Loch Alsh, to the north, or down on the Kyle Rhea, or perhaps in this wee burn that trickled past her father's old ruin.

This was her land. Hers, where she should have grown up, meshed in the traditions and customs that now had to be explained. The Gaelic should've been her natural tongue, with English sounding strange and foreign to her ears. If her kin had not been cleared, she would have married and borne her babes here, in this meadow, in a blackhouse that no longer existed. Lifting her head, Morrigan closed her eyes and listened. She heard sparrows chattering, and breezes through the grass. She drew in air, and more. A thwarted life. If the clearings hadn't ravaged Glenelg, perhaps Douglas wouldn't have become that violent, horrible thing she'd known.

With her eyes closed, Morrigan allowed in a silence that echoed, bringing her castrated life into focus. Wee Nicky playing with his boat. Douglas ploughing his strips. Hannah stirring porridge over a fire.

Her legs gave way. She fell to her knees. Crimson cartwheels leaped across a fathomless black background. Almost able to step into it, the smells, the sounds, the life, she pressed the boat to her cheek and breathed in the scent of earth and wet wood. "Why did you do it?" she whispered. "You knew this would happen. You let it. You caused it. You're a cruel god."

Ibby knelt beside her. "Lord love you, child, forgive me. I shouldn't't've brought you here."

Morrigan couldn't open her eyes. It was frightening, how her blood pounded. She knew weeping would bring relief, but her eyes refused to part with a single tear. They were there inside, locked away. Perhaps the wild, hidden Morrigan held them prisoner.

"This is more emotion than I've seen in you since…well, as long as I can mind," Ibby said. "I thought your heart had gone stone hard, or something inside you had been killed. But you must not hold back. Don't be afraid to mourn. Sometimes, it's all we can do."

"I want to be alone, Auntie."

"Don't be daft. Let's go to Kilgarry. We'll have tea and you can cuddle the wean."

"No. I want to think. I need time."

"I will no' go off without you—"

"*Leave me alone.*"

Ibby paused. She looked stricken. But, after a moment, she nodded. "Very well." Rising, she brushed at her habit and blotted her eyes with her handkerchief before handing it to Morrigan. "We all need time alone now and again. If you forget the way, Glenelg is that direction. Go to the top of the hill and you'll see it."

"I won't forget."

"You're sure?"

"Aye."

After Ibby and her mare disappeared, Morrigan ran her fingertips over the miniature boat, feeling the splinters and warped roughness of her dead brother's toy as she held a one-way conversation with God.

I know what love is now, because of my Livvy. But you'll destroy it, won't you? Like you did to Papa. The toy wavered into a dancing brown water spot and for an instant Morrigan thought she might weep after all. *Why did you hate me, Papa? God did those things, not me.*

"Well, what have we here? Lady Eilginn."

Morrigan scrambled to her feet, blinking frantically. "M-Mr. Hawley." Of all the people who might have come upon her this way, it had to be him—the cold, oppressive Englishman who made her flesh crawl. "I-I thought you were traveling."

He wrapped his mount's reins loosely around one of the tree stumps. "I returned just now. No luck today, I'm afraid."

Averting her face, she stared at the Kyle Rhea. Damn him. She'd only wanted a minute, one brief moment in time, to think.

A curlew called, wretched and lonely.

"Why are you alone out here?" His clipped accent sounded harsh to her ears. "Something is wrong, Mrs. Ramsay."

"I'm simply feeling sorry for myself, Mr. Hawley."

"May I ask why?" His words were solicitous, but his manner mocking.

She shrugged. "I was imagining how things might've been, if the world were different."

"I will not stand for this." He extended his hand. "Come, I'll see you home."

"No, thank you, Mr. Hawley. Women may be delicate, but surely we can have a moment of solitude every so often."

"Not if it makes you sad. Please, sit at least. I insist." He clasped her forearm and led her to a stone that was tilted vertically, its flattened crown offering a likely seat.

She didn't want to display bad manners. Manners were so important to the upper class. Yet, what of his own? She hadn't forgotten the way he'd leered at her.

His touch, even through her sleeve, made her shudder. Thank God, today she wore a high-necked, long-sleeved, full-skirted riding habit, along with a cap, jacket, and gloves, not to mention her undergarments. So many layers lent a sensation of safety, as though she resided behind an impenetrable fortress.

He perched on another stone beside her. "Imagine such treasure, hidden away in that backwater village." He crossed one long leg over the other and kicked at the grass. "What was it? Stranraer? Makes me want to explore the entire country, it does!"

"That's kind of you, Mr. Hawley." Though his words were embarrassingly out of bounds, he didn't appear lustful, only attentive. She couldn't expect him to understand how giving such a compliment, especially to a woman he hardly knew, was as demeaning as it was flattering. She sighed. He was simply attempting to lift her spirits, and no doubt assumed the quickest way was to give homage to her features. Curran often said similar things. She must be more patient. But Curran's compliments never made her feel threatened or uneasy.

"Do call me Patrick."

She inclined her head. Did other women ever resent the flattery men tossed about so carelessly? Perhaps, unlike her, they appreciated the admiration. She had heard tales, after all, of lasses forcing their corsets so tight their lower ribs snapped, but wasn't sure if it was true. She'd also heard of ladies drinking arsenic to make their complexions fashionably pale. Were there women who were actually willing to barter their very lives—

Hawley's hand cupped her knee.

Morrigan started. His cheeks were flushed. The man seemed educated, but Scotland's rudest shieling boy knew better than to lay hands on a married woman.

"I was certain one of these days you'd go out by yourself." He sounded breathless. "I'd started to wonder how long I would have to wait, though I would have waited all summer if I had to. Maybe through the winter as well."

"I don't understand."

His gaze veered away. He pushed at his hair with trembling fingers. Abruptly, he stood and seized her arms, forcing her to her feet. "You like to pretend you're standoffish and proper. That never changes." Leaning forward, he burrowed his face against her throat. "I've missed you. I've missed your flesh. I swear you smell the same."

Morrigan tried to escape and lost her balance as her feet tangled against the stone she'd been sitting on. "Let me go," she cried.

Patrick pinned her arms to her sides. His breath was hot against her cheek. "Playing innocent? Again? When you'd put the whores in the Haymarket to shame?"

Morrigan managed to pull one arm free. She slapped him as hard as she could and arched, shoving at him. Nothing had any effect. The man, though thin, possessed a wiry strength far superior to hers.

He laughed. "I'm ready for you, little vixen. You'll not break my nose as you once did."

In the depths of her brain, Douglas formed. *Take down your dress,* he commanded, in that silky, dangerous voice.

No, not again. *Never* again.

Patrick Hawley bit her earlobe, at first gently, then hard enough to hurt, to let her know that if she made him angry, he would inflict real pain—maybe rip it clear off. The way he tongued her flesh implied he was contemplating it.

"Don't worry," he said. "We'll keep the secret from your oblivious husband, unless you think he'd like to watch. Remember Lycus? He watched, though he didn't seem to enjoy it." He rubbed his cheek against her bodice. "Keep your mouth shut and please me, if you want me to leave your husband alone." He fumbled at her buttons.

"*No.*" She wasn't sure why she wasn't screaming. Part of her didn't want to draw the attention of whoever might hear, for fear of what they'd think of her. She was also terrified that if she did scream, he would hurt her grievously, and enjoy doing it. Some inner sense warned that he might want her to fight more than he wanted her to succumb.

He merely laughed and trapped her hand in his. "I swear you're a comely bitch. The way you turn a man hard as rock hasn't changed." His tongue trailed over her jaw. "I like how you make a bustle swing. You know what it does. A man can't think of anything but having you. That's why you do it. Will you beg for mercy? Beg me, my slave-queen."

Rage formed, shifted to terror, and reformed again. *Foisting bastards on innocent men, driving us daft with your shameless ways. You deserve what you get....*

What could she expect from other men if her own father believed such things? "I've done nothing," she cried. "Let me go. Now! *Let me go!*"

He forced her mouth open with his. Pushed his tongue so deep she gagged. Splinters from her brother's toy boat wormed into her palm, stinging like an insistent messenger. She thought she heard Nicky, shouting. *Fight for yourself.*

She bit down as hard as she could, though her instincts warned that it would only enrage him. He gave a muffled scream and released her, leaving her free to spit out his blood.

"You bitch!" He pressed his hand over his mouth. "I'll make you pay for that." His words slurred. "I'll break every bone in your body and send you to Kilgarry naked and bleeding. Ramsay will be a laughingstock, and yes, I'll make certain this tale is heard everywhere."

"Will you?"

He paused, frowning. He scanned the surrounding hills, his sandy lashes descending to protect his eyes from the glare. "All at once you sound quite brave." He picked up the handkerchief Morrigan had dropped, spit, and wiped his lips. "I remember how you used to lead the prince and his bastard brother around by their noses. Now look at you, pretending to be respectable. You won't be so proud when I'm done with you."

Heat radiated against her thigh.

The knife.

"You'll cry for mercy," Hawley said, "or for more. Depends on you."

He grasped the front of her bodice. His grip tightened then flexed, but the fabric was well made and resisted his attempts to tear it. While his attention was focused on that, she dropped Nicky's boat and slipped her hand into her pocket, bringing out the blade.

Sunlight reflected off it, drawing his eye. His face turned sickly grey and he staggered. His arm rose in a defensive gesture.

She sliced swiftly through his coat and into his forearm. The wool darkened as blood saturated it. He tripped over one of the stones and fell, groaning, his face contorted.

Should she stab him again? With her attacker on the ground, moaning, she hesitated.

He scrabbled to his feet, his good hand pressing against the wound, his mouth open, waves of color washing through his cheeks.

"Come away, *Patrick*," she said. "Weren't you going to make me beg for mercy?" She had to fight a strong urge to stab him in the throat. *You're not a murderer,* she told herself grimly. But she lifted the blade.

Hawley stumbled. He dragged himself to his horse and mounted, wheeling the animal, and galloped away as though all of Hell had come out of the ground to chase him.

Morrigan walked to the burn. She knelt on the wet rocks and rinsed her mouth until she no longer tasted Patrick Hawley's blood, then washed the knife. She stood and returned to the ruin of her father's blackhouse.

Douglas Lawton had been obstinate, unforgiving, often cruel, but he'd never shown fear. She'd learned instinctively, by his example, that to show fear was dangerous. Fear stole power. She'd kept her power today. She felt it resound through her.

Her earlier despair evaporated, like smoke rising into the clear spring air. She would keep this knife with its fearsome blade of glass. Never again would she be without it. And if another man proved daft enough to menace her or her child…

…she'd make him regret it.

CURRAN SEARCHED FOR MORRIGAN WHEN HE'D FINISHED UPDATING HIS LEDGERS. Perhaps she'd returned from her ride. Nightfall might find her well, ready for love. He'd missed their intimacy, and God; it'd been so long, three months since Olivia was born, and how long before that? Months and months, if he didn't count that one night of weakness when he'd defied Eleanor's command and nearly caused the deaths of his wife and child.

Morrigan the mother was as enticing as the virgin on Stranraer's moor. She tempted him with every unconscious movement she made. But she had naturally been occupied with her sickly infant, and he wouldn't let himself intrude. Twice in the last three days he'd had to leave the room as she'd nursed their daughter, such was the strength of his need battling determination to be patient.

With the repulsive Patrick Hawley off seeking land and out of the way, the setting was perfect for uninterrupted seduction.

Diorbhail had thrown open the casements in the nursery. The room smelled of warm earth, sea, and pine.

"Have you seen my wife?" he asked as he entered.

"Not since breakfast. Olivia's hungry. I hope she'll soon come home." Diorbhail cooed to the wean and tickled one miniature ear.

Curran was pleased at how their daughter's nanny had blossomed. She was pretty now, with the weight she'd gained, and the color in her cheeks. Being Olivia's caregiver had helped, he could tell. He crossed to a deep-set window and gazed over the wooded countryside. "Did she say where they were going?"

"No, Master Curran. 'Out for a ride' was all I heard."

As he turned, he glimpsed something in her eyes. She lowered her face, but it was too late. He hoped he'd mistaken that look, and that her gratitude wasn't shifting into infatuation.

"If she comes in, would you send word?"

"Of course."

Though always courteous, Diorbhail's manner made him a bit uncomfortable. When he saw her walking outside with Morrigan, he couldn't help wondering what they talked about. Sometimes they appeared to be grimly serious, and other times were laughing uproariously. It gave him a strong inner satisfaction to improve Diorbhail's lot, yet at the same time a part of him wanted to avoid her.

He rambled through Kilgarry's corridors and rooms, studying the priceless paintings his father had collected and his mother had so lovingly hung. Janet, who'd started the midday meal, asked if Lady Eilginn would join them.

"I don't know. I hope so." The house seemed too quiet. Empty. Somehow, without its mistress, not right.

An obviously irritated Fionna caught up to him outside the bedroom. "Master, d'you see what one of those dogs has done? I found it beneath your bed, up against the wall." She held out a doll he'd bought for Olivia. The poor thing was a mess, its head almost severed from its body. Stuffing billowed from its mangled torso.

"This is the end," Fionna cried. "That doll was the bonniest thing. Why, a few months ago one of those worthless beasts tore up a pillow. I still find feathers when I dust. If ever I catch which one is doing it, I'll have its tail under the butcher knife, so help me."

"What could interest them about pillows and dolls?"

"I suspect it's Antiope. She'll chew on anything. Sometimes I do think she wasn't worth the good sterling you spent on her." She sighed her disgust. "Give it to me, and I'll throw it out."

"No," Curran said, though he wasn't sure why. "I wager Mrs. Ramsay's aunt could fix it." He entered the bedroom and laid the doll on Morrigan's dressing table.

Bored and restless, he flung himself onto the bed. Speckled light through the stained-glass window in the sitting room threw variegated colors over the doll's face. A shadow marred the cheek like a bloodstain. The glass eyes regarded him, unblinking. He found his gaze returning to it again and again. At last he jumped up and knocked the doll into the chair where he could no longer see it.

As it fell, something dropped out of its torn chest. He picked it up. It was a bit of metal, black filigree patterning one edge. The fragment seemed familiar. Bothersome, that he couldn't place it. He left it on the table and went into the sitting room where his book lay.

He read the same page of *The Talisman* three times, distracted by the thumps and bangs of a big, busy house. He stared at the freshly swept fireplace, and next to it, on the stones, his wife's untidy sewing basket. Typical of her impatience with the ladylike art, it was an explosion of tangled thread and crushed material.

Her talents lay in less tangible directions—in her ability to interact wholly, unashamedly, with their daughter. There was wariness in her love for him, but Olivia received all of her without reservation. Then there was the unconscious way she had of absorbing and reflecting the quiet throb of life, making him intensely aware of his own heartbeat. He'd always sensed an inner turmoil within her, which somehow deepened her beyond other women he'd known, and filled him with a desperate need to give her peace.

He relived the vivid images that had overpowered him while Morrigan gave birth. He saw himself running up an endless set of stairs to save the child. She was bleeding profusely, but she watched his face with an expression of such transfixed awe it left him confident he could work miracles.

Sighing wearily, Curran forced his attention back to the book.

He'd never considered himself particularly imaginative or visionary, though he had recurring dreams so vivid they seemed like real experiences.

Last night he'd dreamed of a child named Rosabel. He was the girl's father, or brother, or guardian. They were picking raspberries in an alpine setting, and she was eating more than she was putting in her basket. He had to warn her about making herself sick. Later, when he put her to bed, he knew she would ask for another story about her dead mother.

A black filigree pattern....

Oh, aye. The sewing basket. Morrigan had a pair of scissors with a black filigree pattern, and a little wood figure dangling from the handle on an emerald green ribbon. Curran dropped his book and picked up the basket, digging through the fabric, pins, and thread. Shock jolted through him at what he saw buried at the bottom. The scissors were bent, broken. One point was missing. Fetching the piece from the bedroom, he fit it against the jagged edge and sat on his heels.

I lose control, she'd told him after Michaelmas. *My temper consumes me.*

Certainty gripped him. The dogs hadn't destroyed the doll.

Morrigan had.

Chapter 24

Morrigan didn't know what caused such gratifying exhilaration—warmth and sunlight, the scent of spring, or Patrick Hawley's subjugation. She didn't care. Stoirmeil caught her mood and danced from one narrow rut to the other, arching her neck and flinging her black mane from side to side like a flirtatious debutante enjoying the attention of ten different swains.

The sun climbed almost to the center of the sky. She would ride home, carry Olivia into the garden, and nurse her beneath the oak.

As Stoirmeil clambered onto Glenelg's main track, Morrigan saw Kilgarry's gig pulled off to the side next to the kirk's dry stone fence. Agnes stood next to it, conversing with a seated Diorbhail. Morrigan kicked her mare to a gallop, her heart thudding. "Diorbhail?" she said, bringing Stoirmeil to a snorting halt.

"No need to fret." Diorbhail lifted a blanket-clad bundle out of a basket beside her. "Your daughter's hungry. I thought fresh air and a ride would distract her, and also we might find you."

Morrigan took the child. Olivia, who lately had discovered the sound of her own voice, was chattering and waving her hands. At the sight of her mam she gurgled and grinned, but soon her mouth curled into a sulky frown and the gurgle switched to vexed hiccups.

"Master Curran was looking for you as well," Diorbhail said. "Why not tie your mare to the gig and we'll go home together?"

"Aye, that's what I was thinking," Morrigan said, but as she glanced towards the kirk, a movement distracted her. She squinted.

Someone was walking along the track. She was sure by the height and lean-ness that it was Mackinnon, his hands shoved into his jacket pockets and his face turned down as though refusing to give the bonny day any credence.

"But I confess I'd like to stay out awhile longer," she said impulsively, giving silent thanks to Aunt Ibby for the specially made nursing corset she'd purchased for her niece. "It's such a braw day. Here." She returned Olivia to Diorbhail, dismounted, and tied Stoirmeil's reins to the rear of the gig, keeping her face averted from her perceptive friend, who had made her distrust of Mackinnon clear, and who would not hesitate to voice many protests if she discerned what Morrigan was contemplating. "I've been locked up so long." She was careful not to glance Mackinnon's way again as she came around, holding out her arms for the babe. "I think I'd like to take her for a walk. Will you tell Curran? I promise to be back for tea."

Diorbhail snapped the reins. Somehow, fortune had conspired and she hadn't noticed Mackinnon, or if she had, failed to recognize him. The glare off the water was almost unbearably bright, casting the figure into silhouette. "I understand," she said. "I'd feel the same if I were you. But mind, the wean's hungry."

"I'll feed her beneath the yews by the kirk."

Diorbhail nodded and looked pleased. She turned the gig and headed towards Kilgarry, Stoirmeil trotting along behind.

"A bonny day indeed," Agnes said. "But don't spend too much time in the sun, or you'll be burned red as a savage, and you'd best keep the wee one covered."

Morrigan agreed, and headed towards the water, trying to appear casual, but Agnes reached out and stopped her long enough to say, low, "Don't look in his eyes."

"I don't know what you mean," Morrigan said, laughing. "The sun's eyes?"

She picked up speed the farther she got from Agnes, and soon was trailing close behind her objective, who walked on, oblivious it would seem. "Mackinnon," she said.

At the sound of his name, he lifted his face and turned. Had he truly not heard her approach? His surprise said he hadn't.

"It's a braw day," she said.

He smiled so warmly it sparked a fire inside her. "Aye."

"Where are you going?" she asked.

"Home. Where are you going?"

"Hold Olivia, would you?" she asked by way of an answer.

He took the baby rather gingerly. Morrigan removed her cap and, one by one, pulled the pins out of her hair and threw them into the grass. Her braid fell free of its staid round knot.

Aodhàn's brows lifted.

"Olivia and I are having a walk." She took off her jacket, hooking it over one shoulder before retrieving her child. "I'd rather die than stay inside." She laughed. "Look at the sea, Mackinnon. Look how it glitters!"

His gaze followed her pointing finger, but the more familiar somber expression replaced that instant of pleasure.

No matter. It was too late for him to pretend it hadn't been there. He was pleased to see her.

"I saw what was left of my father's home today," she said.

"Still delving into your past, then?"

"A man found me there. He's an Englishman Curran invited to stay at Kilgarry while he searches for Highland property."

He waited.

"I don't believe he has any sense of gratitude for my husband's hospitality."

"Why?"

"He thought to frighten me."

"Frighten you?" He stopped walking and faced her. When she didn't speak, he gripped her upper arm. "Would you care to elaborate?"

Her heart tore into an impromptu race, born not of fear, but fascination. There was the tingling that his touch seemed to cause. Curran's had, too, once, but not in a long while. She blushed, feeling alive in a way she'd almost forgotten. Months of abstinence and a difficult labor had blurred the reckless intimacy birthed on the moor above Stranraer.

What if Mackinnon put his arms around her? Light would catch in his eyes, and he would draw her in, claiming their love would outlive the pyramids.

She smiled up at him. Light flared in his eyes exactly as she had imagined. Slow upon slow, grave curving into merry, he returned her smile.

Robert Burns had no category for a man like this.

She untangled her tongue. What had they been talking about? Patrick Hawley. "N-now I must decide whether to tell Curran, or pretend nothing happened, for the sake of peace and harmony."

"What did this man do?"

"Well…he seemed to think…he tried to take…liberties." Her face grew hot as she struggled with how to say such a thing. "He meant to force himself on me."

As she spoke, she remembered some of the incomprehensible and sickening things the bastard had said. *I've missed you. I've missed your flesh. Will you beg for mercy?*

Mackinnon's smile faded. Grave returned full force, along with a tightening of his grip. "Did he harm you?"

"No. I cut him."

He frowned, obviously puzzled.

"I had a knife. Diorbhail gave it to me." Tucking Olivia into the crook of her arm, she reached into her pocket and pulled out the weapon.

His reaction was strange. For a moment, he appeared nearly as shocked as Patrick Hawley had. He blinked as she held it up. She saw his jaw clench repeatedly.

"I was lucky, wasn't I?" she said, suddenly unsure. "To have it, I mean?"

Mackinnon took the blade from her. "Diorbhail gave you this? Where did she get it?"

"She had a dream of it, and then she found it, somewhere along the river."

"You say you wounded him?"

She nodded. "He lost all interest in me after that. He couldn't get away fast enough. It's beautiful, isn't it? Have you ever seen anything like it? The blade —it looks like glass."

"Obsidian," he said.

She regarded him with interest. "Aye? What is that?"

"It's created by the heat of volcanoes." He looked up from the blade. "You must tell Curran. Today."

She nodded.

"Give me your promise."

"Aye, Mackinnon. I'll tell him today. Are…are you vexed?"

"You could have been hurt. Are you certain he didn't—"

"I'm quite certain. He's the one hurt. He was bleeding all over himself."

"D'you want me to keep this? It's sharp. It should have some kind of sheath."

"No, I don't want to be without it. Put it in my pocket, would you? It'll be fine."

He seemed reluctant, but then shrugged and returned the knife to her pocket. They walked again, the quiet bulk of the kirk on their right. Morrigan fancied eyes were watching, hidden behind threadbare curtains, and kept her distance.

His lips twitched as though he knew her thoughts and found them amusing. "How is your wean these days?" he asked.

"Spoiled half to death. Smiling. And she's gained ever so much weight."

"Good." But he didn't look particularly happy. What was that shadow in his eyes? Loneliness? Yearning? Morrigan wished she could take a spade and excavate his brain.

"Would you like to have children?" she asked.

"I doubt it," he said, after a too-long pause. "What sort of father would I make?"

"I don't know. Maybe a fine one."

"Maybe," he said, glancing into the sky. "But I'm fair particular about the mother."

His brief grin suggested a game. "Well?" she asked. "What d'you require? Wealth? A title?"

"Red hair." He glanced at hers. "Hair so dark red it fools everyone into thinking it a prim and proper brown, except in the sun, when its true wickedness shines forth." He added lightly, "Though in the Highlands there's nothing that carries more bad luck than a lass with red hair, and they do say dark red's the worst."

"So Nicky used to tell me, all the time." For an instant, it had been Nicky's mocking voice she'd heard.

"Nicky?" he asked. "Oh, aye, your brother."

"What else?" she asked.

"Eyes as rich and dark as a Highland tarn, eyes so deep I could fall in and drown."

She reprimanded herself for the idea that he was making love to her in front of every person who spied on them, in a way that circumvented any hint of scandal. "Aye?" she said, hoping for more.

His gaze turned to the Sound, which dazzled beneath the sun like a vast, trembling field of diamonds. "But that woman eludes me," he said.

Morrigan felt a brief stab of fear, mixed with compassion.

Then, in defiance, his next words tumbled from him, tantalizing and seductive. "What do I require? A woman who speaks to eagles."

Silence lengthened. She remembered the day in the secret glen, thinking she was quite alone. Yet she also recalled feeling as though she was being watched. Had he been there? Had he seen her?

"I'll settle for nothing less," he said. "So you see, I want too much. There is no female for me in poor Glenelg or anywhere, for that matter."

"Are you certain you've looked hard enough? Maybe she's right under your nose."

His eyes transformed from frosty glacier to iridescent warmth.

A shout roused them and she freed her gaze from his with difficulty, wondering how long it had been since they'd stopped walking. Agnes would be apoplectic if she saw the way they'd been staring at each other.

It was Seaghan, waving as he released the tiller of Curran's Loch Fyne pleasure skiff, the *Endeavor*. He lashed the boat to a buoy and leaped off into the dinghy that floated behind.

Morrigan propped Olivia on her shoulder and patted her as she and Aodhàn walked onto the creaking pier. Aodhàn steadied the dinghy as it approached, caught the line, and tied it off.

"Mistress Ramsay." The giant climbed out of the boat, causing it to bob frantically. "Has Aodhàn abducted you? And see here, 'tis wee Olivia! At last!" He clasped Morrigan's hand and squeezed.

Morrigan, sucking in a breath at the overwhelming strength in his grip, said, "I must away home, though. The wean is hungry, and her hippins need changing." Olivia concurred with a whimper.

"Oh, no." His grin vanished. "You needn't go clear to Kilgarry. Let us take you out on Curran's boat."

"She'll screech any minute," Morrigan warned, "and she won't stop till she's fed and changed."

"You have the means to feed her," Seaghan said, shrugging.

Morrigan blushed and looked away.

"D'you think a mother feeding her child is something to be ashamed of?" Seaghan shook his head, solemn as a preacher. "This daft world tries to drain the glory out of everything, but we're no' in England, lass. Here in the Highlands, the mean-minded white-collars will never succeed."

She hadn't expected such forthrightness. Mackinnon stood by, his face revealing nothing.

"Come, we'll away to sea," Seaghan ordered. "You've never had the chance to explore, and it's an uncommon afternoon."

"Well...."

"If your husband loses his temper, he'll have to face me, and I'll tell you, lass, he knows better." He added, canny-like, "I've got fresh-baked bannocks, cheese, and a bottle of fine Bowmore. It slips down the throat like sunlight."

She laughed. "I suppose I'll go home at your pleasure then, Seaghan. But what about the hippins?"

He snorted. "You think fishermen have no cloth or the means to clean a baby?"

She could only laugh again, and beg forgiveness for her ignorance.

Morrigan and Olivia were transported to the *Endeavor* with as much care as if they were royalty. Once she and the baby were comfortably settled, the men unfurled the sails and the boat swept towards open water.

Away to the right was Seaghan's fishing boat, its long, low hull painted green and white, its mast, yard, and sail stowed. *Hannah* was outlined in neat black letters at the prow.

Aodhàn busied himself adjusting the sails, furling lines, and stowing several creels and the toolbox. Seaghan sat at the tiller, holding the baby in the bend of his free arm. He was expert at distracting her with his deep voice and vigorous bouncing, and soon had her making happy giggling sounds.

Morrigan watched them, laughing whenever her baby did. Seagulls veered past, shrieking. Whitecaps crested, subsided, and rose again elsewhere.

The wind died as they neared Skye. Seaghan relinquished Olivia and lit his pipe. "The *Endeavor*'s like a well-bred mare," he said, stretching out his legs. "Curran designed her himself, and had her constructed at his yard in Glasgow. He and his shipwright sailed her here when she was finished. The man told us how Curran directed every detail, sometimes doing the work himself." He ran his fingers along the shiny brass rail. "He lends her out generously. It's one of the benefits of being friends with the laird."

While he chatted, Morrigan took off her gloves. She draped the blanket over her shoulder, and, under its cover, unbuttoned her bodice and the first three hooks of the corset. The chemise was easily pushed aside and Olivia's fretful whimpering faded. Oh aye, she was breaking a hundred different rules of etiquette, but these weren't ordinary men, were they? And hadn't she and Mackinnon gone past such tiresome restrictions anyway, the night of Saint Brigit's Eve? Stealing a glance at Seaghan's face, she was reassured to see that he didn't appear to be in the least offended, or even interested.

Olivia kicked so forcefully she knocked the blanket clear off Morrigan's shoulder. "I know little of boats," Morrigan said, blushing as she retrieved it. "The one we passed in the bay. Is it yours?"

Seaghan kept his face tactfully averted. "Aye, the *Hannah* is mine and Aodhàn's. We catch a fair amount of mackerel, a few saithe, and some red fish. Sometimes in the spring we drift for herring. Our labors don't make us wealthy, but we don't starve, and the township always has a fresh catch. The *Hannah* was Curran's idea as well. He had her built on the isle of Lewis; she's a *Sgoth Niseach*, designed especially for these western seas. I pay him, as I can, but he says he considers it an investment for the prosperity of the village."

"Curran's rescued us all," she said, and wondered what he was doing with his afternoon. She remembered her promise at breakfast, and his reaction. He'd blushed and spilled his tea like an embarrassed schoolboy.

She wanted to see him suddenly, and regretted not going home.

They watched Aodhàn edge onto the bowsprit, his bare feet sure and steady. He did something with a line then lay on his stomach, perfectly balanced, dangling his arms and catching water on his palms, at ease and at one with the docile movement of the boat. A pod of dolphins swept around the prow, leaping and calling, and Morrigan decided, as she cleaned Olivia and tucked her into a new cloth, that they and the man were communing.

"Did you two argue?" Seaghan seemed fair intent on his pouch of tobacco.

"Mackinnon and I? No," she said, surprised.

"You appeared dead serious when I saw you there on shore."

She laughed. "We were picking his perfect wife."

Giving her a startled glance, Seaghan said, "Wife," as though he couldn't believe it.

"I fear my Aunt Ibby might have instilled an inclination towards matchmaking in me, much as I hate to admit it."

"And did he show any interest in being married off?"

"No," she said. "He claims he's too particular." She added no more from that strange conversation.

Seaghan paused quite a long time, frowning as he refilled his pipe. "Aodhàn's a queer man." He paused again, scratching his beard. "I'll no' beat around the bush like a damned *Sasannach*," he said gruffly, and gestured at a low cloudbank. "Not to put too fine a point on it, Aodhàn is like rain, lass. What happens if you try to hold water in your fist?"

"It escapes between your fingers, I suppose."

"Leaving naught but a memory of dew."

She gazed at him.

"Then there's Curran. He's the rock that makes up the Hebrides. Gneiss, it's called. One of the hardest rocks the earth has ever conceived."

Morrigan heard Diorbhail's voice. *Who is the mountain? Who is the seal?*

"Your husband is a patient man." Seaghan's gaze was penetrating. "But it wouldn't be right to test him."

"You're saying Mackinnon is inconstant?" The breeze seemed abruptly chilly.

Seaghan frowned. "Perhaps that word better fits you, Lady Eilginn."

She knew the flush climbing through her cheeks was damning.

Heaving a sigh, he said, "Here's what I think. You're a lass who's been yanked out of everything she's ever known and thrust into a strange place, with demands she's never been prepared for. And you have a romantic bent, *àilleag nan nighean*—no, don't scowl at me. There's naught to be ashamed of. Romance is part and parcel of every Highland-bred heart. What I'm saying is that I do no' believe you're as worldly as you try to appear. I'd not tell you Aodhàn's business if I thought otherwise. He's a man with a devil on his back." He nodded. "Aye, it's the truth. He and I have lived together as comrades and partners since that moment I hauled him onto the deck of the *Bristol*. That's nigh on twenty years. Don't you think if anyone knew him, it'd be me? But I don't. He's stubborn, moody, and hard; whatever damaged him out there in the sea has never released him. I don't think it ever will. I know the day is coming where he'll walk away and none of us will see him again. He'll disappear into the sea like he appeared out of it all those years ago."

Running his hand over a nearby lanyard, he added, "Truth is, I don't want you hurt."

Morrigan lifted a corner of the blanket. Her daughter had fallen asleep.

First Diorbhail, then Eleanor, now Seaghan. Agnes too. And since Michaelmas, Curran had hardly spoken Mackinnon's name.

Yet this deluge of warnings sparked more of an offended loyalty than distrust. She glanced at Mackinnon, alone on the bowsprit but for the dolphins. An angry inner voice shouted. *My Mackinnon.* Her jaw clenched. She didn't realize she'd thought this for a moment, and when she did, she turned her face down, tightening her hold on Olivia. *My Curran,* she told herself. Running the tip of her index finger over the wean's cheek, she repeated it. *My Curran.*

"There's something about the two of you," Seaghan was saying. "These many years he's never bothered with women, though a few have tried to win him. And you, a bride. A new mother. I've seen how your husband looks at you. You're the love of his life. You've been blessed, Morrigan, in a way few can claim, yet still you look at Aodhàn like a fallow field calling for sun and seed…and rain."

Morrigan kept her face down, wanting to hide the confusing emotions she knew she wouldn't properly disguise.

"You are married, you know," he said. "Though you seem in danger of forgetting it."

"No. Never. That is *not* true."

"Well, then, perhaps I'm wrong, and have said things I shouldn't've. If so, I ask your forgiveness."

Morrigan thought of Nicky, how he'd teased her for reading the tales of Greece, and mockingly called her Helen of Troy. That poor married woman had surrendered to infidelity. How many deaths had it caused?

"You loved my mother, didn't you?" She peeked at him through her lashes.

It was his turn to flush. After a long hesitation, he growled, "I did."

Determined to push through shyness and fear, she said, "And you've gone on loving her these many years."

"I have." He rubbed his forehead and sighed.

For longer than she'd been alive, he'd loved Hannah and remained faithful to her memory, though Hannah had wed another, and borne another man's child. "Mackinnon isn't the only one who should put his past to rest."

Seaghan squinted over the sparkling water. He gave a helpless shrug and nodded.

Sunlight gifted them with languorous warmth. Water lapped against the shore. Olivia released a milky sigh and rubbed a fist over her cheek. The boat's drowsy rocking soothed Morrigan into a near doze. She lay down with Olivia on the stern thwart next to Seaghan, her legs tucked against her stomach, her head cushioned on a neatly folded plaid. From the corner of her eye she saw Aodhàn's white sark billowing in intermittent breezes. "I mind when I was small," she said. "I'd lie on the grass beside Loch Ryan. I saw many things in the clouds. Great gods, rearing unicorns, dragons blowing fire."

"Tell me about your life."

"And bore you senseless."

"I'd not be bored. I want to know."

So she described the Wren's Egg, how folk stopped on their way to Ireland, or to the Highlands to shoot the deer. She told him about Nicky's poetry, and her private game, taken from Robert Burns, of categorizing men grave or merry. She related the forbidden early morning rides, and how Aunt Ibby had hired a woman, over Douglas's protests, to teach her to play the piano. "She tricked him into agreeing by telling him it would bring more guests." She sighed. "I'll always be grateful for what she did. There's little I love more than playing. Chopin, especially."

"D'you know," Seaghan said, "if you'd grown up here, you wouldn't've learned that. We're a poor, hard-working lot. You probably wouldn't've had much if any schooling. I didn't think I'd ever say such a thing, but something right came out of the clearings."

"The dominie told me my brain was quick, and it was a pity that because I wasn't a man, I couldn't go to university. But Aunt Beatrice called education a fool's waste on women. She said what was the use, when women's lives are spent cooking, cleaning, and bearing children?"

Seaghan scowled. She noticed, but decided she had pressed enough for one day.

"Did you have any swains before Curran?" he asked.

"I did fancy one of my brother's friends, but he didn't want to marry."

"Young and foolish, was he?"

"He wanted to travel and paint. He was an artist. But he got a lass in trouble and ended up having to wed after all."

His eyes narrowed. "That's who painted you."

"Oh, aye," she said, blushing again. "I forgot you saw it."

"So he was your first love?"

She shrugged. "Papa didn't approve. He never would've given his blessing, even if Kit had been willing, which he wasn't."

"I cannot say I'm disappointed." Seaghan took a long drag off his pipe. The tobacco crackled in the bowl, and the aromatic smoke he released hung in the still air. "About all that...."

"I saw the flowers on my mother's grave, Seaghan."

"Oh, well, that's nothing."

"Nothing?" she said. "Hannah died giving me life. Papa never forgave me for that. It wasn't until after he died that I realized he wasn't evil. He was hurt, and doing the best he could. Of course, my understanding came too late. Do you hate me too, for what I did? I took her away from you as well as Papa."

"Hate?" He rested his hand briefly on her boot. "Hannah lives again in you."

Morrigan couldn't quite suppress the tremor in her laugh. "I'm sorry. There's been too much death, and near death this last year. I'm not accustomed yet to Papa and Nicky being gone, to almost losing Olivia, to the pure chanciness of life. It's made me gloomy."

"I've been unfair, and judgmental as a damned missionary. You're no' inconstant, and I apologize for saying it. But I'm certain Douglas did not hate you over Hannah. You can't know what lay between your da and mam before you were born. My feeling is his anger was directed elsewhere, and you got in the way."

She shrugged. "He had to've suffered, to be so furious all the time. Part of me comprehends that too well. Forgive me, I didn't mean to scunner you. Were you going to tell me something?"

He hesitated. "No," he said. "No. And you've no' scunnered me."

A rolling wave caused the boat to sway. The hull grated against a submerged rock. Seaghan turned his gaze to the bowsprit. "We're drifting in."

"Aye," Aodhàn said.

Neither raised their voices. Morrigan realized Mackinnon must've overheard every word she and Seaghan had exchanged.

She sat up and looked about. They weren't far from the rocky coastline. To her left was an islet holding a lighthouse, to her right a larger hunk of land, bleak and barren.

"Eilean Sionnach." Seaghan used his pipe to point at the isle with the lighthouse. "And that one is Ornsay."

"Would you care to walk about?" Aodhàn asked her. "Have a look at the seals?"

"Aye," she said.

Aodhàn dropped the anchor. Seaghan pulled the dinghy close and helped Morrigan clamber in, handing Olivia down to her when she had her balance.

They landed on a smooth patch of earth on the shore of Ornsay, where they had a fine view of the looming, silent lighthouse. She wondered if Louis's family had built it.

Olivia continued to sleep, not even waking when her mother called out that she'd found a cache of perfect scallop shells.

Seaghan spread out the plaid then presented his basket of bread, cheese, and whisky. There was so much Morrigan wondered if he'd foreseen her coming along. They ate and drank with the sort of appetite Seaghan claimed always accompanied being on the water.

As Aodhàn promised, a harem of sleek grey seals were sunning on the rocks by the lighthouse. More bobbed in the water, and a few swam closer, traversing the expanse between Eilean Sionnach and their picnic spot. They seemed unafraid, and with good reason, as she'd been told time and again that no one on Skye ever killed seals.

The three of them sat near the water's edge to watch the creatures. The largest bull of all raised his mighty head and scrutinized them.

"He's sizing us up," she said.

"Aye." With the barest quirk of a brow and hint of a smile, Mackinnon said, "Sing. He'll come nearer, and his wives will follow."

She searched his face for the jest.

"A woman's singing enchants them," he said. "Didn't you know? They can't resist it."

Seaghan's regard was mockingly stern. "Have you forgotten the legend already?"

"You mean from my wedding day?" She was half-sure they were playing tricks, trying to make her look foolish. "About seals being human? Curran made that up." She glanced at Aodhàn, but thought perhaps she shouldn't mention the part about him being Glenelg's resident selkie.

Aodhàn cleared his throat, cracked his knuckles, and in the space of a breath transformed into a *seanchaidh*, the classic storyteller, his voice rich and resonant, every word and inflection carefully chosen to evoke the image of an ancient bard entertaining his king and court.

"In Scotland," he said, "in the time of King Arthur, before there were castles or clans, many tribes warred and competed for power. Kings and chiefs built forts with high palisades, nestled on hills and rocky cliffs, where they could be easily defended.

"One chief had holdings near land's edge at Cape Wrath. With him in his fortress lived his wife, two doughty sons, and one daughter of marriageable age. The lass was a beauty, with hair that fell like sheets of copper, a mouth red as autumn-ivy, and skin as pure as moonlight."

He paused and his gaze rested on Morrigan. He blinked then looked away to the restless water.

"Her name was Eamhair," he said. "Men throughout the land heard of her, and of her father's wealth. Highland men are impetuous, then even more than now. They traveled the length and breadth of the country, meeting whatever adventures came their way, in hopes of gaining her favor. What they didn't know was that the chief's daughter had already given away her heart. No one knew. Even if the chief had proved willing to indulge her, Eamhair's choice never came forward to claim her.

"She knew this man well and loved him, but he was born of the night, and the long secret hours lasses spend alone in their beds."

Eamhair. A girl immersed in fantasy like Morrigan, pining over a Greek barbarian with shaggy blond hair and a sword that rarely left his side.

But she must listen to her bard, or she would miss something she was beginning to respond to, and to feel was of great importance.

"Whenever a horse brought a man to the gates, she came running, hopeful that this time, it would be her lover. But it never was. She grew despondent, and spent more and more time alone on the cliffs, singing to the gannets, the sunset, and the wind.

"Her father wanted the matter resolved. His wife nagged him to find a kind man, who would treat their daughter well, but he was far more interested in how her beauty could benefit him. Judging from the number of rival suitors loitering about the fort, drinking his ale and consuming his meat, he figured he could make a tidy profit selling her to the highest bidder. Whether the winning man was kind mattered not to Eamhair's father.

"Though he preferred hunting and reaving cattle to the tedious business of women, he spent an evening or two studying the latest set of suitors. Which would bring prestige? Who would give loyalty, silver, and warriors if needed? Several seemed likely, but he hesitated, hoping for more.

"One day, while Eamhair was walking, she was disturbed and frightened by a great horde of men on horseback. One of them was more richly dressed than the others. His mount's bits and saddle were highly polished. His face held an arrogance that put her on guard.

"Several of the men made ribald comments as they crowded around her. But the leader lifted one hand and they all fell silent. He dismounted and approached her. He kissed her hand and asked her name.

"Though he was all charm, Eamhair saw the men exchange glances. Their expressions warned her he was not as he seemed.

"He escorted her to the fort and introduced himself to her father. The two men closeted themselves in order to speak privately.

"That night Eamhair's father notified her that she was to be married. No one knew what the stranger offered or threatened, but Eamhair's father did not seem pleased.

"The lass wept into her pillow. Her father had auctioned her off without a thought or care to what her life would be. She pictured the triumphant suitor, who she could hear shouting and reveling in the great hall. No doubt the morrow would find him gruff and bleary-eyed from too much drink. His eyes offered not the slightest breath of poetry. She feared a man who would set out to purchase her would prove to be hard-hearted and cold. Would he see the majesty of the heavens when a storm blew in, or taste snowflakes on his tongue? Who would laugh with her by the waterfalls? To whom would she sing in his faraway land? Who would walk along the cliffs with her in the gloaming and call to the seals?

"She heard a voice speak from the darkest corner of her chamber. *Why do you weep?* She sat up, never to know how she looked in that moment, her hair tangled about her shoulders, her nightdress reflecting the glow of moonlight shining through the casement."

Mackinnon stopped. His frowning gaze traveled over her, but it was distant, preoccupied. Morrigan wasn't sure he saw her at all. Abruptly he pressed his hands against his eyes and scraped over his temples. He arched his face towards the blue sky as though trying to release a nagging ache. When he again took up his tale, his voice was hoarse.

"*My father has promised me to the Pictish king of Innse Orc, she said. Will you not come to him tomorrow and claim me?*

"He twined her hair in his hands. *I have nothing to recommend me but love.*

"*I am yours and you are mine. Would you see me wed to another?*

"He silenced her with kisses, and promised to love her forever, *for as long as the pyramids stand in Egypt.*"

Morrigan's attention faltered. She'd heard that phrase when daydreaming about Ariadne, the queen from her Greek book of myths, or Aridela, as she preferred to call her. She'd believed it her own private invention, yet here was Mackinnon, repeating it. She stared at him, wondering if he had found a way to *see* her fantasies. He returned her stare intently, missing nothing.

"The next day," he said, "Eamhair was told that the king had gone at sunrise, giving the excuse of pressing matters on his home isle. He left behind a man he trusted to carry out a proxy wedding and escort her north.

"Certain her lover would come and save her, she waited impatiently, fearful yet eager for his rescue. Her father wrapped silk around her wrist and the wrist of the proxy. He made the announcement, sent for musicians, and ordered a feast.

"When would he come? The longer he waited the worse would be the uproar, the anger and protests. Daylight faded into gloaming.

"Eamhair left the celebration. She found land's edge, where mist washed the precipices and salt surf eroded the cliffs.

"She sang as the sun dipped into the ocean, leaving vast purple streaks across the sky. Beneath her feet, the earth trembled against the onslaught of the sea.

"She could submit to her father's choice and live in the far north, where summer sparkled briefly between long months of bitter cold and sunless skies. Refuse, and he would doubtless force her, at the point of a sword if necessary. Or she could die. Everyone would believe it an accident, and there would be no shame on his house.

"Keeping her gaze centered on the clouds, speaking a prayer for her soul and family, she jumped."

Morrigan's hands flexed, relaxed, and flexed again. *Falling. Water cold as knife-blades.*

"The sea surged around her, yet almost immediately, something pushed her to the surface, to a glint of watered rubies and starlight. She saw the face she loved. The face she never saw in the day. The one who existed, yet, perhaps, did not.

"He carried her from the sea and placed her on the sand. *The songs you sang brought me to you,* he said. *I thought no harm would come of it, and I could not keep away. But I was wrong. Now we love each other and you have chosen death.*

"For Eamhair, his voice merged into the towering rocks and blackening sky. She heard the music, not the words.

"*You and I can never marry,* her lover said. *We can never live as other people do.*

"Eamhair brushed his warning away like grains of sand from her skin. *This path is marked by my unknowable destiny*, she said. *I cannot escape it.*

"Her lover was also a king. He ruled over the vast, spraying ocean. Though he'd proven himself wise, strong, a ferocious warrior when necessary, he hadn't the strength or ferocity to leave her, nor could she leave him. She pledged herself to him there, near the ocean at the tip of Scotland.

"When she returned to the fort, she stood before her father's council and refused his decree. For days after, he and her brothers threatened her, shut her away without food, and made excuses to the northland man. But he saw she would never submit. The ill-concealed giggles of serving maids and the mockery of the other suitors rankled. He gave his host an ultimatum. Either the beauteous Eamhair would apologize by the following morning and accept that she was now married to his master, or he would return home and inform his king that the offer had been rebuffed. *He is proud*, the man warned. *He will likely declare war with you over this, and he will lay waste to everything you possess.*

"The chief whipped his daughter. He threatened starvation, and, with fair imagination, described the lives of slave women in far-away godless lands, hinting that she might meet a similar fate.

"But Eamhair would not be moved. *I have given away what you think is most valuable about me. I will love no other, and I will die before another touches me.*

"The northern king's surrogate left. So did the other would-be suitors. They were no longer interested in Eamhair, calling her *used goods*, and *spoiled*.

"Eamhair's father raged over his willful daughter's defiance. She had made him a buffoon. Now he must go to bed at night terrified the northern king would appear at the head of an avenging army. His life was turned upside down, because of a *woman*. His wife pleaded for mercy, and received his fist in her face.

"Eamhair's lover, in his magical way, passed through the thick oak doors and high walls of her tower prison. He waited in shadows, waking her with his thoughts, his need.

"Before long, a child quickened within her."

Ah, Morrigan thought. The imprudent girl could no longer make choices for herself alone. She would have to consider the helpless, dependent one growing inside her. Eamhair might be willing to die rather than be sold to the northern king, but now, if she died, so would this child.

If her father but knew it, he possessed the most powerful weapon that could be conceived to force his daughter's obedience.

"It was an offense to Eamhair's father that she continued to breathe," Mackinnon said. "Since beating and whipping had no effect, the chief gave the order for his sons to kill her. They dragged Eamhair down the stairs and out of the fort. They forced her to the precipices and threw her over, laughing as she plummeted, and went home to receive their father's praise.

"Eamhair lay on the rocks, bleeding. After some time she heard a seal bark, and managed to turn her head and look towards the sea. There was a currach on the beach, and beside it eight seals. Her arms were not broken, though both legs were. She was able, slowly and with great pain, to pull herself to the boat and lift herself inside. The seals pushed her out onto the water.

"Currents swept Eamhair far from land. Storm clouds built and the wind rose, but the seals guided the boat to an uninhabited island.

"One of them swam closer. As he drew near he transformed in the ancient way. He became a man, her lover. The king of the seal clans.

"He placed his hand on Eamhair's stomach and felt the movement of his child. She saw his joy, and though she was suffering, she felt joy as well.

"*You will be free and happy*, the seal-king promised. *Our child will inherit my kingdom.*

"In the secret way no human knows, the seal changed Eamhair, and in the changing, healed her wounds and broken bones. Together the lovers swam away, and were never seen upon the land again."

"I've not heard that particular tale before, Aodhàn." Seaghan drank a swig of whisky and passed him the cup. Aodhàn only shrugged.

Seaghan turned to Morrigan. "Do you understand now why it's such bad luck to kill a seal? One can never know which might be beast, and which might be human, and we Scots do love a good romance."

Morrigan stared at the dark-eyed, long-whiskered creature in the water. She imagined him stepping out of the ocean, water running off his pale skin, regarding her from eyes like sunlight through waves. He seized her in his wet, cold arms and pulled her down to his sea kingdom.

Mackinnon's tale spun a web that left the actual world little more than a dry, colorless shell.

The seals swam away. Seaghan poured the final dregs of whisky and gave Morrigan the last bannock. Morrigan fondly contemplated her companions. Seaghan was an enormous man with hands capable of inflicting fatal damage, yet he also owned a most gentle voice and kind eyes. He reminded her of a sweet-tempered Clyde. Mysterious Aodhàn told a story so well she wished she could slip into his fantasy. He seemed a dark member of the *daoine sìth*. Didn't legend say they were taller than human men, with skin like ivory? And hadn't she clearly seen the faery luminescence emanating from him more than once?

"You're a grand *seanchaidh*, Mackinnon," she said unevenly. "Your tale was so real, I saw you living it, and me as well."

Mackinnon's regard remained unsmiling, yet there was something in his eyes—Agnes would scraich that he was casting his glamour. Oh aye, Morrigan felt it worming through her flesh, seeking her soul. At this moment Curran seemed far away, not of her world or Mackinnon's.

Seaghan laughed, breaking through the spell. "It's *shen-a-chee*. You must learn how to speak properly if you want to live in these mountains."

He leaned back on his elbows, stretching out his legs, and sang:

I am a man upon the land.
I am a selkie in the sea,
And when I'm far from any strand,
My home is in Sule Skerry.

Chapter 25

T HE REVERBERATING BOOM OF THE FOG-BELL AT THE LIGHTHOUSE WOKE M ORRIGAN from a serene, dreamless nap. For one careening moment, she had no memory of where she was, and no amount of blinking could clear her vision. Mist concealed everything except the blanket on which she and Olivia lay.

Someone had covered them with the free side of the plaid, cocooning them in warmth. Giving Olivia a reassuring kiss on the forehead, she stood, putting her daughter against her shoulder and draping the plaid over them both.

She heard nothing but water lapping against the shore, and the muffled cry of a seabird. "Mackinnon?" she ventured. "Seaghan?"

Trepidation began to make its uneasy way through her backbone before she heard Seaghan's voice, singing the seal-song, and felt her way towards it.

Aodhàn appeared, phantom-like, the mist feathering around him. "I don't know how we'll get home in this," he said, his voice clipped.

Seaghan's big comforting form materialized. He sent her a surreptitious warning glance from beneath his bushy brows.

She frowned. Aodhàn growled and vanished into the mist as though he'd stepped through a portal and closed the door. The fog swirled and danced, filling in the space where he'd stood.

Seaghan led her to the dinghy. A dead seal lay next to it, half-beached, its skull splintered and crushed, sodden torso undulating with the movement of the water.

"Aye lass." He steadied her with one great hand. "It's this has blackened his mood. He admires the beasts more than most."

"What happened?" She settled into the boat. "It wasn't here before."

"Possibly an orca." He gave the dinghy a mighty shove and joined her. "The tide probably carried it in."

Aodhàn waded into the water and climbed into the boat. The fog-bell repeated, rumbling through Morrigan's chest.

When they were on board the *Endeavor*, Aodhàn lit the lamps, port and starboard, and all three sails were unfurled in hopes of catching any wind. Seaghan worked the tiller to no avail, so they broke out the oars and rowed into open water.

Seaghan tucked the plaid more securely around Morrigan's shoulders.

"You're worried for Curran, aren't you?" she asked, struck by his expression of guilt.

"Aye."

Since she'd come home from the mountain bothy, Curran had been intensely protective. If only she could send him her thoughts. *I'm with braw men who'd give their lives to see me home safely.* "So am I," she said.

He laughed. "You're to blame for this, you and your red hair. The old superstition is proven. Oh lass, I was only teasing."

"But it's true," said Aodhàn, who sat in the prow, smoking.

"Hist." Seaghan patted Morrigan's hand.

"I-I'm sorry," she said. "I should've gone home."

"It's not your fault," Aodhàn said. "Seaghan's the one who insisted on bringing you out today. It's his."

"The wind will come." Seaghan went up front to smoke with Aodhàn, and give Morrigan privacy to nurse.

They waited, listening to the wash of water. The thick sea haar swirled; the red and green fog-lights winked slyly. Olivia whined, warning her mother not to hold her so tightly.

Wind did stir with the onset of darkness. Seaghan rose, saying unnecessarily, "Here's our breeze. Look, it's clearing."

She'd already felt it, a swell underneath that caused the boat to roll. The mainsail gave a ponderous flap.

Morrigan stared out at torn wisps of fog and an intermittent star or two as they made their way home. The boat's sweet-tempered movement and rippling of the waves, accompanied by the murmur of male voices, lulled her into fanciful visions of selkies and wild, copper-haired lasses who loved unwisely.

Mackinnon's voice came unexpectedly out of the darkness beside her. "You've a great trust in us, haven't you?" As she turned and looked into his face, he added, so quietly she hardly heard, "I cannot bear him having you." He traced her upper lip with one finger. "But sorrow and death bind you to me."

At that moment the boat keeled then acquiesced to the pull of the buoy.

"Stop your dreaming, we're home." Aodhàn jumped away from her before she could ask what he'd meant.

Seaghan helped her into the dinghy and soon, Morrigan stood once again on Glenelg's pier.

"Come away, lass," Seaghan ordered. "We'll get you and Livvy warm and dry before sending you to Kilgarry."

He escorted Morrigan to his blackhouse and into a chair near the fireplace. Aodhàn handed her a dry plaid and lit the fire while Seaghan brewed tea. Olivia clasped at the air, gripped Morrigan's finger, and let her mother know she was again hungry. With the plaid piled high around her and no light but what the blue peat fire offered, Morrigan felt secure enough to accommodate her, yet when she looked up from the baby she caught Aodhàn watching from the shadows by the door. Those colors she'd seen at her wedding feast swirled around him, making her blink as she questioned her sight. Red, aye, dark red, almost brown at the edges, and the red did seem angry, as Diorbhail had described it, throwing showers of sparks.

She was surprised to feel no shame or embarrassment. "Our fine day abandoned us," she said, needing to break the spell for fear of falling so deeply into it that she could never climb out. "Was it dangerous?"

The colors faded as Aodhàn dropped to the floor and crossed his long legs. "It can be, but Seaghan and I know what we're doing."

"Admit it, Aodhàn," Seaghan said. "You would've enjoyed spending the night on that wee rock." He handed their guest tea, served in what must be the man's finest cup.

"I might have," Aodhàn said, and he met Morrigan's gaze.

She sipped, thinking for some reason of the poor dead creature abandoned against Skye's coast. Other animals would eat it. Nothing would remain but bones, and finally, not even that.

"I'll take you home," Aodhàn said.

"Best let me," Seaghan said quickly, but Aodhàn shook his head. There was an instant of strained silence as the two men communicated without speaking. Morrigan tensed. Seaghan turned away with a shrug and a barely suppressed hiss.

Mist still clung to the coastline and caught like cotton in the trees. Aodhàn led her with unhesitating sureness, his hand gripping her forearm. He must know every stone and blade of grass around Glenelg.

"How did you meet Curran?" he asked.

"Aunt Ibby brought him to the inn."

"And why did you marry him? Because he's wealthy?"

She started to make a retort about his manners, but instead swallowed hard and said, "Because I love him, of course. We fell in love."

"It wasn't the child?"

Embarrassment rippled. "Everyone told me I must," she said and inwardly cursed. Now he would think her not only a female without morals, but a daftie, who had to be ordered, molded, and guided.

His face remained expressionless. Even in the happiest of times, she knew his face would be difficult to read. His distrust was clear, though. What had scarred him?

"Tonight you're more nymph than girl. One of the *Meliae*." He picked a primrose, brushed back her hair, and tucked it above her ear.

She felt the contact of his fingers through her whole body. "Meliae. What is that?"

"They live in ash trees. The Greeks called the honey from those trees *méli*. That's how they got their name."

"Really?"

"They're the sweeter sisters to the Erinyes, the crones of vengeance."

"Mackinnon, how do you know these things?"

"You were so certain you had me all puzzled out, neat and tidy, simply from the way I live."

It was true. She couldn't deny it. "I've been obsessed with the stories of Greece since I learned to read."

"Of course." He shrugged as though she'd said something patently obvious. He lifted his brow, slightly mocking, slightly suggestive.

Inside, fear bloomed. Her female senses told her he was deliberately charming her. Though in some shamed part of her imagination she'd secretly wished for it, now that it had come she fought a desire to run away to Curran, her bastion.

"Seaghan told me you vanish for days," she said. "Traipse the hills, stare out to sea. You forget to eat and fall ill."

"Seaghan tells more than he should."

She sensed a withdrawal but continued. "You know the glen? With the cave?"

They stopped. "I saw you there," he said.

She heard his voice reciting the tale as she met his gaze. *This path is marked by my unknowable destiny. I cannot escape it.*

Olivia stirred and yawned. Mist created unworldly chambers of privacy, muffling requirements and rules as it did sound. Perhaps the faeries had whisked them through a magical threshold and they were no longer in the ordinary world at all.

"Have you heard the Mackinnon clan motto?" His voice was low. "It's older than the clan. Almost as old as Earth itself."

She shook her head.

"'Fortune favors the bold.'"

He bent then and kissed her, gripping her shoulders to keep her from fleeing, as part of her wanted to do.

Why did the image of that poor murdered seal flash again through her thoughts?

He might respect Curran Ramsay. He might like him. But in this matter, he could no more restrain himself than he could the sunrise. Mackinnon kissed her because death lay around the next corner; if one gave in to timidity, or respect, or social requirements, one's only chance might be forever lost.

She closed her eyes and rose up on her toes. But Diorbhail's face invaded relentlessly. *Against the mountain, the seal is powerless.*

If Mackinnon is the seal, does that make Curran the mountain?

This is wrong.

Only Olivia separated them, a delicate thread stringing her to Curran, to solemn oaths, and days, weeks, months of shared intimacy.

Once, long ago, Kit had kissed her. At first she'd enjoyed it, but all too soon revulsion had sent her scrabbling away. She still remembered that hurt expression on his face. No such thing happened now, though by rights it should—especially as she was a married woman. Instead she felt herself capitulating, wanting more, no matter the cost. Her legs grew weak and shaky and her breathing shortened. His arms lowered, holding her securely as she started to soften and diffuse.

His mouth moved to her cheek. "You and I," he said. "For as long as the pyramids stand in Egypt. They've always been there. And so will we."

He cradled the back of her head in one hand and kissed her again. For some reason, this man loved her. He loved her with ferocity and reverence. Aye, she sensed lust in his grip, sensed the effort to hold it in check, but there was more, something deeper, desperate, consuming. It made no sense. Yet it did. His age no longer mattered. His gruffness, his coldness, his reserve. None of it mattered.

Aodhàn Mackinnon loves me.

He had repeated that phrase, the one she thought was hers alone. She remembered the day she'd first met braw, beautiful Curran. She'd been lying in the grass by Loch Ryan, half-asleep, daydreaming of Theseus, imagining herself as Queen Aridela.

Shortly after, riding her fat mare along the cliffs, she'd lost her hat and envisioned a man standing near the water.

The color of his hair might have changed. He might now be a lowly fisherman rather than a great warrior, but it was he. She'd found him.

Surfaces could no longer fool her. Faces couldn't fool her.

Aodhàn Mackinnon had the same eyes, exactly, as that blond champion.

The dull thud of hoof-beats penetrated the mist. They separated. Aodhàn plucked the primrose from behind her ear and dropped it to the ground.

Curran loomed on his stallion, Augustus, Stoirmeil in tow.

Morrigan lowered her face, knowing if her husband looked into her eyes just then, he would see.

A terrible mistake has been made.

"There you are," he said. "Finally. Thank God." He swung off his mount.

"*Feasgar math,*" Mackinnon said.

"*Oidhche mhath, ciamar a tha sibh?*" Curran replied, not bothering to mask his irritation.

Mackinnon paused. His left brow lifted, and there was an edge to his reply. "*Tha mi toilichte.*"

Curran frowned. His eyes narrowed.

Morrigan understood this common salutation, but their reactions warned her that the deceptively simple words were hiding something, and she sensed it had to do with her.

She froze, wondering what might happen next, but they seemed to relax slightly, like two adversaries circling. Mackinnon explained how he and Seaghan had taken her out on the *Endeavor,* and how the sea haar had trapped them.

Morrigan stroked Stoirmeil's nose and said nothing.

Aodhàn held Olivia while Curran helped Morrigan into the saddle. She mounted, reached down, and took her child.

"Thank you," she said, and spurred the mare quickly away.

"*Oidhche mhath,* Aodhàn." Curran tipped his cap. "Thank you for bringing her safely through this." He sent his horse after Morrigan, and when he caught up, said almost apologetically, "I was worried. Here, let me take her."

She handed the baby to him and caressed his shoulder. "I should've come home with Diorbhail," she said. "I had no plan to be gone so long. I know you were fashed. Forgive me, Curran."

Later, in the big master bed, her husband drew her close, his hands trailing over her nightgown.

Morrigan closed her eyes and tried to respond, but at the last instant, she jerked away, gasping, fighting a sense that she was suffocating.

"Be patient." She heard the tremble in her voice. "I overdid things today. I'm stiff and sore."

He murmured his sympathies. She watched the dying fire long after he'd fallen asleep, his cheek against her chest.

Curran loved three things: Kilgarry, Morrigan, and Olivia. He'd eagerly sought to unite them, the mother of his child with his beloved home. She would never have come to Glenelg but for him.

Yet, in bringing her here, he might have destroyed whatever chance of love they'd had.

MORRIGAN FELT MORE TIRED THAN REFRESHED WHEN SHE WOKE, AND YAWNED repeatedly as Violet helped her dress. Curran had eaten his breakfast but was having coffee in the dining room.

"How are you, *a ghràidh?*" he asked, pouring tea.

"Sleepy," she said, and clasped his hand. *Could I betray you, Curran Ramsay? Could I do such a thing?*

Daughters of whores usually turn out whores themselves, Enid Joyce had taunted. Had she seen some awful truth Morrigan had blinded herself to?

No. She nearly said it out loud, but caught herself. *Curran loves me. I think Seaghan loves me. Eleanor loves me. Diorbhail loves me. Most of all, Olivia loves me. Enid lied. Papa lied. I am not a whore!*

"Rest today," he said. "Why don't you read in the garden?" He bent his head, a mischievous smile playing about his mouth. "I want you. Do you know how long it's been?"

A flush heated her cheeks. Some part of her, perhaps the part bespelled by Mackinnon's selkie gaze, wanted to shout, *Leave me alone!*

Had Curran made her pregnant to keep her from the man who had been searching for her? No. Morrigan had seduced Curran, not the other way around. And Mackinnon had never met her. It made no sense to think he'd been searching for her, no matter what he said.

"Is something else bothering you?" Curran asked.

Morrigan closed her eyes, trying to block the events that in one short day had ripped gaping holes in the fabric of her shiny new life. "I saw my father's burned home. It sickens me to think of those days, of how much was destroyed. And...and I...I have to tell you about Patrick Hawley."

"What of him?"

"I wanted to be alone, so I sent Aunt Ibby away. He found me there. He attacked me."

Curran went as stiff, straight, and still as iron. A long moment passed. "You're joking," he said.

She shook her head.

"Why didn't you tell me this last night?"

"I forgot."

"You forgot. You *forgot?*" He stared at her. "Did he, did he...."

"No. He meant to, though." She fanned her face with one hand. "I...I don't want to speak of this. Fionna or Tess might hear."

"I'll have his heart."

"Just send him away."

He stood, reaching for his coat.

"Where are you going?"

Cold fury hardened his face, much like the expression he'd had the day he'd seen the whip marks on her back. The crescent scar by his brow undulated over the *clench*-release, *clench*-release of his jaw. It was terrifying.

"Curran, what are you going to do? Promise you won't—"

He turned and seized her arm. An odd light glittered in his eyes. "Why were you so free with me? I find it difficult to believe you were a virgin when I met you. Were you? Well?" He shook her.

She gasped. "You blame me for what he did!"

"This has nothing to do with him. Answer me. You'd never been with a man?"

The memory of the night in the barn with Kit, his hands under her nightgown, left her mute. Should she confess?

He released her. "It's no wonder they think they can have you. Aodhàn, now Hawley. I was right when I said I'd need to keep you pregnant." He laughed without humor. "But even that didn't work. Why do you do what you do? Look at men that way?"

"What way?"

He shoved his hair off his forehead. "Like you're in their beds. Like any moment you'll beg them to take you."

"I don't...I have *never* done that! I can hardly stand to be in the same room as Patrick Hawley!"

He paced, his loose-limbed strides, swinging arms, and tawny hair reminiscent of a restless lion. "I've never understood why I forgot myself on the moor that day. I knew I'd taken unforgivable advantage. But the way you acted, like you wanted it more than anything, wanted me to do it." He glared at her. "Like you knew what you were doing."

"Are you saying you're sorry you married me?"

"Answer me. Did you plan what happened that day?"

"No one ever told me about men and women. It felt good, and it took me away from my life for a moment. Away from my father. You were handsome. You said kind, flattering things. That's why I didn't want you to stop. I didn't think about what could happen, that a child could come of it. Not till after."

He regarded her, filtering her words through some inner judgmental sieve. After a long pause, he spoke in a lower voice, as if to himself. "You were a virgin."

Her hands balled into fists. "Why do you want me to feel shame over that day? You don't. What man ever feels shame over the things he does?" She laughed. "Were *you* a virgin?"

He blinked. "I'm sorry. I've a...damnable jealousy of you." He paced again, like he couldn't contain his energy. "They're trying to steal you right out from under me. Even Aodhàn, my friend these last ten years. I thought we respected each other."

"You're wrong about him." She strained any emotion but resentment from her voice. "I told you, I went outside with him on Michaelmas to make you jealous." She gave him a one-sided smile. "Damn thorough job I did of it, too. I wish I could undo it, but I can't."

"Did you ever stop to think what that would do to him? You say you wanted to make me jealous. But you've started something, Morrigan. You've made him think you have feelings for him. Now he wants you for himself. Every man here does. I've seen Malcolm's face light up at a glimpse of you. And Seaghan. Maybe I should put you in rags, smear dirt on your face."

"You're daft."

"You may be right about that." He shrugged into his coat.

"Where are you going?"

"To find Patrick Hawley."

"I'm afraid of him." She rose, working her napkin in one fist. "He'll kill you, Curran. He has no guilt. No mercy. He's inhuman."

He shrugged. "Well, then...."

"Curran!"

In two strides he reached her, pulling her against him fiercely, holding her face at his throat. "Morrigan, Morrigan." She felt the tremors running through him, and clung, understanding now that fear had birthed the words of anger.

He spoke into her hair. "What might have happened...what he might have done. I thought you were safe here, in my Glenelg. I thought you were safe in this place I love."

"I'm not hurt. He didn't hurt me. I swear it. I had a knife. I cut him. It was only a small cut in the arm, but it hurt him, and he ran away."

His eyes were so dark. She sensed the murderous rage filling his body in great, overwhelming waves. "You're wrong to think I didn't feel shame over what I did that day," he said, low. "But I would have married you, pregnant or not. I would have married you if I'd never touched you. From the moment I saw you, at the train station, I knew. You're the only woman for me. I don't know why, but it's true. The only one."

He turned then and strode out of the dining room, not pausing as she cried, "Curran!" She heard the heavy front portal slam behind him.

Morrigan's anxiety increased as the hours passed. She finally ordered Logan to go and find Curran, but he refused, saying he was not the master's warden and could be banished if he did what she wanted.

She tried to read. She paced. She avoided Diorbhail's questioning worry while she nursed Olivia, who seemed to sense Morrigan's fear and cried inconsolably.

The sun lowered, and still he did not return. Fionna brought a tea tray filled with tempting refreshments, but Morrigan's nerves had stolen any hunger and she left it untouched.

She went to their bedroom and attempted Eleanor's hypnotism. She lay on the bed, staring at the flourishes on the mirror, but her thoughts went right on whirling, woven through with guilt. Violet came and helped her with her nightgown, then went away for the night. Morrigan took one of Curran's shirts from his wardrobe and lay on the bed, holding it against her cheek, breathing the scent of him.

The mantel clock ticked quietly. She listened with all her might for the sound of the door downstairs, but finally drifted off.

The night had grown old when he slipped into bed, still chilled from being outdoors, and slid his arms around her. She murmured, "Where have you been?" only half-waking, and returned to sleep at his, "Don't worry, *a ghaoil.* Everything will be all right."

EARLY MORNING BIRDSONG BROUGHT MORRIGAN OUT OF SLEEP. CURRAN WAS GONE, and Violet hadn't yet come to help her dress. She lay in a place between slumber and waking, not thinking or fretting, just remembering Curran's embrace and his promise, and allowing herself to believe him.

But the quiet of the morning and the melancholy bird drew her down again, and another voice floated through her head.

I'll build you a summer house here, since you love it so much.

Aodhàn Mackinnon reached for her hand. Morrigan heard the breakers far below. The air was thick with the screeching of birds.

Gradually, the busy sounds of Mallaig's harbor intruded. Men shouting, boat whistles, women laughing, raucous birds foraging.

Mallaig's pier.

Morrigan bolted upright, staring into her dim bedroom. She was not in Mallaig. She was in Glenelg, at Kilgarry.

Shall we force his hand?

You will marry me, Lilith.

She tried to discredit the revelation, but the more she examined it, the surer she grew. She had dreamed of walking along a high black cliff with a young Aodhàn Mackinnon.

Before she'd ever taken any witch's cap, before the hypnotism, before she came to Glenelg. She'd dreamed it while living in Ibby's small quarters above her shop in Mallaig, mashed into a narrow bed with Beatrice.

It wasn't surprising that she'd forgotten, not when she considered all the strange dreams that invaded her sleep, but it had waited, tucked away in her memories, for this moment of quiet reflection.

How could it be? How could she have dreamed of him before she became Curran's wife? Before she looked, for the first time, into his face at her wedding cèilidh?

It was…impossible, *impossible* to dream of a real person before meeting him or knowing he existed.

She jumped out of bed, rang the bell, and paced until Violet entered, and hardly heard her chatter as the maid helped her dress and arranged her hair. Impatience thrummed through her body, or was it fear?

She had to speak to someone. It couldn't be Curran, not with everything else that had happened. Nor could it be Diorbhail, with her animosity. Perhaps Eleanor. But no. Eleanor saw too much, sometimes.

Who could she turn to? Who would listen without judgment?

Chapter 26

FATHER DRUMMOND PERFORMED MASS AND LISTENED WITH GRAVE ATTENTION IN the confessional, though he had heard it all many times. Later, after his parishioners had gone off to their dinners, he knelt before the crucifix on the altar and gazed upon his savior.

Shouldn't he try, at least try, to emulate such pure humility?

But my life has been wasted.

"Forgive me." He crossed himself. The old unwelcome complaint often intruded, even after these many years. What did he think he could do, at sixty-one, to make a difference in this world? Though he scoffed at his fancies, the yearning remained, like a gnawed-out hole in the heart.

When he'd taken his vows, he'd expected his superiors to send him to a foreign land, maybe to India or heathen Persia. He'd prepared himself for adversity and hostility.

His corner of the West Highlands could almost be compared to a foreign land. It was cut off from the rest of Scotland by those lofty mountains affectionately dubbed the Five Sisters of Kintail. From the east, it remained nearly unassailable. Horses labored with the ascent from Loch Duich, especially if pulling any sort of load. Then there was the steep descent to accomplish. To the west roiled the Kyle Rhea, that treacherous stretch of water between the mainland and the Isle of Skye, where currents collected and intensified, to spill free farther south into the Sound of Sleat.

Time here was almost suspended, ruled by primitive superstition. These folk would be shocked, horrified, by London's favored pastime of adultery, by the romantic scandals that hounded Prince Edward like a gadfly. Many in those circles believed even stuffy Queen Victoria was having an affair with her rough Scots servant, John Brown. *Punch*, the satirical city magazine, had caricatured Prime Minister Gladstone's Christian charity when he invited prostitutes into his home, ostensibly to help them find other ways of feeding themselves.

Some things did make a body wonder, but the masses, in Hugh's experience, were too eager to embrace the worst about their fellow human beings. What if Victoria was having a liaison? She'd been in mourning for many years. Would the people expect a king to live without female companionship so long? Women and men were different, of course. No sense comparing kings with queens. God-fearing Christians expected more decorum in a female and that was that.

Glenelg's villagers could never comprehend the subtle complexities of human nature, the passions that drove some against reason and upbringing. The worst sins he heard in the confessional were vexations with a spouse, impatience with a wayward child, or perhaps envy at a neighbor's richer catch or crop. These contemporary times couldn't compare with the late forties and early fifties. Hugh had never questioned his role during those terrible years, with blight on the potato, children starving, and landlords exiling tenants in favor of sheep.

But would God never ask anything else of him? For the last twenty years he'd done little more than perform Mass in a half-empty church.

Lethargy sapped his strength. He rested his forehead on his folded hands. "Breathe into me, Holy Spirit, attract my heart, Holy Spirit, that I may love only what is holy—"

Hesitant footsteps and the swish of a woman's skirts interrupted his gloomy thoughts.

Although he knew the voices and sins of every one of his parishioners, he didn't move, in case some penitent wished to enter the confessional in anonymity. Someone no doubt felt compelled to confess gluttony because she'd enjoyed an extra helping of fish or had indulged in unkind gossip.

Whoever it was, she stopped and waited. Hugh bowed his head, crossed himself, and stood.

A shocked breath escaped him. His sight degenerated into leaping spots and his eardrums hummed. Hannah Stewart Lawton stood before him, washed in varied color from the stained-glass window. A dead woman.

"Father?" Her timid voice broke the spell. No, Hannah hadn't returned from death. This was Morrigan, Hannah's daughter.

"Father Drummond?" she repeated.

He smiled. "You gave me a start, my dear. For a moment I thought your mother was standing before me! You are so like her."

"I'm sorry." She held her hands clasped together in a tightly clenched manner that alarmed him.

"Don't apologize, you have no control over it. I've been hoping you would visit. Come away to my rectory. How is our wee Olivia?"

Before he could arm himself against it, the part of his brain he'd muzzled these last forty years thought, *Her mouth is formed for kissing.*

"She's well. Could I speak to you, Father?"

He thrust away his disgusting fancies and led her to his sitting room without another word, gesturing her over to the comfortable old armchair by the fire.

"Tea, m'lady?"

"No, thank you."

She stared into the corner for such a long while he wondered if she ever would speak.

"I'm not of your faith," she said at last. "I hope I'm not breaking some rule in coming here like this."

"Is something troubling you?"

"I've been reading your…the Bible." She glanced at her hands, encased in black leather gloves that looked as soft as butter. "Trying to learn what's expected of us."

"You could choose worse literature."

"I've broken your…the commandments. I feel I've sinned. I don't want my child to suffer because of anything I have done."

He curbed the urge to smile. "And what have you done?" Some small transgression must have migrated wildly out of proportion.

"I got myself with child when I should not have, didn't I, and trapped Curran, giving him no choice but to marry me, and me an innkeeper's daughter."

He shoved away another unwelcome thought about how tempted Curran must have been. "Fornication is a sin, but all too common. If you feel true penance, I can absolve you—"

"I hated my father," she said as though he hadn't spoken. "And never thought about what my hate did to him, not until after he was dead and I had a child of my own." Lower, she added, "I would die to protect Olivia. I would kill." Her hands fisted in her lap. "Such fear comes over me; I fear she'll get sick. I fear her dying. If she did I swear I'd kill myself so I can hold her hand when she goes wherever it is folk go when they die. Even if I have to stop at the entrance into Heaven, at least I'll have gone with her that far. And if the dead don't go anywhere, we can be buried together."

A surprising rush of tears raked the back of his eyelids. "Through the years I've learned there is no love on earth comparable to a mother's. Do you believe this love is a sin? It isn't. Killing yourself, aye, that is. But loving? God created that love in you, and it moves my heart mightily." Gently, he said, "I want to help."

Light from the fire glinted in her eyes. "I should be alone, but Curran, Curran should be happy." She rubbed at a fine set of worry-lines in her forehead. "I suspect he'll come to hate me in the end, and I don't blame him. I don't want to be responsible for ruining his life, and Olivia's."

Why did she believe she should be alone? Hugh shook his head, confused. He had always prided himself on his instinctive wisdom of folk, yet he'd not guessed at the pain this lass was hiding. At her wedding cèilidh she'd looked a little frightened, aye, but happy, no different from any other bride.

Everyone thought Douglas had won. He'd found a way to steal Hannah from Seaghan and make off with her. Hugh had never considered the idea that Douglas's triumph might end in a curse.

"D'you believe in ghosts, Father?"

Hugh scratched his jaw, considering. "I've seen things, gods and goddesses floating among these clouds. The rules, the laws of the outside, don't work, not here, where Time has never quite advanced. I've often thought our corner of Scotland is enchanted."

Memories of those long-gone days sharpened. Everyone eagerly gossiping about that unhappy love triangle, wondering how surly Douglas Lawton managed to win the heart of Hannah Stewart, when they all thought her so loyal and in love with joyous Seaghan. In this mediaeval spot, almost anything could happen—even impossible things. "There are ghosts," he said. "Faeries too, no doubt, though my superiors wouldn't approve me saying so."

She frowned, then threw out a question he found himself completely unprepared for. "Someone told me your church believes women are products of the Devil. That we lead men away from God—that we caused Christ to be crucified."

He heard himself stutter. Clamping his mouth shut, he worked to regain his composure as harsh statements written by long-dead Church leaders ran through his brain. *Every woman is defective. Wives are lower than slaves.* He shook his head to clear it.

"The Church has changed through the centuries, like everything does," he said carefully. "Wisdom is gained. Enlightenment occurs. In the beginning, we were fighting to kill off older religions—cruel, savage faiths, headed by women who used blood sacrifice. The Church now acknowledges the help and joy women give to men. Who told you such things, child?"

Her face hardened. Her eyes narrowed. He knew she wouldn't say. She was protecting someone. Surely not Curran?

The best course was to move them past an airy, philosophical debate. This woman had come to him for help. "Let us keep to the matter at hand," he said. "Please tell me why you hated Douglas."

Her anger seemed to dissipate, thank goodness. She blinked several times, as if unprepared for the question, or overwhelmed by the emotions it caused.

"He…he hit us." She lowered her head. "I was always sneaking off to the moor instead of doing my chores, most every day, if I'm honest about it. It vexed him. It vexed him very much."

"Hit you. He hit you?" Hugh had a great deal of experience reading faces and unsaid words. Everything about her demeanor cried out that *he hit us* meant Douglas beat them, and badly.

She shrugged. "Nicky and my Aunt Beatrice often had to do my chores, because I was off somewhere hiding. Daydreaming."

He covered his face with his hand. "*Mea culpa.* I cannot believe it."

"I'm not lying."

"Oh, child, I know you're not. If only I had known. I'd never have allowed him to take you away."

"How could you have stopped him?"

"I would have found a way."

She continued in a rush. "I used to wish he would die, and he did. It's a sin to want someone to die, isn't it? I know it is. Everything is different now that Olivia has come. I want to make peace with my father, but I can't, because he's dead."

"In the name of God." Hugh shut his mouth and tried to gather his thoughts. After a moment, he said, more calmly, "Douglas was devoted to his first wife, Neala, and to Nick. At least, I always believed he was."

"He loved my mother too. I think he never forgave me for causing her to die. Was it that, Father? Or was it something else, something I haven't yet learned?"

Hugh didn't know what to say. She spoke from instinct; she couldn't know that Douglas had lost his wits over Hannah long before she was born. He had to have, to willingly betray Seaghan.

"Do you blame yourself for his death?" he asked. "Curran told me it was his heart."

She started to answer but instead pressed the back of her hand against her mouth. Her throat worked, her lashes fluttered, and her face reddened.

"Stop," he said and rose. "Not another word. You're going to have some tea."

He went away to the kitchen, surprised to see the teapot steaming under a quilted cozy. "Bless you, Agnes," he murmured. She took care of him with such quiet efficiency he hardly knew she was there.

He arranged the pot and two cups on a tray, adding a dish of sugar, tongs, and a pitcher of milk.

Morrigan appeared more composed when he returned. She relieved him of the tray and poured.

"My father tried to kill me." She met his gaze without any sign of flinching.

"He called me 'Hannah.' I think sometimes, when the anger took over, he mistook me for my mother."

"Then he was mad!" Hugh leaped to his feet. "Oh, God! What stopped him?"

"My aunts fought him off. Then he…grabbed his chest and fell. There was a sliver of glass. I wanted it to fall into him. I wished it to fall, and it did. Then he died."

Hugh rubbed at a piercing throb in his right temple. Dropping into the chair, he labored to regain control over his heavily lurching heart. "Douglas is one thing," he said at last. "He is dead and gone, and we can do nothing about him now." He drew in a deep breath. "Why did you ask me if I believe in ghosts?"

"I have unco dreams. You won't…you won't have me locked away if I tell you?"

"Locked away? What do you mean? In a madhouse?"

She nodded. "You said my father was mad. Does madness run in families, Father? Could I be…d'you think I could be—"

"No!" He felt his own skin blanch. "Of course not." In truth, he had heard that such was the case, but he would not add to her fears. Not today. Besides, as he and everyone else who'd lived in Glenelg twenty years ago knew, there was a strong possibility Morrigan wasn't even related to Douglas.

"Dreams are not a sign of madness. Tell me."

She wrung her handkerchief and closed her eyes. "I dream of a seal. He becomes a man, and tears me away from everything, from Curran, from Olivia. I feel as though I love him, but I'm frightened of him too."

He gritted his teeth to keep from interrupting.

"I dream I'm a wife," she continued, her eyes still shut tight. "To someone else, not Curran. I don't know what crime I've committed, but men force their way into my house and murder my babies in front of me." Her voice broke. "And they cut my throat." One hand lifted, brushing against that fragile flesh. "Before they kill me, they call me a witch. I dream this, over and over."

Hugh jumped to his feet again. He couldn't hear any more. He seized her hands, pulling her from the chair, and embraced her. "My God, my God!"

She resisted his touch. He felt her stiffness, the tenseness in her neck. "Is God sending these dreams as a punishment to me for not giving my father obedience and respect?"

Pain flashed like a bullet through his temple. Morrigan's eyes opened and she stared at him as he sprawled on the floor. He was shuddering, and feared he would vomit.

"Father Drummond!"

An eternity seemed to pass before he gained control over the desperate gasping. He became aware that she was crouched beside him, clutching his hand. "I'll fetch help," she said, rising, her expressive face betraying her anxiety.

"No, no, wait." How hoarse he sounded. Not himself at all. "Give me a moment." He'd never felt like this. His head throbbed in time with his heartbeat, though the piercing bolt of agony was ebbing.

She brought his teacup, helped him sit, and held the cup to his lips. She patted his forehead with her handkerchief. "Can you make it to the chair?"

He nodded and allowed her to help him to his feet. He dropped thankfully into the comforting familiarity of stuffed material scented with years of pipe smoke.

She poured milk into a cup then added tea and extra sugar, as he liked it. Hugh kept his eyes focused on her hands. Minute by minute, he felt the pain subsiding, and several deep breaths settled his stomach.

The serviceable china rattled when he grasped it. Morrigan started to take it from him, but he shook his head. "I can manage," he insisted, and to prove it, lifted the cup and sipped. "Forgive me, child." He placed the cup in its saucer and set it on the table. "I've been no help to you at all." As he drew in a deep, calming breath, he shoved away remnants of horror at what she'd described. "Sit down, my dear, and tell me what's happened between you and Curran. I feel perfectly fine now." Gently, he asked, "You said before that someone has told you the Church teaches men to hate women. Is this what you fear? That Curran hates you, or will, in time?"

Concern disintegrated into despair on her face.

"He, I...." Those flawless, translucent cheeks flamed red. It made him think of an invisible pitcher of wine spilling its contents.

"You mustn't think of me as an ordinary man. I'm a priest of God, and I hear confessions every day."

She dropped into the other chair. "I won't let him touch me. Three months have passed since Olivia was born, yet I...I can't...I cannot be a wife to him, a proper wife. I used to...I used to love...but now, I don't know. He may not hate me yet, but he's bound to."

Drawing off her gloves, she placed them on her lap and smoothed them with her fingertips. "He could have so easily denied being Olivia's father. He didn't have to marry me. I owe everything to him. We were happy. Now I want to run away. I'm ashamed to say it. I...I'm so ashamed. I feel like I'm being strangled."

"This is sorry news," Hugh said, as he tried to understand her disjointed sentences. All young wives and husbands needed time to adjust, but this one had more than her share of hurts to overcome. "What changed? Surely not Olivia."

She shook her head, keeping her gaze on the gloves. "It's because of...I think I...I'm afraid I...."

He knew then, with a terrible sinking sensation, what she couldn't say. The pendulum clock began its hourly chime as he found his voice. "Oh, Morrigan. Oh, no."

Her gaze met his. "You hate me."

"No." He reached across the table and clasped her hand. "I love you, dear lass," he said, as it blazed and invigorated him. "I'll always be your friend." He frowned, thinking over everything she'd said. "Is this because of your dreams? D'you think you're in love with this seal who turns into a man?"

She kept her face downcast as she nodded, every aspect filled with shame. "He makes me feel sad, guilty, wrong. There's not one thing about him that makes me happy. He threatens me, my family, my child, everything. And yet I think of him all the time. I imagine us together. Why, Father? Why?"

Aodhàn Mackinnon. He knew it as though she'd said the name aloud, and not only because everyone in Glenelg had heard the selkie stories. If Hugh realized it, then so must Curran.

The man must not take her from her husband. There would be a catastrophic outcome if that happened. He didn't want to contemplate the repercussions.

Coming to him proved Morrigan wanted to do the right thing. She but needed a guiding hand.

And Aodhàn. Alone so long, chewed up by his mysterious past. From their first meeting, Hugh had been fascinated by the somber fellow. Many times, he had attempted to draw the fisherman into the Church, thinking if Aodhàn could only give his burdens to God, he'd find peace. Aodhàn continued to resist. But if the man were human, if blood flowed in his veins, he could never resist this lovely, equally tormented girl.

It was easy to understand why that poor devil would be drawn to her. But what did Aodhàn have that would attract Morrigan? Could it be his sadness and seclusion, his similarity to her morose father? Did she unconsciously believe she could make up for her past offenses, real or imagined, by destroying her life with Curran and following in Aodhàn's dark wake? The reasons folk did and felt were much more complex than what lay on the surface, sometimes more complex than what they themselves could understand. God alone could delve so deep.

"I am your friend," he repeated, determined to do a better job with this woman who might well be Seaghan's child.

"Thank you, Father." Morrigan gave him a grateful smile.

He patted her hand. "Lass, you've blamed yourself for things you had no say over. Aye, Hannah died giving birth to you. But I won't have you thinking that was your fault. She was fine and healthy until the day Randall Benedict cleared Glenelg. Shock sent her into labor before her time."

Ah, but was it? Was it before her time?

"Glenelg's midwife boarded the *Bristol* that day. No one remained with knowledge to help. Douglas would have been right to hate Randall Benedict, right to hate the men carrying out the laird's orders, but not you, a helpless babe. You're not to blame for being born, or for the resemblance you bear to your mother. Is Douglas the ghost you fear? D'you think he is bringing you these nightmares?"

"I don't know."

"Before you read any more of the Bible, promise you'll talk it over with me. We must make certain you get its proper meaning." He tapped the surface of the table. "Did your father have you baptized?"

She shook her head.

He sighed. "We must see to it." Poor wee thing. If she were to die, her soul couldn't enter Heaven.

He mulled over his next words before speaking. In his majestic pulpit voice, the one he reserved for brimstone and punishment, he said, "Adultery is a fearful sin. A mortal sin. It will devastate you. It will destroy your family." He glared at her. "Curran can take Olivia away from you. The law will enforce it. You say you love your daughter? If you continue down this road, if you do anything that puts your marriage in jeopardy, you'll never see her again. You'll be cast out. Homeless. No decent man or woman will give you a crust of bread."

Morrigan covered her face with her handkerchief, her fingers shaking violently. The other hand, on her lap, wadded her gloves. "I know it," she said. "The world hates women who step off the path men have carved for them."

He was startled by such insight, but refused to waver. "You are Morrigan Ramsay," he said, unrelenting. "You've made a holy vow. Don't you forget it. Don't you dare risk all you've been given, especially the child, to satisfy warped and base desires. It's unworthy of you."

"Oh," she whispered, "I can't bear this."

Hiding how well he understood, he rose, took her hands, and pulled her up. He enclosed her in a soothing embrace. "Shhh, shhh, poor wee thing. I promise you, everything will turn out as it should."

He said it to give her comfort, but inside, he wasn't so sure. He stroked Mistress Ramsay's hair, and wondered.

Would Aodhàn Mackinnon do the right thing and step away?

Hugh doubted it. It was much more likely he would destroy this fragile family without remorse.

Chapter 27

IN HIS CALM, AUTHORITATIVE WAY, FATHER DRUMMOND MADE EVERYTHING SIMPLE and clear. Dreams, no matter how powerful or inexplicable, didn't matter. Nothing mattered but her husband, her child, and her duty. Life might descend into blankness, like a sheet of paper before it's been written on, but unsullied paper held purity and possibility, like a virtuous wife. Though they fit together in ways she didn't understand, she would put Mackinnon from her, for Olivia, and for Curran. Her path was illuminated, well-traveled by countless other women.

But first she must have an answer. Before she turned her back on Mackinnon, she would confront him; she would ask him how she could have dreamed of him before she'd ever met him, and she would watch his eyes to see if he told her the truth. For there was one thing she was certain of—Mackinnon knew something he wasn't sharing.

Hidden at the edge of a copse of trees, Morrigan sat upon her horse and watched Mackinnon's home by the bay, hoping he would see her and Seaghan would not.

She waited a long time, close to two hours, and had almost given up when Mackinnon appeared, coming around the side of the blackhouse, a spade in one hand.

Stoirmeil pricked her ears and nickered, drawing Mackinnon's attention. He frowned. Morrigan beckoned and pointed behind her, to the east, then turned her horse, directing Stoirmeil towards the eagle's glen, hoping he would understand.

Sunlight filtered through the tree branches, blinding then dim, contributing to Morrigan's sense of stumbling unbalance.

For five days, since the night Mackinnon had walked her through the mist, her muscles had remained stubbornly tense and every unexpected sound caused her to jump. She'd spent more nighttime hours in the library, reading or staring at the wall, than she had sleeping. A catapult drove her, one she could no longer ignore or deny. He had devised it by sharing a mythical tale of tragic love. He'd cemented it when he'd led her through a white, formless world and handed her to her husband, doubtless knowing he'd profoundly changed her, knowing she would, from that moment, be torn, unhappy, imprisoned in a cage of his making.

Light showered the open patch of ground in the clearing. She dismounted and paced, crumpling dried leaves.

It didn't take long. The sunlight was so blinding that for an instant, as he approached, he resembled the phantasm she had often dreamed of. Then she blinked and the fancy vanished. The man before her was Mackinnon, pale and thin like the *daoine sìth*, down to the suggestion of a reddish glow issuing from his fingertips.

She faced him. "Why do I feel we know each other...*have* known each other, since before I was born?"

He stopped. "You're mine and I am yours," he said, "no matter what separates us. No matter what fool you marry."

It was not an answer, nothing anyway that explained what she needed to know, and she was determined to have it out. "I dreamed of you...months ago, before I came to Glenelg. You were young, and I.... You called me Lilith. You were arguing with me. I hadn't met you yet!"

He opened his mouth then closed it. With a curse, he picked up a rock and threw it savagely, striking the trunk of a tree.

"Mackinnon! How could that happen? Can you explain it?"

"I don't know," he said. His voice and his eyes were cold and mocking, causing her to blush with shame. He shrugged. "Dreams. You're asking me to explain your dreams, Lady Eilginn. No one can explain such things."

Why was he angry? If her question was truly daft, then why?

The lines etched in his face spoke of more than age, more than the mark of sun and wind. They told a story of long years filled with loneliness and grief.

Pity, that's what she felt, for him or anyone who lived such a sad, solitary life. But it didn't matter. "I'll never be separated from my child," she said. She dug her nails into her palms. "I've given Curran my vow. Leave us alone, Mackinnon."

The repeated clamp of his jaw and his white-knuckled fists betrayed his faltering control.

She had to be careful not to make the same mistake. He mustn't see any hint of the hurricane inside her. She stared into his eyes, not blinking, not allowing any movement or expression to give her away.

"I have done nothing but leave you alone," he said softly. "And yet, here you are."

"I mean…." She gestured at her head, "in here."

The slightest arc of a smile passed over his mouth, making her think about what she'd said. She cursed silently.

She had loved Curran, of the bright hair and brighter smile, of tenderness and talk and kisses. Part of her loved him still, adored him, and longed to restore the joy they'd shared. She hated Mackinnon for destroying it.

No! Mackinnon could destroy nothing without her consent. It was weakness to give him that power. It was what he wanted.

She *would* return to the happy times with Curran. With distance and resolve, Mackinnon would be no more than a memory.

He stepped closer. "I miss you," he said. "I miss you…so much. It's like a wild animal, eating me alive."

She clenched her jaw to keep from responding.

That muted smile returned. His eyes flickered.

"My child is all that matters," she said.

The smile died, to be replaced with a black frown.

"I brought this." She turned her face down to break that bewitching gaze, and fished in her pocket for the driftwood box. She held it out. "I cannot keep it."

"It was a gift," he said. He sounded, for the first time, hurt. He cursed again. "Give me the bloody ring." He took the box from her. "It changes nothing. It won't stop what is between us."

She backed away, fighting off waves of remorse, hating the pain she clearly saw beneath his anger.

"You'll see," he said. "I never give up what's mine." He didn't blink. "And you are mine."

She felt like a butterfly stuck with a pin behind a glass frame, wings fluttering helplessly.

"My marriage lines say differently," she said, but he merely laughed.

Tearing free of his stare, she stumbled to her mare, climbing onto a stone and heaving herself into the saddle. She fled the clearing, kicking Stoirmeil onward, not letting herself crumple against the warm mane until she'd gone far enough that he would never know.

Curran saddled Augustus, his mood so churlish that Logan disappeared into the shadows and didn't show his face again.

Happiness had flowed through every facet of life, from the walls of his beloved manor house to the crofters' pleased faces when he rode up to chat. Now he fancied his crofters' expressions had grown furtive, and his home seemed little more than the discarded husk of a mayfly.

Had Morrigan ever really come with him to Kilgarry? Her body had, but her soul resided elsewhere. Maybe beside the graves of her father and brother.

Maybe with Aodhàn Mackinnon.

He galloped from the courtyard, giving the stallion his head.

He could have believed Aodhàn's tale of bringing her home because of the mist if it hadn't been for the silence, the sadness, the distance, that had built between them like a fortress wall ever since.

He kept waking at night, alone, and twice had gone searching for her. He'd found her in the library, sitting with no light but a candle, staring at the tamped fire. Both times he'd gone away silently.

Has she given herself to him?

He thought of the doll's poor, ripped body. Why had she done that? Was it Olivia she wanted to ravage? Was his baby safe? He shuddered, pushing away the thought.

He found himself at the ancient ruin, Dùn Trodan. Growing up, this was where he'd come when troubled, to these monuments where he and his father discovered the last survivors of the Glenelg clearings.

The remnants of the tower silently proclaimed the inevitability of endings, no matter how strong or thick the walls.

This was where his wife had entered the world and fought to survive. Others who had sheltered here hadn't been so fortunate. Beth Dunbar had died of starvation and cold. So had Padraig's wife and child, and Fionna's husband, Morrigan's grandmam, and Kyle's mother.

Dismounting, he rested his forehead against the stones and closed his eyes, feeling the curse of the place sink into his bones.

A breeze ruffled through the leaves in the nearby trees, bringing the voices to life. *I'm so hungry.*

Few men wed for pleasure or love. Marriage was an institution, designed to provide money, titles, land, or prestige. Many never experienced a single day of harmony with their wives. Yet he and Morrigan had enjoyed an instinctive rapport from the moment they'd met.

Now she seemed to think he could shut off his passion like the valve on a steam engine. He remembered her spiteful expression when she'd inquired about his virginity. She knew he'd been with other women, half-forgotten though they were. But never had he known anyone like her. It had struck him, that day on the moor, how artlessly she'd given herself, without thought or care to consequences, decency, or the fleshly sins Christianity dwelled upon and tried to deny.

She should be grateful for his rescue. He'd given her everything, but damn it, in the end, it hadn't been enough. She preferred the penniless fisherman!

After the wedding, Ibby confessed that Douglas died while attempting to murder his daughter. When Curran thought of those bloody marks on Morrigan's back, still discernable as narrow white stripes, impotent rage left him shaking.

Yet life had flowed from that girl, the one who lived under her father's iron thumb in Stranraer. Her fiery spirit had sucked him in. Now she was quiet. Her spirit had gone hollow, fragile as a champagne flute.

He wanted his Amazon. He wouldn't give her up.

His jaw clenched at the unwelcome thought that perhaps her fascination for Aodhàn fit perfectly with the warrior he craved. That woman didn't care about being rescued. He suspected a ferocious matching of souls was more enticing to her than a manor house, silk gowns, or jewelry.

He longed for his wild, selfish, pagan lass, the one he'd fallen in love with. The one who'd vowed never to be a man's possession.

Resentment conjured images of Aodhàn's death. Curran could shoot him and throw his corpse in the sea. Folk always said Mackinnon would vanish one day. No one would suspect.

"Why can't you die?"

Faint mocking laughter brushed through the pines. *Do you want me to, my brother?*

Aye!

It was time for truth. He wanted Morrigan's uncontrollable qualities only when it suited him. But could wildness be bottled, released at his convenience? Life was never so neat. His wife's undomesticated spirit was tearing their lives apart like a lion bringing down a gazelle, painful to watch, sad, yet natural. Even necessary.

No. I don't wish you to die, brother. No matter the cost.

He slid to the ground, the ruin at his back.

Curran had searched until he found Patrick Hawley in Glenelg's pub. He pulled the man up by his lapels and broke his nose with one blow.

The other men's shocked silence lasted but an instant before they pushed off their stools and stood, forming a half-moon around their laird.

Working his way to his feet and giving Curran a blood-smeared smile, Hawley said, "What lies did she tell you? You've married a whore, in case you haven't realized it yet. She'll cuckold you every time you're not looking. It's what she's always done. And you'll let her, you spineless cunt!"

Curran smashed Hawley's cheekbone. The man flew, crashing into a table. "I'll kill you right now," he shouted, the lust for blood pounding, blinding him.

Only then, as Hawley again pushed himself to his feet, this time more slowly, did Curran notice the wounds. Hawley's face was swollen, covered with purple blotches. His eyes were puffed—the left one nearly shut. The cheekbone Curran had punched split open, releasing blood and pus. He held one arm against his ribs as though protecting it. Had Morrigan done such damage to him? She'd said she had cut him, but these wounds appeared to be some sort of putrefaction.

Patrick touched his cheek and drew away blood-drenched fingers. More blood dribbled from his nostrils. "We'll see." He put his hands on the table, swaying weakly. "You're like a dog, the way you drool after her. I can't say I wouldn't have done the same if I'd found her first, but unlike you, *Master* Ramsay, I know how to keep that bitch in line."

Curran hadn't killed the man though. The others seized him by the arms and prevented it. They told Hawley to get himself out of Glenelg, or they'd let the master loose.

One of them had tripped Hawley as he tried to leave. "You wait," Hawley shouted. "You'll be sorry." He was jeered at and tripped again for speaking like a paddler.

A drop of rain struck, and another. Soon a downpour soaked Curran's clothes and ran down his face. Augustus nickered, shook his head, and trotted to the shelter of the trees behind the ruin.

A horse and rider cantered past on the track. He was startled to recognize his wife, almost as though his thoughts had conjured her. She held her head upraised, her face turned to the sky. He thought he discerned a smile, as though she enjoyed the warm rain caressing her skin.

A gust of wind blew over the stones and through the pines. *Be strong…it* admonished. *Protect.*

He turned, staring at the trees. He wanted to get away from this place that watched and warned. Too many dead spirits lived here. Another movement caught his eye and he looked up. An eagle was circling. Curran watched it, fascinated by its grace as it descended, landing not far from him on a sturdy branch. He'd always loved the creatures, violent and beautiful beyond words, royalty with wings.

Whistling for Augustus, he rode home, following Stoirmeil's fresh watery hoof prints. For some reason, the eagle had given him a sense of hope.

Father Drummond's gig sat in the graveled drive.

"No, I don't want any," he snapped to Fionna's offer of tea. He brushed aside her concern, her exclamations on his poor dripping self and offers to take his wet clothes.

She shrugged and turned away with the parting statement, "I've put Father Drummond in the west parlor."

Curran glanced at the staircase and sighed. The last thing he needed was a sermon. "Give him something to eat. I'll join him after I change."

He leaped up the stairs and paced into the master bedroom. Morrigan wasn't there. Leaving a dripping trail, he continued his search.

The nursery door was ajar, and he heard low singing. He approached, careful to make no sound.

Down by the burn, where birken buds
Wi' dew are hangin clear, my jo,
I'll meet thee on the lea-rig,
My ain kind Dearie O....

She'd changed into a wrapper and had flung her wet hair behind her shoulders. Olivia lay in her arms, giggling as Morrigan danced her around the room. After a moment she lifted the babe and kissed her forehead, her cheeks, and her chin. "Wee pud," she said, burying her nose against the nape of the child's neck. She touched Olivia's toes and stroked the miniature belly, which expanded and contracted in the easy, guileless way of babies. Dropping into the rocking chair, she opened her robe. Olivia nursed happily, kicking. Morrigan hummed and rocked.

Not a fig had she cared about the widespread fear of a spoiled figure from breastfeeding. "A wet-nurse?" she'd said. "That's for grander ladies than me."

How could he have entertained the idea of her harming Olivia? He longed to stop time, capture this picture and trap it in a box so he could relive it whenever he wished. Every smile, every tender stroke she made, not knowing she was being spied upon, proved her adoration.

She switched the wean to her other breast and leaned her head back, closing her eyes.

"Morrigan," he whispered.

Her eyes opened and she glanced about the room, but he was well hidden in the shadows outside the door. "He haunts me," she said. "I hear his voice everywhere."

Olivia lifted her head. She regarded Morrigan, deeply intent.

"Why, what's this?" Morrigan asked. "D'you want to say something, lassikie?" She lifted her daughter, kissing her naked stomach. Olivia gurgled her delight.

Warned by a slight sound, he swiveled. It was Diorbhail, a cup of tea in one hand, holding up the hem of her skirt in the other. She looked as dismayed as he felt.

"I was bringing mistress her tea," she said, low, as if she knew somehow that he didn't want his presence discovered.

He nodded shortly and gestured to her to go on. She passed him with a shy smile and entered the nursery, setting the tea on a table next to Morrigan. She crossed to the far wall, beside the crib, and folded a blanket.

Protect, the pines had commanded. And he would, with his whole being, with everything he had.

Curran watched Morrigan draw the baby close. "No one will ever take you from me," she said, barely loud enough for him to catch the words. "I'll kill them if they try."

Hugh waited a long time for the laird of Kilgarry.

The priest saw the change in him at once. Shadows darkened Curran's eyes. Irritation etched lines around a mouth that used to curve in easy, near-constant laughter.

"Curran," Hugh said. "How are you?"

"Fine." Curran shrugged. "The lambing is going well."

Hugh decided to waste no time. "Your wife has been to see me."

A glitter flickered then disappeared in Curran's eyes, leaving them flat. "Why?"

"She wanted my help."

Dropping into a chair, the lass's husband drummed the surface of a table and sighed. "With what?"

"What's deviling her. It's not caused by you, Curran."

"Scunner it!" Curran rose and paced, rubbing his forehead. "I've tried my best, Father. Apparently, what I'm offering isn't what she requires."

"It is," Hugh said. "Be patient. She's trying her best too."

Curran stopped. "Is she?" he said. "This is her best?"

"You're her husband. You took her to wife, in good times and bad. If you love her, you'll not give up at the first sign of trouble. You'll protect her, like she deserves."

Hugh's voice was sharper than he'd intended. Too sharp, judging from the way Curran's head reared and his eyes widened. No matter. The point must be cemented while he had the man's attention. "Mind, will you, how young and innocent she was when you got her with child—aye, you didn't think that was still a secret, did you? And her father and brother were not faceless strangers to us but locals, known to nearly everyone here, *and,* not a year has passed since they both died. Before she could properly mourn or make peace with her loss, you pushed her into marriage and transported her across the country, away from everything she's ever known. That's not the least of it, is it? She wasn't raised to be a lady but a simple laboring woman. This life is unfamiliar, and I have no doubt it's terrifying. I know she fears shaming you."

"So it's my fault." Curran wearily rubbed his eyes. "I know it. What I did was unforgivable. But I've done everything I can think of to make it right."

Hugh stood. "Aye, you have. You're a good man, Laird. I wish I could tell you what we spoke of today. I know it would ease your worry. But what is said between a priest and a penitent is sacrosanct. So I'll only ask you to be patient awhile longer."

"Douglas beat her. Did she tell you that?" Curran's pacing resembled an angry carnivore. Hugh half-expected to hear a growl.

Pausing before his wife's portrait, Curran stared at it then pivoted. "Her back was covered in welts, this wide, from one of his whippings." He held out his thumb and forefinger. "They were bleeding. She just shrugged. That's how accustomed she was to it. Eleanor thinks Morrigan has...." He stopped. His teeth gritted and he sucked in a harsh breath. "An injury to her brain, and she said it's likely incurable. She suspects that's why Morrigan swoons, and it may be the cause of her nightmares. Now you're telling me she needed more time to mourn his death? Forgive me, Father, I *don't* understand."

Remorse flooded Hugh's throat with bile, but he made himself continue. "He was her father. The only one she had, even if destroyed by madness. Don't you see she feels responsible? Her nightmares are like pages in a book, telling us the story, if we take the time to read them. Morrigan blames herself for her mother's death too, and...and Nick's." His voice broke as he thought of Douglas's son, that braw lad with his mother's enormous blue eyes. He remembered thinking Nicky's eyes were angelic.

Rain pelted the leaded windows like otherworldly fingernails.

"She had nothing to turn to," Hugh said. "When Douglas died, he left his devils to Morrigan, who knew only *his* strength, *his* omnipotence. Some folk ease their pain with prayer, but she couldn't. And she's never witnessed love between a man and woman." The answer exploded, an interior volcano annihilating doubt. "Love, violence, hatred, failure...they're all the same for Morrigan. That's all she knows." Certainty filled his heart. "Don't you see? It's as clear to me as this vase." Prisms flashed through the crystal as he picked it up.

"No, I don't." But Curran's voice slowed like he did see, too well, though he didn't want to.

Hugh set the vase down. "Let me speak to Beatrice. She's the only one left alive who knows everything. She'll understand what drove Douglas."

"The harpy. She won't help you."

"Let me try. And I beg you, don't disown your marriage. Didn't Browning say:

Truth, that's brighter than gem,
Trust, that's purer than pearl,
Brightest truth, purest trust in the universe—
All were for me
In the kiss of one girl.

"That sounds aye secular, Father." A smile played faintly over the young laird's face. "What would the bishop say if he heard you quote that?"

"He is far away in Inverness, and I've a weakness for poetry." Hugh returned the smile, happy to see any hint, no matter how slight, of the Curran Ramsay he knew and loved.

Without hesitation, Curran replied, "Then you'll mind what Burns said:

Their tricks an' craft hae put me daft,
They've taen me in an' a' that.
But clear your decks, and here's—'The Sex!'
I like the jads for a' that.

Hugh grinned.

So did Curran, though he tried not to. Then he called Fionna and asked her to fetch Beatrice. "I'll leave you," he said. "For she'll never say a word with me here."

"Thank you, Curran." Hugh settled himself to wait, enjoying a fresh surge of confidence. Only this morning, he'd mourned his uneventful, unproductive life. Now he felt certain he could serve once more.

But Beatrice refused to share her secrets. He called upon her love, if she had any. "You know why Douglas acted as he did." He smashed his fist against the table, causing knickknacks to jump and jangle in fragile protest. "Tell me. You do want to see your niece happy, don't you?"

Her lips whitened and her eyes turned black, hard and impenetrable as stones.

Hugh's head was throbbing again. He tried to hide it, to level Beatrice with a calm, commanding regard, but sweat broke out in his armpits. He kept thinking of those terrible days after Glenelg burned. They'd never truly faded into the past. They lived on, warping and molding everyone's lives.

"You know," Hugh muttered as he pressed the heels of his hands against his eyelids. "You know—"

"I do know." Beatrice stared him down. "I know many things. Like how little you did after the clearings. You in your cozy cottage, us in the snow."

Hatred so feral sprang from her face it left him speechless. Her presence worked on him like a rope cinched around his throat. Wrinkled, vindictive woman. Everyone knew that Randall Benedict's hired men had come to his home in the middle of the night with torches. They had heard about him taking in two of the cleared villagers, and made it clear that if he did it again, they would tie him to his bed and burn his manse and church around his ears.

"And it was quite plain what you were thinking every time you looked at Hannah," she added, as emotionless as a viper.

He felt the blood drain out of his head like a blade had sliced his jugular. He stuttered something and left her as swiftly as he would run from a demon.

Not until he'd made it halfway home did the trembling subside. Beatrice's face, stony with old hate, kept materializing. *I know many things. Many things.*

He mopped his forehead with his handkerchief, feeling as though he'd tangled with the Devil. Somehow, perceptive Beatrice had discerned his darkest secret…that those many years ago, he, too, had fallen in love with her sister. He was sure he'd kept it hidden in some shamed part of his heart, but maybe Beatrice had a witchy way of seeing.

Mea culpa, he thought, as he'd done hundreds of times when Hannah walked down the main road through Glenelg, leaving every male she passed wrecked and filled with lustful fantasies.

Lost in his guilty thoughts, Hugh belatedly realized his horse had strayed off the track in search of good grazing.

No matter how furiously he blinked, everything remained a blur. He didn't know where he was. Was that the sound of water flowing? Was it still raining? He felt as though he was rising into the air above his body.

Morrigan's voice echoed through his head. *Your church teaches that women are products of the Devil. That we lead men away from God, and that we caused Christ to be crucified.*

He shuddered. "Forgive us."

Woman is an imperfect male, begotten because her father was ill or in a state of sin. Women are not worthy of life. You are the first deserter of the divine law.

Why did he think of these things now? They were ancient teachings, mostly forgotten.

Blinding pain shot through his head. He moaned.

Then he heard an unfamiliar voice.

I sent you a miracle and you have failed her. You and yours will always fail until you return me.

He heard grass rustling, and again the murmur of flowing water. Where was his gig?

A hand clasped his. A beautiful face swam into his eyesight, long auburn hair, eyes luminous with tears. *Hannah, it's you*, he wanted to say, but he couldn't speak.

His attention was drawn from that celestial vision by movement in the sky. An eagle was circling, coming lower, and lower still. Its beak parted and it released a shrill, cold cry.

Oh, God.

Chapter 28

AGNES AND MALCOLM REPORTED FATHER DRUMMOND'S DISAPPEARANCE. A tearful Agnes said he'd never returned to the rectory after visiting Kilgarry, and she was worried half to death. A search party was formed.

Padraig Urquhart found him, hidden in long grass near the river, halfway to Dùn Teilbh. Something—birds maybe, had taken his eyes and pecked holes in his cheeks. Several of his fingers were torn off.

A messenger was dispatched to notify his bishop, and three priests swiftly converged. Dismissing the villagers' protests, two of the priests removed the body to Dumfries, where Father Drummond's brother lived. The third began an investigation. Days were spent poring through his papers and books. Much of it was packed up and taken away.

Folk from every parish up and down the coast came to mourn him at a memorial service arranged by the Laird of Eilginn and his wife.

TIME SPENT WITH OLIVIA BROUGHT WELCOME PEACE. MORRIGAN TOLD HERSELF SHE could endure anything as long as she could be with her child.

She hadn't realized how thoroughly Father Drummond had knitted himself into her heart until she had to face the fact that she would never speak to him again. Remembering his benevolent smile and twinkling eyes, his unruly white shock of hair, his firm, warm handshake, was agonizing. Knowing animals had feasted upon his corpse sickened her. It seemed so disrespectful to a man who had spent his life helping others.

Life returned to a semblance of normalcy, though an invisible chasm remained, formed of questions, mystery, and the unexpected, harrowing loss of a beloved member of their parish.

Why had he gone to see Curran that day? She was too afraid to ask, especially as several times she caught her husband watching her, his gaze somber. Had the priest revealed what she'd told him? Weren't they required to keep confidences a secret? She thought so, but then, what did she really know?

As the days passed and Curran said nothing, her tense muscles relaxed. Still, her last encounter with Hugh weighed upon her. She wished she hadn't burdened him on his final day of life.

Adultery is a fearful sin. It will destroy your family. You'll never see your child again.

She would honor him by living in a way that would make him proud.

Father Drummond had told her about the Celtic war-goddess, *Morrígu*. Tears had filled his eyes when he'd spoken of Hannah. More than anyone else, he had shown a willingness to speak to her about the past.

I'll never see Mackinnon again, she promised him as she carried Olivia through gardens bursting with blooms. Above them, Kilgarry's central keep appeared to move through the heavens like a great ship, its sails formed of puffy white bannocks in an azure sky.

Kyle had transferred hollyhocks from the hothouse to the entry into the hedge maze. Periwinkles and violets filled the shady spots with color. By the garden's sun-warmed wall, lilacs greened and budded. A Scotch Argus fluttered, searching for nectar, while bumblebees hummed from flower to flower. Kilgarry's gardener, swiping one dirty hand across his brow and leaning on his shovel, told Morrigan he couldn't recall a finer spring, and pointed out where he planned to start a batch of Scottish flame flowers.

Lustrous as alabaster, rosy as the interior of a conch shell, Olivia eclipsed it all.

Morrigan observed the changing color and light from a wicker bench in the gazebo. On one side of the path, a marble lion stretched out a paw as if to touch the unicorn on the other side, which dismissively polished its horn against its rump. At the end of the graveled walk, a naked goddess held an amphora from which water flowed.

Had the unicorn just glanced at the lion? Did the goddess's mouth turn up in a sly smile? Morrigan was beguiled into fantasy.

Kyle broke into song as he worked.

Ae fond kiss, and then we sever
Ae farewell, alas forever.

She found peace within Kilgarry's gardens.

"This will be yours someday," she told her daughter. Olivia would have this legacy, the security provided by Curran's wealth. It would be enough.

Washed in sunlight and latticework shadows, she spent every afternoon reading. In some ways, she found a kindred spirit in Emma Bovary. But the woman's stubborn selfishness enraged her and the ending offered no hope.

When she'd first met Curran, he'd asked what she would do with freedom. Hadn't she said she would never marry? Or that she'd not be a man's possession? The exact memory escaped her. But she was married, and from the instant Olivia began forming inside her, she'd lost any possibility of independence, insubstantial though it had been. Olivia stole Morrigan's longed-for emancipation more completely than any man ever could.

Morrigan could not be sorry for it. She would give her freedom and more, if it brought Olivia happiness.

She would do anything for this child. She'd told Father Drummond as much. Protecting a child was not wrong, yet Morrigan knew her fierceness wasn't shared by all women. Females were expected to be delicate and helpless. They were supposed to swoon at the sight of blood and shrink from harming any living thing. Men must perform the crude work of violence so that women could remain pure ideals.

Yet she had to admit Glenelg had introduced her to a whole new breed, an elite corps of naturally strong and practical women. There simply was no room or time to be anything else. These women were the descendants of Scatach and Aife. She suspected every one of them would flay the skin from any fool who might threaten their offspring.

While the babe cooed and played with her fingers, her mother spun fantasies. She saw herself arrayed in trousers, top boots, and rolled up sleeves, dredging ancient civilizations from sand and soil. Curran had mentioned an ongoing excavation for the city of Troy, making her wonder what it would be like to turn a spade of dirt and find a gold bracelet or bit of pottery thousands of years old. How would it be, to earn her own livelihood, to not be dependent on anyone? She could hardly imagine. It was men's domain, and they kept selfish possession of it.

Kyle sang mournfully.

Had we ne'er loved so blindly,
Never met—or never parted—
We had ne'er been broken-hearted.

During the thick soft nights of May, her husband made love to her. He could still compel a fiery response, though she sometimes wept after, silently.

If she had to, she would hang her existence upon self-control for the next fifty years. If it made Olivia and Curran happy, then all would be well.

BUT FOR TESS'S INADVERTENT SLIP, MORRIGAN WOULD NEVER HAVE KNOWN Mackinnon had vanished again.

She was in the garden, reading a letter from Louis Stevenson. He told her he was pondering the idea of writing a book of poems for children. Inspired by what she'd told him about Nicky and the wind, he'd been playing with a wind poem of his own in a child's viewpoint.

"Mistress?"

It was Tess, holding a thick warm plaid. While Morrigan had been reading, the skies had grown heavy, dark, and chilly. She tucked the blanket around Morrigan's shoulders and, glancing at the heavens, said, "I hope Aodhàn Mackinnon finds his way home before it starts to rain."

"Has he been gone?"

"One of his usual disappearances. It does upset Seaghan though, and that upsets my mother. Seaghan won't stop searching, no matter how many times he does this, and no matter how miserable the weather."

"Is anyone helping?"

Tess shrugged and Morrigan's resolve disintegrated. "I'm just sitting here. I'll lend a hand," she said.

She nursed Olivia, saying nothing of her plan to Diorbhail, dressed warmly, and went to the stables. "Would you saddle Stoirmeil for me?" she asked Logan as she drew on her gloves. When he had, she sent the mare from the courtyard in a clattering gallop.

I'm not doing anything wrong, she reassured herself, tapping the reins against her mare's shoulder. She knew she should have said something to Curran, but he would have argued, maybe refused to let her go. Still, he'd been in his study. She'd crept by the door without saying a word. Shame told her she should have done things differently.

"I owe him this," she said, remembering how Mackinnon had searched for her when she was missing, long into the night, how he'd carried her to spare her ankle.

She searched along the coast, then at the cave clearing where they'd last met. She dismounted and walked the path in the Eilanreach, reliving the night of fog, and how his brief, bright elation was ruined by Curran's appearance.

The skies spattered and the wind rose. When she caught up to Seaghan, he seemed pleased and thanked her, but insisted if it started to rain in earnest, she must promise to stop immediately and come to his blackhouse for tea. About Aodhàn, he tried to sound nonchalant. *He'll return,* the brawny fisherman said, *when he's good and ready,* but his eyes said, *will he?*

Morrigan wondered too. Had he decided to go away for her sake and Curran's? Could he dredge up that kind of selflessness?

Seaghan escorted Morrigan to Kilgarry at sunset, and his gratitude deflected Curran's irritation. The next afternoon, Violet brought Morrigan a note. *He came back on his own after midnight,* it said.

Why did he keep doing this? Morrigan's worry turned to anger. She sent Violet to the stables with the order to saddle her mare again and once she assured herself that Olivia wouldn't need her for a while, whipped the horse and raced from the courtyard as though chased by a moaning *bean-sìth.*

All her furious questions vanished when she saw him. He was feverish, every so often muttering unintelligibly. Rolling up her sleeves, she dropped onto a stool by the bed and took over applying wet cloths to his forehead.

"Don't you fret, darling girl." Seaghan knocked a ball of ash from his pipe and put the kettle on to boil. "Aodhàn's prone to these fevers. He'll recover. He always does."

Morrigan's exasperation rose at his careless attitude. "See how restless and hot he is. This could be miasma."

"I've seen what happens to those infected with cholera, child."

"Malaria. Smallpox."

"It's the same nameless fever he's had many times. It clears up after a day or so like nothing ever happened."

"We should fetch Eleanor at least."

"He wouldn't thank you for it." Seaghan relit his pipe and puffed clouds of smoke. "Mind after your wedding, I told you about pulling him from the ocean?"

Morrigan nodded.

"Near dead he was, and no' only from being half-drowned. There was a knife wound in his chest. We stitched it, covered him, and hoped for the best. He lived through that, didn't he, lass?"

Morrigan folded a fresh cloth and dabbed Mackinnon's temples. "Has he still not told you what happened?"

"Won't say a word." Seaghan pointed the stem of his pipe at her. "There wasn't a plume of smoke or a broken board anywhere." He offered a dramatic shrug, a tilt of the head, a mischievous smile. "I've told myself it's indeed possible for a ship to sink in a storm and never a sliver seen again—especially in the seas south of Berneray."

He handed her a cup of tea, lightly infused with milk, she noticed, just as she liked it. "Yet it did seem strange, him floating, alive, no sign of wreckage, nor any other bodies. Only moments could've passed, or he would've been dead, with such a wound, in frigid water." He returned the stem of his pipe to his mouth, sucked in smoke, and shook his head. "Nothing about it seemed probable to my way of thinking."

"You say he'd been stabbed? Maybe he was attacked and thrown off some ship, then it sailed on without him."

"Aye, and an air of mystery draws women like bees to honey. You needn't scowl at me. You're female. And here you are, aren't you? To this day old women up and down the coast make secret signs of protection when Aodhàn passes. We're no' all that far from the Orkneys."

"What've they to do with it?"

"Where d'you think the legend originated?" he asked with exaggerated patience.

"What legend?" Annoyance sharpened her tone.

"The seal-man. Selkies. Orkney folk claim the seal is descended from a royal line. It's within their power to change form at will. You haven't forgotten already, have you?"

Morrigan's throat constricted.

"I am a practical man, of course, and have never believed such daftness. But there remains the fact that Aodhàn didn't drown that day. And he does vanish. He won't say where he goes or why. No one ever sees him. What do you think? Is it the seals he rejoins, in the briny deep?"

She fell into memories of the dream, of the seal beckoning and transforming. Magic existed in the world; this man lying here, so tortured and ill, gave ample proof of it.

Seaghan was trustworthy. She sensed he would understand this strange bond between his friend and the laird's wife, how difficult it was to ignore or deny.

Yet something in his face made her hesitate. Something different from a second ago. She gasped. "You...you're mocking me."

His mouth stretched into a toothy grin. Morrigan rolled her wet cloth into a whip and snapped it against his scalp.

"Ouch," he cried then grinned again, rubbing at the sting. "There's no need for us both to sit here wiping the great wean's brow. I'll see to the hens. Call if you need me." Chuckling at his own wit, he scooped up his cap and left.

It wasn't long before Mackinnon's fever spiked. Heat rolled off him and he thrashed. Morrigan wanted to fetch Seaghan, but feared her patient might injure himself.

His eyes opened, glinting with unhealthy pinpoints of light. "*A rùin mo chridhe.*" He seized her arms. "Aridela...."

"Shhh, Mackinnon," she said. "It's Morrigan." Again she reeled at the way he seemed to know her inner fantasies. How did he do that?

He lifted up off the bed, squeezing her arms. "I cannot give in. I won't."

"You don't have to," Morrigan said gently, hoping to bring him some kind of peace.

"I will best her...."

"Why can't you just live and be happy, Mackinnon?"

His stare was alternately blank then coherent. "Without you?" He pulled her closer and pressed his face against her throat. It was frighteningly hot.

These ramblings were no doubt caused by fever. But the suffering in his voice made her long to give him relief. She kept her voice calm and low. "Here, Mackinnon. I have beef and barley soup. It will make you feel better."

"I carry the memories. Every life…every death…every moment of torture. She forces them into me, trying to break me. I won't…I won't give in."

"Aye, Mackinnon." She stroked his cheek. "You'll win."

"She's fading. None remember her."

Nicky had fallen ill once and had made similar, nonsensical statements. When he improved, he couldn't remember the things he'd said and accused her of lying about it.

"Morrigan…." Mackinnon's voice trailed off. Then he added that other name. "Aridela. I've missed you." He fell back, limp as a drowned kitten. "Your touch is cool."

It sounded like he was calling *her* Aridela. She dunked the cloth into the water, wrung it out, and placed it on his forehead. As soon as he was himself again, she would ask him where he'd heard that name.

His left hand trailed up his chest. He grabbed at something, a chain around his neck, and pulled a pendant out from under his damp sark. After a moment his hand fell away, revealing a flat silver circle with a beautifully worked design.

A blue stone, embedded between two crescents. The stone winked as it caught the light.

Hesitantly, she touched it, brushing the bead with her fingertips. The resulting shock made her gasp and jerk away.

The pendant seemed familiar. Yet she couldn't recall ever seeing it before.

Perhaps she'd imagined that jolt. She touched it again, and again recoiled.

This was silly. If it was hot it was because of Mackinnon's fever. She lifted the pendant away from his skin, holding it by the chain.

The detail was stunning, the delicate carvings perfect in every way. The dark blue stone in the center was injected with subtle veins of white; it was so shiny she saw her face reflected in it.

Another gasp escaped when Mackinnon spoke. She'd been lost inside the gem. It swam before her eyes, filling her senses with sound.

"Morrigan…."

He stared at her intently.

"Mackinnon." She returned the pendant to his chest, leaving her palm over it.

"Come with me." His voice was unguarded, openly pleading. "We'll start again. D'you love me enough?" He gripped her hand.

"You want me to run away? Abandon my child?"

"Your mother tortures me. The bitch."

"My mother is long dead, Mackinnon. She can't harm you."

"I'm so alone."

"I know."

"God should save me, but he does nothing. He never…does anything."

"Rest now. Sleep."

His hand fell. His eyes closed. In a faltering voice, he said, "Everything is spoiled. We should die and start over somewhere else. Aye, just die and start over."

Who was this female he raved about? The mother, the bitch? And why did he keep repeating *Aridela,* as though it was her name?

Confusion and desire clashed with fear and anger.

Who was this man? What was his true purpose? What did he want of her?

A few minutes later he broke out in a cleansing sweat. His breathing slowed and he fell into peaceful sleep.

MIDNIGHT HAD COME AND GONE BY THE TIME MORRIGAN RETURNED TO KILGARRY, but Diorbhail was waiting for her, sitting on the bottom step of the staircase. Fionna stood next to her.

"Why aren't you sleeping?" Morrigan asked. "Is something wrong?"

Diorbhail waved towards the drawing room's open door. "Master Curran," she said, not meeting Morrigan's eyes. "He's waiting for you."

As Morrigan started towards the door, Diorbhail added, low, "Careful."

Morrigan paused at the warning. She saw apprehension in Fionna's face.

"Morrigan." It was Curran, his voice oddly rough. He must have heard her.

She entered the drawing room, pulling off her gloves. She'd known he wouldn't like the way she'd gone off, twice in two days, without a word, and both times because of Mackinnon. Now they would argue.

The sight of him brought her up short. He stood by the sofa, the lamp casting shadows across his face.

"Where have you been?" he asked.

"Mackinnon has caught some kind of fever. I've been there, helping Seaghan with him."

She caught a scent of whisky, and noticed the empty bottle and an over-turned glass on the table. A dark wet stain marred the carpet.

"They've told me what you've done," he said. "Diorbhail and the rest. Oh, they didn't betray you. It was what they didn't say."

Despair took root, twining down inside, and her palms began to sweat. She may not have cuckolded him with her body, but could she say the same of her heart?

"A woman should never hold herself so cheaply. It goes against the laws of God and man."

Instantaneous fury burned away the guilt. She heard herself speak and was amazed. "God and man. Women count for nothing, and yet we're obliged to follow the laws of God and man."

She thought she heard a gasp from outside the room.

Curran's stare intensified. "What is going on between you and Aodhàn?"

"Am I not expected to help your tenants? He helped you when I was missing. He was ill. Seaghan and I got his fever down, though, if you care."

His mouth worked. She waited, hiding her inner turmoil, not nearly as confident or outraged as she sounded.

He crossed to her. His hands clenched and rose. Shock flooded through her at the all-too-familiar gesture, but he grabbed the bottle from the table, smashed it against the edge, and swiveled away. He dug at his scalp with rigid fingertips and spoke something in Gaelic.

Her own hands curled into fists. Long experience had taught her that men would subjugate women by whatever means necessary, including pain and intimidation. They called women who wanted the same freedoms they took for granted whores, sluts, and a hundred other vile titles, which no doubt he'd just done.

Yet, a quiet thought interjected, even drunk and goaded, Curran stopped himself from striking her. Douglas had never shown such restraint.

Morrigan clutched the table, her arms and legs shaking. The whisky glass rolled and fell to the floor. She followed, dropping onto the carpet.

Curran knelt before her. "Something is different," he said. "You're different."

"Leave me alone." She closed her eyes, blocking out all she couldn't bear to face. Curran was the last person, besides Olivia, that she'd wanted to hurt. Yet she had, and she hated herself for it.

He lifted her in his arms and rose.

She placed her hand over his heart. She didn't know what he would do. Maybe he meant to kill her.

He carried her into the now-empty foyer and up the stairs to their bedroom. Kicking the door closed behind him, he dropped her on the bed.

Low light flickered from a single lamp. At first he glared and paced, but, as she lay there watching him, his shoulders drooped. His hands relaxed.

"What's happened to us?" he asked. "I've frightened you. Christ, what am I becoming?"

Morrigan rose on her knees and put her hands on his shoulders. Awash with sorrow, she brought his face to the curve of her throat.

He grasped her arms. "My Morrigan," he said, shuddering.

Compassion and tenderness poured through her. She pulled him onto the bed and covered his face with kisses.

At first he didn't respond, but soon his grip tightened. He returned her kisses. His body shoved against her in a delirium of passion, and he was again a man.

"Love me," she said, as she had in the old days, before he'd brought her here to this place, to Mackinnon. "Love me, Curran," she pleaded, as his mouth ignited fire in her blood. "Love me forever."

The Pilgrimage

Chapter 1

Twice, on the boat, she'd come to sit beside him, tucking her hand in his, once resting her cheek on his shoulder as she closed her eyes and turned her face to the wind. Still, though, nothing felt right. He continued to long for the girl who had enticed him so thoroughly in Stranraer. He'd suffered no doubts then. Now there was nothing but doubt. Only when she held Olivia did he glimpse any genuine, spontaneous joy. The babe certainly delighted in nothing as much as her doting mother. Morrigan could swiftly coax paroxysms of infectious giggles to replace the most furious tantrum.

Hugh Drummond had accused him of stealing Morrigan's innocence, pushing her into marriage, failing to give her time to mourn the deaths of her father and brother.

Shame soured his dinner. It was too bad, since the haddock was freshly caught, delicately fried, and delicious. He poured another whisky and refilled Morrigan's glass with sherry. The crisp air had stimulated her appetite; she'd swiftly consumed her fish, along with two slightly burned girdle scones.

"Careful," he said, "or we'll run clean out of food, and one fine day they'll find our skeletons covered in moss."

She instantly looked guilty, which made him laugh. "I was teasing. The loch has enough fish for a hundred years, and you'd hurt Tom's feelings if you didn't show proper appreciation for his cooking."

Morrigan glanced over her shoulder. Two of the ghillies were laughing and roughhousing as they finished erecting the third tent. Tom, who'd fried their haddock, was scouring his skillet with sand.

"D'you realize it's been a year since we met?" Curran slid his hand across the table to clasp hers.

"A year and a month," she replied. "I've been thinking of that lately, of the golden god who walked across the moor and forever changed my life." She paused, her lids dropping over her eyes. "So…how d'you feel about it these days?" Her smile started bravely but quickly turned tremulous.

"Remember when I said I'd always felt something was missing, something I needed more than anything else?"

"Aye," she said, her voice husky.

"And d'you mind me telling you that it disappeared that day on the moor?"

"Aye," she said, almost in a whisper, and stole a glance at him.

"It's never returned." He brought her hand up to kiss her fingers and turned it so he could do the same to that mark on her wrist, the one that came to him sometimes in disjointed dreams, but on another woman.

Her smile grew more confident, and her eyes darkened in that unconsciously seductive way she had.

What Hugh accused him of was true. He had pushed her into marriage, but what else could have been done? Her pregnancy stripped them both of choices. Nevertheless, he caught himself thinking, *I caged her, the same as Douglas, and she let me.*

"You'll show me…where you had the dream?" Her question startled him from his oppressive thoughts.

"If you insist." He looked over the deep, cold, blue waters of Loch Torridon. He could scarcely believe he'd dragged her, and Diorbhail, and Olivia to this wild, empty place, and in such a precipitous manner. He hadn't even given them time to pack any clothes.

He had scribbled a note to Quinn, though. *Go to Barra. Discover what you can.* He gave it to Fionna as they were leaving, with instructions to post it without delay.

Morrigan hadn't made a single protest. She hadn't even asked where they were going. Kyle drove them to the ferry, where Curran compelled the ferryman to take them where he wanted to go. On the way, his anger cooled by wind and water, he realized he couldn't simply vanish into the wilderness with nothing but what he wore, like he had as a boy with the alarming Fearghas.

He'd gone on an African safari when he was twenty-one. Using that experience, he had the ferryman dock at Kyle of Lochalsh, where he purchased everything he thought they would need—cloth, buttons, and batting for Olivia's hippins, blankets, sherry, tea, and whisky, bread and cheese, tents, cots, lamps, boots, dresses, shawls, and jackets for the women, rough crofter's clothing for himself. Lastly, he hired three experienced ghillies to go along and take care of the hunting, fishing, and other labor.

Once loaded, the ferry carried them right into the upper loch at Torridon and left them on the south shore, under the watchful gaze of Beinn Alligin, and the majestic, towering bulk of Liathach.

He rubbed the scar by his eye, for it had begun to throb. "Tonight's the full moon," he said.

"I want to find the exact spot and be there, all night, if necessary. I want this."

"If nothing happens, you'll think I made it all up to trick you."

"I mind like it was yesterday you telling me about Fearghas, and diving into the loch." She frowned at the water. "The castle. The lion. The lady it guarded."

"We should set off. It'll be dark soon and this is unforgiving land."

"Let me take care of Olivia first." Diorbhail was entertaining the wean by scooping water and letting it run from her fingers. Morrigan joined them, picking Olivia up and swinging her before disappearing into the tent.

There were three tents, the biggest for himself and Morrigan, the second for Diorbhail and Olivia, and lastly one for the three men, though they scoffed and said it would have to rain enough to raise the level of Loch Torridon to the summit of Beinn Alligin before they would use it.

The moon was rising by the time they left. Diorbhail was settling down for sleep with the baby, a lamp throwing her shadow onto the sides of the tent as she prepared for bed. Curran had even purchased a small cradle, though he wondered, as all this gear was unloaded from the ferry, what they would do when it came time to leave again. He couldn't remember ever doing anything quite so impetuous—well, except for that day on the moor outside Stranraer. As if reading his thoughts, Morrigan slipped her hand into his and smiled, and everything fell into place. It had been a long time since she had responded to him so guilelessly, without another man lurking, shadowy and threatening, in her eyes.

The three ghillies, Tom, Dougal, and Zachary, thought a nighttime hike—especially with a woman—foolhardy, even dangerous. Each offered to come along, but Curran refused. "I know where I'm going," he said. "It's not far."

They grudgingly acceded, though he couldn't be absolutely sure one of them wouldn't sneak along behind at a safe distance.

He took her east, over uneven, rocky terrain, then angled south, between two craggy hills, assisting her where it was slippery. The moon ascended, full and bright, helping them find their way. After a half-hour or so, they topped a barren rise and looked down. Below lay a lochan, a mere tarn really, nothing like grand Torridon. Curran, pleased to have found his objective so quickly, took Morrigan's hand and they descended, sliding a bit on the loose rocks.

They circled around to the far side. "This is it," he said. "The exact spot."

She found an area of flattened stone near the water and sat, wrapping her arms around her knees, gazing at the opaque, motionless surface of the tarn.

He joined her, laughing. "You can't resuscitate my dream by staring at it," he said gently.

"Curran, don't be sensible and dull. Don't spoil the tale. I've never forgotten. Never."

He put his arm around her shoulders. "It's only my foreboding that makes me try," he said, kissing her temple. "It was one thing, to be here alone. It's quite another to be here, with you."

Morrigan rested her head on Curran's shoulder as fog swirled. She saw her breath, and was glad for her jacket and gloves. Curran had brought a blanket; he draped it over them, cocooning them in shared warmth.

Above the impenetrable black horizon of enclosing mountains, stars glittered wildly. Morrigan listened, sure she would hear them, for all their shifting movement, but there was only silence.

She remembered how the mist crept through the window at Diorbhail's bothy, how it had taken Curran's shape. It seemed prophetic that here she was again, watching mist form, Curran warm against her.

He'd done this for no other reason than because she'd asked it of him. She turned into him and drew his mouth to hers. "Thank you," she said.

It was the first time they'd been alone since Glenelg. Their kisses soon turned urgent, demanding. Neither spoke of tenderness and love, nor spoke at all, but for Morrigan at least, it didn't matter.

Afterwards, when they returned from passion, Curran sat up and so did she, grateful to abandon the bed of unyielding rock. He draped his coat over her shoulders and held her, keeping her warm under the blanket and against his body.

It was hard to stay alert. She dozed off, again and again, starting awake each time, until, finally, Curran's stroking made sleep impossible to combat.

Will you come with me?

Curran stood beside the water, holding out his hand. The moonlight reflecting off his clothing created a halo, and flashed against the narrow band circling his head.

Behind him, a plank extended to the deck of a fantastical boat, the like of which she knew didn't exist in Scotland or anywhere. It was crafted of pure white wood, and all around it water foamed as though the boat fought its anchor, impatient to be away. Into the prow was carved a full-breasted woman, who turned her head and gazed at them impassively.

Morrigan took one step, and another. She extended her hand, enthralled. But as her fingers touched his, she woke, jerking up from Curran's lap with a startled intake of breath. He stroked her hair but didn't look at her. He was staring at the tarn. Following his gaze, she gasped again. Three women were floating above the water, holding hands, engulfed in halos as the dream-Curran had been. The first had deep red hair; the second's was white, like the moonlight shining upon it, and the third, black as the heavens. Their gowns were translucent, like pearls, and they wore silver crowns. All three gazed at Curran with clear, unwavering love.

Curran nodded towards the lady with the red hair. "That one is the gate-keeper. She led me into the palace. The woman in the middle cauterized my wounds and spoke to me of my quest." He motioned towards the last, the one with black hair, and his voice roughened. "She was imprisoned by the lion."

Morrigan had already recognized her. She stared, unable to breathe.

The black-haired woman glided towards them. Morrigan was startled to see her own birthmark on this phantom's wrist as she lifted her hand. *Will you come with me?* the woman asked, though Morrigan didn't see her lips move.

Morrigan felt Curran's body straining. She sensed how strongly he wanted to go, how irresistible he found this being. She could hardly blame him. She, too, was compelled.

"Will they take us to the castle?" she asked, but the sound of her voice woke her. She was lying with her head in Curran's lap, and he was looking down at her tenderly.

"Were you dreaming?" he asked.

It took a moment to return to the world, to Scotland, to the wee tarn in the cradle of the mountains, where there were no women, or boat, or youthful haloed god. "Aye," she said, a catch in her voice.

CURRAN HAD WATCHED HER AS SHE SLEPT. HER FACE GLOWED, NOT FROM moonlight but a haze of lavender, and, he'd swear, streaks of purest gold. He knew he must be imagining such a thing, but the colors remained, even after he rubbed his eyes. It wasn't the first time he'd seen the phenomenon. When it happened, there was an accompanying shiver, like the vibration that came of being too close to a lightning strike.

She sat up, drawing the blanket closer. "How long have I been asleep?"

"A few hours. I didn't like to disturb you." He stretched his legs, which had become painfully cramped.

"Did you sleep?" she asked.

"No. I've been watching the moon."

"So you didn't…see anything?"

He hesitated. He wanted to tell her how a woman formed in the mist and placed a cool, damp palm against his cheek. He wanted to tell her that this apparition spoke. *I miss you, Menoetius.* But he couldn't repeat such a thing to his wife. He couldn't expect her to understand the grief and longing that welled through him, or how he knew the apparition and Morrigan were, somehow, the same person. She would be hurt by his overwhelming impulse to rise, fling off his clothes, and dive into the tarn.

So he only said, "The mist takes on shapes, much like clouds."

She frowned. "I wish I hadn't fallen asleep. But I did dream. There were three women standing upon the water, and I-I knew them, as if they were my sisters. No, more than that. Other sides of me." She stood, wrapping the blanket around her like a robe, and walked so close to the water's edge that the toes of her boots were submerged. "There was a boat. A live, living boat. I wanted so much to get on it. It wanted to take me somewhere I've always longed to go. And you, Curran…." She faced him. "You were there, ready to board with me, ready and willing to take one last voyage. A final journey to finish it all."

He stood and joined her at the water's edge.

"But what would be finished?" she asked, her voice muffled against him.

"It's almost dawn. Let's go back." This place left him sad and anxious. Anything could happen here, of that he was certain. He rubbed her arms to get her blood moving. "I predict you'll be starved by the time we reach camp. Tom'll have to catch ten fish for you. Maybe twenty."

"Oh, stop it," she said, but laughed.

He took the blanket from her shoulders and tossed it to the ground. "I rather like you in nothing but my coat."

She turned her face up for his kisses and wrapped her arms around his neck, which caused his coat to gape open. He slid his hands inside, around her waist. "You're warm in here," he said, pulling her close.

But time was passing, and this wasn't getting her dressed. He positioned her chemise and laced her corset. Then he couldn't resist lifting her hair to place a line of kisses under her ear and down her neck.

She leaned against him. "Unlace it again," she whispered, which, of course, he did.

THE SUN WAS PEEKING ABOVE THE REDDISH PEAK OF SGURR RUADH WHEN THEY returned to camp. Two of the ghillies had hiked over to Loch Damph and caught fifteen wild brown trout. The air was fragrant with the scent of frying fish. Diorbhail brought the baby, who grinned at the sight of her mother. Both appeared well rested, which was more than Curran could claim. Morrigan took Olivia and went off towards the water, Diorbhail trailing along, the two of them talking and laughing, thick as thieves, like always. The unplanned abandonment of Kilgarry seemed to agree with Diorbhail, and Olivia. Watching them, Curran's guilt lessened; for the first time, he wondered if the oppression he'd begun to feel there had filtered into them as well.

This sense of freedom was bittersweet. It had always been Kilgarry where he was happiest, in control of his life and destiny. Now it appeared he could only recapture that bliss by leaving Kilgarry behind.

I never want this to end, he thought as he watched the two women and his child cavorting beside the loch, and smelled the mouth-watering aroma of frying fish over an open fire. But what did that mean? That they would gad about Scotland like gypsies for the rest of their lives? He couldn't do that. His tenants at Glenelg relied upon him to make decisions about the land. His business partners in Glasgow needed him as well. His child must be educated. He had obligations.

So, grudgingly, he approached the ghillies after they'd breakfasted and asked them how they might make arrangements to leave Torridon.

CURRAN AND MORRIGAN, WITH OLIVIA IN TOW, WALKED OVER TO LOCH DAMPH.

Olivia was fussy. Morrigan opened her blouse, unfastened the top clasps on the corset, and nursed her child.

She wore no hat. The sunlight glanced against her hair, causing strands of auburn to glint and dazzle. Part of a poem by Wordsworth came to Curran unbidden:

A lovely apparition, sent
To be a moment's ornament.

The composition he'd once considered boringly sentimental suddenly seemed resplendent. Why did he feel he'd loved this woman for as long as clouds had formed in the sky? That he could lose everything without regret if he could keep her? Nothing else mattered in the end, not Kilgarry, not his livelihood. Nothing.

...All things else about her drawn
From May-time and the cheerful dawn;

It was a fair description. Crimsons, greens, bronzes. Dawn colors mixed on an artist's palette to create a masterpiece.

A dancing shape, an image gay,
To haunt, to startle, and waylay.

For as long as he drew breath, he would remember this moment, on this morning, at the edge of this deep blue loch.

A trout leaped and splashed. "It'll be a fine day," he said.

Gently rocking the wean, Morrigan asked, "Which is real?"

He met her gaze. "What?"

"Our world, or the one in there?" She nodded at the water. "The one with the lion you fought?"

"Oh." Half-unconsciously, he traced the scar by his eye.

"Look. There we are, in the water. Are they real? Are we the reflections? Do they laugh, weep, and love? Are their lives like ours, or different?"

"We're real." The wind had pulled some hair loose from the knot at her neck. He tucked it behind her ear.

"How can you be sure?"

"They're only there when we're here."

"You don't know that. When you're not here, how do you know what's in the water? You can't. Maybe *they* imagine *us*. Maybe they're living their lives, and that's where our dreams come from."

"These are deep thoughts."

"You told me you weren't sure that what happened to you was a dream. What if, in every pool of water, there's a castle. Lions. Women so bonny they must be divine." She paused. "Have I ever told you about Diorbhail's life in Stranraer?"

"Just that she lost her child."

"She had no husband, and so she was persecuted. Boys threw rocks and shouted hateful things at her. Awful things. No woman would speak to her. She was reviled by the entire town."

He blinked, and again saw Father Drummond's face. Had Morrigan only married him to escape Diorbhail's fate?

And Diorbhail. The thought of her being pummeled with rocks sent fury boiling through him. He wanted to line up her tormenters and throw stones at *them*.

"Once she approached me." Morrigan smiled as she stroked Olivia's curls. "All I could think of was how much trouble I'd be in if Beatrice or Papa found out I'd talked to the local whore. She said something I've never forgotten."

"What was it?" he asked, when she didn't continue.

"She said men fear the shadows women throw. She said that's why they submerged us." Her expression grew pensive as she stared at the water. "D'you think that's where women's souls are? Shadows trapped in nets, deep in the water where they cannot cause problems?"

"Oh, I don't know. You've caused me a problem or two. Maybe we forgot to trap yours. Maybe you trapped mine instead."

"Did I?" She regarded him somberly. "I wish—"

"What?"

"We didn't trap each other. I wish we, all of us, could escape our shadows and become real."

They were quiet. Curran threw a pebble and watched the ripples spread. "Had you been a man," he said, "you could've been a philosopher."

"But because I have a womb, I can never be more than this." She tilted her chin towards Olivia. "Perhaps," she said, "I'm beginning to understand."

"Aye?" The slight upward curve of her lips made him stupid. He spoke without thinking, not knowing from where the words came. "That men's achievements are nothing in comparison?"

She met his gaze and leaned closer.

He put his arm around her shoulders. She nestled willingly, the old Morrigan returned, if only for a moment.

He cleared his throat, yet still heard subtle unevenness as he said, "Where to next? It's your turn."

She tilted her head inquiringly.

"I don't want to go home," he said. "Do you?"

"No," she said after a moment. "My turn?"

"Aye. Pick a place. Anyplace."

She thought awhile as she dropped stones into the water. Finally, she met his gaze and said, "Cape Wrath."

He started to ask her why but decided against it, not wanting her to feel as though she needed to justify her choice. "Cape Wrath," he said, and nodded. "We'll leave first thing in the morning—if the ghillies can find us a boat."

Chapter 2

Morrigan stood on the high cliffs, fighting to keep her balance in a powerful wind.

Eamhair was her name.

She made out a few lines in the grass, darker green tracings, perhaps all that remained of the ancient stronghold Aodhàn had described. The lighthouse behind her could have been built right over Eamhair's home, interring her voice, and the voice of her lover.

He was born of the night, and the long secret hours lasses spend alone in their beds.

The tale passed through her memory like a physical caress. *I am yours and you are mine. Would you see me wed to another?*

Drops of rain splattered her face, or perhaps it was seawater, flung on the wind. The land dropped away at her feet, so sheer it caused hints of vertigo.

She found land's edge, where mist washed the precipices and salt surf eroded the cliffs.

Eamhair's presence merged with her, placing insubstantial hands on her shoulders. Where had she chosen to jump when she'd tried to kill herself? Morrigan needed to know. She walked back and forth, certain some inner sense would alert her when she found it. There were so many jagged boulders below. Yet Eamhair had found a place that wouldn't crush her.

Hadn't Mackinnon said the seal-lover carried Eamhair out of the sea and placed her on sand? There was no beach that she could see. No sand. Nothing but granite, pointed rocks, and restless tides.

It was a story. Something he made up. There are no selkies. She doused the tale with a frigid downpour of logic. *This proves it. There is no sand, and nowhere to jump where she wouldn't have been shattered on the rocks.*

Morrigan gazed at the enormous, heavy swells. *No place to launch a currach, either.*

Mackinnon had beguiled her with a faery tale. She wished now she hadn't chosen Cape Wrath as their next destination. The chronicle of Eamhair and her wraith-like lover could have lived on, untarnished, unchallenged. Now it was ruined.

Her thoughts were in such turmoil that she didn't hear Diorbhail until the woman was nearly upon her. With one shrewd glance into Morrigan's face, Diorbhail clasped her hand and held it without speaking until Morrigan could breathe again, could return from disappointment and mangled illusions.

"Why d'you stand here, looking as though you've lost your only friend?" Diorbhail asked.

"I was dreaming." Morrigan was ashamed to be caught in such foolishness. "Where's Olivia?"

"With Master Ramsay. He's the one pointed you out up here, and suggested I keep you company. But if you'd prefer to be alone, I can go."

"No. I'm being daft." She remembered something Diorbhail and she had talked about on the long voyage, in the stinking skaffie with its leering, scruff-faced captain, the only one they could find who was willing to ferry them, at, of course, an outrageous fee. "You were born near here."

"Aye, by Durness." Diorbhail cocked her chin to the east.

"D'you know this place?"

"Aye, I came here now and then. No one was ever here but for the light-house keepers. Sometimes they gave me soup and bread."

"I don't suppose there's a beach anywhere?"

"Aye there is, over there." She pointed, east again. "See the stack in the water? Right there. Folk who live around here call it Kearvaig." She turned, gesturing to the south. "There's another beach that way. I loved sitting on the sand, listening to the roar of the sea and the call of the kittiwakes. I've seen whales, too."

"Are they far?"

Diorbhail looked slightly puzzled. "The whales?"

"The beaches. Can we walk to them?"

"Aye," Diorbhail said. "Kearvaig is the closest."

"Would you take me?"

Morrigan followed Diorbhail's unhesitating steps along the coastline. Eventually they descended between several ridges until they found themselves on a sheltered sandy beach, framed at one end by the sea stack, rising offshore like a watchtower, and a great mess of stones, as though a child had thrown its blocks in a fit of rage. Yet, beyond them, Morrigan saw how the cliffs climbed higher, with straight, steep, plummeting precipices, lacking, as far as she could tell, those pulverizing rocks at the bottom.

An uneasy thrill ran through her.

He carried her from the sea and placed her on the sand. 'The songs you sang brought me to you. I thought no harm would come of it, and I could not keep away. But I was wrong. Now we love each other and you have chosen death.'

Clouds of fulmars flew in and out of the cliffs, and the darker shags, and a thousand and one kittiwakes, all making a ruckus in competition with the massive, awe-inspiring boom of the sea.

Her lover was also a king. He ruled over the vast, spraying ocean. Though he'd proven himself wise, strong, a ferocious warrior when necessary, he hadn't the strength or ferocity to leave her, nor could she leave him. She pledged herself to him there, near the ocean at the tip of Scotland.

"Morrigan…Morrigan."

It took her a moment to realize Diorbhail was speaking. "Sorry?" She blushed, for as she'd gazed upon the sand, her imagining of Eamhair, with tresses of copper and a mouth of autumn ivy red, and the selkie, dark-haired and green-eyed, had been erotic.

"I was thinking of one of my visions," Diorbhail said. "That your mam gave birth to you in the forest, by the mountain, so that you'd have the strength of the mountain when you fight the seal."

Morrigan stared. *How does she know what I am thinking? Have I no secrets from her?*

"Aye," Diorbhail said. "It came to me at Torridon. I saw many dead trees on the slopes of Liathach, from a fire, maybe. And I thought of how the tides rise and fall every day in their eagerness to consume the land. Yet the mountains remain, unmoved, unchanged. Snow does no' wear them away, nor wind, nor fire. The seal will try to master you. But he'll fail, unless you turn your back on the mountain and invite him in."

Morrigan blushed again. From the moment she'd approached land's end this morning, she'd been lost in Mackinnon's faery tale. She'd rejected the mountain without realizing it, to reach for the seal.

Diorbhail didn't know Mackinnon's story of Eamhair. Morrigan had never shared it. Yet, somehow the woman sensed that something was wrong, something was trying to rip her away from Curran and Olivia.

"Tell me." Morrigan rubbed her temples, trying to soothe the headache that had plagued her all morning. "Is there a place where the water is gentle enough to launch a wee boat, a coracle or currach?"

"The Kyle," Diorbhail said. "The Kyle of Durness, near where we landed yesterday, as long as the wind is calm. 'Tis so shallow, anything much bigger would run aground. But a coracle would swamp when it reached open water, and a currach too, unless it was built to be seaworthy." She waited, her gaze now questioning.

In the secret way no human knows, the seal changed Eamhair, and in the changing, healed her wounds and broken bones. Together the lovers swam away, and were never seen upon the land again.

Morrigan couldn't meet that expectant gaze. "Are you hungry? Let's go before Curran comes searching."

CURRAN'S LUNGS BURNED, BUT HE COULDN'T STOP RUNNING. IF HE DID, THE CHIEF and his men would catch them. He and the woman, *Eamhair,* had to reach the shore, where a boat was waiting to carry her away from her father and brothers.

Her ankle was injured. Running was hard for her. She began limping. In the end, he had to carry her.

There was the inlet, and the currach, just as Taranis had promised. They'd made it.

He placed her in the boat but she refused to release him. *I won't go without you,* she cried.

Then their pursuers were upon them.

He tried again to make her go, but she wouldn't. She was screaming.

Curran woke. Cold drafts slipped through the cracks into the bothy. The lighthouse keepers had offered it to the travelers, but warned it was old and in bad condition. The chill cleared his head from the life-and-death struggle in his memory.

It was Morrigan screaming.

He pulled her into his arms, though she clawed at him and fought until sense returned. Then she collapsed into his embrace.

"You were dreaming," he said.

She nodded.

"So was I."

She murmured, "It was…."

"Hideous."

Diorbhail came to the bed in her thick woolen nightgown, holding a candle. "What happened?" she asked, setting the candle on the rickety table by the bed. Over in her cradle, Olivia began to fret.

"She had a bad dream," Curran said. "Please, would you see to Olivia?"

Morrigan sat up. "I was being stoned!" Her eyes were huge and stricken. She stared at Curran then pressed her hands against his cheeks, moving them up and down and through his hair, as though to make certain he was real and uninjured. She blinked and drew in a deep breath. All the color fled her face. "No," she cried, and fainted.

Curran extricated himself to fetch the bucket of water, and cooled her hot forehead with a wet handkerchief.

She woke after a moment. "What?" she whispered. "A…nightmare." She glanced jerkily around the cramped room. "I'm so dizzy."

He patted her forehead and cheeks with the handkerchief, saying nothing, though inside he careened at the possibility that they'd each dreamed of the same event. He could almost hear the dull thunk of the first stone striking the sand beside him as he tried to shield the woman.

What had she called him in the dream? *Cailean*….

Nothing but a nightmare, and yet….

"That's bonny," Morrigan said of his ministrations, and soon fell asleep again, her head resting on his shoulder. In the morning she regained her composure, though she was quiet, and ate only a bite or two of bread, washing it down with tea. Diorbhail suggested they walk over to the other beach with Olivia, saying it was pretty. Curran said he wanted to go the opposite way, so they separated after breakfast. Curran watched them until they were out of sight, then he went in search of the lighthouse keepers.

"Aye," said Donald, the grey-bearded senior keeper, "there are legends attached to this place." He drew in a mouthful of smoke and released it appreciatively. "Ghost stories."

"Have you ever heard of the murder of a young woman?" Curran asked. "A stoning?"

The tobacco in the man's pipe crackled again. "There is a tale about that. Folk do say they see her from time to time, floating over the cliffs, weeping. You should speak to my assistant. Jasper claims to have seen her with his own two eyes. He's inside, making a supply list."

Jasper was pleased to share the tale. He and Curran walked to the cliffs, where the murdered woman was most often seen moaning and calling for someone. He described her as young, with a great mass of hair.

"What do they say happened?" Curran made an effort to sound no more than mildly curious.

"A sad but common story. An unmarried woman fallen into shame, worse, supposedly, because her da was chief in these parts. It's said she was stoned to death, and a man killed as well. Perhaps the father of her child, who knows?" With a careless shrug, Jasper added, "Such details never survive the passage of time. Have you heard of our tunnels?"

"No," Curran said, feeling oddly off balance.

"Come with me." Jasper took Curran into the lighthouse and threw open a trap door at the back, revealing a set of stone steps winding into the earth. Once he'd lit a lamp, he descended, motioning to Curran to follow. The air was musty, with a briny tinge of seawater.

At the bottom of the steps, Jasper held up the lamp, sending beams of light down long passageways that extended in three directions. "Unfortunately, they're all blocked nowadays with dirt and sand, but for that one, which takes you to a sea cave. I've found seal bones there." He pointed. "This one leads south a wee way, to what we think was probably a secret escape route in and out of the fortress. Aye, there was once a walled fort somewhere around here. I believe stones from the ruin were used in the making of this lighthouse. That way," he pointed again, "leads to the Kyle of Durness, and we believe it did go all the way at one time, because though it's blocked now, we found the entrance on the Kyle side, and it lines up with this one."

The tunnels were intriguing, but Curran wasn't sure how they tied in with the poor murdered girl. In his dream, he'd known the men coming after them meant to kill her. He'd been desperate to save her, but he'd not had the sense that she was with child.

"There's one more thing to show you." Jasper took him into the tunnel leading to the sea. Curran heard the hollow booming echo of water ahead.

"Here." Jasper held his lamp close to the wall. There was a rock embedded in the dirt. Something was scratched into it.

"Are those words?"

"They're old Celtic names," Jasper said eagerly. "I looked them up in a book at Saint Peter's, in Aberdeen. The script is an ancient version of Welsh."

"You can read this?"

"Aye, it took some doing, but I deciphered it. This top word? It is *Eamhair*. The middle word is *Taranis*. The last line says, *Even in death.*"

"Eamhair," Curran said wonderingly. "Taranis." He stared at the carving as the sea took up a thundering roar in his ears. Was it proof the girl in his dream had actually lived? Did it mean he'd lived too, as *Cailean?* He remembered that other name, *Taranis*. With it had come three impressions: that Taranis was a monk, a criminal, and a liar.

"I believe the words were here for a reason," Jasper said. "To mark this." He pulled the block from the wall, revealing an empty alcove. "Donald told me he came down here once, thirty years ago, not long after he first began as assistant keeper; this slab was lying on the floor and there were footprints in the dirt. He was sure someone had come in during the night and taken something. I wonder every day what was hidden in there."

Curran followed Jasper out of the tunnels and obediently drank the tea, doctored with whisky, which was placed before him. He heard his companion say, "Your color's returning," and a few moments later, "Would you pardon me asking, sir, is the child's fair nanny a maid, wife, or widow?"

CURRAN PONDERED WHETHER TO SHARE WHAT JASPER HAD TOLD HIM. MORRIGAN should know, yet his instincts gave warning. Physically she was healthy and strong, yet he always sensed the fragility of her spirit. How would she take the news that a real woman on Cape Wrath had been stoned to death?

Perhaps he should ask Diorbhail for advice. He didn't like to think his wife was closer to her child's nanny than she was to him, but he suspected she might well be.

The wind was sharp, cutting through his sark. He'd fetch a coat and go find them. But when he entered the bothy he heard their voices through the open window. They must have returned, and were sitting outside in the warmth of the sun. He heard Olivia cooing.

Diorbhail's words stopped him cold.

"—still think that about me and Master Curran?"

"No," Morrigan said. There was silence. Then, "I never thought it. I was out of sorts. But it *was* you in the water. It *was* Curran. It was."

"Aye," Diorbhail said. "I've seen her too, that woman…and that man. They may have been us…once. But long ago."

"Still…it was hard to see. To know he loved you. Don't deny it. I have eyes in my head. He loved you. Eleanor's not here to tell me I'm being daft. It may not make sense, but it feels real."

"Believe me." Diorbhail's voice was so low Curran had to step closer to the window to hear her. "I would *never*…nor would he. He's never taken the mushroom. He has no memories…like we do."

"Why not, though? We remembered things before we used the mushroom. Why doesn't he, if he was there with us in other lives?"

"It could be that bits and snatches come to him, like they have for you, and me, and Eleanor. The mushroom is what hones it. Maybe he does see things, but he can make no sense of them. Maybe he hasn't told anyone."

"He did tell me something, once. On our wedding night."

"What?"

"It was a dream he said he had. Something about a child, and a choice he made." After a moment, she added, "Eleanor isn't sure what we've had are memories, mind. She said they could be nothing, fantasies created by the spirit in the mushroom."

Curran heard Diorbhail make a growling sound. "She wearies me with her arguments and doubts. She knows the truth as well as we do, but like a man, she refuses to accept."

"I want to take it again. I want to see *more*."

"I took some from her when she wasn't looking. I brought it. I'll give it to you, but we'll need to be away from everyone else, including Master Curran, for a whole day. What excuse can we give?"

"I don't know. I'll think of something."

DIORBHAIL OPENED THE BOTHY DOOR. SHE AND MORRIGAN STEPPED INSIDE, BOTH taking a moment to let their eyes adjust to the dimness.

"That was nice." Morrigan kept her voice low, for Olivia was asleep in her arms. "Sitting in the sun, out of the wind. But it made me sleepy."

"Why not lie down?" Diorbhail looked around the bothy's interior. Something was wrong.

"I think I will." Morrigan lay on the narrow bed she shared with Curran, tucking Olivia next to her, and yawned.

Diorbhail covered her with the blanket. "I'm going for a walk," she said. Morrigan nodded and closed her eyes.

As Diorbhail straightened, she smelled a trace of Curran's shaving soap. She stood in the center of the bothy, examining every corner, her instincts alert.

He was not there. But he had been. Her gaze rested on the small leather valise Morrigan had given her. It was not where she had left it. She sighed as she crossed to it.

The drawstring bag holding the dried mushrooms was gone.

JASPER LEAPED UP AT DIORBHAIL'S APPEARANCE. HE TOOK HER ELBOW AS THOUGH she were a grand lady, and led her into the lighthouse. "Aye, Mr. Ramsay said he wanted to explore our tunnels again. He went down oh, about an hour ago. Would you like me to search him out for you?"

"Tunnels? What tunnels?"

"Did he not tell you? I took him down to see them earlier today." At the shake of her head, he continued. "Underground passages. Ancient things. There was a fortress here long ago, and we suspect they were secret ways in and out."

Diorbhail hesitated. "Would you allow me to go down alone? I need to speak to Mr. Ramsay about a personal matter."

He looked disappointed, but obediently showed her the trapdoor and assisted her down the steps. "Take care," he said as she started off. "The ground is quite uneven. If you don't return by the time the tide rises, I'm coming for you, no arguments."

"Thank you," she said, lifting the lantern and turning away.

DIORBHAIL HAD KNOWN THERE WAS SOMETHING DIFFERENT ABOUT THIS PLACE SINCE she was a child. If she had to name it, she would say the veil between worlds was thin here, like a cloud, obscuring yet easily torn. There were legends about the air, about how pure it was. When she stood on the cliffs and looked into the sea mist, she could almost see the other lives she'd lived, without any aid whatsoever. Voices and names floated to her on the wind; she felt them seep into her bones. *Rhalanse. Inis Tearmann.*

How had she never heard of these tunnels? Donald had always been close-mouthed. She remembered him from before. Once he showed her how to bake bread, but when she got pregnant, she stopped coming over to the Cape. She was too ashamed, and fearful his quiet kindness would turn into something else, like it had with all the others.

She stood at the point where the three tunnels converged, trying to decide which direction to try first.

Curran would be unprepared for what the mushroom could do. In this magical place, it would be far more potent. It might rip the veil and open long-buried trenches into the past.

She found him in the sea cavern, sitting near the edge, too close for her comfort. His legs were drawn up to his chest, his arms wrapped round them. His shoulders were slumped in a stance so strikingly vulnerable it made her feel as though her heart was being shredded. He wasn't looking out to the water but had his forehead pressed against his knees. Though the light was dim, she saw him trembling.

Diorbhail waited until she had some semblance of control over her emotions then she set the lantern on the shingle and approached.

Lifting his face from his knees, he glanced at her without surprise then stared at the rolling sea. He was weeping. She knelt beside him.

"I've seen the stoning," he said. His voice was breathless, his pupils enlarged, as Morrigan's had been when she'd used the mushroom. "Like I was there."

In his hands was a bone with a dark claw at one end. It was a seal bone, a toe from a front flipper. Diorbhail had seen many, growing up.

"Did you take it all, Master Curran?" she asked, gripping his forearm.

He smiled, yet tears continued to build and spill down his cheeks. "Aye."

She was frightened. There had been enough mushroom in the bag for three people.

He blinked repeatedly. He grinned then frowned, and his hands restlessly turned the bone, over and over.

"Why couldn't I stop them?" He faced Diorbhail, his expression achingly puzzled. "I fought the Saxons. They were fearsome warriors, but I was never defeated. I was Arcturus's friend, his champion. But when it mattered most, I failed."

The tears in his eyes made them intensely blue, like no blue Diorbhail had ever seen. They were familiar. Beloved. She swayed towards him.

"Selene," he whispered.

Next thing she knew, he'd grabbed her and was kissing her, the desperate kisses of a long lost lover.

"I left you," he was saying. She could hardly hear him through her own need. "I left you, and…our baby. Oh, Selene."

Vaguely she realized he was on top of her, drawing up her skirts.

"No…no," she said weakly. "I promised."

"I've missed you. I need you. Selene."

Diorbhail remembered lying with the boy in her village. She'd known it was wrong, that he wasn't the one for her. As clearly as she had known that then, she knew Curran was the right one.

Morrigan's husband.

She felt herself rising to his caresses, losing all sense but immediate, overwhelming eagerness. His mouth was everywhere, on her neck, over her breast. *Selene,* he said. She knew the name was hers, long ago, somewhere, in some other place and time. Curran, in thrall to the mushroom, must be seeing that place. Diorbhail was torn between wanting to know what he was seeing and simply wanting to join with him, to cast aside questions and problems.

Help me, she thought, not knowing who she cried out to, only knowing she could not do what was necessary on her own.

A new sound invaded their delirious breathing—a shrieking, demanding, imperative call. It pulled her back to the cave. To her vows.

She put her hands against Curran's collarbones. He didn't respond immediately. She had to shove him hard before his eyes opened and he blinked again, almost as though he didn't quite recognize her. He propped his hands on either side of her, pushing himself up.

There was movement off to the side, but it was not the lighthouse keeper. It was an owl, a wee, wee thing, skittering and fluffing its wings, crying insistently as if to say *Do not ignore me!*

Curran stared at it as well. His breathing was labored; he blinked and squinted as though he couldn't focus. He faced her again. His gaze roamed over her. He frowned and rolled off.

"I'm sorry," he said. "I'm not myself." He rubbed his eyes.

She wanted to weep. "Thank you," she said to the little owl. It stopped its mad pacing and tilted its head. Then it flew away.

She sat beside Curran, not touching him as the hours passed and he traveled in and out of vision, speaking then falling into long silences. "Rosabel," he said once, then a moment later, "Rosabel, stop asking me." He wept as though his heart was breaking, and she felt hers break too.

The tide crept higher, splashing just below the lip of the cave, but Curran showed no sign yet of returning to his unaffected self.

"Is she his lover?" he asked. "Aodhàn's? Has she…has she given herself to him?"

"No, Master Curran," Diorbhail said with conviction. "Morrigan is yours. She is faithful to you."

She wasn't completely certain of this, but surely she would know. There was something between Morrigan and Aodhàn, and it was disturbing, but… no. It hadn't gone that far.

Not yet.

He slumped and didn't move or speak for so long she began to doze, sedated by the continuous murmur of the sea. She jerked into wakefulness when he said, after a long silence, "What seems the end is only the beginning."

She clasped his forearm; deep shudders ran through him. How she wished he hadn't taken the mushroom without talking to her. She could have given him a little, just enough to help him remember, not to crash over him like an avalanche.

"The mark…of the bull's horns. Velchanos. The god's mark. Wherever she sends me, I will wait…I will wait for you, Aridela." He breathed in ragged gulps of air.

"Master Ramsay?" She spoke low to keep from startling him. "Curran?" It made her feel strange, trembly and daring, to use his given name.

He faced her but his stare held no recognition. "Where are you?" After a moment, his eyes squeezed closed. "What have I done?"

"Come back," Diorbhail said urgently. "You're in Scotland. Can you hear the sea? Everything is fine…you've a bonny wife and daughter. Be at ease, my love." She stroked his hair. After a moment, he rested his cheek on her shoulder and held her, and seemed to find peace.

Half an hour later, he woke at last, embarrassed and shocked to be holding her in such an inappropriate manner.

"I…I don't remember coming here," he said, his gaze veering away. He blushed endearingly.

Oh, how she loved him. Severing it was like slicing off her hand.

Neither of them must ever suspect.

THE NEXT DAY, CURRAN LED MORRIGAN TO THE CLIFFS. "ARE YOU BETTER?" HE asked.

"Aye," she said. "I don't know what it is about this place. It's affected me in ways I cannot explain. I am sorry, Curran. You've married a madwoman. My brother used to say I was cursed by the color of my hair. I've always felt strange and wrong, with my dreams, the way I faint. My head seems to separate from my neck and float away. Everything echoes, then I wake up and time is gone."

He'd asked Eleanor not to tell Morrigan about the condition she suspected was causing the swoons, headaches, and dizziness. She'd called it "concussion." Curran wanted to think about it first and how it might affect her.

So he said, "Strange? Aye, indeed, if you mean rare or extraordinary."

She smiled. "You always know what to say." But unlike other times, when she'd sounded almost annoyed by that, now she sounded grateful.

They walked on as the sun burnished the water to crimson tips broken up with deep black troughs.

"Diorbhail says my dreams are memories of other lives I've lived," she said. Her gaze was anxious. "She says I'm coming close to the end, and that's why I'm having more of them; that's why they're becoming stronger."

Curran breathed in deeply. The secrets were building into a precarious, leaning tower. Yet he said nothing. He hadn't had time yet to try to make sense of all that had happened to him the day before. He put his arm around her and said, "Maybe we should go."

"Well." Her smile brought out the dimple in her left cheek. "It's your turn. Where to?"

He thought. Since they'd left Kilgarry their lives had been rough and dirty, their food garnished with sand. They'd been hounded by mayflies, and spiders were too often discovered in their bedding. Real bathing had been impossible. Plus there had been a great deal of rumination. He was ready for a complete change of scene.

He grinned. "You're going to need a ball gown."

As she returned his smile and demanded to be told what that meant, he thought, *I will follow you, my Morrigan, wherever you want to wander.*

Chapter 3

"You are to blame and you know it." Seaghan's feet were squarely planted, fists on hips. His face bore a dull red tinge and his lower jaw protruded. "Curran is not the fool you think him."

Aodhàn sighed and stared out the open door. The old tic beneath his eye, that flaw he carried into every life, fluttered annoyingly. "I know," he said. But it didn't matter if he defended himself or agreed: Seaghan wasn't listening.

There was fear beneath the anger in his friend's stance. Glenelg's previous laird had destroyed the entire township on a whim. Could a provoked Curran Ramsay do the same? Curran, the man with no enemies? Who would have thought he could strike—or nearly strike—his young wife? The gossip wasn't clear on that point. He'd packed up his family and carried them off to an unknown destination. There had been no word since until today, a letter in Morrigan's hand, briefly informing Beatrice and the others where they had been, and that they were now on their way to London. *We don't know when we'll return,* it said. Fionna had shared the letter with Seaghan, and Seaghan had told Aodhàn the gist of it, right before blaming him for the entire mess.

Seaghan's voice was hoarse. "Has it been worthwhile, this wee game you've played with Curran's wife? It's no' yourself alone, you know. The shame is on me as well, for I should have put a stop to it and I didn't." He slammed his fist against his open hand. "I wouldn't blame Curran if he never brings her home."

Aodhàn's eyes closed, shutting out the day's miserable gloom. Would she defy her husband and come to him anyway? He pressed his palms against his throbbing temples and succumbed to tortured inner hope.

"Have you nothing to say? No excuse you want to bandy about? Aren't you going to explain again how Morrigan must be free to be her own woman?"

Aodhàn clenched his jaw and gave Seaghan a warning stare. "I've told you you're right. I'm to blame. Not you, not Morrigan, not Curran. If I could change it, I would."

The flush on Seaghan's cheeks deepened. "You should never have started this. Now you'll suffer the same fate as she." One massive fist shot out and collided with Aodhàn's chin, propelling him backward.

Aodhàn landed with such force that for a moment he could do nothing but helplessly gasp. He rose on one elbow and touched his jaw, thinking it might well be broken.

Bright hot rage flared. He leaped to his feet and lunged. Seaghan deflected Aodhàn's right fist, but the left came up at the same time, swift and clandestine, an uppercut that landed against the white scar on the brawny fisherman's cheek.

Seaghan staggered, but quickly reclaimed his balance. With a growl and a stunning punch, he sent Aodhàn tumbling across the table and into a chair, splintering it to bits. Kicking aside the table, creels, and dishes, he crashed like a bull, blind to everything but his need to obliterate.

Cold determination cleared Aodhàn's vision. Anticipating his maddened foe, he struck at Seaghan's face and belly, leaving him bent over, his teeth and lips stained wetly crimson.

In the end, after a bout that virtually destroyed the interior of the blackhouse, the adversaries lay bloodied, bruised, and exhausted. Pain crept out of the shadows, laying a wide assault.

Dragging himself off the floor, Aodhàn spat blood. "Curran brought her to *me*," he said. "She's been mine since the earth began, and she'll be mine when it's done."

Seaghan stared at him, panting.

Aodhàn wheeled and left, heading north.

Clouds scudded before a moaning wind. In time he came to the foot of an incline where a burn expanded into a pool. He splashed cold water on his face and lay there, too tired and sore to rise.

On Barra, before Lilith and their daughters were killed, he'd been an immaculately groomed, expensively garbed man. It was an effective method of keeping the inhabitants at arm's length. Now he looked like one of them, his hair long and unkempt, carelessly drawn into a knot to keep it out of his eyes. His beard was untrimmed, his clothing rough and dirty.

You have much to redress, whispered the voice in his head. The old voice, the one that violated his sleep and spoke from the sea.

"No one knows who you are anymore."

See yourself, the voice said, not without pity.

The pool became a mirror to the past, showing him his original face—Chrysaleon, the Gold Lion of Mycenae, so selfishly brazen he'd tricked a country, thwarted a goddess, and perverted the world's destiny to satisfy his own ends.

A transient breeze disturbed the surface of the pool, transforming the arrogant Chrysaleon into the mysterious Taranis, he who visited a chieftain's daughter in her tower bedchamber, luring her into torment and attempted suicide, which might have been a better death than the one she actually suffered.

We've been at Cape Wrath, Morrigan wrote in her letter. Aodhàn knew why. He'd seen how his story affected her. Some buried part of her was bewitched still.

Had she unearthed any sign of Eamhair, of Taranis? He could only hope she wouldn't discover how much he'd altered the facts.

No matter how brutally their incarnations concluded, they all anchored Aridela closer to him—including this one, where Menoetius seemed to have every advantage.

She wasn't content with her wealthy, handsome husband. If she were, she would not have allowed Aodhàn to kiss her, and she surely wouldn't have kissed him back.

At first, when his memories returned, he'd known true fear. What if Olivia changed her, made her Curran's, body and soul?

But it hadn't happened.

He *was* winning. Slowly perhaps, too slowly, but he felt it in every breath. He would win, if he just kept fighting.

Damn Curran for taking her so far away! Aodhàn had been close to bringing Morrigan around to his way of thinking, but now she was beyond his reach.

His bastard brother had gone beyond forgiveness when he got her pregnant. God, how Aodhàn hated that mewling infant, the constant reminder that Aridela had given herself to another man. Never, ever, in all the thousands of years they'd journeyed this thorny trail, had she borne a child to Menoetius.

Did it mean the end was near? Both relief and fear coursed through him at the possibility. He wasn't ready to give in, yet he was so tired.

His fist struck the reflection, dispersing Taranis in a flurry of ripples. "I'll have your daughter and the entire world," he snarled. "You'll be swept away like a housewife brushes crumbs from her kitchen floor."

All perception of gods and goddesses, of Athene and the old ways, was vanishing. History books patronizingly referred to those deities as myths, and knowledge of lands where women ruled was already lost.

Curran would fail. Athene would fail. A bit more time—that's all he needed. Athene would diminish. At some point, she wouldn't have enough power to bring back Menoetius or those other sycophants, Selene and Themiste. Perhaps Athene herself would die.

Then he would drink sweet revenge, as sweet as the old gods' nectar.

That thought, so like something Harpalycus would say, forced a bitter laugh from Aodhàn's throat.

Drawn-out prickling hunger sent him stumbling, reliving the moment in the forest when he'd breathed in the scent of her skin, a subtle perfume that carried somehow from life to life, one body to the next. The musky aroma made him feel he was plunging into a warm chasm, like a womb, where nothing existed but liquid darkness. Her scent alone brought Crete to life with punishing intensity—right up to the last moment.

He veered away from that memory.

A stone tripped him. He fell into pine branches, trying to silence her rejection as needles scraped his face. *I'll never be separated from my child.*

Of course she would attempt nobility. This era of prudish hypocrisy lent itself to such things. On Crete, she could have as many lovers as she wished. Not here, where women must be chaste and faithful all their lives, to one man alone. Aye, she had to choose, and there was only one choice this culture would accept—Curran, simply because he'd found her first.

Nauseated and dizzy, he pushed away from the sticky trunk. Beyond a stretch of grass there was an embankment of obsidian-like stones, forming a jagged barrier between ocean and land.

Aodhàn crawled onto the edge. Below, the surf roiled like a foam-mouthed pack of wolves.

You want me. You want to suck me into ice and darkness.

Lightning flashed in one blinding arc after another. An almost uncontrollable desire to jump flamed then diffused through his muscles. He clutched the slippery rocks. If he were gone, Morrigan could come home to Glenelg and spend the rest of her life raising wee Currans and Morrigans. Middle age would leave her matronly and stout. Would she remember, or would she bury the name of Aodhàn Mackinnon?

The bitch goddess had done this deliberately. She had guided Curran to Morrigan. She had caused a child to start growing. She had stolen Aodhàn's memories then cruelly brought them back when it was too late.

The cold elegance did not escape him. Lilith had shared the same bonds with him and *their* babies, after Aodhàn had ordered Greyson to kill Daniel, so this life was in every respect an eye for an eye.

Glimpses of joy will be ripped from you.

The sea thundered, launching white tentacles up the rocks. He could jump. A few minutes of sharp pain. Then emptiness, silence, and peace, until the next time. A new start. A fresh, unblemished slate.

But Athene might cause him to be reborn immediately. Then he would grow to manhood as Morrigan became a grandmother, the reverse of what the bitch had done this time. What must he look like to her? No doubt his age made it easier for her to reject him.

He imagined pointing a revolver at Curran, squeezing the trigger, watching blood flow from a hole between lifeless eyes. Aodhàn groaned, reveling in the joy of the fantasy.

But he knew everything that had transpired on Barra and up to this moment was his punishment for ordering Daniel's death. Greyson, his instrument of murder, had gone mad. Lilith and the children moldered in their graves; Aodhàn was merely existing, almost dead himself.

He didn't dare harm Curran. He simply didn't dare.

Promise nothing will come between us, Chrysaleon.

Aridela extracted that vow on Crete, before the blazing autumn star had risen in the heavens, before he thwarted his oath of death. Before he himself came between them.

Yes. Face your truth.

"You caused it!" he shouted into the driving rain. "You're to blame!"

He collapsed against the rocks, suffocating in that moment when Aridela's neck snapped and she slumped, lifeless, against him.

The sound of crashing waves faded. Before him lay not Scotland's green, dewy coast but the arid island in the Mediterranean where it all began.

Flanked by a wary Menoetius, he stepped into the palace courtyard at Labyrinthos. Sunlight beat against the paving; he could feel yet the blinding heat ricocheting from those stones. Sensations and images flooded him, of carved pillars supporting gigantic stone awnings, of vibrant frescoes displaying black bulls and blue flittering birds. He'd heard of Crete's magnificent architecture, but the reality left him awestruck.

A line of women approached, richly garbed in open-breasted blouses and tiered skirts covered with shiny hammered disks and shells. In the center stood Aridela, Queen Helice's daughter.

He would carry that fateful moment with him forever, no matter how many centuries passed. A million couldn't dim it. Her black hair, dusky skin, and enormous eyes were flawless perfection, yet while those surface attributes were what had initially captivated him, it wasn't hair, skin, or eyes that made her unforgettable. It was the innate royalty, the pride and majesty that called to his, the courage, passion, and wit, the spirituality, and most especially, her loyalty—once given, immutable. An amaranthine being, she bound him to this day. He was her willing, eager prisoner.

Legend called her the daughter of Velchanos, Athene's son and lover. *Daughter of the Calesienda.*

And oh, the bull leap, the way she laughed as she landed on its haunches then cast herself into the arms of her half brother.

Prince Chrysaleon had recklessly declared she would be his. He would win her, no matter what he had to do.

Would he, had he known the full price?

He heard again Themiste's echoing prophecy.

Curse the usurper, the changer of the Way. He shall follow without rest, without joy, without relief, until the final devastation of the heavens. He shall follow begging, but love will run from him, and he will receive only sorrow and regret until the world is old and tired, and razed by war.

Alexiare had also tried to warn him. *Selene said you and I would follow, and that we would beg for death.*

Curses mean nothing to me. Chrysaleon's unwavering insolence sent a shudder through the older, wiser Aodhàn. *Have you forgotten my grandfather's motto? Fortune favors the bold.*

Rain beat against the coast. Cold wind buffeted him. Aodhàn's arms strained as his psyche warred, one part trying to thrust over the edge, the other clinging to life and hope.

Yes. For you, I would do it again.

What if Olivia died? Morrigan would be freed of her maternal obligation.

Curse it though; she might never recover from the bothersome child's demise. That wouldn't work.

Fortune favors the bold. Favors the bold.

What if Morrigan died? Aodhàn could kill her then himself. After a hazy interlude of nothingness, both would be reborn somewhere else. They would find each other in the magical way that always happened. Morrigan wouldn't remember Curran or Olivia. She would have a new name, a new body.

Athene's gift of forgetfulness used to his own advantage.

But would it unfold that way? So far, every time he'd tried to trick or defy Athene, it was he who paid, and, indirectly, Aridela.

He had killed her once. For all he knew, that was the act that sent them on this pitiless journey.

In the first life after Crete, the life of flailing ignorance and mistakes that was Cape Wrath, he hadn't known there were limits on what he could do. Remembering his reckless stupidity in that incarnation made him wish he could drive a stake into his brain.

He had done everything wrong that could be done wrong at Cape Wrath. He had worsened the curse upon himself, and her, threefold.

But he'd learned from his mistakes, in that life and every life since. Each blunder and subsequent punishment changed his course, refined his purpose.

There were unbreakable rules to Athene's game, the foremost being that he couldn't kill Menoetius, and he couldn't reveal the past. Those two edicts were embedded in his very soul.

Not since Crete had he killed Aridela, but every instinct warned him that if he couldn't kill Menoetius, then surely the punishment would be a thousand times worse for attempting such a crime against the Goddess's beloved daughter.

In the life on Barra, he'd attempted a different ruse by ordering Greyson to kill Daniel. With Daniel dead, nothing stood between him and Lilith. They married. For eight years, there was no retribution.

But Athene was simply biding her time.

The sanctions continued to this day, with Morrigan married to Curran, separated from Aodhàn by her own incorruptible loyalty.

If he tried any new machination to break that bond, Athene's punishment would undoubtedly descend again, worse than he could imagine.

He wondered sometimes if it was Athene who punished him, or Harpalycus. Was Harpalycus Athene's instrument, or was he unconnected, self-governing?

Aodhàn didn't know. Every existence brought new questions, new doubts, and increasing exhaustion.

What if Seaghan was right and Curran never brought Morrigan home? He could become an absentee landlord. He could hire a steward to live at Kilgarry. There was a distinct possibility Morrigan would never be seen in Glenelg again.

If Aodhàn could put his hands on some currency…but his Barra wealth was gone and his real fortune, the priceless treasure from history, was hidden in the mountains on Crete. He had no way to get to it, and he couldn't go so far anyway, not now. What if Morrigan left Curran to come to him, and he wasn't here? He couldn't take that chance.

He imagined appearing in London a rich man, showing her that he could be as good a provider as Curran.

But Aridela had never been impressed with such things. Loyalty motivated her, and love. Bloody Curran had her loyalty.

Aodhàn was afraid to think she might love him too.

What if he could compel Morrigan to kill herself?

If she took her own life…but he knew it was too fine a line, as ordering Greyson to kill Daniel had been. Such distinctions would not protect him. Athene would blame him, and she would retaliate.

Had that merciless deity really forced him into this corner, with only one safe choice, living in dreary shadows, half-man, half-corpse, ever watching her from afar and too timid to do anything about it?

Perhaps he should jump. Give her to Curran in a selfless act of generosity.

Better that than existing without her, in the living death of the last two decades. Now that he'd seen her, touched her hair, drunk in the taste of her, he couldn't survive that emptiness.

Surely he could end his own life without being punished.

He laughed harshly, for he really didn't know about that, either.

Beyond all this, deeper and more wrenching, was what he had observed since he had regained his memories. He'd seen it on the *Endeavor*, and later, when he kissed her in the forest. He had seen it at the wedding cèilidh, though he hadn't understood then. He saw it the night of Saint Brigit's Eve, when she brandished her sewing scissors at ghosts from nightmares.

Morrigan was different from her predecessors. Where Aridela's courage was woven into every fiber of her being, Morrigan was timid, shy, always trying to mold herself into whatever she thought would gain acceptance and love. Eamhair was willing to die rather than allow her father to sell her, but Morrigan had meekly consented to marry Curran on the orders of her aunts and the demands of the world in which she lived. Caparina had defied the terrifying papal inquisitors; not even the threat of the stake could make her confess to witchcraft, while Morrigan said nothing as William Watson denigrated her from his pulpit, and all of Glenelg listening, watching. Lilith laughed at the sanctimonious gossip of Barra's villagers, to her ruin, while Morrigan shrank from judgment.

Everything that made Aridela unique was decaying. She was slowly being crushed, one life at a time. His proud, ancient queen was nearly lost.

Had he fought all these centuries only to lose her to this world's joyless new order—the world he helped create when he caused the destruction of Crete and the last stronghold that honored women? If he finally succeeded in destroying Athene, would he also destroy the woman he loved?

She could eventually become ordinary and lose the mark of the Goddess. He dreaded the prospect of her looking at him without the subliminal recognition he had always counted on. At some point the revelation of their amazing story might get no reaction from her but blankness, ridicule, or fear.

The rain slackened. Sunlight struggled through breaking clouds.

Perhaps this was the final ending Athene had plotted from the beginning— that as he neared his ultimate moment of victory he would lose Aridela to the same defeated spirit every female the world over endured, sooner or later.

If that possibility existed, then what was he fighting for?

An eagle sailed, stretching its wings to ride the currents. Long ago, Aodhàn had watched Morrigan in the secret glen. She stood before an eagle, possibly the same one who now scrutinized him from one stern eye.

Puny weak human, its sharp glance seemed to say. With one negligent flap of its wings, the raptor circled lower, disappearing over mist-shrouded Skye.

"Aodhàn?"

He turned. Eleanor Graeme stood on the wet, windswept grass, a covered basket on one arm, gazing at him curiously. At the sight of his face she exclaimed, and set her basket on the ground.

"Come here at once," she said. "I cannot climb out there to you."

"Leave me alone."

She placed her hands on her hips. "Either jump into the sea or let me tend you. You're bleeding."

He lowered his face to the black stones, tasting them, absorbing their relentless chill. He realized he was shivering. The burn and throb of his injuries returned.

"Come, Aodhàn," she said.

He obeyed, too worn out to argue.

She took him to her home, threw a blanket around his shoulders, and sat him at her table with tea while she ground herbs in her pestle. Bringing the bowl to the table, she washed his face then applied a stinging mixture of some kind to the cuts.

For a moment she worked in silence, frowning, then she said, "You blame yourself for them going away."

He had long ago recognized the spirit of Themiste inside this woman. Once upon a time, she was the sacred oracle, a woman famed throughout the Mediterranean for her beauty and wisdom.

She was quite different now, large and rather plain, with a telltale greenish aura around her head. But she was still intelligent and intuitive. He hated her, distrusted her, and always avoided her. He regretted the lapse in judgment that had brought him to her cottage.

Queen Helice was here too, in the body of the easily dismissed, frivolous Aunt Ibby, still loyal to her child, always loving, but nowadays, not a reckoning power. He didn't think she had any sense of him, or of Curran, and he detected only the slightest yellow emanation around her. She didn't concern him.

Diorbhail was another matter. The colors surrounding her were strong. That night he'd carried Morrigan off the mountain, they had nearly blinded him. Her unexpected appearance was frightening. Selene was a deadly force. Her loyalty rivaled Aridela's, and she'd stolen the knife. Who knew what could come of that?

The followers didn't appear in every life, and he had never seen all three together like this before, not since Crete. Now here they were, and though none had the memories, they were drawn to Morrigan, and Morrigan was drawn to them. Not an hour passed that he didn't wonder what had taken place between Diorbhail, Eleanor, and Morrigan when they were alone in that bothy for three days.

All of them converging was yet another suggestion that they were near the end.

"Well?" she said, holding his chin.

He jerked free.

"I've seen the way you look at her," Eleanor said. "We have all seen it. Go away, Aodhàn. Let her be happy."

Aodhàn wanted to break her nose. He rose, nearly knocking over the chair. "Thank you for whatever you did," he said tightly. "The pain is much less. I'll be off."

She shrugged and started to let him go, then said, "If you need somewhere to sleep, I have an extra bed," and waved him on his way.

Next thing he knew, he was standing in the clearing. He gazed at the boulder and the cave for a long time.

I dreamed of you, before I came to Glenelg. You were young, and you called me Lilith.

Never, ever, had she excavated memories by herself in such coherency. Dreaming of herself as Lilith, and of him, without the use of the *cara* mushroom or his own prompting…?

Had she found out about the mushroom and used it, or were the memories bubbling up on their own?

Everything about this life was different, and that was terrifying.

She had asked him to explain. He'd wanted to. The need had almost overwhelmed him.

I've given Curran my vow. Leave us alone, Mackinnon.

His heartbeat slowed. He would go to London. To hell with these rules— rules that applied to no one but him. He would do everything in his power to coax her away from Curran. He would use all his knowledge, every cajoling word he'd ever learned.

And if she still wouldn't leave her husband, he would cause a confrontation. He wouldn't kill Curran, much as he longed to. Killing Curran would make Morrigan hate him, and would set the law on him. Let Curran age alone, as *he* had these last twenty years.

He would kill Morrigan, then himself. No matter the punishment. He would defy Athene as he'd done on Crete. While he was at it—he might as well be hanged for a sheep as a lamb—he would tell Morrigan of their past, of every life and all they'd shared—the good parts, of course. He had to see her eyes light up with the magic of it one more time. He wanted to hear her ask for details of their long, long love affair…once more.

If they were truly coming to the end, Athene could choke on her rules. He would seize his boldness; he would do what he should have done long ago; force her hand.

And he would win, once and for all.

Chapter 4

"RAMSAY—CURRAN RAMSAY!"

Curran and Morrigan stopped, searching for the source of the shout.

"Up here," came the call again. "I knew it had to be you. Don't move, I will come down."

The afternoon was sunny, forcing Morrigan to squint as she peered upward.

"What the devil?" Curran said, then louder, "Whistler?"

Morrigan saw a flash of white before the second storey casement banged shut. "Who was that?"

"A friend, I think." Her husband grabbed her hand and grinned. "Prepare yourself."

She followed him through a half open doorway into a dim entry hall tiled in blue and white. Footsteps bounded down the staircase.

"Damnation, Ramsay, how long have you been in London?"

The man stretching out his hand had a compact body, delicate long fingers and a weathered face. A patch of white sprouted at the top of his deeply lined forehead, as though a pigeon's feather had lodged in his hair.

"Only a few days," Curran replied, shaking his hand. "Allow me to present my wife. Morrigan, this is Mr. James Whistler. Do you live here, Jimmy? Have you moved?"

The man gave Morrigan a dismissive nod before returning his attention to Curran. "This place has a large studio and gives me an excellent view of the Thames. Come upstairs."

Merry, she thought. *So merry he's forgotten his manners, or never learned any.*

Whistler led them to the top floor and into a bright chamber crowded with tables, easels, papers, and strewn canvases. The aromas of tobacco and paint, carrying an undertone of the river, permeated the air.

Curran and his friend began catching up, leaving Morrigan to look around the room.

Belatedly, Whistler tugged the bell pull. Soon an enormous fellow shouldered through the door with a tray holding a pitcher of lemonade and glasses.

Morrigan's throat was dry and she was hot. The moment they'd arrived, London had turned torturously muggy. Corsets, bustles, and layers of fabric stuck to perpetually damp skin.

But the men paid no heed to the refreshments. Morrigan waited, then decided she might die of thirst before an invitation came. She poured some and sipped it, pressing the cool glass to her cheeks as she explored, studying the mixture of half-finished portraits and vague seascapes along with reproductions of bridges overlaid in dim, hazy light.

As their host had claimed, there was a good view of the Thames from the window. She leaned on the sill, hoping to catch a breeze. Barges and pleasureboats crowded below, sounding their bells and horns. Laughter floated to her.

Beads of sweat gathered on her neck under the weight of her hair. She relinquished her attempt to follow the conversation behind her and took off her bonnet to use as a fan, gasping when her braided bun was seized from behind.

She straightened and swung around. Without a word of warning or excuse, Whistler moved to her side and pulled out her hairpins, causing her braid to fall.

Curran smiled indulgently as he observed this from the center of the room.

"Divine." Whistler rotated her towards the sunlight. "Skin like mother-of-pearl. I swear I have never seen hair this shade. Mahogany?" He brought up the end of her braid, perusing it intently through his monocle. "No," he said. "True russet. And those highlights. I missed those before. You'll allow me to loosen it, won't you?" he asked, as he removed the band and unraveled her hair, spoiling all the work the maid had gone to that morning.

He was a madman. And so was Curran, from the look of things. Her husband made not a single protest at this assault. Whistler lifted handfuls of her hair and held them out to the light in the window. "I must paint her." He faced Curran. "Has she ever modeled?"

Sullen resentment colored Morrigan's cheeks.

"Didn't you hear?" Curran said. "The lady is Mrs. Ramsay. My wife."

Whistler's gaze boldly traveled the length of her body. "Would you care if she posed naked?"

Anger twined with astonishment, leaving Morrigan speechless. Her fingers tightened on the glass as she considered throwing the lemonade in his face.

"Good Lord, Whistler," Curran said with a half-stifled laugh. "Apologize this minute."

"But why? All the aristocracy wants to be painted. Can you not see it in your Kilgarry, commanding everyone's attention? It will, you know."

"I would imagine." Curran snorted.

Whistler studied her with an indifference she found unfamiliar and disconcerting. He was interested, aye, but not in her. She held no fascination for him except in whatever way her coloring made her useful. Perhaps Kit would have become like this one day, had his dreams not been thwarted by Enid.

"I've already had my portrait painted, thank you," she said, fairly imitating Douglas Lawton in a vile mood.

"Eh? What's that?" Whistler shrugged. "He could not have done you justice." He gave a high, piercing laugh. "Besides, do ladies ever have too many portraits of themselves?"

"We'll talk," Curran said, "and let you know."

"My mother lives with me. She could chaperon, or you could come along yourself if you like."

"We really must go." Curran crossed to Morrigan and patted her fist. "We're late for an appointment."

Whistler rolled a cigarette and struck a match. Smoke curled in acrid waves, stinging the inside of Morrigan's nose. "I'm having a breakfast next Sunday. Do come, Ramsay. Rossetti and Swinburne will be here."

"Morrigan?" Curran's regard was a blend of apology, guilt, and a sparkle of ill-suppressed laughter.

She could only shrug. While they worked out the details, she tried to replait her hair, but without a looking-glass, she couldn't be sure how well she succeeded, and Whistler didn't return the fastener. As she and Curran left, he called after them. "I'll have your promise! I must paint her. *Me*, not Rossetti."

Curran caught Morrigan's hand and they ran down the stairs, laughing.

"No wonder he lives with his mother," she said. "Who else could bear him?"

"Have you never heard of him?"

"No, why? What's he done?"

"He's rather well-known."

She gave another shrug.

"My country lass." He kissed her cheek. "What does it all matter, anyway?"

They strolled along sun-streaked Cheyne Walk. "Whistler's work isn't well received," he told her. "It doesn't fit modern tastes. But I think he has genius. His Nocturnes are exquisite and there's one, of his mistress—Jo is her name, I think—that's inspired. Whistler sees painting as visions of patterns in nature, rather than a rendition of facts."

"He has a mistress?"

Curran laughed. "The more obnoxious artists are, the more ladies they acquire."

"Hmmm."

"Would you like him to paint you?"

"I don't want to see myself staring from every wall at Kilgarry. And I won't pose naked."

"He'd try to seduce you."

She stiffened and struggled to keep her voice as casual as his. "You don't sound vexed. Is he that grand a friend?"

Curran brought her hand to his mouth and kissed it. "I'm not a monster. I don't want to lock you away or throttle every man who admires you."

"Oh, look." She tugged him onto the picturesque Battersea Bridge, pointed at a pretty sailboat, and chattered about boats and picnics and Lily and the baby, determined to divert them from this tender subject they had never yet discussed. She wasn't ready. Her emotions were as snarled as windblown hair.

Fortune favors the bold, the Mackinnon clan motto bravely announced. She wished she could be as bold as whoever chose that saying.

Pink evening light softened the buildings and river. Curran's face held resignation and guilt, but he smiled and said nothing.

His wife reminded him of a doe preparing to bolt. Curran didn't have the heart to force the issue. She'd insisted she was only helping Seaghan tend Aodhàn that day, and he knew for a fact Aodhàn often caught strange fevers. But the way she'd sneaked from Kilgarry without a word had left him snared in visceral anger, and more importantly, alarm. Every instinct had clamored at him to get her away.

The idea of her possible infidelity stung like the bite of an adder, but almost worse was his own self-condemnation, born the moment he'd raised his fist to her. He could think of nothing more heinous than being drunk and striking a woman, and what if she'd done nothing to deserve it? Whisky and an overactive imagination may have conjured those pitying glances from the servants.

He tried never to think of that day in the tunnels at Cape Wrath but for Diorbhail's promise, which always gave him comfort. *Morrigan is yours.* Somehow he didn't think she would lie about that, not even to protect her mistress.

Shortly after they arrived in London, while Morrigan slept off the long, wearying journey, Curran had gone to Quinn's offices, seeking news. Quinn was still out of the city, he was told, but one letter had come for Mr. Ramsay.

He unfolded the missive. Quinn's familiar scrawl, on his official letterhead, jumped out at him.

There is much mystery here, and as I'm not only an outsider but also English, no one wants to confide in me. I have heard rumors of a lycanthrope, or angry ghost, that plagued the area some months ago, killing twelve local men. I'm trying to find out more but most here speak only Gaelic. I often get little more than babbling. The woman I hired to cook and clean speaks English, but often chooses to pretend she doesn't, and I think she's stealing from me. There's no use getting rid of her, as I'm quite certain anyone else I might retain would be the same. I do apologize for not yet having the information you require, but I will persevere.

Diorbhail's promise, and the way Morrigan had taken him into her body and heart since they'd left Glenelg nearly convinced Curran he was wrong in his suspicions. He almost penned a letter telling Quinn to abandon his investigation, but decided to wait a few days.

The two meandered along the Chelsea Embankment. Curran flagged a hansom and gave the driver Richard Donaghue's fashionable address on Arlington Street.

Lily met them at the door. "There you are," she said. "You've been gone so long I started to worry. Has Ramsay kept you entertained?" Clasping Morrigan's arm, she led her guest upstairs, waving Curran away with some blethering about a new gown, pins, and a fitting.

"Your wife is a rare jewel," Lily had told him soon after they'd arrived, then she had instructed him not to keep Morrigan in London overly long, for fear its pervasive taint would infect her.

Curran watched them ascend. Morrigan was making some excuse about her untidy hair. She had no idea what an uncommonly beautiful woman she was, though he inundated her with compliments and every mirror could verify the fact. She often returned his flattery with half-disbelieving glances, and lately, there'd been something more. This morning, he'd said, *English females are a milksop lot next to you.* A fleeting expression had passed across her face, one that left him questioning his eyesight. She'd looked annoyed, and he'd swear her spine stiffened. Pulling away from his embrace, she'd crossed the room, plucked an apple from a bowl, and peeled it with a small silver knife.

When he'd asked her if something was wrong, she'd merely shrugged, sent him an expressionless glance, and said, "The heat."

Every answer lay hidden behind those dark eyes. How she felt about Aodhàn...and Olivia...and her marriage.

Another odd thing happened as he'd watched her peel the apple. The long scarlet spiral of apple-skin dropped to the plate. She lifted one juicy, milk-white sliver to her lips and left it there, holding it between her teeth as she sliced another.

The room, with its unmade bed, discarded clothing, and remnants of breakfast, swirled into a different scene—an orchard. White blossoms swam in apple-scented breezes. Yet he still saw Morrigan as well, beyond the trees. Using her tongue, she took the apple slice into her mouth. Her fingers lifted another, and again placed it tenderly between her teeth.

He wanted to be that fruit. Drawn in, torn, crushed until he lost cohesion and became one with her capillaries and membranes. Truly joined at the most elementary level in an endless dance punctuated by the sound of her breath and beat of her heart.

The throb of the scar next to his eye had disrupted the strange images and returned him to the reality of London and their comfortable bedroom. He'd pressed his fingers against his brow and drew them away drenched with blood.

Morrigan hadn't noticed his moment of insanity. Touching a napkin to her lips, she rose and crossed to the bell pull to call a servant while he slipped behind the dressing screen to examine his reflection in the looking-glass.

He dabbed the blood with his handkerchief but it kept welling, filling in the space he'd blotted.

Everything went black; a rushing sound filled his brain and blinding flashes interfered with his eyesight. His heart wallowed and pitched.

Lily's giggle jerked him out of his reverie. He glanced up in time to see his wife and her new companion vanish into the upstairs corridor, leaving him staring stupidly at the staircase. Only a moment had passed.

Certainty welled like the blood in his old scar, which had congealed and stopped with the use of styptic. Morrigan needed him. Him, not Aodhàn Mackinnon. Not Seaghan, Beatrice, or Ibby. She needed him more than even Diorbhail. Somehow, someday, he would prove necessary to Morrigan in ways neither could yet comprehend.

Chapter 5

Beatrice thought Fionna a fool when the woman complained of a pall hanging over Kilgarry's old stones, and claimed she'd seen the bluish light of a *dead-can'le* twinkling along the sea road.

"Someone's going to die." The housekeeper crossed herself.

"Pish," Beatrice said. Though everyone else seemed despondent, Beatrice rather enjoyed having the master and mistress gone.

The next night the dogs all started howling at the same moment. A grim portent, Beatrice had to admit, and the beasts did act afraid. They whined, skulked, and pressed their tails between their legs. That foolish Antiope stopped eating. She'd always been skinny, but now her ribs stuck out like a rotted boat's.

The master and his bride had been gone nearly a month, yet Fionna, Tess, and Violet still dragged about like the world was caving in. Tess seemed worst affected, skittering with long face and fearful eyes that slid from Morrigan's aunt as though she feared being the victim of some evil spell. *Have your pretty beliefs been knocked to bits?* Beatrice wanted to say. *If your father had lived, you would've learned the pure uselessness of men, no matter how rich they are or kind they seem.*

She thought of the long-ago day when Tess's father had stepped onto a cornice of snow at the edge of an embankment. It had collapsed, taking him down the rough hill until a half-buried boulder crushed his skull.

To Beatrice, it meant one less hungry mouth among the starving survivors of the Glenelg clearings. Logan had been inconsolable. Tess was too young to understand, but Fionna had since raised her daughter on glorious tales of her fine upstanding da. Beatrice snorted whenever she heard those stories. John Dunbar had enjoyed his private diversions, the kind a man would never want revealed to his offspring, and Fionna apparently agreed. She churned out one pretty fabrication after another. She might even believe them herself by now.

Beatrice knew better than most how folk kept their wee secrets, things that could destroy generations of families if they ever came out. Why, the idea of a drunken Master Ramsay threatening physical harm to his child's mother, or the possibility of Aodhàn Mackinnon blithely copulating with his good friend's wife not four months after she'd given birth, had torn these ladies' safe Catholic world asunder.

With Curran and Morrigan away in outlandish places, Beatrice could imagine herself the mistress of this stately house. Freed of the endless chores that had monopolized her days at the Wren's Egg, she sometimes thought she'd go mad from idleness. She spent a good amount of it in the kitchens with Janet, who always had something sweet to nibble. That's where she'd settled, in a rocker by the open window, when Violet burst in waving a letter.

"It's from Mistress Ramsay," she cried, tearing the envelope.

It had been a good while since they'd heard from the couple. The first note had been a cursory three lines, stating that they'd spent a few days at Torridon and Cape Wrath, were on their way to London, and didn't know when they'd return.

This missive was longer and more cheerful, with descriptions of shopping sprees and sightseeing. Still, there was no mention of when they planned to come home.

The letter implied an excess of those aimless delights reserved for rich folk. Matters were improved then, since the ignominious flight at the beginning of June.

"It's like a faery tale," Violet said. "Mistress was an ordinary maid like us. Now look at her. She was lucky she lived in that port town. Nothing'll ever happen to us, stuck here, mountains on one side and the sea on the other. We'll be spinsters all our lives."

"Speak for yourself," Tess murmured.

Beatrice knew the cause of Violet's pessimistic tone. A lass from some wee village on Skye had appeared a few days ago with her father, and had accused Logan of getting her with child. Tears and arguments had spewed between Logan and Violet, Logan and Fionna, Logan and the lass from Skye. Beatrice had overheard him threaten to move someplace where females wouldn't haver a man clean out of his senses.

"I pray Master Curran and his bride will find happiness again," Fionna said. "I've felt sad ever since they went away. I do wish things could be like they were before...."

"She always was a willful hissy," Beatrice said. "Never appreciated what others did for her. The master should have given her a clout or two that night. It might have helped matters."

Fionna set down her embroidery with a bang. "What a thing to say. Mistress Ramsay is a dear sweet lass. Master Curran would not have married her otherwise. And he would never strike her, nor any woman."

"Was it her dear sweetness made him shatter a whisky bottle like he wished it was her head?"

Fionna clamped her mouth shut and turned away.

"Aodhàn Mackinnon's caused this trouble." Violet smoothed the crisp sheets of paper on the worktable.

"Hist, missy," Fionna said. "None of that."

"It's true though." Tess lowered her head over the rolling pin and vigorously flattened a daub of pastry. "It's all due to him. A poor fisherman, hardly able to clothe himself. And he's so much older, and no' friendly, or handsome, or anything. He never even smiles. When she has Master Curran and darling Olivia. And master, so in love with her a blind man could see it. Seaghan knows. Isn't that why he and Aodhàn no longer speak, and why Aodhàn has gone away?"

Beatrice rose heavily. "Have you finished that letter, girl?"

"Aye," Violet replied, her voice squeaking, "but for a postscript saying Mistress Ramsay has seen an elephant."

"Well, I'm away for a walk. I won't listen to this bellyaching over two such spoilt weans." Off she went, slamming the door.

PATRICK HAWLEY FOUGHT THROUGH BOUTS OF SWEATING AND CONVULSIVE SPASMS. He could hardly lift his head. He foggily remembered coming to Glenelg on the ferry from Skye. It seemed like he'd hired a pony so he wouldn't have to walk, but there was no pony now. His clothes were wet, as though he'd been caught in a downpour; mud was caked under his nails, and ground into his palms, and an all-too-familiar stench told him he'd soiled his trousers.

After Curran Ramsay broke his nose and knocked out a tooth, Patrick left Glenelg. He'd wanted to be far enough away to feel safe while he healed, but not too far, for he meant to have his revenge on the bastard who hurt him, and Aodhàn Mackinnon, and finally, most especially, Morrigan Ramsay.

He'd found an inn across the strait in the village of Kyleakin. A healing woman had provided salve for the oozing sores that erupted all over his body after that bitch knifed him. His tongue had swelled, making it impossible to eat anything but the thinnest broth.

It was still swollen, but he no longer felt hungry.

He had improved, though, hadn't he, over on Skye? He was certain of it.

The moment he felt better, he returned to Glenelg and skulked around the outskirts, keeping to the forest cover where he could. He saw Aodhàn Mackinnon, but only at a distance, and never Morrigan Ramsay or her husband. Every thought of her brought him to the edge of insanity. He'd almost had her squirming and bleeding under him again. He would have, too, if it hadn't been for the cursed knife.

This was the second time Aridela of Crete had nearly killed him with that knife. His fever brought the memory into startling clarity...the battle on the shore at Amnisos, between his army and the army of the Mycenaean king. She had pulled the knife from her own chest where he had buried it, and with one clean, quick swipe, cut his throat from ear to ear. He remembered the pain, the terror, the sensation of his life draining swiftly away with the cascade of hot blood. If a warrior hadn't happened to run past, near enough to seize, he wouldn't be here.

Years later, Chrysaleon almost managed to complete what his dead wife started, not with the knife, but simple starvation and a fancy cage. Harpalycus could be seen, mocked, tormented...by all the inhabitants of Knossos, but not touched. The guards had been given strict orders about that.

How much time had passed? Where was he?

He could answer but one of these questions. Every time he woke from feverish stupor, he saw the same curved rock wall rising around him. Vaguely, from better days, he knew he was lying inside one of the ruins near Curran's estate. Dun...something.

You have forced your way into my design.

The voice echoed, bouncing off the fitted stones. He pushed it away. He no longer knew if it belonged to the oracle who had foretold his future, or to Athene, but he couldn't bear the taunt in it, not now.

He needed a physician, medicine, and water. He was so thirsty. But the idea of standing was more than he could bear, and he was afraid. What if Aodhàn Mackinnon found him?

In lucid moments, he fantasized. The first one he'd take his rage out on would be Aodhàn Mackinnon. He could hardly believe his old enemy had survived being stabbed in the chest and dumped in the ocean. Patrick had ferreted out the story in Àrnasdal during one of his property searches, for it was a popular tale up and down the coast. Seaghan MacAnaugh happened along at the perfect moment to rescue poor drowning Aodhàn. So here he was, alive, twenty years older and far poorer. Not only had he survived, he'd found Aridela, and, according to incensed yet exultant gossip, was working hard to separate her from her namby-pamby husband, the loyal hound, Menoetius. Would these three never change? They kept being reborn, living out the same useless existence, over and over again, and for what? Perhaps Athene had expired at some point, leaving her human playthings to forever spin in some self-generating rotation that couldn't be stopped. If so, he was caught up in it with them.

Patrick drifted in the ocean of his delirium. He saw himself as a young prince, the son of Lycomedes of Tiryns. *Every one of your kin, to the lowest bastard you have sired, will perish on my sword,* he'd promised Chrysaleon. His brain dredged up other bodies he had consumed and used, too many to count. He'd learned how to listen to the sensations that warned him of the triad's presence. He'd learned how to follow and find them. At first he'd done what anyone in his position would—killed them. But he quickly realized two things: killing them did not mean they were dead; toying with them, making them suffer, prolonged the thrill and added spice to his very long, often tedious, life.

One of his favorite recollections was as Heinrich Baten, Papal Inquisitor, who forced Chrysaleon to watch without recourse as he'd tortured Aridela.

How he loved Christianity! It lent itself so perfectly to his own goals and passions.

Once he learned that Chrysaleon could look directly at him and not know who he was, that was when he really began enjoying himself. As long as he kept Chrysaleon from smelling him, he was safe.

He had to admit he went too far during the German Inquisition. Confident in his terrifying role and in the protection of his guards, he made sure Chrysaleon recognized him, and that arrogance had come close to finishing him.

"He hasn't succeeded yet," Patrick told himself as he tumbled and pitched on dirt turned to heaving waves. Would it, in the end, be a simple flesh wound that proved his undoing? The fever and hallucinations were worsening. Again and again, he relived the ordeal in the cavern at Lebadeia, on the Greek mainland, where he had gone to receive the oracle's revelation. He heard the voices, felt those unearthly hands upon him, and most especially he saw the eyes glowing out of the darkness.

I shall use you.

One morning, he woke in the ruin outside of Glenelg unusually clear-headed, and knew he was dying.

Groaning, he forced himself to his feet and waited, bent over, for the vertigo and hammering to lessen. When he could see the ground in front of him, he staggered from the ruin intent on one thing. Finding a body, any body, to consume before it was too late.

Chapter 6

Olivia was squalling when Diorbhail brought her into Lily's sitting room, but Morrigan soon had the child giggling with a game of keekaboo, then soothed with the newly available powdered milk formula Lily had convinced Morrigan to try, telling her it was high time Olivia adapted to something other than her mother's breast.

"Did you and Ramsay go to Covent Garden?" Lily asked as she poured tea.

"Aye. I mean yes," Morrigan said.

"A wagon-load of flowers arrived with instructions to put them in your bedroom."

"I swear he bought every bloom I admired until I caught on and made him stop."

"Your husband is the rarest of fabled creatures. A romantic male."

Morrigan had been afraid of embarrassing herself or worse, Curran, with her provincial speech and mannerisms. But after a week with Lily, her nervousness disintegrated. It was a pleasure to put this raven-haired lady in the category of *merry*, and Richard, her husband, as well.

"What else did you do?" Lily offered her a plate of star-shaped biscuits and fancy lemon teacakes.

"We walked in Hyde Park." Morrigan closed her eyes to better enjoy the sweetness of sugar mixed with the tang of lemon. "Mr. Disraeli was there. We saw Buckingham Palace. Then it was off to Piccadilly and Knightsbridge. I bought twelve yards of watered silk from the Orient for my Aunt Ibby, and a collar for my dog, embroidered with rubies—sham of course. Can you imagine, I saw a dog collar with real diamonds! And they were meikle—I mean, large."

"Every taste is catered to in London," Lily said, a bit darkly. "What shall we do tomorrow? We could take Olivia to the zoo in Regent's Park, and afterwards we could picnic, if the weather allows."

"Would you like that, lassikie?" Morrigan asked her daughter. Olivia kicked her plump legs, caught at her toes, and giggled.

Lily begged to hold her. Olivia returned her hostess's smiles for a moment but soon twisted in search of her mama. She had little patience for anyone but Morrigan, Curran, or Diorbhail.

"The Hamiltons are having a ball. They're vulgar money, like us, so we're invited. There's enough time to have a dress made, thanks to my dressmaker. I've never seen anyone sew so fast. And my maid, Hélène, is a genius with hair. What do you think of baby's breath? Sprigs of white against your dark hair would be enchanting."

"Oh, aye. Thank you."

"Ramsay's been so vague about your travels." Lily handed the squirming baby back to her mother. "And he kept blushing like a naughty schoolboy. I could sense mischief was afoot. Ah, now you're blushing. I adore mischief. Tell me what you've been up to."

Of course Morrigan couldn't tell her what had precipitated their flight from Glenelg. "It…was an adventure," she said, as her cheeks grew hotter. "He wanted to show me a place he visited when he was young. Then I wanted to go to Cape Wrath, because I'd heard a story about it. Then he wanted me to meet you." She shrugged. "It grew and grew."

One of Lily's brows lifted. "You make it sound quite ordinary, but I have a feeling there's more to it. In fact, it sounds as though you and Ramsay are on a pilgrimage of sorts."

"I don't know what that is," Morrigan said, and dropped her gaze to Olivia's face, embarrassed.

Lily moved closer so she could stroke Olivia's head then she clasped Morrigan's fingers. Gently, she said, "It's more than an adventure. It's a journey to a spiritual place, a place of meaning. It's something that changes you. Sometimes a pilgrimage happens nowhere but in the heart. Other times, the body comes along, as with you. I know of what I speak, having gone on my own, which brought me out of darkness to Donaghue, and this life." She glanced fondly at the room's opulent furnishings and rich wallpaper.

Morrigan hesitated to ask for details, fearing it might be uncivil.

Lily sipped her tea. "Where will you go after London?"

Morrigan could only blink. She had made no plans. She hadn't allowed herself to hope for anything beyond each unfolding moment. But, if all remained the same, Curran would ask her where she wanted to go, as it would be her turn. "I don't know," she said. "I'll have to think on it."

MORRIGAN WOKE IN THE SILENT HOURS AFTER MIDNIGHT. CURRAN LAY NEXT TO her, breathing evenly, one arm thrown across her stomach.

She donned a robe and padded barefoot through the mansion, thinking how different it was from the daytime, when servants were everywhere.

Surely she could find a novel to keep her company. The sumptuous library was dark inside, but warm. She lit a lamp and picked up a leather-bound volume from the table beside it.

It was a book of poems. Settling into the wing chair, she opened it and scanned until a heading caught her eye.

Tristram and Iseult.

How could I have known that your waist would fit my hands like it was made for them? That your body would mold into mine and mine into yours as though we were twined within the same womb?

"Morrigan? Morrigan, dear?"

Morrigan woke with a start. Lily was bending over her, smiling as she brushed a lock of hair off her face.

"Did you sleep all night down here?"

"I came down to read. I must have dozed off."

"Are you hungry? Breakfast is ready in the dining room. What were you reading?"

Lily picked up the book, still open on Morrigan's lap. "Ah, one of my favorites," she said, glancing at the cover, then turned it to the open pages. "A gorgeous tale."

"Aye." Morrigan fought to extricate herself from the warm, scented dream. In that shadowed place of fantasy, her lover offered seductive confessions that Morrigan knew instinctively were hers alone; he had never said such things to any other woman.

She'd been imagining Tristram and his Irish princess, Iseult, before she fell asleep, and the imagining had entwined with her dreams. It was hard to push away the entreaty in the man's voice, hard to return to dull, bright reality.

"Did you like it?" Lily hooked her arm through Morrigan's and they climbed the stairs so Morrigan could change out of her nightgown.

"I loved it," Morrigan said. "It was braw, so braw. But sad."

The lines returned. *Tristram! —Tristram! —Stay—receive me with thee! Iseult leaves thee, Tristram! Never more.*

Lily stopped on the landing and gestured to a painting, one Morrigan had noticed several times over the last few days. It depicted a woman, a man, and a dog very similar to Antiope. Both the dog and the man regarded the woman adoringly.

"Hugues Merle, a Frenchman, painted this," Lily said. "It is his imagining of Tristram and Iseult. I had to have it, and Richard obliged me."

"It's beautiful," Morrigan said dutifully. But the painted Iseult was remote and expressionless, like a marble statue, her face turned away from the man and the dog. Her left hand rested on the dog's neck, but she didn't seem aware of the man, who touched her arms so lightly he might have been plucking the strings of a lute. Such detachment didn't match the Iseult in the book of poems. That woman was passionate, her grief at the dying Tristram's bedside palpable.

I will always be with thee; I will watch thee, tend thee, soothe thy pain; sing thee tales of true, long-parted lovers, join'd at evening of their days again.

Lily chattered gaily as they continued to Morrigan's bedroom, telling her about the time she, Richard, and Curran had traveled to Munich to see the Wagner opera, *Tristan und Isolde* at its premiere. She described the sets, the orchestra, the women with their opera glasses and lacy gowns. "One of the conductors was so overcome with emotion he had to be committed to an asylum!" she claimed with obvious delight.

It reminded Morrigan of a letter she'd received from Louis Stevenson. He'd written in his fanciful way that he sometimes wished he could live inside an opera.

As the maid draped a morning gown over her head, enveloping her for an instant in a cocoon of darkness and fabric, she felt as though she was falling headlong into the poem, or her dream.

Sometimes, she thought uneasily, she couldn't tell the difference.

She was soon dressed. Lily took her arm again. They left the bedroom and came upon Richard and Curran at the foot of the staircase.

"How I wish you could see the opera," Lily said as they all entered the dining room. "I do wonder if it will ever come here. I would love to watch prim, proper London being bombarded with all that sexual desire and tension, the moment when everything is forgotten in blissful frenzied fulfillment. It's all there, in the singing, the music. Yet it's about escaping our sexual longings as well, through the release of death." She shrugged. "I confess that part makes little sense to me. Why escape our sexual longings? They were molded within us for a reason—to enjoy!"

"Lily, please." Richard gripped his wife's chin sternly, though Morrigan was certain she saw hints of a smile. "Mrs. Ramsay will run screaming from our home if you don't stop talking in this indecent fashion. She's a lady, unlike you, my strumpet. Look at her! Her face is as red as those drapes, and you know you only hung those to scandalize the neighbors."

"Nonsense. Ramsay would never wed one of those long-nosed spinsters who swoon at the sight of a bloomer. You insult Mrs. Ramsay by grouping her with them."

"There is a happy medium, my love, between a long-nosed fainting spinster and a brazen tart, for which you don't allow. Surely our Mrs. Ramsay fits into the vast middle ground."

"Please don't argue," Morrigan said. "I'm no' offended, I swear."

She glanced at Curran, thinking of her life before she'd met him, of the thrashings, the dreadful entertaining of strangers, the soul-numbing chores, and the night Douglas Lawton had sought to end her life…not to mention that other night she couldn't bear to think of at all.

Then she pictured the day she had given this man what propriety claimed was a woman's only asset, if she didn't have land or a title.

He seemed to understand. He twined his fingers between hers and kissed her temple.

"Now, now, Donaghue insists we act with decorum." Lily flicked the back of his hand with her napkin, but her smile was pure benevolence.

Glenelg's scruffy delivery boy perused Aodhàn curiously as he handed over a sealed envelope. The fisherman had never before received a letter.

Aodhàn unfolded the missive, his gaze going first to the signature. It was from Faith, Lilith's aging mother on Barra, and was scrawled in nearly unreadable Gaelic.

An Englishman is staying at the MacNeil house. He is asking questions about you, about Lilith, about what happened. He hired me as cook and maidservant. He does not know who I am. His name is Quentin Merriwether.

It was easy to guess why Curran's solicitor was snooping around on Barra. Curran must have sent him. But why? It could only be because of those careless things he'd said to Seaghan the morning after Curran and Morrigan's wedding, when his memories were freshly returned, burning through him like lightning. Aye, he was almost certain he'd said something about Barra, and his wife. Seaghan must have told Curran.

Aodhàn's long friendship with Seaghan was destroyed. Curran and

Morrigan were gone for the foreseeable future. He hadn't yet determined a way to get to London, but he could find someone to sail him over to Barra for the cost of a red fish or two. Quentin Merriwether needed to be dealt with. It would only take a few days.

The man's blood would be on Curran's hands.

Chapter 7

Morrigan's gown, a mossy green taffeta creation, was finished the very day of the Hamilton ball. Lily's French maid, Hélène, arranged her hair in a beautiful twist, adding a few loose wisps in front of her ears and on the neck. She shocked Morrigan by insisting the already plunging décolletage be coaxed lower. Thankfully the rosettes in the center added a teasing hint of subterfuge to her cleavage.

With a diamond tiara sparkling in her piled black hair and a sapphire-blue gown, Lily resembled a celestial goddess. Her neckline was even lower than Morrigan's, and, far from embarrassed, the saucy wench plumped her breasts higher and gave an irrepressible laugh. "I'll have those gentlemen drooling like infants," she said.

"Do you vex your husband with the things you do?" Morrigan blurted.

For the briefest second, Lily's finely arched brows lifted. Then she smiled and shook her curls. "We have a unique understanding." She dabbed a crystal perfume applicator to the hollow in her throat, and the room was inundated with the tantalizing scent of roses. "Come with me." Lily guided Morrigan to the freestanding looking-glass and rested an arm around her shoulders. "There you are, *cara mia*," she said. "How lovely. I knew that color would be perfect on you. It brings out hints of red in your hair, and complements your skin." She tilted her head. "Do you know how beautiful you are?"

Morrigan blushed. She wanted to pull free of Lily's touch and at the same time, longed to dissolve into it. Was it because she'd never known a mother's embraces that the touch of women moved her so?

"Oh, I dinna ken," she said, nervousness making her forget her attempts to cultivate a more patrician manner of speaking.

Lily smiled and fingered one of the wisps of hair in front of Morrigan's ear. "My darling, that is one of your most delightful aspects. If you did know, you would be a formidable adversary to our blue-blooded witches. Morrigan. The name hardly fits, bella. Somehow it makes me think of a necromancer. Of blood and cauldrons. Definitely worldly. Fearless."

"Then it's a mistake on me," Morrigan said. "Because I sometimes think I'm afraid of everything."

Lily's hand faltered then dropped to Morrigan's shoulder and pressed it. "I think you're quite brave."

"Brave?" It was difficult to remain still. The only other women she'd ever been so close to were Eleanor and Diorbhail.

"I hope you'll forgive us," Lily said. "Ramsay told me about your father. Yet you never ran away."

"Only because I was more afraid of what might happen to me elsewhere."

"And it was also brave," Lily continued without pause, "to accompany Ramsay to Glenelg and become his lady of the manor."

"What other choice did I have? I was…." She caught herself.

"And now," Lily went on, "you're courageous enough to be kind to me."

"Why would that take courage? You're maybe the brawest lady I've ever met."

Were those tears in Lily's eyes? "*Merci, mon amie.*"

"What does that mean?"

"It means 'thank you, my friend.' It's French." The tears vanished as Lily laughed. "I made Donaghue hire French and Italian tutors." They left the mirror and sat together on a damask loveseat. "I wanted to learn the languages of love, but I wasn't interested in irregular verbs and conjugations. *Dieu*, how tedious." She leaned closer, lowering her voice. "I only wanted to learn things like *donne-moi un petit bisou*. That means, 'give me a little kiss.'"

Morrigan giggled.

Lily shook her index finger, demanding solemnity. "Listen carefully, my dear. Tomorrow is your husband's birthday, isn't it? How old will he be?"

"Twenty-seven."

"I believe I have the perfect idea for a gift. Something he would particularly appreciate. Tonight, when you and Ramsay retire, you have my permission to use whatever I teach you. Now repeat after me: *Embrasse-moi*."

"Ahmbrasseh maw."

"Try to give it a French accent, darling, not a Scottish one. That means simply, 'Kiss me.' Ah yes, I have a feeling he would appreciate that. He might give you little kisses in places you'd least expect, eh?"

Morrigan fought the urge to throw her skirts over her face.

"And, since you are a good girl, you must say 'please.' *Embrasse-moi, s'il te plait*. Don't forget to appeal to his vanity. *Délicieux garçon*. That means, 'Delicious boy.' Oh, and we mustn't forget to tell him 'happy birthday.' That is *Joyeux anniversaire*. Although I think he might not hear that one after the other things you'll be saying. Would you care to know more?"

"Aye." Morrigan nodded. "*S'il te plait.*"

Glittering chandeliers, plush carpet, bejeweled guests, and expensive champagne in the thinnest gold-edged crystal left Morrigan shyly awed. Elegant society paraded, gossiped, frittered, and danced, exhibiting a carefully cultivated air of nonchalance while managing to note and discuss every detail of the other guests. Morrigan was introduced to so many people her head began to swirl.

Lily fluttered her fan and smoothed one of Morrigan's curls with lace-covered fingers. Drawing her attention to various personalities, she happily related the current scandals. "There's Rossetti," she said, smiling behind her fan. "If he hears that Whistler has asked to paint you, he'll try to steal you away. His wife died, you know."

"Oh, I'm sorry," Morrigan said, wondering at the glint in Lily's eye.

"She committed suicide over his infidelities. He buried several of his poems with her then regretted their loss. It was Whistler who talked him into exhuming her in order to recover them."

Horrified, Morrigan glanced at the artist, who caught her looking and smiled.

In her other ear, Curran murmured, "She can spend all night doing this, you know, especially if you keep rewarding her with that shocked expression."

"The more I hear of Whistler the more I dislike him."

"He's a bohemian. Bohemians thumb their noses at society's sacred rules. That's the source of their charm."

Lily bent closer to Morrigan's ear, using her fan to disguise her words. "You think Rossetti's adventures disgraceful? They are nothing compared to the composer of *Tristan und Isolde*. Wagner was rumored to be King Ludwig's lover."

Morrigan tried to hide her shock but knew she'd failed by the wide smile on Lily's face.

"You're going to muss your hair, darling, if you keep fanning yourself so vigorously. Now come with me. I have more secrets to teach you. Isn't this fun!"

At close to two o'clock in the morning, Curran covertly loosened his cravat and searched for the ladies. He hadn't glimpsed either Lily or Morrigan in over an hour, and the Hamilton mansion was enormous.

He was pleased he'd chosen London as their next destination, though the journey from Cape Wrath had been arduous. Morrigan enjoyed exploring the great old city. She and Lily had become fast friends, and most of the time she appeared quite happy.

Yet Aodhàn Mackinnon remained like a spectre between them. He would be, until they cleared the air, but every time they came close, she shied away.

He caught sight of her in her beautiful dress, shaped like an opening tulip, the skirts constructed into various layers and folds. The bodice sparkled, due to a scatter of miniature crystals. She stood across the room, gazing straight at him, the lower half of her face hidden behind her lace-edged fan. As soon as their eyes met she fanned it provocatively, disguising all but her eyes. Music, laughter, and the clink of glass faded as she deliberately shut the fan and reopened it. Then she turned and left through a dim alcove, pausing once to deliver one last meaningful look.

The message was obvious, even without the use of the fan. Where had she learned such a ploy? Lily, no doubt. Glancing around to make sure no one else had noticed, he set down his glass and followed.

She was waiting for him on one of the terraces, within the overhanging branches of a magnolia tree. He approached her with a faint smile, which she returned before taking his hand and leading him down a set of steps to the foot of the tree, where a wrought-iron bench kept company with deep shadows, hiding them from the colored lanterns and bright windows framing the dancers inside. The air was intoxicating.

"Curran." She leaned against the tree trunk. Catching hold of his lapels, she pulled him close. It brought that day on the moor outside of Stranraer into sharp focus, the abandoned shieling and sprinkle of rain, the first time he'd kissed her.

She melted bonelessly against him and they descended as one to the bench.

Instead of magnolia blossom his lungs filled with the scent of the soft bracken in the Stranraer hills, and in the distance, perhaps only in memory, he heard a solitary curlew's haunting cry.

Chapter 8

Once again, Aodhàn Mackinnon stood on the bluff above Castlebay, looking out over the southern islands. Heavy fog obscured the farthest two, Mingulay and Berneray.

He kicked at a stone, one of the few that hadn't been carted off, and contemplated the years he'd lived in Bishop House, first with his father, then, later, with Lilith and their weans. For a moment he thought he heard childish laughter, but no, it was only the wind, soughing through the grass.

He was surprised to discover warm tears running down his face, and wiped them away with a hard, angry swipe.

He'd provoked the punishment on Barra, first by having Daniel killed, and later, tipsy on a half-bottle of wine, when he'd given in to Lilith's demands. One look from those eyes of hers and he became a babbling idiot, disgorging the secrets he knew better than to reveal...with certain embellishments, of course, a few necessary omissions. He had broken both of Athene's cardinal rules.

He pictured Curran. The laird of Glenelg had a handsome face and an engaging charm. Both had helped make his life one smooth accomplishment after another. Were he to remember their incarnations, he wouldn't have to omit or embellish facts. He could sleep at night without nightmares. He wouldn't be forced to hear the screams of his murdered children.

This hilltop was a dismal place. It made him burn for vengeance, even now, after he'd killed all twelve men who had forced their way into his home and slaughtered his family.

Quentin Merriwether didn't know it, but he would be Aodhàn's thirteenth, a victim of Curran's meddling. Barra hadn't yet slaked its thirst for the blood of retribution.

FAITH COAXED THE ENGLISHMAN FROM HIS SCRIBBLING BY TELLING HIM SHE'D found a crofter who wanted to speak to him about the murdered family. She led him through the deepening gloaming, up to the ruin of Bishop House, where Aodhàn was waiting with a garrote. Afterward, she helped Aodhàn get the body to a remote cove, where it could be weighted with stones and dumped. Aodhàn didn't really care if the corpse surfaced again. If it did, it would serve as a reminder to Curran—to everyone—that he would not be trifled with.

In the coldest hours of the night, he returned to the MacNeil house with Faith and rummaged through Quinn's belongings. There wasn't much of interest, except at the writing table, where he uncovered a letter from Curran.

Quinn,
Have you found anything? Why have I not heard from you? We're still in
London, but will soon be leaving. Morrigan wants to come there, to Barra. I
could scarcely believe it when she told me, but I have to honor her choice: it's a
pact we made. We'll be in Mallaig on the first of August to fetch her aunt then
will stop at Kilgarry for the other one. C.

This was interesting. Her subterranean memories were leading her to revisit the places she'd lived with *him* in other lives. One day, she might want to travel farther afield, to the German Empire, even to Crete.

Thinking of Crete turned his thoughts to the knife, and his humor instantly dissipated. Diorbhail must have spied on him. She always had been a trouble-maker. He remembered when she'd unearthed damning evidence on Crete, and Alexiare had been forced to kill her. Aodhàn could hardly believe she'd made herself crawl into that wet, suffocating hole, braving mud, cold, and spiders. Selene's courage obviously lived on in Diorbhail Sinclair.

Now Morrigan had the knife. He was glad she'd had a weapon when she needed it, but she didn't know how dangerous this one was.

To distract himself, he broke the lock on the desk drawer and found the reply Quinn must have been drafting before Faith interrupted him.

I have disturbing information I do not want to trust to a letter. When you get
to Mallaig stay there. I will come over on the first of August and meet you at
the Scythe and Swan. Do not come here. It is too dangerous.

He'd underlined "do not come here" several times.

Aodhàn leaned the chair onto its rear legs as he contemplated the fire and worked out his plan. Quinn wouldn't be meeting anyone, or telling any tales of his discoveries, and without this letter to warn him, the laird wouldn't know what a risk he was taking by agreeing to his wife's request.

Curran would bring Morrigan to Barra.

Aodhàn laughed. All he had to do was wait.

Morrigan lay in bed, fast asleep. It was only eight-thirty, and they had stayed at the ball until nearly four. Curran, however, was awake—bleary-eyed and with a pounding head, but awake. He shrugged into his coat and paused to look at her. The covers had shifted during the night, leaving her partially exposed. He ran his index finger along her spine then leaned down and kissed her shoulder, wishing he could strip again and dive back into bed with her.

But Doctor Wietzel was waiting. The entire house seemed to be still asleep, but for a few muffled sounds floating from the kitchens. He let himself out without seeing anyone.

He pondered as the cab carried him to his destination. No matter how close and happy he and Morrigan were now, he knew the problems at Kilgarry hadn't been subdued. He longed to divine the future. Would she abandon him? Would he yield to this newfound rage he hadn't known was lurking inside him, and hurt her?

The mutilated doll haunted him.

He'd always believed he would make a good husband and father. Now he had doubts. He feared his jealousy, and this new hatred for Aodhàn Mackinnon.

He stepped out of the cab into drizzling rain and an unseasonable chill. *Doktor Wietzel*, the bright brass nameplate on the green portal declared. No indication of what sort of doctor he was. The man, a German native, came highly recommended. He'd studied at the famed French *Salpêtrière* hospital with Jean-Martin Charcot, and was considered to be at the forefront of the newly emerging study of mental disorders.

Not until Curran sat in a deep comfortable chair in the elderly alienist's office, a cup of coffee in hand, did he begin to question why he'd made this appointment. What did he hope to discover? That he was afraid he might harm his wife? That he thought her half-mad?

In one numbing instant, he realized what he'd been avoiding. He would pay the cost, whatever it was. He had to protect her. But from what? *You're the biggest threat to her*, he caught himself thinking, and scraped a palm over his tired eyes.

It was chilly enough this morning that someone had lit a fire in the hearth. Its crackle and spark reached out, teasing him into its hot core. Doctor Wietzel's nasal voice faded into the flickering light on the wallpaper. No, the walls were not paper. They were stone. He was in a cave, lying on a pallet, half-covered in animal fur. Beside him reclined a woman, her hair falling over the edge of the pallet like a black river. *Kiss me,* she said, and he did.

She wasn't Morrigan. Yet she was. He knew her by the mark on her wrist, and something else…in her eyes, something invisible that surrounded her. *This* was the woman Curran had dreamed of all his life. It was she, as a child, whom he'd carried from some underground place—she who had been imprisoned by a lion. Most recently he'd envisioned her while caught in the magic of Diorbhail's mushroom at Cape Wrath. He'd seen many things that day, had seen himself making love to this woman, and for the first time, he knew her name.

Aridela.

I am empty as a broken crock, she said. *You should have a woman who can return your love, as Selene does. Vengeance is all that's left of me.*

He drew out the words carefully, so she wouldn't misunderstand. *I will bind you to this pallet until the day of your death.*

You'll tether me like a goat? That is your image of victory?

He threw himself over her, kissing then biting her throat until she cried out, yet still she pulled him closer. *I will have victory, Aridela,* he threatened fiercely.

"Mr. Ramsay?"

Curran blinked. Doctor Wietzel was bending over him with a glass of water.

"I think you are unwell, sir."

"No, no." Curran straightened. Perspiration dotted his forehead.

"You lost consciousness, or seemed to." The physician's voice echoed.

Aridela. Though it made no sense, Curran knew that woman was Morrigan. She'd called him Menoetius. Strange as the vision was, it was also familiar, and as real as this chair he sat in. *I will have victory.* He felt a kinship to that scarred, ugly warrior. The words reverberated through Curran's chest. He took the glass from Doctor Wietzel and drank all the water in three gulps.

I will have victory. The image of Aodhàn Mackinnon materialized. Curran's teeth grated; fire ran through his blood.

You wait and see.

CURRAN WAS BACK IN BED WITH HIS WIFE, OLIVIA ASLEEP BETWEEN THEM. AFTER the chilly rain that morning, the day had gone hot and muggy, and had made everyone sleepy.

He breathed in Morrigan's scent, a musky fragrance he could never identify, though it filled him with contentment. He traced her shoulder, his finger hooking beneath the scrap of lace that held up her chemise. "Won't you tell me what he did?" he asked.

"Who?" Morrigan's eyelids fluttered. Her fingers brushed over the baby's head nestled against her bosom, and moved on to her husband's bare shoulder.

"Your father. What did he do to you?" He wanted to understand. He wanted to know her.

"Drove Nicky away. Tried to…let me sleep." She rubbed her palm against his cheek. Her breathing lengthened.

Neither his wife nor daughter moved, but for the lift and fall of their chests.

It didn't last. Morrigan's head turned towards the pillow. She spoke one unintelligible word, trailing off at the end. "Crisss…."

"Are you awake?" he asked quietly.

For several moments she lay still, then she coughed. One hand lifted and scratched at her throat. Again she coughed. "No. No…."

"Morrigan?"

Her eyes opened. She sat upright, causing the lace to fall off her shoulder. "Let me go, Menoetius," she said, touching his cheek.

Blood pounded in his ears and his vision went spotty. "What did you say?"

She lay down again. Her eyes closed.

"Wake up." He shook her. "Morrigan, wake up."

"What's wrong?" she asked, yawning, blinking.

"What were you dreaming?" Olivia, awakened by her father's low but insistent voice, began a strident protest.

"Look what you've done. Oh, Livvy." She cuddled the baby. "Livvy, Livvy, everything's all right." Swinging her legs off the bed, she paced with the child.

"Can you mind it?" he asked. "You said something. Menoetius."

She paused and regarded him, a tilt to her head. "I was dreaming of you, but that was your name. You threatened me."

"Did I say I'd bind you?"

Her eyes widened. "How did you know that?"

"Because I had the same dream. We were lying beside a fire in a—"

"Cave."

"Aye," he said.

"You were keeping me from someone."

"You had black hair."

"I dreamed of the cave before. The first time we…on the moor, the first time, when I fell asleep."

"What does it mean?"

"I don't know." She returned and lay beside him, her back snuggled against his chest and stomach. He held her close, rubbing her cheek with his while she nursed the wean.

"Stop it," she said, half-smiling. "You need to shave. You're prickly."

"A shared dream." He mused, thinking of Cape Wrath and the dream he'd had simultaneously with her, the one where they were being stoned. A faint shiver started at the base of his spine and traveled to his scalp. "What could cause such a thing?"

"You were different. Your hair was dark, and you were horribly scarred."

"A lion did it."

"How d'you know?"

He shrugged. "I just do."

"A lion."

He knew what she was thinking. He was too. The castle beneath the water. Fighting a lion. The woman chained in the oak.

She pressed closer, rousing him though he tried to ignore it. "When I first saw you in Stranraer," she said, "at the train station, I thought you were Theseus come to life. My Greek hero, the man I always dreamed of when I was unhappy."

"I thought you a wood nymph, sunburned and covered with bracken."

She rolled onto her back, holding the babe on her stomach, and touched the scar beside his eye. "This scar…" she said. "It was there in the dream, but much worse. It started here, but went clear down your face." She trailed the tip of her index finger to his mouth.

He took her hand and kissed her fingertips.

"Don't you think that's odd?" she asked.

"Aye."

"You were kissing me. I wanted to stay there with you in that cave… forever. Forever and ever." Her eyes darkened. "Forever." Her face turned sad and forlorn. "But I don't think it happened."

"We're together now." Deep inside, that phrase formed. He'd heard it first when flying on the wings of whatever alchemy was in Diorbhail's mushroom. *What seems the end is only the beginning.*

He kissed her; she sighed, running her fingers through his hair and making a sound in her throat. "Your kisses are magic," she whispered.

Tell me you love me. It was a never-ending desire, one he never voiced. She had never said it. He'd never wanted to hear anything more.

She traced the scar next to his eye, frowning. "What makes us do the things we do? Why can't we form life the way we want it?" Lifting her hand, she flexed her fingers then closed them into a fist. "Sometimes I feel like the paddle wheel on a ferryboat."

He smiled. "That's an odd bit of a thing to feel like."

"I go round and round, clicking and clacking, churning the water, chopping up plankton and wee sea creatures, never getting anywhere, never finding a place to land. Just senseless spinning."

Dark thoughts behind those luminous eyes. Not wanting to cause her more concern, he kept to himself the certainty that somehow, somewhere, the tableau in the cave had happened. The two of them had been in that cave, though they'd looked different and possessed odd names.

He kissed away her frown. She kept him close, her hand stroking the back of his neck. When she rose to change Olivia's hippins he folded his arms beneath his head and gave himself over to the enjoyment of watching her. She wore nothing but a chemise, lace-edged drawers, and a single petticoat. When she caught him watching, she smiled and blushed like a virgin, this lass who had borne his child, and who once said, *I'm going to come home and ride you, my fine stallion.*

Doctor Wietzel had listened to Curran's concerns and had asked to examine her. "It might be possible to bring out the cause of her nervous disposition," he said, "and perhaps insert more healthy suggestions through the use of hypnotism. I've long wanted to try the method."

Curran was instantly on guard. "What is it?"

Doctor Wietzel frowned as he absently polished a smudge on the corner of his desk with a handkerchief. "Hypnotism?" he said. "It was a popular theory in the '40s and '50s, mostly because of a surgeon in Edinburgh named Braid. He learned about the technique from texts on meditation coming out of India. I read his book on the subject—it was fascinating. Interest faded after his death, but lately, the French have resurrected the idea. Their new work shows promise, especially in the area of suggestion. Hysterical patients like your wife are surprisingly susceptible to new ideas and beliefs being placed into their thoughts. I have read accounts of tremendous changes in outlook and attitude."

In parting, Doctor Wietzel made a list of asylums in England and on the Continent where his wife would be treated with compassion. He'd been quite matter-of-fact about the whole idea, like Morrigan was nothing more than an interesting specimen warranting study. Curran left his offices in a cold sweat.

Bedlam. Even in these modern days, the hospital remained infamous. He shuddered at the thought of committing Morrigan. Never. She would *never* go to one of those places.

Yet the man's final words troubled him. *From what you say, I believe she can be dangerous in her present state, not only to you and the child but also to herself. Aggressive treatment is her best hope. You must not delay.*

Curran thought of the latticework of scars across Morrigan's back, her white-hot fury the night of Michaelmas, and the mangled doll.

Doctor Wietzel had theorized that Morrigan's strange dreams were an outward symptom of an unbalanced mental state.

So if he had the same dream…did it mean he was unbalanced as well?

Chapter 9

Mr. and Mrs. Hamilton had accepted Lily's invitation to dinner and brought their three daughters, Nan, the eldest, who had been feted at the recent ball, Phoebe, and Julia. Henry Leyland, Quinn's law partner, came on his own. One of Richard's business partners, Isaac Osbourne, and his wife Gwyneth, rounded out the party.

Conversation about the Hamilton ball and other society gossip eventually dwindled, and the topic turned to Lily's well-known obsession with the Wagner opera, *Tristan und Isolde.* "None other compares," she said.

Richard grinned as he lifted a spoonful of soup to his mouth. "Will you never get beyond that sentimental tripe, my dear?"

"He's teasing," Lily said to Morrigan. "That opera had him weeping like a baby. Pay no attention to his martyrdom."

Morrigan smiled at the way they loved insulting each other, then was mortified when Lily brought all eyes to her.

"Mrs. Ramsay recently read Matthew Arnold's poem," she said, "and I have a new convert."

"It—it's a wondrous story," Morrigan stammered. She mustn't betray why she found it so enchanting. She never wanted Curran to suspect, though she knew it was too late. He'd suspected since Michaelmas. She glanced surreptitiously at him. He knew the Tristram story better than she, and she couldn't help but wonder if he linked it to them.

Candlelight reflected in his long-lashed eyes, and his smile was pensive. She wished, as she had uncounted times, that she could slice Mackinnon from her heart, where he had no right to reside.

The Hamilton girls didn't know the story. Lily was happy to answer their questions; Morrigan listened intently as well, for the opera version fleshed out many details that hadn't been in the poem.

Lily came to the part in Act II where the lovers deemed daylight an illusion, while night freed them from day's lies.

Morrigan had once compared Mackinnon and Curran to night and day. Curran, a bright golden sun, sat openly beside her while Mackinnon was banished to dark night.

Unaware of the inner storm she was creating, Lily described the scene. "They realize death is the opening of a door where nothing can separate them. Together they will die, and lose themselves into love for all eternity."

Mackinnon's fever-stricken words returned. *Everything is spoiled. We should die and start over somewhere else.*

The air in Morrigan's lungs felt sticky, and Lily's voice faded beneath a swimming dizziness.

"In the final Act," Lily continued, "King Marc accuses Tristan of dishonor, and one of his knights attacks. 'Let the day to death surrender!' Tristan cries. He turns to Isolde and asks her to follow him."

Come with me. D'you love me enough? Morrigan fanned her face as wave after wave of heat flushed her skin. Lily's voice went on relentlessly, telling how Tristan was fatally wounded, and Isolde willed herself to die at his side.

One day, she and Curran must return to Scotland. To Kilgarry. Would this ancient saga reenact, with Curran, Mackinnon, and herself as principal players?

Curran rubbed the birthmark on her wrist, what he called her "witch's mark," though the term caused her creeping disquiet. Morrigan pasted on the required appreciative smile, false though it was, as Lily's tale came to an end. She retrieved her wine and sipped it to hide the tremble of her lips.

The girls were entranced, especially Nan, who was preoccupied with love and marriage.

"It's an epic tragedy," Lily said. "The lovers symbolize emotions so encompassing only death can relieve the pain. Wagner wanted to suggest the ultimate dissatisfaction with this life, and the possibilities of the beyond."

Could love and death, though opposite in many ways, be seen as twins, born of one womb? Did the potion force Tristan and Isolde to fall in love, or did it free the love that was already there? Was this fate beyond their choice? Beyond loyalty to king, kin, country, or marriage?

Morrigan stole another glance at Curran.

Lily sipped her wine and dabbed her lips with a napkin. "Wagner has claimed that one needn't understand German or know the legend to grasp his theme. His intent was to communicate through music alone, and he succeeded.

I do wish someone would bring it to London. It's been eight years. What could be causing this delay?"

"I want to see it," Nan said. "Mama? Take us to Germany!"

Mrs. Hamilton laughed. "You can go with your husband when you marry."

Lily said, "I've heard Wagner described as selfish and petty, but the opera proves the opposite. Such high, noble conceptions. Fulfillment through oblivion. Death granting bliss, since life condemned the lovers to be near, yet always separated."

"In life constant yearning," Morrigan said. "But in death, the destruction of guilt, responsibility, and duty. Death as the shadow of love."

There was an instant of silence. Morrigan realized she'd spoken her contemplation aloud. Horrified, she lowered her face.

"We shall have to toast you for that, my dear," Richard cried, though he didn't fully manage to hide his shock.

They all lifted their glasses but for Curran. Morrigan saw the dismay flash through his eyes, but she couldn't dwell on it, for awareness burst through her like a gun blast.

For days she hadn't given Mackinnon a passing thought. Her husband had muffled the inner call from the north, drowned it in his own magnetic presence. Now the call broke through again. Morrigan felt his suffering crash into her like the sea against the cliffs at Cape Wrath.

I never give up what's mine, he'd said that day in the clearing. *And you are mine.*

She'd recognized the pain beneath his threat, and now, sitting here in London, so far from him, glibly discussing how love could prompt suicide, his words reverberated. Mackinnon was older. He'd experienced much more of life than she. He knew love, death, and want.

"Morrigan."

She blinked. Her head cleared.

"Are you well?" Curran asked. "You have the strangest expression."

"I'm fine." She clasped his hand under the table.

"I think nearly every opera has the same elemental root," Isaac said. "That life will do what it wants with us, no matter how we try to shape it."

THE WOMEN RETIRED TO ONE OF THE DRAWING ROOMS FOR TEA AND SHERRY, leaving the men to smoke cigars, drink brandy, and "do whatever men do," as Lily put it.

They talked again about the ball. Mrs. Hamilton bragged of the calling cards pouring in for her Nan. The two younger daughters wore bored expressions and talked to each other behind their hands as they nibbled on sugary biscuits.

"How long are you staying in London?" Gwyneth Osbourne asked Morrigan as Mrs. Hamilton gushed on about the second son of a baronet who had begun pursuing her daughter.

"Not much longer," Morrigan said. "We've imposed upon the Donaghues enough, I think."

"Nonsense!" Lily said. "You could stay till Christmas. But tell me, *cara mia.* Have you decided where you want to go next?" She leaned closer to Gwyneth to explain. "They're playing a game. One chooses where to go and they go there, no questions asked. Then it is the other's turn to choose."

"That sounds droll!" the younger Hamilton girl cried. *Phoebe,* Morrigan remembered. Her sister said, "I would choose Africa!"

"Nothing so far afield for us," Morrigan said, "at least not yet. I have been thinking about it. I have a strange desire to see Barra. It's an island off Scotland's west coast."

She saw the confusion on the faces of the younger girls. With the entire world to choose from, she wanted to go to one of Scotland's backward islands? Morrigan could barely believe it herself. She knew better than to say, *I dream of it. It calls to me.*

"Do they even speak English there?" Mrs. Hamilton asked.

"I'm not sure," Morrigan had to admit.

"Oh," Lily cried. "I know Barra. I've been there! Donaghue's family owns a cottage on a tiny island south of it. We spent a week there once, years ago when he was trying to convince me to live in Scotland, and no, *nobody* spoke English!" She seized Morrigan's arm. "The cottage sits on a hill, apart from the village, if there is still a village. Mostly what the island has are birds and cliffs. Stupendous cliffs. According to Donaghue, the original cottage was owned by the Catholic Church, but it had fallen into ruin. A wealthy gentleman from Barra demolished what was left and built a new one for his wife. After they died, Donaghue's family acquired it, which isn't as strange as it sounds, because his great-grandmother was born there. It's surprisingly comfortable, with large windows, and hmm, four bedrooms, I think. You're most welcome to stay as our guests, for as long as you like, and that would save Richard from worrying what's happened to it. It's a desolate spot, to be sure, but it sounds as though that's what you and Ramsay prefer!" She laughed. "Give me the opera, the ballet, shopping, and balls any day."

"Where is it?" Morrigan asked. "Does this island have a name?"

"Yes of course. Forgive me. Mingulay."

Chapter 10

TENTATIVELY CALLING HIS WORK *WOMAN RECLINING ON THE BANK OF THE THAMES,* Whistler declared his masterpiece needed no more than a few final touches, and it would be finished.

"We have worked hard and must celebrate," he said. "When I'm in an especially good mood, I like to upset the classes of a local art instructor. Come, I'll give you a lesson."

Morrigan no longer considered Whistler a boor. She'd designated him merry, as well as incorrigible.

She soon discovered what he meant by "upsetting the classes." His appearance put the students in turmoil. They clustered and fawned over Whistler, and the poor instructor lost any semblance of order.

Whistler accepted it all as his due and encouraged Morrigan to try her hand at sketching. Giving her chalk and a sheet of brown paper, he demonstrated the curve of the model's back and legs.

Morrigan spent a good twenty minutes at the attempt, but her lines were crooked and childish. She finally gave up, crushing her paper into a ball.

"Don't feel sorry for yourself," Whistler said with a perceptive glance. "For if art were easy, we would all make our livings at it, wouldn't we?" He rolled a cigarette. "Would you care for one?"

"No," she said, still gloomy. "I couldn't."

"Timidity does not suit you." Snapping his chair upright, he leaned forward, his white forelock falling over his forehead. "You must live, girl. You have one chance to accomplish everything you're destined to do before your life is over."

His words sank in far deeper than he could know.

"You've been over-sheltered in Scotland. Here you can experience life in full measure. Stay in London."

"Very well," she said.

"You're going to stay?"

"No, but I'll try one of those things."

He laughed, rolled another cigarette, and lit it.

When the smoke entered her lungs she nearly exploded in a fit of violent coughing. "That's awful," she gasped, dropping it on the ground.

"It's an acquired taste, my dear, as is much in life."

The sun dipped westward, illuminating long streaks of cloud, like a deity stretching out a mighty hand. Whistler coaxed Morrigan into joining him for dinner, and sent a message to Curran to meet them at Rules.

The wine was delicious, plus it had the added benefit of making life more amusing and colorful. Oh, my. Whistler had no money? So that's why he asked Curran to come. Morrigan suspected her husband knew this even before he arrived, but he took care of the matter without a trace of annoyance.

A gentleman and three ladies happened by, causing a wave of murmuring and a frenzied rush of waiters. The well-dressed gentleman had thinning cotton-fuzz hair that couldn't completely cover a pink scalp, and a prominent swooping nose, like a craggy cliff.

Curran told her she was looking at Mr. Gladstone, the Prime Minister. The lady on his arm was Gladstone's wife—he didn't know the other two. One was a hollow-eyed woman, thin and delicate, with a nose remarkably similar to the Prime Minister's. What struck Morrigan was the feverish intensity, not only in the woman's eyes, but her entire face. Her companion was a lady of middle age, as plump as the other was thin.

As they passed, Morrigan overheard the thin lady say, "Mrs. Crewler and I have other obligations this evening, sir. If you will promise us your sponsorship, we can leave you and your good wife to enjoy your meal."

"I cannot do that," Morrigan heard Gladstone reply. She continued to observe them as they were seated at a nearby table. Gladstone snapped open a napkin and smoothed it in his lap. "Your sentimental efforts are admirable, but really, Mrs. Butler, I must insist we conduct this discussion another time. It is far too intimate a subject for open discourse in a public arena."

Gladstone's regard left the woman and landed upon Morrigan. He smiled and inclined his head, making her realize she was staring. She turned away, red-faced. Whistler's foot pressed against hers, letting her know her social blunder had not gone unnoticed. She dared not look at him, knowing he'd make some face and cause her to giggle.

When next she peeked at the Gladstone table, she saw the gaunt Mrs.

Butler close her eyes and press her lips together. The other lady, Mrs. Crewler, shook her head, frowning, as though in denial of something.

Last summer, Olivia had barely been conceived. Morrigan had fancied herself in love with Kit. Nicky and Douglas were very much alive, and she'd been certain her tiresome daily routine would never change. How wrong she had been. She'd married, become mistress of a grand manor, given birth, and fallen under the spell of a selkie. And here she sat, at one of London's foremost eating establishments, within speaking distance of the Prime Minister of England. Any moment now, Queen Victoria would enter and complete the scene.

"I do not understand you, Mr. Gladstone," said Mrs. Butler as she rose. "Our cause is decent. You've shown an interest. We were certain you would help. This is most disappointing."

She pressed a handkerchief to her lips. Mrs. Crewler took Mrs. Butler's elbow and guided her from the restaurant.

Gladstone and his wife spoke in hushed voices, shaking their heads.

Whistler left soon after. Morrigan's eyelids felt heavy as sinkers; she tried to hide a second yawn behind her hand, but Curran noticed. He instantly rose, holding her shawl for her, and they went out into the night. The lively hum of countless conversations and clink of glassware faded into the soothing drip of an earlier rain shower. London's streets loomed dark and empty; the air felt cool and fresh.

"Shall we walk halfway?" Curran asked. "It's a beautiful night."

"A Whistler night," Morrigan agreed. "I'll wager he's gone right back to the Thames to continue painting. Curran, how do you know these folk?"

"My father struck up many alliances during his lifetime. I merely carry on tradition. The queen, for instance, favors the portraits of my ancestor, Allan Ramsay. It's given us something to discuss."

She stopped. "You've spoken to the queen?"

"A few times, at Braemar. You'd think she would appreciate Gladstone. They're more alike than different, but she hates him. It's peculiar. Propriety is so important to her, and she strictly observes class distinctions. Yet at Braemar, I saw her allow her Scots ghillie all sorts of indiscretions. He spoke to her like a sailor and she simply blushed and giggled. May I smoke?" He lit a cigar at her nod. "The papers constantly lampoon them."

"They're lovers?"

"Who knows?"

They hailed a cab and soon arrived at Richard Donaghue's tall white mansion.

"I'll see to Olivia," Morrigan said. Curran nodded and followed the sound of male voices into the smoking parlor.

The child was fast asleep, thumb hooked in her mouth. Morrigan started to her own room but as she passed the stairs, she noticed Lily welcoming a group of women in the vestibule below.

Gwyneth Osbourne was there, and behind her, Morrigan was astonished to see one of the ladies who had fled Rules after being snubbed by the Prime Minister. All were speaking at once, making it impossible to decipher anything but a word or two.

Lily spotted Morrigan as she handed a wrap to the maid. "Here is Mrs. Ramsay," she said to the group. "Morrigan, join us, please."

"Well," Morrigan replied, a little unsettled by the anger she sensed. "I...." She descended the staircase hesitantly.

"Mrs. Crewler." Lily placed her hand on the woman's arm. "This is Mrs. Ramsay."

"I saw you earlier tonight," Morrigan said. "At Rules."

The lady looked surprised. "Oh, were you there? You witnessed our humiliation, then. Josephine and I failed to accomplish anything with Mr. Gladstone. He's spent hours on street corners, personally attempting to reform prostitutes. He established a refuge for them in Soho. I believed he would back us. This is a severe defeat."

"Shall we, ladies?" Lily gestured to the open door of a nearby drawing room. Everyone settled into comfortable wing chairs and loveseats, with cups of tea and plates piled with their choice of biscuits, wedges of cake, or pastries.

Lily introduced the other women to Morrigan, who almost instantly forgot most of their names.

"If you ask me, it's hypocritical," said one, a stout matron dressed in the same shade of half-mourning as Morrigan herself wore. "Why does he not want to help?"

"If we were a group of crusading men," Lily said, "he would have already thrown all his weight behind us." But she waved a hand, adding, "Oh, that isn't fair. We do have a large number of valuable male allies."

"What do you want from him?" Morrigan asked.

"His endorsement," said Gwyneth. "It would help so much if we're to have any hope of success."

At Morrigan's puzzlement, Lily said to the group at large, "We have all heard how much more advanced they are about this issue in Scotland. Please, enjoy your tea while I catch her up." As the others chatted, she said, "These women and I, and many others, are members of the Ladies National Association. We work with child prostitutes and orphans, and we're fighting for women to be given the vote. Tonight we're discussing the Contagious Diseases Acts. That's a set of laws Parliament passed about ten years ago. It's the goal of the LNA to have these laws repealed." She added, lower, "Speaking for myself, I often feel we accomplish little more than beating our heads uselessly against the walls raised against us." She sighed wearily. "It has been a very long battle, and we've made hardly a dent."

"You want to disband laws against contagious diseases?" Morrigan shook her head, baffled.

"Yes. They are cruel, unjust, and…silly! The truth is as slimy as the bottom of the Thames. In the beginning, the Acts were only enforced in a few military towns, because the surface aim is to halt the spread of venereal disease, which obviously runs rampant among soldiers. But, much like the diseases, the laws keep spreading, engulfing more places, and ever more women."

Lily gave Morrigan a perceptive glance. "Do you know what venereal disease is?"

Morrigan reluctantly shook her head. "Ague?" Thankful she had her fan, she employed it to cool her embarrassment. She hated being so unworldly. Once she'd been proud of having gone to school. The dominie had praised her and told her it was a shame she couldn't attend university. She'd thought herself quite stuffed with knowledge, but since coming to London, she'd been forced to realize she actually knew very little about anything.

"Do you see?" Mrs. Crewler had overheard. She nodded at Lily, who shook her head. "She doesn't even know what this crime is for which she could be imprisoned."

"Don't be ashamed," Lily said to Morrigan. "You aren't the only woman who has never heard of it. Most gently brought up ladies haven't, by design. I will explain, but you must prepare yourself. It's indelicate."

Morrigan nodded.

"The most serious disease in question is syphilis. It is passed along somehow between couples during the act of love. It's very bad—mortally so, in fact."

Half-suspecting they were playing a joke on her, Morrigan glanced around at the other ladies, but every expression was somber. "And women cause it?"

"No, no." Mrs. Crewler's voice was slightly hoarse and her nose was red, suggesting a recent bout with illness. "I suspect it is quite the opposite, though I keep that opinion to myself, for we need the good will of men. Only women are held to *blame*, which is a different thing altogether."

"No woman is safe any longer," said one of the other ladies, dressed in muted beige. "No woman, except perhaps the queen herself, and her daughters. Any of us can be arrested with impunity and coerced into the most humiliating physical examination you can imagine. We can be locked away on a doctor's say-so, against our will, without warning, and kept imprisoned for as long as they decide, undergoing their forced treatments."

"But why would they do that?" Morrigan asked. What was this disease? Did all women have it? Did she have it?

"You must understand," Lily said. "Men are not held accountable in the slightest measure. They are never locked away, infected or not. They are never examined or questioned. We did everything we could during the last Royal Commission to rectify this injustice, but they would not listen. They stubbornly cling to the idea, whether they actually believe it or not, that ladies of the night alone cause these diseases, and that controlling and locking up the women—alone—will solve the problem. At first, years ago, it was the intent to examine and treat the soldiers as well, and had they done so, they might have accomplished something. But the men protested and refused, and so that side of the matter was simply dropped."

"Ladies of the night..." Morrigan said. "You mean...fallen women."

"Oh, I didn't make that clear, did I?" Lily said. "Yes. I mean prostitutes."

"You would think our learned governors would be wise enough to perceive that all who engage in these unsavory pastimes play an equal part in the spread of the diseases," the woman in half-mourning said. "My husband says that when both are infected, either one will give it to the next person they are intimate with, including their wives. He is a physician," she added with some pride, "specializing in women's ailments. *He* is not afraid to support us."

"If men were suddenly subjected to such examinations," said one of the others, "you can be certain these laws would be instantly repealed. Instead, they claim that prostitution is a necessary part of a soldier's life. They do nothing to one half of the equation, and treat the other half like little more than animals or slaves. The prostitutes are condemned as degraded human beings with no rights, evil in fact for what they do, while the men are allowed to believe their use of a prostitute is completely natural. Ah, it irks Josephine to no end, no end!"

Morrigan thought of beloved Diorbhail and her sad-faced daughter. Stranraer's righteous populace had vilified them. No one had been punished for the child's murder. And she hadn't been a prostitute. Simply being called one was enough to cast her into a wasteland where anything could be done without repercussion.

Lily went on. "The laws began as a way to inspect and restrain only those who were infected. But they have expanded to a fearful degree. Now policemen walk around in anonymous clothing, granted complete authority to apprehend any female they wish, because according to them, every woman who steps outside her home might be a prostitute."

"It would be so easy to falsely accuse an innocent woman, just to make her suffer for some slight or rejection," said the lady in beige. "And I am quite sure that has happened."

"But it isn't only the wrongdoing towards decent wives and daughters that appalls us," Mrs. Crewler said. "This is just as despicable when it's done to a prostitute—to any person in a supposedly free society."

A woman who had been quiet spoke up. "But the stories of what's done to decent women and children will have the most impact." She was young and pretty, with thick blonde hair and blue eyes, but they were unquiet, and her hands trembled.

"Tell her, Honoria," Lily said, gently.

The lady set her teacup on a table and placed her hands on her lap. "I grew up in Portsmouth," she said. "When I was fourteen, my mother gave me a shilling and sent me off to purchase thread. The police surrounded me as I was entering the dressmaker's. They asked me questions I...I had no answer for. They bound my wrists and made me go with them to a nearby building, where they laced me into a straitjacket and...and performed this examination of theirs. I cannot describe it. I cannot tell you."

Mrs. Crewler rose and crossed to the girl, who had begun to weep. She said, over her shoulder, "She should have been taken to a magistrate, who might have had the intelligence to see she was no prostitute, but that part of the law is often ignored. In Honoria's case, one of the policemen who arrested her has been suspected of other crimes against women."

"They restrain the woman on a table," Lily said, low. "They clamp her legs apart, making her absolutely helpless. Then they examine her with instruments, looking for symptoms of disease. In Miss Collins's situation—Honoria's —they discovered, of course, that she was innocent, a virgin. She was given a few shillings, a bribe, to keep her quiet. She has never recovered, though four years have passed. Her parents cannot convince her to have a season. Instead she has committed herself to our cause."

Morrigan opened her mouth but couldn't speak. The story brought back in horrible clarity what had happened when she'd taken witch's cap. She heard the grate of the rope through the pulley, felt the leather straps tightening on her legs, the cold iron and sharp prongs of that nameless device Heinrich Baten had shoved into her.

She almost felt it now, tearing and stretching. Sweat broke out on her palms and temples. Hoping to conquer the vertigo swirling behind her eyes, she took several deep breaths.

"There are many other stories. I have heard of women having cloth shoved into their throats to stifle their screams, and I know of at least one woman who killed herself after being examined. It is rape, no matter what lofty medical name they give it."

Last August, Morrigan and Louis Stevenson sat on the ground by the pond near the Wren's Egg. *Why do folk hate weans who have no say in being born?* she'd asked him. *Hate women who mean no harm?*

But of course, those who wrote these laws did believe women meant harm. Maybe they were right.

"Didn't Ramsay tell you?" Lily met Morrigan's gaze with cool composure. "I come from Windmill Street. I was nothing so fine as a member of the demi-monde. I was a whore who gave myself to men in alleys for the price of bread. My mother was strangled by a drunken stevedore. I never knew my father. London teems with such children. There isn't much they can do to survive but sell their bodies. It's the only thing they own. I was twelve when I sold myself the first time—old by some measures. Imagine your Olivia, accidentally separated from you in the street. She could be snapped up before you could find her and carted off to a brothel. There, men might offer a hundred pounds or more for the privilege of being the first to have her. This fair city boasts many such places."

Morrigan's teacup fell as though in a dream. Tea splashed over Lily's slippers and the carpet. "Oh! I'm sorry," she cried, seizing a napkin to wipe at the spill.

"Leave it." Lily grabbed Morrigan's hand. "That was cruel of me. I wanted you to feel it as I do, but I should not have used Olivia as an example. Forgive me, *cara mia*."

"I didn't realize."

"Of course you didn't. Who knows where I would be now, if not for Donaghue? Prostitutes, contrary to popular moral sentiment, are people. If they could conjure another way to put food in their stomachs, they would do it. Each morning my first thought is to thank God for Richard—Richard *is* my god, really. He's suffered abuse for being my champion, yet he shrugs it off. He's even had to give up his dream of having children, for I cannot conceive, probably due to one disease or another I had when I was on the streets."

"Lily…."

She smiled sadly. "He is the dearest man, along with your husband. Donaghue has a saying for those who chastise him: *advienne que pourra.* 'Happen what may.' You cannot fathom the depth of what that means to me, the knowledge that he will always stand by me."

"I thought you a born aristocrat."

Lily laughed. "Truly? I don't fool many so easily. Does this change your opinion of me? Can we still be friends?"

There was the barest hint of forlorn resignation in her voice, making Morrigan wonder how many others called "friend" had abandoned her.

Morrigan again saw Diorbhail's face. *I love you,* she'd said. *I'd die for you.*

She put out her hand to cover Lily's. "*Je t'aime,*" she said ardently. "*Crevettes et toujours.*"

"*Très bien.*" Lily tried to stifle a smile. "I'm not sure about the reference to shrimps, though, darling."

"Bloody hell!" Morrigan cried, before remembering where she was. She asked their pardon, adding to Lily, "I should give up trying to learn that language."

Lily brushed at her eyes and leaned closer. "I treasure your friendship too," she said. "*Aujourd'hui et toujours.*" She pressed her cheek to Morrigan's.

Morrigan felt the wetness of her hostess's tears and experienced an instant of enraptured fulfillment. Romance was fine and exciting, but nothing satisfied as much as being understood, or being able to give one's trust and know it would never be betrayed.

Lily sat up and smiled mistily. "Miss Collins and I have opened two homes for orphans," she said. "We feed and clothe about three hundred children a year, and we have several ladies who teach them various ways of earning money so they don't have to resort to selling themselves."

"How do you pay for it?" Morrigan asked.

"Investors. Donaghue contributes of course, and he has brought in others from his club. Miss Collins has a brother who is set to inherit. He also makes generous contributions." She smiled again. "I can see you did not know your husband is one of our investors. It's so like him, to keep his good works quiet."

Morrigan pondered all this as Lily returned her attention to the others and revisited the business of the evening. "So. Gladstone will not help. Does Josephine have another plan up her sleeve?"

Mrs. Crewler bunched her handkerchief in a fist. "She never loses heart. She will probably dash off another colorful speech, and rally a thousand new recruits to the cause. I wish I had her optimism. I confess I often feel we are mere objects of ridicule, a pitiful band of women shouting into the darkness, ignored or laughed at by those we must persuade."

"Why has this been done?" Morrigan asked quietly.

"Men create regulations to benefit themselves," Lily said. "You are aware that Ramsay enjoys complete legal authority over you and Olivia? You are his property, though he might never intimate such a thing. Were he so inclined, he could take Olivia from you, using almost any reason, and you would have very few legal means to fight him. This is what happens when women are excluded from lawmaking and the vote."

Father Drummond had forced her to hear that unbearable truth, and it had changed the way she viewed everything. True, she was the wife of the whisky-voiced laird, a man known for his kindnesses. Yet she had seen his anger unleashed. When goaded, Curran Ramsay was far from perfect, and she would be wise to never forget it.

"We are kept out of universities," Mrs. Crewler added. "We cannot earn a living in any professional way. This compels us to rely on men for everything, a fact that is not happenstance, I assure you."

"Several medical professionals have spoken up, rejecting the Commission's theory that there would be no syphilis if not for the female sex, but so far, it hasn't helped," the physician's wife said. "And it won't, not as long as the military keeps telling them that detaining prostitutes will stamp out these diseases, and that forcing examinations upon the soldiers will demoralize them. There is the added invisible benefit of making all women, fallen or not, realize how little sovereignty they possess. We are dismissed, and in fact condemned for publicly speaking of these matters." A deep furrow appeared between her brows. "I wonder what would happen if there were no prostitutes? My husband believes that many men would find more degrading or violent methods of satisfying those needs they attempt to keep hidden from us."

"Needs?" Lily said. "Perversions, you mean. I still see the faces of children I knew. No one would do a thing to protect them. No one cares about orphans anyway. This, from the most advanced, civilized country on earth."

Sweat formed on Morrigan's forehead. She blotted it with a handkerchief, inwardly recoiling as the old, terrifying flash of light blinded her for an instant, followed by nausea, stabbing pain through the temples, and the hum that filled her ears like a swarm of wasps.

Lily's voice sounded as though it was muffled in cotton. "There's a lucrative business in torturing children here," she said. "They're locked inside brothels with soundproofed rooms, and windows so the customers can watch."

Morrigan fought the urge to get up and run. Her body filled with an awful sensation, like a clot of spiders had erupted from the pit of her stomach and were scattering through her body, suffocating her, filling her lungs with their horrible hairy legs.

Her ribs curved, sharp as knives, making each breath excruciating. She tugged at her collar. If she couldn't breathe, she would die, but better that than weak-willed disgrace before these brave women who were willing to risk mockery and censure in order to assist the humblest, most helpless human beings.

Children tortured for sexual pleasure? Such a thing was madness. A crime so evil would surely bring a death-curse upon the entire world.

Hell is what Earth becomes without her Mother. Morrigan felt Diorbhail's presence, saw her eyes, blazing with unbridled rage.

"You saw this, Diorbhail." She squeezed her eyes closed. "You knew this would happen."

"Morrigan," Lily cried. "Morrigan?"

She dimly realized she was gasping. The room was so hot. She wanted to die of embarrassment. The black cloud swirled closer.

"What can we do?" she heard below the roar in her ears. She sensed the women crowding around.

Lily's face was pale. "Get her husband. He's here somewhere. Try the smoking room."

Chapter 11

LILY DIPPED A HANDKERCHIEF IN HER TEACUP AND PRESSED IT TO MORRIGAN'S cheeks. "Forgive me, *mon amie*," she said.

Honoria Collins brought Curran and Richard. Curran fell to his knees.

Morrigan's eyelids fluttered and she seized the edge of his coat. "The paddle wheel is chopping me to bits," she whispered. "I'm flying everywhere."

"Has she had too much to drink?" Richard asked.

"Only tea," Lily said defensively.

"I'll take her upstairs. Get a doctor." Curran picked her up and carried her out of the room.

"He's wed a damnably vaporish female," Richard said.

"It's not her." Lily stared at the empty doorway. "It's us. We've become walking, talking corpses, filling the silence with Wagner, and hothouse flowers, and balls, while two streets away...." She clasped Mrs. Crewler's hand. "But for a few, like Josephine, and you, and in her way, Morrigan. They shine a light on how dead we are."

She and Richard left the drawing room. Lily instructed one of the maids to send for a doctor, and after she'd gone, said, "I'm so accustomed to London's atrocities I've grown the shell of a turtle. You're right in a way, Donaghue. She is high-strung. But this is no simple honeymoon. There's something we don't know."

Richard nodded. "I confess at first I thought he'd fallen in love with her simply because she's beautiful, young, and malleable. But there is some-thing...." He trailed off, frowning. "Her eyes are ancient."

"And weary," Lily said.

The doctor's wife came out and joined them, wringing her handkerchief. "Did I cause this with what I said? I do forget myself. Dear Lord, I wish the men we appeal to had half as much feeling."

"You didn't do anything," Lily said. "Send the physician up when he arrives, would you please, Donaghue? I'll go and check on her."

She hurried upstairs, knocked, and entered the bedroom.

Morrigan lay on the bed. Curran had removed her dress and corset, and sat slumped in a chair, staring at her.

"How is she?" Lily kept her voice low.

"Sleeping, or fainted." He motioned and they went out into the sitting room. "What happened?"

"I was telling her about London's orphans. It obviously shocked her. I forgot how unsophisticated she is."

"I forget too, sometimes. It's easy to forget."

"Do you know why it affected her so badly?"

He drew in a deep breath. "She's as deep as the ocean, and I've only been introduced to the surface ripples."

"Oh, Ramsay."

"She was a virgin. I ruined her." With a mirthless laugh, he said, "She asked me if she would have a baby after, but she had things…wrong." He laughed again, quietly. "I'd forgotten that till now. I thought, growing up on a farm of sorts, she'd have seen the cows and horses—that she'd know, but she didn't. Not really."

Lily guided him to the love seat and settled beside him. "Did you want to marry her?"

"I couldn't wait. She's unique in ways I can't even describe, innocent as a child one minute, speaking the deepest philosophy I've ever heard the next. I'd be the happiest man alive if she loved me. I don't know if she does, she's never said. If I could hear her *say* it, just once."

"She'd be a fool not to."

"I think she might be…having an affair."

"Indeed." Lily was shocked to her core. She would never have thought such a thing of that shy, easily embarrassed girl.

"From the moment she met him our lives changed. I'd swear she was happy with me, until him. If I'd let her take Olivia, I suspect she'd leave me for him. Maybe I should, but I can't. Even if Olivia's the only thing keeping her with me, I'll use her. I'll use my own child like a cage."

Lily's eyes filled with tears. "You can't blame yourself. You've done nothing wrong."

"I almost hit her." Curran's cheeks reddened. "I wanted to. I was so daft with jealousy. See what I've become?" He covered his eyes with his hands.

Curran Ramsay? No, never. Yet his misery revealed the truth. "Don't you remember how many of the fair sex you had swooning at your feet before you married?" she asked.

No reaction.

"Ramsay." Grasping his arm, she said, "You had your pick of London's finest, decent and otherwise. Don't you know?"

His hands fell to his lap and he regarded her blankly.

"Even me, Curran," she said, "and God knows I love my husband."

Such beautiful blue eyes. She had never seen anything quite like them. If one looked closely enough, purple and minute flecks of green could be detected within the blue. Sometimes she thought she saw infinitesimal motes of silver.

Surprise widened them. He'd never suspected then, how that smile he threw around so carelessly left her breathless, ridden with guilt and fantasies.

"You've changed," she said. "You were happy. Now your eyes follow her, and they are always sad." She stroked the side of his face. Touched his lips with her fingers.

He kissed them. His hand caught at hers, holding on desperately, like she was the only thing keeping him sane and human.

Morrigan woke to flickering candlelight.

Why was she in bed? There was a blurry memory of Lily, her expression growing hard as she described barrenness caused from years of prostitution.

Distant murmuring roused her further. The deeper resonance sounded like Curran. She needed him. When everything grew hopeless and awful, Curran could always soothe her. Sweet, braw Curran. He would take away this sensation of falling into a fathomless hole. "Curran," she whispered. But there was no reply. He wasn't there.

When she stood, the room spun like a dervish, but she gritted her teeth and crossed to the doorway, where shock congealed into frozen, disbelieving horror.

They were pressed together. Touching. Lily was stroking her husband's face. He held her fingers against his lips and kissed them. *Kissed* them.

Morrigan gripped the doorjamb. *He'd* done this, got her with child. Trapped her. Now he thought he could do as he pleased while exploding with jealousy if she even smiled at a man. No, by God. He'd see.

Lily had seduced her with fraudulent kindness. How she and Curran must have laughed at her!

Her body liquefied into a crushing wave. Her mouth opened, ready to spew poison and hatred.

You've changed. You were happy. Now your eyes follow her, and they are always sad.

Morrigan's wrath froze. It hung, rigid and immobilized, then splintered around her in a storm of echoing silence. Stumbling backward, she reached for something to keep her from falling. She grabbed the brass bedpost and slid to the floor.

Lily gave a hushed laugh. "What's the word she used about *Tristram and Iseult?* Braw. Yes. You're braw as toast and jam."

Curran's mouth curved into a slight smile. Maybe there was hope yet.

"Could she be pregnant?"

He stared. "Why d'you ask that?"

"This fainting, for one thing. And she lost her breakfast the other day. Think about it. Has she had her monthly courses?"

He frowned. "I…don't remember."

Lily gave him a moment then wrapped both her hands around his. "If, as you say, she is having an affair—"

"No."

"Oh, darling, you have to face this. Has she ever told you you're braw? Let her go, if she wants, with this man. Perhaps it isn't worth the pain and trouble."

"We've been together nearly every night. She and I…we…." His eyes closed. Tearing free of her grasp, he bent his head and buried his face in his palms, digging his fingertips into his scalp. "Olivia…."

Could she be pregnant?

Curran made some shocked reply, but Lily's voice wouldn't relent. *If she is having an affair….*

Let her go with this man.

She was saying everything that couldn't be said, all that would destroy their lives, annihilate any trust that might remain.

This wasn't Lily's fault. Morrigan had done it herself with the way she'd allowed Aodhàn Mackinnon to infest her imagination.

She heard Curran's desperate *No.* But Lily would convince him. In a matter of moments, Curran would believe. At that point there would be no use telling him she hadn't been unfaithful, even if she could say it without blushing.

All at once, in a rush that felt like a swooping gust of wind, Morrigan knew.

She cupped her hands over her breasts. They were tender, so tender she could hardly bear the pressure of her own touch.

Curran would take Olivia and this new babe away from her. He would install Lily at Kilgarry. Somehow they would rid themselves of Richard. Morrigan would never be allowed to see her babies. She would never again disperse into pliant delirium under Curran's touch.

She'd held his heart in her hand. He'd freely given it. In nurturing that gift, maybe she could have healed herself. But look what she'd done instead. She'd been more Mackinnon's than Curran's before they'd left, even if she hadn't succumbed to the final indignity of physical betrayal. When they returned to Glenelg, how long would it be before that changed? Could she and Mackinnon live together in the same wee village and never surrender to this thing that was so palpable between them? Some part of her knew he would never stop until he got what he wanted.

My children will never know me. They'll think Lily is their mother...Lily, who cannot have children, so she'll take mine!

Just tonight she had congratulated herself for having a friend who would never betray her.

Stupid...stupid.

Behind tightly squeezed eyelids a picture materialized. The pool near the Wren's Egg. Louis Stevenson, chewing a stem of wild grass.

What of the father? he'd asked. *Do you love him?*

She had done the honorable thing by marrying her child's father. That path had taken her to safety and redemption. Her thoughts had carried her no farther.

Needing to escape Curran and Lily and all the terrifying things they were plotting, Morrigan crawled across to the open window. She grasped the sill and pulled herself to her knees.

I've a notion your heart will steer you rightly, Louis had ventured. How wrong he'd been.

The luminescent moon hovered in a starry midnight heaven.

Night and day. Shadow and sun. No, Curran wasn't the sun, so intense one couldn't bear to look at it. He was the softly mesmerizing face of the moon. A quiet steadfast presence, showering her with, with....

Freedom, sang the Judas-wench inside her.

She had thrown joy aside in order to embrace enigmatic sorrow. Now she'd had enough sorrow and wished joy back, like a spoiled child whose long-neglected doll had been thrown into the rubbish, who sobbed, broken-hearted, at the loss and demanded Time be rewound.

She wanted both joy and sorrow to be hers forever in a world that never allowed such things.

Another stark image materialized. She saw herself seizing the horns of an angry bull. Her laughter flew high as she used the jerk of the bull's head to propel herself into the wind.

A breeze stirred the lace curtains. They brushed her face as though in encouragement.

Roaming the earth with no need to rest, eat, or sleep, unhampered by mountains, oceans, cities, or love, unmoved by bullets or despair, wind bolted from zephyr to hurricane on its own momentary impulse, utterly invulnerable to attack or entrapment.

The wind spoke in her throat with Nicky's voice. *Feel me. I am with you.*

She wanted to leap from this window and become wind, join Nicky, spread out invisibly across the earth, scratch her spine in pine trees and send ripples over lochs with her breath.

There was another image from Torridon, of the living boat with the goddess sculpted into the prow. It swayed as the wind played with its sails, coaxing Morrigan to climb aboard. *I will take you to a warm island, to endless peace,* the goddess said. *You are tired, my daughter, and you have suffered for me.*

A movement off to one side brought her swinging around with a gasp, but it was only her reflection in the looking-glass, cast in moonlight and shadows.

Something flitted across the face in the mirror, an overlay of another woman's features. She was older. Her hair was dark, her eyes, haunted. She was both familiar and unknown.

No more children. No more love. Not until they all lie dead. Then we will begin again.

"Begin again." Morrigan pitied the woman in the mirror, who had seen too much, endured too much.

She unbuttoned the pocket in her petticoat and pulled out the knife Diorbhail had given her. It felt hot.

The woman in the looking-glass seemed to stare at it too, then she lifted her gaze to Morrigan's. *See.*

Morrigan blinked and the face in the mirror was her own again.

Her thoughts cleared into distinct separate drops, falling one by one into blank silence.

She would go to Barra. To Mingulay. Oh aye, she'd seen how much Curran hated the idea, though he'd said nothing. But she would go. She would discover why those places called to her. She would search until she found the reason those islands and Mackinnon were connected.

It seemed too much a coincidence, something akin to fate, that Richard would have a cottage on Mingulay. Everything was pulling her there, and she was done fighting her instincts. It was not only fate, but fatality.

Anger again boiled, scalding away her shame. She had done nothing. *Nothing!* Yet at this moment, her husband sat in the next room making love to another woman—a prostitute, by her own admission.

Damn him. Was *this* what she had to look forward to? She had put Mackinnon away from her. She'd vowed to be faithful and honorable. And *this* was what she received for her efforts.

She would confront Mackinnon. This time, there would be no humiliating her into silence. He must tell her why she was so important that he was willing to destroy his long friendship with the laird of Kilgarry in order to have her. And Curran? Never again would he deceive her. She would turn herself into a wind-being. Transparent. Distilled. Untouchable. Nothing different to the outside eye, but inside, pure and blank. A thing without form or substance. A mirage none of them could harness or control.

Lily knew what she had to say, but the words stuck like tar in her throat. "Yes, my darling. Olivia. You could keep her."

Curran shook his head. He met her gaze and drew in a deep breath. "I will never separate them."

"Do you know what this means?" How it ached to keep saying the things she knew he couldn't bear to hear. "You could find yourself raising—"

"Stop." He took another ragged breath. "I know what it means."

"I adore you." She kissed him on the mouth.

"No, Lily, I can't. Don't. Don't ask me."

"Of course not." She smiled. "Like Donaghue says. *Advienne que pourra.* You'll stand by Morrigan, no matter what, and I love you for it. Let me talk to her. We're friends, your wife and I. She'll tell me the truth. I'll help you repair this trouble. Your marriage will be wonderful again. I promise, Curran."

Make it happen, those divine eyes pleaded as the doctor came in.

<hr>

Chapter 12

<hr>

Violet looked up as Eleanor Graeme entered the kitchen at Kilgarry, her hands stuffed with letters, saying she'd run into the delivery boy.

Separating one from the others, she waved it exuberantly. "I believe this must be from the laird, or his wife."

They all ran to Eleanor's side, but for Beatrice. She stayed in the rocking chair, a surly frown on her face.

Violet, who needed the most practice with her English, read the letter out loud. Apparently, the couple had been busy dining, dancing, and meeting people—artists, politicians, even Prince Edward, when they went riding in Rotten Row. Oh, and Whistler was painting her.

"Her head'll be too swollen to thole," Beatrice said.

"'Tis grand." Tess sighed. "Meeting the Prince of Wales. And to have her portrait painted."

"Have you forgotten the picture in the drawing room? How many portraits d'you think a glorified scullery maid needs?" Beatrice snapped.

"This is different," said Violet. "I've heard of Whistler. He's famous. We don't know who painted the one we've got." She frowned as she stared at the letter. "There's one more thing," she said. "It says that...." She paused as she read. Her brows elevated and she blinked.

"What?" Fionna and Tess asked together.

"It says they're coming home, but they plan to leave again right away. They're going across the water to Barra. It says if you want to go along, Miss Stewart, you'd be welcome. They're bringing Mistress Ramsay's Aunt Isabel."

Beatrice snorted. "Barra," she said. Then, "Barra," she repeated, her eyes narrowing. She laughed. Everyone stared at her as she rose heavily to her feet and left the kitchen, snorting one great, indelicate belly laugh after another.

No matter what anyone said, Violet knew Beatrice had changed. She'd never been easy or kind, but now she was angry, cold, and insulting. She hardly ever came out of her room, and when she did, spent most of her time eating or walking, who knew where. Her appetite had increased, and so had her taste for Master Ramsay's brandy.

She also had a new, unpleasant smell, an acrid odor that made Violet's nose itch. Fionna made excuses for the woman, saying she probably missed Morrigan. After all, her niece had been gone a long time, leaving Beatrice with no one for company but Kilgarry's servants. Besides, Morrigan was married now, preoccupied with her husband and baby. Beatrice probably felt as though she was no longer needed.

"I'm passing by Seaghan's on the way home," Eleanor said into the silence. "I'll share the news with him."

"What about Aodhàn Mackinnon?" Tess asked. "Should he be told?"

"Neither Seaghan nor I have any idea where he's gone," Eleanor said. "Besides, isn't he the cause behind this long absence? Why in the name of all that's holy would he have any right to know?"

"It's just hard not to think of one without the other. Everything is so changed."

Eleanor agreed and took her leave.

Violet helped Tess fill shortbread pastry with currants, walnuts, and sugar. She hoped the mistress's homecoming would return Beatrice to her old self, but in the next breath hoped Beatrice would go away with them to Barra.

As if reading her thoughts, Tess glanced at the door. "It's pleased I am God didn't make me kin to Beatrice Stewart."

Violet snickered, but the minding of her own troubles soon etched the frown back into her forehead. *Logan, I believed I'd changed you. You promised I was the only one.*

"I do wish the laird and his mistress would stay awhile when they come home." Janet sliced potatoes into a pot of simmering water. "I want to make tempting dishes again."

"Amen." Fionna nodded.

"Tess?" Janet held up a towel filled with raw turnips. "Help me with these. Did you lasses remember to put whisky in the tart?"

THE NEXT SEVERAL DAYS WERE BUSY WITH COOKING AND CLEANING. VIOLET FELL into bed at night exhausted, almost too exhausted to dwell on Logan.

Kilgarry felt wretchedly forlorn with no Curran, barging into the kitchen, begging in that endearing way for a bite of some delicacy, bringing the smell of heather and wind along with his dogs, who snuffled with wide canine grins and wagging tails. Violet couldn't help smiling as she thought of how he'd always put his arm around Janet and kiss her cheeks to make her blush.

The foursome gathered in the kitchen again a few days after the arrival of the letter, cleaning potatoes, cutting onions, and baking bread. Kilgarry was spotless, ready for the master's return, and the larder was well stocked.

"I miss wee Olivia," Janet grumbled. "I'd just got her smiling, aye, and I miss the perfume the mistress uses. They have been gone too long."

A door slammed distantly. "Watch yourself, that'll be Beatrice," Tess said.

"Mind your tongue." Fionna rose. "Kyle, no doubt, tracking mud again. I'll give him a thrashing so help me." She left.

The remaining three heard the sound of muffled laughter.

"What's happened?" Tess asked.

"Let's go see," Violet replied.

She and Tess ran through the corridor, their excitement mounting. Frantic joyous barking bounced off the walls. As she burst into the polished entry, Violet glimpsed Curran's bright head of hair. Pòl, the deerhound, rose on hind legs and licked his master's face.

An invasive wash of sunlight sent Morrigan's hair blazing. Dressed in an elegant striped costume so narrow-skirted Violet was surprised she could move, Mistress Ramsay fended off Antiope and two eager Border collies, waving her bonnet and crying *Shoo!* as she tried to move out of the way for the ever-increasing pile of crates, boxes, and trunks. Logan carried in more while Fionna brushed at her tears.

"Oh, mistress." Violet ran forward. At the last second her wits returned and she drew up short. She'd never hugged the laird's wife, or touched her in any way other than to help her bathe and dress.

Morrigan laughed and pulled her into a quick embrace, filling Violet's senses with her honey-musk scent. Though she'd tried, Violet never could put a name to that wonderful aroma. It didn't match any of the fragrances sitting upstairs in wee crystal bottles on the mistress's lace-edged dressing table. And she'd know, wouldn't she? Often enough she'd smelled them when tidying, and once placed a drop between her breasts, knowing Logan would find it later.

She should've let Logan do all he'd wanted. Then she'd be the one carrying a child and making demands. It hadn't done the mistress any harm, had it?

Over the barking dogs, clatter of boxes, and Curran's gruff, "Get off me, ye daft beast," the mistress cried, "I've missed you." She let go, gesturing. "See who we brought."

In walked her Aunt Ibby, holding Olivia and directing Logan's every move.

"Aye, they abducted me." Ibby tickled the babe's ear, adding, "And how could I resist such temptation? Logan, d'you know what you're doing? Don't pile that trunk on top of the other. You'll break the lid."

"Auntie," Morrigan said, "leave him be. Has anyone seen Beatrice?"

Violet couldn't help flushing. "She might've gone for a walk. She often does."

"Oh." Morrigan frowned.

Violet wondered at the closeness between those two. It made no sense. What was there to love in that dour, sour woman? Well, she must try to be generous. After all, Beatrice was the only mother Mistress Ramsay had ever known.

"You've brought home my wee one?" Janet, slow from weight and gout, limped through the rear hall door.

Ibby handed Olivia to her. Janet tickled the babe under the chin until she received the required giggles.

"She's a right wee replica of you, Master Curran," Janet cried. "Look at all these curls, and the same color!"

"Aye, she's his, no doubt about that," Morrigan said.

Kyle opened the door. He hailed Curran, shyly tipped his cap to Morrigan, and gathered boxes to carry upstairs.

"Wait." Curran lifted the lid on a trunk and brought out parcels tied with ribbons, handing one to each lady. Fionna cried out over a beautiful fringed shawl in the iridescent shades of a peacock. She draped it across her bodice, extolling the master's generosity. Violet received an original Whistler etching, his butterfly signature in the right-hand corner. Accompanying it were paints and fine sable brushes. Janet flushed crimson over a crate of preserves, smoked oysters, apples, roasted chestnuts, sugared rose-petals, chocolate, and other delicacies seldom found in these mountainous regions. Tess's gift was perhaps the finest of all: a rosewood clàrsach, accented with mother-of-pearl and gold leaf. She touched the strings, sending a thrum of music through the vestibule.

They'd brought gifts for the townsfolk as well, baskets of medicinal herbs and tonics for Eleanor, shawls, caps, and necklaces for the women, pipe tobaccos and whisky for the men.

Logan and Kyle hauled the rest of the luggage upstairs to the master bedroom.

"Tea is what you need," Fionna said. "Violet, help the mistress change while Janet and I set it to brew."

Morrigan dropped her parasol in the umbrella stand and started up the stairs. Violet watched Curran bound to her side over a pile of boxes. Their heads, close together, caught shafts of sunlight from the high mullioned window at the landing.

"What a bonny sweet pair," Fionna said. "I feel I couldn't wipe the smile from my face if I tried." She mopped her eyes. "Ah, it's fine, then. They've reconciled and are happy. Pray God now they're home, nothing'll happen to be mucking it up."

Leaving the unspoken name of *Aodhàn Mackinnon* hanging like a spectre, she went off to see to the tea.

Violet banished a dark thought or two about the odd fisherman and followed the couple upstairs. She'd always observed more of life than folk gave her credit for. In the bedroom, she saw the mistress release the master's hand without a glance in his direction, then crawl onto the window seat where she scrutinized the gardens and the Sound.

Curran, with an almost indecipherable shake of the head, tugged at his cravat and walked the other direction. Logan and Kyle finished with the luggage. To keep herself occupied, Violet opened a trunk and began unpacking.

Morrigan came off the seat. "I want a wrapper," she said. "This corset's cut me to the bones."

Tongue-tied at the unfamiliar frosty note she heard, Violet nodded and fetched a robe, a slender green sheath she knew the lady favored.

The master often said if he couldn't dress or wash himself he oughtn't to be breathing. Unconcerned with Violet's presence, he shrugged out of his coat and trousers and went into his dressing room. When he returned he'd pulled on a pair of rough breeks, top boots, and a homespun sark. He tucked it in as he left, banging the door; she couldn't tell if from exuberance or vexation.

"Did you enjoy your holiday, mistress?" Violet asked as she took Morrigan's corset.

"Oh, aye," came the muffled reply from behind the Chinese screen. "'Twas fair the round, never a moment to catch your breath. If Curran wasn't dragging me to some fine, fancy thing, it was Lily." Glancing around the edge, she impaled her maid with a somber examination. "Have the Donaghues ever come to Kilgarry?"

"Aye, m'lady, many times, Christmases mostly."

"Do you know her well?"

Violet wrinkled her brows. "Mrs. Donaghue? I've helped her dress."

Morrigan stepped out from behind the screen. Freed from the form-fitting skirts, her petticoat floated like a cloud of fluff. "I don't want that one," she said. "I've been bound up like a prisoner all day. Get me the lavender one. I want something that lets me breathe, and it's cold in here."

Violet tossed the green robe on the bed and began digging through the wardrobe. How could she be cold? Impossible! 'Twas August! She pulled out the lavender creation. It was full from the waist down, with long sleeves, buttons up the front, and a high collar. She fancied she glimpsed goosebumps on that alabaster flesh as Morrigan shrugged into the garment and drew her hair free. "Leave it loose," she said, but allowed Violet to brush it as she fastened the buttons. "I'll have tea in the sitting room. Would you tell Fionna?"

Violet bobbed a quick curtsy and started to leave.

"Please send Beatrice when she comes in," Morrigan called after her.

"Aye, m'lady." Violet went downstairs. Perhaps Master Curran's wife was pregnant. That would explain this change of mood and shivering. Tales of expectant women's foibles abounded in the Highlands.

Fionna hummed and smiled as she arranged cups on a silver tray. How long would it be before the housekeeper discovered all wasn't well between the laird and his wife, and her prayers hadn't been answered?

Violet pressed her lips together and said nothing.

CURRAN COLLECTED THE DOGS AND WENT OFF TO WALK HIS LAND. AH, HE'D MISSED this. He hadn't realized how much. The air had a scent, of heath and leaves, mixed with the sea, that he'd never smelled anywhere else.

For him, it was the aroma of home, and had always offered comfort and peace, but today the peace was fleeting, as his thoughts immediately returned to Morrigan. She had inexplicably turned against him, after he'd come to believe all was healed. It had happened so abruptly, the night she had swooned. At first she clung to him like a boat in a storm, but later, he could have been an offensive stranger. She rebuffed any gesture and spent hardly any time in his company, always finding a way to leave. Once or twice he'd caught her staring at him, her eyes brooding, but she would not explain. She almost seemed to be waiting for *him* to say something, but he didn't know what.

As of yet, she'd said little about expecting. Maybe she hated it. That prospect made him recoil, but he couldn't blame her. It had only been six months since she nearly died giving birth to Olivia. Not many women would be overjoyed at the thought of going through that again.

And why, of all the places in the world he would gladly take her, had she chosen Barra as their next destination? His teeth ground together as he stabbed the wet grass with his stick.

Two nights before they left London to come home, he'd asked her. She'd gazed at him narrowly, almost accusingly. *It doesn't matter why. I want to go there.*

He'd convinced himself that Aodhàn Mackinnon was a fading smudge in their lives, but since that moment, he'd returned like a sneering devil, even invading Curran's dreams.

Well, they would go. With any luck they would find themselves confronted with Aodhàn's wife, a living, breathing wife. Children, too. Grown children. Maybe Aodhàn the grandfather would put an end to her fantasies.

But the fact that he hadn't heard from Quinn worried him. There had been nothing in all these weeks, no letter, no messenger. Curran had finally written, but that letter, too, had gone unanswered. Where could he be? What could be taking so long?

He didn't realize he wasn't alone until Seaghan grabbed his forearm. Blinking, he looked up to see not only Seaghan but Eleanor as well. Both were staring at him.

"Curran Ramsay," Seaghan said. "Wake up, man."

"Oh, I...I didn't see you," Curran said.

"That is clear!" Seaghan released a thunderous laugh. He enveloped Curran in a great, suffocating embrace. "It's been too long, damn you! Too damned long!" He belatedly turned to Eleanor, apologizing for his crudeness, which she waved away.

"Welcome home, Master Ramsay," she said, smiling. "Is your wife up at the house?"

"Aye," Curran said. "Unpacking, and packing again, I'm sorry to say."

Seaghan's expression dropped into palpable disappointment. "It's true? You're leaving again?"

Curran sighed and nodded. "Morrigan wants to see the isle of Barra."

"You weren't merely playing with me, then," the fisherman said, glancing at Eleanor, who shook her head.

"Your letter arrived a few days ago," Eleanor explained.

"Well, that settles it." Seaghan clapped his hand on Curran's shoulder. "Can I go along?"

"Well...." Curran couldn't hide his surprise. "I've no objection. But why would you want to?"

"Really? Why? Well, I'll tell you why. Because I have no' seen either of you since the beginning of June, that's why. And while I do just fine without a glimpse of your pretty face, I would like to see your wife's now and then. It appears as though I'll have to chase you all over the country to do it!"

Curran laughed. "You're more than welcome," he said, realizing it was true. He would be glad of Seaghan's common sense. Turning to Eleanor, he added, "I know Morrigan would like it if you came along as well."

"I don't think I can. I've a lass giving birth down by Àrnasdal in a week or two. I should stay here."

"Speaking of that," Curran said, "Olivia might be gaining a brother or sister. Don't say anything, for Morrigan hasn't announced it yet, and it's very early."

"Another babe!" Eleanor's face lit up.

"That is bonny news!" Seaghan added, his grin widening.

"What do you mean, 'might be'?" Eleanor's gaze was perceptive. "Is she, or not?"

Curran's mood darkened as he remembered that awful night, and Morrigan collapsing. "She fainted one evening in July, and I brought in a physician. He said he couldn't be certain, but there were a few early signs. She refused to see him after that, but as far as I know, nothing has changed to rule it out."

"Hmm." Eleanor's brows lifted. "Refused to see him, you say? Any number of things could cause the fainting, as you and I have discussed. I should examine her. She trusts me, Master Curran. Are you sure you don't want me to ask her about it?"

"Better wait, I think—especially if I'm wrong." He knew he was flushed, and he knew Eleanor noticed. The woman missed nothing. Why did he feel so guilty? He hadn't done anything to be ashamed of, so why did he feel as though he had?

Seaghan broke into his thoughts. "There's other news you probably haven't heard. Aodhàn is gone."

"What?"

"Aye." It was Seaghan's turn to blush. "We had a…disagreement. Eleanor sheltered him for a few nights, but now he seems to have left Glenelg altogether."

Curran was so astounded he could only stare.

"He said nothing to me of leaving." Eleanor shook her head, her annoyance clear. "I came home one day and he was gone. Apparently he told no one of his plans. He's simply…gone."

Seaghan and Eleanor continued on their way, excited to see Morrigan. Curran walked with his entourage of dogs until he came to Dùn Teilbh, where he sat awhile in contemplation, allowing the voices of the glen, the clouds, earth, and wind to refill his soul.

Aodhàn is gone.

Hope ran through him as he imagined it—the rest of their lives, freed of Aodhàn Mackinnon.

The dogs soon roused him. They'd found something by the edge of the forest and were digging at it. The deerhound whined. Curran got up to investigate, stopping some distance away because of the stink and swarm of flies. Something had died and was rotting in the long grass. No wonder the dogs were intrigued. Rummaging for his handkerchief, he held it over his nose and stepped closer.

His blood chilled as he realized he was looking at the remains of a person. A man, judging by the clothing. At once he thought of Father Drummond before remembering the priest had been found and taken away. This was someone else. A pinkish jelly-like substance slimed the cadaverous face.

Antiope licked at it and Curran prodded her away with his stick. The corpse was little more than bones at this point, covered by matted clothing.

Could it be Aodhàn? It was a gruesome thing to look upon, but he forced himself to search for anything that could identify the dead man. The remains seemed to be about the same height as Aodhàn, but he couldn't be certain.

What was left of the corpse's hair finally gave him the answer he sought. Though the pinkish ooze had infiltrated it, Curran saw that it was light; when a ray from the sun struck it, the strawberry-blond highlights he remembered were still there. This was Patrick Hawley.

He remembered Morrigan's account of cutting Hawley with a knife back in the middle of May, but she'd said it was only a flesh wound in the arm. Then he remembered how diseased Hawley had appeared in the tavern.

Maybe the wound had festered. It was impossible to muster distress over the bastard's sorry end. He would fetch some men and have the corpse removed to the graveyard. That was as far as he would go. And he would keep this from his wife. She didn't need to be reminded of the day Patrick Hawley attacked her, especially if she was pregnant.

He wanted no repeat of the harrowing labor Morrigan had endured giving birth to Olivia.

During their journey home, he'd given the matter much thought, and had resolved to keep his suspicions and jealousy to himself. He would not argue with her, confront her, or make demands. He would enclose her in a chrysalis of perfect calm and serenity. He would allow nothing to upset her, even if it killed him.

But he had to admit these resolutions would be much easier to keep with Aodhàn gone. It felt as though a hundredweight had been lifted from his shoulders.

For the first time in a long while, Curran smiled without reservation.

Chapter 13

Where were Nicky and Papa? In an enchanted forest, populated with unicorns and doves?

It would be nice if true, but Morrigan couldn't stop picturing them simply rotting in wood coffins, Nicky's life snuffed out by one never punished for the crime, Douglas a victim of his heart. Everything, for them, over and done, finished.

Father Drummond would say they were in Heaven, singing with angels. She stifled a laugh. Douglas Lawton...singing with angels? That was indeed impossible to picture, though it gave her comfort to think of Father Drummond there.

Making herself comfortable on the window seat, the sunset warming the glass behind her, she opened her leather-bound diary.

An Indian princess named Jamini had given Morrigan the diary at one of Whistler's bohemian dinners, along with a warning. *You are dousing your fire. You must set your fire free.* She had suggested writing in the book to help Morrigan explore what she needed to learn.

Morrigan contemplated the blank pages. Behind her, breezes keened against the casement, whispering of the vastness of the earth and heavens, of how small she was, she and all people.

She dipped her pen in ink.

Nicky used to tell me unicorns were happiness that just escapes us.
Once in a lifetime, we might catch a glimpse of them out of the corner of the
eye, yet when we look, they are gone. We don't know the secret of taming them.

*Or is it that we gain too much wisdom as we get older, and become blind to
their magic? My bones feel the truth. If we recognize our mistake and repent,
can we find them again?*

Solitude allowed her a welcome respite from maintaining the wind-wall
she'd constructed around her soul, though whenever she relived the picture of
Lily pressing her fingers to Curran's lips, of seeing her husband kiss them,
anger and guilt wormed hotly through the fissures. They were the two
emotions she'd found most difficult to eradicate in her quest to become as
coldly indifferent as a wintertime tempest.

You had your pick of London's finest, decent and otherwise. Even me.

A furious blaze raged through her chest.

Let her go with this man. Oh aye, that would be convenient, wouldn't it?
Lily's betrayal was unforgivable. How could she have trusted such a villainous
wench?

Though her friendship with Lily had been a lie, the woman had started
something inside Morrigan, and she couldn't let go of it. Lily, for all her faults,
had stepped out of her safe, wealthy world to help prostitutes and orphans.
She had a close-knit circle of women aiding her.

Morrigan wanted to help those children too, all of them, if it were only
possible. But how? She had no talents, no gifts, no real understanding of the
world. All she knew how to do was dust, cook, and wash linens. What if she
tried and failed? What if she was laughed at or rejected?

She rested her cheek against the glass then wrote again, feeling her way.

*All my life, I've taken the easiest path. I gave away the courage I was born
with. Papa told me I was useless and I've kept his voice inside me, repeating it.
Everything about this world, every law and tradition, forbids women from
striking out. We must be delicate, helpless beings, like rose petals. If we try to
escape our cages, we are punished, sometimes horribly.*
*But what if those laws and traditions are no more than mist, and can be torn
away? Lily is defying them. So is poor damaged Miss Collins. Diorbhail, after
all she was subjected to, resolved to find me, and did. Why am I so convinced I
can do nothing?*

She listened to the muffled honking of geese as they flew past. "Where are
you, Mama?" she asked softly. "Heaven, Hell, Purgatory? Or nowhere at all?"

Perhaps there was another answer. After dinner, Jamini's brother had gone
off to chat and smoke with the men, leaving the princess and Morrigan alone
in a separate parlor for quite a while. Morrigan tried to make polite conversation, but it was difficult because Jamini, though proficient with English, didn't

seem interested. She only became animated when Morrigan, desperate to find something they could talk about, brought up the subject of reincarnation.

"We believe all people are souls in possession of bodies," Jamini said, at last smiling. "Bodies perish, but every soul continues, learning, growing, and purifying, until eventually the liberation and union of moksha is achieved." She paused. "There are many religions and faiths in this world. All you need do is find one that speaks to your soul, and give yourself to it."

She explained that there were other beliefs far older than Christianity's idea of Heaven and Hell, and brought out a female figurine carved of stone.

It had tapered legs and a crude head without features. The breasts were prominent and the arms curved up like horns, antlers, or, as Jamini suggested, the moon in its crescent form. "She never leaves my side," the Indian woman said. "She is sacred, older than you can imagine. She was found in Egypt. Do you feel her power?"

How did she know? The instant Morrigan touched the figure, shock radiated through her fingertips and along her arm. "Tell me more," she'd said.

Jamini's eyes were luminous, seductive, and the gown she wore, a *phiran*, looked much more comfortable than Morrigan's own frock, which as usual was tight and stifling. Jamini's hair was covered with a flowing headdress, and she wore massive amounts of silver jewelry. The effect was charming. Exotic.

"Everything flows from the divine source of Shakti," Jamini said. "She is the restless energy behind all creation. Fire birthed the Goddess—the same fire I see within you."

Morrigan stared at her.

"Yes." Jamini nodded. "An avatar's fire-heat burns within you. I see it in your aura. You possess strength you have not yet recognized, but it will come. Your lessons will end and your sacred heat will burst free. Though you have feared it, it is the necessary force to achieve miracles."

"Aura? What is that?"

"The radiance that surrounds each of us. The corona of our souls. Yours is lavender, fermented with gold." She extended her hand, scooping the air around Morrigan's shoulder then brushing at her palm with her other hand as though she were sorting grains of sand. "You are a dreamer. The gold tells me you are spiritual, and that you have wisdom. But it says more as well. It is rare to see this color. Gold is a manifestation of the divine. You are being guided and protected."

"Curran...." Morrigan remembered the colors around him on their wedding day.

"Yes, I have seen his. You are well suited."

"I saw swirls of blue and purple around him, then they ran together and turned white."

"He is a visionary." Jamini shrugged; her smile turned a bit regretful. "I have fallen a little in love with your husband. I hope you will forgive me."

"I understand." That was before Lily's betrayal, of course. Lily was a liar, a cheat, where Jamini was straightforward. Lily conspired behind Morrigan's back to seduce her husband, while Jamini spoke with honest admiration.

"I've seen color around three others," Morrigan said. "Two women and a man. Diorbhail's is white, hazy like a cloud, and delicate, with the slightest pink. Eleanor's is like the green shadows in a forest."

"And the man?"

"Reddish orange, a dark, simmering fire."

"Hmm." Jamini's gaze grew intent. "Now your colors are changing. They are becoming redder."

"What does it mean?"

"You are drawn to this man." Jamini frowned. "He sparks excitement in you. As far as his colors, orange can be amiable. It is energy, strength. It is the mark of courage and adventure. Red, though...."

"Is bad?"

"It is a forceful, sexual aura. I have seen this color around those who become obsessed by their desires. Artists, revolutionaries, ascetics. If this nature is kept under control, it can manifest creatively. If not, well then...." She shrugged.

"You're not sleeping, are you, isoke?"

Morrigan straightened. With a dull *thump* the diary fell off her lap to the floor. She had been almost asleep, halfway immersed in Jamini's prophetic visions. "No, Auntie." She reached down to retrieve her book. "Come in, have a cup of tea."

Ibby made herself comfortable and arranged her skirts. "Thank you." She poured tea and stirred in a lump of sugar. "What are you doing?"

"Nothing." Morrigan left the window seat, tucking the diary beneath one of the cushions. "Thinking, I suppose. I've had many strange thoughts lately." She dropped into the stuffed chair opposite Ibby and studied the neglected dish of fruit and cake.

"Curran asked me not to say anything, but when has that ever stopped me? I must know. Are you going to have another child?"

Morrigan flushed. "Aye." She drummed her fingers on the arm of her chair and added, "Please, Auntie. Let me tell everyone."

Ibby's gaze was penetrating, but after a moment, she sighed. "I'll respect your wishes. Truthfully, I am torn about this. I would have preferred that you have a year at least to recover from Olivia's birth. I often think of Nicky's mam.... She only had two months before she was again expecting." She sipped the tea and made a face. "Still, it's a blessing. Curran couldn't be prouder."

"He loves children, and wants many."

Ibby handed her a cup. "Are you exhausted from your long holiday?"

"A bit." Morrigan sipped. The tea had been left too long and was barely warm.

"What are these thoughts you've been having?"

The truth would shock and frighten her. Yet perhaps Ibby could provide answers to some questions. "When we were in London," Morrigan said, "I wondered if I do anything well. I'm no' artistic. Not a poet. I play the piano but I could never compose. Everything I do is by ear. What use am I? What can I offer? Why am I here?"

Ibby set her cup on the table. "I'm surprised you would say that when you must know how important you are to Olivia and your husband."

"But shouldn't there be something more? I met some women in London, Auntie. They stand up to important men—even the Prime Minister. They want women to be treated fairly, and they speak as a man would, giving speeches and working to change laws. They remind me of the queen you told me about. Boudicca. Goats and pigs give birth. I've heard wolves mate for life. Most creatures make fine mothers. Shouldn't a human be more? What can I do? Is there something only I can give? If not, then I'm no more than 'an abuse of space,' as Curran puts it."

Ibby made no immediate comment, which surprised Morrigan. She'd expected her loyal aunt to burst into a torrent of trite reassurances, yet the woman turned her face away and studied the Whistler portrait, which was propped against the wall.

At last she rubbed her eyelids and, still avoiding Morrigan's gaze, spoke.

"Someone once said, a long time ago, that you were the finest miracle I would ever see."

The words seemed familiar. "Have you told me that before?"

Ibby nodded. "I wrote it—"

"In my *Translated Greek Mythology*. I'd forgotten. Papa took it from me the day you brought Curran to the Wren's Egg. I never saw it again. Who said that, Auntie?"

Ibby smoothed a wrinkle in her skirt. "A dream came to me the night you were born." With a deep breath she added, "A lady appeared. She called you a holy child."

This was daftness. People kept telling her she was special. What were they seeing that she could not? "You've often promised to tell me of that time," she said quietly, "yet you never have. Would you now?"

Ibby, in the process of inserting a forkful of cake into her mouth, stopped. She looked comical, her mouth open and her eyes as startled as a burglar's caught stealing the silver. She carefully returned the fork to the plate and wiped her lips with a napkin. "You do have the right." Clearing her throat, she added, "You've always had the right. I never understood why Douglas was against it. Maybe he wanted to protect you." She brushed crumbs from her lap and settled more comfortably. "For surely, this tale is not fit for children."

Ibby finished an hour later.

"I cannot tell you," she said, "why Hannah chose Douglas over Seaghan. It flies in the face of reason. But she did, and moreover, somehow talked Douglas and Beatrice into abandoning Glenelg in the middle of the night, saying nothing to anyone. That was in June, and we heard not a word from them until November. They reappeared as suddenly as they'd left, a fortnight before the clearings. They'd been living in Ireland, and knew nothing of Randall Benedict's eviction order.

"I could tell right away things were bad between them. Douglas was cruel, and she very obviously hated him. They called each other the vilest names. But I could not twist the story from either of them, so I cannot tell you why, or what happened to sour their marriage.

"They were there with us when the mercenaries burned the village. Hannah might still be alive, had they stayed in Ireland."

Ibby leaned forward and drank from her cup. Her voice had grown hoarse over the last twenty minutes or so.

"Let me ring for fresh tea," Morrigan said.

"No, isoke." Ibby placed the cup on its saucer. "It's late. I wouldn't want to wake anyone. I needed something wet is all. This helped."

She frowned and fiddled for a moment with one of her ruffles. "I don't think any of us believed it would really happen. So, when the day came—'The Day of the Burning,' as I've always called it—our homes, our possessions, were put to the torch and we were unprepared. We could have boarded the *Bristol* and sailed to Nova Scotia, but Douglas refused, I think simply because of Seaghan. Douglas would not give Seaghan that satisfaction."

Morrigan glanced at the mantel clock. It was close to midnight.

"As I said, one of the soldiers pushed Hannah because she attacked him. She fell and landed on her stomach. Her water broke shortly after. The ferries took most of the villagers to the *Bristol,* and those of us left sought shelter in the forest. Hannah could hardly walk by then. I mind Beatrice saying that it looked to be a hard labor, and it was. It was so hard, it stole your mam's life."

For a few moments, nothing but the ticking of the clock broke the silence. Morrigan rubbed her eyes. She studied the sitting room, picturing Randall Benedict warming his hands at this fireplace, maybe on the same night Hannah perished.

Now the child she'd given birth to lived in his house.

"I'm ashamed to admit that while Hannah suffered, I fell asleep," Ibby said.

"You were exhausted."

"'Tis my only excuse. That's when the dream came."

Silence stretched into minutes. Morrigan resisted the urge to prod her.

"She was beautiful," Ibby said. "Long black hair and a shining silver crown. The purest face. She asked me how I could sleep when a miracle was coming."

"Me?"

"Aye. She said your name was the forgotten title of a Greek goddess, Goddess Athene. I didn't understand that, since every child in Scotland over the age of two has heard of the Morrígan. She's as Celtic as they come."

"This dream told you my name?"

"Aye. That was strange, but stranger still was when she told me I once gave life to you." Ibby smiled. "Truly, you've always felt more like a daughter to me than a niece."

Morrigan returned her smile.

Sobering, Ibby added, "She said you came to save us, but that first you must suffer as her Mother's children had suffered."

Morrigan shook her head. "It was a dream, Auntie. A daft dream."

"Your life's hardly begun. I've always felt there was something special about you, Morrigan. Haven't you?"

It was hard to speak such deep, private thoughts out loud, but she tried. "I've thought I had feelings and thoughts like no one else's, except maybe… maybe Curran. And…a few others. I see things—hear things sometimes. But tell me the end of your story. What else happened that night?"

"Your mam gave birth to you and slipped away." Ibby sat back in her chair and rubbed her forehead. "Douglas cleaned her face with a blanket. Everything was a struggle for them, but I believe Douglas did love Hannah, and longed for her to love him." Pouring another cupful of cold tea, Ibby drank like she was uncommonly thirsty. "He wasn't evil, not in those days."

Morrigan bit down on the protest that rose inside.

"There was blood everywhere," her aunt continued. "Blood, death, and sorrow because Randall Benedict wanted his land free of folk. Because he wanted to replace us with sheep."

"What about the others? Why didn't we all die?"

"Many did. We buried them as best we could. It was so cold, you can't imagine. We used everything the soldiers left, even rebuilt a shack or two, but they came again and burned them. When we tried to shelter in the old barracks they called us trespassers and threatened us with prison. We had no guns. You would've starved for sure if Wynda Urquhart hadn't agreed to nurse you along with her son. His name was Hearn. Oh, the men made traps to catch rabbits. Sometimes they did, but it seemed like when the folk left, so did the beasts. Hearn sickened and Wynda refused to share her milk any longer. She said she needed it for him. I couldn't blame her. Her milk dried up soon enough. Beth Dunbar got frostbite. Her toes turned white and she couldn't feel them. Later, they turned black. John, her father, stepped in a snowdrift. It collapsed and a boulder crushed his head. It was Logan who found him."

"Logan. He doesn't act like he endured such horror. He's so—"

"Logan was a hero. Eight years old, yet he saved three children that day. He ran into their burning home and brought them out. When his da died, he took it hard. His spirit started to go. He'd sob for hours. It may not seem like it, but Logan remembers. I think it molded him into the man he is. Tess was two. She has no real memories, yet when she sings, I hear those days in her voice."

"Her songs are always of pain and loss."

"Father Drummond tried to help. His is a poor parish, so there wasn't much, but he begged for money, which he used to buy food and material for tents. He took two ill women to his manse, and for that, they threatened to burn it down. He wrote many a letter demanding assistance, all of which Randall Benedict, who by then had moved to Edinburgh, ignored. Mam came down with lung fever. Soon she couldn't breathe, and we'd no medicines, no knowledge of herbs or roots. With the ground frozen, we couldn't bury her. Our blankets and clothing fell apart."

Ibby stopped, her face turning white. "The weans' cries of hunger," she said, "the way they begged for food, was more than I could…more than any of us…I wonder we didn't all go mad as Wynda. I'll hear those voices till the day I die."

"Auntie," Morrigan cried. "Stop! Don't speak of it anymore."

A knock startled them both. The door swung open and there stood her husband, dandling a squirming Olivia. "Am I interrupting?" He took in Ibby's tear-stained cheeks.

"Of course not," Ibby said. "Come in, dear." She wiped her eyes. "I was telling Morrigan of the clearings. She wanted to know, and I thought she had the right."

He stepped inside and closed the door. "The wee one misses her mama," he said quietly, and gave their daughter to Morrigan. Then he straightened and held out his arms. Ibby entered them willingly.

Over the top of Ibby's head, Curran frowned at his wife. She looked away.

"My recollections are confused after Mam died." Ibby stepped back, brushing away fresh tears. "You tell her the rest." She faced Morrigan. "He surely has better memories than I, though he was, oh I cannot mind. How old were you, Curran?"

"Seven." Curran nodded. "I do remember. My father discussed it with me many times. It was important to him that I never forget. It made the greatest impression on him of anything in his life. I'd be glad to tell you what happened, if you like." His tone was diffident, and he didn't meet Morrigan's gaze.

The image of Lily and Curran, kissing on the loveseat while Morrigan watched, materialized forcibly. Curran had not defended her. He'd allowed Lily to criticize her, to accuse her of reprehensible acts.

Morrigan had agonized over the intimacies she and Mackinnon had shared. She had separated herself from him, had vowed never to be alone with him again. She had cared about harming her marriage.

She wanted to strike out, to stamp her feet and scream. Mackinnon had made it clear, that night in the forest, that he loved her, that all she had to do was speak, and he would be hers. And she hadn't! Instead she'd gone to see Father Drummond. She'd resisted with all her might, for Olivia's sake, for Curran's, only to be betrayed by him like she meant nothing, like Olivia meant nothing. "I do want to know," she said, hearing her voice so rigidly controlled she hardly recognized it, "but I'm tired. Maybe tomorrow."

Curran opened his mouth as if to speak, but, in the end, he only nodded. His jaw clenched. Then he left them, Ibby, his daughter, and his wife.

Chapter 14

CURRAN LED HIS BAND OF TRAVELERS FROM THE PIER TO THE MACNEIL HOUSE. Impossible to miss, it squatted in the middle of Castlebay, a stone structure that seemed out of place among the smaller, ruder buildings. He felt the eyes of the locals observing this strange, and therefore suspicious, troop of foreigners with the squalling baby. He could hardly blame them, but at least, unlike Quinn, his companions were all Scots.

A tired-looking woman met them at the door. She didn't smile or welcome them, or even seem surprised, but merely said, in heavily accented English, that yes, they could let the place, and that she was the housekeeper. Curran tried to put her at ease by replying in Gaelic, but she didn't seem impressed.

They soon determined that with only three bedrooms, Ibby and Beatrice would have to sleep together, as would Curran and Seaghan. Morrigan, Diorbhail, and Olivia would take the third room. The housekeeper, who reluctantly told them her name was Faith Kelso, and only after being asked twice, produced an ancient cradle from somewhere.

Curran waited until the women were busy unpacking before going in search of Mrs. Kelso. He found her making tea in the kitchen. "Has an Englishman stayed here recently?" he asked.

He'd never seen a face so unreadable. "Aye," she said.

"What happened to him, d'you know?"

This question merely made one of her brows lift.

"He's a friend," Curran said impatiently. "I expected to hear from him, but I haven't. He's disappeared."

"He left."

"Was he in good health?"

"As far as I know." She stopped speaking, and Curran's jaw clenched with the effort to keep from grabbing her and shaking her to forcibly loosen her tongue.

"The night before he left," she said, "he was writing something. He was always writing. He cursed Barraigh. Said he could reach London faster than his letter. He left the next morning."

"Please show me where he wrote his letters."

She led him to a cramped, unremarkable study and pointed to the writing desk.

Curran thanked her and sent her away before he began rummaging. His own letter to Quinn was inside the drawer. There was nothing else but a few sheets of blank stationery, a blotter, and a couple of scraps with unintelligible notes. Only after he slammed the drawer closed did he notice a crumpled ball of paper on the floor under the desk, almost invisible in the shadows. He retrieved it and smoothed it out, his gut churning with worry at what he read.

I have disturbing information I do not want to trust to a letter. When you get to Mallaig stay there. I will come over on the first of August and meet you at the Scythe and Swan. Do not come here—it is too dangerous.

"Curran?"

"Seaghan." Curran waved in the fisherman. "Look what I've found." He explained briefly about Quinn and read the letter out loud.

"What will you do?" Seaghan asked.

Curran rubbed his eyes, feeling as weary as he could ever remember. "I wonder if he was at the Scythe and Swan? If only I had known. But how could I, since he never mailed this? Nor did he come to London that I know of, though the housekeeper says that's what he intended."

"Why don't you go and see if you can find him. If his information is that important, surely he'll go up to Kilgarry since he missed you in Mallaig. I'm here, I'll watch over the lasses. You need to know what the man discovered, I think."

"But the letter says it's dangerous here. We should go home."

"That isn't necessary. Besides, your wife told me she wants to visit the isle of Mingulay. She said your London friends offered you a cottage there. Why don't I escort the ladies to this island while you find Quinn? We'll all be gone from Barra, and whatever danger he was speaking of."

"Well...."

"D'you really think anyone can get through me to harm Morrigan or your wean?"

Curran laughed. "I don't know what Morrigan would do to me if I forced her to go home, and I can't tell her I sent Quinn here to investigate Aodhàn. She'd never forgive it."

"I won't tell her. Come; let's walk down to the pier while the women are doing their female things. We'll see about finding a willing captain to ferry you to the mainland and the rest of us to the southern isles."

Curran left early in the morning, and while waiting for the fisherman who had agreed to transport them to Mingulay, Morrigan decided to walk around the village. Diorbhail wanted to go with her, so they left Olivia with Ibby and Beatrice.

"'Tis odd, Master Ramsay leaving again," Diorbhail said as they paused to admire the medieval castle in the bay.

"Aye." Morrigan kept her relief to herself. Since the moment Barra had come into view, she'd had a peculiar sense that she'd been here before. With Curran gone, she didn't feel as guilty or angry, and it was nice to not sense his gaze always upon her, as though he'd like to peel away her skin and bones and tear into her brain. "Something to do with his shipping company. I'm no' going to fret about it. Do you think you could beat me to the top of that mountain? The housekeeper called it *Sheabhal*."

"Let's see what being a lady of leisure has done to you."

They spent the next two hours panting and laughing their way to the summit of the hill behind the village, and when they got there, fought the wind to keep standing, and stuffed themselves with cheese and bread.

"Which one of those islands d'you think is Mingulay?" asked Diorbhail.

Morrigan shrugged. "I don't know," she said, but her gaze locked on the western one, half shrouded in clouds. Could that be it? She felt it was, but didn't know why.

"You dreamed of it, did you not, a long while ago? Do you remember asking me if I knew what it was?"

"I have so many dreams, I can hardly remember." Diorbhail was looking at her searchingly, obviously hoping Morrigan would say more, but Morrigan knew better. Diorbhail might well go off and shoot or stab the man she considered such a threat to her beloved Curran.

Diorbhail said nothing for a moment. She just looked at Morrigan in that way she had, making Morrigan feel like her secrets were displayed on her forehead.

"Maybe you lived there once, in another body," she said finally, "and that's why you want to go there."

"I promised Lily and Richard that we would check on their cottage, that's all," Morrigan said. "What's on that hill over there? A ruin? Let's go see."

"I DON'T LIKE THIS PLACE," DIORBHAIL SAID, LOW.

Morrigan felt too ill to reply, and could only shake her head.

Stones were scattered around the hilltop haphazardly, many still blackened with old soot stains. The wind sounded like soft, mournful wailing.

Both jumped when someone behind them spoke. "What are you doing?" It was their housekeeper, staring at them coldly. "None come here, unless they prefer the company of ghosts to men."

"Ghosts?" Morrigan asked.

"Here, where the murders took place." Faith wore an odd, satisfied expression, but there was something else there, as well. "My daughter was butchered, and my grandchildren."

Morrigan felt more than heard Diorbhail's gasp. With each passing moment, she felt more nauseated, and had to resist the urge to rub her throat, which had begun to itch and burn. Sparkles burst before her eyes and the ground rushed towards her face. Diorbhail seized her arms and supported her.

"Aye," Faith said, narrow-eyed. "My youngest grandchild was but four."

"Don't...don't," Morrigan whispered.

Ignoring her, the woman said, "They burned the house. This is all that's left. Go away. This place is no' for outsiders. You defile it by coming here."

Diorbhail pulled Morrigan off that sad, awful hill. Morrigan looked back once, and saw Faith swipe at her eyes.

SEAGHAN LECTURED MORRIGAN AS THE BOAT PASSED THE CASTLE IN THE BAY AND headed into open water. "Your husband left you in my care," he said. "I'll thank you to no' make my work harder." When she said nothing, he put his hand on her forearm. "D'you understand? You will tell me where you're going from now on."

"Aye, Seaghan."

Their captain, Mr. Cameron, spoke only Gaelic, so Seaghan had to translate. Apparently the man seldom saw such calm seas around Mingulay, and said the Virgin Mary must be blessing their visit. He suggested a boat tour of the island, promising they would never forget the western cliffs.

Up and up and up Morrigan stared, transfixed. Mr. Cameron laughed, quite gratified. *Bual na Creige*, he called the rock face, sheer, black, ominous, like something from myth. Only the kittiwakes and guillemots dared touch it. The water was so soft he decided to venture into the sharp cleft slicing into the island; they dropped into deep, cold shadow beneath the towering ebony wall.

"I want to stand on the summit and look down," she said.

The grizzled old man laughed again, and uttered something.

"He says to make certain you haven't been drinking," Seaghan told her. "He hates to think how many have fallen off."

Their guide carried them past several towering sea stacks: Lianamuil, with its mysterious yawning caves, and Arnamuil, and through the chilly narrow arch separating the island from another stack he called Gunamuil.

She imagined being in a small boat like this when the waters were not calm. No doubt the boat and its passengers would be shattered to bits against the rock and sucked into fathomless graves. Tales abounded of lighthouse keepers and fishermen, lost mysteriously, leaving no clues as to what might have happened.

Mr. Cameron dropped his dinghy on the east side and they put to shore without incident beside a white sandy beach. They asked him to point out the Donaghue house and he did, with the stem of his pipe. It was hard to miss, a multicolored fieldstone cottage with a slate roof, perched in solitary magnificence above the humble village, halfway up a steep hill where green beach grass and sea holly turned to moorland scrub and peat.

When he mentioned it was locally called Taigh na Gaoithe, "Windy House," a sharp shock coursed through Morrigan, causing her breath to catch. She saw again the woman smashing a bottle of champagne against those stones and wiping her wet, sticky hands on Aodhàn Mackinnon's face.

Her vision degenerated into wildly bursting spots of color; her ears hummed so loudly she hardly heard Mr. Cameron telling them they would have no trouble finding women to clean and cook.

Two village lasses, eager to earn extra coin, led the group up the hill to their new home and went about dusting and digging out the teapot and cups. It was as Lily had described, a pleasant cottage with four bedrooms, two parlors, and a well-equipped kitchen, the whole drawing in light from large casement windows. Stuffed couches, chairs, and loveseats were preserved beneath sheets, which the hired women whisked away. Ibby and Beatrice took the east bedroom, Diorbhail chose one in the middle for herself and Olivia, and Seaghan the next, leaving Morrigan and Curran the largest, with the biggest bed, at the west end. A fire was soon burning cheerily in the west parlor, chasing away the chill that lingered from being shut up and empty for so long.

The interior of the cottage didn't seem familiar. Morrigan told herself she was giving an old dream too much importance and was no doubt wrong about the name she remembered hearing.

In the morning, with only starlight to guide her, she stole out of Taigh na Gaoithe. Seaghan would be angry, but she knew she could get around him. To ward off the worst of a lecture, she scribbled a note. He had only demanded she tell him where she was, and she'd done so.

Knowing already where she wanted to go, she paused no more than a moment on the slope outside the house. She meant to be on those western cliffs when the sun came up. Summiting the hill wasn't difficult; before long she was descending again. She detoured briefly to explore an abandoned shepherd's hut, but as dawn pushed back the blackness of night, she made her way to the precipice she'd seen the day before, and looked down. It was dizzying, like staring into a bottomless abyss, and she heard Seaghan's voice as he translated Mr. Cameron's warning. *I hate to think how many have fallen off.*

She perused the coastline, noting the nearby promontory called Dùn Mhiughalaigh, hazy with morning mist. She walked to it and crossed to the far end, where she could look out as if she were at the prow of a ship, over unbroken ocean. The rising sun lit the endless expanse, catching on the wings of the kittiwakes. The sea was loud as it threw itself against these rock walls, and the cry of birds seemed in the thousands. She walked from one side to the other and turned her head up, staring into the depthless blue sky at an eagle circling over her head.

Though she'd halfway convinced herself she was wrong about the cottage, there remained a conviction that she'd been here before. She saw herself breathing this air, scented of salt sea and bird droppings, and walking these high crags, holding hands with Aodhàn Mackinnon, but not as she knew him now. The man in her imagination was young.

Something moved at the edge of her sight. She turned with a gasp, expecting Seaghan, but it was not the grizzled giant. This form, almost in silhouette with the sun behind him, was taller, leaner. She blinked, and blinked again.

"Morrigan," he said, stopping a few steps away.

It was Aodhàn Mackinnon.

Beatrice Stewart settled into a rocking chair by the window and clumsily tried to separate red yarn from blue.

"I was a prince," she muttered. "I sacked cities. I killed legions. I bathed in blood. Now look at me."

She peered at the tangled yarn, wondering if anyone would notice if Beatrice, who had always enjoyed needlework, suddenly gave it up.

Females and their daft, useless occupations. All the menial tasks, the world's free labor. They were like slaves, but stupider. Slaves knew they were slaves. Women didn't seem to grasp that fact.

Why couldn't a man have happened by the ruin outside Glenelg? Anyone other than this ugly, stumpy witch with legs like telegraph poles.

There was some amusement in imagining Ibby's horror if she were to find out she was changing her clothes and sleeping with a man in truth, rather than her sister-in-law's sister.

Harpalycus snickered.

He had determined many things through the centuries. Early on, he'd observed that neither Aridela nor Menoetius retained any memories of their previous lives. But, for some reason, Chrysaleon did, and that made him formidable.

A knock interrupted his plotting. "Who is it?" he barked.

The door was thrust open with such force it thudded against the wall. Seaghan MacAnaugh stood there, looking hard, almost dangerous.

Finally. A diversion. Though he had made the body of this stinking female his, Harpalycus could still call out Beatrice's memories, and he had none of that woman's reticence.

He slipped into character. "What d'you want with your banging and scowling?"

"Morrigan, you old crone. Have you seen her?"

"So far, Seaghan, you've done a bloody poor job of watching her. What will the master say?"

"Have you seen her or not?" Seaghan's hands clenched.

"Ask that whore from Stranraer where she's gone. They have no secrets from each other."

"Morrigan left before she woke."

Beatrice shrugged. "Maybe she caught the eye of one of the village men and went off for a bit of enjoyment. But you'd know more about such things than me, wouldn't you?"

He hardly blinked. "Now that you bring it up, there's something that's been troubling me. Why is it you've let her believe these many years that Douglas was her father?"

"Who would her father be in your eyes, then?"

"I am. You know it. And I also want to know why Hannah ran away with him."

She laughed, and laughed again at the anguish he didn't quite manage to disguise. "What pretty wee notions you've got rolling around in your head. Hannah was near her time to deliver when you sailed to Nova Scotia to begin a new life."

"Which proves what I say. They hadn't been together six months, but Hannah looked to be full term."

"Women are different, some carry high, some low. Some women grow large and some don't. If you were so certain the wean was yours, why did you board the ship without her?"

"You know Douglas tricked me. You were there. I thought all of you were getting on the ferry right behind me. I tried to stay, when I saw what Douglas was doing." Flicking a hand impatiently towards his cheek, he added, "And received a truncheon in the face."

"I know nothing but how she wept when you sailed away. Thank God Douglas was there to care for her."

"Aye. He took such good care of her she died that night."

"At least he was there. There's more to being a father, you know, than planting seed in soil. Douglas cared for the child when you wanted nothing to do with her or her mam. Hannah wrote to you, asking your forgiveness, begging you to come for her. If you had, she'd be alive today and you'd have your precious Morrigan. You'd have had her all along. But you chose to let Hannah suffer, and Morrigan as well. Hannah's death is on your shoulders, and I will never help you with Morrigan, or with anything else in this life."

"Wrote to me? When? What are you talking about?"

"What daft game d'you think to play now? I helped her write that letter. I posted it. Lies won't serve you, not with me."

"What letter? Damn you! She wrote to me? When?"

Beatrice shook her head. "You don't fool me."

Seaghan slammed his fist into the wall. "I never got any letter from Hannah!"

Beatrice saw the truth in his face. This was amusing. Hannah had believed Seaghan purposely didn't answer, that he hated her and was leaving her to her fate. But he'd never received the letter that told him he was Morrigan's father, the letter beseeching him to save her, the letter begging his forgiveness.

She rubbed her hand over her mouth to hide a smirk. "Well, she sent you one, from Ireland. She quickened, and went to see the midwife, who told her she was five months gone. That's when Hannah realized it was your child she was bringing into the world, and not a rapist's."

"Rapist's?" Seaghan's face paled.

"Aye, she claimed she was attacked and forced." Harpalycus remembered the night he had assaulted Seaghan's lovely betrothed. He'd been Charles Kelly then, a homeless vagabond.

Following that mad sense of his, the one that always led him to the triad, he'd journeyed to Glenelg, but not one of them had been there and none ever appeared, though he waited a good three months. It had simply been a crime of opportunity when he'd come across Hannah and Seaghan having one of their trysts in the forest on a warm night in June. He'd watched and waited, and when Hannah went off, telling Seaghan she didn't need an escort to get home safely, he'd proven her wrong. He might not have done it, but Seaghan MacAnaugh had been rude to him on more than one occasion, and Harpalycus never let a slight go unpunished. Afterward, he deserted Glenelg and consumed another man, the fiery religious zealot, Owen Anderson. Following a new inner call, he caught a boat to Barra, and there found success at last: Chrysaleon, Aridela, and a long-overdue night of revenge.

He pushed Beatrice to the forefront again. "Of course, Hannah was not exactly virtuous, was she? So it's anyone's guess on that detail."

Now, so many years later, and with Beatrice Stewart's memories, Harpalycus was able to see the rest of that story.

A devastated and bloody Hannah had staggered home, where Beatrice met her and gave her comfort. Believing she was ruined for Seaghan, Hannah had turned to Douglas Lawton. She'd made up a story of being overwhelmed by love for him, and convinced him to run away with her.

"She…she was raped?" Seaghan wilted. "Who in Glenelg would do such a thing?"

When Harpalycus found Chrysaleon and Aridela, living as Aodhàn Mackinnon and his wife, Lilith, he'd employed one of his favorite, most effective pastimes—a carefully plotted destruction, which culminated in November of the same year. Harpalycus convinced twelve devout men that the Mackinnon house was a haven to Satan and the black arts. When they were good and drunk he sent them in, inflamed and ready to slaughter. The children were easily dispatched; Aridela, hidden away in the body of Lilith Mackinnon, took surprisingly more effort. His men bound Aodhàn, threw him in a fishing boat, stabbed him, and dumped him overboard off the cliffs of Berneray. But fate, or Athene, intervened, sending Seaghan MacAnaugh to pluck the man out of the water and save his life.

Mere hours later, it would seem, Aridela returned as Morrigan, daughter to Hannah Stewart Lawton, outside the burned village of Glenelg. And eventually, after years of wandering, Chrysaleon found his way to that place too, and settled there with Seaghan.

Beatrice's memories revealed the chain of events. Menoetius appeared in Glenelg in the body of the seven-year-old boy, Curran Ramsay. Soon after, Douglas took Nicky, Morrigan, and Beatrice away to Stranraer. Years later, Curran Ramsay was reintroduced to Morrigan and promptly fell in love, which the dowf could be counted on to do in every life. He wed her and carted her back to Glenelg and Chrysaleon, and it all started again, all over again, with the three of them finally rejoined.

Now Harpalycus understood why he'd been drawn to Glenelg in the first place. Some part of him had sensed that the triad would gather there. He'd just been too early.

Only now could he see the full extent of that whole Barra episode. It was, without a doubt, one of his brightest achievements. Chrysaleon had come so close to death, was so traumatized by what happened, that he'd lost his ability to recall anything for two decades. His memories returned when it was too late —after his beloved Aridela was married.

Making those three suffer offered incomparable satisfaction. It was better, so much more *amusing,* than simply killing them.

A new game took root inside him. He couldn't consume Curran—the only times he'd ever attempted to consume one of the triad, first Aridela then Chrysaleon, a handmaid of Athene had nearly speared him through. He'd never risked it since, but there was nothing to prevent him from consuming Seaghan. He studied the brawny fisherman. Anything was an improvement over Beatrice, and Seaghan, though he was surely in his fifties, was still a strong, vital male.

Beatrice rose, tossed the yarn into the chair, and went right up to Seaghan, forcing him to meet her gaze. "What about when Douglas brought her back to Glenelg before the clearings? Again she begged you to take her away. If you had, she wouldn't have given birth in the forest. But no. You refused. You would hardly speak to her. Poor, poor Seaghan's wounded pride. And what about these last twenty years? It wouldn't have been hard to find us. Your daughter could not have been all that important to you, since you never bothered. You really expect me to believe you care about her?"

Seaghan's hands clenched and he grimaced. "It's true, I was angry, and I sent Hannah away, to my shame. I know I should have searched for Morrigan when I came home. I made mistakes. I was wrong. I'm going to tell her the truth. I'm her father. Not Douglas."

He retreated. She fancied he didn't trust his self-control. Either that or he didn't like her smell.

"Will you?" Her lifted brows expressed doubt. "She'll hate you if you do. I'll make sure of it. Douglas Lawton is the only father she ever knew, and she's riddled with guilt because she robbed him of his beloved wife. She'll become Aodhàn Mackinnon's whore, too, if she hasn't already. Oh aye, I know all about it. And why d'you think she'll do that? Because Aodhàn is like Douglas, with his black, tortured ways. Well, I'll help her, and I'll help her keep the secret. That is, until I want the truth known."

"You've filled her head full of lies all these years!"

"Douglas and I together did that. Hannah gave you a second chance—and a third—but you threw her away. Now you're sorry. It's too late—d'you understand? There'll never be another man to match the father Morrigan knew. Because he was there, through the years. Always there, while you were off in the New World, proud you'd saved yourself from being cuckolded. Well, you hold onto that pride of yours, Seaghan. See how it cares for you in your dotage."

Seaghan stared at her. Helpless rage and grief wrenched his face into an ugly mask.

"Get out," Beatrice said, fully enjoying her triumph.

Chapter 15

MORRIGAN THREW HERSELF INTO MACKINNON'S ARMS, LAUGHING, PRESSING HER cheek against his neck. But he only allowed that for a moment before lifting her face and kissing her, his mouth demanding all he'd waited for these many months. She returned his kisses, pulling him closer, until at last, after a lost interlude of time, he finally held her at arm's length.

"Mackinnon," she said, feeling as though her heart had risen up through her throat and was shining from her eyes.

He looked older, as if it had been years instead of months. *"Mo rùn,"* he said, low.

"Am I dreaming? How…why…how can you be here?" He'd kissed her so hard her cheeks were burning from the scrape of his beard.

"I knew you would come. I watched you land yesterday."

"But how…oh, I don't care." She grabbed his neck and drew him close. When he maneuvered her to the ground she acquiesced willingly, ripping away the buttons on his sark and sliding her hands over his bare chest.

It wasn't until he'd opened her bodice and was pushing the chemise from her shoulders that she remembered Olivia. Olivia would be up by now, and she always wanted to see her mother when she woke. They would all be awake. Seaghan might even now be searching for her.

"Stop," she said. "I have to go. Seaghan will find us."

His jaw clenched. His eyes narrowed. His hand lay possessively over her pounding heart, and she feared he might refuse to release her. "Why Seaghan?" he asked. "Where is Curran?"

"He had business on the mainland that couldn't be put off. He means to join us here tomorrow or the next day."

"Ah," he said, and sighed as she stroked the hair off his cheek. He put his hand over hers and kissed her palm. Then, so suddenly it made her gasp, he caught her around the waist and rolled over so she lay on his chest. "You are maddening," he said. "Like absinthe in my soul."

She traced his lips so he would kiss her fingers, then decided she might die if she didn't taste him again.

"*An tig thu thugam a-nochd?*"

"What does that mean?"

"Come to me. Tonight."

"Where?"

"You passed a bothy on the hill."

"Aye, I went inside. Does it belong to someone?"

"Not any longer. *An tig thu thugam a-nochd?* Say you will, or I won't let you go."

"Aye, aye." She rolled off him to lie at his side. "I will come to you tonight."

Above them, high in the sky, the eagle watched and circled.

SHE WAS HALFWAY TO THE DONAGHUE HOUSE BEFORE IT SANK IN. MORRIGAN rubbed her palms over her cheeks, hoping to cool this feverish heat.

Curran. Curran! The unexpected sight of Mackinnon had wiped him away like he didn't exist. It was unforgivable. How could she be so cruel and thoughtless to the man who had given her Olivia, and this new babe, just begun…to he who had married her though he could easily have turned away?

She deliberately recalled the image of Lily, pressed against him, stroking his face, and of Curran's response, but her anger refused to burn as hotly as it had, and no wonder. Hadn't she just now done the exact same thing?

"Morrigan!" She looked up to see Seaghan and Diorbhail climbing towards her. Seaghan was panting. "Where the devil have you been this time?" He sounded truly vexed.

"Walking. Exploring." She took a deep breath, knowing she needed to quickly become an accomplished actress, for Seaghan MacAnaugh was perceptive, and Diorbhail Sinclair even more so. Gritting her teeth, she willed away the fierce ardor Mackinnon had ignited inside her.

"Walking!" He came closer. Whipping out a handkerchief, he mopped his forehead. "Damn it, and damn you! You are the most vexatious female I've ever known!"

"Forgive me," she said. "I lost track of time, and I did leave a note. Maybe you could punish me later? I think I hear Olivia."

"I'm certain of that!" he said, but she thought with alarm that his gaze grew more acute, even puzzled. She wondered if her cheeks were as red as they felt.

Diorbhail stood at his side, reminding Morrigan of an albumen print the dominie had showed her of the Great Sphinx of Giza.

Late in the afternoon, Morrigan asked for a bath to be drawn, saying she felt grimy after the sea crossing and strenuous walk. She begged out of the evening meal with the excuse of being tired.

After Olivia had been put down for the night, she sat at the dressing table in her bedroom, combing her hair, trying to recall more details from the dreams she'd had that seemed to take place on this island. She saw herself running barefoot along the cliffs, a man laughing as he chased her, a man her imagination fashioned into Mackinnon. She let the dream unfold, and embellished it.

What of her resolve to do whatever she must for the sake of her husband and child? She thought of Emma Bovary, of Iseult. Were all adulteresses condemned to tragic ends? What of men who were unfaithful to their vows?

The golden heart locket winked at her in the lamplight. *Whither thou goest, I will go. Where thou diest, I will die, and there will I be buried.*

It had been placed in the wedding cake for Curran, not Mackinnon, yet it was Mackinnon's voice she heard. Tonight she would ask him to explain, if he could, what he'd said when trapped in fever. She had to know, especially after reading *Tristram and Iseult*. Was it death he wanted, or had his words been meaningless delirium?

It's the only way.

Sin never escaped punishment. Father Drummond, the Bible, and Jamini had confirmed it. Jamini had described how humans were reborn, hopefully to ascend higher and higher, becoming purer and purer, until no more lives were required, and eternity was spent in the sweet liberation of moksha.

If her belief was truth, then death was not the end. It was a doorway to new possibilities.

She heard the others climbing the stairs, retiring to their rooms for the night. If she was careful, she could sneak away and be home before daybreak. Before the guard dog Seaghan woke. Before Olivia clamored for her breakfast. Curran was gone. No one would ever know.

Was she really contemplating this?

Beside the wee loch at Torridon that night in June, she'd dreamed of a boat. She remembered the carved lady in the prow turning, regarding her. Curran, glowing with moonlight, had offered to lead her up the plank. She'd wanted to go. She'd reached out to him…but then she'd awakened.

Every time she tried to shut out Mackinnon's face it returned more vividly. There had been desperation in his eyes when he'd asked her to meet him.

He'd told her the motto of his clan. *Fortune favors the bold.* Could she venture into the realm of boldness? *You have to,* whispered the inner Morrigan, *or you will always regret, and wonder.*

She removed her wedding ring and placed it gently beside her hairbrush. *Fortune favors the bold.*

What if she climbed the hill to that abandoned hut and he was nothing more than an echoing laugh upon the wind? It did seem fantastic that he would be here, on this obscure island. How had he known she would come? Maybe she'd had some kind of dream or vision on the cliffs and he wasn't here, not really. It might be a good thing if she went to the bothy and found nothing but mice and mold. Then she could put these longings out of her head and get down to her duty—being a decent wife, a good mother, and vanishing into oblivion when she died.

At last she crept down the stairs to the side door off the kitchen. The night sparkled and for once, the wind had subsided. She climbed the slope behind the house, stumbling in hidden divots and over treacherous stones.

As she ran up to the bothy, holding her skirts, a shadow separated from it. Aodhàn pinned her against the wall and kissed her, on her mouth, her face, and neck, kisses that made his long-restrained passion clear.

My Mackinnon. Her hands told her he was real and solid, no dream to scatter at the sound of Beatrice calling her to her chores.

He pulled her inside. She waited, blind in the dark, listening to him move about. The hearth fire caught, leaping, giving off curls of blue aromatic smoke that funneled upward through a hole in the thatch. Its light revealed a pile of blankets and peat stacked against the wall.

"You planned this," she said. None of it had been here earlier, except for the old trunk in the corner, which had been padlocked.

He crossed to the trunk and opened it, bringing out his treasures—sheepskins, pewter goblets, a bottle of whisky, fat white candles, which he lit, salted mutton, a crusty loaf of oat bread, a hunk of cheese, a knife, and a large cloth.

She pictured him collecting these things, placing them in the trunk, preparing for this moment. A terrible fear rose up within her and she heard Diorbhail's voice. *He is not what he seems.*

"Why am I here?" She backed away towards the door. "Why are you such a part of me? What of Curran?"

In two long strides he reached her and gripped her arms. "Don't. Tonight, you're mine."

The intensity in his voice and eyes sparked an image, so fleeting she received only the barest impression of falling through starlit air, of a pounding sea, of strong hands, and rocks yawning like black teeth.

She knew instantly it was Eamhair, jumping to her death.

"No," she said. "I cannot do this." She twisted, trying to free herself.

"Why did you come here?" He spoke furiously, and his grip only tightened.

Did he mean to force himself upon her? If so, she had only herself to blame.

"I…I don't know. I don't know, Mackinnon! I shouldn't have!"

His lips tensed. His regard narrowed then sharpened. "You're afraid of me?" he said, low, and released her.

She rubbed her arms. She could go no farther. The rough, splintery door pressed against her spine.

He raked through his hair, hissing *"Mhic an Diabhail."*

"I'll go," she said, reaching for the latch.

He sighed and fisted his hands. "Don't do this to me, Morrigan." He closed the space between them. "If you don't want to be with me that way, it will not happen. I don't care. All I ask is that you stay. I need…I need to be with you. I've waited a long time." He held out his hand.

She considered. At last she put her hand in his and let him lead her to the fire.

OUTSIDE IT WAS MISTY AND COLD, WITH THE VAST ATLANTIC CHILLING THE AIR, BUT in the bothy the warmth of the peat fire kept them comfortable.

Mackinnon rolled up his sleeves. Earlier that day she had ripped most of the buttons off his sark, so it hung open. Morrigan sat on one of the sheepskins, watching him as he cut a slice of bread and topped it with cheese.

When he handed it to her, she asked, "Is that the scar Seaghan told me about?"

Looking down, he pulled the material away, revealing it—a raised, rough line resembling a snake. It wound from his collarbone to the middle of his chest.

"Aye, Seaghan stitched it up for me. He decided I shouldn't die that day."

"I must thank him."

He poured her whisky and took some himself. There was no tension now, no fear. He obediently maintained space between them, though not much, and seemed perfectly content to feed her bread and cheese, to fill her goblet with amber whisky and keep the fire going. She began to feel as relaxed as if she were sitting with Diorbhail.

"Shall we toast?" He held out his goblet.

"To what?"

He thought a moment. "To cheese."

She laughed, but struck her cup to his and drank. "Mackinnon."

"What? Cheese was a good invention."

"I was expecting something profound."

"To beauty, then." He waited, holding up his goblet. "Well?" he said, when she didn't respond. "Is beauty not profound enough for you?"

"No."

"You're beautiful. Don't you want to hear me say it?"

She drained her cup without toasting. "Is that why you're here? Because of how I look?"

His regard didn't change. "Do you think so?"

"You don't know me. I could be ugly inside. Would it matter?"

He laughed. "You have no idea what ugly is."

Morrigan shrugged. "Folk talk about my face like it's the only thing I possess of value. Yet to me it seems the least important. What does any woman have that breaks through to a man's heart other than beauty?" She caught herself before blurting, *My own father wanted to lie with me*. Sickened, she turned her face away. Beauty was a curse if it could make a father want to do such a thing.

Placing two fingers on her cheek, he brought her gaze back to his.

"Understanding."

Aye, true understanding was a braw thing, especially if accompanied by acceptance. Braw, aye, and rare. She remembered the time she'd spent alone with Diorbhail on the mountain, and how the woman's instinctive understanding made her feel whole, and strong, and valuable.

"Every man, woman, and child craves to be understood," he said. "Communion. It's more nourishing than bread, for everything that breathes." He leaned forward. "There's none on this earth who understands me like you. Every time you look into my face, you free me of my demons. You say I don't know you? You're aye wrong about that. You and I know each other. Look into your heart. I am there."

She studied him, absorbing his statement, shredding it in a private search to determine its truth.

"Curran doesn't know your soul. He doesn't understand. You're here with me because I do."

He frowned. "*What did it mean when I lost the soft hills*," he quoted. "*Time melts into mine, jewels and ancient forgiveness*."

"That's the song I heard," she said.

"It was my wife's song. She sang it to our children."

"Wife? You've a wife?" Morrigan's heart stopped, or seemed to, before wallowing sickly in her chest. "Where is she?"

The skin around his eyes tightened and his jaw clenched. "Dead."

Silence stretched between them. Then she asked, lower, "Your children?"

"Dead."

This was what tortured him, made him so quiet and withdrawn. "Mackinnon."

Fear, doubt, and guilt washed out of her.

"What was her name?" she asked, taking his hand.

She knew before he said it.

Lilith.

"THEY CAME IN THE NIGHT." HIS VOICE CAUGHT. "SPLINTERED THE DOOR. OUR children were screaming. I looked at her. I saw by her face she knew what would happen. They had plenty of men. Six it took and a rope to keep me, and another six could hardly hold her. My Lilith bloodied the nose of one of them with her forehead. But they were mad, full of whisky and righteous piety. One of the bastards slit my daughter's throat—she but seven, and another threw my four-year-old against the hearthstones."

His lips drew back and his hands, violently shaking, closed upon themselves. "I couldn't stop—I couldn't stop them—"

Morrigan seized his wrists. "Oh, Mackinnon. Mackinnon."

"They killed them. All three of them. Left their bodies on the floor. Gave me a good long while to look before they dragged me out on their boat. They cut me open and threw me overboard, laughing about how I'd still be alive when the fish came to eat me. She did it to punish me for being happy. *You will follow and follow without end. Glimpses of joy will be ripped from you.* That was the curse she laid upon me, and God, how she loves making it happen...."

Morrigan knew she had to deliver him from whatever hell he was drowning in. "You would've given your life to save them, but you couldn't."

"Would I? History proves my truth." He seized a fistful of her hair and stared into her face. His eyes were greener now, as green as that Greek warrior's she dreamed of. "If you knew what I've done, you would hate me. You might kill me yourself. Whenever I start to forget, she proves all over again what I really am. For me, there is no redemption."

Morrigan held his face. "I don't know what to say. I'm so sorry this happened to you. I think I love you more, more than I did."

He reared up and put the fire between them, clenching and unclenching his hands. His shadow leaped across the floor and climbed the wall, rippling in the firelight.

"They were murderers." Morrigan kept her voice calm and controlled, knowing she hadn't yet reached him. "And they paid for what they did. Imagine what they thought when they woke the next morning, sober. It had to be with them always, every minute."

Mackinnon turned and stared at her, his face as colorless as a skeleton's, but he was listening at last. His fists uncurled.

She stood and stepped around the fire, taking his cold hands in her own. "I would weep for you, my Mackinnon…if I could."

He looked down into her face for a long moment then drew her tightly against him, murmuring something in Gaelic, his voice breaking.

He raised his head. His lashes were clumped and a sheen of tears made his eyes as brilliant as the emeralds Curran had given her. "I will weep for both of us," he said softly, before picking her up and laying her on the sheepskins. He pressed his mouth to her neck, until she could no longer think about stopping him, or think at all.

He kissed the pulses in her throat and at her wrists, telling her how much he'd missed her, ached for her, longed for her. "'*S tusa gaol is rùn mo chridhe.* Thou art my love, my heart. *Gu bràth.* Forever. *M' ulaidh bhuaireanta.* I'm not sure I want you to know what that means."

But he remembered his promise, and made no attempt to remove her clothing, nor did he touch her in a sexual way. Somehow, that made his kisses, and the heat of his hand against hers, far more intimate than any sexual act could have been.

He regarded her, his face at last tranquil. His eyes, for the first time, were open and relaxed, no longer squinting. "You love me, Morrigan?" He kissed her knuckles. "You said it. I won't let you take it back now."

"I do." It was such a betrayal. It broke her heart, but she couldn't deny it, not after what he'd endured.

He spoke against her mouth. "Your skin calls to me with the voices of all the women you have been and will be. It brings me back, over and over, when all I want to do is give up."

Smoke from Aodhàn's pipe tickled Morrigan's nose. His head was pillowed on her stomach and she lay, half-reclining, supported by the stack of blankets. For the last hour, they'd watched the fire and listened to the wind pick up outside. He seemed more content than she had ever seen him, but her thoughts were whirling.

"We've been together before, somewhere," she said, taking his hair out of its knot and combing it with her fingers.

She felt him tense and sat up, dislodging him so she could look into his face. "There's something. I can almost catch it, but not quite. Why do I feel I knew you had a wife and children, and that they were dead?"

Still he said nothing, but she sensed him withdraw in some intangible fashion.

"That woman...the housekeeper on Barra, she said her daughter and grandchildren were murdered on the hill outside of Castlebay. She said her youngest granddaughter was four."

His jaw clenched and he turned away, but she wouldn't allow it, not again. "Look at me, Mackinnon," she said. "Is she Lilith's mother?"

"Aye."

She pictured that hard, bitter woman, but she couldn't pause, not with so many questions. "The night when you were ill. The night before Curran and I left Glenelg...."

"Aye." He kissed her palm. "Your hands were cool."

"You said you wanted us to die."

He threaded his fingers with hers. "Is death really the end? Not for me. Not for you, either. Sometimes, death is the easiest way to start over."

"What the bloody hell does that mean?"

He frowned. "I've said too much."

"I've dreamed of the woman named Lilith, the slaughter of the girls. You know it. It was them I saw on Saint Brigit's Eve."

He closed his eyes. She discerned the trembling that came over him. He made a sound in his throat, a hoarse, harsh sound of pain. "Damn it!" he said, and shoved his fists against his eyes. "You always do this. You keep pushing and pushing, and I never can resist telling you."

She pried his hands away. "I have to know."

He ran the tips of his fingers over her forehead, closing her eyelids, and put his mouth next to her ear. "I remember the lives I've lived," he said. "And you...you're always there. I always find you. The only reason it took so long this time was because of this...." He touched the scar on his chest, "and the deaths. It was all barricaded behind a wall I could not breach until you came back to me. *You* were my Lilith, and Taigh na Gaoithe is the summer cottage I built for you, because you loved Mingulay. You gave it its name. We conceived both our children here, on Dùn Mhiughalaigh."

She stared at him. He was deadly serious. He drew her back down again, holding her between his arm and chest as he kissed each of her fingertips.

The dreams...were memories. She had broken champagne against the wall of the cottage. She had laughed on the cliffs at Mackinnon's demand that she marry him.

"Do you want to see yourself?" Mackinnon rose, fetched his coat, and brought something out of the pocket. He handed her a miniature portrait of a woman with very dark hair, black, or almost, pulled up and off her face. Her eyes were dark too, far seeing, enigmatic, full of mystery, of secrets, and her skin was as pale as the moon. She stared out from the portrait solemnly, and Morrigan found herself wishing she could talk to her.

"You and I return," he said. "Can't you feel our long history? We've loved each other, lived as husband and wife, and you've borne my weans. You were my Lilith. You were the mother of Claire and Evie. *Mo bhean*. My wife."

She was full of questions. *How did we meet? Where did we live? On Barra, in that burned ruin?* But the one that came from her mouth was, "Did you love me?"

"Always you, you alone, since the beginning of time. Does knowing that make it better? There's no use judging yourself. If you were an ordinary woman, and I an ordinary man, you wouldn't be here. You would never betray anyone—loyalty is your cornerstone, and always has been. But what we have…goes beyond all that."

Before she could decide whether she agreed with this or not, he added, "I've sealed my fate, but I don't care. Trust me, Morrigan. Believe me. Can you?"

"Aye," she said.

Later, when she was alone, without those intoxicating eyes and storyteller's voice…that's when the questions would come.

In a moment, after she finished a reviving bite or two of cold mutton, Mackinnon would put out the fire and take her to Taigh na Gaoithe. It wasn't yet dawn, but dawn was close.

"That ring you gave me," she said. "It was my wedding ring?"

"Aye." He rubbed his eyes wearily.

"What does the inscription mean? I was afraid to ask."

"You know Gaelic. It was your first language. If you think about it, it will come to you."

She smiled and took a deep breath. "It said *Gaol mo chridhe*. Love is *gaol*. *Mo* is my."

He nodded, offering no assistance.

"So…*my love*." She pondered as he rolled up the sheepskins and put them in the trunk. "*Chridhe*," she said again, listening, looking inside for the answer. "Heart."

He turned from the trunk, watching her.

"Love of my heart," she said.

He smiled and returned, going down on one knee. "I have something else of yours." Digging once more into his coat pocket, he brought out the delicate chain and pendant, and placed it over his fingertips so it was illuminated in the firelight. There was the dark blue stone, the crescent moons and wavy lines.

"You were wearing this when you had the fever," she said.

He traced the engraving. "The moon, waxing and waning, with the holy star between them, means hope for paradise. The lines speak of the labyrinth, the center of things, where truth is found and love, reborn. Will you take it? Keep it against your skin to remind you of this night?"

She hesitated. Was he suggesting this was all they would ever have?

Not trusting her voice, she nodded, and he fastened it around her neck. For a moment the reddish-orange color appeared around him, and the ornament seemed to respond with emanating warmth.

He tilted his head and smiled, then rose and kicked the fire out. They left the bothy and walked down the hill, holding hands, until Taigh na Gaoithe loomed before them.

The moon dangled low in the west. Their one night, their bold fortune, was nearly over.

The air was sharp and clear. Stars glittered, so close Morrigan thought she could reach up and pluck one. The wind sang in the grass, a nearby burn bubbled in accompaniment, and one solitary tern made a heartbreaking entreaty.

Anything could happen on such an enchanted night. The earth waited with her, holding its breath. Perhaps Aodhàn was really a god from Greek Olympus. If so, he'd be Dionysos, with the power to transform her blood to wine.

Closing her eyes, she felt herself revolve, round and round in perfect harmony with the earth. She placed a hand over her stomach, wanting to sense the new child. She would go to Olivia. She wanted to hold her baby as dawn saturated the heavens.

Rustling disturbed the brush. Aodhàn's head turned and she heard the scraich of a cat close in the darkness, followed by a squeal.

Did he change in some subtle way? For an instant she believed the primal challenge had come from his throat. Would he shake his head and revert to true form? Would he devour her here in this wild, windswept place? The illusion vanished into the dour, somber, familiar Mackinnon, though the likeness to a feral beast remained in the alert angle of his head.

"There's your cottage," he said. He gazed down at her, his eyes suffused with moonlight.

She glanced at the house but was far more intrigued by the way the light carved patterns over his face, changing him from ordinary man to something supernatural—again she thought of the *daoine sìth*. After so many strange visions, how could she know for certain what was real? Any second, he might give a crazed laugh and vanish, leaving her alone with the unhappy tern and the ever-soughing sea, or she might wake alone in her bed, victim of yet another bodiless dream.

"Go home to Glenelg," she said. "I need to think, and when I'm with you, I can't. Whatever I do, from now on, I mean to do with a clear head."

He put his hands on her waist. She felt he knew, in the fearsome way they had, every queer thought running through her brain.

"Should I...should I go and visit that woman...Faith?" she asked. "She was Lilith's mother."

"No." He shook his head. "Don't. She wouldn't understand or believe you. She has grown accustomed to her loss now. It would reawaken her suffering. You can't go back in time, only forward."

She thought for a moment. "Promise me, promise," she said, almost involuntarily.

"What, *m' eudail.*"

"Promise nothing will come between us, no matter what happens."

He paused. "This isn't the first time you've demanded that vow of me. And I have kept it, for over three thousand years."

The strangest words floated within as she gazed into his face.

Until the rise of Iakchos.

The number slowly sank in. "Three *thousand* years?"

He turned his face up and laughed, the sound full and joyous. "Fortune favors the bold," he shouted, with no regard for secrecy, wrongdoing, or the sleeping inhabitants of Mingulay. Away in the grass, the cat hissed.

Could she allow him to see her worries, her fears? No. She'd be invincible, a moon goddess to his wine god.

"Why do I call you Mackinnon instead of Aodhàn?"

"Because I always kissed you when you called me Aodhàn." He placed his thumb on her lower lip. "Always. Because of the shape your mouth makes when you say it. You had to call me Mackinnon so I wouldn't make love to you at inopportune moments."

"Aodhàn," she said.

He rested his hand on her shoulder then let it trail down to her backside, where it pressed, drawing her inexorably closer. She raised her face and he kissed her for a long while before releasing her. "We'll see if you can give me up," he said.

She went down the hill, pausing at the door. There. A dark figure hidden in the shadows. Morrigan caught a quick flash of silver, like a star had fallen to the earth.

An ocean of rainbows filled her mouth, bursting with the flavor of strawberries.

With one last look at the deeper shadow in a world of shadows, she went indoors to dream of lost sisters, of the women she had been.

But now she felt them surrounding her. She even knew what one looked like, and they did not seem quite as lost.

Chapter 16

Curran visited every tavern in Mallaig, searching for Quinn. He checked every lodging house. He inquired at the pier of all the ferryboat captains and fishermen who hired out boats for a fee.

No one remembered seeing a dignified older Englishman with bushy steel-colored sideburns.

Throughout his search, Curran had to fight a constant urge to jump onto the next boat heading west. The itching anxiety, the need to find something, he knew not what, reappeared. During this last year with Morrigan he'd almost forgotten it. Morrigan had filled him to overflowing even as she'd driven him halfway down the road towards madness.

What was she doing? Was she safe? Was Olivia? Was Seaghan watching over them as he'd promised? He needed to be there, with them, not here, searching for a man who seemed to have vanished from the earth. He was furious with Quinn, for writing that letter and not mailing it, for not detailing what he'd discovered, for not being where he'd promised to be.

Finally, after making the circuit of Mallaig three times, Curran was forced to admit Quinn was not here, and may never have been.

He would sail up to Kilgarry. If Quinn wasn't there, he would set off immediately for Mingulay.

Morrigan sat on a blanket looking out at the Atlantic, listening to the thunder of the waves against the cliffs far, far below. Olivia lay next to her, laughing joyously at a foraging grey-winged gull that seemed intent on entertaining her.

A village boy had delivered a note from Mackinnon this morning. Morrigan pulled it out of her pocket.

Nam chridhe gu bràth, it said. She'd worked it out, smiling at the challenge. *In my heart forever*. Below that, it read, *Once more. Tonight. Dùn Mhiughalaigh*.

He claimed she was his wife, reborn. It might sound outrageous, but she knew it was true, partly because of the dreams she'd had even before Curran introduced her to Aodhàn Mackinnon. Their disparate ages also fit.

You're mine and I am yours, he'd stated. *No matter what separates us*.

She wasn't a whore, or a weak woman recklessly succumbing to shallow passions. She wasn't even an adulteress. It was her husband she'd spent the night with, a husband she'd shared a home and children with. She hadn't left him. She'd been murdered. It changed everything.

Of course she wouldn't meet him. All her instincts ordered her to tear up the note. Justifications aside, she was now married to a different man, a man who also deserved respect and honor. The way her bones seemed to vibrate at the mere thought of Aodhàn told her she could never resist him if she saw him again. He muddled her clarity. She had told him she would not meet him, and she must stand firm.

Hearing footsteps, she turned to find Seaghan approaching. He dropped onto the blanket and swooped up Olivia with a sound kiss. She giggled in a baby's fresh, free-spirited way, unspoiled as yet by life's inevitable humiliations and disappointments.

Morrigan returned the note to her pocket.

"Lass," he said, "I have things I want to say."

He'd been watching her, observing the nuances of every expression, for two days. She'd done her best to act as though nothing had changed, but she probably hadn't succeeded.

"What things?" she asked.

"Aodhàn's been my comrade and confidant for twenty years. Long ago, I might've killed myself if he hadn't been there. I was so far from home. I didn't know what had happened to Hannah." He sighed. "I was grateful he was with me when I learned of her death."

He gestured at the heaving Atlantic swells. "There's something about the sea that tears at him. He goes coarse and moody and disappears. He's suffered with something. You'd think it would have driven him mad to never find relief. To never speak of it, not to anyone, even me." He paused. "Only those who understand the dark can hear the heartbeat of the night...of God, I like to think. Aodhàn understands the dark better than most."

Seaghan waited until Morrigan stopped contemplating the ocean and faced him again. "Sometimes I think Aodhàn *is* mad," he said. A frown deepened the creases around his mouth. "I know I'm stepping beyond my boundaries to say these things, but he's married. I've never seen her, but no' so long ago, the day after your wedding in fact, he claimed she's alive. If that's true, neither of you are free."

She thought of the murders, and the secret Mackinnon had told her. "No, Seaghan," she said. "His wife is dead."

"You knew of it?"

She nodded, and his shoulders relaxed. "Be that as it may, I think you're going to be hurt. Somehow this will end badly. Aodhàn's no' meant to love a lass. Not the way Curran can."

Aching over his concern, she decided to be as honest as she could. "You speak of madness? I know it well, and Mackinnon understands that. He understands me in a way Curran can't. As braw as Curran is, as much as he loves me, he can't understand me. I know he would if he could, but Mackinnon... Mackinnon is the only one." She rubbed her arm across her forehead. "I don't want to hurt my husband. What's he ever been but decent and good?" Her gaze turned to the granite precipice that fell away, sheer and implacable. She felt like she was sitting at the summit of Mount Olympus, in the company of all the great gods and goddesses, looking out over the world of mortals. "Curran and Olivia have taken over my heart," she said softly. "Do I give up my heart, or my soul?"

"You're no' alone," he said. "Not ever, my darling. I...I...."

She smiled and squeezed his hand. "You remind me of a man I saw once in Stranraer. He came out of a dress shop with his daughter; she'd near buried him under boxes and bags. They were laughing. He spoke to her. He listened like he was interested in everything she said. I followed them awhile, and went home in misery because of the way my papa hated me. I wished I had a father like that man. I wished it all the time. I think that old wish has been granted... in you. Oh, I know I sound like a spoiled child. I'm not saying I'd exchange Douglas Lawton. If I could have a moment with him right now, I'd thank him for all he did. Maybe he needed to hear me say it. Maybe he needed to believe I cared. But you're my honorary father. If I could help it, I'd never do anything to shame you. I don't think Mackinnon would either. But we're dragged like leaves in a windstorm, aren't we? Do we ever have as much control over events as we think we do?"

Seaghan pulled her head to his great chest and held her there, the slow beat of his powerful heart lending her brief hope that everything might yet turn out as it should.

FIONNA HANDED CURRAN A PILE OF LETTERS AFTER DISAPPOINTING HIM WITH HER reply that no, Quinn had not come to Kilgarry, not since Olivia had been christened. Then she pointed to the envelope on top. He saw it had been forwarded from the man's law office in London.

Ripping it open, Curran went off to his study so he could read in private.

I do hope to see you soon, but I mail this letter in case something prevents it. You were right to be concerned. With the help of shillings, whisky, and a lonely old man's love of sad tales, I at last have the information you sent me here to discover.

This entire island was sold to a Colonel Gordon in the thirties. He apparently had no real interest in the place, and sent a factor, Kenneth Mackinnon, to see to his interests. Kenneth, a widower, had one child, a son, Aodhàn, who was twelve when his father brought him here.

Aodhàn was sent away to Eton soon after, with the assumption he would go on to Oxford, but his father's worsening consumption forced him back to Barra when he was nineteen, and he took up with a local girl. The old man only remembers her Christian name: Lilith. There was apparently another man who was interested in the same girl. I mention it because he may have been murdered. My informant says one of Kenneth Mackinnon's servants was likely the perpetrator, but no one was ever arrested as evidence could not be found, and the official cause of death was cholera.

Aodhàn Mackinnon married this girl and Aodhàn's father died not long after their first child was born. Aodhàn assumed the factor's duties and was hated every bit as much by the natives as his sire. His wife gave birth to a daughter in 1846, and another in 1849. In 1851, Gordon ordered the clearing of most of Barra's populace, and this was carried out, according to my informant, with heartless brutality. Some time after this, Aodhàn Mackinnon and his wife adopted a European child, an abandoned orphan girl named Romhilde.

In 1853, there was some kind of scandal. The old man did not know the details, and could only tell me the gossip he'd heard, that the youngest Mackinnon child had revealed to someone that her mother and father worshipped the Devil, and that her mother was a witch. The rumors claimed she had the power of never ending life, which she had gained by selling her soul.

It took much more whisky to coax the man into sharing what happened next, and he wept as he told it. Twelve men broke into the Mackinnon house. They murdered Aodhàn's wife and daughters before his eyes. They threw him into the ocean, from where, if I have the story right, Seaghan MacAnaugh dredged him. I say that because I heard it from you. The old Barra man of course did not know that part.

I hope you received my first letter, where I mentioned the latest murders: twelve men killed by some wolf-like creature or ghost. It turns out those murdered men

*were the very ones who broke into the Mackinnon home and killed Mistress
Mackinnon and her daughters. The slayings occurred during the two months
you told me Aodhàn Mackinnon disappeared from Glenelg, in October of last
year, after, as you said, his lost memories were restored to him.*

*It is my belief that your Aodhàn Mackinnon came here and killed those men. It
may not be Christian of me to say so, but I hardly blame him.*

*Here are the bare facts: he was married, but his wife is long dead, as are his
offspring, all but the adopted girl. I understand she survived the attack and was
sent back to her homeland.*

*I would be most happy to sit down with you and discuss what you want to do
next, my friend. I hope to meet with you in Mallaig*

—Quinn

Curran stared at the letter a long while as he imagined the horror of what
Aodhàn had suffered. Then he raced to the kitchen tell Fionna he was leaving
immediately.

"I'm sorry, m'lord, but there will be no landing today." The wizened
fisherman tapped the bowl of his pipe against the boat rail. "It would be
suicide."

"I have to land." Every muscle in Curran's body clenched. "We're here. The
shore's right there in front of us. It's urgent."

"D'you see that?" The fisherman pointed, a bit too patiently, at the way the
heavy swell climbed up then dipped into a fathomless trough, over and over.
"D'you see how the waves are hitting the rocks? They're moving too fast. You
cannot race them and win, no' to mention the dinghy would be swamped as
soon as we put her in the water. Is landing so important you're ready to
drown, or have your head bashed in? Now, I'm willing to wait awhile. Things
could calm down after sunset."

"No." Curran knew the old sailor was right. There was nothing to be done,
no way to get to Morrigan, not with these waves. But everything within him
shouted that he must reach her, no matter the cost. He could hardly breathe
through the compulsion.

Before the captain could discern what this young fool meant to do and grab
him, Curran seized the rail and leaped overboard.

Pleading a headache, Morrigan retired to her bedroom. She wanted to be
free of all the eyes, especially Seaghan's, that watched her so closely. Some-

thing new had appeared in his gaze since their talk. It seemed almost possessive, and made her uncomfortable.

Sinking with a sigh into the armchair beside the window, she looked upon the village below, folk going about their business unaware that someone in the big house was watching them.

She couldn't bear to think of Mackinnon waiting for her. She had Olivia, Curran, Diorbhail, Seaghan, and the aunts. Mackinnon had no one. No one but her, and she remained set on denying him. How long would he wait before he gave up?

Come with me. Do you love me enough? Those words replayed, along with Lily's voice, reciting what a grief-stricken Tristan had shouted in the Wagner opera. *Let the day to death surrender!*

She fetched the black-bladed knife from her cupboard and held it, turning it over and over in her hands. In the dimmer light of her bedroom, a nearly transparent red glow around it brought Jamini's face into focus.

She suspected this knife had lived many lives. It grew and changed as she did. There was savageness in the blade, and definite heat. As she held it, she fancied its destiny was weaving into her own.

Somehow, this weapon gave her confidence, as though a warrior's blood coursed through her veins, as though she could do what was required of her, if that time ever came. She put it into a deep pocket in her apron and buttoned the flap.

Chapter 17

The water was so frigid that for an endless moment, Curran couldn't breathe. Then he was shoved under. Cold sliced like razors. The water rolled his body as though he was a weightless fragment of seaweed. Rocks lunged out of the deep black and struck him everywhere. All he could do was put his hands over his head and pray for a quick death.

He couldn't tell which way was up. The swells kept coming, each bigger than the last, pushing him farther from air and light, mighty godlike fists set to annihilate him.

His knuckles struck sand. He was so desperate, so close to drawing water into his screaming lungs, he tried to seize it. It disintegrated but he grabbed at more, and, little by little, dragged himself out of the bottomless shelf until the swells spewed him onto the beach where he lay, a senseless, sodden lump. A village man came across him at some point. He turned Curran over and expertly pumped the water from his lungs, pulling him back from the chasm of death.

Curran choked and vomited. His lungs burned as though they'd been set afire. He gasped a long while, and had to accept the man's support so he could stagger off the beach and into the village, but gradually, a little strength returned to his legs and he remembered his purpose. Thanking his rescuer in a voice so rough and hoarse he didn't recognize it, he left him and stumbled, like an old, old man, up to the Donaghue house.

MORRIGAN JUMPED TO HER FEET AS THE BEDROOM DOOR FLEW OPEN. SHE GASPED AT who, or what, stood there. Curran…soaking wet, emanating a strong aroma of the sea. His forehead was swelling and dribbling blood from a gash. His arms, hands, and knuckles were scraped and raw. His lips were blue and he shuddered uncontrollably. She yanked the blanket off the bed and ran to him, throwing it over his shoulders, and rubbed him with it, trying to get his blood moving. "Bring tea and coal!" she called down the stairs, and pushed him into the armchair.

The aunts and Seaghan came running, but Morrigan could tell by the way he turned from them that he didn't want them there. She sent them off, saying he needed rest and quiet. They left after she assured them she would tell them everything as soon as she knew it.

The fire was lit and a tea tray brought. She had to hold the cup for him, and much of it was spilled due to his pained coughing before he finally began to lose the tinge of blue and his shudders diminished.

When he'd had two cups of tea, she cleaned his cuts and abrasions then sat on a footstool by the chair, one hand on his knee.

After a long while, light began to glimmer in his eyes. He lifted his hand and cupped her cheek. "Are you well?" he asked, his voice weak and hoarse.

She couldn't help laughing. "Much better than you, I think. What happened?"

"I…I fell overboard." She heard the lie in his voice, but his condition certainly made it believable.

"Curran, you might've drowned."

"Is there more tea?"

"A whole pot."

He held the cup himself now, drinking voraciously to get the taste of the ocean from his throat. "Is Olivia well?"

"Happy as a puffin. Island life agrees with her."

He brushed a hand through her hair. "I missed you," he said.

His tenderness made her remember what she'd done. She dropped her gaze. Would it be like this for the rest of their lives? Seeing him, hearing all that was in his voice and his face, made it so much worse.

She glimpsed the future, saw her guilt grinding and chewing until it devoured everything but itself.

HE DIDN'T WANT TO SLEEP. HE SAID HE WOULD HAVE NIGHTMARES OF DROWNING. He asked Morrigan to keep him company while he bathed.

"I'll tell you about the winter my father brought me to Glenelg. The winter you were born."

"But your throat...."

He shook his head. "I kept thinking of it as I was sinking, how much I wanted to share it with you. Besides, I'm sure Ibby's already told you most of it. I only have my father's bit to add."

The housemaids had gone to their homes in the village, so she made him another pot of tea and carried up buckets of hot water from the copper boiler while he dragged out the cast iron tub.

When he was comfortably installed in a steaming, soapy bath, a cup of tea next to him on a stool, she settled into the armchair to listen.

"My father knew how to make a profit," he said. "He was ingenious at that sort of thing. He came home one day and told us he'd purchased an estate in the Highlands, overlooking the Sound of Sleat. We were going to live there and raise sheep. He promised we would make a fortune.

"Mother was less enthusiastic. She said she'd read about whole populations being forced from their homes. My father assured her that the Highlanders were starving, that because of the potato blight they couldn't grow food enough to survive on. He claimed landowners were paying passage for these people to relocate to America, or moving them to villages on the coast, which offered better livelihoods as herring fishermen. He said the parcel he bought was already empty anyway, ready for a good Lowland shepherd.

"He didn't want to wait until spring, and moved us immediately, promising us a fine new home at the end.

"We arrived on the first of February, 1854, just after a bad snowstorm. I mind him standing in Kilgarry's vestibule, laughing as my mother ran from room to room, yanking sheets off furniture and shouting about how bonny it was. She made us both dance with her."

Curran paused, squinting at the fireplace. "I still feel her there," he said. "In the tables, the chairs, the kitchen, the walls. Everywhere. She's part of why I love Kilgarry."

"I feel my mother in Glenelg," Morrigan said, nodding. "Especially in the forest. I don't know why."

Curran traced his fingertips over her knee and smiled. "The next morning, my father and I explored. Our horses frightened a red grouse. I've never forgotten it because when it flew up, it shrieked. It sounded like it was warning us. *Go go go go!* From that moment, I felt ill at ease."

"Shall I rinse the soap from your hair?" Morrigan asked.

"Aye," Curran said, and tilted his head for her.

When she finished and handed him a towel, he continued. "We followed an old track inland from the sea, which took us past Dùn Teilbh. I asked him what it was. He didn't know, so we rode over."

Curran stopped again, frowning. "A man was lying on the ground beside the stones. At first, I thought he was dead. He was little more than a skeleton, and he didn't move. There was an awful stench in the air. My father jumped off his horse like he'd been bitten by a snake. He bent over the man and said, 'Sir, what are you doing here?'

"The old fellow pointed up the hill and said, 'Help the babies. Help.' We could see the top of Dùn Trodan. I thought he was daft, but my father climbed to the other pile of stones. I followed on horseback.

"That's where the rest were. Children scattered in the snow, the mud. Three women, so still and colorless I was sure they were gone. I admit I wanted to turn my horse and ride away, pretend it never happened. But when my father's boots scraped against the stones, one of the women opened her eyes, and one of the children coughed. All those weans put together wouldn't weigh as much as I did.

"My father told the woman not to be afraid, and took the baby she was holding. He glanced at me, and I knew it was dead. The woman begged him not to take her son. She hadn't enough strength to lift her hand in protest.

"My father told her he'd never do such a thing, and put the baby in her arms. He walked over to a lass, and asked her what her name was. She told him she was Tess.

"The next child was Beth Dunbar, Fionna's other daughter. She was dead, her skin white as porcelain.

"Father rolled a boy over, and nodded to let me know he was alive. That was Logan. Then he stood and stared. I'd never seen him look like that before, like he'd lost everything.

"Fionna was there and Ibby, both barely able to speak or keep their eyes open. While we were checking these people, a man came out of the forest. He accused us of coming to burn them out. He had only rags to protect his feet from the snow, and could barely stand, yet he awed me. He meant to fight us both, no matter that he was starved and weak. Of course you know who it was. Your own father. There were more with him. Beatrice, Nicky, Kyle. Padraig, leading a half-starved goat. And you. Beatrice had you strapped to her chest with strips of cloth.

"My father asked Douglas how many more there were. I remember what Douglas said. 'Not so many as before. Soon we'll be dead, and your land will be empty for your damned sheep.'

"I'd never seen my father so angry. He shouted, 'Not one more will die!' and he asked Douglas if he could take you to Kilgarry right then and there. He promised to bring wagons, to have all the rest moved to our home, where they would be fed and treated by a doctor.

"At first Douglas refused. 'Over my dead body. Don't you touch her,' he said. My father swore before God that he wanted to help, that not one more would die if he could prevent it. But he told Douglas it was up to him.

"They stared at each other, and finally, Douglas allowed it. My father wrapped his coat around you and took you onto his horse. We rode home like madmen and he rounded up drivers and wagons, and all the rest were brought to Kilgarry."

"Your father saved us," Morrigan said.

Curran had finished his bath while he talked. He'd dried himself and dressed, and looked nearly recovered.

"I was jealous," he said. "Once you came along, nobody else seemed to exist for my mother. She'd rock you and sing lullabies for hours. I held you myself a time or two."

Diorbhail knocked and came in with Olivia, saying she'd been crying for her mother. She went out again, sending Curran an anxious glance. Olivia cooed and played for a few minutes, but soon fell asleep on Morrigan's shoulder.

Curran leaned forward. "You were the first female in my life besides her. Maybe that's why I never married. I was waiting to find you again. That's what I think, because of how I felt the moment I saw you from that train. Like I was complete at last."

Morrigan kept her face expressionless, but inside, Lily's last words reverberated.

I don't understand you. Do you love your husband? Why won't you talk to me? She'd stormed from the room with the parting remark, *Curran deserves better.*

Aye, he did. She would never argue that fact. But she tightened her grip on Olivia and recited her litany.

I am made of wind. I am as cold as winter stars. I am formless as the Aurora.

"Here, let me put her in the cradle," he said, sighing. He carried it from the wall over to Morrigan's chair and tucked Olivia in, covering her with a light blanket. Then he dropped, loose-limbed, into his chair and resumed the tale, idly rubbing the scar beside his eye.

"My father brought a surgeon from Fort William in time to save you and most of your kin. But that first old man we saw died. I cannot remember his name now. Wynda Urquhart died. Beatrice told my da she wouldn't let anyone take Hearn, and never stopped speaking to him as though he lived. We had them buried together. Your grandmother died, John Dunbar, and Kyle's mam. His father had died years before, so the clearings made him an orphan. And, of course, your mother."

Morrigan thought she glimpsed the faintest reflective sheen pass through his eyes, but he continued without pause. "My mother asked Douglas how they kept you from starving, and he told her about the goat."

Morrigan rocked the cradle with one hand. "I've always wondered about these things." She felt light-headed, like she had at the beginning of her first pregnancy. Something about the way their lives had woven into each other's from the start seemed dreamlike…unreal yet almost planned. She most certainly would have died if not for Curran's father.

"Ibby told me how Douglas never let anyone speak of those days," he said.

"I'm glad I finally know it all. I'm not a child any longer, who must be sheltered and protected."

The second pot of tea had grown cold. Olivia sighed in her sleep. "That's why you were afraid of the forest," Morrigan said.

He glanced away and ran a hand through his hair.

"No wonder," she said. "That's why your father sent you with Fearghas. To get over finding us."

"But finding you was worth any amount of fear or nightmares. You lived. What if we hadn't gone riding that day?"

She stared at the cradle.

"Will you talk to me, Morrigan?" he said.

She gritted her teeth, refusing to look at him.

"I can't get anything out of you anymore," he went on. "You're not here. You're a ghost. Where have you gone?"

"Nowhere." She fanned her anger by reliving the picture of Lily kissing him. She added, "I'm right where you want me." Damn it, she *was* angry. Fury flowed like white-hot lava.

His head jerked as though she'd slapped him. The scar by his eye whitened. "Is it the pregnancy that makes you this way?" His gaze bored into her. "Are you sorry to be carrying another child of mine?"

She turned away and stared at the fireplace.

"Bloody hell." He rose and bent over her, imprisoning her between his arms. "Look at me."

Douglas had done that once, furious over some transgression—made bars out of his arms. He bent over her and proceeded to threaten in his hateful, quiet voice. Though she'd forgotten his words, the fear and powerlessness returned, undiminished by time.

Curran couldn't understand. Had he grown up seeing himself as hated, a child who enraged his parent merely by breathing? No. Thomas Ramsay had loved and honored his son. His mother had adored him. Curran could never comprehend her devils. *Every man, woman, and child craves to be understood,* Mackinnon had said. Mackinnon did, because of his suffering. It wasn't Curran's fault, but he didn't; he couldn't.

"You think you can browbeat me?" she said. "I learned from the best."

"By God, you'll speak to me if I have to keep you here all night…." the hoarseness resurfaced, making his voice rough.

Balling her hands into fists, she struck, throwing herself into the old rage, welcoming it, for it camouflaged the voice deep inside that wanted to *hold him, tell him how sorry I am, how much I wish—*

He took blows to the jaw, temple, and nose before managing to pin her wrists. She kicked him in the shin.

"Morrigan!" He dragged her from the chair, forced her arms behind her and secured them with one hand. The other held her against him, deliberately off-balance to prevent her from kicking again. How could he still be so much stronger than she after what he'd gone through? It wasn't fair.

"Talk to me," he said.

At least he was breathing hard. Morrigan hadn't felt so infuriatingly helpless since before Douglas died. "Let...me...go...."

She would've screamed, but Olivia was asleep. It was almost amusing, the way they carried out this battle in quiet undertones. More like proper *Sasannaich* than a pair of tempestuous Scots.

"Why are you acting like this?" His eyes, so close to hers, narrowed. "Ever since that night when you fainted at Richard's. We were happy before then. What changed?"

Don't let him make you feel. Feeling makes you weak.

But it was so hard when he was this close. Her defenses were unraveling. If only she could slip through his fingers and climb into the heavens—wind in truth.

"Christ," he said. "Love me, hate me, but don't ignore me. Damn you, don't ignore me." He bent and kissed her in a way he'd never done before, a kiss that held nothing of gentleness, tenderness, or affection, but it had plenty of demand. She felt every last fragment of his repressed frustration in that kiss. He held nothing back.

Time vanished. When had she stopped fighting? When had he released her? Her arms were around his neck, but she couldn't remember putting them there.

Fear sparked.

If she allowed him to carry her to the bed as his eyes said he meant to, it would be like stabbing him and filching the rings off his fingers as he bled to death. He didn't know what she'd done while he was gone. He didn't know Mackinnon was now on Mingulay, waiting for her to come to him.

She stiffened and managed to escape his grip, quickly constructing an expression of cold blankness.

Curran's arms dropped to his sides. The dark triumphant seduction in his eyes slowly faded. He sighed.

"D'you think I didn't see what happened that night?" she said. "You were kissing Lily. You thought I was unconscious, but I wasn't. I saw everything. If I hadn't been there, if you'd had more time before the doctor came, you would've stripped her naked and had her, right there on the floor. I saw how much you wanted to."

She watched him startle. He blinked. Realization dawned on his face.

"She told me what she was before she married Richard. A whore. If you need a woman, she'll oblige. She made that clear enough. Maybe I'll make friends with Richard."

"You might, if Aodhàn Mackinnon will let you. What about that man in Stranraer who painted you? You blush every time his name comes up. Shall I list the others who've tried to bed you since we married? Tell me. Which ones succeeded?"

What was going on with the creature inside her, the wild, selfish girl? *I only want to be with you*, she whispered. *Only you. You may not be the Greek Theseus, but you are my hero.*

Shoving the traitorous liar down where she couldn't be heard, Morrigan said, "They all did. Every one. Lily has nothing on me."

"Damn you. Morrigan. Damn you. You're a witch."

Horror and helpless resignation flooded her.

Olivia woke, flailed, and whimpered.

He came forward and caught her hands, but she pushed him away. Words tumbled out of her mouth, words she didn't plan to say, or know had been inside her. "You think you can do whatever you want. Have whatever you want. Everything is so easy for you, so bonny and blithe. But it isn't for me. I'm...tired. So tired. One thing I know. No one will force me again. No one. Not you. Not my father. No one, not ever again."

His expression changed. Anger transformed into shock then comprehension. "Morrigan," he said, aghast.

As she realized what she'd said, her hands rose and covered her mouth. But it was too late. The words could not be rolled back into her throat. This would be the final death-knell. Disgust would trounce any lingering sentiment. She bent over the cradle and lifted Olivia, pressing her face to the baby's cheek, closing her eyes, blocking out Curran and breathing in the fine, clean scent of her child. *I love you Olivia*, she thought. *You have made me better.*

"I'm going for a walk," she said.

"We're not finished."

She expected to see loathing when she opened her eyes, but the only thing she discerned beyond doubt in his expression was weariness. "You're exhausted, and we've both said too much. I need to be alone for a while. I'll be back before dark. Mingulay is perfectly safe."

His jaw clenched several times, but in the end, he sighed and let her go.

Chapter 18

Harpalycus of Tiryns couldn't ignore Beatrice Stewart's foibles and ailments. The woman suffered from intermittent waves of flushing heat that left her drenched in sweat and unable to sleep. She often left her bed and wandered through the night, weather permitting, and now, Harpalycus found he was obliged to do the same.

In an effort to overcome the irritating habit, he'd been wearing out the body by walking to exhaustion in the evenings. After the Laird of Eilginn appeared, sopping wet from his ill-advised swim in the bay, Harpalycus set out. He circled the village, trudged through the sand at the water's edge, and hiked to an overlook on the east coast. There he rested, drinking brandy from a flask as he read through Morrigan's diary, which he'd noticed on her dressing table while she was tending to her husband. He'd filched it when no one was looking.

Hot, hungry, and well on his way to drunk, he eventually returned to Taigh na Gaoithe. Climbing up the hill from the village, cursing the old woman's weak lungs and heavy skirts, he was nearly there when he spotted Morrigan coming out of the cottage, holding her baby. She walked the opposite direction, climbing the hill towards the western cliffs. He stopped. Shouldn't she still be with her half-drowned husband? She lifted the baby above her head, making her shriek with laughter, but never looked back. Curran emerged a moment later, his hair wet and his collar open, but he remained on the steps, merely watching until she was out of sight. Then Diorbhail joined him.

"Where is Morrigan going?" The whore asked in her timid voice.

"For a walk." Curran sounded tired, resigned. In truth, quite unhappy.

Harpalycus, in the body of Beatrice Stewart, grinned. The master's tone said it all. They were at odds again. Those two could find something to fight about every day of the week. It wasn't all that surprising that Beatrice's niece suffered from a deep mistrust, and in some cases, hatred, of men. It was obvious to the outside eye. But the twit had always denied this truth, and continued trying to mold herself into a proper lady. Like she could ever be anything close.

A strange flash blinked around Diorbhail's head, there then gone, probably sunlight catching on a pin in her hair. But Harpalycus's instincts sharpened. He stared at Diorbhail Sinclair, wondering for the first time if she could be one of the followers. Just in case, he would be on his guard around her. He didn't know if they had the same protections as the others, and he didn't want to find out.

Ibby stuck her head out the door. "Curran, why are you out here? Seaghan's built a fire in the parlor, and you still look a bit chilled to me."

With a last glance towards the hilltop, Curran allowed himself to be pulled inside. The door closed.

Groaning a little at the painful rheumatism in Beatrice's joints, Harpalycus approached the steps. He paused before entering, and looked again at the scrap of paper he'd found tucked in the pages of the diary.

Nam chridhe gu bràth. *Once more. Tonight. Dùn Mhiughalaigh.*

He reread the last entry. She always made things so easy.

Harpalycus, with the benefit of Beatrice's memories, would wager his last coin on the willful besom's destination. Pools, lochs, seas, and oceans. Water drew her like she was part fish. Aye, she loved to stand on cliffs, didn't she? Right on the edge.

The note was from Aodhàn Mackinnon, obviously—*Chrysaleon*. So he had followed her here. That must be where the chit sneaked off to three nights ago. Harpalycus had been standing at the window, unable to sleep for the sweating. She'd witnessed Morrigan running off into the night. Now it made sense. She had cuckolded her husband.

No doubt Aodhàn Mackinnon had conjured up a plan to have the bitch and humiliate Curran Ramsay at the same time.

It would give Harpalycus much pleasure to thwart his old enemy's schemes.

"Let's see if we can start some excitement," he said. "You want Morrigan to meet you? And what if Curran comes after her? What will happen then?"

Harpalycus had perfected the art of making weak-willed men jump to his whim like they were marionettes and he the puppeteer. The lies he'd told were awe-inspiring, and now he'd invent one of the best. Using Beatrice's memories and her old, bitter resentment, he'd stoke Curran Ramsay's frustration into a fevered rage, and once he had him boiling, he would send the fool off to shoot

Aodhàn Mackinnon dead, right before his lover's eyes. Considering the master of Kilgarry's present mood and ill-controlled passion for his wife, it would be easy. Curran had no idea how many thousands of years of buried obsession were egging him on.

It seemed poetic. Chrysaleon had slaughtered Menoetius on Crete, and then there was that betrayal at Cape Wrath. No doubt he'd played a part in Daniel's death on Barra. Menoetius was long overdue a day of recompense.

If Harpalycus managed his lies well, he would soon be free. He could hardly wait to be rid of this disgusting body, with its drooping paps and belly.

"Someday you'll learn, Chrysaleon of Mycenae," he said. "When you least expect it, there I'll be, staring at you from your nightmares."

Beatrice opened the door and entered.

Curran came swiftly out of the parlor, his face hopeful. "Oh, it's you," he said. "Where have you been? Have you seen Morrigan?"

"I have." Beatrice smiled. "But she didn't see me."

Curran sighed and raked back his hair. The man was at the end of his wits over that wench. But he had much more to endure this night…maybe near as much as what he'd suffered the night he gave himself to the barley, on Crete, all for love of that country's queen.

Seaghan stepped into the hall, glaring. Behind him, stupid Ibby was blubbering, and Diorbhail was trying to soothe her.

"It's my fault," Ibby cried. "I should've refused. Beatrice, I told Morrigan of the clearings at Glenelg."

"Why?"

"She wanted to know." Ibby wrung her hands. "I thought she had the right. Now Curran has told her his da's part in it. It was too shocking. It's upset her."

Beatrice snorted. "She doesna care about that old history. She's just gone off to be with her paramour."

Curran stared at her, eyes widening, while Beatrice removed her shawl and shook the sand from it.

"Worthless hussy!" Seaghan growled. "What are you on about?"

"How am I a hussy?" Her laugh faded to a glower. "You'd be more honest to call your dear Hannah that."

Seaghan stepped towards her, fists clenching, but Curran placed a restraining hand on his forearm. "Wait," he said, frowning.

"Aye." Beatrice nodded. "You'll not want to miss what I've got to tell. But first, I'd like a cup of tea." Dropping the shawl on a table, she moved past them into the parlor.

Diorbhail helped Ibby to a chair and remained at her side, staring at Beatrice, saying nothing, but taking it all in.

"She's naught but lies and tricks," Seaghan said. "Throw the witch out. You don't know her like I do, Curran."

"There's fear in you, Seaghan," Beatrice said, "and every one of us can hear it."

"Leave her be, Seaghan," Curran said. "She obviously has something to say."

Ibby looked confused. Seaghan leaned against the doorjamb, scowling.

"You've always got tea, hot and ready to drink." Beatrice took a cup and settled in the rocking chair. "It's one of the best things about living in the Laird of Eilginn's home."

Would Aodhàn be prepared for a husband so blinded by rage that nothing short of cold-blooded murder would satisfy him? The prince of Mycenae had always been shortsighted, caring only for the moment, a night's pleasure, having whatever female he'd taken a fancy to. He probably wished to humiliate Curran by flaunting Morrigan's infidelity. But, using a bit of well-turned imagination, Beatrice would see to it that Aodhàn had trouble enough of his own to deal with.

"My Douglas enjoyed his tea," she said. "I made it dark and strong. He hated a watery brew. Hannah now, she preferred the *uisge-beatha*. That lass could drink like a stevedore. Sit, Master Ramsay."

"I warn you," Curran said. "I've had a trying day, and I've no patience at the moment for idle blethering."

"Stop me whenever you wish. This tale's waited over twenty years to be shared, and there's none left alive who know it but me. I think you'll find it interesting. I know Seaghan will."

"Should it wait for Morrigan? She promised she'd be back by sundown."

"Well, let's begin. If she returns, she can hear the end of it."

Curran stared at her. She waited. His eyes narrowed and his hands clenched, but after a long pause, he sighed and sat in one of the other chairs.

"You never knew Hannah," she began, "or how men went mad over her. Her daughter's given you a taste though, hasn't she?"

The stubborn lout said nothing but, "Are you drunk?"

She snorted. "Hannah inherited all the beauty. Makes a body wonder if we didn't have different fathers. If I'd received even a small portion, well...." She shrugged. "Who knows?"

"You're a cow, and you always will be," Seaghan said.

Beatrice flushed. "Hannah used folk for her own ends. She didn't care what it did to them. We'll see if you still think she's so lovely when I'm finished."

"You bloody bitch. You couldn't change what I think about anything."

"Seaghan." Curran waved sharply. "Let her get on with it."

Beatrice sipped tea and examined her audience—Ibby's baffled innocence, murderous Seaghan, a strangely alert Diorbhail, and lastly the exhausted, scunnered Curran Ramsay.

"Hannah stole everything from me. I can't mind when I began to hate her."

"I thought you were inseparable," Ibby cried. "You always took such care of her."

"Aye, well, Mam didn't like her much either," Beatrice replied scornfully, "so she made Hannah my fee, in a manner of speaking. Of course, I didn't get paid to change her hippins and feed her. Da seemed to think I was born to be her maidservant. Like that's all I was good for."

She inspected her fingernails then lifted her gaze to Curran's. "Your wife is planning a change in her circumstances tonight, Master Ramsay," she said. "If you want to know what it is, you'll hear me out."

Chapter 19

MORRIGAN AMBLED ALONG THE PRECIPICES, KEEPING A SAFE DISTANCE FROM THE edge. The breeze, the ocean, the scent of wildflowers and call of seabirds—all helped cool her panic. Olivia, ever a trusting baby, was content in her mother's arms.

Soon she stood at Dùn Mhiughalaigh, the hulking promontory that thrust into the sea like a giant's great nose, which must be why they called the far end of it Sròn an Dùin, Nose of the Dun. She crossed over the wide, sinking dip where it linked to the main part of the island.

"Let's sit here awhile, eh dablet?" she said. "Then we'll go home to your papa." She settled on the northern edge of the dip, crossing her legs, her full skirts forming a hammock for the babe to lie in.

The ocean sang. Below her feet it was angrier, thundering as it funneled into the narrow space between her resting spot and Gunamuil, the lower outcropping next to it. A storm skulked on the northern horizon, bringing coolness that teased her ankles and calves. Two quick flashes of blue-white lightning streaked through the clouds.

Olivia shoved strands of her mother's hair in her mouth. She cooed, kicked, and played with her blanket. Morrigan held her child close, soothed by her sweet smell, the smoothness of her flesh, the grip of her miniature fingers.

But Olivia didn't want to be hugged. She protested until Morrigan propped her in the pool of fabric where she could stare at the birds and the ocean, and play with her mother's delicious long hair.

Morrigan had imagined herself a wind creature, and perhaps she'd succeeded too well. For were not hurricanes, mistrals, monsoons, and cyclones all examples of wind, leaving destruction in their wake?

Why had she said such terrible things to Curran? What Douglas had done was her deepest, darkest secret; one she'd believed would go with her into death. Why had she revealed it? She couldn't be certain. The workings of the heart and brain seemed beyond her understanding.

She glanced at far-off lightning, fast-moving clouds, and the sun, making its way down to the sea. She'd promised Curran she would be back before dark, but she didn't want to leave this landscape. The cottage offered only arguing, unhappiness, and pain.

Even so, there was a niggling, uneasy conviction that part of her had remained behind with him, and that more was breaking off even now, rolling back over the hill towards him.

"Mama," she said. "What have I done? What should I do?"

She dropped her gaze to the sea.

Diorbhail had once claimed that women could cause their own pregnancies, using the north wind or water.

Water is the beginning and the end of all things, and woman is water's guardian.

Washed in sea breezes, Morrigan experienced an instant of connection to the water. She sensed how it would feel to break down, bones dissolving, rising and falling according to the whim of the moon. The cadence stole into her, glimmering like fired oil.

The wind's breath carried a rumble of thunder, but a swift examination convinced her the cloudbank was retreating, blowing off to the northwest.

She stayed in the furrow between Dùn Mhiughalaigh and the main island, observing the myriad faces of the water as it stretched into an unknowable beyond. Waves edged with foam, curling, sliding, lost in vastness, murmuring then pounding like bass drums.

"See, *a leannan?*" Supporting Olivia under her arms, she helped the wean stand upright. Olivia's legs stiffened in the instinctive primal rush to grow and be independent. Lightning flashed, followed by thunder, and the baby laughed as though it was a puppet show put on for her enjoyment.

"*Yonder Clouden's silent towers,*" Morrigan sang. Olivia turned her head up to her mother's face, wide-eyed.

Where at moonshine's midnight hours,
O'er the dewy bending flowers,
Fairies dance sae chearie.

It was enticing to imagine stepping off this cliff and onto that sparkling pathway created on the surface of the water by the setting sun. They would be forgotten, nothing to mark their passing, lost yet joined with immense magnificence. Finally they would descend to the underwater castle and live for eternity among pearls and lost gold from sunken galleons.

She helped Olivia take a few stumbling steps.

If things were different, the idea of death might overwhelm me, she'd written that morning in her diary. *I might turn it into magic and poetry, and succumb to it as Iseult did. But I choose life. Life for my babies. My weans will grow up with their mother, knowing they are loved.*

And when death comes, somewhere, somehow, Mackinnon and I will find each other, we two who understand the darkness in the other's soul.

She picked Olivia up, kissed her temple, and to quiet the beginnings of a sulk, sang again.

Fair and lovely as thou art,
Thou hast stown my very heart;
I can die—but canna part,
My bonny bonny dearie.

Only then, as the last words whisked away on a playful breeze, did she realize where she was, and what it meant. Mackinnon had asked her to meet him here. She had forgotten in the anxiety of Curran's injuries, then their argument. Or had she? Had she come here in unconscious acquiescence to her lover's demand?

She rose and turned…and there he was, standing a few steps away.

"Mackinnon," she breathed. The selkie. Dionysos. Theseus. Fisherman. Tristram.

Husband.

He had many names and faces, all merging into one word. *Beloved.* Though she'd been determined to keep her distance, she was happy to see him. It gave her the chance to explain why this had to be the end.

"Morrigan." He squatted and smiled.

They clasped hands. His felt cool and strong and reassuring. "I wasn't sure you'd come."

"I didn't mean to," she felt compelled to say.

He paused. "Yet you did."

"Curran's back from the mainland," she said. "We argued and I ran away."

He said nothing to that.

"I promised him I'd return by sundown," she said. "I should go. I must go. But I am glad to see you…." She hesitated. It was hard to say *for the last time.* The words stung her throat.

He stood, reaching down to help her up. "There's a place I want to show you before you go. We'll have to do some juggling though, with the child."

"I don't know…. Olivia should not be here, with us."

"Stay a wee while," he said. "I've something to ask you. We'll make do." He nodded towards the west. "There's still time." He led her along the crags a bit, north of Dùn Mhiughalaigh. "We can climb down," he said. "It'll be an adventure."

She resisted. "It's straight down. We can't."

"There's a ladder." He knelt and pulled up a portion of it to show her. "See?"

She knelt too. It was woven of something rope-like, maybe horsehair. "Is it strong enough?" she asked doubtfully.

"I've been up and down it many times. I'll go first." Grasping the rope, he maneuvered over the edge.

"Do we have to do this?"

"It's not far." He climbed down a few more rungs. "Here, see? Solid ground. Hand her down to me." He lifted his arms.

Morrigan lay on her stomach and held Olivia out, wrapped in her blanket. Mackinnon took her. She made a curious inquiring sound, and turned her head in search of her mother.

"Be careful," Morrigan said.

"You too." He stepped away from the ladder, turned, and went off through the scrub, out towards the overhang.

He's a trickster, that one, Diorbhail's voice whispered as Morrigan watched him walk away with her child. She heard a disturbance all around, as though the breezes were adding to the warning by bringing the wildflowers and bracken to life.

"Mackinnon?" She tamped down irrational fright as she heard Diorbhail again. *I fear him. He is not what he seems.*

She took a deep breath, trying to keep calm. "Wait for me, Mackinnon." Not giving herself time to panic, she found the ladder's rungs and propelled herself over the edge, cursing the hem of her skirt when it caught beneath her toes and pulled her off balance.

He wouldn't harm Olivia, not Olivia, not her baby. Diorbhail didn't like any men other than Curran. It had simply been a meaningless sigh of wind she'd heard.

We should die. It's the only way. Mackinnon's words formed a litany as she stumbled down the ladder.

What if he decided Olivia could die as well?

She jumped off the ladder onto solid ground and turned, searching for the man and child, but they'd vanished. She took a few steps, stumbling over exposed roots. Unfounded terror was making her clumsy. She mustn't think about how far they could all fall, or how many rocks lay below, or how cold and deep the Atlantic was.

I'm coming. I'm coming, my braw girl. An interior avalanche of clarity exploded through her. She didn't want to die, not tonight or any night, with Mackinnon. She would never abandon her children, born, newly conceived, and yet to be imagined, not them and not Curran. As she scrambled for footing, a tiger's ferocity flooded her. She would not be thwarted.

Her hem caught on something and ripped as she refused to pause.

Olivia wailed in the distance, a thin, desperate sound. Morrigan had no idea how she maneuvered the last expanse between them. She dimly realized the ground slanted upward steeply. She climbed, using her hands and feet, gasping, tasting mud. Her body felt numb, separated, smashed beneath intent. There they were. Mackinnon was holding Olivia on the flat surface of a rock scoured by wind of all flora, bleached like bone from the sun. He stood at the edge, nothing beyond his boots but cool swirling air, a mouthful of Earth's sharp teeth, and endless depths of water.

"A CHANGE IN HER CIRCUMSTANCES? WHAT DOES THAT MEAN?" CURRAN ASKED impatiently. "If you know something, then tell me!"

"I'm getting ahead of myself." Beatrice smiled. "I meant to begin with Hannah."

"What the hell does she have to do with anything?" Had the witch gone mad? She appeared to be on the verge of dissolving into laughter, and her eyes didn't seem properly focused.

"She's Morrigan's mother. I'd think you'd be interested to know who raped her that night in June when she ran off and abandoned poor Seaghan."

A dark flush bloomed across Seaghan's face.

"Hannah was raped?" Curran gripped the arms of the chair, hoping she would say whatever she had to say, and that his patience would last that long.

"That's why she left Glenelg the way she did. But I'm the only one who knows who did it. It was Douglas. Douglas Lawton."

"Oh no, no," Ibby moaned. Diorbhail put a reassuring hand on her shoulder.

The color ran out of Seaghan's face but he seemed more devastated than surprised. Curran frowned. He wanted to comfort Seaghan and Ibby, but he forced himself to remain quiet. Morrigan was all that mattered now.

"Our da brought us to Glenelg that year, just for the summer. He wanted to become familiar with the place Hannah would be living once she married Seaghan. He wanted her to see it too, so she could decide if she was really willing to give up the city. We stayed at Kilgarry with Randall Benedict and his wife. That's how we met Douglas. He was Benedict's gamekeeper. Like all men, Douglas wanted her, but she refused him. So he followed her. He knew Randall Benedict's land far better than she. One night, finding her alone in the forest," she quirked a brow at Seaghan, causing him to flush again, "he attacked her. He covered her head so she could never identify him. When he was done he left her there and hid himself until she managed to get to her feet. Then he approached her, full of sympathy and care and tenderness, and made her believe he'd come across her by accident. He carried her to Kilgarry. She was out of her senses, saying all kinds of daft things. She asked Douglas to take her away and he agreed, of course. She never knew her attacker was the same man she ran off with."

Curran's grip tightened in his struggle to keep himself from leaping to his feet and throttling the bitch. "If you knew this, why have you never told anyone?"

She shrugged. "Why should I? Would it have helped Morrigan to know? Hannah was grateful to Douglas at first. He was willing to marry her, a ruined woman. When he discovered, much later, she was already pregnant before he attacked her, and that her child was Seaghan's, not his, he was, shall we say, not happy."

Seaghan's eyes slitted. Curran heard his teeth grind.

She's making this up. Maybe—who cares! What does it matter?

"Come now." Beatrice nodded. "You've no secrets from your good friend the Laird of Eilginn, do you?"

"Why have you kept this from me all these years, you bitch!" Seaghan rushed forward, fists raised. "You stole my daughter from me with your lies."

She showed no sign of fear, Curran had to give her that. "I stole nothing from you. You're the one who sailed away to Nova Scotia. You threw it away. Without Morrigan, Douglas wouldn't have needed me. He couldn't take care of an infant and a three-year-old boy. She's what kept us together, and by that time, as you know, my da had killed himself, and his wealth was lost in the search for his missing daughter."

"You pathetic slut," Seaghan said. "Douglas used you. And you let him."

Though she gave a flippant shrug, Beatrice's face bloomed with angry color. "In every way but name I lived as his wife. I do wish he'd kissed me though. I used to pray to God to make him kiss me, but God's never answered my prayers."

"Beatrice...." Ibby sighed, shaking her head.

Seaghan was scarlet, his mouth a white sneer.

"What of Morrigan?" Curran asked.

"Aye, Morrigan. I didn't expect you to keep her after she cuckolded you in your own township, and you the laird. You've served your pride to her on a plate for the whole world to see."

"You hate her," Curran said. "Why?"

"She doesn't deserve all that's been given to her. If I hadn't been there, no doubt Douglas would've loved her too. Her aunt clothed her in fine dresses though she was no more than a maidservant." Beatrice grimaced at Ibby. "Nick watched out for her, took her skelpings. Kit Lindsay adored her. Then you came along with your wealth and fine house, giving her flowers, treating her like a queen. You had to have her though your rich comrades would judge you for it. I lay that at your door as well." She sent Ibby another scowl. "You brought him and ruined my plans."

"What were your plans?" Ibby cried. "She didn't suffer enough to suit you?"

"Morrigan had everything and worked for none of it. Hannah's beauty lived on in her, and her brain was quick. She was like a cherry tart to every male who saw her. The biggest difference between Hannah and her daughter was that Morrigan never turned cold. By the end, Hannah had no feeling left for anyone or anything, but Morrigan grew up innocent and feeling-hearted. The beatings never hardened her. She never learned what folk truly are."

"Thank God." Ibby struck the arm of her chair with a closed fist. "Thank God she's stayed the way she is. It shows her strength, not her weakness, as you'd have us believe."

"D'you not want to know what I've got to tell?" Beatrice rose. "I'll not waste your time, if you are so much wiser than me."

Curran saw her sway. Aye, Beatrice was drunk. He smelled the brandy. But no matter. He couldn't let her leave now. He had to know what she was withholding. "Don't go," he said.

"Aye," she replied. "The master wants to know about his dearie. Well, I'll tell you, though I doubt you'll be thanking me once I'm done." Heavily, she resumed her seat.

"Get on with it, I beg you," Curran said. The sun was lowering; Morrigan hadn't yet returned. His anxiety was building, but he held himself still, his instincts warning him he needed to know what Beatrice had finally decided to tell. Who knew when or if she would ever be so loose-tongued again?

"It was easy to make Douglas hate Morrigan," Beatrice said. "She reminded him of Hannah, of Hannah's duplicity, of her many lies. Hannah tried to foist Seaghan's bastard on him. Well, Douglas was a proud man. He never forgave that. There's always another side of the coin, though. He saw Hannah in Morrigan and lusted after her."

"Bloody fucking hell." Curran clenched his hands. It felt as though the icy, heavy swells in the bay were washing over him again, paralyzing him. He knew this was the truth, and he wasn't sure he could bear to hear it.

Seaghan leaped forward once more. "Curran, you've got to stop this!"

Curran rose wearily. He grasped Seaghan by the arms, hauling on him with all his strength. "Seaghan, let her speak," he said. "Please. For Morrigan's sake."

At first it didn't seem Seaghan heard. He strained and fought to break free.

But Curran refused to release him, and gradually Seaghan acquiesced. He retreated again to the wall, where he crossed his arms and stared coldly.

"I don't believe this," Ibby said. But she sounded as though she did.

"Be strong," Diorbhail returned quietly.

"Nobody knew the truth but me." Beatrice wiped her nose with her knuckles. They came away wet, but she didn't seem to notice.

"My God." Ibby's face was white and her plump fingers trembled. Her shoulders slumped and she wept. "Oh my God. I would've…I would've—"

"Being cleared, losing his home and Hannah nearly drove Douglas into madness, which worked in my favor. I thought, what if he decides to marry again? I couldn't have that, and I knew he would never marry me. So I used the bad part of him, that buried sickness what can be dredged out of most men. I made it grow. It's easy if you know how. You don't need herbs or potions. You use what's in their black hearts already, shape it how you want. I started when Morrigan was a baby, marveling how much she resembled her sweet mam. Maybe Hannah had come back to life in her. 'Leave me alone,' he'd say. But I caught him staring at her, and I knew. I knew what he was thinking. One night…she was about fourteen, as I mind…I woke and he wasn't in bed. I found him in her room, fair panting in his madness. I made him leave and I watched Morrigan close for I knew if once he had her, I'd lose my power over him. But I nurtured the sickness. While this guilt lived in him along with wanting her, a girl barely out of childhood and his daughter in the eyes of the world, he'd need me, wouldn't he? He'd think himself too low for other lasses. Men are thrawn creatures."

"Not all men," Seaghan growled.

"Aye? Really? If what you say is true, the good ones would put a stop to those who are bad, but they never do. The punishment's worse for a man what lies with other men than it is for those who harm women and children." She paused. "Are you a good man, Master Ramsay?"

What he'd said to Lily returned with taunting clarity. *I'll use my own child like a cage.*

Beatrice lifted her brows. "I know more about men than you might imagine. What bad men do, good men want to do, and sometimes will."

"This is making me sick," Seaghan said. "You cannot listen to her, Curran."

Curran fought off the sense that he was falling. Seaghan's voice echoed as though it came from a great distance.

Beatrice's regard betrayed nothing but calm calculation. She smiled as though she relished his misery. "I knew Douglas wanted Morrigan. Every year that passed Morrigan became more like Hannah, in body if not spirit. Douglas knew he wouldn't be breaking any Biblical laws if he had her. Still, some part of him understood how wrong it was. She ripened, and it was no' so obvious that she wasn't yet a grown woman. Knowing she wasn't his blood kin kept him on the knife-edge, lust constantly battling his scruples. I believe he thought it a way to have Hannah again, but young, untouched, an innocent he could mold to his pleasure. He wanted the Hannah in her. Sometimes he called her name in his sleep. He hated though, the part of her that reminded him of Seaghan. I fancied when he beat her, he saw Seaghan under the strap. Who knows? Maybe he punished Hannah too, for what she'd done. As for himself?" She laughed, shaking her head. "He took no responsibility for the things he did, no blame for the way he treated her."

Curran shuddered. He covered his face with both hands and drew in a shaking breath. His hair spilled over his fingers, brushing like insect wings. "You did it, didn't you?" he said, dropping his hands to his lap. "Somehow, *you* started this thing with Aodhàn Mackinnon."

"Oh, no," she said. "No, you cannot blame that on me. First of all, it's Morrigan's nature to be a whore. It's in her blood. But it's more. Those two have an uncanny way of knowing about each other. It's like a force of nature, impossible to resist. Only death will separate them. Only death Master Ramsay, and I suspect he's convinced her he has a way to thwart that as well."

"I would've helped her if I'd known." Ibby's voice broke. She seized Diorbhail's hand.

"Pretend all you want," Beatrice said, "but you knew."

Seaghan's boot tapped against the floor. It took up the beat of Curran's heart and reverberated through his skull.

Beatrice was lying about some or all of this. Morrigan had no strange urge to be unfaithful. She was a virgin before that day on the moor by Stranraer. Somehow, Aodhàn had overwhelmed her loyalty. If it weren't for Aodhàn, she'd be happy, content to be Curran's wife, mother to his children.

If Beatrice was lying about Morrigan, she could be lying about Hannah as well. But what good could come of spreading such falsehoods? It wasn't as though they would harm Hannah. Everyone involved except Seaghan and Morrigan was dead.

His spinning thoughts halted at the sound of Beatrice's voice. She was staring at him, her eyes watchful. "And now here we are again," she said, almost gently. "Morrigan is pregnant, just like Hannah, and no way of telling who the father is. Not until the babe is born, and we see the color of its hair."

"Do you know where Morrigan has gone? If so, tell me. What is this 'change in circumstances'?" Curran pinched the arms of his chair in an effort to maintain control.

"Don't you understand?" Beatrice waved at him. "She's away to Aodhàn Mackinnon. He's waiting for her. She'd rather die his penniless whore than live in your fine manor house as your wife."

"Aodhàn is here, on Mingulay?" Curran's heart began to pound sickeningly, and his blood grew fiery hot in his veins. No, this couldn't be. She had to be lying.

"He's been having his fill of your wife while you've been gone, and before you took her away as well. Since your wedding, in fact." She laughed. "He won't give her back. It's a pledge they made. Do you recognize this?" Holding up the diary, she thumbed the pages and read aloud.

I can see why Mackinnon longs for death. Perhaps that is the lesson in all great, tragic love stories. Tristram and Iseult knew this secret, and agreed to its demands. If there is reincarnation, as Jamini claims, then death is not a terrible thing. It offers peace from suffering, new beginnings and possibilities.

She looked at Curran. "Have you worked it out yet, Master Ramsay? Your daft, daft wife intends to kill herself—and your precious Olivia. He's convinced her that's the only way they'll be together. And it's clear Morrigan won't be separated from the wean. Why else would she take her?"

Beatrice threw the diary on the floor between them. It fell on its spine, open, the pages covered with Morrigan's handwriting. "You'll find naught when you go searching but bodies, maybe no' even that, for if I know Morrigan, she'll jump into the sea. That's where she was headed. You saw it yourself. And she'll take your child with her, Master Ramsay. An offering to the old gods."

Ibby gasped. She covered her mouth, moaned, and burst into sobbing.

Curran didn't realize he'd leaped to his feet until he was standing over Beatrice, staring down into her face, which was at first startled, then oddly triumphant. The glow in her watery blue eyes suggested satisfaction. Had she orchestrated this scene? Was it playing out as she wished? Her expression chilled him. She looked from him to Seaghan, smiling.

Curran seized her wrists, meaning to drag her out of the chair, but a hard shove sent him sprawling. Ibby's piercing scream bounced through his ears. Her chair crashed against the mantel as she stumbled from it and nearly fell.

Seaghan had pushed him and taken his place. The fisherman stood hunch-shouldered, his meaty hands reaching towards Beatrice's throat.

"Come to me, Seaghan MacAnaugh," she said, like a lover. Seaghan complied almost eagerly.

"No!" It was Diorbhail. She ran forward and tried to pull Seaghan away. "No, it's what she wants!"

Curran jumped to his feet and barreled into his old friend, but the giant didn't flinch. His eyes were locked on the woman's, who returned his stare as her tongue protruded and she made horrible gagging sounds. Her breasts convulsed.

"You're killing her!" Curran yanked on those massive arms, pried at the whitened fingers biting into Beatrice's fleshy throat. He punched Seaghan in the cheekbone three times, but the man remained impervious. Nothing could reach him. Diorbhail had no better luck. Seaghan was like an immovable mountain.

The two were locked in a strange, macabre embrace. Beatrice's eyes bulged. One of Seaghan's legs was thrust between hers and her hands gripped his forearms, scrabbling to no avail.

Curran's fists dropped to his sides as a greenish black cloud floated from her mouth. An awful stench made him gag. She must have lost hold of her bowels.

Seaghan released her. He stumbled away, groaning, gagging, coughing, but he'd achieved his goal. Freed at last of his hands, Beatrice slumped, her arms dropping over the arms of the rocking chair. Her eyes glared sightlessly. Purple splotches in the shape of her killer's fingers marred her throat. Drool seeped from her gaping mouth.

Seaghan fell to his knees and vomited. Curran knelt beside him. "What can I do?" he asked.

The man was shuddering. His flesh dripped sweat. He heaved in one breath after another, then vomited again and collapsed.

Curran rose. "Ibby, can you fetch the brandy?"

She was shaking uncontrollably, but nodded. She went off and soon brought the decanter and a glass. Curran poured some and, lifting Seaghan's head, helped him sip.

Diorbhail stood nearby, one hand on her throat, staring at Seaghan.

After he'd taken in a measure of spirits, Seaghan gave a weak, dismissive wave, and rose to his feet. His eyes opened and closed as though he was having a hard time remaining conscious. "Where am I?" He lifted his hands and stared at them. "It's over," he said, his voice barely discernable through the roar in Curran's ears. "I'm a man, at least."

He stared at Beatrice's body. His eyes narrowed and he sneered. Before Curran or Ibby could intervene, he was standing above her again, unbuttoning his trousers. He pissed all over her, splattering her dress and face.

"Oh my God," Ibby screamed. She retreated, stumbling, squeezing her eyes closed.

"Seaghan!" Curran pulled the fisherman from the corpse.

"He is not Seaghan," Diorbhail said quietly, but Curran dismissed it as hysterics.

"I...I'm sorry." Seaghan pushed his tadger back into his trousers. But he didn't look sorry or embarrassed.

Curran let it go. The woman had brought it on herself, after all, with her merciless goading. "What have we done?" he said, half to himself. "We've murdered Morrigan's aunt. Did she deserve it?" He knew he was rambling, making no sense. He rubbed his hands against his thighs, but as he'd fought to pry Seaghan's fingers loose, spittle had flown from the dying woman's mouth, spattering over him, and he couldn't seem to rub it off.

Seaghan stood motionless, breathing hard. After a moment, he lifted his gaze and stared fixedly at Diorbhail, who stood her ground and returned his stare somewhat defiantly, Curran thought.

"It's over," Curran said. "Seaghan? D'you hear me?"

Seaghan bent and picked up a slip of paper that had fallen out of the diary. He read it, and handed it to Curran.

Nam chridhe gu bràth. *Once more. Tonight. Dùn Mhiughalaigh.*

Curran's breath shortened, igniting into rage. *In my heart forever.* "We'll see about that," he said. It would seem Beatrice, the bloody bitch, had been telling the truth about one thing, at least. These were the words of a lover. He balled the paper in his fist and threw it into the fire.

Ibby stumbled closer. "Find Morrigan," she cried. "Curran, she can't be dead. And Olivia." Her voice rose. "Bring them home, please, I beg you." Her eyes closed as she crumpled. Seaghan caught her.

"I could come with you," he said, grasping Ibby around the shoulders and waist.

"No." *The worst is still to come.* "This is between me and him. It's my fight."

Seaghan nodded. "Aye," he said. He guided Ibby towards the loveseat. "No matter what we think of Beatrice, I believe one thing she said. Aodhàn wants Morrigan, and he'll kill anyone who stands between them." He speared Curran with a grim stare. "I'd advise you to take a gun."

Chapter 20

Curran's soul swelled and strained. Without Morrigan, did anything matter? If she and Olivia died....

He couldn't be too late. He couldn't.

The revolver's hard cold grip, shoved beneath his belt, reminded him that the fight he intended to wage would end in death.

She'd rather die his penniless whore than live in your fine manor house as your wife.

Diorbhail stumbled out of the cottage, running after him and grabbing his elbow. "Master Curran."

"Get away. I've no more time for talk."

"Be careful. Something…something isn't right. And, Master Curran…."

"What?"

"I'd swear on my life she was lying. Please, please, Master Curran!" This last was shouted as he stalked off.

"I know that," he muttered. By the time he stood at the summit of Càrnan, the sky was dimming, but he could still make out the isle of Berneray to the east, the cliffs where the lighthouse stood resembling the open jawed mouth of a gigantic dragon, drinking its fill of the ocean, and the lighthouse itself a distant white pillar.

Images flickered one after the next, always returning to that moment after he'd kissed her. Everything was so clear on her face a baby could read it. She didn't hate him. She was terrified. Her words, designed to convince him she didn't care, were the opposite of what he saw. She cared too much, and feared drowning in the torrent.

He'd never been sure before; now he had no doubt. She loved him. Yet whatever triumph he might have felt at that knowledge a month ago was edged with black certainty that she would do almost anything to stop feeling that way.

Love, violence, hatred, and failure...they're all the same for Morrigan. That's all she knows. Father Drummond had seen the truth far more quickly than Curran. How he missed the old priest and his wisdom.

Urgency sent his heels gouging into the springy peat. *What would you do with freedom?* he'd asked when he and Morrigan trekked the moor above Stranraer.

I'd be pagan. No man would own me.

Why remember that now? Were his fears trying to prepare him for the worst?

Before anything else, he'd fallen in love with the half-hidden siren beneath that veneer of malleability, the inner Morrigan whose eyes flashed when the outer lass smiled. He'd wanted to draw that girl into the light and sun. "Don't take her from me," he said out loud, not knowing if he spoke prayer or premonition, to God or Aodhàn.

She'd given him a glimpse of her true self, long before they lay together. What sort of man would he be to carp now, when the thing became a challenge?

His wife was a labyrinth, with sharp corners and blind curves, long dark passages leading into an unknown future.

"Morrigan!" he shouted as he approached the promontory of Dùn Mhiughalaigh. There was no answer but the wash of the sea and the shrill cacophony of seabirds.

He cupped his hands around his mouth. "Morrigan!" A lone puffin swerved off warily after glancing at him.

Curran pulled the gun from his belt. He saw nothing, no matter which direction he looked, though there seemed no place to hide. It gave weight to Beatrice's claim that the lovers would throw themselves into the ocean, and take Olivia with them.

No way of telling who the father is, not until the babe is born and we see the color of its hair.

He stared at the empty promontory, shaking with fear and rage.

Tonight. Dùn Mhiughalaigh, Mackinnon's note said. But there was no one on Dùn Mhiughalaigh.

She'll jump into the sea.

"No," he said roughly. Lifting his face to the sky's dimming glow, he shouted, "Where are you?"

It was shocking to realize that Seaghan, not Douglas, was Morrigan's father. But what difference did it make? He didn't care if the Devil himself had fathered her. Beatrice's evil intent had no power, and had brought her nothing but her own end.

And no matter what Aodhàn had done, knowing his awful past changed everything for Curran. No wonder he'd lost his memories. The only surprise was that he'd managed to go on living after they returned.

When Curran met Morrigan, he'd too easily assumed she was a typical country girl, experienced rather than innocent. He thought of how ethereal she'd looked in her wedding dress, how dark and enormous her eyes had been. He relived how close she'd come to dying after giving birth, and how she'd fought her way back. There had been that incredible insight at Torridon, and later in London, when Lily gushed over the Wagner opera.

Fulfillment through oblivion, Lily had said. *Death granting bliss, since life condemned the lovers to be near, yet always separated.*

Morrigan had added something. What was it? *In life constant yearning, but in death the destruction of guilt. Death as the shadow of love.* She'd seemed almost in a trance.

The bloody damnable legend had reawakened, with him in the role of the gullible King Marc.

Curran shuddered. She might well convince herself that death would bring her the elusive peace she longed for.

Terror seared. "Damn it!" he shouted. "Damn you! Why can't I get you out of my blood!"

Then, carried on the wind, he heard Morrigan's echoing shout. *"No, Mackinnon!"*

His head jerked one way then the other. He couldn't tell where the scream came from. It floated from the clouds, the ocean. "Morrigan!" he shouted again, hoarsely, but there was no answer. "Morrigan! Where are you?"

The landscape mocked him. He floundered, seeing nothing but impervious black granite and a hungry ocean. "I'll find you," he said, shoving away his fear. "You're alive, and I'm going to find you."

When Aodhàn saw Morrigan climbing down to the cliffs, he smiled. He'd been working out what to say, how to convince her to run away with him. The fact that she was coming, after telling him she wouldn't see him again, gave him hope. But his smile faded when he saw what she was carrying. The *infant.*

What was he supposed to do with that?

After she'd wandered some distance along the edge, he left the bothy and followed her. She sat at the crux where Dùn Mhiughalaigh met the main island, and played with her baby. He crept closer, unconcerned that she might hear his approach. How could she hear something as slight as footsteps over the continuous thunder of the sea against the cliffs and the shrieking of seabirds?

He listened to her sing, as enchanted as the child by the sound of her voice. The fading sun haloed her in gold and bronze light. He heard her say, *What should I do, Mama?* and wanted to weep at her grief and longing for a mother.

What if she won't leave with me?

He had vowed he would kill her. He wouldn't allow her to be slaughtered by outsiders again, and he feared it now that he'd told her the truth about Lilith. Athene might send Harpalycus after them. He could be on Mingulay right now, in any one of the villagers' bodies, or on his way, plotting how to best cause torture and mayhem. Or she could do something else. There were ten thousand ways for an inventive goddess to destroy them.

I will pick the time and method of our death, he thought defiantly. *Not you. Not again.*

But what was he supposed to do with Olivia?

I'll kill her too.

The idea was repellent. Maybe they could put the child in the heath somewhere. Someone would find it, surely.

She turned then and saw him, and he was gratified at the flash of happiness on her face. Even the baby smiled. But his sense of triumph didn't last. She hadn't come to meet him after all. It was mere coincidence, apparently, all due to a fight with Curran, who had inconveniently returned.

Understanding came in a crushing landslide so overwhelming he had to grit his teeth to keep from shouting at her. He would never convince Morrigan to run away. There were no words he could construct that would pull off such a trick. The instant she said *Olivia should not be here with us,* he knew.

That left only one other choice.

Fighting to hide his miserable jealousy, he coaxed her into handing him her child and walked to the edge of the precipice. He felt the tremble of earth beneath his feet as the heavy ocean swells crashed against it. He could easily toss the bothersome thing over. She would fall into the sea or be broken on the rocks, far, far below. He could kill Morrigan too. She would never remember. She would love him again in the next life.

Only he would remember. It would be one more awful memory, just one more, bleeding into all the others.

"No, Mackinnon!" Morrigan stopped an arm's length away. Her face was transparent, illuminating her terror. She didn't dare force his hand by grappling with him, but she wanted to. She'd read his thoughts somehow, and knew what he contemplated.

He looked at her then down at the baby, reclining securely in the crook of his left arm.

One slow step at a time she approached, staring at Olivia rather than the yawning drop beyond their feet. Mackinnon put his arm around her shoulders, feeling her icy stiffness and the underlying shudder.

"I know what's in your heart," she said. "You want us to die. But so help me, if you harm my child, I will curse you until the end of my days."

He tilted his head and his brows rose. "Those are words I would be stupid to ignore." Olivia started whimpering so he removed his arm from Morrigan's shoulder and brought the baby against his chest, her head near his throat, one hand holding her securely, the other patting her back—exactly as he used to hold Claire and Evie when they fretted. "A curse sent me on this journey. I know better than anyone the power of a woman's curse." He was silent for a long moment. Olivia quieted, soothed by his confident embrace, or the vibrations his voice made against her cheek, or both.

He had to do it. Throw the child over. Then, quickly, he must do the same to Morrigan, so the torment of watching her baby hurtle to its death wouldn't last too long. Then himself. And it would be over…until the next time, if there were a next time.

But his arms remained rigid. They would not move, no matter how he willed it.

He saw himself breaking Aridela's neck on Crete, thousands of years ago. He heard the snap of her bones. He felt her body slump against him.

He saw his arm lift, the moonlight race along his skin to reflect off the bone knife as it descended, ripping Menoetius from throat to groin.

He saw Eamhair and Cailean trapped on all sides at the edge of the Kyle. He saw Caparina being dragged to the stake. He heard the drunken village men laughing as they swarmed into his house on Barra, his daughters' childish screams, and he heard the silence that followed, a silence that had filled him with its emptiness ever since.

Harpalycus had played a part in the last three of these atrocities, but he couldn't blame the prince of Tiryns for the first two. That blood was on his hands.

He couldn't do it. No matter if he lost everything, even if he lost this woman for all eternity.

He realized, with astonishment, that he didn't want to harm Curran either. Not this time. He simply…couldn't.

How interesting. Perhaps there was a reason the Bitch was known as the Goddess of Wisdom.

This wasn't like him. He fought to construct a new plan, like a girl hastily pulling up her clothes after being caught in a compromising position. He would *allow* her to stay with Curran, but she would never quite belong to him.

Mackinnon would build such an impenetrable wall around her that Curran would end up bashing himself to bits against it. Her life would be one of contentment, but deep inside, it would be Aodhàn Mackinnon she secretly hungered for. That longing would carry over into death, branding itself into the intangible part of her that never really died.

In the next life, he would fan those banked embers and claim her, forever.

Some small part of him laughed. *You're justifying your weakness.*

"You mistake me," he said. "I don't want to hurt Olivia, or you, Morrigan. Never."

She said nothing, but her eyes said much. *You're lying. You'd kill her to make Curran suffer.*

"I've had time to think while you've been gone," he said.

Olivia held out her hands to Morrigan and whined.

"Here. It's you she wants."

He saw her joy as the baby's arms fastened around her neck. She gasped. Olivia put her face against Morrigan's throat and sucked her thumb.

"Thank you," she said brokenly. "I'm sorry."

He saw something then that touched his ancient, rotted soul. At first it hurt, as it would if someone put a finger on an open wound, but then warmth spread like healing ointment.

She was *weeping*.

She, who hadn't shed a tear, according to Seaghan, who'd heard it from Ibby, since she was a small child.

He brushed the tears from her cheeks with his thumbs. "Will you sit with me for a few minutes? Then I'll go."

She nodded. He helped her sit, there at the edge of land, as the sun dipped halfway into the sea, flooding the ocean with crimson, blue, and yellow fire.

"I'm not returning to Glenelg," he said.

She stared into his face. "Why?"

"This is Curran's time. Olivia's. I fought it. I've always been a selfish man, and I wanted you. I wanted you back. I wanted to recreate the past. But the truth is I owe him—Curran. There's a debt, a very long, very old debt, and like I told you, we can only go forward."

"So you'll leave your home. Your livelihood. Seaghan. Everything you know. Because of me."

"Because I want you to be happy. Will you ever be happy if I'm there?"

She didn't answer.

"She speaks to me, you know," he said. "Sometimes I feel like she wants to forgive. She beckons. Beyond her, everything is bonny. When I have that dream, I know it wasn't her on Barra. It was the men. Just men. And they are my creation. Mine and other men like me."

"Oh, Mackinnon. I don't understand."

Above them, the sky shifted from blue to purple, and the ocean fell into shadow. The storm was now no more than a faraway bruise on the horizon.

In August, on these isles, this was as dark as it would get all night. He remembered it from his years on Barra.

He felt younger somehow, like his decision had released him from shackles. Words poured out, things he'd been holding in for too long. "I'll never forget the first time we met. You were Aridela, a young visionary, full of hope and loyalty and courage. The reckless one, the 'Taker of Chances,' the firm believer in good. You grew into a wondrous ruler; your spirit and strength triumphed over catastrophe. There was magic in you. The heart of a long line of queens. It runs in your blood still—if I will only step out of the way."

"Aridela is real? I thought…all my life I thought I'd dreamed her." Her gaze intensified. "I was Aridela? Like I was Lilith?" She paused. Her voice hitched. "Eamhair?"

"Aye."

She waited impatiently. When he remained silent, she finally asked, "There are more, surely, with three thousand years. What of Caparina Naske?"

He knew he hesitated an instant too long. "No, there was no Caparina," he said. "There were no others." Inside he reeled. How was she remembering so much outside of his guidance? Was it the influence of Selene and Themiste? Could it be Athene herself?

Quickly, before she could challenge him, he said, "You're right to choose life. You do tend to make the right choices." *Defiance,* he thought. *That is what brings us back, over and over. My defiance. If I submit, that's when it will end. As long as I defy her, I'll have another chance.*

"I'm ashamed of what I thought earlier," she said. "I should have known you would never harm someone I love."

His throat closed, but he managed to say, "I don't blame you, not after the things I've done."

"I've been lost, tired of being certain that no one could ever love me. I was so sure of it that I've pushed away everyone who wanted to."

"You are loved." He clasped her hand. His jaw clenched so hard it locked, and he had to forcibly release it. "And you will be happy. I promise."

She stared at him, unblinking, motionless but for the breezes playing through her hair. Olivia made no sound as she gazed from one to the other.

"I'll always remember our night." She pulled the crescent moon necklace out from under her collar. The silver glinted, as violet as the sky.

He glanced down at the child. Her eyes were achingly blue, replicas of Curran's.

"Aodhàn…."

He leaned forward and kissed her, following the command of her mouth.

Just as he started to forget his resolve, to feel the old fantasy begin to reform, he heard a noise. A scatter of pebbles. He jerked away from her, turning his head sharply, staring behind them.

Curran's golden head appeared then his torso as he hoisted himself over the incline and joined them on the bare rock.

"Morrigan!" His shout was furious, and he brandished a revolver.

Aodhàn's senses plunged into scarlet-black rage. His body exploded like a ball of magma from the summit of a volcano.

Leaping to his feet and emitting a wordless roar, he barreled across the rock and flung himself on his old adversary.

Chapter 21

"Curran!" Morrigan held tight to Olivia as the baby threw out her arms, shrieking.

Mackinnon's fist smashed into her husband's jaw before he had time to take in the scene. Curran flew. The gun dropped from his hand, clattering and skidding.

"No!" Morrigan cried. "What are you doing? Stop it, Mackinnon!"

Curran rose and struck, his fist connecting with Mackinnon's left eye.

Blood spurted from his eyebrow, but Mackinnon instantly reengaged. The two men joined in a ferocious, cursing tangle.

An almost godlike strength seemed to imbue Mackinnon. Swinging both fists together, he cracked Curran's jaw. Blood spattered over the rock face.

Morrigan didn't dare go closer, not with Olivia. "Stop!" she screamed again, uselessly. Curran would die. Olivia would witness her father's murder. Then she and the baby would be at Mackinnon's mercy. He'd showed regret and compassion before, but this mad rage seemed bestial. She feared it wouldn't subside until everyone within his reach was dead.

"Curran," she whispered. "Curran, oh Curran."

Her husband slid past Mackinnon's fists long enough to punch him in the stomach. Mackinnon doubled over. Morrigan's hopes rose, but, overcoming the pain somehow, he lunged, battering Curran's face and making him stumble. One fist lowered, opened, and chopped sideways into the area of his enemy's kidney. Curran fell, writhing.

"Help me," Morrigan cried. "Diorbhail, you said men face a great She when they die. Who is She? Will She help me now?"

This blade can right an ancient wrong.

Morrigan brought the knife from her pocket. Gloaming light sparkled along the blade.

"I'm a woman," she said. "I can't kill."

She saw Louis shaking his head. *Respect the strength inside you.*

What else had he said? *You've a bit of Penthesilea in you.*

Lifting her gaze from the knife to the men, Morrigan shoved away her terror. Mackinnon was on top of Curran. She heard a horrifying cracking sound.

This be a woman's resolve! As for men, they may live and be slaves. Who had shouted that? Ibby, quoting the Celtic queen, Boudicca.

There was that other queen, too. Aridela. Would she be timid, or would she do what was necessary?

I can kill. I will kill to save my husband and child. I am Penthesilea, Boudicca, Aridela.

Securing Olivia between her left arm and her body, she ran forward, lifting the blade in her right hand, eyeing a spot halfway down the side of Mackinnon's ribcage where she meant to bury it.

But at that moment, a desperate thrust of Curran's knee propelled Mackinnon backward. He flailed, striking Morrigan's arm, and his shoulder hit her in the chest. The knife flew out of her hand as she lost her balance, and all her attention veered to Olivia. She twisted to keep from falling on the baby, and instead landed hard on her right elbow.

Pain erupted. Olivia was wailing; Morrigan sat up, biting off a curse, and attempted to soothe her.

Mackinnon stood, but instead of renewing his attack he stepped away. His hands opened, palms up.

Curran reached for the revolver, grabbed it, and fired, all in one motion. The explosion reverberated, frightening a colony of kittiwakes into screeching flight. The act seemed to take all his remaining will. He collapsed and lay motionless.

Mackinnon staggered. A small spot of blood appeared on his sark, below his ribs, and quickly expanded. He pressed his hand against the wound and looked down at it. Blood seeped over his fingers.

His gaze rose, meeting Morrigan's, and he smiled.

Then, releasing a stifled groan, he crumpled, so close to the precipice that one out-flung arm dangled in empty space.

Olivia sobbed and clung to her mother. Neither man moved.

Morrigan patted the baby and rocked, automatically wiping Olivia's nose with her sleeve. "You're fine, jo, my wee jo. You're not hurt."

Screeches subsided into hiccups. As Olivia calmed, Morrigan rose and crossed to Curran, praying to any deity who would listen to spare him. She closed her eyes and drew in a deep breath when she placed her hand under his jaw. He had a pulse. He was alive. There was blood everywhere, but she didn't think it was enough to make him die. He was unconscious, and she was glad. For this moment at least, he felt no pain.

"Morrigan." Mackinnon lifted himself on his elbows.

They lived. Both still lived.

"Morrigan," he repeated. "Will you speak to me?"

As much as she hated him in this moment, she couldn't forget those two other children she'd borne. How they were murdered. How that murder and his failure to save them had tortured him these many years. Their names flowed over her tongue like whisky. She could almost see their faces.

"No." She kept her gaze locked on Curran. Using the edge of her sleeve, she mopped at the blood.

"Please, Morrigan. Let me say goodbye."

She looked at him then. His face was grey. Sweat dampened his hair and ran down his temples. He clenched his jaw repeatedly, grimacing.

A kaleidoscope of bright, tear-sparkled images flared behind Morrigan's eyes as Mackinnon reached out to her. Would he ask forgiveness? After nearly killing Curran, whose only crime had been to marry, in innocence, the woman he wanted? Sorrow and fury trampled one over the other. She sighed. Then she went to him and knelt.

Olivia made a noise like a kitten's inquiring meow and outstretched a hand, splay-fingered, towards Mackinnon. He hesitated, then lifted his own. The baby patted it, much like her mother patted her when she was upset.

"You didn't have to do that," Morrigan said. "He wouldn't have shot you. You're a monster."

"I know what I am." His hand moved to Morrigan's forearm and grasped with surprising strength. "I wanted you to run away with me, but...." Pain drew him rigid, left him panting, then seemed to relent. "I'd kill anyone...I'd tear this world apart to be with you. But not this time. There's that debt. And not...not after the others. You can't lose Olivia too." His jaw clenched and his grip tightened. "I love you, Morrigan." He sighed and glanced at Olivia, then at the motionless Curran.

"Are you saying you planned it this way? That you knew Curran would come looking for me?"

"Of course he would. He always comes. As soon as you told me he was on Mingulay, I knew."

"Why? Why?"

"You think...you think I can go on living, always knowing where you are, never…able to see you, speak to you? Worse…far worse than death, believe me. And….” Unbelievably, he smiled again. “He always shows up at the worst moments. Right when I'm kissing you. The bastard.”

“Oh, Mackinnon.”

He regarded her, eyes half-closed, hot bright with pain. One shaking hand hovered over the wound. “You always called me that,” he said. Then he added, “Be happy.”

Now that he'd said his piece, his eyes closed and he lay quietly. Tears streamed over his temples.

Whatever happened now, part of her heart and soul would remain on this terrible rock, bled into this stone with her lover's. The lover who was willing to die in order to set her free.

The sea's murmur blended with a final, distant clamor of thunder.

“Morrigan?”

“Aye, Mackinnon.”

“I will find you,” he said faintly.

“Morrigan!” It was Diorbhail. She ran towards them, then stopped and bent. When she straightened, she had the knife.

Half the blade was missing. It must have shattered on the rock when it was knocked from Morrigan's hands.

Diorbhail would not be stopped. She would waste no thought on guilt or fear, right or wrong. One glimpse of Curran and she would sink that blade into Mackinnon, no matter that he stood at the gate into death already.

Diorbhail paused beside Curran. When she looked up, her face bore nearly as much rage as Curran's had earlier. She ran forward, lifting the knife, baring her teeth exactly the way Morrigan had pictured Boudicca when she attacked the Romans.

Mackinnon seized Morrigan's arm. “Don't let her touch me with that. I… don't think I can come back if she does.”

Morrigan jumped to her feet. “No!” she cried, placing herself between them. “Stop!”

Diorbhail had no choice but to obey or stab Morrigan. “Move,” she shouted. “If you won't do it, I will!”

“He's dying anyway.” Morrigan dropped to her knees. “Just wait. Please just wait.”

Mackinnon ran his fingertip over the pendant. He looked into her eyes. “Take care of it for me.”

There was no color left in his face. “Next time,” he said, soft as a voice in a dream, “*I* will win.”

She could only shake her head.

“*Gus am faic mi a-rithist thu,*” he said.

He shoved her backward and rolled off the edge.

Chapter 22

"Why are you laughing?" Ibby asked Seaghan. "I fail to see the humor in anything that's happened here."

Harpalycus was reveling in this feeling of strength, the deepness of his voice. He flexed his biceps. "I'm picturing the scene. Aodhàn and Morrigan, naked maybe, and along comes Curran. I'd give much to see it!"

"I don't know what's come over you this night, Seaghan MacAnaugh. Oh, how I wish you hadn't told him to take a gun!" She glanced at Beatrice then quickly away. "And here lies Beatrice, dead at your hands, and what you...you did to her after! I know you didn't like her much—truth to tell, nor did I, but it wasn't Christian. You should be ashamed. Have you thought about what you're facing? You'll be brought up on murder charges."

The fisherman glanced at Beatrice, still sprawled in the chair and stinking of his piss. "If you don't let me be," he said, "I'll do the same to you, Isabel."

She drew in a sharp, offended breath, but said nothing, obviously believing him. Instead she pulled a blanket out of one of the cupboards and threw it over the corpse.

He felt himself growing hard. For too long he'd been trapped in that noxious female. It felt good to be a man again, and it would feel better yet to celebrate by forcing his will upon some hapless woman, though Ibby would be his last choice. He'd rather have one of the kitchen wenches, or Diorbhail—he'd enjoy humbling that bitch, and he'd wager she would put up an entertaining fight—but they were gone and she was here. In the end he discarded the idea. She'd scream, and she was a dried-up old woman. He'd had enough of that. Besides, someone was bound to turn up shortly. He'd love to see who had won this round, Chrysaleon or Menoetius, but he'd best be off. His sense of self-preservation was strong, and if Chrysaleon came through the door and recognized him, nothing would stop him from murder, no matter the consequences. Seaghan MacAnaugh was far too conspicuous a body to remain in for long. He plucked his cap from the hook on the wall then went to the scullery, found a sharp butcher knife, and came back, opening the front door.

"Where are you going?" Ibby asked. He heard the hesitancy in her voice. She was afraid of him, as she should be.

"To see what's what," he replied and went off, heading for the village. Several boats floated in the bay. He dug in his pocket and brought out some coins, counting them carefully. He'd buy his way off Mingulay. When he got to Barra or the mainland, he'd pick a victim—a man—and use the knife to fatally injure himself so he could consume him. He'd be damned if he'd take another female's body.

He'd always been good at knowing when to leave, though sometimes he was sorry to miss the final outcomes of his plots.

There was a woman in France, one who found pleasure in pain. They had enjoyed several encounters. Perhaps he would go to Paris and see if she was still there. He'd had enough of Scotland to last several lifetimes.

As it happened, he crossed paths with a solitary man who was younger than Seaghan, and who looked healthy. So be it.

The man nodded politely and tipped his cap. Seaghan smiled and fingered the knife stuck under his belt. He took a deep breath of the cool night air. Life was a gratifying thing, when one wasn't afraid to make it turn in one's favor.

MORRIGAN SCRAMBLED TO HER FEET, SCREAMING, "*MACKINNON!*"

Diorbhail grabbed her shoulders and pulled her from the edge. "Don't look. Don't," she cried, and would not let go.

Gradually Morrigan stopped fighting. "Aodhàn," she whispered.

They stood together in silence, Diorbhail holding onto Morrigan steadfastly. "The sea claims final possession," she said, and pressed her cheek against the side of Morrigan's head.

"And leaves nothing behind."

"Come, *a bhrònag*." Diorbhail led Morrigan further from the edge. "Everything will turn out as it's meant."

"Will it?" Morrigan couldn't stop her teeth chattering, or the shudders, racing one upon the next as though she'd caught a fever.

"Aye, see, Master Curran is moving."

"Curran," Morrigan said. "Aye, Curran. Curran is alive." She gave Olivia to Diorbhail and ran to him.

He looked like an altogether different man. His eyes opened and closed without focusing. One leg bent at the knee. His face was covered in blood, and this somehow made him appear harder, colder. Morrigan was reminded of the dream they'd shared of the cave. That man's face had possessed a similar hardness. The man in the cave dream was a killing force. Here, in the present, on this rock above Scotland in the modern age, Curran was again that warrior, his scar standing out as white as a slivered moon.

Rapidly swelling skin kept him from opening his eyes properly. His nose was broken, and his right cheekbone seemed…not right. Blood caked his bright hair. Had Mackinnon sought to destroy Curran's beauty on purpose? If so, he'd succeeded.

"Morrigan? Olivia?"

"I'm here," she said. "We're here."

"Aodhàn…." His voice faded.

"He can't hurt us now, or ever again."

Curran allowed her to help him sit. He groaned, pressed a hand against his side, and stared past her to the edge of the cliff. His face suffused with fury. "Damn you, Morrigan. Beatrice told the truth, didn't she?"

"Truth?"

Curran looked from his child to her. His tone was accusing; so was his gaze. "She said you and Aodhàn meant to kill yourselves, and Olivia, that you've been his lover for months, that the babe you're carrying may well be his."

Beatrice? How…why…. No wonder Curran was so angry. "*None* of that is true. Why would she say that?" Trembling cascaded through her limbs and her teeth started chattering again. "Whether you believe me or not, I would never let anyone hurt Olivia. Never."

His stare was relentless. The redness and swelling around his eyes intensified the blue, making them appear hard as sword blades. "But…you?" The demand in his voice brooked no lies. "If Olivia hadn't been here?"

"No. No. I've had thoughts, I admit, but I want to live."

She ran shaking fingertips over her brows, her lashes and cheekbones. Seabirds squealed and the ocean soughed. The smell of fish and bird and salt water was strong.

Life. *Life* as she had seldom felt it, immediate and all encompassing.

"Give me Olivia," Curran said.

Diorbhail brought the babe and handed her over then retreated, turning away to give them privacy.

Dark, sad peace replaced fear. Olivia was safe with her father. Mackinnon was dead. Everything worked out, set as though the universe had conspired to draw them into this final juncture.

"I was his lover," she said. "Not before, but here on Mingulay. I won't make excuses."

Had she really believed death to be somehow noble? All because of a legend, true or not, that had come through the centuries, no doubt embellished and romanticized. She'd pictured herself and Mackinnon joined in death's embrace, to be reincarnated in some other place and time. "Divorce me. Marry a woman who will give you all you deserve." The words stuck and suffocated. "Lily, or someone. There must be hundreds who would love the chance to make you happy."

"Lily again?" Impatience chilled his voice. "You're wrong about her, and clear daft to think I'd stoop so low as to steal a friend's wife. I'm not Aodhàn."

She had no desire to defend Mackinnon. He had been selfish, until the end. Fear rose in her throat, but she knew she must defeat it and make one last request. She dabbed at her forehead with a torn sleeve. "I'll go away. I'll never cause you another problem. You'll never see me again." She thought of the sickle knife, of what it was designed for. *You'll know when to use it*, Diorbhail had promised. But events had turned from their designed course. Some part of her, awakened by Diorbhail and her potions, suspected a rare opportunity had been missed, and this failure would bring unimaginable consequences.

"Diorbhail," Morrigan said. "May I have the knife?"

"It's yours," Diorbhail said, and gave it to her.

A little less than half of the blade was sheared off. The broken edge was jagged, and possibly sharper now than it had been.

"Would you give this to Olivia when she's old enough? And maybe tell her I loved her? She'd believe it from you." She held out the blade, forcing herself to meet that hard, uncompromising gaze. "She shouldn't think her mother didn't care."

He glanced at the knife and his frown intensified. "Where did you get that?"

"Diorbhail found it and gave it to me. This is what I used on Patrick Hawley."

"That's the knife from my vision…by Torridon. I killed the lion with it."

They regarded each other, and the knife, and Olivia. Morrigan wondered what it could mean, and saw that he wondered the same thing.

His brows lowered. He looked well and truly enraged enough to strike, but he swiped at the blood running from his torn lip and grabbed Morrigan's chin. "There's no woman on this earth for Olivia and me but you," he ground out, as though he hated the admission. "You. Now you want to abandon us. Christ, Morrigan, will you run your whole life, from everything?"

She tamped down the instantaneous spark of hope and tried again. "There's something inside me. Something wrong. I don't fit anywhere, and I don't know how to change. It's like I am this knife, made of glass, and I've been thrown against a wall. There's no mending me. I think I'll never do anything but bring you unhappiness. The kindest thing I can do, the *only* thing that makes sense, is for me to go away."

"My children need their mother. Here. Hold her and tell me again how you're going to leave."

She handed him the knife and took Olivia. Amazing, how this child filled her with such confidence, strength, and resolve. How could she go on living without her?

Curran ran his hand over the hilt. "I remember using this like it happened today. And here it is. Real." He looked at her. "How? How could this knife be real? It's hot."

She nodded. "Aye, it seems to carry some kind of heat."

"Why did Aodhàn attack me like that…like he'd gone mad?"

The trembling started again. She stared at the ground. "I suppose he had a hard time accepting his fate."

Olivia played with her mother's fingers. Silence stretched until Morrigan lifted her gaze.

"When I first met you," Curran said, "I mind thinking you could revive the heart of a drowned sailor. He was never alive until you came."

She stared at him, certain she'd heard wrong. That note of compassion in his voice was her imagination. *My children need their mother*, he'd said. No, she couldn't hope. When he had time to think, and wasn't consumed by pain, he would hate her.

"Diorbhail," he said, "Could you help get me to the cottage? I don't think I can make it on my own."

"Aye, Master Curran, of course." She approached, sending Morrigan an encouraging smile.

In a few nights the moon would grow fat and full, but right now it was a lopsided hunchback. Its light spilled over them as they worked to get Curran to his feet. Silver-white phosphorescence trailed across the sea like a road, beckoning to an invisible, magical place. Avalon, perhaps, or some other long forgotten sunken city.

Moon-glade, she'd once heard this path of light called.

They put their shoulders under his arms and helped him, step by slow step. The worst was the incline, where they needed to prevent him from stumbling while not dropping Olivia. No, the worst was the rope ladder where he was forced to climb, with them pushing at him from below while holding a baby. When he finally stood on Mingulay proper, he was white, shaking, and drenched in sweat, pressing his left arm tightly against his ribs.

As they passed over the central hill, Curran nearly lost consciousness, wheezing that his ribs were stabbing through his lungs. They made him sit down and rest.

Morrigan wiped her arm across her forehead and looked into the night sky. *Aunt Ibby said I was a miracle. Mackinnon claimed I was Aridela, a great queen. Can it be?*

At first there was no answer. Then a star soared, shimmering, across the high heavenly arc.

"Ah, 'tis bonny," Diorbhail said. "And a blessing to you."

"I hope for all of us," Morrigan said.

Eventually Curran said he could go on. By the time they reached the cottage, his limp was much worse and his breathing had again degenerated into gasping.

Oddly, there was light in the windows, though it was late. Perhaps someone had left a lamp burning. The women assisted Curran carefully through the door.

"Morrigan," Curran said through harsh, struggled breathing. "There's something else I have to tell you. Something has happened."

Ibby came out of the parlor. When she saw the state of the Laird of Eilginn, she blinked rapidly and swayed. Diorbhail went to her quickly, catching her.

"Auntie?" Morrigan said. "Would you bring your laudanum?"

Ibby rallied. She patted Diorbhail's hand. "I'm fine, dear," she said. "Let's get you upstairs, Curran. Leave the other, for now. I think we've all had enough for today." She paused and added, "There's nothing that needs to be done or said right at the moment, not by you anyway. Diorbhail can help me with what needs taking care of."

Mystified, Morrigan looked from one to the other, but Curran only nodded. Diorbhail returned, taking Curran's other arm. Together they maneuvered him up the stairs and finally into bed, where he heaved a constricted, grimacing sigh.

Ibby brought her bottle of laudanum and a spoon. She looked at Curran anxiously. "Two spoonfuls, I think. I'm so blessedly glad you're here with us, Curran Ramsay. Blessedly glad, and I thank you for bringing my niece and great-niece home safely."

"Get some sleep, Ibby," he said. "I'll be fine."

She kissed an uninjured place on his forehead and left as Diorbhail came in with a basin of hot water, cloths, strips for bandages, needles, and thread.

"If you don't need me," she said, "I'll see to your aunt."

"Of course." Morrigan gave Curran a spoonful of bitter elixir, then another. "What does she need help with?"

Diorbhail only shrugged and left them.

Morrigan cleaned his face and assessed the damage. "You need stitches. I can do it. I used to stitch Nicky up when he drank and brawled."

"Press on," he said.

She brought the lamp over and set to work, making neat, close stitches on his eyebrow then his cheekbone. That hurt, she could tell, but he kept still except for one or two muffled groans.

Diorbhail brought tea and set the tray on the table by the fireplace. She and Curran exchanged glances and Diorbhail nodded once before leaving.

After a few minutes of silence, while Morrigan finished the last stitch on his cheekbone and wrung out a cloth in the basin to cool his flesh and dab away the last of the blood, he said, his voice beginning to slow and slur as the laudanum took effect, "I wanted to protect him."

She paused, drew in a breath, and replied, "You had to do it."

"I climbed that hill," he said, "and saw you, at the edge, with him."

Now he would ask, *Why did you go to him? Why were you unfaithful to me?*

The breath left her lungs so thoroughly it seemed to carry away her essence. She'd never felt so drained, not even when she finally woke after giving birth. "He was saying goodbye."

"Then why did he attack me?" Almost immediately, he added, "To force me to shoot him."

She couldn't tell him the truth, nor could she lie.

"He tried to talk you into abandoning me." Curran's stare missed nothing. Again, he answered his own question. "You refused."

Was her face so easy to read?

"He chose death rather than life without you." Curran's voice was flat.

Aodhàn Mackinnon was mystery, agony, a knot she would no doubt attempt to unravel for the rest of her life.

They were silent, avoiding each other's gaze. She gently prodded the massive dark red discoloration over his ribs, reassured when they didn't shift beneath her hands. "I'm not sure what to do about this," she said. "Nicky broke his ribs once, and I asked the apothecary what to do. He said not to wrap them, and that Nicky must breathe as deeply as he could. Otherwise he might catch lung fever."

"I'll try," he said.

He was quiet a moment, watching her roll the bandages she hadn't used. When he spoke, he sounded as if he'd had an evening of too much whisky. "My father told me that throughout my life, men would hold me to the fire and women would heal the burns. And that's exactly how it's been."

She had to turn away to hide a smile.

His eyelids drifted shut and she sat, watching him. He startled suddenly and his eyes opened wide, as though he was back on that cliff battling for his life.

"You're safe." She smoothed his hair. "You're safe now, *'ille.*"

"Been learning some Gaelic, I see," he replied, but his words were slurred, and she knew he wouldn't remember when he woke. His eyes closed and his breathing became more regular.

The lamplight magnified the damage. Curran Ramsay would carry scars from this night for the rest of his life. It was possible he would never again be touted as the handsomest man in Inverness-shire. But he would always be beautiful to her.

She busied herself cleaning up the mess she'd made then stood by the bed, looking at him, knowing at last that she loved Curran Ramsay, loved his loyalty and determination, his kindness and generosity, his smiles and easy affection, his efforts to heal the damage left by Douglas Lawton. At last, when it was too late, she understood it and there was no doubt of it in her heart, no fear of facing it, no need to deny it. In that moment when she'd believed Mackinnon meant to throw Olivia over the cliff, all doubts and fears had sharpened into a blazing arrow of crystallized focus. Curran. Olivia. It was not guilt or duty she felt for them. It was love, and she would feel it for the rest of her days, no matter if she ever saw either one again.

She took his hand and held it against her cheek.

Even with a mangled face and untold other injuries, even after hearing the awful things Aunt Beatrice had said, even after her admission of being another man's lover, he'd still offered her comfort.

Mackinnon would never have granted such charity. Yet, his last day on earth, he'd told her to go and be happy with Curran. For that final sacrifice that went so contrary to his nature, one small secret corner of her heart would love him too, for as long as she drew breath.

She dropped into the chair by the fireplace, mesmerized by the way the lamplight gleamed against Curran's hair.

I should be gone when he wakes. Then he won't feel obligated. He can divorce me. He'll recover, and be glad he's rid of me.

But she was exhausted, and in a few moments had fallen asleep.

Chapter 23

AT DAWN, AFTER AN INTERLUDE OF NIGHTMARES WHERE SHE WATCHED MACKINNON rolling off the edge of the cliff over and over again, always trying to catch him and never succeeding, Morrigan rose from the chair. She felt Curran's forehead; it was cool and his breathing was even, so she went along to Diorbhail's room, not surprised to discover her friend was also awake.

"I mean to walk to the cliffs," Morrigan said, rubbing her sprained elbow. "I must try to find him."

"He would've sunk," Diorbhail said gently. "What could you do if he was there? There's no way to get to him."

"I have to try. If I do see him, I can ask one of the fishermen to…retrieve his body, so he can be buried."

Diorbhail was shaking her head. "Is Master Curran awake? Did you tell him?"

"He's asleep. That's why I want to go now. You can tell him where I've gone if need be."

"Oh, no, if you're bent on doing this, I'm going with you."

"I have to, whether there's any hope or not." The thought of him, lying broken upon the rocks, cold and alone, was more than she could endure.

Ibby promised to watch over Olivia and Curran, though it required an argument and repeated vows to not take any chances on those devil cliffs.

They made their way down the rope ladder and up the incline. To the west, beyond the cliffs, a low-riding moon glistened with the brilliance of a newly minted coin. Morrigan stood at the edge, looking down, but the sun wasn't yet high enough; darkness shrouded the water below.

"We'll wait a bit." Diorbhail rested her hand on Morrigan's shoulder.

Morrigan sought to think of something, anything, other than what sunlight might reveal. "What were you, Curran, and Aunt Ibby hiding from me last night?" she asked.

Color rose in Diorbhail's face, but she answered. "Master Curran should no doubt be the one to tell you." She paused, frowning. "There's no easy way to say it. Your Aunt Beatrice is dead."

"What!" Morrigan stared, wondering if this was a terrible joke, but the grave sorrow on Diorbhail's face told her it wasn't. "Does...does this have something to do with...with those things she accused me of?"

Diorbhail nodded. "After you went out yesterday, she came back from a walk. She was drunk. She insisted Master Curran and all of us listen to a story about your dead mother, and...she had your diary. She forced Master Curran to listen to her for near on an hour, and then she told him you'd gone off to kill yourself, and Olivia, and that you'd been...Aodhàn Mackinnon's whore. He was furious, but no' so furious as Seaghan MacAnaugh. Seaghan...he...choked her. He choked her to death." She had more to say, Morrigan could see it on her face, but she drew in a breath and fell silent.

Morrigan heard the words, but it was impossible to believe. "Aunt Beatrice...dead?" Dead. The woman who had raised her. She turned her face away to stare blankly at the setting moon. Dead by violence at Seaghan's hand.

"One more of my family dead."

"I am your family. I am your kin, and so is Eleanor." Diorbhail embraced her, offering comfort, and Morrigan was comforted, but she noted that Diorbhail didn't say Curran's name. She must know there was no hope for kinship there, not now.

Mackinnon was dead. Curran was horribly injured, and Seaghan had murdered her aunt. Morrigan closed her eyes, inwardly tumbling, and wondered if things would have been better if she *had* killed herself.

Yesterday, she had wept for the first time in memory. She knew she should weep now—it seemed only right, a sign of respect to her aunt. Tears clogged her throat, but her eyes remained dry. Perhaps that brief ability had gone over the cliff with Mackinnon.

"Something changed in her while we were away," Diorbhail said. "I felt the difference when we returned from London, and when I looked at her I saw a man's face—a cruel face. She wanted to hurt Master Curran last night, and she did. But I know you loved her, and I'm sorry."

"Where...where is she now?"

"We wrapped her in bedclothes while you took care of Master Curran. Ibby said that one of the housemaids is the undertaker's daughter. She said she would send for him today."

"I should see her," Morrigan said, but reluctantly.

"I don't advise it," Diorbhail said. "Mind her as she was."

Morrigan realized what she was saying. Beatrice had been throttled to death, and that would no doubt be evident. Seaghan…Seaghan would have to face the law.

"Seaghan murdered my aunt," she said. "Seaghan…the gentlest man I think I've ever met."

"There was long-standing hatred between them. From when your mother was alive. I felt it. I saw it."

Morrigan rested her cheek on Diorbhail's shoulder. "I should never have come to Glenelg. How I wish I could go back in time and undo it."

"How could you have known?"

"Where is Seaghan? I just realized I haven't seen him."

"Ibby said he left the cottage last night, after…and he never returned."

"He's probably beside himself at what he's done."

"Maybe." Diorbhail didn't sound so sure about that. "Look, *a charaid,* it's getting lighter."

They walked along the edge, examining every speck as best they could, but they saw nothing. It was too far. There was too much spray, obscuring everything beneath it.

"It's no use," Morrigan said.

"Come," Diorbhail said. "We'll pay a fisherman to bring us round in his boat."

"I suppose there's nothing else we can do."

They made their way down the incline and crossed to the rope ladder. Then Diorbhail said, "What's that?" and pointed.

Off to the right the frayed end of another rope was whipping in the wind, and beside it was a square, faded flag.

They went over and discovered a manmade path. It descended, terrifyingly steep and narrow, as far as could be seen, the lower reaches hidden in spray mist. A rope was nailed into the rock, to use as a handhold when the wind blew, which it always did on Mingulay.

"I wager this leads to the water," Morrigan said.

"What are you thinking?"

"We could go down, try to find him."

Diorbhail eyed the threadlike, crumbling path. But she nodded. "Lead the way."

They set out. Morrigan half-stumbled, half-slid along the path that in places was no wider than her foot, keeping such a tight grip on the rope that her hands cramped. She avoided looking over the drop to her right, or thinking how any misstep could send her plummeting. The uncertain pathway, little more than slippery rock covered with a thin layer of slimy mud, eventually broadened onto a shelf of rough sand. The sea boomed and echoed.

There was a dinghy, roped into an iron ring, rising and dipping in the morning swells, tugging against its restraining line. Morrigan shaded her eyes and examined the cliffs; she saw nothing, no body of a drowned man, but there were many recesses that could be hiding him.

Even as she wondered if this boat was Mackinnon's, she saw the driftwood box on the center thwart.

She pulled on the line to draw the boat nearer, and stepped onto a ledge beneath the water's surface. Icy seawater foamed over her ankles and drenched through her shoes. The boat tipped precariously as she climbed in, then recovered its balance.

She opened the box. The ring was there, winking in the sunlight. Mackinnon's presence surrounded her. Her hands shook as she closed the box and put it in her pocket.

"What is it?" Diorbhail asked.

"Mackinnon's boat," Morrigan said.

Again, methodically, she examined the cliffs and sea. As her gaze traveled to the south, she discerned what looked like a large cave, carved into the side of Dùn Mhiughalaigh, near the water line. Her heartbeat sped up, thinking she saw a person standing there, but it never moved, and she decided it must be a tall rock, or maybe a standing stone.

There was a threatening roar amongst these cliffs. The swell was powerful. But the need to search was more urgent.

"The tide is ebbing," she said. "If we hurry, we can make use of it before it gets too strong."

"It'll pull us out," Diorbhail said, "but I've rowed in worse." She climbed into the boat, untied it, and pushed off with one of the oars. Immediately the current swept them away towards open sea. They both grabbed oars and fought to gain control. Slowly, laboriously, they reversed course.

"We must hurry," Diorbhail warned.

The water calmed a bit as they rowed between a ring of rock monoliths and along the cliffs as close as they dared, but still they saw nothing, no glimpse of a corpse, only a few dead fish and bird carcasses.

Morrigan gazed up at the towering stacks. Impassive, invisible eyes seemed to return her stare from within these primordial observers to uncounted eons of history. Water surged and retreated, making eerie sounds —*pock-whaup, pock-whaup*—like smithies hammering with rubber mallets, or fingers drumming hollow wood. The sun, showering upon the summit above, could send no more than a few misty rays into this elemental spot.

They reached the cave. Diorbhail rowed hard onto a sliver of wet shingle. Morrigan jumped over the side, dragged the prow farther up on the sand, and tied the rope to a stone.

The tall form was a cairn, constructed from smooth, rounded rocks, a marvel, each stone placed to give those around it strength.

Had Mackinnon made it? Had he known this enigmatic place? He and Lilith had spent time on Mingulay, long enough to build Taigh na Gaoithe and conceive their children. If Agnes Campbell were here, she would claim he used this spot to rejoin his seal kin, and there was, indeed, evidence of footprints around the cairn.

At the rear there was a crate. Inside were blankets, a coat, and flint.

"He must have lived here," Diorbhail said. "It's barely above tide level. In a storm, I'd wager it floods." She perused the echoing space. "I would not want to be here then."

"Look," Morrigan said. She picked up a skull from the sand beside the crate. "A seal?"

"No," Diorbhail said. "That's a lamb's skull."

"I wonder why it's here."

They returned to the edge. Morrigan saw more caves, hollows, and arches along the cliffs. He could have washed into any of them, or out to sea, or into a trough.

Diorbhail took off her shoes and waded along the lip. "It reminds me of Durness," she said.

Morrigan sat on a rock, arms around her knees. Light filtered in a soft, golden haze, creeping further and further then vanishing as the sun rose higher. The cavern turned chilly.

Diorbhail stopped. She stood still, staring.

Morrigan followed her gaze. A short distance away a seal watched them, nothing visible but the top of its smooth head, wet black nose, and fluid eyes.

As though it knew it had been spotted, it barked and ducked underwater, revealing itself again farther out towards the open sea, its bullet-shaped head a silhouette against glassy waves. Striking its right flipper against the water with a resounding *slap*, it disappeared.

She looked at Diorbhail. Diorbhail returned her gaze, brows lifted.

"He has sunk, or been carried out," Diorbhail said. "And we'd best get back to the path."

Morrigan approached the ledge where land gave way to sea. She removed the driftwood box from her pocket, opened it, and took out the ring.

Gaol mo chridhe, it said. *Love of my heart.*

Quickly, before weakness could stop her, she threw the ring towards the spot where the seal had been. It arced outward, glittering, hit the water soundlessly, and vanished.

"*Gus am faic mi a-rithist thu*," she said.

Until I see you again.

Curran was sitting outside in the sun, a blanket over his legs. Olivia played with a set of wooden blocks on the ground beside his wicker chair.

He asked the question without speaking.

No. Morrigan shook her head.

"Sit with me." He held out his hand.

Diorbhail went inside, leaving them alone.

"How are you?" She bent over him to inspect the stitches.

"I slept."

The bruises had turned blackish purple and the swelling was worse, but there was no new bleeding or streaks of infection.

"Don't fuss." He pulled away from her examination, so she sat on the ground at his feet and picked up Olivia.

"All my life I've lived with pain," he said after a few moments. "No, a hole, like something was missing. I was always searching, even when I wasn't thinking about it, every new face; places, too. I never escaped that feeling until the day on the moor when you and I made Olivia." He turned a meditative stare to her. "It disappeared like that—" he snapped his fingers. "I had my first experience of peace. It felt like coming home after war, seeing your wife running to meet you. Your weans shouting *Papa!* It was a feeling like some old illness was finally done."

She could only gaze at him. The faint smile on his face told her he saw all she had no words to express.

Olivia cooed and patted her mother's cheek.

Morrigan thought she glimpsed the aura that Jamini had spoken of. On their wedding day, it had showed itself as a mingling of blue and violet. She saw those again, but now interspersed with a sparkle of gold.

"Let's walk," he said. "I cannot abide this idleness."

She paused. *He wants to get me away from the others, so he can tell me I'm to leave.* But she said only, "Should you?"

"It might help the stiffness. And I have this cane Ibby found." He brandished it with a rueful smile.

They left Olivia with Diorbhail and walked into the village, then past it to the roaring sea.

Several women near the water were weaving creels and cleaning fish. They stared at the two outsiders and spoke among themselves. By now, of course, they would know about Beatrice.

Curran grasped her hand, drawing her attention from the gossips. "Shall we walk along the beach?" He nodded the opposite direction from the women. "It looks as though it continues on past the headland."

Once they'd passed the crag, they were out of sight and alone. His walk was slower now, his breathing noticeable. "That was a fair labor, I admit," he said. "I've a mind to cool off." He threw down the cane. "Sit here and wait for me?"

She nodded, unable to speak for the dread churning inside. She sat on sand so fine it could rise in the air and dance, and put her knees against her chest.

He removed his coat, his shirt, and his boots, and waded in, splashing water over his shoulders. The discoloration on his ribs had expanded overnight, and he still favored his left arm. It worried her, but she knew he didn't want her to speak of it.

She watched him, thinking back over their time together. She'd convinced herself she had chosen the easier path when her womb quickened and Curran wanted to marry her.

Now she knew better. Love was capable of ripping one's heart out, exposing it to all manner of injury. Love was the most dangerous path of all.

He seemed more ancient myth than mere man as he came up out of the sea and crossed to her. Swift sailing clouds illuminated him in silver and dark-gold, streaming shadows and planes of pearl. He shook water from his hair and put his shirt on, not bothering to button it. Reaching into a pocket in his coat, he brought out a cigarette and lit it. Then he sat beside her.

They watched the sea; it was as trance-inducing as Eleanor's hypnotism, and Morrigan almost forgot to fear what was coming. Green, black, and purple, the water wore a veil yet at the same time could blind…like people, the surface an illusion, hiding what lay beneath, speaking in that not-quite-under-stood language. No matter what small humans suffered, the sea, always changing, stayed the same.

Who assigns women their place? Louis had asked. *What happens to you, to your daughters, if you allow it?*

For a moment she had believed Penthesilea was directing her. She'd run forward on that rock, resolved to save Curran. Would she have stabbed Mackinnon if the blade hadn't been knocked from her hand?

Since leaving London, she'd thought, again and again, of those ladies in Lily's drawing room, and their leader, Josephine Butler. One of the last things she had done before they left was to slip out of the townhouse and find one of the rallies where Josephine was speaking. She'd listened, enraptured, to her stirring call for justice.

Here, on a remote Scottish island in the Atlantic, far from civilization and politics, she still saw that impassioned face, heard the fervent words. Brave and determined, Josephine and her compatriots flouted society's rules and restrictions. Her empathy was inspiring. How easily she could have reviled the fallen women as most did, or simply ignored their plight. Instead, Josephine and her partners worked to help those they had never met, women with no voice.

Women helping women. Decent women helping prostitutes.

On her wedding day, Morrigan had tried to banish the old desire for freedom. She'd told herself it was an impossible wish; she must settle and conform to the role of proper wife and mother.

Josephine Butler, that devout and delicate woman, was also a wife and mother. Yet she had pulled herself out of the kitchen and thrown off the expectations. She still lived and breathed. She walked the streets of London, made speeches, confronted Parliament and whoever else stood in her way.

She hadn't been branded or tossed in gaol. Certainly, she was ostracized, but she didn't seem to care.

Such was the power of boldness, of devotion to something beyond oneself.

Morrigan wondered if she could return to London and join those women in their fight. Maybe they wouldn't reject her. Maybe she could find a small garret somewhere.

She shivered. This was the great lesson of her life. Everything had built to it, especially having a child...a daughter. If women went on allowing themselves to be tethered, then nothing would change. If they made themselves blind to the bars around them because of mollifying words spoken by husbands and lawmakers, if they were frightened into compliance because of what they saw awaiting them if they dared rebel, then no doors would open. Change would only come when those who were numbed and fettered were willing to fight. And if Josephine Butler could fight, then so could Morrigan Ramsay.

She might fail, or be laughed at. She could even be harmed. Maybe it didn't matter. Perhaps the fight was what mattered, and if she was harmed, others might rise up in her place.

"Morrigan?"

She turned to Curran, seeing both that embittered dark warrior and the young, golden god.

He rose and stepped behind her. He untied her hair and drew it over her shoulders, combing through it gently. "Whistler was right," he said. "It is true russet."

She looked up at him and so caught the grief clouding his face. *Mackinnon,* she thought. *He'll miss the friend and life he had before I came along.*

He rubbed his eyes and his shoulders slumped. Coming around, he knelt before her and placed his hands on her knees. "I loved Aodhàn. I know he cared for me too, in his way. And we both loved you."

She heard the past tense and knew what it meant. "I understand," she said. "I don't blame you, Curran. No one blames you. I've killed what could have been. You must hate me, who wouldn't?"

"I don't hate you."

"But...what I've done—"

"It doesn't matter."

She must have gone mad, to hear him say such a thing. "I've hurt you and disappointed you, again and again. In the worst ways."

"No." Curran shook his head. "And there's part of me that knows, sure as I know my own hand, it was the same for Aodhàn. You're a wild, free spirit, a child of Artemis, who belongs to the seas and mountains." He raised a lock of her hair and let it run off his palm. "I thought I had to turn you into a tame lady, a drawing room figurine. I thought that was my obligation as a man. It shames me to admit I wanted to cage you, or, as you put it, bind you at the bottom of the sea. I won't ever try to break you or change you again, my Morrigan."

Why was she surprised? Long ago she'd realized Curran Ramsay wasn't like other men. She touched his temple, where the bright hair sprang as it dried, feeling his acceptance wash over her.

His understanding.

She almost laughed. She'd had it all along. She'd had it from the moment she looked up into that train car in Stranraer. Canny, selfish Mackinnon hadn't wanted her to see it. He'd almost convinced her he was the only one who could accept and understand her.

Her gaze turned to the rolling sea. Once more, soft and gauzy, she saw herself plunging into a deep blue ocean, water bubbling like champagne. She remembered the story Mackinnon had told of the selkie and his human love, Eamhair.

It had happened somewhere along this odyssey of lives they'd lived. Somehow, Aodhàn remembered. Curran was there as well, in the body of…*Cailean*, but she didn't think he remembered his past lives any better than she. They came in broken images and dreams, as they did for her.

Perhaps, with Diorbhail and Eleanor's help, they could find a way to retrieve those shared memories.

And if they were thorough, maybe…maybe they could make a difference in lives to come, for she knew it wasn't yet finished, though an inner voice— Eleanor's voice—kept insisting there was only one more.

The dreams…were they part of what Aodhàn told her before he died? *You were Aridela. There was magic in you. It runs in your blood still.*

His words left more questions, more mystery.

She would sort through that later. There were more important tasks that needed tending now. "D'you know what I mind?" she said. "You telling me you loved me before you knew about Olivia."

"Aye, well." He blushed. "That might have been lust talking. I knew I couldn't stop thinking about you all the bloody time. You were like an itch I couldn't get to." The embarrassed, quirky smile faded. "Now I know more of love."

So do I.

Her body hummed with joy. "You don't want to divorce me?"

His gaze remained steady. "Never," he said.

"You love me for me, not because of how I look, or because I'm Olivia's mother?"

A puzzled frown formed between his eyes. "Of course it's for you. I love you, my quicksilver wife. I'll love you when you're eighty, and wrinkled as a dried apple, with brown apple seed eyes that see everything. I knew I was going to marry you the first time I kissed you."

She pressed her palms against his and smiled.

"I know…about Aodhàn's family," he said, still frowning. "What happened to them. I know nothing he did was meant to hurt me. When I think of what he suffered, and for how long…I don't know that I could have borne it. I think I might've forced someone to shoot me, too."

The sobs came without warning. It was mortifying, but she didn't know how to make it stop. Horrible, racking sobs. She pushed her knuckles against her eyes and turned away, wanting to hide, needing to hide, feeling her insides run together like candle wax. She was coming apart.

Then she felt him. He pulled her in against his chest and held her there, one hand on her head, rocking her gently. She clung to him, pressing her mouth to his throat where he tasted of the sea, ashamed and more than a little terrified.

He went on holding her, soothing her as he would Olivia.

Her voice snagged and broke, but she managed to say, "He believed I was his wife, born again."

Curran's rocking paused…then resumed.

She struggled on. "I've told you about my dreams. I see myself being murdered. There are other…other dreams, too. I t-think it's true."

He said nothing. Gradually, her weeping subsided and she simply rested against his damp skin. Every now and then her chest constricted, but the awful shuddering relaxed.

"You were his wife," he said, so quietly she almost didn't hear.

"But now I'm yours, Curran. He accepted it in the end. He wants us to be happy. He was more your friend than it might seem."

One last sob convulsed her throat.

Clasping her upper arms, Curran moved her away from his chest so he could meet her gaze. Gently, he pressed his cool palms to her hot skin. Sunlight struck his face, setting those blue eyes on fire and sparking against the stubble on his jaw.

He wiped her nose with his sleeve.

"I'm sorry I've been so stupid," she said. Love welled up, strong, unwavering, freed of guilt, duties, of unfinished lives and lifetimes to come. "I've been very, very stupid."

Indeed, Curran's smile could melt the Devil's heart. "Come away, Lady Eilginn," he said. "Have you been drinking? I have never in my life heard a female admit to stupidity."

"I could use a drink, if you want to know the truth." Tracing the crescent scar curving from brow to cheekbone, she drew him towards her and kissed that ridge of flesh.

He turned his face and kissed her on the mouth. It was profound, undoing her, reaching inside her, filling her with hope and peace. It said everything, yet beneath lay a delicate thread of loss. No doubt those opposite emotions would plait, like complementary ribbons, around her soul for the rest of her life. But she could bear it.

Until next time.

"I want to make love to you," he said.

"In time." She took his hand and placed it on her stomach. "This baby happened that night at Torridon, in the moonlight. I think those three women had a hand in it."

His smile was as dazzling as the sparkle of sunlight against a pristine field of snow. "I knew Beatrice was lying." He held her hands. "Morrigan, Seaghan is your father. Not Douglas Lawton."

"What?"

"It's true, *a ghràidh.*"

At first she was dismayed. She wasn't sure how to feel. The man who had killed her Aunt Beatrice? But it was only the unexpectedness of it. As the moments passed, she realized the news made her happy. She remembered the day she'd met Seaghan at the Mallaig Games, how huge he was, how loud, boisterous, and friendly, like a great Clydesdale. She pictured his face, so pleased that day he'd talked her into sailing with him on the *Endeavor*, how he'd watched over her, and had spoken plainly about Mackinnon, like a real father would. A *real* father. "Why didn't he tell me?"

"I suspect he was afraid you might be disappointed."

She blinked and tried to absorb that. He was afraid he would be worse, in her eyes, than Douglas? She needed to set that right as soon as possible. "I hope he comes back soon," she said. "I want to give my father a kiss, and thank him."

Life is what gives new beginnings...not death.

She contemplated what the orphans in London had to do to survive, and how they were manipulated, abused, tortured.

Why couldn't she and Curran bring some of those sad, starving children to Kilgarry? After the squalor and stink of the city, to run along Glenelg's coast, to help in the birthing of lambs, to play in clean mountain snow and swim in the bay, would be heaven for a child, and there was plenty of room. She could involve the village. She knew the Campbells and the Urquharts would be enthusiastic. Seaghan could teach them how to fish. Curran would enjoy it too. He loved children.

They would help heal Glenelg. The spectre of the clearings couldn't survive the laughter of so many children.

Mackinnon gave his life so I could stay with Curran and be happy. I will make his gift mean something. I will do this, in part, for Mackinnon.

And she must apologize to Lily for her nonsensical doubts and jealousy. Together, they would prove that women could support, trust, and encourage each other, and cause miracles to happen.

I will make myself a reckoning.

"I took Diorbhail's mushroom," Curran said, brushing hair off her face. As she met his gaze, startled and wary, he added, "At Cape Wrath."

"You know about that?"

"I heard the two of you talking about it, and found it in Diorbhail's bag. It cleared up a few mysteries. I'd like to share what I saw with you."

She nodded eagerly. "Aye. Please, Curran. And I'll tell you what I've seen."

Caressing her shoulder, he said, "We've found each other before, my Morrigan, in other lives. We always find each other. Aodhàn is part of it as well. We three have been together, I think, for a long time. We're woven together somehow. I have no doubt you were his wife. What I don't understand is how he manages to remember more than we do."

"Why is this happening? Diorbhail thinks I'm meant to do something, but..." she shrugged. "I don't know what."

"Maybe, together, we can puzzle it out."

"Diorbhail can help." Blushing, she added, "So can Eleanor. She's used the mushroom too."

He snorted and grinned. "I should have known. You and Diorbhail and Eleanor. The Three Graces."

Her emotions were almost too strong to contain. She rose and went to the water, taking off her shoes so she could squish her toes in the wet sand. A velvety August breeze skimmed past with the promise of a fine day, and for an endless moment, time and space shimmered.

"Curran," she said. "It's time to go home, don't you think?"

"Finally."

"There is something about Douglas Lawton I don't want to forget."

He met her gaze, and his frown returned.

"He fed me goat's milk, though he could've let me die. A man who would do that had goodness. There's never light with no dark, good with no evil." Her voice lowered. "Never wind without stillness." She wondered, through a quick wrench of fear, if Curran could exist without Mackinnon any better than he had with him. "I think, I think...he did...the best he could."

Curran came to her. How warm he was—warm and brash and vigorous. "Aye," he said.

Hell is what Earth becomes without her Mother. So Diorbhail had stated in her simple yet profound fashion. Douglas had writhed in the desert men made of their souls. But Diorbhail had prophesied something else. *One day,* she'd said, *we women will rise again. Our Mother will open our hearts and we will have thousands upon thousands of years of joy, not just men, and not just women, but all of us, together.*

Movement brought Morrigan's gaze to the sky. An eagle was drifting, silent and watchful. She felt its shadow pass over her face as it flew between her and the sun.

She breathed deeply. This sea air tasted like wine. "'Tis braw to be alive, sometimes."

Curran made no immediate reply, and she glanced at him.

"D'you mind when you told me you felt like the paddle wheel on a steamer?" he asked.

She smiled sheepishly. "Spinning and spinning, never accomplishing anything."

"Oh, you're wrong there."

"I am?"

"Aye, Morrigan." He smiled again, that incandescent Curran Ramsay smile. "The wheel is what moves the boat along, my darling. The wheel is what gets us to our destination. Do you still think that's such a bad thing to be?"

Above them, the eagle spread its wings and circled, higher, higher.

Warm, bright Curran, splashing rainbows into the dullest corners of life.

The End

Due to the sheer size of this book, I did not include the three companion epilogues in this volume. Please visit my website, where you can read them, AND view a high resolution zoomable map that shows the locations in this book more clearly.

To find the website, simply type rebeccalochlann dot com into your search engine. Specific link addresses below.

https://rebeccalochlann.wordpress.com/category/epilogues/

https://rebeccalochlann.wordpress.com/category/map-the-sixth-labyrinth/

Glossary

Bannock: flat bread

Batting: cotton quilting (in this case, for diapers)

Bauld and ferlie: bold and wondrous. Ferlie: strange, unusual, causing wonder: "a marvel"

Besom: can be a broom, but in this case it's a silly, tiresome girl

Boak: to vomit

Bogle: like a bogey-man, a ghost, a demon or supernatural thing

Braes: a steep bank or hillside

Braw: fine, beautiful, grand

Cheviot: a breed of sheep

Clishmaclaver: gossip

Close: a narrow place like an alley, a path, a passage

Cockerdecosie: piggy-back riding

Currach: a very small boat, similar to a coracle, but shaped differently: currachs could be sea-worthy

Dawless: lazy

Dead-can'le: a mystical bluish light that would appear around a house where someone was soon to die

Deiseal: the direction of the sun as it travels through the sky every day: to walk deiseal is to walk following the sun's movement, and is believed to give powerful protection

Dirk: a dagger

Dominie: a schoolteacher

Dowf: dull and stupid
Dowp: backside
Dreich: wet, cold, miserable weather
Dulse: a salty dark red seaweed
Fashing, or fash: to be annoyed, worried, or stressed
Fee: a job
Gawpus: a clumsy stupid lout
Glaikit: thoughtless, stupid, foolish
Glengarry: a traditional men's cap
Greet, greeting: weeping
Haar: a sea-haar is a thick sea mist
Half-mark church: a church that performs clandestine or unconventional weddings
Hippins: baby diapers
Hissy: Beatrice uses this as a way of saying "hussy," which is a mischievous girl, a problem child
Jillet: a flirt
Jo: "dear" or "sweetheart"
Keek: to peek
Kirk: a Presbyterian church
Kist: the bride's kist: her hope chest, in which she stores linens and other things she's made for when she marries
Kye: cattle
Lief: "rather," "happily." "I would as happily buy a dog."
Mince: rubbish. Nonsense
Moolet: to whine
Mucker: while this can be used in place of "friend," it can also be derogatory. Kit uses it on Douglas to mean a coarse man, a jerk
Mutchit: said to children when annoyed with them or when one doesn't think much of them
Paddler: a child just beginning to walk. A toddler
Sark: shirt
Scunner: there are several ways to use this word. It describes many different emotions: angry, frustrated, annoyed, dislike.
Shieling: a rude hut or stone shelter up in sheep grazing lands, usually only occupied in the summer
Skaffie: a versatile Scottish fishing boat
Sonsie: another word with many uses and meanings, like "healthy," "good-natured," "attractive."
Thole: bear, tolerate, endure: (I cannot bear it any longer)
Thrawn: perverse, twisted, crooked

Thwart: a bench on a boat
Unco: strange, weird, extraordinary
Wambly: trembling, shaky
Wame: stomach
Wynd: an alleyway, a narrow lane between buildings

Gaelic & Greek Translations

a bhrònag: you poor thing
    a charaid: my friend
    a ghaoil: my darling
    a ghràidh: my love
    àilleag nan nighean: jewel of the girls
    a leannan: sweetheart, to a baby or child
    a luaidh: an endearment. "Beloved"
    a-mach às mo shealladh: get out of my sight
    a nighean: my lass
    an tig thu thugam a-nochd: will you come to me tonight
    Arnamuil, Gunamuil, Lianamuil: sea stacks at Mingulay
    a rùin mo chridhe: my greatest love
    a shiùrsach: whore, or "you whore"
    Bàgh a' Chaisteil: Castlebay, a village on the island of Barra
    Barraigh: Gaelic for the island of Barra
    beannachd leat a ghràidh: goodbye, my love
    beannachd leat, mo nighean: goodbye, my daughter
    bean-nighe: water-wraith
    bean-sìth: female spectres
    bean-uasal: a Highland lady
    cait fhiadhaich: the Scottish wildcat
    caileag: girl
    Cailleach an Dùdain: "The Old Woman of the Mill-Dust," or "The Old Wife,"

a traditional harvest-time dance from ancient times, with specific movements and symbolism

Càrnan: the highest hill on Mingulay

cèilidh: a visit, a get-together, a party

chan fhaca mi a leithid: "I never saw the like"

ciamar a tha thu, a ghràidh: how are you, my love

crioslachan: a bag, sometimes used to hold the Michaelmas carrots

curran: carrot

daoine sìth: a supernatural race of faery-like people from Ireland. Described in various ways, as spirits of nature, gods and goddesses, faery people

Dòmhnach Curran: Carrot Sunday (at Michaelmas)

Dùn Mhiughalaigh: a promontory on Mingulay

Earsaraidh: a village on Barra

feasgar math: good evening

fèilidhean: kilts

gaol mo chridhe: love of my heart

gille: boy

glaistig: a fearsome grey creature

gu bràth: forever

gus am faic mi a-rithist thu: until I see you again

Innse Orc: the Orkney Islands

Là Fèill Bhrìghde: St. Brigit's Feast Day

madainn mhath: good morning

m' eudail: my darling

mhic an Diabhail: son of the Devil

mìos nam pòg: month of kisses

mo bhean: my wife

Mo rùn: my love

Morrigan/Morrígan: I kept the acute accent when I referenced the goddess, to differentiate between my character and the deity. There is some argument about whether it would have the accent. Various sources show it both ways, so I made that literary choice.

m' ulaidh bhuaireanta: bhuaireanta has different connotations. On the one hand, it means "tempting," "enticing," and maybe the most telling, "enflaming." But it also means "annoying," "irritating," "argumentative." All of which can go together in many ways. It is the perfect, most sublime word in this instance

Nam chridhe gu bràth: in my heart forever

oda: the Michaelmas horse race

oidhche mhath, ciamar a tha sibh: good evening (or good night), how are you? (spoken formally)

pìobaireachd: the piping (bagpipes)

Sasannach: an Englishman
Sasannaich, na Sasannaich: the English
seanchaidh: storyteller
sìthean: a faery hill
Sgoth Niseach: a type of fishing boat built on the isle of Lewis
Sgurr Mhic Bharraich: mountain (or hill, really) east of Glenelg
Slàinte, or slàinte mhath: good health
Sròn an Dùin: Nose of the Dun
strùan: the Michaelmas cake
's tu mo bhean is mo rùn: thou art my wife and my love
's tusa gaol is rùn mo chridhe: thou art my love, my heart
tadger: penis
tha gaol agam ort: I am in love with you
tha ise bòidheach: she is beautiful
tha mi toilichte: I am happy
tha thu gam chur às mo chiall: you're driving me daft
Taigh gun chù, gun chat, gun leanabh beag. Taigh gun ghean, gun ghàire: "A house without a dog, a cat, or a little child is a house without joy or laughter"
Taigh na Gaoithe: Windy House
taigh-tughaidh: thatched house
Tuatha Dé Dannann (Danaan) or *Tuath Dé*: Tribe of the gods, or of the goddess Danu. Kings, queens, and heroes with supernatural powers. Worshipped as gods originally: Robert Graves thought they originated in the Mediterranean
uisge-beatha: whisky
ùruisg: part goat, part human with tangled hair and protruding eyes

Lebadeia: site of an ancient sanctuary on the Greek mainland, north of Athens, where people sought prophecy from oracles
Zoi mou…agapi mou. T'aste'ri mou: Greek. Zoi mou: my life. Agapi mou: my love. T'aste'ri mou: my star

Historical Notes

The Sixth Labyrinth is a complicated weave of truth and fantasy: Yes, liberties were taken. Following are notes, both about the liberties and truths, for those who might be interested.

The maiden voyage of the *Princess Louise* was July 1, 1872. I moved this date back to May, for the purposes of the story. (I wanted Morrigan to be married and in Glenelg by Michaelmas.)

I was thrilled to discover some maps of Stranraer as it was in the 1850s. I used those to help describe the city, as well as my own memories from staying there.

I have an extensive library of books and other media detailing the Scots language and dialects. I have studied these, off and on, for about twenty-five years. This has equated into me understanding some but still being able to authentically speak almost none. I was extremely fortunate to receive the help of two native Gaelic speakers for this book, and I will always be grateful for their assistance and patience.

One of my favorite dictionaries is the *Chambers Scots Dictionary*, (compiled by Alexander Warrack, M.A.), which I purchased while in Scotland years ago. It was first published in 1911, and I've noticed it contains many words that apparently have been dropped from newer publications. Perhaps those words have gone out of favor, but I was happy to have access to words that were likely common in the 1800s. Here is the subtitle:

Serving as a glossary for Ramsay, Fergusson, Burns, Scott, Galt, minor poets, kail-yard novelists, and a host of other writers of the Scottish tongue.

I'm sure I fit in there somewhere!

Beannachd leat, mo nighean: I understand this isn't the way Gaelic speakers would say this, but I chose it because I wanted Morrigan to be able to question Curran later about those words. (Goodbye, my daughter.)

Castle Kennedy, the ruin that Curran and Morrigan explore outside Stranraer, still stands. It was built by the clan of that name who controlled the area in the distant past. When I was there, it was off by itself in an empty field; we had to climb over a fence and were alone in exploring it, which no doubt added to its ghostly feel. I think now there's a parking lot nearby, but there wasn't then.

Lighthouses:

The description of *Dhu Heartach* was taken from *A Star for Seamen*, by Craig Mair. Work on *Dhu Heartach* was completed in November 1872.

Corsewall was built in 1817, Cape Wrath in 1828, Berneray in 1833, and Cairn Point in 1847, all by the Stevenson family of engineers.

The Glenelg Clearances: My descriptions of the Glenelg Clearances are an amalgam of evictions over the years, from various areas. In reality, Glenelg was cleared more than once, with the biggest eviction (500 people) occurring in 1849, and it did not happen exactly how I've portrayed it. The anguish I describe encapsulates almost every account I studied of people being cleared from their ancestral homes, but some were done in a more humane fashion than others, and in some instances, it was the crofters themselves who petitioned to be cleared. There are arguments about the Clearances, whether they were good or bad, kind or cruel, and I am not putting myself into those arguments. I had a vision of being a crofter in those days, of living on land my family had lived on for generations, of having everything fall apart, and of being relocated to a far away country, and that's what I wrote.

Randall Benedict, the story's landowner at the time of the Glenelg clearings, is my fictional invention, and bears no resemblance to any true-life landowners.

In the late eighteen hundreds, the Highlands of Scotland were gradually converted from sheep farms to open parks for killing deer and birds. The pastime was popular among the wealthy British.

The Macleods did own the land around Glenelg in the 1600s, and would have been the builders of Kilgarry, (if Kilgarry existed. Which it didn't—doesn't. Kilgarry is my invention.)

My descriptions of Glenelg are not exactly what one would see these days, because I was trying to envision what the area might have looked like in the 1870s. I think there would have been more forest and less agriculture.

The Five Sisters of Kintail: it's a nice label, although not used in Gaelic, and much easier than listing each one individually:
Sgùrr nan Spàinteach (The Peak of the Spaniards)
Sgùrr na Ciste Duibhe (The Peak of the Black Chest)
Sgùrr Fhuaran (The Peak of the Springs)
Sgùrr nan Saighead (The Peak of the Arrows)
Sgùrr na Càrnach (The Peak of the Stony Place)

In August of 1872 a sea serpent was indeed sighted and documented swimming through the straits of Kylerhea off Glenelg's coast.

I've never actually heard that selkies have a magic "gaze" that will bewitch any they turn it upon. That was my invention.

Syncope and concussions have obviously been around for a long time (as long as we have had brains?) The word syncope has two meanings: it appears that the word as it pertains to fainting has been around since about the 1400s. There was work being done in the Victorian era on concussions, but no one knew the depth of details that we have today. So diagnosing Morrigan's fainting would have been mostly guesswork. The aura she often sees before fainting is a symptom of concussion as well as other medical conditions, and there is speculation that concussions can sometimes cause nightmares (although I think it's safe to say there are other powers at work with Morrigan's nightmares!)

Origin of syncope:
The American Heritage Dictionary: "Middle English *sincopis*, from *sincopene*, from Late Latin *syncopēn*, accusative of *syncopē*, from Greek *sunkopē*, from *sunkoptein, to cut short : sun-, syn- + koptein, to strike.*"
The word "concussion" has been around since ancient times, but came into general use in the 16th century, along with descriptions of some of the common symptoms.
A few people who have had concussions continue to experience symptoms for the rest of their lives—dizziness, headaches, mood changes, etc, and often stress or anxiety will bring on the symptoms. Current theory suggests that post

concussion syndrome is more likely to persist in those who have suffered several concussions, as Morrigan has.

Hypnotism: as I mentioned in the book, hypnotism was developed by James Braid, a Scot. He coined the term "hypnotism" in the 1850s and used self-hypnotism to alleviate pain. After Braid's death in 1860, interest in the procedure died out in England, and was later revived in France.

Readers might detect similarities between Heinrich Baten, my fictitious Papal Inquisitor, and Konrad Marburg, a historical figure. Yes, I did think of him as I wrote the Inquisition scenes. Klaus Berthold, however, is completely fictitious: I did no reading about any historical archbishops, and all I know about the Archbishops of Cologne is the title.

As noted, Curran is not a true laird, but is called "Laird" by his crofters as a sign of their respect. The "Eilginn" title is my invention, an honorary moniker given by the locals, and hearkens to the area around Glenelg, the Pictish Ruins, and the forest over to Shiel Bridge. Curran is not landed gentry and so it is proper for people outside of his little world to call him "Mr. Ramsay."

Dun Troddan and Dun Telve are two of the most well preserved brochs (ancient stone buildings) left in Scotland.

Only Clydesdales are used in the oda? No. My invention. The part about the horses being stolen the night before is real though.

Don't go up to Cape Wrath thinking you'll find tunnels under the lighthouse, or the remains of a fort! (This is all detailed in *Falcon Blue*.) They live only in my imagination. The higher oxygen content of the air at Cape Wrath is documented, and the *Clo Mor* cliffs at Cape Wrath are the highest on the British mainland, at over nine hundred feet.

I also made up the MacNeil house in Castlebay, on Barra, and of course Bishop House as well.

Anachronisms: Not. The setting of The Sixth Labyrinth runs parallel to the work women were starting to undertake in Britain to obtain equal rights. Obviously, women were thinking the things that are brought up in my book. Many might not have, and many more who did might never have breathed a word about it, but change was on the horizon. Additionally, Morrigan, who possesses the subconscious memories of Aridela, has at this point five previous lives influencing her thoughts and the way she sees the world.

• See Elizabeth Clarke Wolstenholme, John Stuart Mill, and others.

I could go on and on about Josephine Butler, Elizabeth Wolstenholme, and the efforts of the Ladies National Association in trying to repeal the Contagious Diseases Acts. It's true that prostitutes were seen in a different light than the men who had sex with them. The women were perceived as unclean, "degraded," and it was believed that they alone carried syphilis (at least that's what the lawmakers said they believed). The men were not considered unclean or degraded, nor were they bothered with exams after they protested the idea. And it's true that women who were not prostitutes were pulled into this net of forced examination. The Acts were at last repealed in 1886. The LNA continued their work and were instrumental in getting the age of sexual consent increased from 12 to 16.

The actual 1871 Commission Report can be read here: https://archive.org/details/b21365945

The LNA was a real team effort and a role model for me: the group had many committed male supporters as well as female. This concept is of passionate personal interest, as I feel we will never get anywhere unless we're all willing to leave gender prejudices behind and achieve it together. The discerning reader will see that as Aridela lives her various incarnations, she receives support and assistance not only from her reincarnated female followers, but men and women in the current time periods. In *The Sixth Labyrinth*, she is helped and influenced not only by those you might expect, but also her brother Nicky, Robert Louis Stevenson, Seaghan MacAnaugh, James Whistler, Lily Donaghue, Jamini, and Hugh Drummond.

Separate but connected: I reject the idea that love and feminism are mutually exclusive.

White bread was available by the 1820s, but it wasn't exactly what modern people might think. It wasn't pre-sliced, and the term simply meant that it was baked from a more finely ground flour, not modern bleached flour.

Poetry and Songs:
My Love She's But a Lassie Yet, lyrics by Robert Burns
Bonny Wee Thing, lyrics by Robert Burns
I'll Meet Thee on the Lea-Rig, lyrics by Robert Burns
Ae Fond Kiss, lyrics by Robert Burns
Ca' the Yows to the Knowes, lyrics by Robert Burns
My Heart's in the Highlands, by Robert Burns
Ode to the West Wind, by Percy Bysshe Shelley
She Was a Phantom of Delight, by William Wordsworth

Tristram and Iseult, by Matthew Arnold, published 1852

Master McGrath did win the Waterloo cup in the years mentioned.

The builder and owner of the famous *Cutty Sark* was Jock Willis, who built her in 1869. The race between the two clippers *Cutty Sark* and *Thermopylae* happened as described in the summer of 1872.

At the time of Nicky's death (August 10, 1872), RLS was in Frankfurt. I used my authorial license to have him come back briefly to attend the funeral.

RLS did agree, reluctantly, to study law, though he wanted to write. Louis's father attempted creative writing when young, but hid that fact from his son, and pressured him to become an engineer. Thomas believed that women should be able to divorce their husbands, but that husbands shouldn't be allowed the same privilege.

RLS wrote that he thought he would never be great or rich. He did want his own children very much. He loved opera, and stated that he wished he could live his life inside one.

I used the older spelling for the May 1 festival of Beltain. The spelling "Beltane" appears to have been adopted from James Frazer's *The Golden Bough,* which wasn't published until after my story. The spelling I use is from Anne Ross's wonderful book *The Folklore of the Scottish Highlands,* which I highly recommend to anyone wanting to read more about the early customs, traditions, and beliefs of Scotland.

I made up the Catholic Church at the estuary in Glenelg.

Queen Victoria loved Scotland; she made it a popular place to go on holiday. She and Albert purchased Balmoral Castle and she often attended the Highland Games at Braemar.

As everyone knows by now, gossip ran rampant in the years after Albert's death that Victoria was having an affair with her Scottish servant, John Brown. She even had statues made of him.

Gladstone was lampooned for trying to rescue the prostitutes of London from their sins, but he was actually quite generous and helpful in that regard, when he certainly did not need to be.

James McNeill Whistler was a well-known figure in 1870s London. Whistler often went to Victor Barthe's art classes in order to disrupt them.

The rumor that Richard Wagner may have been King Ludwig's lover is an old one that is no doubt rumor by association, and is doubtless untrue. Why can men never be friends with other men without being accused of homosexuality? Ludwig may have been gay—Wagner was not. Ludwig helped Wagner financially and was his patron. Without Ludwig's patronage, much of Wagner's music might not have become a reality. (I'm grateful to King Ludwig for this.)

As far as the conductor—Lily has heard wrong. It was one of Hans von Bülow's assistants who had a breakdown and had to be institutionalized.

The place where the denouement occurs is loosely based on Gunamuil, the lower promontory next to Dun Mingulay, but is really a composite of the various cliffs, arches, and caves on the west coast of Mingulay, adapted for the story's benefit.

St. Brigit: the name of this important saint of both Ireland and Scotland has several different spellings. I chose to use the one Anne Ross used in her book *Folklore of the Scottish Highlands*.

About the word "all right." Apparently it wasn't coined yet in the 1870s. I used it anyway, for convenience, clarity, and modern ears, but I tried not to use it very often.

Did Scots put on mourning clothes after the death of a loved one? I can find no evidence that they did NOT, except for a mention in *Scottish Customs From the Cradle to the Grave*, where there are 5 or 6 mentions of YES on the mourning, and one mention of NO, and that was offered by a woman in 1988, not the Victorian period. I searched and searched for a definitive decision on this: most of what I found suggests that Victorian Scotswomen did put on mourning: besides, Queen Victoria made the white wedding dress popular, so she probably made the widow's weeds popular as well.

I did read in *The Pictorial History of Scotland: From the Roman invasion to the close of the Jacobite Rebellion. A, Volume 1,* by James Taylor, published in 1859, that mourning dress was not known in Scotland until 1537.

I didn't want my book to be as long as Clavell's *Shogun*, so I had some people speak English who probably would not have in real life, like Kilgarry's servants.

Lebadeia was a shrine in Greece, north of Delphi; Pausanias tells a story about seeking prophecy from the oracle there, and how terrifying it was.

Titles in The Child of the Erinyes series

Book One: *The Year-god's Daughter*
Book Two: *The Thinara King*
Book Three: *In the Moon of Asterion*
Book Four: *The Moon Casts a Spell* (a novella)
Book Five: *The Sixth Labyrinth*
Book Six: *Falcon Blue*
Book Seven: *When the Moon Whispers, First Chronicle*
Book Eight: *When the Moon Whispers, Second Chronicle*
Book Nine: *Swimming in the Rainbow*

About the Author

Early on, Rebecca Lochlann began envisioning an epic story, a new kind of myth, one built upon the foundation of the Greek classics and continuing through the centuries right up to the present and future.

This became her life's work, though she didn't exactly intend it to be that way when she started.

The Child of the Erinyes series is mythic fantasy, inspired by the Greek tale of Ariadne, Theseus, and the Minotaur. As one reader put it, "Loads of testosterone, slaughter, and crazy magic," with a love story (of course.)

Though the story is fiction-fantasy, it still took about fifteen years to research the Bronze Age segments of the series, and encompassed rare historical documents, mythology, archaeology, ancient religions, and volcanology.

The Year-god's Daughter is her debut novel: Book One of *The Child of the Erinyes* series. It has been utilized as a study guide in an American university, named a B.R.A.G. Medallion honoree, and was a finalist in the Chaucer Historical Fiction awards. Book Two, *The Thinara King*, a First Place winner in the Ancient History category of the Chaucer Historical Fiction awards and a Next Generation Indie Book Awards finalist, continues the saga. Book Three, *In the Moon of Asterion*, wraps up the Bronze Age segment of the series and leads into the middle trilogy, set in Scotland. These are: Book Four, *The Moon Casts a Spell*, Book Five, *The Sixth Labyrinth*, and Book Six, *Falcon Blue*, which jumps backward in time to the Early Medieval Era.

The denouement comes in the final three books: *When the Moon Whispers, First and Second Chronicles*, and *Swimming in the Rainbow*.

Rebecca has always believed that certain rare individuals, either blessed or tortured, voluntarily or involuntarily, are woven by fate or the Immortals into the labyrinth of time, and that deities sometimes speak to us through dreams and visions, gently prompting us to tell their lost stories. Who knows? It could make a difference.

Connect with Rebecca at her website, BookBub, Facebook, or in a review at your point of purchase.

Attributions

Interior and cover design: Rebecca Lochlann, Erinyes Press
   Original front cover figure: Eve Ventrue, eve-ventrue.com

Les Trois Grâces 2.jpg: https://commons.wikimedia.org/wiki/File:Les_Trois_-Gr%C3%A2ces_2.jpg {{Information |Description=Les trois grâces,par James Pradier,1831,musée du Louvre.(Image détourée) |Source=Own work |Date=11/03/07 |Author=Vassil |Permission=PD-self }} <u>Category:French sculptures in the Louvre - Room 32.</u> I, the copyright holder of this work, release this work into the **public domain**. This applies worldwide.
   Big Crescent Moon with Triple Moon, Infinity Loop and Little Goddess. Pagan and Wicca: Christine Krahl, Shutterstock
   Design Elements: A-R-T-U-R, Depositphotos
   Beautiful red haired girl in white dress standing in river with water lilies: Boiko Olha, Shutterstock
   Woman on tropical island: sergey_causelove, Depositphotos
   Mature businessman: prostooleh, Depositphotos
   6 circuit labyrinth illustrated stone wall: EcOasis, Shutterstock
   Labrys Axe graphic © "Labrys-symbol" Licensed under Public domain via Wikimedia Commons http://commons.wikimedia.org/wiki/File:Labrys-symbol.svg#mediaviewer/File:Labrys-symbol.svg
   Crescent moons, necklace image, & Erinyes Press logo: Lance Ganey freelanceganey.com/
   Mountain elements on map created by StarRaven, aka Daphne Arcadius, at DeviantArt. Other design elements: Shutterstock. Map layout and design—Rebecca Lochlann, Erinyes Press

Thanks to the following:
   Thalia Proctor, who helped me shape my characters, structure, and description. Not only that, but lucky for me, she also knows Greek and French.
   Eve Ventrue created the original image you see on the cover of *The Sixth Labyrinth*. This fellow perfectly captures my gloomy Aodhàn Mackinnon. She

also created the original image for Lilith Kelso Mackinnon on the cover of *The Moon Casts a Spell,* and the original image for Cailean on the cover of *Falcon Blue*. What a divine threesome they are!

My Speakers of Gaelic, who did not make fun of my language errors: they simply helped me fix them.

www.ingramcontent.com/pod-product-compliance
Lightning Source LLC
Chambersburg PA
CBHW020511110726
47899CB00004B/1079